THE PENGUIN BOOK OF MODERN FANTASY
BY WOMEN

Richard Glyn Jones trained and worked as a psychologist before entering the world of publishing. In the late 1960s he was an editor of the controversial magazine *New Worlds*, which at one point was banned by W. H. Smith and caused questions to be asked in the House of Commons. He ran his own small press for ten years, where he published Christine Keeler's bestselling *Scandal!*, as well as Jorge Luis Borges's *The Book of Fantasy*. He currently works as a writer and editor, and has compiled more than twenty anthologies, including *Killer Couples*, a study of *folie à deux* in murderers, and, with A. Susan Williams, *The Penguin Book of Erotic Stories by Women*. His most recent anthology is *Cybersex*.

A. Susan Williams is a senior researcher at the Institute of Education, University of London. She has published extensively on literature and history, with a particular focus on women's lives and work. Recent publications include *The Penguin Book of Classic Fantasy by Women*, a companion to this volume. She is currently completing a book on the development of maternity services over the twentieth century.

THE PENGUIN BOOK OF
MODERN FANTASY
BY WOMEN

EDITED BY A. SUSAN WILLIAMS
AND RICHARD GLYN JONES

WITH AN INTRODUCTION BY JOANNA RUSS

PENGUIN BOOKS

PENGUIN BOOKS

Published by the Penguin Group
Penguin Books Ltd, 27 Wrights Lane, London W8 5TZ, England
Penguin Books USA Inc., 375 Hudson Street, New York, New York 10014, USA
Penguin Books Australia Ltd, Ringwood, Victoria, Australia
Penguin Books Canada Ltd, 10 Alcorn Avenue, Toronto, Ontario, Canada M4V 3B2
Penguin Books (NZ) Ltd, 182–190 Wairau Road, Auckland 10, New Zealand

Penguin Books Ltd, Registered Offices: Harmondsworth, Middlesex, England

First published by Viking 1995
Published in Penguin Books 1996
1 3 5 7 9 10 8 6 4 2

Printed in England by Clays Ltd, St Ives plc

Contents

Sources and Acknowledgements

'MARMALADE WINE' by Joan Aiken, first published in *Argosy*, 1964, collected in *A Bundle of Nerves* (London: Gollancz, 1976). Copyright © 1964 by Joan Aiken, reprinted by permission of the author.

'WHEN IT HAPPENS' by Margaret Atwood, first published in *Chatelaine*, 1975, collected in *Dancing Girls and Other Stories* (Toronto: McClelland & Stewart, 1977). Copyright © 1975, 1982 by O. W. Toad, reprinted by permission of the author and the author's agent, Phoebe Larmore.

'THE FALL OF FRENCHY STEINER' by Hilary Bailey, first published in *New Worlds*, 1964. Copyright © 1964 by Hilary Bailey, reprinted by permission of the author.

'THE DEMON LOVER' by Elizabeth Bowen, first published in *The Listener*, 1941, collected in *The Demon Lover and Other Stories* (London: Jonathan Cape, 1945). Copyright © 1941 by the Estate of Elizabeth Bowen, reprinted by permission of the Estate of the Author and Random House UK Ltd.

'THE LAKE OF THE GONE FOREVER' by Leigh Brackett, first published in *Thrilling Wonder Stories*, 1949. Copyright © 1949 by Leigh Brackett, reprinted by permission of the Author's Estate and the agents for the Estate, Blassingame, McAuley & Wood.

'THE FOOT' by Christine Brooke-Rose, first published in *The Unlikely Ghosts*, ed. James Turner (London: Cassell, 1967). Copyright © 1967 by Christine Brooke-Rose, reprinted by permission of the author.

'THE EVENING AND THE MORNING AND THE NIGHT' by Octavia E. Butler, first published in *Omni* magazine, 1987. Copyright © 1987 by Omni Publications International, reprinted by permission of the author.

'MY FLANNEL KNICKERS' by Leonora Carrington, written *circa* 1955 in Mexico City, first published in *The Seventh Horse and Other Tales* (London: Virago, 1989). Copyright © 1989 by Leonora Carrington, reprinted by permission of Virago.

'PETER AND THE WOLF' by Angela Carter, first published in *Firebird 1*, 1982, revised and collected in *Black Venus* (London: Chatto & Windus, 1985). Copyright © 1982, 1985 by the Estate of Angela Carter, reprinted by permission of the Estate of Angela Carter, c/o Rogers, Coleridge & White, 20 Powis Mews, London W11 1JN.

'BOOBS' by Suzy McKee Charnas, first published in *Isaac Asimov's Science Fiction Magazine*, 1989, revised for *The Skin of the Soul: New Horror Stories by Women*, ed. Lisa Tuttle (London: The Women's Press, 1990). Copyright © 1989, 1990 by Suzy McKee Charnas, revised version reprinted by permission of the author.

'(LEARNING ABOUT) MACHINE SEX' by Candas Jane Dorsey, first published in *Machine Sex . . . and Other Stories* (Canada: Tesseract (Porcépic) Books, 1988). Copyright © 1988 by Candas Jane Dorsey, reprinted by permission of the author.

'THE OLD MAN' by Daphne du Maurier, first published in *The Apple Tree: a Short Novel and Some Stories* (London: Gollancz, 1952). Copyright © 1952 by Daphne du Maurier, reprinted by permission of Curtis Brown Ltd, London, on behalf of The Chichester Partnership.

'IF THE WORD WAS TO THE WISE' by Carol Emshwiller, first published in *The Start of the End of it All and Other Stories* (London: The Women's Press, 1990). Copyright © 1990 by Carol Emshwiller, reprinted by permission of the author and Virginia Kidd, Literary Agent.

'RELICS' by Zoë Fairbairns, first published in *Despatches from the Frontiers of the Female Mind: an Anthology of Original Stories*, eds. Jen Green and Sarah Lefanu (London: The Women's Press, 1985). Copyright © 1985 by Zoë Fairbairns, reprinted by permission of Zoë Fairbairns and the publisher.

1982, collected in *The Compass Rose* (New York: Harper & Row, 1982). Copyright © 1982 by Ursula K. Le Guin, reprinted by permission of the author and the author's agent, Virginia Kidd.

'THE SHIP WHO SANG' by Anne McCaffrey, first published in the *Magazine of Fantasy and Science Fiction*, 1961, collected in *The Ship who Sang* (New York: Ballantine, 1970). Copyright © 1961, 1989 by Anne McCaffrey, reprinted by permission of the author and the author's agent, Virginia Kidd.

'FIREFLOOD' by Vonda N. McIntyre, first published in the *Magazine of Fantasy and Science Fiction*, 1979, collected in *Fireflood and Other Stories* (Boston: Houghton Mifflin, 1979). Copyright © 1979 by Vonda N. McIntyre, reprinted by permission of the author.

'PRODIGAL PUDDING' by Suniti Namjoshi, first published in *The Blue Donkey Fables* (London: The Women's Press, 1988). Copyright © 1988 by Suniti Namjoshi, reprinted by permission of the author.

'DEATH IN THE EGG' by Ann Oakley, first published in this collection. Copyright © 1995 by Ann Oakley, printed by permission of the author.

'NIGHT-SIDE' by Joyce Carol Oates, first published in *Night-Side: Eighteen Tales* (New York: Vanguard Press, 1977). Copyright © 1977 by Joyce Carol Oates, reprinted by permission of John Hawkins & Associates, Inc.

'TRIAL BY TEASPOON' by Lynda Rajan, first published in this collection. Copyright © 1995 by Lynda Rajan, printed by permission of the author.

'CYNOSURE' by Kit Reed, first published in the *Magazine of Fantasy and Science Fiction*, 1964, collected in *The Killer Mice* (London: Gollancz, 1976). Copyright © 1964, 1976 by Kit Reed, reprinted by permission of the author.

'THE SECOND INQUISITION' by Joanna Russ, first published in *Orbit 6*, ed. Damon Knight (New York: Berkley, 1970), collected in *The Adventures of Alyx* (New York: Simon & Schuster, 1983).

Copyright © 1970, 1983 by Joanna Russ, reprinted by permission of the author.

'THE WALL' by Josephine Saxton, first published in *Science Fantasy*, 1966, collected in *The Power of Time* (London: Chatto & Windus, 1985). Copyright © 1966 by Josephine Saxton, reprinted by permission of the author.

'MISS PINKERTON'S APOCALYPSE' by Muriel Spark, first published in *The Go-Away Bird and Other Stories* (London: Macmillan, 1958). Copyright © 1958 by Muriel Spark, reprinted by permission of the author and David Higham Associates.

'KAY AND PHIL' by Lucy Sussex, first published in *Alien Shores*, eds. Peter McNamara and Margaret Winch (Adelaide: Aphelion, 1994). Copyright © 1994 by Lucy Sussex, reprinted by permission of the author.

'THE MILK OF PARADISE' by James Tiptree, Jr [Alice Sheldon], first published in *Again, Dangerous Visions*, ed. Harlan Ellison (New York: Doubleday, 1972), collected in *Warm Worlds and Otherwise*, introduced by Robert Silverberg (New York: Ballantine, 1975). Copyright © 1972 by James Tiptree, Jr, reprinted by permission of the Author's Estate and the Estate's agent, Virginia Kidd.

'WIVES' by Lisa Tuttle, first published in the *Magazine of Fantasy and Science Fiction*, 1979, collected in *A Spaceship Built of Stone and Other Stories* (London: The Women's Press, 1987). Copyright © 1979 by The Mercury Press; Copyright © 1983 by Lisa Tuttle, reprinted by permission of the author and the author's agent, A. P. Watt Ltd.

'ANGEL, ALL INNOCENCE' by Fay Weldon, first published in *The Thirteenth Ghost Book*, ed. James Hale (London: Barrie and Jenkins, 1977), collected in *Watching Me, Watching You* (London: Hodder & Stoughton, 1981). Copyright © 1977 by Fay Weldon, reprinted by permission of Sheil Land Associates Ltd.

'BABY, YOU WERE GREAT' by Kate Wilhelm, first published in *Orbit 2*, ed. Damon Knight (New York: Berkley, 1967). Copyright © 1967 by Kate Wilhelm, reprinted by permission of the author.

Introduction

BY JOANNA RUSS

Fantasy is reality. Aristotle says that music is the most realistic of the arts because it represents the movements of the soul directly. Surely the mode of fantasy (which includes many genres and effects) is the only way in which some realities can be treated. I grew up in the United States in the 1950s, in a world in which fantasy was supposed to be the opposite of reality. 'Rational', 'mature' people were concerned only with a narrowly defined 'reality' and only the 'immature' or the 'neurotic' (all-purpose put-downs) had any truck with fantasy, which was then considered to be wishful thinking, escapism and other bad things, attractive only to the weak and damaged. Only Communists, feminists, homosexuals and other deviants were unsatisfied with Things As They Were at the time and Heaven help you if you were one of those.

I took to fantasy like a duckling to water. Unfortunately for me, there was nobody around then to tell me that fantasy was the most realistic of the arts, expressing as it does the contents of human souls directly.

The impulse behind fantasy I find to be dissatisfaction with literary realism. Realism leaves out so much. Any consensual reality (though wider even than realism) nonetheless leaves out a great deal also. Certainly one solution to the difficulty of treating experience that is not dealt with in the literary tradition, or even in consensual reality itself, is to 'skew' the reality of a piece of fiction, that is, to employ fantasy.

Sometimes authors can't face the full reality of what they feel or know and can therefore express that reality only through hints and guesses. Fantasies often fit this pattern, for example, Edith Wharton's fine ghost story, 'Afterwards'. Wharton can't afford to investigate too explicitly the assumptions and values of the society which provided her with money and position; so although the story 'knows' in a sense that the artistic culture of the wealthy depends on devastatingly brutal commercial practices, none of this can be as explicit as, say, Sylvia Townsend Warner's wonderful historical novel, *Summer will Show*, in which the mid-nineteenth-century heroine ends by reading the *Communist Manifesto*.

But there are other stories, quite as 'Gothic' in method and tone, which do not fit this pattern. Authors may know what their experience is and yet be unable to name it, not because it is unconscious or unfaceable, but because it is not majority experience. Shirley Jackson strikes me as a writer who does both: for example, clearly portraying Eleanor (in *The Haunting of Hill House*) as an abused child long before the phrase itself was invented, occasionally using material she doesn't really seem to have understood; and sometimes dislocating reality because conventional forms simply will not express the kind of experience she knows exists. After all, reality is – collectively speaking – a social invention and is not itself really real. Individually, it is as much something human beings do as it is something refractory that is prior to us and outside of us. Some artists, like Angela Carter, even use flamboyant appeals to 'unconscious' content to conceal very non-psychological meanings . . . and giggle as they do so.

And sometimes, of course, authors write fantasy because the punch is clearer and harder that way. It would take a bold critic, for example, to read *unconscious* content into some of the stories in this book, for example, Suzy McKee Charnas's 'Boobs' or the irony of the last line of Ursula Le Guin's 'Sur'. They are very conscious.

This brings us to the subject of women.

When I was seventeen and in a writing class in college, I learned that the kind of things I wrote about – things that came out of my experience as a seventeen-year-old girl – were not serious literary subjects. My realism wouldn't do. So I decided at some point to write fantasy and science fiction. (I did love them!) Nobody could pull me up on the importance or the accuracy of those. The stories in this book are here because they are good stories and because they are part of a fascinating tradition of fantasy. But they are also here (I suspect) because many fine writers who are women have discovered that fantasy, fantastic elements and methods, or simply even the tone of fantasy, give them the method to handle the specifically female elements of their experience in a way that our literary tradition of realism was designed not to do.

And I once thought I was the only one!

Editors' Note

In this book we have taken a broad view of what constitutes fantasy. There are stories from various different literary genres, as well as 'fantastic' departures from mainstream fiction. But since lines have to be drawn somewhere, we have confined our choices to stories that were written originally in English.

The stories are arranged in chronological order, from the Second World War to the present day. We make no claim that the selection is exhaustive or 'representative'; with such a pervasive element as fantasy, that would be impossible – even in a volume of this size. Rather, the book offers a sampling of the diverse ways in which women writers have used the fantastic in their writing in modern times.

For their special help, advice and support, we should like to thank Tendayi Bloom, Luigi Bonomi, David R. Hartwell, Virginia Kidd, Ursula K. Le Guin, Ann Oakley, Joanna Russ, Lucy Sussex and Howard Watson.

A. S. W. and R. G. J.

The Demon Lover

(1941)

ELIZABETH BOWEN

Towards the end of her day in London Mrs Drover went round to her shut-up house to look for several things she wanted to take away. Some belonged to herself, some to her family, who were by now used to their country life. It was late August; it had been a steamy, showery day: at the moment the trees down the pavement glittered in an escape of humid yellow afternoon sun. Against the next batch of clouds, already piling up ink-dark, broken chimneys and parapets stood out. In her once familiar street, as in any unused channel, an unfamiliar queerness had silted up; a cat wove itself in and out of railings, but no human eye watched Mrs Drover's return. Shifting some parcels under her arm, she slowly forced round her latchkey in an unwilling lock, then gave the door, which had warped, a push with her knee. Dead air came out to meet her as she went in.

The staircase window having been boarded up, no light came down into the hall. But one door, she could just see, stood ajar, so she went quickly through into the room and unshuttered the big window in there. Now the prosaic woman, looking about her, was more perplexed than she knew by everything that she saw, by traces of her long former habit of life – the yellow smoke-stain up the white marble mantelpiece, the ring left by a vase on the top of the escritoire; the bruise in the wallpaper where, on the door being thrown open widely, the china handle had always hit the wall. The piano, having gone away to be stored, had left what looked like claw-marks on its part of the parquet. Though not much dust had seeped in, each object wore a film of another kind; and the only ventilation being the chimney, the whole drawing-room smelled of the cold hearth. Mrs Drover put down her parcels on the escritoire and left the room to proceed upstairs; the things she wanted were in a bedroom chest.

She had been anxious to see how the house was – the part-time caretaker she shared with some neighbours was away this week on his holiday, known to be not yet back. At the best of times he did not look in often, and she was never sure that she trusted him. There were some cracks in the structure, left by the last bombing, on which she was anxious to keep an eye. Not that one could do anything –

A shaft of refracted daylight now lay across the hall. She stopped dead and stared at the hall table – on this lay a letter addressed to her.

She thought first – then the caretaker *must* be back. All the same, who, seeing the house shuttered, would have dropped a letter in at the box? It was not a circular, it was not a bill. And the post office redirected, to the address in the country, everything for her that came through the post. The caretaker (even if he *were* back) did not know she was due in London today – her call here had been planned to be a surprise – so his negligence in the manner of this letter, leaving it to wait in the dusk and the dust, annoyed her. Annoyed, she picked up the letter, which bore no stamp. But it cannot be important, or they would know . . . She took the letter rapidly upstairs with her, without a stop to look at the writing till she reached what had been her bedroom, where she let in light. The room looked over the garden and other gardens: the sun had gone in; as the clouds sharpened and lowered, the trees and rank lawns seemed already to smoke with dark. Her reluctance to look again at the letter came from the fact that she felt intruded upon – and by someone contemptuous of her ways. However, in the tenseness preceding the fall of rain she read it: it was a few lines.

Dear Kathleen: You will not have forgotten that today is our anniversary, and the day we said. The years have gone by at once slowly and fast. In view of the fact that nothing has changed, I shall rely upon you to keep your promise. I was sorry to see you leave London, but was satisfied that you would be back in time. You may expect me, therefore, at the hour arranged. Until then . . . K.

Mrs Drover looked for the date: it was today's. She dropped the letter on to the bed-springs, then picked it up to see the writing again – her lips, beneath the remains of lipstick, beginning to go white. She felt so much the change in her own face that she went to the mirror, polished a clear patch in it and looked at once urgently and stealthily in. She was confronted by a woman of forty-four, with eyes starting out under a hat-brim that had been rather carelessly pulled down. She had not put on any more powder since she left the shop where she ate her solitary tea. The pearls her husband had given her on their marriage hung loose round her now rather thinner throat, slipping in the V of the pink wool jumper her sister knitted last autumn as they sat round the fire. Mrs Drover's most normal expression was one of controlled worry, but of assent. Since the birth of the third of her little boys, attended by a quite serious illness, she had had an intermittent muscular flicker to the left of her mouth, but in spite of this she could always sustain a manner that was at once energetic and calm.

Turning from her own face as precipitately as she had gone to meet it, she went to the chest where the things were, unlocked it, threw up the lid and knelt to search. But as rain began to come crashing down she could not keep from looking over her shoulder at the stripped bed on which the letter lay. Behind the blanket of rain the clock of the church that still stood struck six – with rapidly heightening apprehension she counted each of the slow strokes. 'The hour arranged . . . My God,' she said, '*what* hour? How should I . . .? After twenty-five years . . .'

The young girl talking to the soldier in the garden had not ever completely seen his face. It was dark; they were saying goodbye under a tree. Now and then – for it felt, from not seeing him at this intense moment, as though she had never seen him at all – she verified his presence for these few moments longer by putting out a hand, which he each time pressed, without very much kindness, and painfully, on to one of the breast buttons of his uniform. That cut of the button on the palm of her hand was, principally, what she was to carry away. This was so near the end of a leave from France that she could only wish him already gone. It was August 1916. Being not kissed, being drawn away from and looked at intimidated Kathleen till she imagined spectral glitters in the place of his eyes. Turning away and looking back up the lawn she saw, through branches of trees, the drawing-room window alight: she caught a breath for the moment when she could go running back there into the safe arms of her mother and sister, and cry: 'What shall I do, what shall I do? He has gone.'

Hearing her catch her breath, her fiancé said, without feeling: 'Cold?'

'You're going away such a long way.'

'Not so far as you think.'

'I don't understand.'

'You don't have to,' he said. 'You will. You know what we said.'

'But that was – suppose you – I mean, suppose.'

'I shall be with you,' he said, 'sooner or later. You won't forget that. You need do nothing but wait.'

Only a little more than a minute later she was free to run up the silent lawn. Looking in through the window at her mother and sister, who did not for the moment perceive her, she already felt that unnatural promise drive down between her and the rest of all human kind. No other way of having given herself could have made her feel so apart, lost and foresworn. She could not have plighted a more sinister troth.

Kathleen behaved well when, some months later, her fiancé was reported missing, presumed killed. Her family not only supported her but were able to praise her courage without stint because they could not regret, as a husband for her, the man they knew almost nothing about. They hoped she would, in a year or two, console herself – and had it been only a question of consolation things might have gone much straighter ahead. But her trouble, behind just a little grief, was a complete dislocation from everything. She did not reject other lovers, for these failed to appear: for years she failed to attract men – and with the approach of her thirties she became natural enough to share her family's anxiousness on this score. She began to put herself out, to wonder; and at thirty-two she was very greatly relieved to find herself being courted by William Drover. She married him, and the two of them settled down in this quiet, arboreal part of Kensington: in this house the years piled up, her children were born and they all lived till they were driven out by the bombs of the next war. Her movements as

Mrs Drover were circumscribed, and she dismissed any idea that they were still watched.

As things were – dead or living the letter-writer sent her only a threat. Unable, for some minutes, to go on kneeling with her back exposed to the empty room, Mrs Drover rose from the chest to sit on an upright chair whose back was firmly against the wall. The desuetude of her former bedroom, her married London home's whole air of being a cracked cup from which memory, with its reassuring power, had either evaporated or leaked away, made a crisis – and at just this crisis the letter-writer had, knowledgeably, struck. The hollowness of the house this evening cancelled years on years of voices, habits and steps. Through the shut windows she only heard rain fall on the roofs around. To rally herself, she said she was in a mood – and, for two or three seconds shutting her eyes, told herself that she had imagined the letter. But she opened them – there it lay on the bed.

On the supernatural side of the letter's entrance she was not permitting her mind to dwell. Who, in London, knew she meant to call at the house today? Evidently, however, this had been known. The caretaker, *had* he come back, had had no cause to expect her: he would have taken the letter in his pocket, to forward it, at his own time, through the post. There was no other sign that the caretaker had been in – but, if not? Letters dropped in at doors of deserted houses do not fly or walk to tables in halls. They do not sit on the dust of empty tables with the air of certainty that they will be found. There is needed some human hand – but nobody but the caretaker had a key. Under circumstances she did not care to consider, a house can be entered without a key. It was possible that she was not alone now. She might be being waited for, downstairs. Waited for – until when? Until 'the hour arranged'. At least that was not six o'clock: six has struck.

She rose from the chair and went over and locked the door.

The thing was, to get out. To fly? No, not that: she had to catch her train. As a woman whose utter dependability was the keystone of her family life she was not willing to return to the country, to her husband, her little boys and her sister, without the objects she had come up to fetch. Resuming work at the chest she set about making up a number of parcels in a rapid, fumbling-decisive way. These, with her shopping parcels, would be too much to carry; these meant a taxi – at the thought of the taxi her heart went up and her normal breathing resumed. I will ring up the taxi now; the taxi cannot come too soon: I shall hear the taxi out there running its engine, till I walk calmly down to it through the hall. I'll ring up – But no: the telephone is cut off . . . She tugged at a knot she had tied wrong.

The idea of flight . . . He was never kind to me, not really. I don't remember him kind at all. Mother said he never considered me. He was set on me, that was what it was – not love. Not love, not meaning a person well. What did he do, to make me promise like that? I can't remember – but she found that she could.

She remembered with such dreadful acuteness that the twenty-five years since then dissolved like smoke and she instinctively looked for the weal left by the button on the palm of her hand. She remembered not only all that he said and did but the complete suspension of *her* existence during that August week. I was not myself – they all told me so at the time. She remembered – but with one white burning blank as where acid has dropped on a photograph: *under no conditions* could she remember his face.

So, wherever he may be waiting, I shall not know him. You have no time to run from a face you do not expect.

The thing was to get to the taxi before any clock struck what could be the hour. She would slip down the street and round the side of the square to where the square gave on the main road. She would return in the taxi, safe, to her own door, and bring the solid driver into the house with her to pick up the parcels from room to room. The idea of the taxi driver made her decisive, bold: she unlocked her door, went to the top of the staircase and listened down.

She heard nothing – but while she was hearing nothing the *passé* air of the staircase was disturbed by a draught that travelled up to her face. It emanated from the basement: down there a door or window was being opened by someone who chose this moment to leave the house.

The rain had stopped; the pavements steamily shone as Mrs Drover let herself out by inches from her own front door into the empty street. The unoccupied houses opposite continued to meet her look with their damaged stare. Making towards the thoroughfare and the taxi, she tried not to keep looking behind. Indeed, the silence was so intense – one of those creeks of London silence exaggerated this summer by the damage of war – that no tread could have gained on hers unheard. Where her street debouched on the square where people went on living, she grew conscious of, and checked, her unnatural pace. Across the open end of the square two buses impassively passed each other: women, a perambulator, cyclists, a man wheeling a barrow signalized, once again, the ordinary flow of life. At the square's most populous corner should be – and was – the short taxi rank. This evening, only one taxi – but this, although it presented its blank rump, appeared already to be alertly waiting for her. Indeed, without looking round the driver started his engine as she panted up from behind and put her hand on the door. As she did so, the clock struck seven. The taxi faced the main road: to make the trip back to her house it would have to turn – she had settled back on the seat and the taxi *had* turned before she, surprised by its knowing movement, recollected that she had not 'said where'. She leaned forward to scratch at the glass panel that divided the driver's head from her own.

The driver braked to what was almost a stop, turned round and slid the glass panel back: the jolt of this flung Mrs Drover forward till her face was almost into the glass. Through the aperture driver and passenger, not six inches between them, remained for an eternity eye to eye, Mrs Drover's mouth hung open for some seconds before she could issue her first scream. After that she continued to scream freely and to beat with her gloved hands on the glass all round as the taxi, accelerating without mercy, made off with her into the hinterland of deserted streets.

The Tooth

(1948)

SHIRLEY JACKSON

The bus was waiting, panting heavily at the curb in front of the small bus station, its great blue-and-silver bulk glittering in the moonlight. There were only a few people interested in the bus, and at that time of the night no one passing on the sidewalk: the one movie theatre in town had finished its show and closed its doors an hour before, and all the movie patrons had been to the drugstore for ice cream and gone home; now the drugstore was closed and dark, another silent doorway in the long midnight street. The only town lights were the street lights, the lights in the all-night lunch-stand across the street, and the one remaining counter lamp in the bus station where the girl sat in the ticket office with her hat and coat on, only waiting for the New York bus to leave before she went home to bed.

Standing on the sidewalk next to the open door of the bus, Clara Spencer held her husband's arm nervously. 'I feel so funny,' she said.

'Are you all right?' he asked. 'Do you think I ought to go with you?'

'No, of course not,' she said. 'I'll be all right.' It was hard for her to talk because of her swollen jaw; she kept a handkerchief pressed to her face and held hard to her husband. 'Are you sure *you*'ll be all right?' she asked. 'I'll be back tomorrow night at the latest. Or else I'll call.'

'Everything will be fine,' he said heartily. 'By tomorrow noon it'll all be gone. Tell the dentist if there's anything wrong I can come right down.'

'I feel so funny,' she said. 'Light-headed, and sort of dizzy.'

'That's because of the dope,' he said. 'All that codeine, and the whisky, and nothing to eat all day.'

She giggled nervously. 'I couldn't comb my hair, my hand shook so. I'm glad it's dark.'

'Try to sleep in the bus,' he said. 'Did you take a sleeping pill?'

'Yes,' she said. They were waiting for the bus driver to finish his cup of coffee in the lunchstand; they could see him through the glass window, sitting at the counter, taking his time. 'I feel so *funny*,' she said.

'You know, Clara,' he made his voice very weighty, as though if he spoke more seriously his words would carry more conviction and be therefore more comforting, 'you know, I'm glad you're going down to New York to have Zimmerman take care of this. I'd never forgive myself if it turned out to be something serious and I let you go to this butcher up here.'

'It's just a *toothache*,' Clara said uneasily, 'nothing very serious about a *toothache*.'

'You can't tell,' he said. 'It might be abscessed or something; I'm sure he'll have to pull it.'

'Don't even talk like that,' she said, and shivered.

'Well, it looks pretty bad,' he said soberly, as before. 'Your face so swollen, and all. Don't you worry.'

'I'm not worrying,' she said. 'I just feel as if I were all tooth. Nothing else.'

The bus driver got up from the stool and walked over to pay his check. Clara moved toward the bus, and her husband said, 'Take your time, you've got plenty of time.'

'I just feel funny,' Clara said.

'Listen,' her husband said, 'that tooth's been bothering you off and on for years; at least six or seven times since I've known you you've had trouble with that tooth. It's about time something was done. You had a toothache on our honeymoon,' he finished accusingly.

'Did I?' Clara said. 'You know,' she went on, and laughed, 'I was in such a hurry I didn't dress properly. I have on old stockings and I just dumped everything into my good pocketbook.'

'Are you sure you have enough money?' he said.

'Almost twenty-five dollars,' Clara said. 'I'll be home tomorrow.'

'Wire if you need more,' he said. The bus driver appeared in the doorway of the lunchroom. 'Don't worry,' he said.

'Listen,' Clara said suddenly, 'are you *sure* you'll be all right? Mrs Lang will be over in the morning in time to make breakfast, and Johnny doesn't need to go to school if things are too mixed up.'

'I know,' he said.

'Mrs Lang,' she said, checking on her fingers. 'I called Mrs Lang, I left the grocery order on the kitchen table, you can have the cold tongue for lunch and in case I don't get back Mrs Lang will give you dinner. The cleaner ought to come about four o'clock, I won't be back so give him your brown suit and it doesn't matter if you forget but be sure to empty the pockets.'

'Wire if you need more money,' he said. 'Or call. I'll stay home tomorrow so you can call at home.'

'Mrs Lang will take care of the baby,' she said.

'Or you can wire,' he said.

The bus driver came across the street and stood by the entrance to the bus.

'Okay?' the bus driver said.

'Goodbye,' Clara said to her husband.

'You'll feel all right tomorrow,' her husband said. 'It's only a toothache.'

'I'm fine,' Clara said. 'Don't you worry.' She got on the bus and then stopped, with the bus driver waiting behind her. 'Milkman,' she said to her husband. 'Leave a note telling him we want eggs.'

'I will,' her husband said. 'Goodbye.'

'Goodbye,' Clara said. She moved on into the bus and behind her the driver swung into his seat. The bus was nearly empty and she went far back and sat down at the window outside which her husband waited. 'Goodbye,' she said to him through the glass, 'take care of yourself.'

'Goodbye,' he said, waving violently.

The bus stirred, groaned, and pulled itself forward. Clara turned her head to wave goodbye once more and then lay back against the heavy soft seat. Good Lord, she thought, what a thing to do! Outside, the familiar street slipped past, strange and dark and seen, unexpectedly, from the unique station of a person leaving town, going away on a bus. It isn't as though it's the first time

I've ever been to New York, Clara thought indignantly, it's the whisky and the codeine and the sleeping pill and the toothache. She checked hastily to see if her codeine tablets were in her pocketbook; they had been standing, along with the aspirin and a glass of water, on the dining-room sideboard, but somewhere in the lunatic flight from her home she must have picked them up, because they were in her pocketbook now, along with the twenty-odd dollars and her compact and comb and lipstick. She could tell from the feel of the lipstick that she had brought the old, nearly finished one, not the new one that was a darker shade and had cost two-fifty. There was a run in her stocking and a hole in the toe that she never noticed at home wearing her old comfortable shoes, but which was now suddenly and disagreeably apparent inside her best walking shoes. Well, she thought, I can buy new stockings in New York tomorrow, after the tooth is fixed, after everything's all right. She put her tongue cautiously on the tooth and was rewarded with a split-second crash of pain.

The bus stopped at a red light and the driver got out of his seat and came back toward her. 'Forgot to get your ticket before,' he said.

'I guess I was a little rushed at the last minute,' she said. She found the ticket in her coat pocket and gave it to him. 'When do we get to New York?' she asked.

'Five-fifteen,' he said. 'Plenty of time for breakfast. One-way ticket?'

'I'm coming back by train,' she said, without seeing why she had to tell him, except that it was late at night and people isolated together in some strange prison like a bus had to be more friendly and communicative than at other times.

'Me, I'm coming back by bus,' he said, and they both laughed, she painfully because of her swollen face. When he went back to his seat far away at the front of the bus she lay back peacefully against the seat. She could feel the sleeping pill pulling at her; the throb of the toothache was distant now, and mingled with the movement of the bus, a steady beat like her heartbeat which she could hear louder and louder, going on through the night. She put her head back and her feet up, discreetly covered with her skirt, and fell asleep without saying goodbye to the town.

She opened her eyes once and they were moving almost silently through the darkness. Her tooth was pulsing steadily and she turned her cheek against the cool back of the seat in weary resignation. There was a thin line of lights along the ceiling of the bus and no other light. Far ahead of her in the bus she could see the other people sitting; the driver, so far away as to be only a tiny figure at the end of a telescope, was straight at the wheel, seemingly awake. She fell back into her fantastic sleep.

She woke up later because the bus had stopped, the end of that silent motion through the darkness so positive a shock that it woke her stunned, and it was a minute before the ache began again. People were moving along the aisle of the bus and the driver, turning around, said, 'Fifteen minutes.' She got up and followed everyone else out, all but her eyes still asleep, her feet moving without awareness. They were stopped beside an all-night restaurant, lonely and lighted on the vacant road. Inside, it was warm and busy and full of people. She saw a seat at the end of the counter and sat down, not aware that she had fallen asleep again when someone sat down next to her and touched her arm. When she looked around foggily he said, 'Travelling far?'

'Yes,' she said.

He was wearing a blue suit and he looked tall; she could not focus her eyes to see any more.

'You want coffee?' he asked.

She nodded and he pointed to the counter in front of her where a cup of coffee sat steaming.

'Drink it quickly,' he said.

She sipped at it delicately; she may have put her face down and tasted it without lifting the cup. The strange man was talking.

'Even farther than Samarkand,' he was saying, 'and the waves ringing on the shore like bells.'

'Okay, folks,' the bus driver said, and she gulped quickly at the coffee, drank enough to get her back into the bus.

When she sat down in her seat again the strange man sat down beside her. It was so dark in the bus that the lights from the restaurant were unbearably glaring and she closed her eyes. When her eyes were shut, before she fell asleep, she was closed in alone with the toothache.

'The flutes play all night,' the strange man said, 'and the stars are as big as the moon and the moon is as big as a lake.'

As the bus started up again they slipped back into the darkness and only the thin thread of lights along the ceiling of the bus held them together, brought the back of the bus where she sat along with the front of the bus where the driver sat and the people sitting there so far away from her. The lights tied them together and the strange man next to her was saying, 'Nothing to do all day but lie under the trees.'

Inside the bus, travelling on, she was nothing; she was passing the trees and the occasional sleeping houses, and she was in the bus but she was between here and there, joined tenuously to the bus driver by a thread of lights, being carried along without effort of her own.

'My name is Jim,' the strange man said.

She was so deeply asleep that she stirred uneasily without knowledge, her forehead against the window, the darkness moving along beside her.

Then again that numbing shock, and, driven awake, she said, frightened, 'What's happened?'

'It's all right,' the strange man – Jim – said immediately. 'Come along.'

She followed him out of the bus, into the same restaurant, seemingly, but when she started to sit down at the same seat at the end of the counter he took her hand and led her to a table. 'Go and wash your face,' he said. 'Come back here afterward.'

She went into the ladies' room and there was a girl standing there powdering her nose. Without turning around the girl said, 'Costs a nickel. Leave the door fixed so's the next one won't have to pay.'

The door was wedged so it would not close, with half a match folder in the lock. She left it the same way and went back to the table where Jim was sitting.

'What do you want?' she said, and he pointed to another cup of coffee and a sandwich. 'Go ahead,' he said.

While she was eating her sandwich she heard his voice, musical and soft, 'And while we were sailing past the island we heard a voice calling us . . .'

Back in the bus Jim said, 'Put your head on my shoulder now, and go to sleep.'

'I'm all right,' she said.

'No,' Jim said. 'Before, your head was rattling against the window.'

Once more she slept, and once more the bus stopped and she woke frightened, and Jim brought her again to a restaurant and more coffee. Her tooth came alive then, and with one hand pressing her cheek she searched through the pockets of her coat and then through her pocketbook until she found the little bottle of codeine pills and she took two while Jim watched her.

She was finishing her coffee when she heard the sound of the bus motor and she started up suddenly, hurrying, and with Jim holding her arm she fled back into the dark shelter of her seat. The bus was moving forward when she realized that she had left her bottle of codeine pills sitting on the table in the restaurant and now she was at the mercy of her tooth. For a minute she stared back at the lights of the restaurant through the bus window and then she put her head on Jim's shoulder and he was saying as she fell asleep, 'The sand is so white it looks like snow, but it's hot, even at night it's hot under your feet.'

Then they stopped for the last time, and Jim brought her out of the bus and they stood for a minute in New York together. A woman passing them in the station said to the man following her with suitcases, 'We're just on time, it's five-fifteen.'

'I'm going to the dentist,' she said to Jim.

'I know,' he said. 'I'll watch out for you.'

He went away, although she did not see him go. She thought to watch for his blue suit going through the door, but there was nothing.

I ought to have thanked him, she thought stupidly, and went slowly into the station restaurant, where she ordered coffee again. The counter man looked at her with the worn sympathy of one who has spent a long night watching people get off and on buses. 'Sleepy?' he asked.

'Yes,' she said.

She discovered after a while that the bus station joined Pennsylvania Terminal and she was able to get into the main waiting-room and find a seat on one of the benches by the time she fell asleep again.

Then someone shook her rudely by the shoulder and said, 'What train you taking, lady, it's nearly seven.' She sat up and saw her pocketbook on her lap, her feet neatly crossed, a clock glaring into her face. She said, 'Thank you,' and got up and walked blindly past the benches and got on to the escalator. Someone got on immediately behind her and touched her arm; she turned and it was Jim. 'The grass is so green and so soft,' he said, smiling, 'and the water of the river is so cool.'

She stared at him tiredly. When the escalator reached the top she stepped off and started to walk to the street she saw ahead. Jim came along beside her and his voice went on, 'The sky is bluer than anything you've ever seen, and the songs . . .'

She stepped quickly away from him and thought that people were looking at her as they passed. She stood on the corner waiting for the light to change and Jim came swiftly up to her and then away. 'Look,' he said as he passed, and he held out a handful of pearls.

Across the street there was a restaurant, just opening. She went in and sat down at a table, and a waitress was standing beside her frowning. 'You was asleep,' the waitress said accusingly.

'I'm very sorry,' she said. It was morning. 'Poached eggs and coffee, please.'

It was a quarter to eight when she left the restaurant, and she thought, if I take a bus, and go straight downtown now, I can sit in the drugstore across the street from the dentist's office and have more coffee until about eight-thirty and then go into the dentist's when it opens and he can take me first.

The buses were beginning to fill up; she got into the first bus that came along and could not find a seat. She wanted to go to Twenty-third Street, and got a seat just as they were passing Twenty-sixth Street; when she woke she was so far downtown that it took her nearly half an hour to find a bus and get back to Twenty-third.

At the corner of Twenty-third Street, while she was waiting for the light to change, she was caught up in a crowd of people, and when they crossed the street and separated to go different directions someone fell into step beside her. For a minute she walked on without looking up, staring resentfully at the sidewalk, her tooth burning her, and then she looked up, but there was no blue suit among the people pressing by on either side.

When she turned into the office building where her dentist was, it was still very early morning. The doorman in the office building was freshly shaven and his hair was combed; he held the door open briskly, as at five o'clock he would be sluggish, his hair faintly out of place. She went in through the door with a feeling of achievement; she had come successfully from one place to another, and this was the end of her journey and her objective.

The clean white nurse sat at the desk in the office; her eyes took in the swollen cheek, the tired shoulders, and she said, 'You poor thing, you look worn out.'

'I have a toothache.' The nurse half-smiled, as though she were still waiting for the day when someone would come in and say, 'My feet hurt.' She stood up into the professional sunlight. 'Come right in,' she said. 'We won't make you wait.'

There was sunlight on the headrest of the dentist's chair, on the round white table, on the drill bending its smooth chromium head. The dentist smiled with the same tolerance as the nurse; perhaps all human ailments were contained in the teeth, and he could fix them if people would only come to him in time. The nurse said smoothly, 'I'll get her file, doctor. We thought we'd better bring her right in.'

She felt, while they were taking an X-ray, that there was nothing in her head to stop the malicious eye of the camera, as though the camera would look through her and photograph the nails in the wall next to her, or the dentist's cuff buttons, or the small thin bones of the dentist's instruments; the dentist said, 'Extraction,' regretfully to the nurse, and the nurse said, 'Yes, doctor, I'll call them right away.'

Her tooth, which had brought her here unerringly, seemed now the only part of her to have any identity. It seemed to have had its picture taken without her; it was the important creature which must be recorded and examined and gratified; she was only its unwilling vehicle, and only as such was she of interest to the dentist and the nurse, only as the bearer of her tooth was she worth their immediate and practised attention. The dentist handed her a slip of paper with the picture of a full set of teeth drawn on it; her living tooth was checked with a black mark, and across the top of the paper was written 'Lower molar; extraction.'

'Take this slip,' the dentist said, 'and go right up to the address on this card; it's a surgeon dentist. They'll take care of you there.'

'What will they do?' she said. Not the question she wanted to ask, not: What about me? or, How far down do the roots go?

'They'll take that tooth out,' the dentist said testily, turning away. 'Should have been done years ago.'

I've stayed too long, she thought, he's tired of my tooth. She got up out of the dentist's chair and said, 'Thank you. Goodbye.'

'Goodbye,' the dentist said. At the last minute he smiled at her, showing her his full white teeth, all in perfect control.

'Are you all right? Does it bother you too much?' the nurse asked.

'I'm all right.'

'I can give you some codeine tablets,' the nurse said. 'We'd rather you didn't take anything right now, of course, but I think I could let you have them if the tooth is really bad.'

'No,' she said, remembering her little bottle of codeine pills on the table of a restaurant between here and there. 'No, it doesn't bother me too much.'

'Well,' the nurse said, 'good luck.'

She went down the stairs and out past the doorman; in the fifteen minutes she had been upstairs he had lost a little of his pristine morningness, and his bow was just a fraction smaller than before.

'Taxi?' he asked, and remembering the bus down to Twenty-third Street, she said, 'Yes.'

Just as the doorman came back from the curb, bowing to the taxi he seemed to believe he had invented, she thought a hand waved to her from the crowd across the street.

She read the address on the card the dentist had given her and repeated it carefully to the taxi driver. With the card and the little slip of paper with 'lower molar' written on it and her tooth identified so clearly, she sat without moving, her hands still around the papers, her eyes almost closed. She thought she must have been asleep again when the taxi stopped suddenly, and the driver, reaching around to open the door, said, 'Here we are, lady.' He looked at her curiously.

'I'm going to have a tooth pulled,' she said.

'Jesus,' the taxi driver said. She paid him and he said, 'Good luck,' as he slammed the door.

This was a strange building, the entrance flanked by medical signs carved in stone; the doorman here was faintly professional, as though he were competent to prescribe if she did not care to go any farther. She went past him, going straight ahead until an elevator opened its door to her. In the elevator she showed the elevator man the card and he said, 'Seventh floor.'

She had to back up in the elevator for a nurse to wheel in an old lady in a wheelchair. The old lady was calm and restful, sitting there in the elevator with a rug over her knees; she said, 'Nice day' to the elevator operator and he said, 'Good to see the sun,' and then the old lady lay back in her chair and the nurse straightened the rug around her knees and said, 'Now we're not going to worry,' and the old lady said irritably, 'Who's worrying?'

They got out at the fourth floor. The elevator went on up and then the operator said, 'Seven,' and the elevator stopped and the door opened.

'Straight down the hall and to your left,' the operator said.

There were closed doors on either side of the hall. Some of them said 'DDS', some of them said 'Clinic', some of them said 'X-Ray'. One of them, looking wholesome and friendly and somehow most comprehensible, said 'Ladies'. Then she turned to the left and found a door with the name on the card and she opened it and went in. There was a nurse sitting behind a glass window, almost as in a bank, and potted palms in tubs in the corners of the waiting-room, and new magazines and comfortable chairs. The nurse behind the glass window said, 'Yes?' as though you had overdrawn your account with the dentist and were two teeth in arrears.

She handed her slip of paper through the glass window and the nurse looked at it and said, 'Lower molar, yes. They called about you. Will you come right in, please? Through the door to your left.'

Into the vault? she almost said, and then silently opened the door and went in. Another nurse was waiting, and she smiled and turned, expecting to be followed, with no visible doubt about her right to lead.

There was another X-ray, and the nurse told another nurse: 'Lower molar,' and the other nurse said, 'Come this way, please.'

There were labyrinths and passages, seeming to lead into the heart of the office building, and she was put, finally, in a cubicle where there was a couch with a pillow and a wash-basin and a chair.

'Wait here,' the nurse said. 'Relax if you can.'

'I'll probably go to sleep,' she said.

'Fine,' the nurse said. 'You won't have to wait long.'

She waited, probably, for over an hour, although she spent the time half-sleeping, waking only when someone passed the door; occasionally the nurse looked in and smiled; once she said, 'Won't have to wait much longer.' Then, suddenly the nurse was back, no longer smiling, no longer the good hostess, but efficient and hurried. 'Come along,' she said, and moved purposefully out of the little room into the hallways again.

Then, quickly, more quickly than she was able to see, she was sitting in the chair and there was a towel around her head and a towel under her chin and the nurse was leaning a hand on her shoulder.

'Will it hurt?' she asked.

'No,' the nurse said, smiling. 'You know it won't hurt, don't you?'

'Yes,' she said.

The dentist came in and smiled down on her from over her head. 'Well,' he said.

'Will it hurt?' she said.

'Now,' he said cheerfully, 'we couldn't stay in business if we hurt people.' All the time he talked he was busying himself with metal hidden under a towel, a great machinery being wheeled in almost silently behind her. 'We couldn't stay in business at all,' he said. 'All you've got to worry about is telling us all your secrets while you're asleep. Want to watch out for that, you know. Lower molar?' he said to the nurse.

'Lower molar, doctor,' she said.

Then they put the metal-tasting rubber mask over her face and the dentist said, 'You know,' two or three times absentmindedly while she could still see him over the mask. The nurse said 'Relax your hands, dear,' and after a long time she felt her fingers relaxing.

First of all things get so far away, she thought, remember this. And remember the metallic sound and taste of all of it. And the outrage.

And then the whirling music, the ringing confusedly loud music that went on and on, around and around, and she was running as fast as she could down a long horribly clear hallway with doors on both sides and at the end of the hallway was Jim, holding out his hands and laughing, and calling something she could never hear because of the loud music, and she was running and then she said, 'I'm not afraid,' and someone from the door next to her took her arm and pulled her through and the world widened alarmingly until it would never stop and then it stopped with the head of the dentist looking down at her and the window dropped into place in front of her and the nurse was holding her arm.

'Why did you pull me back?' she said, and her mouth was full of blood. 'I wanted to go on.'

'I didn't pull you,' the nurse said, but the dentist said, 'She's not out of it yet.'

She began to cry without moving and felt the tears rolling down her face and the nurse wiped them off with a towel. There was no blood anywhere around except in her mouth; everything was as clean as before. The dentist was gone, suddenly, and the nurse put out her arm and helped her out of the chair. 'Did I talk?' she asked suddenly, anxiously. 'Did I say anything?'

'You said, "I'm not afraid,"' the nurse said soothingly. 'Just as you were coming out of it.'

'No,' she said, stopping to pull at the arm around her. 'Did I *say* anything? Did I say where he is?'

'You didn't say *anything*,' the nurse said. 'The doctor was only teasing you.'

'Where's my tooth?' she asked suddenly, and the nurse laughed and said, 'All gone. Never bother you again.'

She was back in the cubicle, and she lay down on the couch and cried, and the nurse brought her whisky in a paper cup and set it on the edge of the wash-basin.

'God has given me blood to drink,' she said to the nurse, and the nurse said. 'Don't rinse your mouth or it won't clot.'

After a long time the nurse came back and said to her from the doorway, smiling, 'I see you're awake again.'

'Why?' she said.

'You've been asleep,' the nurse said. 'I didn't want to wake you.'

She sat up; she was dizzy and it seemed that she had been in the cubicle all her life.

'Do you want to come along now?' the nurse said, all kindness again. She held out the same arm, strong enough to guide any wavering footstep; this time they went back through the long corridor to where the nurse sat behind the bank window.

'All through?' this nurse said brightly. 'Sit down a minute, then.' She indicated a chair next to the glass window, and turned away to write busily. 'Do not rinse your mouth for two hours,' she said, without turning around. 'Take a laxative tonight, take two aspirin if there is any pain. If there is much pain or excessive bleeding, notify this office at once. All right?' she said, and smiled brightly again.

There was a new little slip of paper; this one said, 'Extraction,' and underneath, 'Do not rinse mouth. Take mild laxative. Two aspirin for pain. If pain is excessive or any hemorrhage occurs, notify office.'

'Goodbye,' the nurse said pleasantly.

'Goodbye,' she said.

With the little slip of paper in her hand, she went out through the glass door and, still almost asleep, turned the corner and started down the hall. When she opened her eyes a little and saw that it was a long hall with doorways on either side, she stopped and then saw the door marked 'Ladies' and went in. Inside there was a vast room with windows and wicker chairs and glaring white tiles and glittering silver faucets; there were four or five women around the wash-basins, combing their hair, putting on lipstick. She went directly to the nearest of the three wash-basins, took a paper towel, dropped her pocketbook and the little slip of paper on the floor next to her, and fumbled with the faucets, soaking the towel until it was dripping. Then she slapped it against her face violently. Her eyes cleared and she felt fresher, so she soaked the paper again and rubbed her face with it. She felt out blindly for another paper towel, and the woman next to her handed her one, with a laugh she could hear, although she could not see for the water in her eyes. She heard one of the women say, 'Where we going for lunch?' and another one say, 'Just downstairs, prob'ly. Old fools says I gotta be back in half an hour.'

Then she realized that at the wash-basin she was in the way of the women in a hurry so she dried her face quickly. It was when she stepped a little aside to let someone else get to the basin and stood up and glanced into the mirror that she realized with a slight stinging shock that she had no idea which face was hers.

She looked into the mirror as though into a group of strangers, all staring at her or around her; no one was familiar in the group, no one smiled at her or looked at her with recognition; you'd think my own face would know me, she thought, with a queer numbness in her throat. There was a creamy chinless face with bright blonde hair, and a sharp-looking face under a red veiled hat, and a colorless anxious face with brown hair pulled straight back, and a square rosy face under a square haircut, and two or three more faces pushing close to the mirror, moving, regarding themselves. Perhaps it's not a mirror, she thought, maybe it's a window and I'm looking straight through at women washing on the other side. But there were women combing their hair and consulting the mirror; the group was on her side, and she thought, I hope I'm not the blonde, and lifted her hand and put it on her cheek.

She was the pale anxious one with the hair pulled back and when she realized it she was indignant and moved hurriedly back through the crowd of women, thinking, It isn't fair, why don't I have any color in my face? There were some pretty faces there, why didn't I take one of those? I didn't have time, she told herself sullenly, they didn't give me time to think, I could have had one of the nice faces, even the blonde would be better.

She backed up and sat down in one of the wicker chairs. It's mean, she was thinking. She put her hand up and felt her hair; it was loosened after her sleep but that was definitely the way she wore it, pulled straight back all around and fastened at the back of her neck with a wide tight barrette. Like a schoolgirl, she thought, only – remembering the pale face in the mirror – only I'm older than that. She unfastened the barrette with difficulty and brought it around where she could look at it. Her hair fell softly around her face; it was warm and reached to her shoulders. The barrette was silver; engraved on it was the name, 'Clara'.

'Clara,' she said aloud. '*Clara*?' Two of the women leaving the room smiled back at her over their shoulders; almost all the women were leaving now, correctly combed and lipsticked, hurrying out talking together. In the space of a second, like birds leaving a tree, they were all gone and she sat alone in the room. She dropped the barrette into the ashstand next to her chair; the ashstand was deep and metal, and the barrette made a satisfactory clang falling down. Her hair down on her shoulders, she opened her pocketbook, and began to take things out, setting them on her lap as she did so. Handkerchief, plain, white, uninitialled. Compact, square and brown tortoise-shell plastic, with a powder compartment and a rouge compartment; the rouge compartment had obviously never been used, although the powder cake was half-gone. That's why I'm so pale, she thought, and set the compact down. Lipstick, a rose shade, almost finished. A comb, an opened package of cigarettes and a package of matches, a change purse, and a wallet. The change purse was red imitation leather with a zipper across the top; she opened it and dumped the money out into her hand. Nickels, dimes, pennies, a quarter. Ninety-seven cents. Can't go far on that, she thought, and opened the brown leather wallet; there was money in it but she looked first for papers and found nothing. The only thing in the wallet was money. She counted it; there were nineteen dollars. I can go a little farther on *that*, she thought.

There was nothing else in the pocketbook. No keys – shouldn't I have keys? she wondered – no papers, no address book, no identification. The pocketbook itself was imitation leather, light grey, and she looked down and discovered that she was wearing a dark grey flannel suit and a salmon pink blouse with a ruffle around the neck. Her shoes were black and stout with moderate heels and they had laces, one of which was untied. She was wearing beige stockings and there was a ragged tear in the right knee and a great ragged run going down her leg and ending in a hole in the toe which she could feel inside her shoe. She was wearing a pin on the lapel of her suit which, when she turned it around to look at it, was a blue plastic letter C. She took the pin off and dropped it into the ashstand, and it made a sort of clatter at the bottom, with a metallic clang when it landed on the barrette. Her hands were small, with stubby fingers and no nail polish; she wore a thin gold wedding ring on her left hand and no other jewelry.

Sitting alone in the ladies' room in the wicker chair, she thought, The least I can do is get rid of these stockings. Since no one was around she took off her shoes and stripped away the stockings with a feeling of relief when her toe was released from the hole. Hide them, she thought: the paper towel wastebasket. When she stood up she got a better sight of herself in the mirror; it was worse than she had thought: the grey suit bagged in the seat, her legs were bony, and her shoulders sagged. I look fifty, she thought; and then, consulting the face, but I can't be more than thirty. Her hair hung down untidily around the pale face and with a sudden anger she fumbled in the pocketbook and found the lipstick; she drew an emphatic rosy mouth on the pale face, realizing as she did so that she was not very expert at it, and with the red mouth the face looking at her seemed somehow better to her, so she opened the compact and put on pink cheeks with the rouge. The cheeks were uneven and patent, and the red mouth glaring, but at least the face was no longer pale and anxious.

She put the stockings into the wastebasket and went bare-legged out into the hall again, and purposefully to the elevator. The elevator operator said, 'Down?' when he saw her and she stepped in and the elevator carried her silently downstairs. She went back past the grave professional doorman and out into the street where people were passing, and she stood in front of the building and waited. After a few minutes Jim came out of a crowd of people passing and came over to her and took her hand.

Somewhere between here and there was her bottle of codeine

pills, upstairs on the floor of the ladies' room she had left a little slip of paper headed 'Extraction'; seven floors below, oblivious of the people who stepped sharply along the sidewalk, not noticing their occasional curious glances, her hand in Jim's and her hair down on her shoulders, she ran barefoot through hot sand.

The Lake of the Gone Forever

(1949)

LEIGH BRACKETT

1. Landing on Iskar

In his cabin aboard the spaceship *Rohan*, Rand Conway slept – and dreamed.

He stood in a narrow valley. On both sides the cliffs of ice rose up, sheer and high and infinitely beautiful out of the powdery snow. The darkling air was full of whirling motes of frost, like the dust of diamonds, and overhead the shining pinnacles stood clear against a sky of deepest indigo, spangled with great stars.

As always, the place was utterly strange to Conway and yet, somehow, not strange at all. He began to walk forward through the drifting snow and he seemed almost to know what he was seeking around the bend of the valley.

Fear came upon him then but he could not stop.

And as always in that icy place his dead father stood waiting. He stood just as he had years ago, on the night he died, and he spoke slowly and sadly the words he had spoken then to his uncomprehending small son.

'I can never go back to Iskar, to the Lake of the Gone Forever.'

Tears dropped slowly from under the closed lids of his eyes and the echo went to and fro between the cliffs, saying, '. . . Lake of the Gone Forever . . . Gone Forever . . .'

Conway crept on, trembling. Above him the golden stars wheeled in the dark blue sky and the beauty of them was evil and the shimmering turrets of the ice were full of lurking laughter.

He passed into the shadows under the sheathed rocks that hid the end of the valley and as he did so the dead man cried out in a voice of agony, 'I can never go back to Iskar!'

And the cliffs caught up the name and shouted it thunderously through the dream.

Iskar! Iskar!

Rand Conway started up in his bunk, wide awake, shaken and sweating as always by the strangeness of that vision. Then his hands closed hard on the edge of the bunk and he laughed.

'*You* couldn't go back,' he whispered to the man dead twenty years. 'But *I'm* going. By heaven, I'm going, at last!'

It seemed to him that the very fabric of the ship murmured the name as it rushed on into deep space, that the humming machines purred it, that the thundering jets bellowed it.

Iskar! Iskar!

A savage triumph rose in Conway. So many times he had awakened from that dream to hopelessness – the hopelessness of ever reaching his goal. So many times, in these years of hard dangerous spaceman's toil, the lost little world that meant power and riches had seemed remote beyond attainment.

But he had hung on, too stubborn ever quite to give up. He had waited and planned and hoped until finally he had made his chance. And he was on his way now to the place that his father had lost and never regained.

Iskar!

Conway started up, his face swiftly losing its brooding look. That wasn't just an echo of his dream. Someone was shouting the name outside his cabin door.

'Conway! Rand Conway! We've sighted *Iskar*!'

Of course! Why else would the jets be thundering? He had been half asleep still, not to know it at once. He sprang up and crossed the dimly lighted cabin, a tall man, very lean and hard, yet with a certain odd grace about him, a certain beauty in the modeling of his bones. His eyes, of a color somewhere between grey and blue, were brilliant with excitement and full of a wolfish hunger.

He flung open the door. The glare from the corridor set him to blinking painfully – an inherited sensitivity to light was his one weakness and he had often cursed his father for passing it on to him. Through a dancing haze he saw Peter Esmond's mild good-looking face, as excited as his own.

Esmond said something, but Conway neither heard it nor cared what it was. He pushed past him and went with long strides down the passage and up the ladder to the observation bridge.

It was dark up there under the huge port. Immediately everything came clear to his vision – the blue-black sky of the Asteroid Belt, full of flashing golden stars where the little worlds caught the light of the distant Sun.

And ahead, dead ahead, he saw the tiny misty globe that was Iskar.

He stood for a long time, staring at it, and he neither moved nor spoke except that a deep trembling ran through him.

Close beside him he heard Charles Rohan's deep voice. 'Well, there's the new world. Quite a thrill, eh?'

Instantly Conway was on his guard. Rohan was no fool. A man does not make forty million dollars by being a fool and it was going to be hard enough to get away with this without tipping his hand to Rohan now.

Inwardly he cursed, not Rohan, but his daughter Marcia.

It was she who had talked her father into going along to see about opening up trade with Iskar. Rohan controlled the lion's share of trade with the Jovian Moons and the idea was logical enough. Marcia's interest, naturally, was not financial. It was simply that she could not bear to be parted from Esmond and there was no other way for her to go with him.

Conway glanced at Marcia, who was standing with her arm around her fiancé. A nice girl. A pretty girl. Ordinarily he would have liked her. But she didn't belong here and neither did Rohan – not for Conway's purposes.

Esmond alone he could have handled easily. Esmond was the Compleat Ethnologist to his fingertips. As long as he had a brand-new race to study and catalogue he would neither know nor care what other treasures a world might hold.

Now that he looked back on it the whole chain of circumstances seemed flimsy and unsure to Conway – his meeting with Esmond on a deep-space flight from Jupiter, the sudden inspiration when he learned of Esmond's connection with the Rohans, the carefully casual campaign to get the ethnologist interested in the unknown people of Iskar, the final business of producing his father's fragmentary notes to drive Esmond quite mad with longing to see this inhabited world that only one other Earthman had ever seen.

Esmond to Marcia Rohan, Marcia to her father – and now here they were. Esmond was going to get a Fellowship in the Interplanetary Society of Ethnologists and Rand Conway was going to get what he had lusted for ever since he had stumbled upon his father's notes and read in them the story of what lay in the Lake of the Gone Forever, waiting to be picked up by the first strong pair of hands.

That portion of the notes he had never shown to anyone.

Here they were, plunging out of the sky toward Iskar, and it had all been so easy – too easy. Conway was a spaceman and therefore superstitious, whether he liked it or not. He had a sudden feeling that he was going to have to pay for that easiness before he got through.

Esmond had pressed forward in the cramped space, staring raptly out at the distant glittering of silver light that was Iskar.

'I wonder what they're like?' he said as he had said a million times before. Marcia smiled.

'You'll soon know,' she answered.

'It *is* odd,' said Rohan, 'that your father didn't tell more about the people of Iskar, Conway. His notes were strangely fragmentary – almost as though he had written much more and then destroyed it.'

Conway tried to detect an edge of suspicion in Rohan's voice, but could not.

'Perhaps he did,' said Conway. 'I never could find any more.'

With that one exception it was the truth.

Marcia's face was thoughtful and a little sad, in the dim glow of that outer sky.

'I've read those notes over and over again,' she said. 'I think you're right, Dad. I think Mr Conway wrote his whole heart into those notes and then destroyed them because he couldn't bear to have them read, even by his son.'

She put a sympathetic hand on Conway's arm.

'I can understand your wanting to know, Rand. I hope you'll find your answer.'

'Thanks,' said Conway gravely.

He had had to account for his own interest in Iskar and he had been able to do that too without lying except by omission. The story of his father was true enough – the dark brooding man, broken in health and spirit, living alone with a child and a dream. He had died before Rand was ten, by his own hand and with the name of Iskar on his lips. *I can never go back, to the Lake of the Gone Forever!*

Conway himself had never doubted what his father's secret tragedy was. He had found a fortune on Iskar and had not been able to go back to claim it. That was enough to drive any man mad.

But it was easy, out of his childhood memories and those strangely incoherent notes, to build a romantic mystery around the lonely prospector's discovery of an unknown world and his subsequent haunted death. Marcia had found it all fascinating and did not doubt for a moment Conway's statement that he was seeking to solve that mystery which, he said, had overshadowed his whole life.

And it had. Waking or sleeping, Rand Conway could not forget Iskar and the Lake of the Gone Forever.

He watched the misty globe grow larger in the sky ahead, and the beating of his heart was a painful thing. Already his hands ached with longing to close around Iskar and wring from it the power and the wealth that would repay him for all the bitter years of waiting.

He thought of his dream. It was always unpleasantly vivid, and remained with him for hours after he woke. But this time it was different. He thought of the vision of his father, standing in the crystal valley, alone with his dark sorrow, and he said to the vision, 'You should have waited. You should have had the courage to wait, like me.'

For the first time he was not sorry for his father.

Then he forgot his father. He forgot time and Esmond and the Rohans. He forgot everything but Iskar.

The *Rohan* shuddered rhythmically to the brake-blasts. Iskar filled the port, producing a skyline of shimmering pinnacles so like his dream that Conway shuddered too in spite of himself.

The pinnacles shot up swiftly into a wall of ice and the *Rohan* swept in to a landing.

2. The White City

The spaceship lay like a vast black whale, stranded on a spotless floe. Behind it the icewall rose, its upper spires carved by the wind into delicate fantastic shapes. Spreading away from it to the short curve of the horizon was a sloping plain of snow, broken here and there by gleaming tors. In the distance other ranges lifted sharply against the deep dark blue of the sky.

Rand Conway stood apart from the others. His face had a strange look. He slipped the warm hood back, lifting his head in the icy wind.

Great golden stars wheeled overhead and the air was full of dancing motes of frost. The wind played with the powdery snow, whirling it up into shining veils, smoothing it again into curious patterns of ripples.

The plain, the sky, the frozen spires, had a wondrous beauty of color, infinitely soft and subtle. There was no glare here to plague Conway's eyes. Iskar glimmered in a sort of misty twilight, like the twilight of a dream.

Iskar – the bulk of it solid under his feet at last after all these years. Conway trembled and found it difficult to breathe. His eyes, black and luminous as a cat's now with the expansion of the pupils, glistened with a hard light. Iskar!

Quite suddenly he was afraid.

Fear rushed at him out of the narrow valleys, down from the singing peaks. It came in the wind and rose up from the snow under his feet. It wrapped him in a freezing shroud and for a moment reality slipped away from him and he was lost.

The shadows were deep under the icy cliffs and the mouths of the valleys were black and full of whispers. It seemed to him that the lurking terror of his dream was very close, close and waiting.

He must have made some sound or sign, for Marcia Rohan came to him and took him by the arm.

'Rand,' she said. 'Rand, what is it?'

He caught hold of her. In a moment everything was normal again and he was able to force what might pass for a laugh.

'I don't know,' he said. 'Something came to me just then.' He could not tell her about the dream. He told her instead what he knew must be the cause of it.

'My father must have told me something about this place when I was a child, something I can't remember. Something ugly. I –' He paused and then plunged on. 'I thought for a moment that I had been here before, that I knew . . .'

He stopped. The shadow was gone now. To the devil with dreams and subconscious memories. The reality was all that mattered – the reality that was going to make Rand Conway richer than the Rohans. He stared away across the plain. For a moment his face was unguarded and Marcia was startled by the brief cruel look of triumph that crossed it.

The others came up, Rohan and young Esmond and Captain Frazer, the well-fed but very competent skipper of the *Rohan*. They were all shivering slightly in spite of their warm coveralls. Esmond looked at Conway, who was still bare-headed.

'You'll freeze your ears off,' he said.

Conway laughed, not without a faint edge of contempt. 'If you had kicked around in deep space as many years as I have you wouldn't be bothered by a little cold.'

He pointed off to where the distant ranges were, across the plain.

'According to my father's maps, the village, or what have you, lies between those ranges.'

'I think,' said Marcia, 'that we had better break out the sledges and go before Peter bursts something.'

Esmond laughed. He was obviously trembling with eagerness.

'I hope nothing's happened to them,' he said. 'I mean, since your father was here. You know – famine, plague or anything.'

'I imagine they're a pretty hardy lot,' said Rohan, 'or they couldn't have survived at all in this God-forsaken place.' He turned to Frazer, laughing. 'For heaven's sake, get the sledges.'

Frazer nodded. The crew had come tumbling out and were rollicking like schoolboys in the snow, glad to be released from the long confinement of the voyage. The Second Officer and the engineer were coming up and Frazer went to meet them. The Second turned back to round up his men.

The sledges came presently out of the cargo hatch. There were three of the light plastic hulls – two to carry the exploring party, one to be left with the ship in case of emergency. They were fully equipped, including radio and the efficient Samson riot guns, firing shells of anaesthetic gas.

Rohan looked at his daughter. 'I want you to stay here, Marcia.'

The girl must have been expecting that, Conway thought, because her only reaction was to set her jaw so that she looked ridiculously like her father – smaller and prettier but even more stubborn.

'No,' said Marcia.

Esmond said, 'Please, darling. These people may not be friendly at first. You can go next time.'

'No,' said Marcia.

'Marcia,' said Rohan pleasantly. 'I don't want any foolishness about this. Go with Frazer, back to the ship.'

Marcia studied him. Then she turned and kissed Esmond lightly on the cheek and said, 'Good luck, darling.' She went off with Frazer. Conway saw that there were tears in her eyes. He warmed to Marcia. She hadn't been trying to show off. She just wanted to be with Esmond in case anything happened.

Rohan said, 'I guess we might as well go.'

They climbed in, six men to a sledge, all burly spacehands with the exception of Rohan and the ethnologist and Conway, who had sweated his way up from the ranks to Master Pilot.

The small jets hissed, roared and settled down to a steady thrumming. The sledges shot out across the trackless plain like two small boats on a white sea, throwing up waves of snowy spray.

Conway was in the leading sledge. He leaned forward like a leashed hound, impatient to be slipped. Part of him was mad with excitement and another part, completely cool and detached, was making plans.

The spaceship began to grow smaller. Almost imperceptibly the gleaming pinnacles of ice lengthened into the sky.

Presently the pace of the sledges grew slower and slower still. Tors, half rock, half ice, rose up out of the snow and here and there a reef, mailed and capped with the shining armor, was scoured clear by the wind. The man at the controls thrust his head forward, squinting.

'What's the matter?' asked Conway. 'Why the delay?'

The man said irritably, 'I'm afraid of ramming into something, sir. It's so bloody dark and shadowy, I can't see.'

'Is that all!' Conway laughed and shoved him aside. 'Here – let an owl do it.'

He took the controls and sent the sledge spinning ahead. Every reef and tor, every ripple in the snow, was as clear to him as it would have been to most men in broad daylight. He laughed again.

'I'm beginning to like Iskar,' he said to Rohan. 'I think I'll start a colony for people with hemeralopia, and we can all be as happy as bats in the dark. My father must have loved it here.'

Rohan glanced up at him. Conway had forgotten to put his hood back up. The wind was whipping an icy gale through his hair and there was rime on his lashes. He seemed to be enjoying it. Rohan shivered.

'I'm nyctalopic myself,' he said. 'I'll stick to plenty of sunlight – *and* heat!'

Esmond did not bother to listen to either one of them. His dream was as strong as Conway's and at this moment he had room for nothing else.

The sledges rushed on across the plain, the one following the tiny jet-flares of the other. The spaceship was lost in the white distance behind them. Ahead the twin ranges grew against the stars. Nothing stirred but the wind. It was very lovely, very peaceful, Conway thought. A cold, sweet jewel of a world.

The words sang in his ears, the words that had themed his father's death and run through his own life as a promise and a challenge. 'The Lake of the Gone Forever – Gone Forever . . .'

He had long ago ceased to wonder what that name meant. Only in his nightmare dream did it have the power to frighten him. He wanted what was there and nothing else mattered.

The Lake of the Gone Forever. Soon – soon – soon!

Yet it seemed a very long time to Conway before they entered the broad defile between the twin ranges.

He was forced to slow his breakneck pace because here the ground was broken and treacherous. Finally he stopped altogether.

'We'll have to go on foot from here,' he said.

In a fever of impatience he waited while the men climbed out, shouldering the Samson guns. They left two to guard the sledges and went on, scrambling in single file over the tumbled rocks. The wind howled between the mountain walls so that the air was blind with snow. There was no sight of the city.

Conway was in the lead. He was like a man driven by fiends. Where the others slipped and stumbled he went over the rough ground like a cat, swift and sure-footed even among the deceptive drifts. Several times he was forced to stop and wait lest he leave the party too far behind.

Suddenly, above the organ notes of the wind, there was another sound.

Conway lifted his head to listen. Clear and sweet and strong he heard the winding of horns from the upper slopes. They echoed away down the valley, calling one to the other with ringing voices that stirred Conway's blood to a wild excitement. He shook the snow out of his hair and plunged on, leaving the rest to follow as best they could.

A jutting shoulder of the mountains loomed before him. The wind blew and the deep-throated horns called and called again across the valley. The blown drifts leaped at him and the icy screes were a challenge to his strength but they could not slow him down. He laughed and went on around the shoulder and saw the white city glittering under the stars.

It spread across the valley floor and up the slopes as though it grew from the frozen earth, a part of it, as enduring as the mountains. At Conway's first glance, it seemed to be built all of ice, its turrets and crenellations glowing with a subtle luminescence in the dusky twilight, fantastically shaped, dusted here and there with snow. From the window openings came a glow of pearly light.

Beyond the city the twin ranges drew in and in until their flanks were parted only by a thin line of shadow, a narrow valley with walls of ice reaching up to the sky.

Conway's heart contracted with a fiery pang.

A narrow valley – *the* valley.

For a moment everything vanished in a roaring darkness. Dream and reality rushed together – his father's notes, his father's dying cry, his own waking visions and fearful wanderings beyond the wall of sleep.

It lies beyond the city, in a narrow place between the mountains – the Lake of the Gone Forever. And I can never go back!

Conway said aloud to the wind and the snow and the crying horns, 'But *I* have come back. I have come!'

Exulting, triumphant, he looked again at the city, the white beauty of it, the wind-carved towers bright beneath the golden stars.

It was a strong place, walled and fortified against whatever enemies there might be on this world of Iskar. Conway ran toward it and as he did so the braying of horns rose louder and then was joined by the shrill war-cry of pipes.

They went skirling along the wall and through the snow-mist he saw that men were there above him looking down. The glitter of their spears ran like a broken line of silver from both sides of the great stone gate.

3. The Fear

Conway's blood leaped hot within him. The pipes sent him mad and he flung up his arm and shouted at the men, a long hail. He could see them clearly now. They were tall lean men with bodies tough as rawhide and strong bone in their faces and eyes like the eyes of eagles. They wore the white fur of beasts kilted about them, thrown loosely over their naked shoulders, and they were bareheaded and careless of the cold.

Their spears rose up and menaced him.

He stopped. Once again he cried out, a cry as wild and shrill as the martial pipes. Then he stood still, waiting.

Slowly behind him came Rohan and the others. They formed into a sort of knot around him. Some of the men reached nervously for their riot guns and Rohan spoke sharply. The pipes fell silent and the sounding horns. They waited, all of them.

There was movement on the wall and an old man came forward among the warriors, a cragged gnarled old man with a proud face and fierce eyes, standing strong as a granite rock.

He looked down at the alien men below him. His hair and his long beard blew in the bitter wind, and the white furs whipped around him, and for a long time he did not speak. His eyes met Conway's and there was hatred in them and deep pain.

Finally he said, very slowly, as though the words came haltingly from some long-locked vault of memory. 'Men of Earth!'

Conway started. It had not occurred to him that his father might have left some knowledge of English behind him.

'Yes,' he answered, holding out his empty hands. 'Friends.'

The old man shook his head. 'No. Go, or we kill.'

He looked again at Conway, very strangely, and a little chill ran through the Earthman. Was it possible that the old man saw in him some resemblance to the Conway he had known before? He and his father had not looked alike.

Esmond stepped forward. 'Please,' he said. 'We mean you no harm. We only want to talk to you. We will obey you, we will bring no weapons – only let us in!'

He was very like a child pleading, almost on the verge of tears. It was unthinkable that he should be denied now.

The old man said again, 'Go.'

Rohan spoke. 'We have gifts, many things for your people. We want nothing. We come as friends.'

The old man flung up his head and laughed, and his mirth was like vitriol poured on the wind.

'*Friend!* Conna was my friend. In my house, as my own son, lived Conna, my friend!'

He cried out something in his own harsh tongue and Conway knew that was a curse and he knew that Conna was his own name. They had not forgotten his father on Iskar, it seemed.

He was suddenly angry, more terribly angry than he had ever been in his life. Beyond the city, almost within reach, lay the valley of the Lake and nothing, not all their spears, not death itself, was going to stop him now.

He strode up under the wall and looked at the old man with eyes as black and baleful as his own.

'We know nothing of this Conna,' he said. 'We come in peace. But if you want war we will make war. If you kill us others will come – many others. Our ship is huge and very terrible. Its fire alone can destroy your city. Will you let us in, old man, or must we . . .'

After a long time the other said slowly, 'What is your name?'

'Rand,' said Conway.

'Rand,' repeated the old man softly. 'Rand.' He was silent for a time, brooding, his chin sunk on his breast. His eyes were hooded and he did not look again at Conway.

Abruptly he turned and issued orders in his own tongue. Then, to the Earthmen, he shouted, '*Enter!*'

The great stone was rolled away.

Conway went back to the others. Both Esmond and Rohan were furious.

'Who gave you the right –' Rohan began, and Esmond broke in passionately.

'You shouldn't have threatened them! A little more talk would have convinced them.'

Conway looked at them contemptuously.

'You wanted in, didn't you?' he demanded. 'All right, the gate's open and they'll think twice about getting tough with us after we're through it.'

He unbuckled his gun belt and tossed it, holster and all, to a man on the wall. It was a gesture and no more because he had hidden a small anaesthetic needle-gun under his coverall in case of need – but it would look good to the Iskarians.

'I'd do the same if I were you,' he said to the others. 'Also, I would send the men back. They're not going to do us any good inside the wall and they might do us harm. Tell them to bring the trade goods and one of the radios from the sledges and then return to the ship – and stand by.'

Rohan scowled. He did not like having the command taken from him. But Conway's orders made sense and he relayed them. Then he tossed his own gun to one of the warriors. Esmond did not carry one. The men went away, back to the sledges.

'Remember,' said Conway, 'you never heard of "Conna", or his son.'

The others nodded. They turned then and went into the city and the stone gate was closed behind them.

The old man was waiting for them, and with him a sort of honor guard of fifteen tall fighting men.

'I am Krah,' said the old patriarch. He waited politely until Esmond and Rohan had said their names and then he said, 'Come.'

The guard formed up. The Earthmen went – half guest, half captive – into the streets of the city.

They were narrow winding streets, rambling up and down over the broken ground. In some places they were scoured clean to the ice by the whistling wind, in others they were choked by drifts. Conway could see now that the buildings were all of solid stone, over which the cold shining mail had formed for centuries, except where the openings were kept clear.

The people of the city were gathered to watch as the strangers went by.

It was a strangely silent crowd. Men, women and children, old and young, all of them as stalwart and handsome as mountain trees, with their wide black pupils and pale hair, the men clad in skins, the women in kirtles of rough woolen cloth. Conway noticed that the women and children did not mingle with the men.

Silent, all of them, and watching. There was something disquieting in their stillness. Then, somewhere, an old woman sent up a keening cry of lament, and another took it up, and another, until the eerie *ochone* echoed through the twisting streets as though the city itself wept in pain.

The men began to close in. Slowly at first, now one stepping forward, now another, like the first pebbles rolling before the rush of the avalanche. Conway's heart began to pound and there was a bitter taste in his mouth.

Esmond cried out to the old man, 'Tell them not to fear us! Tell them we are friends!'

Krah looked at him and smiled. His eyes went then to Conway and he smiled again.

'I will tell them,' he said.

'Remember,' said Conway harshly. 'Remember the great ship and its fires.'

Krah nodded. 'I will not forget.'

He spoke to the people, shouting aloud, and reluctantly the men drew back and rested the butts of their spears on the ground. The women did not cease to wail.

Conway cursed his father for the things he had not written in his notes.

Quite suddenly, out of a steep side lane, a herd boy drove his flock with a scramble and a clatter. The queer white-furred beasts milled in the narrow space, squealing, filling the air with their sharp, not unpleasant odor.

As though that pungency were a trigger, a shutter clicked open somewhere in Conway's mind and he knew that he had seen these streets before, known the sounds and smells of the city, listened to the harsh staccato speech. The golden wheeling of the stars overhead hurt him with a poignant familiarity.

Conway plunged again into that limbo between fact and dream. It was far worse this time. He wanted to sink down and cling to something until his mind steadied again but he did not dare do anything but walk behind the old man as though nothing on Iskar could frighten him.

Yet he was afraid – afraid with the fear of madness, where the dream becomes the reality.

Beads of sweat came out on his face and froze there. He dug his nails into his palms and forced himself to remember his whole life, back to his earliest memory and beyond, when his father must have talked and talked of Iskar, obsessed with the thought of what he had found there and lost again.

He had not spoken so much of Iskar when his son was old enough to understand. But it seemed that the damage was already done. The formative years, the psychologists call them, when the things learned and forgotten will come back to haunt one later on.

Conway was a haunted man, walking through that strange city. And old Krah watched him sidelong and smiled and would not be done with smiling.

The women wailed, howling like she-wolves to the dark heavens.

4. 'Go Ask of Her . . .'

It seemed like centuries to Conway, but it could not have been so long in actual time before Krah stopped beside a doorway and pulled aside the curtain of skins that covered it.

'Enter,' he said and the Earthmen filed through, leaving the guard outside, except for five who followed the old man.

'My sons,' said Krah.

All grown men, far older than Conway, and scarred, tough-handed warriors. Yet they behaved toward Krah with the deference of children.

The ground floor of the house was used for storage. Frozen sides of meat and bundles of a dried moss-like stuff occupied one side. On the other was a pen and a block for butchering. Apparently there was no wood on Iskar, for the pen was built of stone and there were no doors, only the heavy curtains.

Krah lifted another one of these, leading the way up a closed stair that served as a sort of airlock to keep out the draughts and the extreme cold of the lower floor. The upper chamber was freezing by any Earthly standards but a small, almost smokeless fire of moss burned on the round hearth and the enormously thick walls were perfect insulation against the wind. Immediately Conway began to sweat, probably from sheer nervousness.

A girl sat by the hearth, tending the spit and the cooking pot. Obviously she had only just run back in from the street, for there was still snow in her silvery hair and her sandals were wet with it.

She did not lift her head when the men came in, as though such happenings were not for her to notice. Yet Conway caught a sidelong glance of her eyes. In the soft light of the stone lamps her pupils had contracted to show the clear blue iris, and for all her apparent meekness, he saw that her eyes were bright and rebellious and full of spirit. Conway smiled.

She met his gaze fairly for a moment with a curious intensity, as though she would tear away his outer substance and see everything that lay beneath it – his heart, his soul, his innermost thoughts, greedily, all in a minute. Then the old man spoke and she was instantly absorbed in the turning of the spit.

'Sit,' said Krah, and the Earthmen sat on heaps of furs spread over cushions of moss.

The five tall sons sat also but Krah remained standing.

'So you know nothing of Conna,' he said and Conna's son answered blandly,

'No.'

'Then how came you to Iskar?'

Conway shrugged. 'How did Conna come? The men of Earth go everywhere.' Unconsciously he had slipped into Krah's ceremonial style of phrasing. He leaned forward, smiling.

'My words were harsh when I stood outside your gate. Let them be forgotten, for they were only the words of anger. Forget Conna also. He has nothing to do with us.'

'Ah,' said the old man softly. 'Forget. That is a word I do not know. Anger, yes – and vengeance also. But not forget.'

He turned to Rohan and Esmond and spoke to them and answered them courteously while they explained their wishes. But his gaze, frosty blue now in the light, rested broodingly on Conway's face and did not waver. Conway's nerves tightened and tightened and a great unease grew within him.

He could have sworn that Krah knew who he was and why he had come to Iskar.

Reason told him that this was ridiculous. It had been many years since Krah had seen his father and in any case they were physically dissimilar. Nor did it seem likely that he should have preserved intact any of his father's mannerisms.

Yet he could not be sure and the uncertainty preyed upon him. The old man's bitter gaze was hard to bear.

The five sons neither moved nor spoke. Conway was sure that they understood the conversation perfectly and he reflected that, according to Krah, they had lived with Conna as his brothers. They seemed to be waiting, quite patiently, as though they had waited a long time and could afford to wait a little longer.

From time to time the girl stole a secret smoldering look at Conway and in spite of his uneasiness he grew very curious about her, wondering what devil of unrest lurked in her mind. She had a fascinating little face, full of odd lights and shadows where the glow of the fire touched it.

'Trade,' said Krah at last. 'Friendship. Study. They are good words. Let us eat now, and then rest, and I will think of these good words, which I have heard before from Conna.'

'Look here,' said Rohan rather testily, 'I don't know what Conna did here but I see no reason to condemn us for his sins.'

'We speak the truth,' said Esmond gently. He glanced at

Conway, waiting for him to ask the question that was his to ask. But Conway could not trust himself and finally Esmond's curiosity drove him to blurt out,

'What was Conna's crime?'

The old man turned upon him a slow and heavy look.

'Do not ask of me,' he said. 'Ask of her who waits, by the Lake of the Gone Forever.'

That name stung Conway's nerves like a whiplash. He was afraid he had betrayed himself but if he started no one seemed to notice. The faces of Esmond and Rohan were honestly blank.

'The Lake of the Gone Forever,' Esmond repeated. 'What is that?'

'Let there be an end to talk,' said Krah.

He turned and spoke to the girl in his own tongue and Conway caught the name Ciel. She rose obediently and began to serve the men, bringing the food on platters of thin carved stone. When she was done she sat down again by the fire and ate her own dinner from what was left, a slim, humble shadow whose eyes were no more humble than the eyes of a young panther. Conway stole her a smile and was rewarded by a brief curving of her red mouth.

When the meal was finished Krah rose and led the Earthmen down a corridor. There were two curtained doorways on each side and beyond them were small windowless cells, with moss and furs heaped soft to make a sleeping place.

Ciel came quietly to light the stone lamps and it seemed to Conway that she took special note of the cubicle he chose for his own.

'Sleep,' said Krah, and left them. Ciel vanished down a narrow back stair at the end of the hall.

The Earthmen stood for a moment, looking at each other, and then Conway said sullenly, 'Don't ask me any questions because I don't know the answers.'

He turned and went into his chamber, dropping the curtain behind him. In a vile mood he sat down on the furs and lighted a cigarette, listening to Rohan's low half-angry voice telling Esmond that he thought Rand was acting very strangely. Esmond answered soothingly that the situation would be a strain on anyone. Presently Conway heard them go to bed. He blew out his lamp.

He sat for quite a while, in a terrible sweat of nerves, thinking of Krah, thinking of the narrow valley that lay so nearly within his reach, thinking of his father, hating him because of the black memories he had left behind on Iskar, so that now the way was made very hard for his son.

Heaven help him if old Krah ever found out!

He waited for some time after everything was still. Then, very carefully, he lifted the curtain and stepped out into the hall.

He could see into the big main room. Four of Krah's brawny sons slept on the furs by the embers. The fifth sat crosslegged, his spear across his knees, and he did not sleep.

Conway glanced at the back stair. He was perfectly sure that it led to the women's quarters and that any venturing that way would bring the whole house around his ears. He shrugged and returned to his cell.

Stretched out on the furs he lay frowning into the dark, trying to think. He had not counted on the hatred of the Iskarians for Earthmen. He wondered for the hundredth time what his father had done to make all the women of Iskar wail a dirge when they were reminded of him. *Ask of her who waits, by the Lake of the Gone Forever . . .*

It didn't really matter. All that mattered was that they were under close watch and that it was a long way through the city for an Earthman to go and stay alive, even if he could get away from Krah.

Quite suddenly, he became aware that someone had crept down the hall outside and stopped at his door.

Without making a sound, Conway reached into the breast of his coverall and took hold of the gun that was hidden there. Then he waited.

The curtain moved a little, then a little more, and Conway lay still and breathed like a sleeping man. Faint light seeped in, outlining the widening gap of the curtain, showing clearly to Conway's eyes the figure that stood there, looking in.

Ciel, a little grey mouse in her hodden kirtle, her hair down around her shoulders like a cape of moonbeams. Ciel, the mouse with the wildcat's eyes.

Partly curious to see what she would do, partly afraid that a whisper might attract attention from the other room, Conway lay still, feigning sleep.

For a long moment the girl stood without moving, watching him. He could hear the sound of her breathing, quick, and soft. At last she took one swift step forward, then paused, as though her courage had failed her. That was her undoing.

The big man with the spear must have caught some flicker of movement, the swirl of her skirt, perhaps, for she had made no noise. Conway heard a short exclamation from the main room, and Ciel dropped the curtain and ran. A man's heavier footfalls pelted after her.

There was a scuffling at the other end of the hall and some low intense whispering. Conway crept over and pulled the curtain open a crack.

Krah's son held the girl fast. He seemed to be lecturing her, more in sorrow than in anger, and then, deliberately and without heat, he began to beat her. Ciel bore it without a whimper but her eyes glazed and her face was furious.

Conway stepped silently out into the hall. The man's back was turned, but Ciel saw him. He indicated in pantomime what she should do and she caught the idea at once – or perhaps only the courage to do it.

Twisting like a cat, she set her teeth hard in the arm that held her.

The man let her go from sheer astonishment rather than pain. She fled down the woman-stair and he stood staring after her, his mouth wide open, as dumbfounded as though the innocent stones he walked on had risen suddenly and attacked him. Conway got the feeling that such a thing had never happened before in the history of Iskar.

He leaned lazily against the wall and said aloud, 'What's going on?'

Krah's son turned swiftly and the look of astonishment was replaced instantly by anger.

Conway made a show of yawning, as though he had just waked up. 'Was that Ciel you were thrashing? She's a pretty big girl to be spanked.' He grinned at the marks on the man's arm. 'By the way, who is she – Krah's granddaughter?'

The answer came slowly in stumbling but understandable English.

'Krah's fosterling, daughter of my sister's friend. Ciel drank wickedness with mother's milk – wickedness she learn from my sister, who learn from Conna.'

Quite suddenly the big man reached out and took Conway's jacket-collar in a throttling grip. Amazingly there were tears in his eyes and a deep, bitter rage.

'I will warn you, man of Earth,' he said softly. 'Go – go swiftly while you still live.'

He flung Conway from him and turned away, back to the big room to brood again by the fire. And the Earthman was left to wonder whether the warning was for them all or for himself alone.

Hours later he managed to fall into an uneasy sleep, during which he dreamed again of the icy valley and the hidden terror that waited for him beyond the wall of rock. It seemed closer to him than ever before, so close that he awoke with a strangled cry. The stone cell was like a burial vault, and he left it, in a mood of desperation such as he had never known before. Outside, the wind was rising.

He came into the big room just as Krah entered from the outer stair. Behind him, very white-faced and proud, came Marcia Rohan. Her cheek was bleeding and her lovely dark hair was wet and draggled and her eyes hurt Conway to look at them.

'Marcia!' he cried and she ran to him, clinging with tight hands like a frightened child. He held her, answering her question before she could gasp it out.

'Peter's safe,' he said. 'So is your father. They're quite safe.'

Old Krah spoke. There was a strange stony quality about him now, as though he had come to some decision from which nothing could shake him. He looked at Conway.

'Go,' he said. 'Call your – friends.'

5. *Warrior of Iskar*

Conway went, taking Marcia with him. Rohan came out at once but Esmond was sleeping like the dead. Apparently he had worked for hours by the light of the stone lamp, making notes on the people of Iskar.

Conway wondered, as he shook him awake, whether any of that data was going to get safely back to Earth. He knew, as certainly as he knew his own name, that their stay here was ended and he did not like the look in Krah's eyes.

'It's nobody's fault,' Marcia was saying, over and over. 'I couldn't stand it. I didn't know whether you were alive or dead. Your radio didn't answer. I stole a sledge.'

'Did you come alone?' asked Rohan.

'Yes.'

'My God!' said Esmond softly, and picked her up in his arms. She laid her bleeding cheek against his and sobbed out. 'They stoned me, Peter, the women did. The men brought me through the streets and the women stoned me.'

Esmond's mild face became perfectly white. His eyes turned cold as the snow outside. He strode down the hall bearing Marcia in his arms, and his very step was stiff with fury. Rohan followed, crowding on his heels.

Old Krah never gave them a chance to speak. His five sons were ranged behind him and there was something very formidable about them, the five tall fair men and the tall old one who was like an ancient dog-wolf, white with years but still leader of the pack.

Krah held up his hand, and the Earthmen stopped. From her place by the fire Conway saw that Ciel was watching, staring with fascinated eyes at the alien woman who had come alone across the snow-fields to stand beside her men. The wind piped loud in the window embrasures, coming down from the high peaks with a rush and a snarl that set Conway's nerves to quivering with a queer excitement.

Krah spoke, looking at Marcia.

'For this I am sorry,' he said. 'But the woman should not have come.' His frosty gaze rose then to take in all of them. 'I offer you your lives. Go now – leave the city, leave Iskar and never return. If you do not I cannot save you.'

'Why did they stone her?' demanded Esmond. He had one thing on his mind, no room for any other thought.

'Because she is different,' said Krah simply, 'and they fear her. She wears the garments of a man and she walks among men and these things are against their beliefs. Now, will you go?'

Esmond set the girl on her feet beside him, leaving his arm around her shoulders.

'*We* will go,' he said. 'And I will kill the first one who touches her.'

Krah was gentleman enough to ignore the emptiness of that very sincere threat. He bowed his head.

'That,' he said, 'is as it should be.'

He looked at Rohan.

'Don't worry,' Rohan snapped. 'We'll leave and may you all go to the devil. This is a fit world for wolves and only wolves live in it!'

He started toward the door with Esmond and his daughter and Krah's eyes turned now to Conway. He asked softly, 'And you, man who is called Rand?'

Conway shrugged, as though the whole thing were a matter of no importance to him. 'Why should I want to stay?' His hands were shaking so that he thrust them into his pockets to conceal it and little trickles of sweat ran down his back. He nodded toward the window opening.

'There's a white wind blowing, Krah,' he said. He drew himself erect, and his voice rose and rang. 'It will catch us on the open plain. The woman will surely die and perhaps the rest of us also. Nevertheless we will go. But let it be told through the city that Krah has laid aside his manhood and put on a woman's kirtle, for he has slain by stealth and not by an honest spear!'

There was silence. Esmond stopped and turned in the doorway, the girl held close in the circle of his arm. Rohan stopped also, and their faces showed the shock of this new thought.

Conway's heart beat like a trip-hammer. He was bluffing – with all the resources of the sledge, he thought, their chances of perishing were fairly small, but there was just that germ of truth to pitch it on. He was in agony while he waited to see if the bluff had worked. Once outside the city walls he knew that the Lake was lost to him as it had been to his father.

After what seemed a very long time, Krah sighed and said quietly, 'The white wind. Yes, I had forgotten that the Earth stock is so weak.'

A subtle change had come over the old man. It was almost as

though he too had been waiting tensely for some answer and now it had come. A deep, cold light crept into his eyes and burned there, something almost joyous.

'You may stay,' he said, 'until the wind drops.'

Then he turned sharply and went away down the stair and his sons went with him.

Esmond stared after them and Conway was amused to see the wolfish fury in his round, mild face.

'He would have sent us out to die,' said Esmond, as though he wished he could kill Krah on the spot. Danger to Marcia had transformed him from a scientist into a rather primitive man. He turned to Conway.

'Thanks. You were right when you threatened them on the wall. And if anything happens to us I hope Frazer will make them pay for it!'

'Nothing's going to happen,' said Conway. 'Take Marcia back to the sleeping rooms – it's warmer there and she can lie down.' He looked at Ciel and said sharply, 'Can you understand me?'

She nodded, rather sullenly.

Conway pointed to Marcia. 'Go with her. Bring water, something to put on that cut.'

Ciel rose obediently but her eyes watched him slyly as she followed the Earthfolk out and down the hall.

Conway was left quite alone.

He forced himself to stand still for a moment and think. He forced his heart to stop pounding and his hands to stop shaking. He could not force either his elation or his fear to leave him.

His way was clear now, at least for the moment. Why was it clear? Why had Krah gone away and taken his sons with him?

The wind swooped and screamed, lifting the curtains of hide, scattering snow on the floor. The white wind. Conway smiled. He had this chance. He would never have another.

He turned and went swiftly into the second corridor that opened opposite the one where the others had gone. It too contained four small sleeping rooms. One, however, was twice as large as the others and Conway was sure it belonged to Krah.

He slipped into it, closing the curtain carefully behind him.

All that he needed was there. All that he needed to make possible this one attempt that he could ever make upon the hidden valley of his dream.

He began to strip. The coverall, the thin jersey he wore underneath, the boots – everything that was of Earth. He must go through the city and he could not go as an Earthman. He had realized that there was only one way. He was glad of the white wind, for that would make his deception easier.

It would be cold and dangerous. But he was contemptuous of cold and beyond caring about danger. He was not going to eat his heart out and die, as his father had, because his one chance was lost forever.

In a few minutes Rand Conway was gone and in the stone chamber stood a nameless warrior of Iskar, a tall fair man wrapped in white furs, shod in rough hide boots and carrying a spear.

He retained two things, hidden carefully beneath his girdle – the little gun and a small vial, sheathed and stoppered with lead.

He turned, and Ciel was standing there, staring at him with wide astonished eyes.

She had slipped in so quietly that he had not heard her. And he knew that with one loud cry she could destroy all his plans.

In two swift angry strides he had caught her and put one hand hard over her mouth.

'Why did you come here?' he snarled. 'What do you want?'

Her eyes looked up at him, steady and fierce as his own. He said, 'Don't cry out or I'll kill you.' She shook her head and he took his hand away a little, not trusting her.

In slow painful English she said, 'Take me with you.'

'Where?'

'To Earth!'

It was Conway's turn to be astonished.

'But why?'

She said vehemently, 'Earth-woman proud like man. Free.'

So that was the smouldering anger she had in her. She was not patient like the other women of Iskar, for she had had a glimpse of something else. He remembered what Krah's son had said.

'Did Conna teach this?'

She nodded. 'You take me?' she demanded. 'You take me? I run away from Krah. Hide. You take me?'

Conway smiled. He liked her. They were the same kind, he and she – nursing a hopeless dream and risking everything to make it come true.

'Why not?' he said. 'Sure, I'll take you.'

Her joy was a savage thing. 'If you lie,' she whispered, 'I kill you!' Then she kissed him.

He could tell it was the first time she had ever kissed a man. He could also tell that it was not going to be the last.

He thrust her away. 'You must help me then. Take these.' He handed her the bundle of his discarded clothing. 'Hide them. Is there a back way from the house?'

'Yes.'

'Show it to me. Then wait for me – and talk to no one. *No one.* Understand?'

'Where you go?' she asked him. The look of wonder came back into her eyes, and something of fear. 'What you do, man of Iskar?'

He shook his head. 'If you don't help me, if I die – you'll never see Earth.'

'Come,' she said, and turned.

Esmond and Rohan were still with Marcia, still full of their fears and angers – too full to worry about Conway, the outsider. The house of Krah was empty and silent except for the wind that swept through the embrasures with a shriek of laughter, like the laughter of wolves before the kill. Conway shivered, an animal twitching of the skin.

Ciel led him down a little stair and showed him a narrow passage built for the taking of offal from the slaughtering pen – woman's work, unfit for warriors.

'I wait,' she said. Her fingers closed hard on the muscles of his arm. 'Come back. Come soon!'

Her fear was not for him but for herself, lest now in this last hour her hope of freedom should be snatched away. Conway knew how she felt.

He bent and gave her a quick rough kiss. 'I'll come back.' Then he lifted the curtain of hide and slipped out into the darkness.

6. Echoes of a Dream

The city was alive and vocal with the storm. The narrow streets shouted with it, the icy turrets of the houses quivered and rang. No snow was falling but the thick-blown whiteness drove and leaped and whirled, carried across half of Iskar in the rush of the wind. Above the tumult the stars burned clear and steady in the sky.

The cold bit deep into Conway's flesh, iron barbs reaching for his heart. He drew the warm furs closer. His heartbeat quickened. His blood raced, fighting back the cold, and a strange exaltation came over him, something born out of the wild challenge of the wind. His pupils dilated, black and feral as a cat's. He began to walk, moving at a swift pace, setting his feet down surely on the glare of ice and the frozen stones.

He knew the direction he must take. He had determined that the first time he saw the city and it was burned into his memory for all time.

The way to the Lake, the Lake of the Gone Forever.

There were not many in the streets and those he passed gave him no second look. The white wind laid a blurring veil over everything and there was nothing about Conway to draw attention, a lean proud-faced man bent against the wind, a solitary warrior on an errand of his own.

Several times he tried to see if he were being followed. He could not forget Krah's face with its look of secret joy, nor cease to wonder uneasily why the old man had so suddenly left the Earthfolk unwatched. But he could see nothing in that howling smother.

He made sure of the little gun and smiled.

He found his way by instinct through the twisting streets, heading always in the same direction. The houses began to thin out. Quite suddenly they were gone and Conway stood in the open valley beyond. High above he could distinguish the shining peaks of the mountains lifting against the stars.

The full sweep of the wind met him here. He faced it squarely, laughing, and went on over the tumbled rocks. The touch of madness that had been in him ever since he reached Iskar grew into an overwhelming thing.

Part of his identity slipped away. The wind and the snow and the bitter rocks were part of him. He knew them and they knew him. They could not harm him. Only the high peaks looked down on him with threatening faces and it seemed to him that they were angry.

He was beginning to hear the echoes of his dream but they were still faint. He was not yet afraid. He was, in some strange way, happy. He had never been more alone and yet he did not feel lonely. Something wild and rough woke within him to meet the wild roughness of the storm and he felt a heady pride, a certainty that he could stand against any man of Iskar on his own ground.

The city was lost behind him. The valley had him between its white walls, vague and formless now, closing in upon him imperceptibly beyond the curtain of the storm. There was a curious timelessness about his journey, almost a spacelessness, as though he existed in a dimension of his own.

And in that private world of his it did not seem strange nor unfitting that Ciel's voice should cry out thinly against the wind, that he should turn to see her clambering after him, nimble-footed, reckless with haste.

She reached him, spent with running. 'Krah,' she gasped. 'He go ahead with four. One follow. I see. I follow too.' She made a quick, sharp gesture that took in the whole valley. 'Trap. They catch. They kill. Go back.'

Conway did not stir. She shook him, in a passion of urgency. 'Go back! Go back now!'

He stood immovable, his head raised, his eyes questing into the storm, seeking the enemies he only half believed were there. And then, deep and strong across the wind, came the baying of a hunter's horn. It was answered from the other side of the valley. Another spoke, and another, and Conway counted them. Six — Krah and his five sons around and behind him, so that the way back to the city was closed.

Conway began to see the measure of the old man's cunning and he smiled, an animal baring of the teeth.

'You go,' he said to Ciel. 'They will not harm you.'

'What I do they punish,' she answered grimly. 'No. You must

live. They hunt you but I know trails, ways. Go many times to Lake of the Gone Forever. They not kill there. Come.'

She turned but he caught her and would not let her go, full of a quick suspicion.

'Why do you care so much about me?' he demanded. 'Esmond or Rohan could take you to Earth as well.'

'Against Krah's will?' She laughed. 'They are soft men, not like you.' Her eyes met his fairly in the gloom, the black pupils wide and lustrous, looking deep into him so that he was strangely stirred. 'But there is more,' she said. 'I never love before. Now I do. And – you are Conna's son.'

Conway said, very slowly, 'How did you know that?'

'Krah know. I hear him talk.'

Then it had been a trap all along, from the beginning. Krah had known. The old man had given him one chance to go from Iskar and he had not taken it – and Krah had been glad. After that he had withdrawn and waited for Conway to come to him.

The girl said, 'But I know without hearing. Now come, son of Conna.'

She led off, swift as a deer, her skirts kilted above her knees. Conway followed and behind and around them the horns bayed and answered with the eager voices of hounds that have found the scent and will never let it go.

All down the long valley the hunters drove them and the mountain walls narrowed in and in, and the ringing call of the horns came closer. There was a sound of joy in them, and they were without haste. Never once, beyond the white spume of the blowing snow, did Conway catch a glimpse of his pursuers. But he knew without seeing that old Krah's face bore a bleak and bitter smile, the terrible smile of a vengeance long delayed.

Conway knew well where the hunt would end. The horns would cry him into the throat of the cleft, and then they would be silent. He would not be permitted to reach the Lake.

Again he touched the little gun and his face could not have been less savage than Krah's. He was not afraid of spears.

The girl led him swiftly, surely, among the tangled rocks and the spurs of ice, her skirt whipping like a grey flag in the wind. High overhead the cold peaks filled the sky, leaving only a thin rift of stars. And suddenly, as though they were living things, the walls of the valley rushed together upon him, and the shouting of the horns rose to an exultant clamor in his ears, racing, leaping toward him.

He flung up his head and yelled, an angry, defiant cry. Then there was silence, and through the driven veils of snow he saw the shapes of men and the dim glittering of spears.

He would have drawn the gun and loosed its bright spray of instant sleep into the warriors. The drug would keep them quiet long enough for him to do what he had to do. But Ciel gave him no time. She wrenched at him suddenly, pulling him almost bodily into a crack between the rocks.

'Hurry!' she panted. '*Hurry!*'

The rough rock scraped him as he jammed his way through. He could hear voices behind him, loud and angry. It was pitch dark, even to his eyes, but Ciel caught his furs and pulled him along – a twist, a turn, a sharp corner that almost trapped him where her smallness slipped past easily. Then they were free again and he was running beside her, following her urgent breathless voice.

For a few paces he ran and then his steps slowed and dragged at last to a halt. There was no wind here in this sheltered place. There were no clouds of blowing snow to blur his vision.

He stood in a narrow cleft between the mountains. On both sides the cliffs of ice rose up, sheer and high and infinitely beautiful out of the powdery drifts. The darkling air was full of whirling motes of frost, like the dust of diamonds, and overhead the shining pinnacles stood clear against a sky of deepest indigo, spangled with great stars.

He stood in the narrow valley of his dream. And now at last he was afraid.

Truth and nightmare had come together like the indrawn flanks of the mountains and he was caught between them. Awake, aware of the biting cold and the personal sensation of his flesh, still the nameless terror of the dream beset him.

He could almost see the remembered shadow of his father weeping by the sheathed rocks that hid the end of the cleft, almost hear that cry of loss – *I can never go back to the Lake of the Gone Forever!*

He knew that now he was going to see the end of the dream. He would not wake this time before he passed the barrier rocks. The agonizing fear that had no basis in his own life stood naked in his heart and would not go.

He had known, somehow, all his life that this time must come. Now that it was here he found that he could not face it. The formless baseless terror took his strength away and not all his reasoning could help him. He could not go on.

And yet he went, as always, slowly forward through the drifting snow.

He had forgotten Ciel. He was surprised when she caught at him, urging him to run. He had forgotten Krah.

He remembered only the despairing words whispered back and forth by the cold lips of the ice. *Gone Forever . . . Gone Forever . . . !* He looked up and the golden stars wheeled above him in the dark blue sky. The beauty of them was evil and the shimmering turrets of the ice were full of lurking laughter.

Nightmare – and he walked in it broad awake.

It was not far. The girl dragged him on, drove him, and he obeyed automatically, quickening his slow pace. He did not fight. He knew that it was no use. He went on as a man walks patiently to the gallows.

He passed the barrier rocks. He was not conscious now of movement. In a sort of stasis, cold as the ice, he entered the cave that opened beyond them and looked at last upon the Lake of the Gone Forever.

7. Black Lake

It was black, that Lake. Utterly black and very still, lying in its ragged cradle of rock under the arching roof where, finally, the mountains met.

A strange quality of blackness, Conway thought, and shuddered deeply with the hand of nightmare still upon him. He stared into it, and suddenly, as though he had always known, he realized that the Lake was like the pupil of a living eye, having no light of its own but receiving into itself all light, all impression.

He saw himself reflected in that great unstirring eye and Ciel beside him. Where the images fell there were faint lines of frosty radiance, as though the substance of the Lake were graving upon itself in glowing acid the memory of what it saw.

Soft-footed from behind him came six other shadows – Krah and his five sons – and Conway could see that a great anger was upon them. But they had left their spears outside.

'We may not kill in this place,' said Krah slowly, 'but we can keep you from the thing you would do.'

'How do you know what I mean to do?' asked Conway and his face was strange as though he listened to distant voices speaking in an unknown tongue.

Krah answered, 'As your father came before you, so you have come – to steal from us the secret of the Lake.'

'Yes,' said Conway absently. 'Yes, that is so.'

The old man and his tall sons closed in around Conway and Ciel came and stood between them.

'Wait!' she said.

For the first time they acknowledged the presence of the girl.

'For your part in this,' said Krah grimly, 'you will answer later.'

'No!' she cried defiantly. 'I answer no! Listen. Once you love Conna. You learn from him good things. His mate happy, not slave. He bring wisdom to Iskar – but now you hate Conna, you forget.

'I go to Earth with Conna's son. But first he must come here. It is right he come. But you kill, you full of hate for Rand – I come to save him.'

She stood up to Krah, the little grey mouse transfigured into a bright creature of anger, blazing with it, alive with it.

'All my life – hate! Because of Rand you try to kill memory of Conna, you teach people hate and fear. But my mother learn from Conna. I learn from her – and I no forget! Rand happy, free. My mother know – and I no forget.'

It came to Conway with a queer shock that she was not speaking of him but of another Rand. He listened to the girl and there was a stillness in him as deep and lightless as the stillness of the Lake.

'You not kill, old man,' Ciel whispered. 'Not yet. Let him see, let him know. Then kill if he is evil.'

She swung around.

'Son of Conna! Look into the Lake. All the dead of Iskar buried here. They gone forever but memory lives. All come here in life, so that the Lake remember. Look, son of Conna, and think of your father!'

Still with that strange quiet heavy on his heart Rand Conway looked into the Lake and did as Ciel told him to do. Krah and his sons looked also and did not move.

At first there was nothing but the black infinite depth of the Lake. *It is semi-liquid*, said his father's notes, the notes he had kept secret from everyone – *and in this heavy medium are suspended particles of some transuranic element – perhaps an isotope of uranium itself that is unknown to us. Incalculable wealth – incalculable pain! My soul is there, lost in the Lake of the Gone Forever*.

Rand Conway stood waiting and the thought of his father was very strong in him. His father, who had died mourning that he could never come back.

Slowly, slowly, the image of his father took shape in the substance of the Lake, a ghostly picture painted with a brush of cold firs against the utter dark.

It was no projection of Rand Conway's own memory mirrored there, for this was not the man he had known, old before his time and broken with longing. This man was young, and his face was happy.

He turned and beckoned to someone behind him, and the shadowy figure of a girl came into the circle of his outstretched arm. They stood together, and a harsh sob broke from old Krah's throat. Conway knew that his father and the pale-haired lovely girl had stood where he stood now on the brink of the Lake and looked down as he was looking, that their images might be forever graven into the heart of the strange darkness below.

They kissed. And Ciel whispered, 'See her face, how it shines with joy.'

The figures moved away and were gone. Conway watched, beyond emotion, beyond fear. Some odd portion of his brain even found time to theorize on the electrical impulses of thought and how they could shape the free energy in the unknown substance of the Lake, so that it became almost a second subconscious mind for everyone on Iskar, storehouse from which the memories of a race could be called at will.

The eye of the Lake had seen and now, at the urging of those intense minds, it produced the pictures it had recorded like the relentless unreeling of some cosmic film.

Rand Conway watched, step by step, the disintegration of a man's soul. And it was easy for him to understand, since his own life had been ruled by that same consuming greed.

Conna came again and again to the Lake, alone. It seemed to hold a terrible fascination for him. After all he was a prospector, with no goal before him for many years but the making of a big strike. Finally he brought instruments and made tests and after that the fascination turned to greed and the greed in time to a sort of madness.

It was a madness that Conna fought against and he had reason. The girl came again. With her this time were Krah and his sons, all younger and less bitter than now, and others whom Conway did not know. It was obviously a ritual visit and it had to do with the newborn child the girl held in her arms.

Rand Conway's heart tightened until it was hardly beating. And through the frozen numbness that held him the old fear began to creep back, the nightmare fear of the dream, where something was hidden from him that he could not endure to see.

Conna, the girl, and a newborn child.

I cannot escape. I cannot awake from this.

Conna's inward struggle went on. He must have suffered the tortures of hell, for it was plain that what he meant to do would cut him off from all he loved. But he was no longer quite sane. The Lake mocked him, taunted him with its unbelievable wealth, and he could not forget it.

The last time that Conna came to the Lake of the Gone Forever, he had laid aside the furs and the spear of Iskar, and put on again his spaceman's leather and the holstered gun. He brought with him a leaden container, to take back proof of the Lake and what it held.

But while he worked to take his sample – the sample that would, in the end, mean the destruction of the Lake and all it meant to Iskar – the pale-haired girl came, her eyes full of pain and pleading, and the child was with her, a well-grown boy now, nearly two years old.

And Conna's son cried out suddenly and swayed so that Ciel put out her hand to him, and he clung to it, with the universe dark and reeling about him.

I know now! I know the fear behind the dream!

Within the Lake the shadowy child watched with uncomprehending horror how his mother snatched the little heavy box from his father's hands – his father who had grown so strange and violent and was dressed so queerly in black.

He watched how his mother wept and cried out to his father, pleading with him, begging him to stop and think and not destroy them all.

But Conna would not stop. He had fought his fight and lost and he would not stop.

He tried to take the box again. There was a brief moment when he and the girl swayed together on the brink of the Lake. And then – quickly, so very quickly that she had only time for one look at Conna as she fell – the girl fell over the edge. The disturbed cold fires of the Lake boiled up and overwhelmed her and there was no sight of her ever again.

The child screamed and ran to the edge of the rock. He too would have fallen if his father had not held him back.

For a long while Conna stood there, holding the whimpering child in his arms. The girl had taken the leaden box with her but Conna had forgotten that. He had forgotten everything except that his mate was dead, that he had killed her. And it was as though Conna too had died.

Then he turned and fled, taking the boy with him.

The surface of the Lake was as it had been, dark and still.

Rand Conway went slowly to his knees. He felt dully as though he had been ill for a long time. All the strength was gone out of him. He stayed there on the icy rock, motionless and silent, beyond feeling, beyond thought. He was only dimly aware that Ciel knelt beside him, that he was still clinging to her hand.

Presently he looked up at Krah.

'That was why you gave me my chance to leave Iskar. I was Conna's son – but I was the son of your daughter, too.'

'For her sake,' said Krah slowly, 'I would have let you go.'

Conway nodded. He was very tired. So many things were clear to him now. Everything had changed, even the meaning of the name he bore. Rand. It was all very strange, very strange indeed.

Ciel's hand was warm and comforting in his.

Slowly he took from his girdle the little gun and the leaden vial, and let them drop and slide away.

'Father of my mother,' he said to Krah, 'let me live.' He bowed his head and waited.

But Krah did not answer. He only said, 'Does Conna live?'

'No. He paid for her life, Krah, with his own.'

'That is well,' whispered the old man. And his sons echoed, 'That is well.'

Conway stood up. His mood of weary submission had left him.

'Krah,' he said, 'I had no part in Conna's crime and for my own – you know. I am of your blood, old man. I will not beg again. Take your spears and give me mine and we will see who dies!'

A ghost of a grim smile touched Krah's lips. He looked deeply into his grandson's eyes and presently he nodded.

'You are of my blood. And I think you will not forget. There will be no taking of spears.'

He stepped back and Conway said, 'Let the others go. They know nothing of the Lake and will not know. I will stay on Iskar.'

He caught Ciel to him. 'One thing, Krah. Ciel must not be punished.'

Again the grim smile. Some of the frosty cold had gone from Krah's eyes. In time, Conway thought, the old bitterness might vanish altogether.

'You have stood together by the Lake,' said Krah. 'It is our record of marriage. So if Ciel is beaten that is up to you.'

He turned abruptly and left the cavern and his sons went with him. Slowly, having yet no words to say, Rand Conway and Ciel followed them – into the narrow valley that held no further terrors for the man who had at last found his own world.

Behind them, the Lake of the Gone Forever lay still and black, as though it pondered over its memories, the loves and hatreds and sorrows of a world gathered from the beginning of time, safe there now until the end of it.

The Old Man

(1952)

DAPHNE DU MAURIER

Did I hear you asking about the Old Man? I thought so. You're a newcomer to the district, here on holiday. We get plenty these days, during the summer months. Somehow they always find their way eventually over the cliffs down to this beach, and then they pause and look from the sea back to the lake. Just as you did.

It's a lovely spot, isn't it? Quiet and remote. You can't wonder at the old man choosing to live here.

I don't remember when he first came. Nobody can. Many years ago, it must have been. He was here when I arrived, long before the war. Perhaps he came to escape from civilization, much as I did myself. Or maybe, where he lived before, the folks around made things too hot for him. It's hard to say. I had the feeling, from the very first, that he had done something, or something had been done to him, that gave him a grudge against the world. I remember the first time I set eyes on him I said to myself, 'I bet that old fellow is one hell of a character.'

Yes, he was living here beside the lake, along of his missus. Funny sort of lash-up they had, exposed to all the weather, but they didn't seem to mind.

I had been warned about him by one of the fellows from the farm, who advised me, with a grin, to give the old man who lived down by the lake a wide berth – he didn't care for strangers. So I went warily, and I didn't stay to pass the time of day. Nor would it have been any use if I had, not knowing a word of his lingo. The first time I saw him he was standing by the edge of the lake, looking out to sea, and from tact I avoided the piece of planking over the stream, which meant passing close to him, and crossed to the other side of the lake by the beach instead. Then, with an awkward feeling that I was trespassing and had no business to be there, I bobbed down behind a clump of gorse, took out my spy-glass, and had a peep at him.

He was a big fellow, broad and strong – he's aged, of course, lately; I'm speaking of several years back – but even now you can see what he must have been once. Such power and drive behind him, and that fine head, which he carried like a king. There's an idea in that, too. No, I'm not joking. Who knows what royal blood he carries inside him, harking back to some remote ancestor? And now and again, surging in him – not through his own fault – it gets the better of him and drives him fighting mad. I didn't think about that at the time. I just looked at him, and ducked behind the gorse when I saw him turn, and I wondered to myself what went on in his mind, whether he knew I was there, watching him.

If he should decide to come up the lake after me I should look pretty foolish. He must have thought better of it, though, or perhaps he did not care. He went on staring out to sea, watching the gulls and the incoming tide, and presently he ambled off his side of the lake, heading for the missus and home and maybe supper.

I didn't catch a glimpse of her that first day. She just wasn't around. Living as they do, close in by the left bank of the lake, with no proper track to the place, I hardly had the nerve to venture close and come upon her face to face. When I did see her, though, I was disappointed. She wasn't much to look at after all. What I mean is, she hadn't got anything like his character. A placid, mild-tempered creature, I judged her.

They had both come back from fishing when I saw them, and were making their way up from the beach to the lake. He was in front, of course. She tagged along behind. Neither of them took the slightest notice of me, and I was glad, because the old man might have paused, and waited, and told her to get on back home, and then come down towards the rocks where I was sitting. You ask what I would have said, had he done so? I'm damned if I know. Maybe I would have got up, whistling and seeming unconcerned, and then, with a nod and a smile – useless, really, but instinctive, if you know what I mean – said good day and pottered off. I don't think he would have done anything. He'd just have stared after me, with those strange narrow eyes of his, and let me go.

After that, winter and summer, I was always down on the beach or the rocks, and they went on living their curious, remote existence, sometimes fishing in the lake, sometimes at sea. Occasionally I'd come across them in the harbour on the estuary, taking a look at the yachts anchored there, and the shipping. I used to wonder which of them made the suggestion. Perhaps suddenly he would be lured by the thought of the bustle and life of the harbour, and all the things he had either wantonly given up or never known, and he would say to her, 'Today we are going into town.' And she, happy to do whatever pleased him best, followed along.

You see, one thing that stood out – and you couldn't help noticing it – was that the pair of them were devoted to one another. I've seen her greet him when he came back from a day's fishing and had left her back home, and towards evening she'd come down the lake and on to the beach and down to the sea to wait for him. She'd see him coming from a long way off, and I would see him too, rounding the corner of the bay. He'd come straight in to the beach, and she would go to meet him, and they would embrace each other, not caring a damn who saw them. It was touching, if you know what I mean. You felt there was something lovable about the old man, if that's how things were between them. He might be a devil to outsiders, but he was all the world to her. It gave me a warm feeling for him, when I saw them together like that.

You asked if they had any family? I was coming to that. It's about the family I really wanted to tell you. Because there was a tragedy, you see. And nobody knows anything about it except me. I suppose I could have told someone, but if I had, I don't know ... They might have taken the old man away, and she'd have broken her heart without him, and anyway, when all's said and done, it wasn't my business. I know the evidence against the old man was strong, but I hadn't positive proof, it might have been some sort of accident, and anyway, nobody made any inquiries at the time the boy disappeared, so who was I to turn busybody and informer?

I'll try and explain what happened. But you must understand that all this took place over quite a time, and sometimes I was away from home or busy, and didn't go near the lake. Nobody seemed to take any interest in the couple living there but myself, so that it was only what I observed with my own eyes that makes this story, nothing that I heard from anybody else, no scraps of gossip, or tales told about them behind their backs.

Yes, they weren't always alone, as they are now. They had four kids. Three girls and a boy. They brought up the four of them in that ramshackle old place by the lake, and it was always a wonder to me how they did it. God, I've known days when the rain lashed the lake into little waves that burst and broke on the muddy shore near by their place, and turned the marsh into a swamp, and the wind driving straight in. You'd have thought anyone with a grain of sense would have taken his missus and his kids out of it and gone off somewhere where they could get some creature comforts at least. Not the old man. If he could stick it, I guess he decided she could too, and the kids as well. Maybe he wanted to bring them up the hard way.

Mark you, they were attractive youngsters. Especially the youngest girl. I never knew her name, but I called her Tiny, she had so much go to her. Chip off the old block, in spite of her size. I can see her now, as a little thing, the first to venture paddling in the lake, on a fine morning, way ahead of her sisters and the brother.

The brother I nicknamed Boy. He was the eldest, and between you and me a bit of a fool. He hadn't the looks of his sisters and was a clumsy sort of fellow. The girls would play around on their own, and go fishing, and he'd hang about in the background, not knowing what to do with himself. If he possibly could he'd stay around home, near his mother. Proper mother's boy. That's why I gave him the name. Not that she seemed to fuss over him any more than she did the others. She treated the four alike, as far as I could tell. Her thoughts were always for the old man rather than for them. But Boy was just a great baby, and I have an idea he was simple.

Like the parents, the youngsters kept themselves to themselves. Been dinned into them, I dare say, by the old man. They never came down to the beach on their own and played; and it must have been a temptation, I thought, in full summer, when people came walking over the cliffs down to the beach to bathe and picnic. I suppose, for those strange reasons best known to himself, the old man had warned them to have no truck with strangers.

They were used to me pottering, day in, day out, fetching driftwood and that. And often I would pause and watch the kids playing by the lake. I didn't talk to them, though. They might have gone back and told the old man. They used to look up when I passed by, then glance away again, sort of shy. All but Tiny. Tiny would toss her head and do a somersault, just to show off.

I sometimes watched them go off, the six of them – the old man, the missus, Boy, and the three girls, for a day's fishing out to sea. The old man, of course, in charge; Tiny eager to help, close to her dad; the missus looking about her to see if the weather was going to keep fine; the two other girls alongside; and Boy, poor simple Boy, always the last to leave home. I never knew what sport they had. They used to stay out late, and I'd have left the beach by the time they came back again. But I guess they did well. They must have lived almost entirely on what they caught. Well, fish is said to be full of vitamins, isn't it? Perhaps the old man was a food faddist in his way.

Time passed, and the youngsters began to grow up. Tiny lost something of her individuality then, it seemed to me. She grew more like her sisters. They were a nice-looking trio, all the same. Quiet, you know, well-behaved.

As for Boy, he was enormous. Almost as big as the old man, but with what a difference! He had none of his father's looks, or strength, or personality; he was nothing but a great clumsy lout. And the trouble was, I believe the old man was ashamed of him. He didn't pull his weight in the home, I'm certain of that. And out fishing he was perfectly useless. The girls would work away like beetles, with Boy, always in the background, making a mess of things. If his mother was there he just stayed by her side.

I could see it rattled the old man to have such an oaf of a son. Irritated him, too, because Boy was so big. It probably didn't make sense to his intolerant mind. Strength and stupidity didn't go together. In any normal family, of course, Boy would have left home by now and gone out to work. I used to wonder if they argued about it back in the evenings, the missus and the old man, or if it was something never admitted between them but tacitly understood – Boy was no good.

Well, they did leave home at last. At least, the girls did.

I'll tell you how it happened.

It was a day in late autumn, and I happened to be over doing some shopping in the little town overlooking the harbour, three miles from this place, and suddenly I saw the old man, the missus, the three girls and Boy all making their way up to Pont – that's at the head of the creek going eastward from the harbour. There are a few cottages at Pont, and a farm and a church up behind. The family looked washed and spruced up, and so did the old man and the missus, and I wondered if they were going visiting. If they were, it was an unusual thing for them to do. But it's possible they had friends or acquaintances up there, of whom I knew nothing. Anyway, that was the last I saw of them, on the fine Saturday afternoon, making for Pont.

It blew hard over the week-end, a proper easterly gale. I kept indoors and didn't go out at all. I knew the seas would be breaking good and hard on the beach. I wondered if the old man and the family had been able to get back. They would have been wise to stay with their friends up Pont, if they had friends there.

It was Tuesday before the wind dropped and I went down to the beach again. Seaweed, driftwood, tar and oil all over the place. It's always the same after an easterly blow. I looked up the lake, towards the old man's shack, and I saw him there, with the missus, just by the edge of the lake. But there was no sign of the youngsters.

I thought it a bit funny, and waited around in case they should appear. They never did. I walked right round the lake, and from the opposite bank I had a good view of their place, and even took out my old spy-glass to have a closer look. They just weren't there. The old man was pottering about as he often did when he wasn't fishing, and the missus had settled herself down to bask in the sun. There was only one explanation. They had left the family with friends in Pont. They had sent the family for a holiday.

I can't help admitting I was relieved, because for one frightful moment I thought maybe they had started off back home on the Saturday night and got struck by the gale; and, well – that the old man and his missus had got back safely, but not the kids. It couldn't be that, though. I should have heard. Someone would have said something. The old man wouldn't be pottering there in his usual unconcerned fashion and the missus basking in the sun. No, that must have been it. They had left the family with friends. Or maybe the girls and the Boy had gone up country, gone to find themselves jobs at last.

Somehow it left a gap. I felt sad. So long now I had been used to seeing them all around, Tiny and the others. I had a strange sort of feeling that they had gone for good. Silly, wasn't it? To mind, I mean. There was the old man, and his missus, and the four youngsters, and I'd more or less watched them grow up, and now for no reason they had gone.

I wished then I knew even a word or two of his language, so that I could have called out to him, neighbour-like, and said, 'I see you and the missus are on your own. Nothing wrong, I hope?'

But there, it wasn't any use. He'd have looked at me with his strange eyes and told me to go to hell.

I never saw the girls again. No, never. They just didn't come back. Once I thought I saw Tiny, somewhere up the estuary, with a group of friends, but I couldn't be sure. If it was, she'd grown, she looked different. I tell you what I think. I think the old man and the missus took them with a definite end in view, that last week-end, and either settled them with friends they knew or told them to shift for themselves.

I know it sounds hard, not what you'd do for your own son and daughters, but you have to remember the old man was a tough customer, a law unto himself. No doubt he thought it would be for the best, and so it probably was, and if only I could know for certain what happened to the girls, especially Tiny, I wouldn't worry.

But I do worry sometimes, because of what happened to Boy.

You see, Boy was fool enough to come back. He came back about three weeks after that final week-end. I had walked down through the woods – not my usual way, but down to the lake by the stream that feeds it from a higher level. I rounded the lake by the marshes to the north, some distance from the old man's place, and the first thing I saw was Boy.

He wasn't doing anything. He was just standing by the marsh. He looked dazed. He was too far off for me to hail him; besides, I didn't have the nerve. But I watched him, as he stood there in his clumsy loutish way, and I saw him staring at the far end of the lake. He was staring in the direction of the old man.

The old man, and the missus with him, took not the slightest notice of Boy. They were close to the beach, by the plank bridge, and were either just going out to fish or coming back. And here was Boy, with his dazed stupid face, but not only stupid – frightened.

I wanted to say, 'Is anything the matter?' but I didn't know how to say it. I stood there, like Boy, staring at the old man.

Then what we both must have feared would happen, happened.

The old man lifted his head, and saw Boy.

He must have said a word to his missus, because she didn't move, she stayed where she was, by the bridge, but the old man turned like a flash of lightning and came down the other side of the lake towards the marshes, towards Boy. He looked terrible. I shall never forget his appearance. That magnificent head I had always admired now angry, evil; and he was cursing Boy as he came. I tell you, I heard him.

Boy, bewildered, scared, looked hopelessly about him for cover. There was none. Only the thin reeds that grew beside the marsh. But the poor fellow was so dumb he went in there, and crouched, and believed himself safe – it was a horrible sight.

I was just getting my own courage up to interfere when the old man stopped suddenly in his tracks, pulled up short as it were, and then, still cursing, muttering, turned back again and returned to the bridge. Boy watched him, from his cover of reeds, then, poor clot that he was, came out on to the marsh again, with some idea, I suppose, of striking for home.

I looked about me. There was no one to call. No one to give any help. And if I went and tried to get someone from the farm they would tell me not to interfere, that the old man was best left alone when he got in one of his rages, and anyway that Boy was old enough to take care of himself. He was as big as the old man. He could give as good as he got. I knew different. Boy was no fighter. He didn't know how.

I waited quite a time beside the lake but nothing happened. It began to grow dark. It was no use my waiting there. The old man and the missus left the bridge and went on home. Boy was still standing there on the marsh, by the lake's edge.

I called to him, softly. 'It's no use. He won't let you in. Go back to Pont, or wherever it is you've been. Go to some place, anywhere, but get out of here.'

He looked up, that same queer dazed expression on his face, and I could tell he hadn't understood a word I said.

I felt powerless to do any more. I went home myself. But I thought about Boy all evening, and in the morning I went down to the lake again, and I took a great stick with me to give me courage. Not that it would have been much good. Not against the old man.

Well . . . I suppose they had come to some sort of agreement, during the night. There was Boy, by his mother's side, and the old man was pottering on his own.

I must say, it was a great relief. Because, after all, what could I have said or done? If the old man didn't want Boy home, it was really his affair. And if Boy was too stupid to go, that was Boy's affair.

But I blamed the mother a good deal. After all, it was up to her to tell Boy he was in the way, and the old man was in one of his moods, and Boy had best get out while the going was good. But I never did think she had great intelligence. She did not seem to show much spirit at any time.

However, what arrangement they had come to worked for a time. Boy stuck close to his mother – I suppose he helped her at home, I don't know – and the old man left them alone and was more and more by himself.

He took to sitting down by the bridge, humped, staring out to sea, with a queer brooding look on him. He seemed strange, and lonely. I didn't like it. I don't know what his thoughts were, but I'm sure they were evil. It suddenly seemed a very long time since he and the missus and the whole family had gone fishing, a happy, contented party. Now everything had changed for him. He was thrust out in the cold, and the missus and Boy stayed together.

I felt sorry for him, but I felt frightened too. Because I felt it could not go on like this indefinitely; something would happen.

One day I went down to the beach for driftwood – it had been blowing in the night – and when I glanced towards the lake I saw that Boy wasn't with his mother. He was back where I had seen him that first day, on the edge of the marsh. He was as big as his father. If he'd known how to use his strength he'd have been a match for him any day, but he hadn't the brains. There he was, back on the marsh, a great big frightened foolish fellow, and there was the old man, outside his home, staring down towards his son with murder in his eyes.

I said to myself, 'He's going to kill him.' But I didn't know how or when or where, whether by night, when they were sleeping, or by day, when they were fishing. The mother was useless, she would not prevent it. It was no use appealing to the mother. If only Boy would use one little grain of sense, and go . . .

I watched and waited until nightfall. Nothing happened.

It rained in the night. It was grey, and cold, and dim. December was everywhere, trees all bare and bleak. I couldn't get down to the lake until late afternoon, and then the skies had cleared and the sun was shining in that watery way it does in winter, a burst of it, just before setting below the sea.

I saw the old man, and the missus too. They were close together, by the old shack, and they saw me coming for they looked towards me. Boy wasn't there. He wasn't on the marsh, either. Nor by the side of the lake.

I crossed the bridge and went along the right bank of the lake, and I had my spy-glass with me, but I couldn't see Boy. Yet all the time I was aware of the old man watching me.

Then I saw him. I scrambled down the bank, and crossed the marsh, and went to the thing I saw lying there, behind the reeds.

He was dead. There was a great gash on his body. Dried blood on his back. But he had lain there all night. His body was sodden with the rain.

Maybe you'll think I'm a fool, but I began to cry, like an idiot, and I shouted across to the old man, 'You murderer, you bloody God-damned murderer.' He did not answer. He did not move. He stood there, outside his shack with the missus, watching me.

You'll want to know what I did. I went back and got a spade, and I dug a grave for Boy, in the reeds behind the marsh, and I said one of my own prayers for him, being uncertain of his religion. When I had finished I looked across the lake to the old man.

And do you know what I saw?

I saw him lower his great head, and bend towards her and embrace her. And she lifted her head to him and embraced him too. It was both a requiem and a benediction. An atonement, and a giving of praise. In their strange way they knew they had done evil, but now it was over, because I had buried Boy and he was gone. They were free to be together again, and there was no longer a third to divide them.

They came out into the middle of the lake, and suddenly I saw the old man stretch his neck and beat his wings, and he took off from the water, full of power, and she followed him. I watched the two swans fly out to sea right into the face of the setting sun, and I tell you it was one of the most beautiful sights I ever saw in my life: the two swans flying there, alone, in winter.

My Flannel Knickers

(c. 1955)

LEONORA CARRINGTON

Thousands of people know my flannel knickers, and though I know this may seem flirtatious, it is not. I am a saint.

The 'Sainthood', I may say, was actually forced upon me. If anyone would like to avoid becoming holy, they should immediately read this entire story.

I live on an island. This island was bestowed upon me by the government when I left prison. It is not a desert island, it is a traffic island in the middle of a busy boulevard, and motors thunder past on all sides day and night.

So . . .

The flannel knickers are well known. They are hung at midday on a wire from the red green and yellow automatic lights. I wash them every day, and they have to dry in the sun.

Apart from the flannel knickers, I wear a gentleman's tweed jacket for golfing. It was given to me, and the gym shoes. No socks. Many people recoil from my undistinguished appearance, but if they have been told about me (mainly in the Tourist's Guide), they make a pilgrimage, which is quite easy.

Now I must trace the peculiar events that brought me to this condition. Once I was a great beauty and attended all sorts of cocktail-drinking, prize-giving-and-taking, artistic demonstrations and other casually hazardous gatherings organized for the purpose of people wasting other people's time. I was always in demand and my beautiful face would hang suspended over fashionable garments, smiling continually. An ardent heart, however, beat under the fashionable costumes, and this very ardent heart was like an open tap pouring quantities of hot water over anybody who asked. This wasteful process soon took its toll on my beautiful smiling face. My teeth fell out. The original structure of the face became blurred, and then began to fall away from the bones in small, ever-increasing folds. I sat and watched the process with a mixture of slighted vanity and acute depression. I was, I thought, solidly installed in my lunar plexus, within clouds of sensitive vapour.

If I happened to smile at my face in the mirror, I could objectively observe the fact that I had only three teeth left and these were beginning to decay.

Consequently . . .

I went to the dentist. Not only did he cure the three remaining teeth but he also presented me with a set of false teeth, cunningly mounted on a pink plastic chassis. When I had paid a sufficiently large quantity of my diminishing wealth, the teeth were mine and I took them home and put them into my mouth.

The Face seemed to regain some of its absolutely-irresistible-attraction, although the folds were of course still there. From the lunar plexus I arose like a hungry trout and was caught fast on the sharp barbed hook that hangs inside all once-very-beautiful faces.

A thin magnetic mist formed between myself, the face, and clear perception. This is what I saw in the mist. 'Well, well. I really was beginning to petrify in that old lunar plexus. This must be me, this beautiful, smiling fully toothed creature. There I was, sitting in the dark bloodstream like a mummified foetus with no love at all. Here I am, back in the rich world, where I can palpitate again, jump up and down in the nice warm swimming pool of outflowing emotion, the more bathers the merrier. I Shall Be Enriched.'

All these disastrous thoughts were multiplied and reflected in the magnetic mist. I stepped in, wearing my face, now back in the old enigmatic smile which had always turned sour in the past.

No sooner trapped than done.

Smiling horribly, I returned to the jungle of faces, each ravenously trying to eat each other.

Here I might explain the process that actually takes place in this sort of jungle. Each face is provided with greater or smaller mouths, armed with different kinds of sometimes natural teeth. (Anybody over forty and toothless should be sensible enough to be quietly knitting an original new body, instead of wasting the cosmic wool.) These teeth bar the way to a gaping throat, which disgorges whatever it swallows back into the foetid atmosphere.

The bodies over which these faces are suspended serve as ballast to the faces. As a rule they are carefully covered with colours and shapes in current 'Fashion'. This 'fashion' is a devouring idea launched by another face snapping with insatiable hunger for money and notoriety. The bodies, in constant misery and supplication, are generally ignored and only used for ambulation of the face. As I said, for ballast.

Once, however, that I bared my new teeth I realized that something had gone wrong. For after a very short period of enigmatic smiling, the smile became quite stiff and fixed, while the face slipped away from its bonish mooring, leaving me clutching desperately to a soft grey mask over a barely animated body.

The strange part of the affair now reveals itself. The jungle faces, instead of recoiling in horror from what I already knew to be a sad sight, approached me and started to beg me for something which I thought I had not got.

Puzzled, I consulted my Friend, a Greek.

He said: 'They think you have woven a complete face and body and are in constant possession of excess amounts of cosmic wool. Even if this is not so, the very fact that you know about the wool makes them determined to steal it.'

'I have wasted practically the entire fleece,' I told him. 'And if anybody steals from me now I shall die and disintegrate totally.'

'Three-dimensional life,' said the Greek, 'is formed by attitude. Since by their attitude they expect you to have quantities of wool, you are three-dimensionally forced to "Sainthood", which means you must spin your body and teach the faces how to spin theirs.'

The compassionate words of the Greek filled me with fear. I am a face myself. The quickest way of retiring from social Face-eating competition occurred to me when I attacked a policeman with my strong steel umbrella. I was quickly put into prison, where I spent months of health-giving meditation and compulsive exercise.

My exemplary conduct in prison moved the Head Wardress to an excess of bounty, and that is how the Government presented me with the island, after a small and distinguished ceremony in a remote corner of the Protestant Cemetery.

So here I am on the island with all sizes of mechanical artifacts whizzing by in every conceivable direction, even overhead.

Here I sit.

The Anything Box

(1956)

ZENNA HENDERSON

I suppose it was about the second week of school that I noticed Sue-lynn particularly. Of course, I'd noticed her name before and checked her out automatically for maturity and ability and probable performance the way most teachers do with their students during the first weeks of school. She had checked out mature and capable and no worry as to performance, so I had pigeonholed her – setting aside for the moment the little nudge that said, 'Too quiet' – with my other no-worrys until the fluster and flurry of the first days had died down a little.

I remember my noticing day. I had collapsed into my chair for a brief respite from guiding hot little hands through the intricacies of keeping a Crayola within reasonable bounds and the room was full of the relaxed, happy hum of a pleased class as they worked away, not realizing that they were rubbing 'blue' into their memories as well as onto their papers. I was meditating on how individual personalities were beginning to emerge among the thirty-five or so heterogeneous first graders I had, when I noticed Sue-lynn – really noticed her – for the first time.

She had finished her paper – far ahead of the others as usual – and was sitting at her table facing me. She had her thumbs touching in front of her on the table and her fingers curving as though they held something between them – something large enough to keep her fingertips apart and angular enough to bend her fingers as if for corners. It was something pleasant that she held – pleasant and precious. You could tell that by the softness of her hold. She was leaning forward a little, her lower ribs pressed against the table, and she was looking, completely absorbed, at the table between her hands. Her face was relaxed and happy. Her mouth curved in a tender half-smile, and as I watched, her lashes lifted and she looked at me with a warm share-the-pleasure look.

Then her eyes blinked and the shutters came down inside them. Her hand flicked into the desk and out. She pressed her thumbs to her forefingers and rubbed them slowly together. Then she laid one hand over the other on the table and looked down at them with the air of complete denial and ignorance children can assume so devastatingly.

The incident caught my fancy and I began to notice Sue-lynn. As I consciously watched her, I saw that she spent most of her free time staring at the table between her hands, much too unobtrusively to catch my busy attention. She hurried through even the fun-est of fun papers and then lost herself in looking. When Davie pushed her down at recess, and blood streamed from her knee to her ankle, she took her bandages and her tear-smudged face to that comfort she had so readily – if you'll pardon the expression – at hand, and emerged minutes later, serene and dry-eyed. I think Davie pushed her down because of her Looking. I know the day before he had come up to me, red-faced and squirming.

'Teacher,' he blurted. 'She Looks!'

'Who looks?' I asked absently, checking the vocabulary list in my book, wondering how on earth I'd missed 'where', one of these annoying 'wh' words that throw the children for a loss.

'Sue-lynn. She Looks and Looks!'

'At you?' I asked.

'Well –' He rubbed a forefinger below his nose, leaving a clean streak on his upper lip, accepting the proffered Kleenex and putting it in his pocket. 'She looks at her desk and tells lies. She says she can see –'

'Can see what?' My curiosity pricked up its ears.

'Anything,' said Davie. 'It's her Anything Box. She can see anything she wants to.'

'Does it hurt you for her to Look?'

'Well,' he squirmed. Then he burst out. 'She says she saw me with a dog biting me because I took her pencil – she said.' He started a pell-mell verbal retreat. 'She *thinks* I took her pencil. I only found –' His eyes dropped. 'I'll give it back.'

'I hope so,' I smiled. 'If you don't want her to look at you, then don't do things like that.'

'Dern girls,' he muttered, and clomped back to his seat.

So I think he pushed her down the next day to get back at her for the dog-bite.

Several times after that I wandered to the back of the room, casually in her vicinity, but always she either saw or felt me coming and the quick sketch of her hand disposed of the evidence. Only once I thought I caught a glimmer of something – but her thumb and forefinger brushed in sunlight, and it must have been just that.

Children don't retreat for no reason at all, and though Sue-lynn did not follow any overt pattern of withdrawal, I started to wonder about her. I watched her on the playground, to see how she tracked there. That only confused me more.

She had a very regular pattern. When the avalanche of children first descended at recess, she avalanched along with them and nothing in the shrieking, running, dodging mass resolved itself into a withdrawn Sue-lynn. But after ten minutes or so, she emerged from the crowd, tousle-haired, rosy-cheeked, smutched with dust, one shoelace dangling, and through some alchemy that I coveted for myself, she suddenly became untousled, undusty and unsmutched.

And there she was, serene and composed on the narrow little step at the side of the flight of stairs just where they disappeared into the base of the pseudo-Corinthian column that graced Our Door and her cupped hands received what ever they received and her absorption in what she saw became so complete that the bell came as a shock every time.

And each time, before she joined the rush to Our Door, her hand would sketch a gesture to her pocket, if she had one, or to the tiny ledge that extended between the hedge and the building. Apparently she always had to put the Anything Box away, but never had to go back to get it.

I was so intrigued by her putting whatever it was on the ledge that once I actually went over and felt along the grimy little outset. I sheepishly followed my children into the hall, wiping the dust from my fingertips, and Sue-lynn's eyes brimmed amusement at me without her mouth's smiling. Her hands mischievously squared in front of her and her thumbs caressed a solidness as the line of children swept into the room.

I smiled too because she was so pleased with having outwitted me. This seemed to be such a gay withdrawal that I let my worry die down. Better this manifestation than any number of other ones that I could name.

Someday, perhaps, I'll learn to keep my mouth shut. I wish I had before that long afternoon when we primary teachers worked together in a heavy cloud of Ditto fumes, the acrid smell of India ink, drifting cigarette smoke and the constant current of chatter, and I let Alpha get me started on what to do with our behaviour problems. She was all raunched up about the usual rowdy loudness of her boys and the eternal clack of her girls, and I – bless my stupidity – gave her Sue-lynn as an example of what should be our deepest concern rather than the outbursts from our active ones.

'You mean she just sits and looks at nothing?' Alpha's voice grated into her questioning tone.

'Well, I can't see anything,' I admitted. 'But apparently she can.'

'But that's having hallucinations!' Her voice went up a notch. 'I read a book once –'

'Yes.' Marlene leaned across the desk to flick ashes in the ash tray. 'So we have heard and heard and heard!'

'Well!' sniffed Alpha. 'It's better than *never* reading a book.'

'We're waiting,' Marlene leaked smoke from her nostrils, 'for the day when you read another book. This one must have been uncommonly long.'

'Oh, I don't know.' Alpha's forehead wrinkled with concentration. 'It was only about –' Then she reddened and turned her face angrily away from Marlene.

'Apropos of *our* discussion –' she said pointedly. 'It sounds to me like that child has a deep personality disturbance. Maybe even a psychotic – whatever –' Her eyes glistened faintly as she turned the thought over.

'Oh, I don't know,' I said, surprised into echoing her words at my sudden need to defend Sue-lynn. 'There's something about her. She doesn't have that apprehensive, hunched-shoulder, don't-hit-me-again air about her that so many withdrawn children have.' And I thought achingly of one of mine from last year that Alpha had now and was verbally bludgeoning back into silence after all my work with him. 'She seems to have a happy, adjusted personality, only with this odd little – *plus*.'

'Well, I'd be worried if she were mine,' said Alpha. 'I'm glad all my kids are so normal.' She sighed complacently. 'I guess I really haven't anything to kick about. I seldom ever have problem children except wigglers and yakkers, and a holler and a smack can straighten them out.'

Marlene caught my eye mockingly, tallying Alpha's class with me, and I turned away with a sigh. To be so happy – well I suppose ignorance does help.

'You'd better do something about that girl,' Alpha shrilled as she left the room. 'She'll probably get worse and worse as time goes on. Deteriorating, I think the book said.'

I had known Alpha a long time and I thought I knew how much of her talk to discount, but I began to worry about Sue-lynn. Maybe this *was* a disturbance that was more fundamental than the usual run of the mill that I had met up with. Maybe a child *can* smile a soft, contented smile and still have little maggots of madness flourishing somewhere inside.

Or, by gorry! I said to myself defiantly, maybe she *does* have an Anything Box. Maybe she *is* looking at something precious. Who am I to say no to anything like that?

An Anything Box! What could you see in an Anything Box? Heart's desire? I felt my own heart lurch – just a little – the next time Sue-lynn's hands curved. I breathed deeply to hold me in my chair. If it was *her* Anything Box, I wouldn't be able to see my heart's desire in it. Or would I? I propped my cheek up on my hand and doodled aimlessly on my time schedule sheet. How on earth, I wondered – not for the first time – do I manage to get myself off on these tangents?

Then I felt a small presence at my elbow and turned to meet Sue-lynn's wide eyes.

'Teacher?' The word was hardly more than a breath.

'Yes?' I could tell that for some reason Sue-lynn was loving me dearly at the moment. Maybe because her group had gone into new books that morning. Maybe because I had noticed her new dress, the ruffles of which made her feel very feminine and lovable, or maybe just because the late autumn sun lay so golden across her desk. Anyway, she was loving me to overflowing, and since, unlike most of the children, she had no casual hugs or easy moist kisses, she was bringing her love to me in her encompassing hands.

'See my box, Teacher? It's my Anything Box.'

'Oh, my!' I said. 'May I hold it?'

After all, I have held – tenderly or apprehensively or bravely – tiger magic, live rattlesnakes, dragon's teeth, poor little dead butterflies and two ears and a nose that dropped off Sojie one cold morning – none of which I could see any more than I could the Anything Box. But I took the squareness from her carefully, my tenderness showing in my fingers and my face.

And I received weight and substance and actuality!

Almost I let it slip out of my surprised fingers, but Sue-lynn's apprehensive breath helped me catch it and I curved my fingers around the precious warmness and looked down, down, past a faint shimmering, down into Sue-lynn's Anything Box.

I was running barefoot through the whispering grass. The swirl of my skirts caught the daisies as I rounded the gnarled apple tree at the corner. The warm wind lay along each of my cheeks and chuckled in my ears. My heart outstripped my flying feet and melted with a rush of delight into warmness as his arms –

I closed my eyes and swallowed hard, my palms tight against the Anything Box. 'It's beautiful!' I whispered. 'It's wonderful, Sue-lynn. Where did you get it?'

Her hands took it back hastily. 'It's mine,' she said defiantly. 'It's mine.'

'Of course,' I said. 'Be careful now. Don't drop it.'

She smiled faintly as she sketched a motion to her pocket. 'I won't.' She patted the flat pocket on her way back to her seat.

Next day she was afraid to look at me at first for fear I might say something or look something or in some way remind her of what must seem like a betrayal to her now, but after I only smiled my usual smile, with no added secret knowledge, she relaxed.

A night or so later when I leaned over my moon-drenched window sill and let the shadow of my hair hide my face from such ebullient glory, I remembered the Anything Box. Could I make one for myself? Could I square off this aching waiting, this outreaching, this silent cry inside me, and make it into an Anything Box? I freed my hands and brought them together, thumb to thumb, framing a part of the horizon's darkness between my upright forefingers. I stared into the empty square until my eyes watered. I sighed, and laughed a little, and let my hands frame my face as I leaned out into the night. To have magic so near – to feel it tingle off my fingertips and then to be so bound that I couldn't receive it. I turned away from the window – turning my back on brightness.

It wasn't long after this that Alpha succeeded in putting sharp points of worry back in my thoughts of Sue-lynn. We had ground duty together, and one morning when we shivered while the kids ran themselves rosy in the crisp air, she sizzled in my ear.

'Which one is it? The abnormal one, I mean.'

'I don't have any abnormal children,' I said, my voice sharpening before the sentence ended because I suddenly realized whom she meant.

'Well, I call it abnormal to stare at nothing.' You could almost taste the acid in her words. 'Who is it?'

'Sue-lynn,' I said reluctantly. 'She's playing on the bars now.'

Alpha surveyed the upside-down Sue-lynn whose brief skirts were belled down from her bare pink legs and half covered her face as she swung from one of the bars by her knees. Alpha clutched her wizened, blue hands together and breathed on them. 'She looks normal enough,' she said.

'She *is* normal!' I snapped.

'*Well*, bite my head off!' cried Alpha. 'You're the one that said she wasn't, not me – or is it "not I"? I never could remember. Not me? Not I?'

The bell saved Alpha from a horrible end. I never knew a person so serenely unaware of essentials and so sensitive to trivia.

But she had succeeded in making me worry about Sue-lynn again, and the worry exploded into distress a few days later.

Sue-lynn came to school sleepy-eyed and quiet. She didn't finish any of her work and she fell asleep during rest time. I cussed TV and Drive-Ins and assumed a night's sleep would put it right. But next day Sue-lynn burst into tears and slapped Davie clear off his chair.

'Why, Sue-lynn!' I gathered Davie up in all his astonishment and took Sue-lynn's hand. She jerked it away from me and flung herself at Davie again. She got two handfuls of his hair and had him out of my grasp before I knew it. She threw him bodily against the wall with a flip of her hands, then doubled up her fists and pressed them to her streaming eyes. In the shocked silence of the room, she stumbled over to Isolation and seating herself, back to the class, on the little chair, she leaned her head into the corner and sobbed quietly in big gulping sobs.

'What on earth goes on?' I asked the stupefied Davie who sat spraddle-legged on the floor fingering a detached tuft of hair. 'What did you do?'

'I only said "Robber Daughter,"' said Davie. 'It said so in the paper. My mama said her daddy's a robber. They put him in jail cause he robbered a gas station.' His bewildered face was trying to decide whether or not to cry. Everything had happened so fast that he didn't know yet if he was hurt.

'It isn't nice to call names,' I said weakly. 'Get back into your seat. I'll take care of Sue-lynn later.'

He got up and sat gingerly down in his chair, rubbing his ruffled hair, wanting to make more of a production of the situation but not knowing how. He twisted his face experimentally to see if he had tears available and had none.

'Dern girls,' he muttered, and tried to shake his fingers free of a wisp of hair.

I kept my eye on Sue-lynn for the next half hour as I busied myself with the class. Her sobs soon stopped and her rigid shoulders relaxed. Her hands were softly in her lap and I knew she was taking comfort from her Anything Box. We had our talk together later, but she was so completely sealed off from me by her misery that there was no communication between us. She sat quietly watching me as I talked, her hands trembling in her lap. It shakes the heart, somehow, to see the hands of a little child quiver like that.

That afternoon I looked up from my reading group, startled, as though by a cry, to catch Sue-lynn's frightened eyes. She looked around bewildered and then down at her hands again – her empty hands. Then she darted to the Isolation corner and reached under the chair. She went back to her seat slowly, her hands squared to an unseen weight. For the first time, apparently, she had had to go get the Anything Box. It troubled me with a vague unease for the rest of the afternoon.

Through the days that followed while the trial hung fire, I had Sue-lynn in attendance bodily, but that was all. She sank into her Anything Box at every opportunity. And always, if she had put it away somewhere, she had to go back for it. She roused more and more reluctantly from these waking dreams, and there finally came a day when I had to shake her to waken her.

I went to her mother, but she couldn't or wouldn't understand me, and made me feel like a frivolous gossip-monger taking her mind away from her husband, despite the fact that I didn't even mention him – or maybe because I didn't mention him.

'If she's being a bad girl, spank her,' she finally said, wearily shifting the weight of a whining baby from one hip to another and pushing her tousled hair off her forehead. 'Whatever you do is all right by me. My worrier is all used up. I haven't got any left for the kids right now.'

Well, Sue-lynn's father was found guilty and sentenced to the State Penitentiary and school was less than an hour old the next day when Davie came up, clumsily a-tiptoe, braving my wrath for interrupting a reading group, and whispered hoarsely, 'Sue-lynn's asleep with her eyes open again, Teacher.'

We went back to the table and Davie slid into his chair next to a completely unaware Sue-lynn. He poked her with a warning finger. 'I told you I'd tell on you.'

And before our horrified eyes, she toppled, as rigidly as a doll, sideways off the chair. The thud of her landing relaxed her and she lay limp on the green asphalt tile – a thin paper doll of a girl, one hand still clenched open around something. I pried her fingers loose and almost wept to feel enchantment dissolve under my heavy touch. I carried her down to the nurse's room and we worked over her with wet towels and prayer and she finally opened her eyes.

'Teacher,' she whispered weakly.

'Yes, Sue-lynn.' I took her cold hands in mine.

'Teacher, I almost got in my Anything Box.'

'No,' I answered. 'You couldn't. You're too big.'

'Daddy's there,' she said. 'And where we used to live.'

I took a long, long look at her wan face. I hope it was genuine concern for her that prompted my next words. I hope it wasn't envy or the memory of the niggling nagging of Alpha's voice that put firmness in my voice as I went on. 'That's play-like,' I said. 'Just for fun.'

Her hands jerked protestingly in mine. 'Your Anything Box is just for fun. It's like Davie's cow pony that he keeps in his desk or Sojie's jet-plane, or when the big bear chases all of you at recess. It's fun-for-play, but it's not for real. You mustn't think it's for real. It's only play.'

'No!' she denied. '*No!*' she cried frantically, and hunching herself up on the cot, peering through her tear-swollen eyes, she scrabbled under the pillow and down beneath the rough blanket that covered her.

'Where is it?' she cried. 'Where is it? Give it back to me, Teacher!'

She flung herself toward me and pulled open both my clenched hands.

'Where did you put it? Where did you put it?'

'There is no Anything Box,' I said flatly, trying to hold her to me and feeling my heart breaking along with hers.

'You took it!' she sobbed. 'You took it away from me!' And she wrenched herself out of my arms.

'Can't you give it back to her?' whispered the nurse. 'If it makes her feel so bad? Whatever it is —'

'It's just imagination,' I said, almost sullenly. 'I can't give her back something that doesn't exist.'

Too young! I thought bitterly. Too young to learn that heart's desire is only play-like.

Of course the doctor found nothing wrong. Her mother dismissed the matter as a fainting spell and Sue-lynn came back to class next day, thin and listless, staring blankly out the window, her hands palm down on the desk. I swore by the pale hollow of her cheek that never, *never* again would I take any belief from anyone without replacing it with something better. What had I given Sue-lynn? What had she better than I had taken from her? How did I know but that her Anything Box was on purpose to tide her over rough spots in her life like this? And what now, now that I had taken it from her?

Well, after a time she began to work again, and later, to play. She came back to smiles, but not to laughter. She puttered along quite satisfactorily except that she was a candle blown out. The flame was gone wherever the brightness of belief goes. And she had no more sharing smiles for me, no overflowing love to bring to me. And her shoulder shrugged subtly away from my touch.

Then one day I suddenly realized that Sue-lynn was searching our classroom. Stealthily, casually, day by day she was searching, covering every inch of the room. She went through every puzzle box, every lump of clay, every shelf and cupboard, every box and bag. Methodically she checked behind every row of books and in every child's desk until finally, after almost a week, she had been through everything in the place except my desk. Then she began to materialize suddenly at my elbow every time I opened a drawer. And her eyes would probe quickly and sharply before I slid it shut again. But if I tried to intercept her looks, they slid away and she had some legitimate errand that had brought her up to the vicinity of the desk.

She believes it again, I thought hopefully. She won't accept the fact that her Anything Box is gone. She wants it again.

But it *is* gone, I thought drearily. It's really-for-true gone.

My head was heavy from troubled sleep, and sorrow was a weariness in all my movements. Waiting is sometimes a burden almost too heavy to carry. While my children hummed happily over their fun-stuff, I brooded silently out the window until I managed a laugh at myself. It was a shaky laugh that threatened to dissolve into something else, so I brisked back to my desk.

As good a time as any to throw out useless things, I thought, and to see if I can find that colored chalk I put away so carefully. I plunged my hands into the wilderness of the bottom right-hand drawer of my desk. It was deep with a huge accumulation of anything – just anything – that might need a temporary hiding place. I knelt to pull out leftover Jack Frost pictures, and a broken beanshooter, a chewed red ribbon, a roll of cap gun ammunition, one striped sock, six Numbers papers, a rubber dagger, a copy of the *Gospel According to St Luke*, a miniature coal shovel, patterns for jack-o'-lanterns and a pink plastic pelican. I retrieved my Irish linen hankie I thought lost forever and Sojie's report card that he had told me solemnly had blown out of his hand and landed on a jet and broke the sound barrier so loud that it busted all to flitters. Under the welter of miscellany, I felt a squareness. Oh, happy! I thought, this *is* where I put the colored chalk! I cascaded papers off both sides of my lifting hands and shook the box free.

We were together again. Outside, the world was an enchanting wilderness of white, the wind shouting softly through the windows, tapping wet, white fingers against the warm light. Inside, all the worry and waiting, the apartness and loneliness were over and forgotten, their hugeness dwindled by the comfort of a shoulder, the warmth of clasping hands – and nowhere, nowhere was the fear of parting; nowhere the need to do without again. This was the happy ending. This was –

This was Sue-lynn's Anything Box!

My racing heart slowed as the dream faded – and rushed again at the realization. I had it here! In my junk drawer! It had been here all the time!

I stood up shakily, concealing the invisible box in the flare of my skirts. I sat down and put the box carefully in the center of my desk, covering the top of it with my palms lest I should drown again in delight. I looked at Sue-lynn. She was finishing her fun paper, competently but unjoyously. Now would come her patient sitting with quiet hands until told to do something else.

Alpha would approve. And very possibly, I thought, Alpha would, for once in her limited life, be right. We may need 'hallucinations' to keep us going – all of us but the Alphas – but when we go so far as to try to force ourselves, physically, into the Never-Never-land of heart's desire –

I remembered Sue-lynn's thin rigid body toppling doll-like off its chair. Out of her deep need she had found – or created? Who could tell? – something too dangerous for a child. I could so easily bring the brimming happiness back to her eyes – but at what a possible price!

No, I had a duty to protect Sue-lynn. Only maturity – the maturity born of the sorrow and loneliness that Sue-lynn was only beginning to know – could be trusted to use an Anything Box safely and wisely.

My heart thudded as I began to move my hands, letting the palms slip down from the top to shape the sides of –

I had moved them back again before I really saw, and I have now learned almost to forget that glimpse of what heart's desire is like when won at the cost of another's heart.

I sat there at the desk trembling and breathless, my palms moist, feeling as if I had been on a long journey away from the little schoolroom. Perhaps I had. Perhaps I had been shown all the kingdoms of the world in a moment of time.

'Sue-lynn,' I called. 'Will you come up here when you're through?'

She nodded unsmilingly and snipped off the last paper from the edge of Mistress Mary's dress. Without another look at her handiwork, she carried the scissors safely to the scissors box, crumpled the scraps of paper in her hand and came up to the wastebasket by the desk.

'I have something for you, Sue-lynn,' I said, uncovering the box.

Her eyes dropped to the desk top. She looked indifferently up at me. 'I did my fun paper already.'

'Did you like it?'

'Yes.' It was a flat lie.

'Good,' I lied right back. 'But look here.' I squared my hands around the Anything Box.

She took a deep breath and the whole of her little body stiffened.

'I found it,' I said hastily, fearing anger. 'I found it in the bottom drawer.'

She leaned her chest against my desk, her hands caught tightly between, her eyes intent on the box, her face white with the aching want you see on children's faces pressed to Christmas windows.

'Can I have it?' she whispered.

'It's yours,' I said, holding it out. Still she leaned against her hands, her eyes searching my face.

'Can I have it?' she asked again.

'Yes!' I was impatient with this anticlimax. 'But –'

Her eyes flickered. She had sensed my reservation before I had. 'But you must never try to get into it again.'

'Okay,' she said, the word coming out on a long relieved sigh. 'Okay, Teacher.'

She took the box and tucked it lovingly into her small pocket. She turned from the desk and started back to her table. My mouth quirked with a small smile. It seemed to me that everything about her had suddenly turned upwards – even the ends of her straight taffy-colored hair. The subtle flame about her that made her Sue-lynn was there again. She scarcely touched the floor as she walked.

I sighed heavily and traced on the desk top with my finger a probable size for an Anything Box. What would Sue-lynn choose to see first? How like a drink after a drought it would seem to her.

I was startled as a small figure materialized at my elbow. It was Sue-lynn, her fingers carefully squared before her.

'Teacher,' she said softly, all the flat emptiness gone from her voice. 'Any time you want to take my Anything Box, you just say so.'

I groped through my astonishment and incredulity for words. She couldn't possibly have had time to look into the Box yet.

'Why, thank you, Sue-lynn,' I managed. 'Thanks a lot. I would like very much to borrow it some time.'

'Would you like it now?' she asked, proffering it.

'No, thank you,' I said, around the lump in my throat. 'I've had a turn already. You go ahead.'

'Okay,' she murmured. Then – 'Teacher?'

'Yes?'

Shyly she leaned against me, her cheek on my shoulder. She looked up at me with her warm, unshuttered eyes, then both arms were suddenly around my neck in a brief awkward embrace.

'Watch out!' I whispered, laughing into the collar of her blue dress. 'You'll lose it again!'

'No I won't,' she laughed back, patting the flat pocket of her dress. 'Not ever, ever again!'

Miss Pinkerton's Apocalypse

(1958)

MURIEL SPARK

One evening, a damp one in February, something flew in at the window. Miss Laura Pinkerton, who was doing something innocent to the fire, heard a faint throbbing noise overhead. On looking up, 'George! come here! come quickly!'

George Lake came in at once, though sullenly because of their quarrel, eating a sandwich from the kitchen. He looked up at the noise then sat down immediately.

From this point onward their story comes in two versions, his and hers. But they agree as to the main facts; they agree that it was a small round flattish object, and that it flew.

'It's a flying object of some sort,' whispered George eventually.

'It's a saucer,' said Miss Pinkerton, keen and loud, 'an antique piece. You can tell by the shape.'

'It can't be an antique, that's absolutely certain,' George said.

He ought to have been more tactful, and would have been, but for the stress of the moment. Of course it set Miss Pinkerton off, she being in the right.

'I know my facts,' she stated as usual, 'I should hope I know my facts. I've been in antique china for twenty-three years in the autumn,' which was true, and George knew it.

The little saucer was cavorting round the lamp.

'It seems to be attracted by the light,' George remarked, as one might distinguish a moth.

Promptly, it made as if to dive dangerously at George's head. He ducked, and Miss Pinkerton backed against the wall. As the dish tilted on its side, skimming George's shoulder, Miss Pinkerton could see inside it.

'The thing might be radioactive. It might be dangerous.' George was breathless. The saucer had climbed, was circling high above his head, and now made for him again, but missed.

'It is not radioactive,' said Miss Pinkerton, 'it is Spode.'

'Don't be so damn silly,' George replied, under the stress of the occasion.

'All right, very well,' said Miss Pinkerton, 'it is not Spode. I suppose you are the expert, George, I suppose you know best. I was only judging by the pattern. After the best part of a lifetime in china –'

'It must be a forgery,' George said unfortunately. For, unfortunately, something familiar and abrasive in Miss Pinkerton's speech began to grind within him. Also, he was afraid of the saucer.

It had taken a stately turn, following the picture rail in a steady career round the room.

'Forgery, ha!' said Miss Pinkerton. She was out of the room like a shot, and in again carrying a pair of steps.

'I will examine the mark,' said she, pointing intensely at the saucer. 'Where are my glasses?'

Obligingly, the saucer settled in a corner; it hung like a spider a few inches from the ceiling. Miss Pinkerton adjusted the steps. With her glasses on she was almost her sunny self again, she was ceremonious and expert.

'Don't touch it, don't go near it!' George pushed her aside and grabbed the steps, knocking over a blue glass bowl, a Dresden figure, a vase of flowers and a decanter of sherry; like a bull in a china shop, as Miss Pinkerton exclaimed. But she was determined, and struggled to reclaim the steps.

'Laura!' he said desperately. 'I believe it is Spode. I take your word.'

The saucer then flew out of the window.

They acted quickly. They telephoned to the local paper. A reporter would come right away. Meanwhile, Miss Pinkerton telephoned to her two scientific friends – at least, one was interested in psychic research and the other was an electrician. But she got no reply from either. George had leaned out of the window, scanning the rooftops and the night sky. He had leaned out of the back windows, had tried all the lights and the wireless. These things were as usual.

The news man arrived, accompanied by a photographer.

'There's nothing to photograph,' said Miss Pinkerton excitably. 'It went away.'

'We could take a few shots of the actual spot,' the man explained.

Miss Pinkerton looked anxiously at the result of George and the steps.

'The place is a wreck.'

Sherry from the decanter was still dripping from the sideboard.

'I'd better clear the place up. George, help me!' She fluttered nervously, and started to pack the fire with small coals.

'No, leave everything as it is,' the reporter advised her. 'Did the apparition make this mess?'

George and Miss Pinkerton spoke together.

'Well, indirectly,' said George.

'It wasn't an apparition,' said Miss Pinkerton.

The reporter settled on the nearest chair, poising his pencil and asking, 'Do you mind if I take notes?'

'Would you mind sitting over here?' said Miss Pinkerton. 'I don't use the Queen Annes normally. They are very frail pieces.'

The reporter rose as if stung, then perched on a table which Miss Pinkerton looked at uneasily.

'You see, I'm in antiques,' she rattled on, for the affair was beginning to tell on her, as George told himself. In fact he sized up that she was done for; his irritation abated, his confidence came flooding back.

'Now, Laura, sit down and take it easy.' Solicitously he pushed her into an easy chair.

'She's overwrought,' he informed the pressmen in an audible undertone.

'You say this object actually flew in this window?' suggested the reporter.

'That is correct,' said George.

The camera-man trained his apparatus on the window.

'And you were both here at the time?'

'No,' Miss Pinkerton said. 'Mr Lake was in the kitchen and I called out, of course. But he didn't see inside the bowl, only the outside, underneath where the manufacturer's mark is. I saw the pattern so I got the steps to make sure. That's how Mr Lake knocked my things over. I saw inside.'

'I am going to say something,' said George.

The men looked hopefully towards him. After a pause, George continued, 'Let us begin at the beginning.'

'Right,' said the reporter, breezing up.

'It was like this,' George said. 'I came straight in when Miss Pinkerton screamed, and there was a white convex disc, you realize, floating around up there.'

The reporter contemplated the spot indicated by George.

'It was making a hell of a racket like a cat purring,' George told him.

'Any idea what it really was?' the reporter enquired.

George took his time to answer. 'Well, yes,' he said, 'and no.'

'Spode ware,' said Miss Pinkerton.

George continued, 'I'm not up in these things. I'm extremely sceptical as a rule. This was a new experience to me.'

'That's just it,' said Miss Pinkerton. 'Personally, I've been in china for twenty-three years. I recognized the thing immediately.'

The reporter scribbled and enquired, 'These flying discs appear frequently in China?'

'It was a saucer. I've never seen one flying before,' Miss Pinkerton explained.

'I am going to ask a question,' George said.

Miss Pinkerton continued, 'Mr Lake is an art framer. He handles old canvases but next to no antiques.'

'I am going to ask. Are you telling the story or am I?' George said.

'Perhaps Mr Lake's account first and then the lady's,' the reporter ventured.

Miss Pinkerton subsided crossly while he turned to George.

'Was the object attached to anything? No wires or anything? I mean, someone couldn't have been having a joke or something?'

George gave a decent moment to the possibility.

'No,' he then said. 'It struck me, in fact, that there was some sort of Mind behind it, operating from outer space. It tried to attack me, in fact.'

'Really, how was that?'

'Mr Lake was not attacked,' Miss Pinkerton stated. 'There was no danger at all. I saw the expression on the pilot's face. He was having a game with Mr Lake, grinning all over his face.'

'Pilot?' said George. 'What are you talking about – pilot!'

Miss Pinkerton sighed. 'A tiny man half the size of my finger,' she declared. 'He sat on a tiny stool. He held the little tiny steering-wheel with one hand and waved with the other. Because, there was something like a sewing-machine fixed near the rim, and he worked the tiny treadle with his foot. Mr Lake was not attacked.'

'Don't be so damn silly,' said George.

'You don't mean this?' the reporter asked her with scrutiny.

'Of course I do.'

'I would like to know something,' George demanded.

'You only saw the under side of the saucer, George.'

'You said nothing about any pilot at the time,' said George. 'I saw no pilot.'

'Mr Lake got a fright when the saucer came at him. If he hadn't been dodging he would have seen for himself.'

'You mentioned no pilot,' said George. 'Be reasonable.'

'I had no chance,' said she. She appealed to the camera-man. 'You see, I know what I'm talking about. Mr Lake thought he knew better, however. Mr Lake said, "It's a forgery." If there's one thing I do know, it's china.'

'It would be most unlikely,' said George to the reporter. 'A steering-wheel and a treadle machine these days, can you credit it?'

'The man would have fallen out,' the camera-man reflected.

'I must say,' said the reporter, 'that I favour Mr Lake's long-range theory. The lady may have been subject to some hallucination, after the shock of the saucer.'

'Quite,' said George. He whispered something to the photographer. 'Women!' Miss Pinkerton heard him breathe.

The reporter heard him also. He gave a friendly laugh. 'Shall we continue with Mr Lake's account, and then see what we can make of both stories?'

But Miss Pinkerton had come to a rapid decision. She began to display a mood hitherto unknown to George. Leaning back, she gave way to a weak and artless giggling. Her hand fluttered prettily as she spoke between gurgles of mirth. 'Oh, what a mess! What an evening! We aren't accustomed to drink, you see, and now oh dear, oh dear!'

'Are you all right, Laura?' George enquired severely.

'Yes, yes, yes,' said Miss Pinkerton, drowsy and amiable. 'We really oughtn't have done this, George. Bringing these gentlemen out. But I can't keep it up, George. Oh dear, it's been fun though.'

She was away into her giggles again. George looked bewildered. Then he looked suspicious.

'It's definitely the effect of this extraordinary phenomenon,' George said firmly to the Press.

'It was my fault, all my fault,' spluttered Miss Pinkerton.

The reporter looked at his watch. 'I can quite definitely say you saw a flying object?' he asked. 'And that you were both put out by it?'

'Put down that it was a small, round, flattish object. We both agree to that,' George said.

A spurt of delight arose from Miss Pinkerton again.

'Women, you know! It always comes down to women in the finish,' she told them. 'We had a couple of drinks.'

'Mr Lake had rather more than I did,' she added triumphantly.

'I assure you,' said George to the reporter.

'We might be fined for bringing the Press along, George. It might be an offence,' she put in.

'I assure you,' George insisted to the photographer, 'that we had a flying saucer less than an hour ago in this room.'

Miss Pinkerton giggled.

The reporter looked round the room with new eyes; and with the air of one to whom to understand all is to forgive all, he folded his notebook. The camera-man stared at the pool of sherry, the overturned flowers, the broken glass and china. He packed up his camera, and they went away.

George gave out the tale to his regular customers. He gave both versions, appealing to their reason to choose. Further up the road at her corner shop, Miss Pinkerton smiled tolerantly when questioned. 'Flying saucer? George is very artistic,' she would say, 'and allowances must be made for imaginative folk.' Sometimes she added that the evening had been a memorable one, 'Quite a party!'

It caused a certain amount of tittering in the neighbourhood. George felt this; but otherwise, the affair made no difference between them. Personally, I believe the story, with a preference for Miss Pinkerton's original version. She is a neighbour of mine. I have reason to believe this version because, not long afterwards, I too received a flying visitation from a saucer. The little pilot, in my case, was shy and inquisitive. He pedalled with all his might. My saucer was Royal Worcester, fake or not I can't say.

A Bright Green Field

(1958)

ANNA KAVAN

In my travels I am always being confronted by a particular field. It seems that I simply can't escape it. Any journey, no matter where it begins, is apt to end towards evening in sight of this meadow, which is quite small, sloping, and in the vicinity of tall dark trees.

The meadow is always beautifully green; in the dusk it looks almost incandescent, almost a source of light, as though the blades of grass themselves radiated brightness. The vividness of the grass is always what strikes people first; it takes them a moment longer to notice that, as a matter of fact, the green is rather too intense to be pleasant, and to wonder why they did not see this before. The observation once made, it becomes obvious that for grass to be luminiferous is somewhat improper. It has no business to advertise itself so ostentatiously. Such effulgent lustre is unsuited to its humble place in the natural order, and shows that in this meadow the grass has risen above itself – grown arrogant, aggressive, too full of strength.

Its almost sensational, inappropriate brightness is always the same. Instead of changing with the seasons, as if to underline the insolence of the grass, the field's brilliance remains constant, though in other ways its aspect varies with the time and place. It is true that, besides being always bright green, the field is always small, always sloping, always near big dark trees. But size and colour are relative, different people mean different things when they speak of a small bright meadow or a big dark tree. The idea of a slope is flexible too, and though a persistent divergence from the horizontal is characteristic of the field, the degree of steepness fluctuates widely.

The slant may be imperceptible, so that one would swear the surface was as flat as a billiard-table. There have been times when I couldn't believe – until it was proved to me by measurements taken with a clinometer – that the ground was not perfectly level. On other occasions, in contrast with what may be called an invisible incline, the meadow appears to rise almost vertically.

I shall never forget seeing it so that thundery summer day, when, since early morning, I had been travelling across a great dusty plain. The train was oppressively hot, the landscape monotonous and without colour, and, during the afternoon, I fell into an uneasy doze; from which I woke to the pleasant surprise of seeing mountain slopes covered with pines and boulders. But, after the first moment, I found that, with the mountains shutting out the sky, the enclosed atmosphere of the deep ravine was just as oppressive as that of the flat country. Everything looked drab and dingy, the rocks a nondescript mottled tint, the pines the shiny blackish-green of some immensely old shabby black garment – their dense foliage, at its brightest the colour of verdigris, suggesting rot and decay, had the unmoving rigidity of a metal with the property of absorbing light, and seemed to extinguish any occasional sunbeam that penetrated the heavy clouds. Although the line kept twisting and turning, the scenery never changed, always composed of the same eternal pine forest and masses of rock, pervaded, as the plain had been, by an air of dull sterile monotony and vegetative indifference.

The train suddenly wound round another sharp bend, and came out into a more open place where the gorge widened, and I saw, straight ahead, between two cataracts of black trees, the sheer emerald wall that was the meadow, rising perpendicular, blazing with jewel-brightness, all the more resplendent for its dismal setting.

After the dim monochrome vistas at which I had been looking all day, this sudden unexpected flare of brilliance was so dazzling that I could not immediately identify the curious dark shapes dotted about the field, still further irradiated, as it was now, by the glow of the setting sun, which broke through the clouds just as I reached the end of my journey, making each blade of grass scintillate like a green flame.

The field was still in full view when I emerged from the station, a spectacular vivid background to the little town, of which it appeared to be an important feature, the various buildings having been kept low, and grouped as if to avoid hiding it. Now that I was able to look more carefully, and without the distorting and distracting effect of the train's motion, I recognized the peculiar scattered shapes I had already noticed as prone half-naked human bodies, spread-eagled on the glistening bright green wall of grass. They were bound to it by an arrangement of ropes and pulleys, that slowly drew them across its surface, and had semicircular implements of some sort fastened to their hands, which they continually jerked in a spasmodic fashion, reminding me of struggling flies caught in a spider's web. This tormented jerking, and the fact that the grotesque sprawling figures were chained to the tackle pulling them along, made me think they must be those of malefactors, undergoing some strange archaic form of punishment, conducted in public up there on the burning green field. In this, however, I was mistaken.

A passerby presently noticed my interest in the mysterious movements outlined so dramatically on the brilliant green, and, seeing that I was a stranger, very civilly started a conversation, informing me that I was not watching criminals, as I had supposed, but labourers engaged in cutting the grass, which grew excessively fast and strongly in that particular field.

I was surprised that such a barbarous mowing process should be employed merely to keep down the grass in a small field, even though in a way, it formed part of the town; and I inquired whether their obviously painful exertions did not jeopardize the health and efficiency of the workers.

Yes, I was told, unfortunately the limbs, and even the lives, of the men up there were in danger, both from the effects of overstrain, and because the securing apparatus was not infrequently broken by the violence of their muscular contractions. It was regrettable, but no alternative method of mowing had so far been discovered, since the acute angle of the ground prohibited standing upon it, or even crawling across on all fours, as had at times been attempted. Of course, every reasonable precaution was taken; but, in any case, these labourers were expendable, coming from the lowest ranks of the unskilled population. I should not pay too much attention to the spasms and convulsions I was observing, as these were mainly just mimicry, a traditional miming of the sufferings endured by earlier generations of workers before the introduction of the present system. The work was now much less arduous than it looked, and performed under the most humane conditions that had as yet been devised. It might interest me to know that it was not at all unpopular; on the contrary, there was considerable competition for this form of employment, which entailed special privileges and prestige. In the event of a fatality, a generous grant was made to the dependents of the victim, who, in accordance with tradition, was always interred *in situ* – a custom dating from antiquity, and conferring additional prestige, which extended to the whole family of the deceased.

All this information was given in a brisk, matter-of-fact way that was reassuring. But I could not help feeling a trifle uneasy as I gazed at the meadow, compelled by a kind of grisly fascination to watch those twitching marionettes, dehumanized by the intervening distance, and by their own extraordinary contortions. It seemed to me that these became more tortured as the sun went down, as though a frantic haste inspired the wild uncoordinated swinging of the sickles, while the green of the grass brightened almost to phosphorescence against the dusk.

I wanted to ask why the field had to be mown at all – what would it matter if the grass grew long? How had the decision to cut it been made in the first place, all those years ago? But I hesitated to ask questions about a tradition so ancient and well-established; evidently taken for granted by everyone, it surely must have some sound rational basis I had overlooked – I was afraid of appearing dense, or imperceptive, or lacking in understanding – or so I thought. Anyhow, I hesitated until it was too late, and my informant, suddenly seeming to notice the fading light, excusing himself, hurried on his way, barely giving me time to thank him for his politeness.

Left alone, I continued to stand in the empty street, staring up, not quite at ease in my mind. The stranger's receding steps had just ceased to be audible when I realized that I had refrained from asking my questions, not for fear of appearing stupid, but because, in some part of me, I already seemed to know the answers. This discovery distracted me for the moment; and when, a few seconds later, my attention returned to the field, the row of jerking puppets had vanished.

Still I did not move on. An apathetic mood of vague melancholy had descended on me, as it often does at this hour of the changeover from day to night. The town all at once seemed peculiarly deserted and quiet, as though everyone were indoors, attending some meeting I knew nothing about. Above the roofs, the mountain loomed, gloomy, with pines flowing down to the hidden gorge, from several parts of which evening mist had begun to rise, obscuring my view of the slopes, but not of the meadow, still vividly green and distinct.

All at once, I found myself listening to the intense stillness, aware of some suspense in the ominous hush of impending thunder. Not a sound came from anywhere. There was no sign of life in the street, where the lights had not yet come on, in spite of the gathering shadows. Already the houses around me had lost their sharp outlines and seemed huddled together, as if nervously watching and waiting, and holding their breath. Mist and twilight had blotted out colours, all shapes were blurred and indefinite, so that the clear-cut bright green field stood out startlingly, mysteriously retaining the light of the departed day, concentrated in its small rectangle, floating over the roofs like a bright green flag.

Everywhere else, the invisible armies of night were assembling, massing against the houses, collecting in blacker blackness beneath the black trees. Everything was waiting breathlessly for the night to fall. But the advance of darkness was halted, stopped dead, at the edge of the meadow, arrested by sheer force of that ardent green. I expected the night to attack, to rush the meadow, to overrun it. But nothing happened. Only, I felt the tension of countless grass blades, poised in pure opposition to the invading dark. And now, in a first faint glimmer of understanding, I began to see how enormously powerful the grass up there must be, able to interrupt night's immemorial progress. Thinking of what I'd heard, I could imagine that grass might grow arrogant and far too strong, nourished as this had been; its horrid life battening on putrescence, bursting out in hundreds, thousands, of strong new blades for every single one cut.

I had a vision then of those teeming blades – blades innumerable, millions on millions of blades of grass – ceaselessly multiplying, with unnatural strength forcing their silent irresistible upward way through the earth, increasing a thousandfold with each passing minute. How fiercely they crowded into that one small field, grown unnaturally strong and destructive, destruction-fed. Turgid with life, the countless millions of blades were packed densely together, standing ready, like lances, like thickets, like trees, to resist invasion.

In the midst of the deep dusk that was almost darkness, the brilliance of that small green space appeared unnatural, uncanny. I had been staring at it so long that it seemed to start vibrating, pulsating, as if, even at this distance, the tremendous life-surge quickening it were actually visible. Not only the dark was threatened by all that savage vitality; in my vision, I saw the field always alert, continually on the watch for a momentary slackening of the effort to check its growth, only awaiting that opportunity to burst all bounds. I saw the grass rear up like a great green grave, swollen by the corruption it had consumed, sweeping over all boundaries, spreading in all directions, destroying all other life, covering the whole world with a bright green pall, beneath which life would perish. That poison-green had to be fought, fought; cut back, cut down; daily, hourly, at any cost. There was no other defence against the mad proliferation of grass blades: no other alternative to grass, blood-bloated, grown viciously strong, poisonous and vindictive, a virulent plague, that would smother everything, everywhere, until grass, and grass only, covered the face of the globe.

It seems monstrous, a thing that should never have been possible, for grass to possess such power. It is against all the laws of nature that grass should threaten the life of the planet. How could a plant meant to creep, to be crushed underfoot, grow so arrogant, so destructive? At times the whole idea seems preposterous, absolutely crazy, a story for children, not to be taken seriously – I refuse to believe it. And yet ... and yet ... one can't be quite certain ... Who knows what may have happened in the remote past? Perhaps, in the ancient archives kept secret from us, some incident is recorded ... Or, still further back, before records even began, something may have deviated from the norm ... Some variation, of which nothing is known any more, could have let loose on the future this green threat.

One simply doesn't know what to believe. If it is all just a fantasy, why should I have seen, as in a vision, that grass, fed on the lives of bound victims, could become a threat to all life, death-swollen, and horribly strong? In the beginning, when the whole thing started, did the threat come before the victim, or vice versa? Or did both evolve simultaneously, out of a mutual need for one another? And how do I come into it? Why should I be implicated at all? It's nothing to do with me. There's nothing whatever that I can do. Yet this thing that should never have happened seems something I cannot escape. If not today or tomorrow, then the day after that, or the next, at the end of some journey one evening, I shall see the bright green field waiting for me again. As I always do.

The Ship who Sang

(1961)

ANNE McCAFFREY

She was born a thing and as such would be condemned if she failed to pass the encephalograph test required of all newborn babies. There was always the possibility that though the limbs were twisted, the mind was not, that though the ears would hear only dimly, the eyes see vaguely, the mind behind them was receptive and alert.

The electro-encephalogram was entirely favorable, unexpectedly so, and the news was brought to the waiting, grieving parents. There was the final, harsh decision: to give their child euthanasia or permit it to become an encapsulated 'brain', a guiding mechanism in any one of a number of curious professions. As such, their offspring would suffer no pain, live a comfortable existence in a metal shell for several centuries, performing unusual service to Central Worlds.

She lived and was given a name, Helva. For her first three vegetable months she waved her crabbed claws, kicked weakly with her clubbed feet and enjoyed the usual routine of the infant. She was not alone, for there were three other such children in the big city's special nursery. Soon they were all removed to Central Laboratory School, where their delicate transformation began.

One of the babies died in the initial transferral, but of Helva's 'class', seventeen thrived in the metal shells. Instead of kicking feet, Helva's neural responses started her wheels; instead of grabbing with hands, she manipulated mechanical extensions. As she matured, more and more neural synapses would be adjusted to operate other mechanisms that went into the maintenance and running of a space ship. For Helva was destined to be the 'brain' half of a scout ship, partnered with a man or a woman, whichever she chose, as the mobile half. She would be among the elite of her kind. Her initial intelligence tests registered above normal and her adaptation index was unusually high. As long as her development within her shell lived up to expectations, and there were no side-effects from the pituitary tinkering, Helva would live a rewarding, rich and unusual life, a far cry from what she would have faced as an ordinary, 'normal' being.

However, no diagram of her brain patterns, no early IQ tests recorded certain essential facts about Helva that Central must eventually learn. They would have to bide their official time and see, trusting that the massive doses of shell-psychology would suffice her, too, as the necessary bulwark against her unusual confinement and the pressures of her profession. A ship run by a human brain could not run rogue or insane with the power and resources Central had to build into their scout ships. Brain ships were, of course, long past the experimental stages. Most babies survived the perfected techniques of pituitary manipulation that kept their bodies small, eliminating the necessity of transfers from smaller to larger shells. And very, very few were lost when the final connection was made to the control panels of ship or industrial combine. Shell-people resembled mature dwarfs in size whatever their natal deformities were, but the well-oriented brain would not have changed places with the most perfect body in the Universe.

So, for happy years, Helva scooted around in her shell with her classmates, playing such games as Stall, Power seek, studying her lessons in trajectory, propulsion techniques, computation, logistics, mental hygiene, basic alien psychology, philology, space history, law, traffic, codes: all the et ceteras that eventually became compounded into a reasoning, logical, informed citizen. Not so obvious to her, but of more importance to her teachers, Helva ingested the precepts of her conditioning as easily as she absorbed her nutrient fluid. She would one day be grateful to the patient drone of the subconscious-level instruction.

Helva's civilization was not without busy, do-good associations, exploring possible inhumanities to terrestrial as well as extraterrestrial citizens. One such group – Society for the Preservation of the Rights of Intelligent Minorities – got all incensed over shelled 'children' when Helva was just turning fourteen. When they were forced to, Central Worlds shrugged its shoulders, arranged a tour

of the Laboratory Schools and set the tour off to a big start by
showing the members case histories, complete with photographs.
Very few committees ever looked past the first few photos. Most
of their original objections about 'shells' were overridden by
the relief that these hideous (to them) bodies *were* mercifully
concealed.

Helva's class was doing fine arts, a selective subject in her
crowded program. She had activated one of her microscopic tools
which she would later use for minute repairs to various parts of
her control panel. Her subject was large – a copy of the *Last Supper*
– and her canvas, small – the head of a tiny screw. She had tuned
her sight to the proper degree. As she worked she absentmindedly
crooned, producing a curious sound. Shell-people used their own
vocal chords and diaphragms, but sound issued through micro-
phones rather than mouths. Helva's hum, then, had a curious
vibrancy, a warm, dulcet quality even in its aimless chromatic
wanderings.

'Why, what a lovely voice you have,' said one of the female
visitors.

Helva 'looked' up and caught a fascinating panorama of regular,
dirty craters on a flaky pink surface. Her hum became a gurgle of
surprise. She instinctively regulated her 'sight' until the skin lost
its cratered look and the pores assumed normal proportions.

'Yes, we have quite a few years of voice training, madam,'
remarked Helva calmly. 'Vocal peculiarities often become excessively irritating during prolonged intranstellar distances and must
be eliminated. I enjoyed my lessons.'

Although this was the first time that Helva had seen unshelled
people, she took this experience calmly. Any other reaction would
have been reported instantly.

'I meant that you have a nice singing voice . . . dear,' the lady
said.

'Thank you. Would you like to see my work?' Helva asked,
politely. She instinctively sheered away from personal discussions,
but she filed the comment away for further meditation.

'Work?' asked the lady.

'I am currently reproducing the *Last Supper* on the head of a
screw.'

'O, I say,' the lady twittered.

Helva turned her vision back to magnification and surveyed her copy critically.

'Of course, some of my color values do not match the old Master's and the perspective is faulty, but I believe it to be a fair copy.'

The lady's eyes, unmagnified, bugged out.

'Oh, I forget,' and Helva's voice was really contrite. If she could have blushed, she would have. 'You people don't have adjustable vision.'

The monitor of this discourse grinned with pride and amusement as Helva's tone indicated pity for the unfortunate.

'Here, this will help,' said Helva, substituting a magnifying device in one extension and holding it over the picture.

In a kind of shock, the ladies and gentlemen of the committee bent to observe the incredibly copied and brilliantly executed *Last Supper* on the head of a screw.

'Well,' remarked one gentleman who had been forced to accompany his wife, 'the good Lord can eat where angels feared to tread.'

'Are you referring, sir,' asked Helva politely, 'to the Dark Age discussions of the number of angels who could stand on the head of a pin?'

'I had that in mind.'

'If you substitute "atom" for "angel", the problem is not insoluble, given the metallic content of the pin in question.'

'Which you are programmed to compute?'

'Of course.'

'Did they remember to program a sense of humor, as well, young lady?'

'We are directed to develop a sense of proportion, sir, which contributes the same effect.'

The good man chortled appreciatively and decided the trip was worth his time.

If the investigation committee spent months digesting the thoughtful food served them at the Laboratory School, they left Helva with a morsel as well.

'Singing' as applicable to herself required research. She had, of

course, been exposed to and enjoyed a music appreciation course
that had included the better known classical works such as *Tristan
and Isolde*, *Candide*, *Oklahoma*, and *Nozze de Figaro*, along with the
atomic age singers, Birgit Nilsson, Bob Dylan, and Geraldine
Todd, as well as the curious rhythmic progressions of the Venu-
sians, Capellan visual chromatics, the sonic concerti of the Altairi-
ans and Reticulan croons. But 'singing' for any shell-person posed
considerable technical difficulties. Shell-people were schooled to
examine every aspect of a problem or situation before making a
prognosis. Balanced properly between optimism and practicality,
the non-defeatist attitude of the shell-people led them to extricate
themselves, their ships, and personnel, from bizarre situations.
Therefore to Helva, the problem that she couldn't open her mouth to
sing, among other restrictions, did not bother her. She would work
out a method, bypassing her limitations, whereby she could sing.

She approached the problem by investigating the methods of
sound reproduction through the centuries, human and instrumental.
Her own sound production equipment was essentially more instrumental than vocal. Breath control and the proper enunciation of
vowel sounds within the oral cavity appeared to require the most
development and practice. Shell-people did not, strictly speaking,
breathe. For their purposes, oxygen and other gases were not drawn
from the surrounding atmosphere through the medium of lungs but
sustained artificially by solution in their shells. After experimentation,
Helva discovered that she could manipulate her diaphragmic unit to
sustain tone. By relaxing the throat muscles and expanding the oral
cavity well into the frontal sinuses, she could direct the vowel sounds
into the most felicitous position for proper reproduction through
her throat microphone. She compared the results with tape record-
ings of modern singers and was not unpleased, although her own
tapes had a peculiar quality about them, not at all unharmonious,
merely unique. Acquiring a repertoire from the Laboratory library
was no problem to one trained to perfect recall. She found herself
able to sing any role and any song that struck her fancy. It would not
have occurred to her that it was curious for a female to sing bass,
baritone, tenor, mezzo, soprano, and coloratura as she pleased. It
was, to Helva, only a matter of the correct reproduction and
diaphragmic control required by the music attempted.

If the authorities remarked on her curious avocation, they did so among themselves. Shell-people were encouraged to develop a hobby so long as they maintained proficiency in their technical work.

On the anniversary of her sixteenth year, Helva was unconditionally graduated and installed in her ship, the XH-834. Her permanent titanium shell was recessed behind an even more indestructible barrier in the central shaft of the scout ship. The neural, audio, visual, and sensory connections were made and sealed. Her extendibles were diverted, connected or augmented and the final, delicate-beyond-description brain taps were completed while Helva remained anesthetically unaware of the proceedings. When she woke, she *was* the ship. Her brain and intelligence controlled every function from navigation to such loading as a scout ship of her class needed. She could take care of herself and her ambulatory half, in any situation already recorded in the annals of Central Worlds and any situation its most fertile minds could imagine.

Her first actual flight, for she and her kind had made mock flights on dummy panels since she was eight, showed her to be a complete master of the techniques of her profession. She was ready for her great adventures and the arrival of her mobile partner.

There were nine qualified scouts sitting around collecting base pay the day Helva reported for active duty. There were several missions that demanded instant attention, but Helva had been of interest to several department heads in Central for some time and each bureau chief was determined to have her assigned to *his* section. No one had remembered to introduce Helva to the prospective partners. The ship always chose its own partner. Had there been another 'brain' ship at the base at the moment, Helva would have been guided to make the first move. As it was, while Central wrangled among itself, Robert Tanner sneaked out of the pilots' barracks, out to the field and over to Helva's slim metal hull.

'Hello, anyone at home?' Tanner said.

'Of course,' replied Helva, activating her outside scanners. 'Are you my partner?' she asked hopefully, as she recognized the Scout Service uniform.

'All you have to do is ask,' he retorted in a wistful tone.

'No one has come. I thought perhaps there were no partners available and I've had no directives from Central.'

Even to herself Helva sounded a little self-pitying, but the truth was she was lonely, sitting on the darkened field. She had always had the company of other shells and, more recently, technicians by the score. The sudden solitude had lost its momentary charm and become oppressive.

'No directives from Central is scarcely a cause for regret, but there happen to be eight other guys biting their fingernails to the quick just waiting for an invitation to board you, you beautiful thing.'

Tanner was inside the central cabin as he said this, running appreciative fingers over her panel, the scout's gravity-chair, poking his head into the cabins, the galley, the head, the pressured-storage compartments.

'Now, if you want to goose Central and do *us* a favor all in one, call up the barracks and let's have a ship-warming partner-picking party. Hmmmm?'

Helva chuckled to herself. He was so completely different from the occasional visitors or the various Laboratory technicians she had encountered. He was so gay, so assured, and she was delighted by his suggestion of a partner-picking party. Certainly it was not against anything in her understanding of regulations.

'Cencom, this is XH-834. Connect me with Pilot Barracks.'

'Visual?'

'Please.'

A picture of lounging men in various attitudes of boredom came on her screen.

'This is XH-834. Would the unassigned scouts do me the favor of coming aboard?'

Eight figures galvanized into action, grabbing pieces of wearing apparel, disengaging tape mechanisms, disentangling themselves from bed-sheets and towels.

Helva dissolved the connection while Tanner chuckled gleefully and settled down to await their arrival.

Helva was engulfed in an unshell-like flurry of anticipation. No actress on her opening night could have been more apprehensive, fearful or breathless. Unlike the actress, she could throw no hysterics, china *objets d'art* or grease-paint to relieve her tension. She could, of course, check her stores for edibles and drinks, which she did, serving Tanner from the virgin selection of her commissary.

Scouts were colloquially known as 'brawns' as opposed to their ship 'brains'. They had to pass as rigorous a training program as the brains and only the top 1 percent of each contributory world's highest scholars were admitted to Central Worlds Scout Training Program. Consequently the eight young men who came pounding up the gantry into Helva's hospitable lock were unusually fine-looking, intelligent, well-coordinated and adjusted young men, looking forward to a slightly drunken evening, Helva permitting, and all quite willing to do each other dirt to get possession of her.

Such a human invasion left Helva mentally breathless, a luxury she thoroughly enjoyed for the brief time she felt she should permit it.

She sorted out the young men. Tanner's opportunism amused but did not specifically attract her; the blond Nordsen seemed too simple; dark-haired Al-atpay had a kind of obstinacy with which she felt no compassion: Mir-Ahnin's bitterness hinted at an inner darkness she did not wish to lighten, although he made the biggest outward play for her attention. Hers was a curious court-ship – this would be only the first of several marriages for her, for brawns retired after seventy-five years of service, or earlier if they were unlucky. Brains, their bodies safe from any deterioration, were indestructible. In theory, once a shell-person had paid off the massive debt of early care, surgical adaptation and maintenance charges, he or she was free to seek employment elsewhere. In practice, shell-people remained in the service until they chose to self-destruct or died in line of duty. Helva had actually spoken to one shell-person 322 years old. She had been so awed by the contact she hadn't presumed to ask the personal questions she had wanted to.

Her choice of a brawn did not stand out from the others until Tanner started to sing a scout ditty, recounting the misadventures of the bold, dense, painfully inept Billy Brawn. An attempt at harmony resulted in cacophony and Tanner wagged his arms wildly for silence.

'What we need is a roaring good lead tenor. Jennan, besides palming aces, what do you sing?'

'Sharp,' Jennan replied with easy good humor.

'If a tenor is absolutely necessary, I'll attempt it,' Helva volunteered.

'My good *woman*,' Tanner protested.

'Sound your "A",' laughed Jennan.

Into the stunned silence that followed the rich, clear, high 'A', Jennan remarked quietly, 'Such an "A" Caruso would have given the rest of his notes to sing.'

It did not take them long to discover her full range.

'All Tanner asked for was one roaring good lead tenor,' Jennan said jokingly, 'and our sweet mistress supplied us an entire repertory company. The boy who gets this ship will go far, far, far.'

'To the Horsehead Nebula?' asked Nordsen, quoting an old Central saw.

'To the Horsehead Nebula and back, we shall make beautiful music,' said Helva, chuckling.

'Together,' Jennan said. 'Only you'd better make the music and, with my voice, I'd better listen.'

'I rather imagined it would be I who listened,' suggested Helva.

Jennan executed a stately bow with an intricate flourish of his crush-brimmed hat. He directed his bow toward the central control pillar where Helva *was*. Her own personal preference crystallized at that precise moment and for that particular reason: Jennan, alone of the men, had addressed his remarks directly at her physical presence, regardless of the fact that he knew she could pick up his image wherever he was in the ship and regardless of the fact that her body was behind massive metal walls. Throughout their partnership, Jennan never failed to turn his head in her direction no matter where he was in relation to her. In response to this personalization, Helva at that moment and from then on always spoke to Jennan only through her central mike, even though that was not always the most efficient method.

Helva didn't know that she fell in love with Jennan that evening. As she had never been exposed to love or affection, only the drier cousins, respect and admiration, she could scarcely have recognized her reaction to the warmth of his personality and thoughtfulness. As a shell-person, she considered herself remote from emotions largely connected with physical desires.

'Well, Helva, it's been swell meeting you,' said Tanner suddenly as she and Jennan were arguing about the baroque quality of 'Come All Ye Sons of Art'. 'See you in space some time, you lucky dog, Jennan. Thanks for the party, Helva.'

'You don't have to go so soon?' asked Helva, realizing belatedly that she and Jennan had been excluding the others from this discussion.

'Best man won,' Tanner said, wryly. 'Guess I'd better go get a tape of love ditties. Might need 'em for the next ship, if there're any more at home like you.'

Helva and Jennan watched them leave, both a little confused.

'Perhaps Tanner's jumping to conclusions?' Jennan asked.

Helva regarded him as he slouched against the console, facing her shell directly. His arms were crossed on his chest and the glass he held had been empty for some time. He was handsome, they all were; but his watchful eyes were unwary, his mouth assumed a smile easily, his voice (to which Helva was particularly drawn) was resonant, deep, and without unpleasant overtones or accent.

'Sleep on it, at any rate, Helva. Call me in the morning if it's your opt.'

She called him at breakfast, after she had checked her choice through Central. Jennan moved his things aboard, received their joint commission, had his personality and experience file locked into her reviewer, gave her the coordinates of their first mission. The XH-834 officially became the JH-834.

Their first mission was a dull but necessary crash priority (Medical got Helva), rushing a vaccine to a distant system plagued with a virulent spore disease. They had only to get to Spica as fast as possible.

After the initial, thrilling forward surge at her maximum speed, Helva realized her muscles were to be given less of a workout than her brawn on this tedious mission. But they did have plenty of time for exploring each other's personalities. Jennan, of course, knew what Helva was capable of as a ship and partner, just as she knew what she could expect from him. But these were only facts and Helva looked forward eagerly to learning that human side of her partner that could not be reduced to a series of symbols. Nor could the give and take of two personalities be learned from a book. It had to be experienced.

'My father was a scout, too, or is that programmed?' began Jennan their third day out.

'Naturally.'

'Unfair, you know. You've got all my family history and I don't know one blamed thing about yours.'

'I've never known either,' Helva said. 'Until I read yours, it hadn't occurred to me I must have one, too, someplace in Central's files.'

Jennan snorted. 'Shell psychology!'

Helva laughed. 'Yes, and I'm even programmed against curiosity about it. You'd better be, too.'

Jennan ordered a drink, slouched into the gravity couch opposite her, put his feet on the bumpers, turning himself idly from side to side on the gimbals.

'Helva – a made-up name . . .'

'With a Scandinavian sound.'

'You aren't blonde,' Jennan said positively.

'Well, then, there're dark Swedes.'

'And blonde Turks and this one's harem is limited to one.'

'Your women in purdah, yes, but you can comb the pleasure houses –' Helva found herself aghast at the edge of her carefully trained voice.

'You know,' Jennan interrupted her, deep in some thought of his own, 'my father gave me the impression he was a lot more married to his ship, the Silvia, than to my mother. I know I used to think Silvia was my grandmother. She was a low number so she must have been a great-great-grandmother at least. I used to talk to her for hours.'

'Her registry?' asked Helva, unwittingly jealous of everyone and anyone who had shared his hours.

'422. I think she's TS now. I ran into Tom Burgess once.'

Jennan's father had died of a planetary disease, the vaccine for which his ship had used up in curing the local citizens.

'Tom said she's got mighty tough and salty. You lose your

sweetness and I'll come back and haunt you, girl,' Jennan threatened.

Helva laughed. He startled her by stamping up to the column panel, touching it with light, tender fingers.

'I *wonder* what you look like,' he said softly, wistfully.

Helva had been briefed about this natural curiosity of scouts. She didn't know anything about herself and neither of them ever would or could.

'Pick any form, shape, and shade and I'll be yours obligingly,' she countered, as training suggested.

'Iron Maiden, I fancy blondes with long tresses,' and Jennan pantomimed Lady Godiva-like tresses. 'Since you're immolated in titanium, I'll call you Brunhild, my dear,' and he made his bow.

With a chortle, Helva launched into the appropriate aria just as Spica made contact.

'Waht'n'ell's that yelling about? Who are you? And unless you're Central Worlds Medical go away. We've got a plague. No visiting privileges.'

'My ship is singing, we're the JH-834 of Worlds and we've got your vaccine. What are our landing coordinates?'

'Your *ship* is singing?'

'The greatest SATB in organized space. Any request?'

The JH-834 delivered the vaccine but no more arias and received immediate orders to proceed to Leviticus IV. By the time they got there, Jennan found a reputation awaiting him and was forced to defend the 834's virgin honor.

'I'll stop singing,' murmured Helva contritely as she ordered up poultices for the third black eye in a week.

'You will not,' Jennan said through gritted teeth. 'If I have to black eyes from here to the Horsehead to keep the snicker out of the title, we'll be the ship who sings.'

After the 'ship who sings' tangled with a minor but vicious narcotic ring in the Lesser Magellanics, the title became definitely respectful. Central was aware of each episode and punched out a 'special interest' key on JH-834's file. A first-rate team was shaking down well.

Jennan and Helva considered themselves a first-rate team, too, after their tidy arrest.

'Of all the vices in the universe, I *hate* drug addiction,' Jennan remarked as they headed back to Central Base. 'People can go to hell quick enough without that kind of help.'

'Is that why you volunteered for Scout Service? To redirect traffic?'

'I'll bet my official answer's on your review.'

'In far too flowery wording. "Carrying on the traditions of my family, which had been proud of four generations in Service", if I may quote you your own words.'

Jennan groaned. 'I was *very* young when I wrote that. I certainly hadn't been through Final Training. And once I was in Final Training, my pride wouldn't let me fail . . .

'As I mentioned, I used to visit Dad on board the Silvia and I've a very good idea she might have had her eye on me as a replacement for my father because I had had massive doses of scout-oriented propaganda. It took. From the time I was seven, I was going to be a scout or else.' He shrugged as if deprecating a youthful determination that had taken a great deal of mature application to bring to fruition.

'Ah, so? Scout Sahir Silan on the JS-422 penetrating into the Horsehead Nebula?'

Jennan chose to ignore her sarcasm.

'With *you*, I may even get that far. But even with Silvia's nudging *I* never day-dreamed myself *that* kind of glory in my wildest flights of fancy. I'll leave the whoppers to your agile brain henceforth. I have in mind a smaller contribution to space history.'

'So modest?'

'No. Practical. We also serve, et cetera.' He placed a dramatic hand on his heart.

'Glory hound!' scoffed Helva.

'Look who's talking, my Nebula-bound friend. At least I'm not greedy. There'll only be one hero like my dad at Parsaea, but I *would* like to be remembered for some kudo. Everyone does. Why else do or die?'

'Your father died on his way back from Parsaea, if I may point out a few cogent facts. So he could never have known he was a hero for damning the flood with his ship. Which kept Parsaean colony from being abandoned. Which gave them a chance to discover the antiparalytic qualities of Parsaea. Which *he* never knew.'

'I know,' said Jennan softly.

Helva was immediately sorry for the tone of her rebuttal. She knew very well how deep Jennan's attachment to his father had been. On his review a note was made that he had rationalized his father's loss with the unexpected and welcome outcome of the Affair at Parsaea.

'Facts are not human, Helva. My father was and so am I. And *basically*, so are you. Check over your dial, 834. Amid all the wires attached to you is a heart, an underdeveloped human heart. Obviously!'

'I apologize, Jennan,' she said.

Jennan hesitated a moment, threw out his hands in acceptance and then tapped her shell affectionately.

'If they ever take us off the milk runs, we'll make a stab at the Nebula, huh?'

As so frequently happened in the Scout Service, within the next hour they had orders to change course, not to the Nebula, but to a recently colonized system with two habitable planets, one tropical, one glacial. The sun, named Ravel, had become unstable; the spectrum was that of a rapidly expanding shell, with absorption lines rapidly displacing toward violet. The augmented heat of the primary had already forced evacuation of the nearer world, Daphnis. The pattern of spectral emissions gave indication that the sun would sear Chloe as well. All ships in the immediate spatial vicinity were to report to Disaster Headquarters on Chloe to effect removal of the remaining colonists.

The JH-834 obediently presented itself and was sent to outlying areas on Chloe to pick up scattered settlers who did not appear to appreciate the urgency of the situation. Chloe, indeed, was enjoying the first temperatures above freezing since it had been flung out of its parent. Since many of the colonists were religious fanatics who had settled on rigorous Chloe to fit themselves for a life of pious reflection, Chloe's abrupt thaw was attributed to sources other than a rampaging sun.

Jennan had to spend so much time countering specious arguments that he and Helva were behind schedule on their way to the fourth and last settlement.

Helva jumped over the high range of jagged peaks that surrounded and sheltered the valley from the former raging snows as well as the present heat. The violent sun with its flaring corona was just beginning to brighten the deep valley as Helva dropped down to a landing.

'They'd better grab their toothbrushes and hop aboard,' Helva said. 'HQ says speed it up.'

'All women,' remarked Jennan in surprise as he walked down to meet them. 'Unless the men on Chloe wear furred skirts.'

'Charm 'em but pare the routine to the bare essentials. And turn on your two-way private.'

Jennan advanced smiling, but his explanation of his mission was met with absolute incredulity and considerable doubt as to his authenticity. He groaned inwardly as the matriarch paraphrased previous explanations of the warming sun.

'Revered mother, there's been an overload on that prayer circuit and the sun is blowing itself up in one obliging burst. I'm here to take you to the spaceport at Rosary –'

'That Sodom?' The worthy woman glowered and shuddered disdainfully at his suggestion. 'We thank you for your warning but we have no wish to leave our cloister for the rude world. We must go about our morning meditation, which has been interrupted –'

'It'll be permanently interrupted when that sun starts broiling you. You must come now,' Jennan said firmly.

'Madame,' said Helva, realizing that perhaps a female voice might carry more weight in this instance than Jennan's very masculine charm.

'Who spoke?' cried the nun, startled by the bodiless voice.

'I, Helva, the ship. Under my protection you and your sisters-in-faith may enter safely and be unprofaned by association with a male. I will guard you and take you safely to a place prepared for you.'

The matriarch peered cautiously into the ship's open port.

'Since only Central Worlds is permitted the use of such ships, I acknowledge that you are not trifling with us, young man. However, we are in no danger here.'

'The temperature at Rosary is now 99°,' said Helva. 'As soon as the sun's rays penetrate directly into this valley, it will also be 99°, and it is due to climb to approximately 180° today. I notice your buildings are made of wood with moss chinking. Dry moss. It should fire around noontime.'

The sunlight was beginning to slant into the valley through the peaks and the fierce rays warmed the restless group behind the matriarch. Several opened the throats of their furry parkas.

'Jennan,' said Helva privately to him, 'our time is very short.'

'I can't leave them, Helva. Some of those girls are barely out of their teens.'

'Pretty, too. No wonder the matriarch doesn't want to get in.'

'Helva.'

'It will be the Lord's will,' said the matriarch stoutly and turned her back squarely on rescue.

'To burn to death?' shouted Jennan as she threaded her way through her murmuring disciples.

'They want to be martyrs? Their opt, Jennan,' said Helva dispassionately, 'We must leave and that is no longer a matter of option.'

'How can I leave, Helva?'

'Parsaea?' Helva asked tauntingly as he stepped forward to grab one of the women. 'You can't drag them *all* aboard and we don't have time to fight it out. Get on board, Jennan, or I'll have you on report.'

'They'll die,' muttered Jennan dejectedly as he reluctantly turned to climb on board.

'You can risk only so much,' Helva said sympathetically. 'As it is we'll just have time to make a rendezvous. Lab reports a critical speed-up in spectral evolution.'

Jennan was already in the airlock when one of the younger women, screaming, rushed to squeeze in the closing port. Her action set off the others. They stampeded through the narrow opening. Even crammed back to breast, there was not enough room inside for all the women. Jennan broke out spacesuits to the three who would have to remain with him in the airlock. He wasted valuable time explaining to the matriarch that she must put on the suit because the airlock had no independent oxygen or cooling units.

'We'll be caught,' said Helva in a grim tone to Jennan on their private connection. 'We've lost eighteen minutes in this last-minute rush. I am now overloaded for maximum speed and I must attain maximum speed to outrun the heat wave.'

'Can you lift? We're suited.'

'Lift? Yes,' she said, doing so. 'Run? I stagger.'

Jennan, bracing himself and the women, could feel her sluggishness as she blasted upward. Heartlessly, Helva applied thrust as long as she could, despite the fact that the gravitational force mashed her cabin passengers brutally and crushed two fatally. It was a question of saving as many as possible. The only one for whom she had any concern was Jennan and she was in desperate terror about his safety. Airless and uncooled, protected by only one layer of metal, not three, the airlock was not going to be safe for the four trapped there, despite their spacesuits. These were only the standard models, not built to withstand the excessive heat to which the ship would be subjected.

Helva ran as fast as she could but the incredible wave of heat from the explosive sun caught them halfway to cold safety.

She paid no heed to the cries, moans, pleas and prayers in her cabin. She listened only to Jennan's tortured breathing, to the missing throb in his suit's purifying system and the sucking of the overloaded cooling unit. Helpless, she heard the hysterical screams of his three companions as they writhed in the awful heat. Vainly, Jennan tried to calm them, tried to explain they would soon be safe and cool if they could be still and endure the heat. Undisciplined by their terror and torment, they tried to strike out at him despite the close quarters. One flailing arm became entangled in the leads to his power pack and the damage was quickly done. A connection, weakened by heat and the dead weight of the arm, broke.

For all the power at her disposal, Helva was helpless. She watched as Jennan fought for his breath, as he turned his head beseechingly toward *her*, and died.

Only the iron conditioning of her training prevented Helva

from swinging around and plunging back into the cleansing heart of the exploding sun. Numbly she made rendezvous with the refugee convoy. She obediently transferred her burned, heat-prostrated passengers to the assigned transport.

'I will retain the body of my scout and proceed to the nearest base for burial,' she informed Central dully.

'You will be provided escort,' was the reply.

'I have no need of escort.'

'Escort is provided, XH-834,' she was told curtly. The shock of hearing Jennan's initial severed from her call number cut off her half-formed protest. Stunned, she waited by the transport until her screens showed the arrival of two other slim brain ships. The cortège proceeded homeward at unfunereal speeds.

'834? The ship who sings?'

'I have no more songs.'

'Your scout was Jennan.'

'I do not wish to communicate.'

'I'm 422.'

'Silvia?'

'Silvia died a long time ago. I'm 422. Currently MS,' the ship rejoined curtly. 'AH-640 is our other friend, but Henry's not listening in. Just as well – he wouldn't understand it if you wanted to turn rogue. But I'd stop *him* if he tried to deter you.'

'Rogue?' The term snapped Helva out of her apathy.

'Sure. You're young. You've got power for years. Skip. Others have done it. 732 went rogue twenty years ago after she lost her scout on a mission to that white dwarf. Hasn't been seen since.'

'I never heard about rogues.'

'As it's exactly the thing we're conditioned against, you sure wouldn't hear about it in school, my dear,' 422 said.

'Break conditioning?' cried Helva, anguished, thinking long-ingly of the white, white furious hot heart of the sun she had just left.

'For you I don't think it would be hard at the moment,' 422 said quietly, her voice devoid of her earlier cynicism. 'The stars are out there, winking.'

'Alone?' cried Helva from her heart.

'Alone!' 422 confirmed bleakly.

Alone with all of space and time. Even the Horsehead Nebula would not be far enough away to daunt her. Alone with a hundred years to live with her memories and nothing . . . nothing more.

'Was Parsaea worth it?' she asked 422 softly.

'Parsaea?' 422 repeated, surprised. 'With his father? Yes. We were there, at Parsaea when we were needed. Just as you . . . and his son . . . were at Chloe. When you were needed. The crime is knowing where need is and not being there.'

'But *I* need *him*. Who will supply my need?' said Helva bitterly . . .

'834,' said 422 after a day's silent speeding, 'Central wishes your report. A replacement awaits your opt at Regulus Base. Change course accordingly.'

'A replacement?' That was certainly not what she needed . . . a reminder inadequately filling the void Jennan left. Why, her hull was barely cool of Chloe's heat. Atavistically, Helva wanted time to mourn Jennan.

'Oh, none of them are impossible if *you're* a good ship,' 422 remarked philosophically. 'And it is just what you need. The sooner the better.'

'You told them I wouldn't go rogue, didn't you?' Helva said.

'The moment passed you even as it passed me after Parsaea, and before that, after Glen Arhur, and Betelgeuse.'

'We're conditioned to go on, aren't we? We *can't* go rogue. You were testing.'

'Had to. Orders. Not even Psych knows why a rogue occurs. Central's very worried, and so, daughter, are your sistership. I asked to be your escort. I . . . don't want to lose you both.'

In her emotional nadir, Helva could feel a flood of gratitude for Silvia's rough sympathy.

'We've all known this grief, Helva. It's no consolation, but if we couldn't feel with our scouts, we'd only be machines wired for sound.'

Helva looked at Jennan's still form stretched before her in its shroud and heard the echo of his rich voice in the quiet cabin.

'Silvia! I *couldn't* help him!' she cried from her soul.

'Yes, dear, I know,' 422 murmured gently and then was quiet.

The three ships sped on, wordless, to the great Central Worlds base at Regulus. Helva broke silence to acknowledge landing instructions and the officially tendered regrets.

The three ships set down simultaneously at the wooded edge where Regulus' gigantic blue trees stood sentinel over the sleeping dead in the small Service cemetery. The entire Base complement approached with measured step and formed an aisle from Helva to the burial ground. The honor detail, out of step, walked slowly into her cabin. Reverently they placed the body of her dead love on the wheeled bier, covered it honorably with the deep blue, star-splashed flag of the Service. She watched as it was driven slowly down the living aisle which closed in behind the bier in last escort.

Then, as the simple words of interment were spoken, as the atmosphere planes dipped in tribute over the open grave, Helva found voice for her lonely farewell.

Softly, barely audible at first, the strains of the ancient song of evening and requiem swelled to the final poignant measure until black space itself echoed back the sound of the song the ship sang.

Marmalade Wine

(1964)

JOAN AIKEN

'Paradise,' Blacker said to himself, moving forward into the wood. 'Paradise. Fairyland.'

He was a man given to exaggeration; poetic licence he called it, and his friends called it 'Blacker's little flights of fancy,' or something less polite, but on this occasion he spoke nothing but the truth. The wood stood silent about him, tall, golden, with afternoon sunlight slanting through the half-unfurled leaves of early summer. Underfoot, anemones palely carpeted the ground. A cuckoo called.

'Paradise,' Blacker repeated, closed the gate behind him, and strode down the overgrown path, looking for a spot in which to eat his ham sandwich. Hazel bushes thickened at either side until the circular blue eye of the gateway by which he had come in dwindled to a pinpoint and vanished. The taller trees over-topping the hazels were not yet in full leaf and gave little cover; it was very hot in the wood and very still.

Suddenly Blacker stopped short with an exclamation of surprise and regret: lying among the dog's-mercury by the path was the body of a cock-pheasant in the full splendour of its spring plumage. Blacker turned the bird over with the townsman's pity and curiosity at such evidence of nature's unkindness; the feathers, purple-bronze, green, and gold, were smooth under his hand as a girl's hair.

'Poor thing,' he said aloud, 'what can have happened to it?'

He walked on, wondering if he could turn the incident to account. 'Threnody for a Pheasant in May'. Too precious? Too sentimental? Perhaps a weekly would take it. He began choosing rhymes, staring at his feet as he walked, abandoning his conscious rapture at the beauty around him.

> Stricken to death . . . and something . . . leafy ride,
> Before his . . . something . . . fully flaunt his pride.

Or would a shorter line be better, something utterly simple and heartful, limpid tears of grief like spring rain dripping off the petals of a flower?

It was odd, Blacker thought, increasing his pace, how difficult he found writing nature poetry; nature was beautiful, maybe, but it was not stimulating. And it was nature poetry that *Field and Garden* wanted. Still, that pheasant ought to be worth five guineas.

> Tread lightly past,
> Where he lies still,
> And something last . . .

Damn! In his absorption he had nearly trodden on *another* pheasant. What was happening to the birds? Blacker, who objected to occurrences with no visible explanation, walked on frowning. The path bore downhill to the right, and leaving the hazel coppice, crossed a tiny valley. Below him Blacker was surprised to see a small, secretive flint cottage, surrounded on three sides by trees. In front of it was a patch of turf. A deck-chair stood there, and a man was peacefully stretched out in it, enjoying the afternoon sun.

Blacker's first impulse was to turn back; he felt as if he had walked into somebody's garden, and was filled with mild irritation at the unexpectedness of the encounter; there ought to have been some warning signs, dash it all. The wood had seemed as deserted as Eden itself. But his turning round would have an appearance of guilt and furtiveness; on second thoughts he decided to go boldly past the cottage. After all there was no fence, and the path was not marked private in any way; he had a perfect right to be there.

'Good afternoon,' said the man pleasantly as Blacker approached. 'Remarkably fine weather, is it not?'

'I do hope I'm not trespassing.'

Studying the man, Blacker revised his first guess. This was no gamekeeper, there was a distinction in every line of the thin, sculptured face. What most attracted Blacker's attention were the hands, holding a small gilt coffee-cup; they were as white, frail, and attenuated as the pale roots of water-plants.

'Not at all,' the man said cordially. 'In fact you arrive at a most opportune moment; you are very welcome. I was just wishing for a little company. Delightful as I find this sylvan retreat, it becomes, all of a sudden, a little *dull*, a little *banal*. I do trust that you have time to sit down and share my after-lunch coffee and liqueur.'

As he spoke he reached behind him and brought out a second deck-chair from the cottage porch.

'Why, thank you; I should be delighted,' said Blacker, wondering if he had the strength of character to take out the ham sandwich and eat it in front of this patrician hermit.

Before he made up his mind the man had gone into the house and returned with another gilt cup full of black, fragrant coffee, hot as Tartarus, which he handed to Blacker. He carried also a tiny glass, and into this, from a blackcurrant-cordial bottle, he carefully poured a clear, colourless liquor. Blacker sniffed his glassful with caution, mistrusting the bottle and its evidence of home brewing, but the scent, aromatic and powerful, was similar to that of curaçao, and the liquid moved in its glass with an oily smoothness. It certainly was not cowslip wine.

'Well,' said his host, reseating himself and gesturing slightly with his glass, 'how do you do?' He sipped delicately.

'Cheers,' said Blacker, and added, 'My name's Roger Blacker.' It sounded a little lame. The liqueur was not curaçao, but akin to it, and quite remarkably potent; Blacker, who was very hungry, felt the fumes rise up inside his head as if an orange tree had taken root there and was putting out leaves and golden glowing fruit.

'Sir Francis Deeking,' the other man said, and then Blacker understood why his hands had seemed so spectacular, so portentously out of the common.

'The surgeon? But surely you don't live down here?'

Deeking waved a hand deprecatingly. 'A weekend retreat. A hermitage, to which I can retire from the strain of my calling.'

'It certainly is very remote,' Blacker remarked. 'It must be five miles from the nearest road.'

'Six. And you, my dear Mr Blacker, what is your profession?'

'Oh, a writer,' said Blacker modestly. The drink was having its usual effect on him; he managed to convey not that he was a journalist on a twopenny daily with literary yearnings, but that he was a philosopher and essayist of rare quality, a sort of second Bacon. All the time he spoke, while drawn out most flatteringly by the questions of Sir Francis, he was recalling journalistic scraps of information about his host: the operation on the Indian Prince; the Cabinet Minister's appendix; the amputation performed on that unfortunate ballerina who had both feet crushed in a railway accident; the major operation which had proved so miraculously successful on the American heiress.

'You must feel like a god,' he said suddenly, noticing with surprise that his glass was empty. Sir Francis waved the remark aside.

'We all have our godlike attributes,' he said, leaning forward. 'Now you, Mr Blacker, a writer, a creative artist – do you not know a power akin to godhead when you transfer your thought to paper?'

'Well, not exactly then,' said Blacker, feeling the liqueur moving inside his head in golden and russet-coloured clouds. 'Not *so* much then, but I do have one unusual power, a power not shared by many people, of foretelling the future. For instance, as I was coming through the wood, I *knew* this house would be here. I knew I should find you sitting in front of it. I can look at the list of runners in a race, and the name of the winner fairly leaps out at me from the page, as if it was printed in golden ink. Forthcoming events – air disasters, train crashes – I always sense in advance. I begin to have a terrible feeling of impending doom, as if my brain was a volcano just on the point of eruption.'

What was that other item of news about Sir Francis Deeking, he wondered, a recent report, a tiny paragraph that had caught his eye in *The Times*? He could not recall it.

'*Really?*' Sir Francis was looking at him with the keenest interest; his eyes, hooded and fanatical under their heavy lids, held brilliant points of light. 'I have always longed to know somebody with such a power. It must be a terrifying responsibility.'

'Oh, it is,' Blacker said. He contrived to look bowed under the weight of supernatural cares; noticed that his glass was full again, and drained it. 'Of course I don't use the faculty for my own ends; something fundamental in me rises up to prevent that. It's as basic, you know, as the instinct forbidding cannibalism or incest –'

'Quite, quite,' Sir Francis agreed. 'But for another person you would be able to give warnings, advise profitable courses of action . . .? My dear fellow, your glass is empty. Allow me.'

'This is marvellous stuff,' Blacker said hazily. 'It's like a wreath of orange blossom.' He gestured with his finger.

'I distil it myself; from marmalade. But do go on with what you were saying. Could you, for instance, tell me the winner of this afternoon's Manchester Plate?'

'Bow Bells,' Blacker said unhesitatingly. It was the only name he could remember.

'You interest me enormously. And the result of today's Aldwych by-election? Do you know that?'

'Unwin, the Liberal, will get in by a majority of two hundred and eighty-two. He won't take his seat, though. He'll be killed at seven this evening in a lift accident at his hotel.' Blacker was well away by now.

'Will he, indeed?' Sir Francis appeared delighted. 'A pestilent fellow. I have sat on several boards with him. Do continue.'

Blacker required little encouragement. He told the story of the financier whom he had warned in time of the oil company crash; the dream about the famous violinist which had resulted in the man's cancelling his passage on the ill-fated *Orion*; and the tragic tale of the bullfighter who had ignored his warning.

'But I'm talking too much about myself,' he said at length, partly because he noticed an ominous clogging of his tongue, a refusal of his thoughts to marshal themselves. He cast about for an impersonal topic, something simple.

'The pheasants,' he said. 'What's happened to the pheasants? Cut down in their prime. It – it's terrible. I found four in the wood up there, four or five.'

'Really?' Sir Francis seemed callously uninterested in the fate of the pheasants. 'It's the chemical sprays they use on the crops, I understand. Bound to upset the ecology; they never work out the probable results beforehand. Now if *you* were in charge, my dear Mr Blacker – but forgive me, it is a hot afternoon and you must be tired and footsore if you have walked from Witherstow this morning – let me suggest that you have a short sleep . . .'

His voice seemed to come from farther and farther away; a

network of sun-coloured leaves laced themselves in front of Blacker's eyes. Gratefully he leaned back and stretched out his aching feet.

Some time after this Blacker roused a little – or was it only a dream? – to see Sir Francis standing by him, rubbing his hands, with a face of jubilation.

'My dear fellow, my dear Mr Blacker, what a *lusus naturae* you are. I can never be sufficiently grateful that you came my way. Bow Bells walked home – positively *ambled*. I have been listening to the commentary. What a misfortune that I had no time to place money on the horse – but never mind, never mind, that can be remedied another time.

'It is unkind of me to disturb your well-earned rest, though; drink this last thimbleful and finish your nap while the sun is on the wood.'

As Blacker's head sank back against the deck-chair again, Sir Francis leaned forward and gently took the glass from his hand.

Sweet river of dreams, thought Blacker, fancy the horse actually winning. I wish I'd had a fiver on it myself; I could do with a new pair of shoes. I should have undone these before I dozed off, they're too tight or something. I must wake up soon, ought to be on my way in half an hour or so . . .

When Blacker finally woke he found that he was lying on a narrow bed, indoors, covered with a couple of blankets. His head ached and throbbed with a shattering intensity, and it took a few minutes for his vision to clear; then he saw that he was in a small white cell-like room which contained nothing but the bed he was on and a chair. It was very nearly dark.

He tried to struggle up but a strange numbness and heaviness had invaded the lower part of his body, and after hoisting himself on to his elbow he felt so sick that he abandoned the effort and lay down again.

That stuff must have the effect of a knockout drop, he thought ruefully; what a fool I was to drink it. I'll have to apologize to Sir Francis. What time can it be?

Brisk light footsteps approached the door and Sir Francis came in. He was carrying a portable radio which he placed on the window sill.

'Ah, my dear Blacker, I see you have come round. Allow me to offer you a drink.'

He raised Blacker skilfully, and gave him a drink of water from a cup with a rim and a spout.

'Now let me settle you down again. Excellent. We shall soon have you – well, not on your feet, but sitting up and taking nourishment.' He laughed a little. 'You can have some beef tea presently.'

'I am so sorry,' Blacker said. 'I really need not trespass on your hospitality any longer. I shall be quite all right in a minute.'

'No trespass, my dear friend. You are not at all in the way. I hope that you will be here for a long and pleasant stay. These surroundings, so restful, so conducive to a writer's inspiration – what could be more suitable for you? You need not think that I shall disturb you. I am in London all week, but shall keep you company at weekends – pray, pray don't think that you will be a nuisance or *de trop*. On the contrary, I am hoping that you can do me the kindness of giving me the Stock Exchange prices in advance, which will amply compensate for any small trouble I have taken. No, no, you must feel quite at home – please consider, indeed, that this *is* your home.'

Stock Exchange prices? It took Blacker a moment to remember, then he thought, Oh lord, my tongue has played me false as usual. He tried to recall what stupidities he had been guilty of. 'Those stories,' he said lamely, 'they were all a bit exaggerated, you know. About my foretelling the future. I can't really. That horse's winning was a pure coincidence, I'm afraid.'

'Modesty, modesty.' Sir Francis was smiling, but he had gone rather pale, and Blacker noticed a beading of sweat along his cheekbones. 'I am sure you will be invaluable. Since my retirement I find it absolutely necessary to augment my income by judicious investment.'

All of a sudden Blacker remembered the gist of that small paragraph in *The Times*. Nervous breakdown. Complete rest. Retirement.

'I – I really must go now,' he said uneasily, trying to push himself upright. 'I meant to be back in town by seven.'

'Oh, but Mr Blacker, that is quite out of the question. Indeed, so as to preclude any such action, I have amputated your feet. But you need not worry; I know you will be very happy here. And I feel certain that you are wrong to doubt your own powers. Let us listen to the nine o'clock news in order to be quite satisfied that the detestable Unwin did fall down the hotel lift shaft.'

He walked over to the portable radio and switched it on.

The Fall of Frenchy Steiner

(1964)

HILARY BAILEY

1954 was not a year of progress. A week before Christmas I walked into the bar of the Merrie Englande in Leicester Square, my guitar in its case, my hat in my hand. Two constables were sitting on wooden stools at the counter. Their helmets turned together as I walked in. The place was badly lit by candles, hiding the run-down look but not the run-down smell of home-brew and damp rot.

'Who's he?' said one of the PCs as I moved past.

'I work here,' I said. Tired old dialogue for tired old people.

He grunted and sipped his drink. I didn't look at the barman. I didn't look at the cops. I just went into the room behind the bar and took off my coat. I went to the wash-basin, turned the taps. Nothing happened. I got my guitar out of its case, tested it, tuned it and went back into the bar with it.

'Water's off again,' said Jon, the barman. He was a flimsy wisp in black with a thin white face. 'Nothing's working today . . .'

'Well, we've still got an efficient police force,' I said. The cops turned to look at me again. I didn't care. I felt I could afford a little relaxation. One of them chewed the strap of his helmet and frowned. The other smiled.

'You work here do you, sir? How much does the boss pay you?' He continued to smile, speaking softly and politely. I sneered.

'Him?' I pointed with my thumb up to where the boss lived. 'He wouldn't, even if it was legal.' Then I began to worry. I'm like that – moody. 'What are you doing here, anyway, officer?'

'Making enquiries, sir,' said the frowning one.

'About a customer,' said Jon. He leant back against an empty shelf, his arms folded.

'That's right,' said the smiling one.

'Who?'

The cops' eyes shifted.

'Frenchy,' said Jon.

'So Frenchy's in trouble. It couldn't be something she's done. Someone she knows?'

The cops turned back to the bar. The frowning one said: 'Two more. Does he know her?'

'As much as I do,' said Jon, pouring out the potheen. The white, cloudy stuff filled the tumblers to the brim. Jon must be worried to pour such heavy ones for nothing.

I got up on to the platform where I sang, flicking the mike, which I knew would be dead, as it had been since the middle of the war. I leaned my guitar against the dryest part of the wall and struck a match. I lit the two candles in their wall-holders. They didn't exactly fill the corner with a blaze of light, they smoked and guttered and stank and cast shadows. I wondered briefly who had supplied the fat. They weren't much good as heating either. It was almost as cold inside as out. I dusted off my stool and sat down, picked up my guitar and struck a few chords. I hardly realized I was playing 'Frenchy's Blues'. It was one of those corny numbers that come easy to the fingers without you having to think about them.

Frenchy wasn't French, she was a kraut and who liked krauts? I liked Frenchy, along with all the customers who came to hear her sing to my accompaniment. Frenchy didn't work at the Merrie Englande, she just enjoyed singing. She didn't keep boyfriends long or often, she preferred to sing, she said.

'Frenchy's Blues' only appealed to the least sensitive members of our cordial clientele. I didn't care for it. I'd tried to do something good for her, but as with most things I tried to do well, it hadn't come off. I changed the tune, I was used to changing my tune. I played 'Summertime' and then I played 'Stormy Weather'.

The cops sipped the drinks and waited. Jon leant against the shelves, his narrow, black-clad body almost invisible in the shadow, only his thin face showing. We didn't look at one another. We were both scared – not only for Frenchy, but for ourselves. The cops had a habit of subpoenaing witnesses and forgetting to release them after the trial – particularly if they were healthy men who weren't already working in industry or the police force. Though I didn't have to fear this possibility as much as most, I was still worried.

During the evening I heard the dull sound of far-away bomb explosions, the drone of planes. That would be the English *Luftwaffe* doing exercises over the still-inhabited suburbs.

Customers came and most of them went after a drink and a squint at the constables.

Normally Frenchy came in between eight and nine, when she came. She didn't come. As we closed up around midnight, the cops got off their stools. One unbuttoned his tunic pocket and took out a notebook and pencil. He wrote on the pad, tore off the sheet and left it on the bar.

'If she turns up, get in touch,' he said. 'Merry Christmas, sir,' he nodded to me. They left.

I looked at the piece of paper. It was cheap, blotting-paper stuff and one corner was already soaking up spilled potheen. In large capitals, the PC had printed: 'Contact Det. Insp. Braun, N. Scot. Yd. Ph. WHI 1212, Ext. 615.'

'Braun?' I smiled and looked up at Jon. 'Brown?'

'What's in a name?' he said.

'At least it's CID. What do you think it's about, Jon?'

'You never can tell these days,' said Jon. 'Good night, Lowry.'

''Night.' I went into the room behind the bar, packed my guitar and put on my coat. Jon came in to get his street clothes.

'What do they want her for?' I said, 'It's not political stuff, anyway. The Special Branch isn't interested, it seems. What –?'

'Who knows?' said Jon brusquely. 'Goodnight –'

''Night,' I said. I buttoned up my coat, pulled my gloves on and picked up the guitar case. I didn't wait for Jon since he evidently wasn't seeking the company and comfort of an old pal. The cops seemed to have worried him. I wondered what he was organizing on the side. I decided to be less matey in future. For some time my motto had been simple – keep your nose clean.

I left the bar and entered the darkness of the square. It was empty. The iron railings and trees had gone during the war. Even the public lavatories were officially closed, though sometimes people slept in them. The tall buildings were stark against the night sky. I turned to my right and walked towards Piccadilly Circus, past the sagging hoardings that had been erected around bomb craters, treading on loose paving stones that rocked beneath my feet. Piccadilly Circus was as bare and empty as anywhere else. The steps were still in the centre, but the statue of Eros wasn't there any more. Eros had flown from London towards the end of the war. I wish I'd had the same sense.

I crossed the circus and walked down Piccadilly itself, the wasteland of St James's Park on one side, the tall buildings, or hoardings where they had been, on the other. I walked in the middle of the road, as was the custom. The occasional car was less of a risk than the frequent cosh-merchant. My hotel was in Piccadilly, just before you got to Park Lane.

I heard a helicopter fly over as I reached the building and unlocked the door. I closed the door behind me, standing in a wide, cold foyer, unlighted and silent. Outside the sound of the helicopter died and was replaced by the roar of about a dozen motorbikes heading in the general direction of Buckingham Palace, where Field Marshal Wilmot had his court. Wilmot wasn't the most popular man in Britain, but his efficiency was much admired in certain quarters. I crossed the foyer to the broad staircase. It was marble, but uncarpeted. The bannister rocked beneath my hand as I climbed the stairs.

A man passed me on my way up. He was an old man. He wore a red dressing gown and carried a chamber pot as far away from him as his shaking hand could stand.

'Good morning, Mr Pevensey,' I said.

'Good morning, Mr Lowry,' he replied, embarrassed. He coughed, started to speak, coughed again. As I began on the third flight, I heard him wheeze something about the water being off again. The water was off most of the time. It was only news when it came on. The gas came on three times a day for half an hour – if you were lucky. The electricity was supposed to run all day if people used the suggested ration, but nobody did, so power failures were frequent.

I had an oil stove, but no oil. Oil was expensive and could be got only on the black market. Using the black market meant risking being shot, so I did without oil. I had a place I used as a kitchen, too. There was a bathroom along the corridor. One of the rooms I used had a balcony overlooking the street with a nice view of the weed-tangled park. I didn't pay rent for these rooms. My brother paid it under the impression that I had no money. Vagrancy was a serious crime, though prevalent, and my brother didn't want me to be arrested because it caused him trouble to get me out of jail or one of the transit camps in Hyde Park.

I unlocked my door, tried the light switch, got no joy. I struck a match and lit four candles stuck in a candelabra on the heavy mantelpiece. I glanced in the mirror and didn't like the dull-eyed face I saw there. I was reckless. My next candle allowance was a month off but I'd always liked living dangerously. In a small way.

I put on my tattered tweed overcoat, Burberry's 1938, lay down on the dirty bed and put my hands behind my head. I brooded.

I wasn't tired, but I didn't feel very well. How could I, on my rations?

I went back to thinking about Frenchy's trouble. It was better than thinking about trouble in general. She must be involved in something, although she never looked as if she had the energy to take off her slouch hat, let alone get mixed up in anything illegal. Still, since the krauts had taken over in 1946 it wasn't hard to do something illegal. As we used to say, if it wasn't forbidden, it was compulsory. Even strays and vagabonds like me were straying under licence – in my case procured by brother Gottfried, ex-Godfrey, now Deputy Minister of Public Security. How he'd made it baffled me, with our background. Because obviously the first people the krauts had cleared out when they came to liberate us was the revolutionary element. And in England, of course, that wasn't the tattered, hungry mob rising in fury after centuries of oppression. It was the well-heeled, well-meaning law-civil-service-church-and-medicine brigade who came out of their warm houses to stir it all up.

Anyway, thinking about Godfrey always made my flesh creep, so I pulled my mind back to Frenchy. She was a tall, skinny rake of a girl, a worn out, battered old twenty in a dirty white mac and a shapeless pull-down hat with the smell of a Cagney gangster film about it. I never noticed what was under the mac – she never took it off. Once or twice she'd gone mad and undone it. I had the impression that underneath she was wearing a dirty black mac. No stockings, muddy legs, shoes worn down to stubs, not exactly Ginger Rogers on the town with Fred Astaire. Still, the customers liked her singing, particularly her deadpan rendering of 'Deutschland über Alles', slow, husky and meaningful, with her white face staring out over the people at the bar. A kraut by nationality, but not by nature, that was Frenchy.

I yawned. Not much to do but go to sleep and try for that erotic dream where I was sinking my fork into a plate of steak and kidney pudding. Or perhaps, if I couldn't get to sleep, I'd try a nice stroll round the crater where St Paul's had been – my favourite way of turning my usual depression into a really fruity attack of melancholia.

Then there was a knock.

I went rigid.

Late night callers were usually cops. In a flash I saw my face with blood streaming from the mouth and a lot of black bruises. Then the knock came again. I relaxed. Cops never knocked twice – just a formal rap and then in and all over you.

The door opened and Frenchy stepped in. She closed the door behind her.

I was off the bed in a hurry.

I shook my head. 'Sorry, Frenchy. It's no go.'

She didn't move. She stared at me out of her dark blue eyes. The shadows underneath looked as though someone had put inky thumbs under them.

'Look, Frenchy,' I said. 'I've told you there's nothing doing.' She ought to have gone before. It was the code. If someone wanted by the cops asked for help you had the right to tell them to go. No one thought any the worse of you. If you were a breadwinner it was expected.

She went on standing there. I took her by the shoulders, about faced her, wrenched the door open with one hand and ran her out on to the landing.

She turned to look at me. 'I only came to borrow a fag,' she said sadly, like a kid wrongfully accused of drawing on the wallpaper.

The code said I had to warn her, so I shoved her back into my room again.

She sat on my rumpled bed in the guttering candlelight with her beautiful, mud-streaked legs dangling over the side. I passed her a cigarette and lit it.

'There were two cops in the Merrie asking about you,' I said. 'CID!'

'Oh,' she said blankly. 'I wonder why? I haven't done anything.'

'Passing on coupons, trying to buy things with money, leaving London without a pass —' I suggested. Oh, how I wanted to get her off the premises.

'No. I haven't done anything. Anyhow, they must know I've got a full passport.'

I gaped at her. I knew she was a kraut — but why should she have a full passport? Owning one of those was like being invisible — people ignored what you did. You could take what you wanted from who you wanted. You could, if you felt like it, turn a dying old lady out of a hospital wagon so you could have a joy-ride, pinch food — anything. A sensible man who saw a full passport holder coming towards him turned round and ran like hell in the other direction. He could shoot you and never be called to account. But how Frenchy had come by one beat me.

'You're not in the government,' I said. 'How is it you've got an FP?'

'My father's Willi Steiner.'

I looked at her horrible hat, her draggled blonde hair, her filthy mac and scuffed shoes. My mouth tightened.

'You don't say?'

'My father's the Mayor of Berlin,' she said flatly. 'There are eight of us and mother's dead so no one cares much. But of course we've all got full passports.'

'Well, what the hell are you shambling around starving in London for?'

'I don't know.'

Suspicious, I said: 'Let's have a look at it, then.'

She opened her raincoat and reached down into whatever it was she had on underneath. She produced the passport. I knew what they looked like because brother Godfrey was a proud owner. They were unforgettable. Frenchy had one.

I sat down on the floor, feeling expansive. If Frenchy had an FP I was safer than I'd ever been. An FP reflected its warm light over everybody near it. I reached under the mattress and pulled out a packet of Woodies. There were two left.

Frenchy grinned, accepting the fag. 'I ought to flash it about more often.'

We smoked gratefully. The allowance was ten a month. As stated, the penalty for buying on the black market, presuming you could get hold of some money, was shooting. For the seller it was something worse. No one knew what, but they hung the bodies up from time to time and you got some idea of the end result.

'About this police business,' I said.

'You don't mind if I kip here tonight,' she said. 'I'm beat.'

'I don't mind,' I said. 'Want to hop in now? We can talk in bed.'

She took off the mac, kicked away her shoes and hopped in.

I took off my trousers, shoes and socks, pulled down my sweater and blew out the candles. I got into bed. There was nothing more to it than that. Those days you either did or you didn't. Most didn't. What with the long hours, short rations and general struggle to keep half clean and slightly below par, few people had the will for sex. Also sex meant kids and the kids mostly died, so that took all the joy out of it. Also I've got the impression us English don't breed in captivity. The Welsh and Irish did, but then they've been doing it for hundreds of years. The Highlanders didn't produce either. Increasing the population was something people like Godfrey worried about in the odd moments when they weren't eliminating it, but a declining birthrate is something you can't legislate about. What with the slave labour in the factories, cops round every corner, the jolly lads of the British *Wehrmacht* in every street, and being paid out in food and clothing coupons so you wouldn't do anything rash with the cash, like buying a razor blade and cutting your throat, you couldn't blame people for losing interest in propagating themselves. There'd been a resistance movement up until three or four years before, but they'd made a mistake and taken to the classic methods – blowing up bridges, the few operating railway lines and what factories had started up. It wasn't only the reprisals – on the current scale it was twenty men for every German killed, or

ten schoolkids or five women – but when people found out they
were blowing up boot factories and stopping food trains, a loyal
population, as the krauts put it, stamped out the antisocial Judaeo-
Bolshevik element in their midst.

The birthrate might have gone up if they'd raised the rations
after that, but that might cause a population explosion in more
ways than one.

Anyhow, it was warmer in there with Frenchy beside me.

'Would you mind,' I said, 'removing your hat?'

I couldn't see her, but I could tell she was smiling. She reached
up and pulled the old hat off and threw it on the floor.

'What about these cops, then?' I asked.

'Oh – I really don't know. Honestly, I haven't done anything. I
don't even know anybody who's doing anything.'

'Could they be after your full passport?'

'No. They never withdraw them. If they did the passports
wouldn't mean anything. People wouldn't know if they were
deferring to a man with a withdrawn passport. If you do something
like spying for Russia, they just eliminate *you*. That gets rid of
your FP automatically.'

'Maybe that's why they're after you . . .?'

'No. They don't involve the police. It's just a quick bullet.'

I couldn't help feeling awed that Frenchy, who'd shared my last
crusts, knew all this about the inner workings of the regime. I
checked the thought instantly. Once you started being interested
in them, or hating them or being emotionally involved with them
in any way at all – they'd got you. It was something I'd sworn
never to forget – only indifference was safe, indifference was the
only weapon which kept you free, for what your freedom was
worth. They say you get hardened to anything. Well, I'd had
nearly ten years of it – disgusting, obscene cruelty carried out by
stupid men who, from top to bottom, thought they were masters
of the Earth – and I wasn't hardened. That was why I cultivated
indifference. And the Leader – Our Führer – was no mad genius
either. Mad and stupid. That was even worse. I couldn't understand, then, how he'd managed to do what he'd done. Not then.

'I don't know what it can be,' Frenchy was saying, 'but I'll
know tomorrow when I wake up.'

'Why?'

'I'm like that,' she said roughly.

'Are you?' I was interested. 'Like – what?'

She buried her face in my shoulder. 'Don't talk about it, Lowry,' she said, coming as near to an appeal as a hard case like Frenchy could.

'OK,' I said. You soon learnt to steer away from the wrong topic. The way things, and people, were then.

So we went to sleep. When I woke, Frenchy was lying awake, staring up at the ceiling with a blank expression on her face. I wouldn't have cared if she'd turned into a marmalade cat overnight. I felt hot and itchy after listening to her moans and mutters all night and I could feel a migraine coming on.

The moment I'd acknowledged the idea of a migraine, my gorge rose, I got up and stumbled along the peeling passageway. Once inside the lavatory I knew I shouldn't have gone there. I was going to vomit in the bowl. The water was off. It was too late. I vomited, vomited and vomited. At least this one time the water came on at the right moment and the lavatory flushed.

I dragged myself back. I couldn't see and the pain was terrible.

'Come back to bed,' Frenchy said.

'I can't,' I said. I couldn't do anything.

'Come on.'

I sat on the edge of the bed and lowered myself down. Go away, Frenchy, I said to myself, go away.

But her hands were on that spot, just above my left temple where the pain came from. She crooned and rubbed and to the sound of her crooning I fell asleep.

I woke about a quarter of an hour later and the pain had gone. Frenchy, mac, hat and shoes on, was sitting in my old armchair, with the begrimed upholstery and shedding springs.

'Thanks, Frenchy,' I mumbled. 'You're a healer.'

'Yeah,' she said discouragingly.

'Do you often?'

'Not now,' she said. 'I used to. I just thought I'd like to help.'

'Well, thanks,' I said. 'Stick around.'

'Oh, I'm off now.'

'OK. See you tonight, perhaps.'

'No. I'm getting out of London. Coming with me?'

'Where. What for?'

'I don't know. I know the cops want me but I don't know why. I just know if I keep away from them for a month or two they won't want me any more.'

'What the bloody hell are you talking about?'

'I said I'd know what it was about when I awoke. Well, I don't – not really. But I do know the cops want me to do something, or tell them something. And I know there's more to it than just the police. And I know that if I disappear for some time I won't be useful any more. So I'm going on the run.'

'I suppose you'll be all right with your FP. No problem. But why don't you cooperate?'

'I don't want to,' she said.

'Why run? With your FP they can't touch you.'

'They can. I'm sure they can.'

I gave her a long look. I'd always known Frenchy was odd, by the old standards. But as things were now it was saner to be odd. Still, all this cryptic hide-and-seek, all this prescient stuff, made me wonder.

She stared back. 'I'm not cracked. I know what I'm doing. I've got to keep away from the cops for a month or two because I don't want to cooperate. Then it will be OK.'

'Do you mean you'll be OK?'

'Don't know. Either that or it'll be too late to do what they want. Are you coming?'

'I might as well,' I said. When it came down to it, what had I got to lose? And Frenchy had an FP. We'd be millionaires. Or would we?

'How many FPs in Britain?' I asked.

'About two hundred.'

'You can't use it then. If you go on the run using an FP you'd – we'd never go unnoticed. We'll stick out like a searchlight on a moor. And no one will cover for us. Why should they help an FP holder with the cops after her?'

Frenchy frowned. 'I'd better stock up here then. Then we can leave London and throw them off the scent.'

I nodded and got up and into the rest of my gear. 'I'll nip out and spend a few clothing coupons on decent clothes for you. You won't be so memorable then. They'll just think you're some high-up civil servant. Then I'll tell you who to go to. The cops will check with the dodgy suppliers last. They won't expect FP holders to use Sid's Foodmart when they could go to Fortnums. Then I'll give you a list of what to get.'

'Thanks, boss,' she said. 'So I was born yesterday.'

'If I'm coming with you I don't want any slip-ups. If we're caught you'll risk an unpleasant little telling-off. And I'll be in a camp before you can say Abie Goldberg.

'No,' she said bewilderedly. 'I don't think so.'

I groaned. 'Frenchy, love. I don't know whether you're cracked, or Cassandra's second cousin. But if you can't be specific, let's play it sensible. OK?'

'Mm,' she said.

I hurried off to spend my clothing coupons at Arthur's.

It was a soft day, drizzling a bit. I walked through the park. It was like a wood, now. The grass was deep and growing across the paths. Bushes and saplings had sprung up. Someone had built a small compound out of barbed wire on the grass just below the Atheneum. A couple of grubby white goats grazed inside. They must belong to the cops. With rations at two loaves a week people would eat them raw if they could get at them. Look what had happened to the vicar of All Saints, Margaret Street. He shouldn't have been so High Church – all that talk about the body and blood of Christ had set the congregation thinking along unortho-dox lines.

I walked on in the drizzle. No one around. Nice fresh day. Nice to get out of London.

'Any food coupons?' said a voice in my ear.

I turned sharply. It was a young woman, so thin her shoulder blades and cheek bones seemed pointed. In her arms was a small baby. Its face was blue. Its violet-shadowed eyes were closed. It was dressed in a tattered blue jumper.

I shrugged. 'Sorry, love. I've got a shilling – any use?'

'They'd ask me where I'd got it from. What's the good?' she whispered, never taking her eyes off the child's face.

'What's wrong with the kid?'

'They've cut off the dried milk. Unless you can feed them yourself they starve – I'm hungry.'

I took out my diary. 'Here's the address of a woman called Jessie Wright. Her baby's just died of diphtheria. She may take the kid on for you.'

'Diphtheria?' she said.

'Look, love, your kid's half-dead anyway. It's worth trying.'

'Thanks,' she said. Tears started to run down her face. She took the piece of paper and walked off.

'Hey ho,' said I, walking on.

I crossed the Mall and got the usual suspicious stares from the mixed assortment of soldiery that half-filled it. The uniforms were all the same. You couldn't tell the noble Tommy from the fiendish Hun. I looked to my right and saw Buckingham Palace. From the mast flew a huge flag, a Union Jack with a bloody great swastika superimposed on it. I'd never got rid of my loathing for that symbol, conceived as part of their perverted, crazy mysticism. Field Marshal Wilmot had been an officer in the Brigade of St George – British fascists who had fought with Hitler almost from the start. A shrewd character that Wilmot. He had a little moustache that was identical with the Leader's – but as he was prematurely bald, hadn't been able to cultivate the lock of hair to go with it. He was fat and bloated with drink and probably drugs. He depended entirely on the Leader. If he hadn't been there it might have been a different story.

I walked down Buckingham Gate and turned right into Victoria Street. The Army and Navy Stores had become exactly what it said – only the military elite could shop there.

Arthur was in business in the former foreign exchange kiosk at Victoria Station. I bunged over the coupons. Sunlight streamed through the shattered canopy of the station. There had been some street fighting around here but it hadn't lasted long.

'I want a lady's coat, hat and shoes. Are these enough?'

Arthur was small and shrewd. He only had one arm. He put the coupons under his scanner. 'They're not fakes.' I said impatiently, 'Are they enough?'

'Just about, mate – as it's you,' he said. He was a thin-faced cockney from the City. His kind had survived plagues, sweatshops and the depression. He'd survive this, too. I happened to know he'd been one of Mosley's fascists before the War – in fact he'd kicked a thin-skulled Jew in the head in Dalston in 1938, thus saving him from the gas chambers in 1948. Funny how things work out.

But somehow since the virile lads of the *Wehrmacht* had marched in he seemed to have cooled off the old blood-brotherhood of the Aryans, so I never held it against him. Anyway, being about five foot two and weasely with it, he was no snip for the selective breeding camps.

'What size d'you want?' he asked.

'Oh, God. I don't know.'

'The lady should have come herself.' He looked suspicious.

'Coppers tore her clothes off,' I said. That satisfied him. A cop passed across the station at a distance. Arthur's eyes flicked, then came back to me.

'Funny the way they left them in their helmets and so on,' he said. 'Seems wrong, dunnit?'

'They wanted you to think they were the same blokes who used to tell you the time and find old Rover for you when he got lost.'

'Aren't they?' Arthur said sardonically. 'You should have lived round where I lived mate. Still, this won't buy baby a new pair of boots. What's the lady look like?'

'About five nine or ten. Big feet.'

'Coo – no wonder the coppers fancied her,' he jeered jealously. 'You must feel all warm and safe with her. Thin or fat?'

'Come off it Arthur. Who's fat?'

'Girls who know cops.'

'This one didn't until last night.'

'Nothing dodgy is it?' His eyes started looking suspicious again. Trading licences were hard to come by these days. I thought of telling him about Frenchy's full passport, but dismissed the idea. It would sound like a fantastic, dirty great lie.

'She's OK. She just wants some clothes that's all.'

'If she got her clothes torn off why don't she want a dress? That's more important to a lady than a hat – a lady what is a lady that is.'

'Give me the coupons, Arthur.' I stretched out my hand. 'You're not the only clothes trader around. I came here to buy some gear, not tell you my love life.'

'OK, Lowry. One coat, one hat, one pair of shoes, size seven – and God help you if her feet's size five.' Arthur produced the things with a wonderful turn of speed. 'And that'll be a quid on top.'

I'd expected this. I handed him the pound. As I put the goods in a paper bag I said, 'I took the number of that quid, mate. If the cops call on me about this deal I'll be able to tell them you're taking cash off the customers. They may not nick you, of course – but they may soak you hard.'

He called me a bastard and added some more specific details, then said, 'No hard feelings, Lowry. But I thought all along this was a dodgy deal.'

'You mind your business, chum, I'll mind mine,' I said. 'So long.'

'So long,' he said. I headed back towards the park.

Frenchy was asleep when I got back. She looked fragile, practically TB. I woke her up and handed her the gear. She put it on.

'Frenchy, love,' I said sadly. 'I've got to break it to you – you must have a wash. And comb your hair. And haven't you got a lipstick?'

She sulked but I fetched some water. By some accident Pevensey had missed what was left in the taps. She washed, combed her hair with my comb and we made up her lips with a Swan Vesta.

I stood back. Black coat, a bit short with a fur collar, white beret and black high heeled shoes.

'Honestly, French, you look like Marlene Dietrich,' I said partly to give her the morale to carry off the FP-ing, partly because it was almost true. It was a pity she looked so undernourished, but perhaps they'd think it was natural.

'Get yourself some makeup while you're at it.'

'Here,' she said in alarm, 'I don't know what to do.'

'You mean you've never *used* that passport,' I said.

'You wouldn't if you were me,' she replied. For her that was obviously the question you never asked, like 'where were you in '45?' or 'what happened to cousin Fred?' Her face was dark.

I passed it off. 'You're cracked. Never mind. Just march into the place. Look confident. Tell them what you want. They'll cotton on immediately. You probably won't even need to show it to them. Scoop the stuff up and go. Don't forget they're scared of you.'

'OK.'

'Here's the list of what we want and where to get it.'

'Yeah,' she glanced over the list. 'Brandy, eh?'

I grinned. 'Christmas, after all. You never drink, though.'

'No. It does something bad to me.'

'Uh huh. Use a slight German accent. That'll convince them.'

She left and I went and lay down. I felt tired after all that.

And, lo, another knock at my door. Thinking it was Pevensey wanting me to get him some more quack medicine, I shouted 'come in.'

He stood in the doorway, a vision of loveliness in his black striped coat and pinstriped trousers. He glanced round fastidiously at my cracked lino, peeling wallpaper, the net curtain that was hanging down on one side of the small greasy window. Well, he had a right. He paid the rent, after all.

I didn't get up. 'Hullo, *mein* Gottfried,' I said.

'Hullo, old man.' He came in. Sat down on my armchair like a man performing an emergency appendectomy with a rusty razor blade. He lit a Sobranie.

As an afterthought he flung the packet to me. I took one, lit it and shoved the packet under the mattress.

'I thought I'd look in,' he said.

'How sweet of you. It must be two years now. Still, Christmas is the time for the family, isn't it?'

'Well, quite . . . How are you?'

'Rubbing along, thanks, Godfrey. And you?'

'Not too bad.'

The scene galled me. When we were young, before the war, we had been friends. Even if we hadn't been, brothers were still brothers. It wasn't that I minded hating my brother, that's common enough. It was that I didn't hate him the way brothers hate. I hated him coldly and sickly.

At that moment I would have liked to fall on him and throttle him, but only in the cold, satisfied way you rake down a flypaper studded with flies.

Besides I still couldn't see why he had come.

'How's the – playing?' he asked.

'Not bad, you know. I'm at the Merrie Englande these days.'

'So I heard.'

Hullo, I thought, I see glimmers of light. He saw I saw them – he was, after all, my brother.

'I wondered if you'd like some lunch,' he said.

Normally I would have refused, but I knew he might stay and catch Frenchy coming back. So I pretended to hesitate. 'All right, hungry enough for anything.'

We went down the cracked steps and walked up Park Lane. The drizzle had stopped and a cold sun had come out and made the street look even more depressing. Boarded up hotels, looted shops, cracked facades, grass growing in the broken streets, bent lamp standards, the park itself a tangled forest of weeds. It was sordid.

'Thinking of cleaning up, ever, Godfrey?' I asked.

'Not my department,' he said.

'Someone ought to.'

'No manpower, you see,' he said. I bet, I thought. Naturally they left it. One look was enough to break anyone's morale. If you were wondering how defeated and broken you were and looked at Park Lane, or Piccadilly, or Trafalgar Square, you'd soon know – completely.

Godfrey took me to a sandwich-and-soup place on the corner. A glance and the man behind the counter knew him for an FP holder. So the food wasn't bad, although Godfrey picked at it like a man used to something better.

Conversation stopped. The customers bent their shoulders over their plates of sandwiches and munched stolidly. Godfrey didn't seem to notice. He probably never had noticed. I had to face facts – although a member of my own family, Godfrey had always been a kraut psychologically. Always neat, always methodical, jumping his hurdles – exams, tests and assignments at work – like a trained horse. It wasn't that he didn't care about other people – I can't say I did – he just never knew there was anything to care about.

'How's the department?' I asked, beginning the ridiculous question and answer game again – as if either of us worried about anything to do with the other.

'Going well.'

'And Andrea?'

'She's well.'

She ought to be, I thought. Fat cow. She'd married Godfrey for his steady civil service job and made a far better bargain than she'd thought.

'What about you – are you thinking of getting married?'

I stared at him. Who married these days unless they had a steady job at one of the factories or on road transport, or, of course, in the police?

'Not exactly. Haven't really got the means to keep my bride in the accustomed manner.'

'Oh,' said Godfrey. Watch it, I thought. I knew that expression. 'Oh, they said Sebastian'd been riding Celeste's bike, mother.' 'Oh, father, I thought you'd given Seb *permission* to go out climbing.'

'I mentioned it because they told me you were engaged to a singer at the Merrie Englande.'

'Who are they?'

'Well, my private secretary, as a matter of fact. He's a customer.'

Yeah, I thought, like a rag-and-bone-man's a customer at the Ritz. He'd heard it from some spy.

'Well,' I said. 'I can't think how he managed to get that idea. I'm not sure there is a regular singer at the Merrie . . .'

'This girl was supposed to be like you – a sort of casual entertainer. A German girl I think he said.'

Too specific, chum. That line might just work with a stranger – not with your little brother.

'I think I've met her. In fact I've played for her once or twice. I don't know much about her, though. I'm certainly not engaged to her.'

Godfrey bit into a sandwich. I'd closed that line of enquiry. He was wondering how to open another.

'That's a relief. She sounds a tramp.'

'Maybe.'

'We want to repatriate her – know where she is?'

'Why should I?' I said. 'Apart from that, why should I help you? If she doesn't want to be repatriated, that's her business.'

'Be realistic, Sebby – anyway, she does want to be, or she would do, if she knew. Her aunt's died and left her a lot of money. The other side has asked us to let her know so she can go home and sort out her affairs.'

I went on drinking soup, but I wondered. Perhaps the story was true. Still, I didn't need to put Godfrey on to her – I could tell her myself.

'Well, I'll tell her if I see her. I doubt if I shall. I should leave a message at the Merrie.'

'Yes.'

He looked up broodingly, staring round in that blank way people have when they're bored with their eating companion.

I followed his gaze. My eyes lit on Frenchy. Loaded with parcels, she was buying food and having a flask filled with coffee at the counter. I went rigid. Frenchy had gained confidence – she was buying like an FP holder. And anyone with that amount of stuff on them attracted attention anyway. She was attracting it all right. Godfrey was the only man in the room who wasn't looking at her and pretending not to. He was just looking at her. I couldn't decide if he was watching her like a cat or just watching.

'Heard about Freddy Gore?' I said.

'No,' said Godfrey, not taking his eyes off her.

'He committed suicide,' I said.

'Well I'm damned,' said Godfrey, looking at me greedily. 'Why?'

'It was his wife. He came home one afternoon . . .' I spoke on hastily. Frenchy was still buying. Half the customers were still pointedly ignoring her – apart from anything else she looked quite good in her new gear. She picked up her stuff and left without showing her FP to the man behind the counter. She left without Godfrey noticing. I brought my tale of lust, adultery, rape and murder in the Gore family to a speedy close. A horrible thought had struck me. Godfrey was a high-up. He knew about Frenchy and he knew I knew her. There were a lot of cops on the job and he might have fixed it so that some were watching my hotel. Somehow I had to shift him and catch Frenchy before she got back.

'Shocking story,' said Godfrey, looking at his watch. 'I must be getting back. Like a lift?'

'Not going in that direction,' I said. 'Thanks all the same.'

So he flagged down a passing car and told the sulky driver to take him to Buckingham Palace – the krauts had restored it at huge expense for the Ministry of Security as well as our paternal governor.

I walked slowly down the road, turned off and ran like hell. I caught Frenchy, all burdened with parcels, just in time.

'Better not go back,' I gasped. 'They may be watching the hotel.'

There was a car standing outside a house just down the street. I ran her up to it and tugged at the door. It wasn't locked. I shoved her in, paper bags, flask and all, and got in the driving seat.

A stocky man ran out of the house. He had a revolver in his hand. I started up. Frenchy had the passport out. I grabbed it and waved it at the man with the gun.

'Full passport!' I yelled.

He stood staring at the back of the car. He didn't even dare snarl.

'What makes you think they're watching the hotel?' she asked.

I told her about Godfrey.

She frowned. 'I must be right about having to run.'

'Are you sure it isn't this legacy they say you've inherited?'

'I've only got one aunt and she's broke. Besides, why should your brother get involved in such a silly little business?'

'Because your father's so important. Or perhaps Papa just wants you home and made up the aunt business to cover up the fact that you're his no-good daughter who's drifting about in occupied territory, dragging the family name in the mud behind her.'

'Could be. It's not though. I'm still not sure – you'll have to believe me. In the past I've been – well – important. It's to do with that, I know.'

'What sort of important?'

She began to cry, great, racking sobs which bent her double.

'Don't ask me – oh, don't ask me.'

I got hard-hearted. 'Come on, Frenchy. Why should I break the law for you?'

'I don't want to remember – I can't remember,' she gasped.

'Nuts. You can remember if you want to.'

'I can't. I don't want to.'

I passed her my handkerchief silently. How important could she have been – at twenty years old? She must have been at school until a couple of years ago.

'Where did you go to school?' I asked, more to pass time than anything.

'I was at the Berlin *Gymnasium* for Girls. When I was thirteen, I – they took me away.'

Then the tears stopped and when I glanced at her, she had fainted. I pushed her back so that she was sitting comfortably, and drove on.

As dark came we reached Histon, just outside Cambridge, and spent the night in the car, parked beside a hedge, inside a field.

When I woke next morning there was a rifle barrel in my ear.

'Oh, Gawd,' I said. 'What's this?'

A hand opened the car door and dragged me out. I lay on the ground with the barrel pointing at my belly. Above the barrel was a red face topped by a trilby hat. It wasn't a copper anyway.

I glanced sideways at the car. Inside, Frenchy was sitting up. Outside another man pointed a rifle at her temple, through the open window.

'What's all this about?' I said.

'Who're you?' the man said.

'Sebastian Lowry and Frenchy Steiner,' I said.

'What're you here for?'

'Just riding –'

The gun barrel dropped. The man was looking at his friend.

Then I saw – Frenchy had her passport out.

He touched his hat and retreated quickly, mumbling apologies. So I got back in the car and we snuggled up and back to sleep.

When we woke up, we had coffee from the flask, and a sandwich. Then we walked round the field. One or two birds cheeped from the bare hedges and our feet sank into ploughed furrows. It was silent and lonely. We walked round and round, breathing deeply.

We sat down and looked out over the big, flat field, sharing a bar of chocolate.

Frenchy smiled at me – a real smile, not her usual tense grin. I smiled back. We sat on. No noise, no people, no grimy, cracked buildings, no cops. A pale sun was high in the sky. The birds cheeped. I took Frenchy's hand. It felt strange, to be holding someone's hand again. It was warm and dry. Her fingers gripped mine. I stared at the pale, pointed profile beside me, and the long, messy blonde hair. Then I looked at the field again. We started a second bar of chocolate. Frenchy yawned. The silence went on and on. And on and on.

I was staring numbly across the acres of brown earth when Frenchy's hand clenched painfully on mine.

Slowly, from behind every bush, like the characters in some monstrous, silent film, the cops were rising. On all sides, over the bare bushes came a pair of blue shoulders, topped by a helmet. They rose slowly until they were standing. Then they moved silently forward. They tightened in.

Frenchy and I rose. The circle closed. To keep in the centre we had to move over to the road. Slowly they drove us out of the field, past our car, through the gate and on to the road. No one spoke. All we heard was the sound of their boots on the earth. Their faces were rigid, like cops' faces always are.

Coming through the gate, we saw the reception committee. Three of them. My friend Inspector Braun, all knife-edged creases and polished buttons, and brother Godfrey. And then a short fat man I didn't know. He was wearing a well-cut suit and power, as they say, was written all over him, from his small, neatly shod feet, to his balding head.

Frenchy stepped up to the group. 'Hullo, father,' she said in German.

'Hullo, Franziska. We've found you at last, I see.'

Godfrey smirked. Extra rations for good old Gottfried tomorrow. Maybe the Iron Cross.

So I thought I'd embarrass him. 'Hi, Godfrey, old man.'

'Morning, Sebastian.' How he wished I wasn't shaking his hand. 'We're parked up the road. Come on.'

So we walked up the road to the shiny blue car that would take us back to God knew where – or what.

How silently they must have moved. What bloody fools we'd been not to get away after those two farmers had copped us. Godfrey and friends had probably had bulletins out for us all morning.

I sat at the back, between Godfrey and the Inspector. Frenchy was in front with her father and the driver.

'It's nice to know officialdom has its more human side,' I remarked. 'To think that the deputy security minister, a CID Inspector and fifty coppers should all come out on a cold winter's morning to see a young girl gets the legacy that's rightfully hers.'

Godfrey said nothing. He merely looked important. From the way Braun didn't grip my arm and the driver didn't keep glancing over his shoulder to see who I was coshing, I got the impression this wasn't a hanging charge. There was a sort of alligator grin in the air – cops taking home a naughty under-age couple who had run off to get married – not that cops did that kind of little social service job these days, but, wistfully, they kept trying to make you think so.

But what *was* the set-up? In front Frenchy had given up talking to her father – he cut every remark off at source. Why? No family rows in public? Frenchy, what I could see of her, looked like a girl on a cart bound for the scaffold. Her father looked like a man determined to knock some sense into his daughter's flighty head as soon as he got her home. Godfrey merely looked pontifical. Braun looked official.

Frenchy tried again. 'Father. I *can't* go –'

'Be quiet!' said her father. Godfrey was listening hard. Suddenly I got the picture. *Godfrey and Braun didn't know what it was all about.* And Frenchy's father didn't want them to.

It must be really something, then, I thought.

There was silence all the way back to London. What about me? I thought. I'm just not in this at all. But I bet it's me who takes the rap. The car stopped in Trafalgar Square. Frenchy and her father got out. He hurried her up the steps of the Goering Hotel. Her eyes were burning like coals.

Then Godfrey and Braun pulled me out. 'You'll be in a suite here till we decide what to do with you,' Godfrey said in a low voice. 'Don't worry. I'll do what I can to help.'

I won't say tears came to my eyes – I knew just how far he would go to help. I said goodbye to him and Braun led me up the marble steps. The place was crowded with neat soldiery. We were joined by the hotel manager and two coppers. We went up to the top storey and I was shown my suite. Three rooms and a bathroom. Quite a nice little shack, although somewhat Teutonically furnished. It was elegant, but there was the smell of loot about it. You kept wondering which bit of furniture covered the bloodstains where they'd bayonetted the Countess and her kids one morning.

Then the two policemen stationed themselves, one at the door and one inside with me. That wasn't so pleasant. I wondered when the cop was going to suggest a hand of nap to while away the time before the execution. I looked about appreciatively, sat down on the blue silk sofa and said 'What now?'

A waiter came in with tea and toast. One cup. I asked the cop if he'd like some. He refused. As I went to pour out my second cup I saw why, because the room began to spin. 'This hotel isn't what it was,' I muttered and fell down.

I woke up next morning in a fourposter. Frenchy, in a red silk nightdress and negligee was bending over me with a cup of coffee. I hauled myself up, noticing my blue silk pyjamas, and took the cup.

She sat down at the Louis XIV table beside the bed. She went on eating rolls and butter. Her hair, obviously washed, cascaded down her back like gold thread.

'Very nice,' I said, handing back my cup for a refill. 'If I didn't wonder whose Christmas dinner I was being fattened for. Where's the cop?'

'I sent him outside.'

I began to glance round. The windows were barred.

'You can't get out. The place is heavily guarded and the cops will shoot you on sight.'

'That's new?'

She ignored me. 'You're quite safe as long as you're with me. I've told them I've got to have you with me.'

'That's nice. How long will you be around?'

'I thought you'd spot a snag.'

'Look, Frenchy. I think you'd better tell me what this is about. It's my carcass after all.'

'I will,' she said calmly. 'Prepare yourself for surprises.' She seemed very matter of fact, but her face had the calm of a woman who's just had a baby, the pain and shock were over, but she knew this was really only the beginning of the trouble.

'I told you I was at a *Gymnasium* in Berlin until I was thirteen. Then I began seeing visions. Of course, the tutors didn't make much of it at first. It's not too unusual in girls at the beginning of puberty. The trouble was, they weren't the usual kind of visions. I used to see tables surrounded by German officers. I used to overhear conferences. I saw tanks going into battle, burning cities, concentration camps – things I couldn't possibly know about. Then, one night, my room-mate heard me talking English in my sleep. I was talking about battle plans, using military terms and English slang I also couldn't possibly have known. She told the House Leader. The House Leader told my father, who was then only a captain in the SS. Father was an intelligent man. He took me to Karl Ossietz, one of the Leader's chief soothsayers. A month later I was installed in a suite at headquarters. I was dressed in a white linen dress, my hair was bound with a gold band. I'd become part of the German myth . . .

'I was the virgin who prophesied to Attila, I was thirteen years old and I lived like a ritual captive for four years, officiating at sacrifices and Teutonic Saturnalia, watching goats have their throats cut with gold knives, seeing torchlight on the walls – all that. And I thought it was marvellous, to be helping the cause like that. I went into a kind of mystic dream where I was an Aryan queen helping her nation to victory. And in my midnight conferences with the Leader I prophesied. I told him not to attack Russia – I knew he would be defeated. I told him where to concentrate his forces to use them to their best effect. Oh, and much, much more . . .

'Also only I could soothe him when his attacks of mania came on – by putting my hands on him the way I did for you the other day. I'm not a real healer. I can't cure the body. But I can reach into overtaxed or unstable minds and take away the tightness.

'When the war ended, I just left in a daze. They thought they didn't really need me at that time. There was something in the back of my mind – I don't know what it was – made me come here, with my passport, my safe conducts, my letters of introduction . . . When I saw what I had done to you all – what could I do? I tried to kill myself and failed – maybe I wasn't trying hard enough. Then I tried to live with you, simply because I couldn't think of anything else to do. A stronger person might have thought of practical ways to help – but I'd spent four years in an atmosphere of blood and hysteria, calling on the psychic part of me and ignoring the rest. I was unfit for life. I just tried to forget everything that had ever happened to me.'

She shrugged. 'That's it.'

I stared at her, feeling a horrible pity. She knew she had been used to kill millions of people and reduce a dozen nations to slavery. And she had got to live with it.

'What's it all about now?' I asked.

'They need me again. There must be desperate problems to be solved. Or the Leader's madness is getting worse. Or both. That's why I felt if I could disappear for a month it would be all right. By that time no one could have cleared up the mess.' She lit a cigarette, passed it to me and lit one for herself.

'What are you going to do?'

'I don't know. If I don't help they'll torture me until I do. I'm not strong enough to resist. But I can't, can't, *can't* cooperate any more. If I had the guts I'd kill myself but I haven't. Anyway, they've taken away anything I could use to do it. That's why all the windows are barred – it's not to stop you escaping. It's to stop me from throwing myself out. I don't suppose you'd kill me quickly, so I wouldn't know anything about it?'

In a sense the idea was tempting. A chance to get back at the Leader with a vengeance. But I knew I couldn't kill poor, thin Frenchy.

I told her so. 'I'm too kindhearted,' I said. 'If I killed you, how could I go on hoping you'd have a better life?'

'I won't. If I'm needed they'll cage me again. And this time I'll have known freedom. I'll be back in robes, with incense and torchlight and all the time I'll be able to remember being free – walking in the field at Histon, for example.' I felt very sad. Then I felt even sadder – I was thinking about myself.

'What happens next?' I said.

'They'll fly me to Germany. You're coming too.'

'Oh, no,' I said. 'Not Germany. I wouldn't stand a chance.'

'What chance do you stand here? If I went and you stayed, you'd be shot the moment I left the building. They can't risk letting you go about with your story.'

Her shoulders were bowed. She looked as if she had no inner resources left. 'I'm sorry. It's my fault. I should have left you alone. If I'd never made you run away with me you'd be safe now.'

That wasn't how I remembered it exactly, but I'd rather blame her than me for my predicament. I agreed, oh, how I agreed. Still, once a gent, always a gent. 'Never mind that. I'll come and perhaps we can think of something.' I was dubious about that, but by that time I was too far in.

So at eleven that morning we left the hotel for the airport. From Berlin we went by limousine to the Leader's palace. I've never been so afraid in my life. It's one thing to go in daily danger of being shot, or sent to starve in a camp. It's another thing to fly straight into the centre of all the trouble. I was so afraid I could hardly speak. Not that anyone wanted to hear from me anyway. I was just a passenger – like a bullock on its way to the abattoir.

During the trip, Frenchy's father kept up a nervous machine-gun monologue of demands that she would cooperate and promises of a glorious future for her. Frenchy said nothing. She looked drained.

We arrived in the green courtyard of the palace. On the other side of the wall I heard the rush of a waterfall into a pool. The palace was half old German mansion, half modern Teutonic, with vulgar marble statues all over the place – supermen on super-horses. That's the nearest they'd got to the master-race, so far. A white haired old man led the jackbooted party which met us.

Frenchy smiled when she saw him, a child's smile. 'Karl,' she said. Even her voice was like the voice of a very young girl. I shuddered. The spell was beginning to operate again – that blank face, the voice of the little school girl. Oh, Frenchy, love, I sighed to myself. Don't let them do it to you. She was being led along by Karl Ossietz, across the green courtyard.

We made a peculiar gang. In front, Ossietz, tall and thin, with long white hair, and Frenchy, now looking so frail a breeze might blow her away. Behind them a group of begonged generals, all horribly familiar to me from seeing their portraits on pub signs. Just behind them rolled Frenchy's father, trying to join in. Then me, with two ordinary German cops. I caught myself feeling peeved that if I made a dash for it I'd be shot down by an ordinary cop.

Then Karl turned sharply back, stared at me and said: 'Who's that?'

Her father said: 'He's an Englishman. She wouldn't come without him.'

Karl looked furious and terrified. His face began to crumble. 'Are you lovers?' he shouted at Frenchy.

'No, Karl,' she whispered. He stared long and deeply into her eyes, then nodded.

'They must be separated,' he said to Frenchy's father.

Frenchy said nothing. Suddenly I felt more than concern for her – panic for myself. The only reason I'd come here was because she could protect me. Now she could, but she wasn't interested any more. So instead of being shot in England, I was going to be shot right outside the Leader's front door. Still, dead was dead, be it palace or dustbin.

We entered the huge dark hall, full of figures in ancient armours and dark horrible little doors leading away to who knew where. The mosaic floor almost smelt of blood. My legs practically gave way under me, I saw Frenchy being led up the marble staircase. I felt tears come to my eyes – for her, for me, for both of us.

Then they took me along a corridor and up the back stairs. They shoved me through a door. I stood there for several minutes. Then I looked round. Well, it wasn't a rat-haunted oubliette, at any rate. In fact it was the double of my suite at the Goering Hotel. Same thick carpets, heavy antique furniture, even – I poked my head round the door – the same fourposter. Obviously they picked up their furniture at all the little chateaux and castles they happened to run across on a Saturday morning march.

In the bedroom, torches burned. I took off my clothes and got into bed. I was asleep.

The first thing I saw as I awoke was that the torches were burning down. Then I saw Frenchy, naked as a peeled wand, pulling back the embroidered covers and coming into bed. Then I felt her warmth beside me.

'Do it for me,' she murmured. 'Please.'

'What?'

'Take me,' she whispered.

'Eh?' I was somewhat shocked. People like Frenchy and me had a code. This wasn't part of it.

'Oh, please,' she said, pressing her long body against me, 'It's so important.'

'Oh – let's have a fag.'

She sank back. 'Haven't got any,' came her sulky voice.

I found some in my pocket and we lit up. 'May as well drop the ash on the carpet,' I said. 'Not much point in behaving nicely so we'll be asked again.' I was purposely being irrelevant. Code or no code the situation was beginning to affect me. I tried to concentrate on my imminent death. It had the opposite effect.

'I don't understand, love,' I said, taking her hand.

'I had to crawl over the roof to get here,' she said, rather annoyed.

'It can't just be passion,' I suggested politely.

'Didn't you hear –?'

'My God,' I said. 'Ossietz. Do you mean that if you're not a virgin, you can't prophesy?'

'I don't know – he seems to think so. It's my only chance. He'll make me do whatever he wants me to – but if I can't perform, if it seems the power's gone – it won't matter. They may shoot me, but it will be a quick death.'

'Don't be so dramatic, love.' I put my cigarette out on the bed head and took her in my arms. 'I love you, Frenchy.' I said. And it was quite true. I did.

*

That was the best night of my life. Frenchy was sweet, and actually so was I. It was a relief to drop the mask for a few hours. As dawn came through the windows she lay in our tangled bed like a piece of pale wreckage.

She smiled at me and I smiled back. I gave her a kiss. 'A man who would do anything for his country,' she grinned.

'How are you going to get back?' I said.

'I thought I'd go back over the roof – but now I'm not sure I'll ever walk again.'

I said: 'Have I hurt you?'

'Like hell. I'll bluff my way out. The guards will be tired and I doubt if they know anything. Anyway all roads lead to the same destination now.'

I began to cry. That's the thing about an armadillo – underneath his flesh is more tender than a bear's. Not that I cared if I cried, or if she cried, or if the whole palace rang with sobs. The torches were guttering out.

She stood naked beside the bed. Then she put on her clothes, said goodbye. I heard her speaking authoritatively outside the door, heels clicking, and then her feet going along the corridor.

I just went on crying. Her meeting with the Leader was in two hours' time. If I went on crying for two hours I wouldn't have to think about it all.

I couldn't. By the time the guard came in with my breakfast, I was dressed and dry-eyed. He looked through the open door at the bed and gave a wink. He said something in German I couldn't understand, so I knew the words weren't in the dictionary. I stared at the bed and my stomach lurched. It seemed a bit rude to feel lust for a woman who was going to die.

Then I realized my condition was getting critical, so I ate my breakfast to bring me to my senses. The four last things, that was what I ought to be thinking about. What were they?

Suddenly I thought of the woman with the baby in the park. If Frenchy couldn't help the Leader, perhaps he'd go. Perhaps they'd lead a better life.

I paced the floor, wondering what was happening now.

This was what was happening . . .

Frenchy was bathed, dressed in a white linen robe with a red cloak and led down to the great hall.

The Leader was sitting on a dais in a heavy wooden chair. His arms were extended along the arms of the chair, his face held the familiar look of stern command, now a cracking facade covering decay and lunacy.

On his lips were traces of foam. Around him were his advisors, belted and booted, robed and capped or blonde and dressed in sub-valkyrie silk dresses. The court of the mad king – the atmosphere was hung with heavy incomprehensibilities. Led by her father and Karl Ossietz, Frenchy approached the dais.

'We – need – you –' the Leader grunted. His court held their places by will-power. They were terrified, and with good reason. The hall had seen terrible things in the past year. There were, too, one or two faces blankly waiting for the outcome. As the old pack-leader sickens, the younger wolves start to plan.

'We – have – sought – you for – half a year,' the grating, half-human voice went on. 'We need your predictions. We need your – *health!*'

His eyes stared into hers. He leapt up with a cry. 'Help! Help! Help!' His voice rang round the hall. More foam appeared at his lips. His face twisted.

'Go forward to the Leader,' Karl Ossietz ordered.

Frenchy stepped forward. The court looked at her, hoping.

'Help! Help!' the mad, uncontrollable voice went on. He fell back, writhing on his throne.

'I can't help,' she said in a clear voice.

Karl's whisper came, smooth and terrifying, in her ear: 'Go forward!'

She went forward, compelled by the voice. Then she stopped again.

'I can't help.' She turned to Ossietz. 'Can I Karl? You can see?'

He stared at her in horror, then at the writhing man, making animal noises on the dais, then back at Frenchy Steiner.

'You – you – you have fallen . . .' he whispered. 'No. No, she cannot help!' he called. 'The girl is no longer a virgin – her power has gone!'

The court looked at the Leader, then at Frenchy.

In a moment, chaos had broken out. Women screamed – there was a rush to the heavy doors. Men's voices rose, shouted. Then came the crack of the first gun, followed by others. In a moment the hall was milling and ringing with shots, groans and shouts.

On the dais, the Leader lay, twisting and uttering guttural moans. The pack was at frenzied war. Those who had considered the Leader immortal – and many had – were bewildered, terrified. Those who had planned to succeed him now hardly knew what to do. Several of them shot themselves there and then.

I was lying on the bed smoking when Frenchy ran in, slammed and bolted the doors behind the guards and her pursuers. Her hair was dishevelled, she held the scarlet cloak round her. 'Out of the window,' she yelled, ripping it off. Underneath, her white dress was in ribbons.

I got up on to the window-sill and helped her after me. I looked down towards the courtyard far below. I clung to the sill.

'Go on!'

I reached out and got a grip on a drainpipe. I began to slide down it, the metal chafing my hands. She followed.

At the bottom, I paused, helped her down the last few feet and pointed at a staff car that was parked near the gates. Guards had left the gates and were probably taking part in the indoor festivities. There was only one there and he hadn't seen us. He was looking warily out along the road, as if expecting attack.

We skipped over the lawn and got into the car. I started.

At the gate, the guard, seeing a general's insignia on the car, automatically stepped aside. Then he saw us, did a double take, and it was too late. We roared down that road, away from there.

The road ahead was clear.

True to form, Frenchy had found and put on an officer's white mac from the back seat.

I slowed down. There was no point in doing eighty towards any danger on the road.

'And have you lost your power?' I asked her.

'Don't know,' she gave me an irresponsible grin.

'What was going on below? It sounded like a battlefield.'

She told me.

'The leader's finished. His successors are fighting among themselves. This is the end of the Thousand Year Reich.' She grinned again. 'I did it.'

'Oh, come now,' I protested. 'Anyway I think we'll try to get back to England?'

'Why?'

'Because if the Empire's crumbling, England will go first. It's an island. They'll withdraw the legions to defend the Empire – it's traditional.'

'Can we make it?'

'Not now. We'll get out of Germany and then lie low for a few days until the news leaks out in France. Once things start to break down, the organization will disintegrate and we'll get help.'

We bowled on merrily, whistling and singing.

Cynosure

(1964)

KIT REED

'Now Polly Ann, Mrs Brainerd might not like children, so I want you to go into the bedroom with Puff and Ambrose till we find out.'

Polly Ann pulled her ruffles down over her ten-year-old paunch and picked up the cat, sausage curls bobbing as she went. 'Yes Momma.' She closed the bedroom door behind her and opened it again with a juicy, pre-adolescent giggle. 'Ambrose made a puddle on the rug.'

The three-note door chime sounded: Bong BONG Bong.

Norma motioned frantically. 'Never *mind*.'

'All *right*.' The door closed on Polly Ann.

Then, giving her aqua faille pouf pillows a pat and running her hand over the limed oak television set, Norma Thayer, housewife, went to answer the door.

She had been working at being a housewife for years. She cleaned and cooked and went to PTA and bought every single new appliance advertised and just now she was a little sensitive about the whole thing because clean as she would, her husband had just left her, when there wasn't even an Other Woman to take the blame. Norma would have to be extra careful about herself from now on, being divorced as she was – especially now, when she and Polly Ann were getting started in a new neighbourhood. They had a good start, really, because their new house in the development looked almost exactly like all the others in the block, except for being pink, and her furniture was the same shape and style as all the other furniture in all the other living rooms, right down to the formica dinette set visible in the dining area; she knew because she had gone around in the dark one night, and looked. But at the same time, she and Polly Ann didn't have a Daddy to come home at five o'clock, like the other houses did, and even though she and Polly Ann marked their house with wrought-iron numbers and put their garbage out in pastel plastic cans, even though they had centred their best lamp in the picture window and the kitchen was every bit as cute as the brochure said it was, the lack of a Daddy to put out the garbage and pot around in the yard on Saturdays and Sundays, just like everybody else, had put Norma at a distinct disadvantage.

Norma knew, just as well as anybody on the block, that a house was still a house without a Daddy, and things might even run smoother in the long run without all those cigarette butts and dirty pyjamas to pick up, but she was something of a pioneer, because she was the first in the neighbourhood to actually prove it out.

Now her next door neighbour was paying her first visit and Norma's housewifely heart began to swell. If all went well, Mrs Brainerd would look at the sectional couch and the rug of salt-and-pepper cotton tweed (backed with rubber foam) and see that Daddy or no, Norma was just as good as any of the housewives in the magazines, and that her dish-towels were just as clean as any in the neighbourhood. Then Mrs Brainerd would offer her a recipe and invite her to the next day's morning coffee hour which, if she recollected properly, would be held at Mrs Dowdy's, the lime split-level in the next block.

Patting the front of her Swirl housedress, she opened the door.

'Hello, Mrs Brainerd.'

'Hello,' Mrs Brainerd said. 'Call me Clarice,' she rubbed her hand along the lintel. 'Woodwork looks real nice.'

'Xerox,' Norma said with a proud little smile, and let her in.

'Brassit on the doorknob,' Mrs Brainerd said.

'Works like a dream. I made some coffee,' Norma said. 'And a cake . . .'

'Never touch cake,' Mrs Brainerd said.

'No greasy feel . . .'

'Metrecookies,' Mrs Brainerd said, and her jaw was white and firm. 'And no sugar for me. Sucaryl.'

'If you'll just sit down here.' Norma patted the contour chair.

'Thanks, no.' Mrs Brainerd smoothed *her* Swirl housedress and followed Norma into the kitchen.

She was small, slender, lipsticked and perfumed, and she was made of steel. Norma noticed with a guilty pang that Mrs Brainerd fastened the neck of *her* housedress with a Sweetheart pin.

'Something special,' Mrs Brainerd said, noticing her looking at it. 'Got it with labels from the Right Kind of Margarine.' She brushed past Norma, not even looking at the darling little dining area. 'Hm. Stains even bleach can't reach,' she went on, peering into the sink.

Norma flushed. 'I know. I scrubbed and scrubbed. I even used straight liquid bleach.' She hung her head.

'Well.' Clarice Brainerd reached into the pocket of her flowered skirt and came up with a shaker can. 'Here,' she said. She said it with a beautiful smile.

Norma recognized the brand. 'Oh,' she said, almost weeping with gratitude.

Clarice Brainerd had already turned to go. 'And the can is decorated, so you'd be proud to have it in your living room.'

'I know,' Norma said, deeply moved. 'I'll get two.'

Her neighbour was at the back door now. Norma reached out, supplicating. 'You're not leaving are you, before you even taste my cake . . .'

'You just try that cleanser,' Clarice said. 'And I'll be back.'

'The morning coffee. I thought you might want me to come to the . . .'

'Maybe next time,' her neighbour said, trying to be kind. 'You know, you might have to entertain them here one day, and . . .' She looked significantly at the sink. 'Just use that,' she said reassuringly. 'And I'll be back.'

'I will.' Norma bit her lip, torn between hope and despair. 'Oh I will.'

'Cake,' said Polly Ann just as the back door closed on Mrs Brainerd's mechanically articulated smile. She came into the kitchen with Puff, the kitten, and Ambrose, the beagle, trailing dust and hairs behind. 'I think Ambrose might be sick.' She got herself some grape juice, spilling as she poured. A purple stain began to spread on the sink.

Norma reached out with the cleanser, wanting desperately to ward off the stain.

'He just did it again in the living room,' Polly Ann said.

Norma's breath was wrenched from her in a sob. 'Oh, *no*.' Putting the cleanser in the little coaster she kept for just that purpose, she headed for the living room with sponge and Glamorene.

The next time Mrs Brainerd came she stayed for a scant thirty seconds. She stood in the doorway, sniffing the air. Ambrose had Done It again – twice.

'It really does get out stains even bleach can't reach,' Norma said, flourishing the cleanser can.

'Everyone knows that,' Clarice Brainerd said, passing it off. Then she sniffed. 'This will do wonders for your musty rooms,' she said, handing Norma a can of aerosol deodorant, turned without even coming in and closed the door.

Norma spent four days getting ready for the day she invited Mrs Brainerd to look into the stove. ('I'm having a little trouble with the bottoms of the open shelves,' she confided on the phone. She had just spent days making sure they were immaculate. 'I just wondered if you could tell me what to use,' she said seductively, thinking that when Clarice Brainerd saw that Norma was worried about dirt in an oven that was cleaner than any oven in the block, she would be awed and dismayed, and she would have to invite Norma to the next day's morning coffee hour.)

At the last minute, Norma had to shoo Polly Ann out of the living room. 'I was just making a dress for Ambrose,' Polly Ann said, putting on her Mary Janes and picking up her cloth and pins.

Vacuuming frantically, Norma stampeded her down the hall and into her room. 'Never *mind*.'

'Arient did the job all right,' Mrs Brainerd said, sniffing the air without even pausing to say hello. 'The *rest* of us have been using it for years.'

'I know,' Norma said apologetically.

In the kitchen, she spent a long time with her head in the oven. 'I don't think you have too much trouble,' she said grudgingly. 'In fact it looks real nice. But I would take a pin and clear out those gas jets.' Her voice was muffled because of the oven, and for a second Norma had to fight back wild temptation to push her the rest of the way in, and turn on the gas.

Then Clarice said, 'It looks real nice. And thanks, I will have some of your cake.'

'No greasy feel,' Norma said, weak with gratitude. 'You'll really sit down for a minute? You'll really have some coffee and sit down?'

'Only for a minute.'

Norma got out her best California pottery – the set with the rooster pattern – and within five minutes, she and Mrs Brainerd were sitting primly in the living room. The organdy curtains billowed and the windows and woodwork shone brightly and for a moment Norma almost imagined that she and Mrs Brainerd were being photographed on behalf of some product, in *her* living room, and their picture – in full colour – would appear in the very next issue of her favourite magazine.

'I would so love to do flower arrangements,' Norma said, made bold by her success.

Mrs Brainerd wasn't listening.

'Maybe join the Garden Club?'

Mrs Brainerd was looking down. At the rug.

'Or maybe the Music League . . .' Norma looked down, where Mrs Brainerd was looking, and her voice trailed off.

'Cat hairs,' said Mrs Brainerd. 'Loose threads.'

'Oh, I *tried* . . .' Norma clapped her hand to her mouth with a muffled wail.

'And scuff marks, on the hall floor . . .' Mrs Brainerd was shaking her head. 'Now, I don't mean to be mean, but if you were to entertain the coffee group, with the house looking like this . . .'

'My daughter was sewing,' Norma said faintly. 'She *knew* I was having company, but she came in here. It's a little hard,' she said, trying to smile engagingly. 'When you have kids . . .'

Mrs Brainerd was on her feet. 'The rest of us manage.'

Norma managed to keep the sob out of her voice. '. . . and pets . . .'

'The coffee hours,' Norma said, maundering. 'The garden club . . .'

But Mrs Brainerd was already gone.

Norma snuffled. 'She didn't even mention a *product* to try.'

'I made Ambrose a baby carriage,' Polly Ann said, dragging Ambrose through in a box. 'Is that lady gone?'

'Gone,' Norma said, looking at the way the box had scarred her hardwood floor. 'She may be gone forever,' she said, and began to cry. 'Oh Polly Ann, what can we do? We may have to move to a less desirable residential district.'

'Ambrose tipped over Puff's sandbox and got You Know What all over the floor.' Polly Ann went outside.

Crumbs, hairs, thread, dust and all seemed to converge on Norma then, eddying and swirling, threatening, plunging her into blackest despair. She sank to the couch, too overwhelmed to cry and it was then, looking down, that she spied the magazine protruding from under the rug, and things began to change.

END HOUSEHOLD
DRUDGERY

The advertisement said.

YOUR HOUSE CAN BE
THE CYNOSURE
OF YOUR NEIGHBOURHOOD

Norma wasn't sure what cynosure meant, but there was a picture of a spotless and shining lady, sitting in the middle of a spotless and shining living room, with an immaculate kitchen just visible through a door behind. Trembling with hope, she cut out the accompanying coupon, noting without a qualm that she would have to liquidate the rest of her savings to afford the product, or machine, or whatever it was. Satisfaction was guaranteed and if she got satisfaction it was worth it, every cent of it.

It was unprepossessing enough when it came.

It was a box, small and corrugated, and inside, wrapped in excelsior, was a small, lavender enamel-covered machine. A nozzle and hose, also lavender, were attached. Curious, Norma began leafing through the instruction book, and as she read she began to smile, because it all became quite plain.

'Effects are not necessarily permanent,' she read aloud, to assuage her conscience. 'Can be reversed by using green gauge on the machine. Oh, Puff,' she called, thinking of the white angora hairs which had sullied so many rugs. 'Puffy, come here.'

The cat came through the door with a look of insolence.

'Come here,' Norma said, aiming the nozzle. 'Come on, baby,' she said, and when Puff approached, she switched on the machine.

A pervasive hum filled the room, faint but distinct.

Expensive or not it was worth it. She had to admit that none of her household cleansers worked as fast. In less than a second Puff was immobile – wall-eyed and stiff-backed but immobile, looking particularly fluffy and just as natural as life. Norma arranged the cat artistically in a corner by the TV set and then went looking for Polly Ann's dog. She made Ambrose sit up and beg and just as he snapped for the puppy-biscuit she turned on the machine and ossified him in a split-second. When it was over she propped him on the other side of the television set and carefully put away the machine.

Polly Ann cried quite a bit at first.

'Now, honey, if we ever get tired of them this way, we can reverse the machine and let them run around again. But right now, the house is so *clean*, and see how cute they are? They can see and hear everything you want them to,' she said, quelling the child's sticky tears. 'And look, you can dress Ambrose up all you want, and he won't even squirm.'

'I guess so,' Polly Ann said, smoothing the front of her velvet dress. She gave Ambrose a little poke.

'And see how little dirt they make.'

Polly Ann bent Ambrose's paw in a salute. It stayed. 'Okay, Momma. I guess you're right.'

Mrs Brainerd thought the dog and cat were very cute. 'How did you *get* them to stay so still?'

'New product,' Norma said with a smug smile, and then she wouldn't tell Mrs Brainerd what product. 'I'll get my cake now,' she said. 'No greasy feel.'

'No greasy feel,' Mrs Brainerd said automatically, echoing her, and almost smiled in anticipation.

Moving regally, proud as a queen, Norma brought her coffee tray into the living room. 'Now about the coffee hour,' she said, presuming because Mrs Brainerd took up her cup and spoon with an almost admiring look, poking with her fork at the chocolate cake. ('I got the stainless with coupons. You know the kind.')

'The coffee hours,' Mrs Brainerd said, almost mesmerized. Then, looking down, 'Oh, what on earth is that?'

And already dreading what she would see, Norma followed Mrs Brainerd's eyes.

There was a puddle, a distinct puddle, forming under the bathroom door, and as the women watched it, it massed and began making a sticky trail down the highly polished linoleum of the hall.

'I'd better . . .' Mrs Brainerd said, getting up.

'I know,' Norma said with resignation. 'You'd better go.' Then, as she rose and saw her neighbour to the door, she stiffened with a new resolve. 'You just come back tomorrow. I can promise you, everything just as neat as pie.' Then, because she couldn't help herself, 'No greasy feel.'

'You know,' Mrs Brainerd said ominously. 'This kind of thing can only go on for so long. My time is valuable. There are the coffee hours, and the Canasta group . . .'

'I promise you,' Norma said. 'You'll envy my way with things. You'll tell all your friends. Just come back tomorrow. I'll be ready, I promise you . . .'

Clarice deliberated, unconsciously fingering her Good Luck earrings with one carefully groomed hand. 'Oh,' she said finally, after a pause which left Norma in a near faint from anxiety. 'All right.'

'You'll see,' Norma said to the closing door. 'Wait and see if you don't see.'

Then she made her way through the spreading pool of water and knocked on the bathroom door.

'I was making Kool-Ade to sell to all the Daddies,' Polly Ann said, gathering all the overflowing cups and jars.

'Come with me, baby,' Norma said. 'I want you to get all cleaned up and in your very best clothes.'

They were all arranged very artistically in the living room, the dog and the cat curled next to the sofa, Polly Ann looking just as pretty as life in her maroon velvet dress with the organdy pinafore. Her eyes were a little glassy and her legs did stick out at a slightly unnatural angle, but Norma had thrown an afghan over one end of the couch, where she was sitting, and thought the effect, in the long run, was just as good as anything she'd ever seen on a television commercial, and almost as pretty as some of the pictures she had seen in magazines. She noticed with a little pang that there was a certain moist look about the way Polly Ann was watching her, and so she went to the child and patted one waxen hand.

'Don't you worry, honey. When you get big enough to help Momma with her housecleaning, Momma will let you run around for a couple of hours every day. Momma promises.'

Then, smoothing the front of her Swirl housedress and refastening her Sweetheart pin, she went to meet Mrs Brainerd at the door.

'Well,' said Mrs Brainerd in an almost good-natured way. 'How nice everything looks.'

'No household odour, no stains, no greasy feel to the cake,' said Norma anxiously. 'This is my little girl.'

'What a good child,' Mrs Brainerd said, skirting Polly Ann's legs, which stuck straight out from the couch.

'And our doggy and kitty,' Norma said with growing confidence, propping Ambrose against one of Polly Ann's feet because he had begun to slide.

Mrs Brainerd even smiled. 'How cute, how nice.'

'Come see the darling kitchen,' Norma said, standing so Clarice Brainerd could look into the unclogged drain, the white and pristine sink.

'Just lovely,' Clarice said.

'Let me get the cake and coffee,' Norma said, leading Clarice Brainerd back to the living room.

'Your windows are just sparkling.'

'I know,' Norma said, beaming and capable.

'And the rug.'

'Glamorene.'

'Wonderful.' Clarice was hers.

'Here,' Norma said, plying her with coffee and cake.

'Wonderful coffee,' Clarice said. 'Call me Clarice. Now about the Garden Club, and the morning coffee hours ... We go to Marge on Thursday, and Edna Mondays, and Thelma Tuesday afternoons, and ...' She bit into the proffered piece of cake. 'And ...' she said, turning the morsel over and over in her mouth.

'And ...' Norma said hopefully.

'And ...' Mrs Brainerd said, looking slightly cross-eyed down her nose, as if she were trying to see what was in her mouth. 'This cake,' she said. 'This cake . . .'

'Marvel Mix,' Norma said with elan. 'No greasy feel . . .'

'I'm sorry,' Mrs Brainerd said, getting up.

'You're – *what?*'

'Sorry,' Mrs Brainerd said, with genuine regret. 'It's your cake.'

'What about my cake?'

'Why, it's got that greasy feel.'

'You – I – it – but the commercial *promised* . . .' Norma was on her feet now, moving automatically. 'The cake is so good, and my house is so beautiful . . .' She was in between Mrs Brainerd and the door now, heading her off in the front hall.

'Sorry,' Mrs Brainerd said. 'I won't be seeing you. Now, if you'll just close that closet door, so I can get by . . .'

'Close the door?' Norma's eyes were glazed. 'I can't. I have to get something off the closet shelf.'

'It doesn't matter what you get,' Mrs Brainerd said. 'I can't come back. We ladies have so much to do, we don't have time . . .'

'Time,' Norma said, getting what she wanted from the shelf.

'Time,' Mrs Brainerd said condescendingly. 'Oh. Maybe you'd better not call me Clarice.'

'Okay, Clarice,' Norma said, and she let Mrs Brainerd have it with the lavender machine.

First she propped Mrs Brainerd up in a corner, where she would be uncomfortable. Then she reversed the nozzle action and brought Polly Ann and Puff and Ambrose back to mobility. Then she brought her box of sewing scraps and all the garbage from the kitchen, and began spreading the mess around Mrs Brainerd's feet and she let Puff rub cat hairs on the furniture and she sent Polly Ann into the back yard for some mud. Ambrose, released, Did It at Mrs Brainerd's feet.

'So glad you could come, Clarice,' Norma said, gratified by the look of horror in Mrs Brainerd's trapped and frozen face. Then, turning to Polly Ann's laden pinafore, she reached for a handful of mud.

The Wall

(1966)

JOSEPHINE SAXTON.

It was as if the landscape was divided into two halves, split across by some change in the light, in the atmosphere, in the colours of the air and the earth. It was a great flat valley that rose so shallowly to the summits of the surrounding escarpments that the change in height was scarcely noticeable, but indeed the difference in height between the floor and the horizon was some five hundred feet. A great curving saucer. But the saucer was cracked across from east to west by a difference. The horizon on the north and the horizon on the south when looked at from west or east looked little different from one another when seen in turn, but to bring the eyes forward would have shown how great indeed the difference between these two halves was, and the eyes looking thus would discern a definite line across this area of the world, coming closer, winding upward, until it was close enough to be seen as a wall.

It was a very high wall, thirty feet in height, and it was very ancient in its stone, dark blue, hard, impenetrable, but rough and worn. Crystalline almost, its surfaces sprang this way and that, revealing whole lumps of glittering faceted hardness, with smooth places where mosses and orange lichens had got hold especially on one side, and at its foot many creeping plants, tough twisted vines bearing clusters of ungathered raisins, convolvulus white and pink, and ivy in many colours, thick, glossy, spidery. Here and there stones had fallen from its old structure, two and three feet thick, and in one place, almost halfway across the floor of the valley, there was a hole through the wall, only six inches across its greatest measurement, and three feet from the floor, which was moist red clay on the north side, and dry white sand on the south. The top of the wall was sealed to all climbers by rows of dreadful spikes which curved in every direction, cruel, needle-sharp, glassy metal rapiers set into green bronze. They were impassable in every way, these swords, and stood endless guard between north and south.

The valley was the home of rats and snakes of many kinds, and thousands of spiders ran in the dust at the foot of the leafy creepers, and rabbits burrowed in the clay at the north side and lizards scuttled on the south. There were two sources of water: one a spring which flooded a puddle in the clay – the water here was cold and green and clear – and the other a limpid pool in the sand under a rock, the water therein being warm and slimy and grey except for a slim trickle where it filled. There were no trees to be seen anywhere, only the earth with the sparse grasses, no habitation save the rabbit warrens.

At either side of the hole in the wall lived a man and a woman. The man lived on the north side where it was usually cold and damp, and the woman lived on the south side where it was usually warm and dry. These two were tall and thin and beautiful, strong and lean, but something was to be seen in their way of moving that spoke of inner suffering, some twisted thing which showed on the outside, almost imperceptible, something from the heart. He was fair in colour, with yellow-grey hair to his shoulders and a beard of great length which tangled in curls with blackberry thorns and stains of purple juice in his beard from the raisins he had eaten over the years. His feet and hands were horny with callouses from running and scrabbling for wild rabbits, but his fingernails were specklessly white for in his idle hours, of which there were many, he sat and cleaned them with a little stick of thornwood and rubbed them down to a neat shape on a stone in the wall. He wore a threadbare suit of lovat green thorn-proof worsted, a dark green silk shirt which had been very fine when new, with gilt cufflinks which had only just enough cuff to stay hanging in the threads, and a tie which was not properly tied but which could not be seen for the beard.

The woman was dark and brown like a nut that has been polished. Her hair was very dark and her lashes and brows were dark and full, and her hair fell straight and heavy to her thighs in thick locks with not a wave. Her hands were immaculately clean too, and she had callouses on her knees from kneeling at the side of the pool, washing her hair until it shone. Her breasts were still young and bore the marks of suckling an infant, but that was in another life. She was dressed in a dark blue dress of Courtelle jersey with brass buttons long turned mouldy green. The dress fitted her figure and had a pleat in the back of the skirt, and she showed a little bit of nylon lace from under the dress sometimes, a very dusty white. She always carried a handbag with her. It was a large white plastic beach-bag with bamboo handles, and in it were all manner of bottles containing sun oil, hand lotion, face cream and skin food, handkerchieves, hairpins, dried-up cigarettes, old bills, papers and letters and a paper bag with a clean sanitary pad and two little safety pins wrapped up tight. She also had a brush and comb, a necklace of heavy beads, several photographs, some dried flowers and recipes for the making of home-made wines, Irish soda bread, and potted meat.

These two people were lovers. For most of the day, in their separate climates, they would sit by the hole in the wall exchanging conversation, peeping at glimpses of one another, able to see half a face or a hand in close-up or get a total view at a distance. They made up poetry for one another which only had meaning for themselves alone; sometimes they would hold hands through the rock, although they could only do this for very short periods of time because of the awkward height of the hole and the pain caused by being half bent and by the cold sharp rock rubbing on their arms. They would exchange bits of food – blackberries and raw rabbit meat, ripe grapes and mushrooms – and they would pass bunches of grasses or flowers from around the base of the wall to each other with passionate love messages whispered from the heart and from their deepest feelings. Although they had not properly seen one another or touched each other properly, they felt for one another in the tenderest way, and were swept by full passions that could never be consummated because of the wall. At times like these – especially was it hard when the moon was full – they would sit close to the hole and weep and moan for each other, longing for something the other could give were it not for the cruel wall that parted their starving bodies. Many long tortured hours they passed in this way wishing the wall would melt. But it never melted, it stayed there hard and enduring, as if it had always been there and would always be so. They had no ideas on the subject of how to remedy this terrible situation for it had been like this so long they could hardly remember when it was, the day they had found themselves, each at a side of the wall. Their love had begun on that very day, even before the sound of their singing voices, and with the rapturous discovery of the hole and the first blissful touches of the hands, and with the dreadful realization that they could never come closer together than this. All through the years they had yearned but never thought it could be any different. They knew as if with an inborn knowledge that the wall was too deeply set to be tunnelled under, too long to be walked around, if indeed it had an end anywhere, and much too hideously guarded at its crest.

One day the man began to think that he could not stand it any longer. His body and emotions had taken all they could; he was racked with desire and his head was full of pain with inner weeping. He suggested to the woman that they should part. He explained that the idea had come to him that there might be other lands where a person might live, over the horizon, away to the north and south, things they had neither of them dreamed of, other loves perhaps, other climates and better food. He felt just then that anything would be better than to sit here forever just yearning for something that could never be had. At first, when the woman listened to this idea, she was so deeply shocked inside herself that she became as stone, she neither spoke nor moved for a day and a night, but lay with her head on the stone of the wall in a cold agony such as she had never before experienced. And then she began to weep, silently at first, then with little moans, then louder and from lower in her being, until she screamed in great pain, and cut her forehead on the blue rock and the blood ran into her dark hair, although she felt only the emotions caused by the idea. But the man persisted. He spoke to her soothingly and gently and he explained with a heavy heart that it would cause him an equal pain to be parted forever from her, but that it seemed the only course open to them unless they were to die here without ever having known any other thing than craving.

After twenty-eight days the woman had absorbed this idea into herself; she had turned it over, and tried to visualize the world beyond, without the man, perhaps with strangers, other women, more food, another dress, but she could feel none of it and gave up as the pictures refused to take shape. But she knew also that it would be thus, she had accepted the idea, and so she finally bent her head down to the hole and agreed with him that they should part. They decided to begin their separate journeys the very next day.

They spent the rest of the day gathering food; the woman tore off her petticoat and wrapped it around heaps of dried grapes, mushrooms and meat that the man had given her, and he took off his shirt and did the same. They spent a sleepless and silent night of unspoken doubts leaning against the hole, and at dawn they clasped hands through the hole, said quiet goodbyes and turned around to walk, he with his bundle, she with a bundle and a handbag.

They each walked for several hours, with such a weight of dread and despair in their hearts as they had never known; their feet dragged, their backs bent, tears ran gently down their faces, and they each tried to recall the feel of the other's hand through the wall, but already the impression was fading, and it was very difficult to feel anything. So, grieving, they walked slowly towards the perimeter of the north and south sides of the valley, and there in the distance they each heard strange sounds, smelt strange smells, and felt strange changes in the atmosphere. They were miles apart by now and it was not yet noon, and the way had been uphill.

At exactly the same moment in time, the man in the north and the woman in the south met strangers of the opposite sex, and these two asked them the same questions. They inquired who they were, where they lived, and where they were going. Sadly they both told the same tale, and the woman who now faced the man in the north asked him to touch her long fair hair and she made kissing mouths at him. He was immediately impassioned by this brazenness and, full of unspent vigour from the many dry years, he held her in his arms and began to make love to her, clumsily and fiercely, his own dark woman already forgotten. At the other side of the valley, she was just then succumbing to the advances of a dark man, a person more handsome than she could have visualized, raven and brown like herself, strong and passionate, and she was so filled with admiration and physical hunger that entering the embrace was easy. And then the two couples parted, after long kisses and greedy sighing. As they stood up they chanced to look back across the valley, and in the distance saw one another, infinite specks, but each speck duplicated, and because each had just then been unfaithful with a stranger, they each knew that the other had, too.

They were immediately filled with remorse at what they had done, and longed for each other again as much as before, and because they could now see each other even though it was at such a distance, they wished to be close again. Having tasted full physical contact with others they now knew that no bliss in the world could match what they would feel for one another, could it be achieved. They had the idea that they would run to each other across the sinking plain, and somehow against all reason overcome the obstacle of the wall, which, from this distance, looked very small indeed. So they set off running without even saying goodbye to their lovers-that-were-not-lovers, running and breathing heavily from the unaccustomed effort.

When they were about one mile apart they could see each other clearly in the sharp white air which lit this part of the valley giving an illusion of clarity and nearness. They paused, then, and staring in wonder each at the other, a pure brave kind of love lighted them up from within, and it was as if they could see the pool that was the hidden soul. They began to run again, and as the ground levelled off, the sight of them was almost lost behind the top of the wall; but this made them run the last few hundred yards even harder. At last they came up to the wall, and ran up and down at its base in joyous haste, seeking the hole. Soon they stood opposite, and the woman shouted to the man that she was going to climb the wall and the man shouted to the woman that he was going to climb the wall, but they were so out of breath with running that their words were all muddled up and lost, and together they dropped the bundles and the bag at the base of the wall and began to climb. It was easy to find hand- and toe-holds in the rock and the old vines and in minutes they were near the top where the cruel spikes stood waiting. If they looked upwards they could see the tops shining bright. They wanted each other. Together they made one last desperate push towards the top and saw themselves close together at the narrow summit; as the spikes pushed into their bodies and as the blood ran down they stared in horror, not at the pain of Death but at what was really in the heart and soul of the other. In terror they clung to one another, closer and closer, hoping that it was not true, as they embraced breast to breast across the spikes, their cheeks pressed close with blood and tears; it was then that they noticed all the other lovers impaled on the spikes.

Some were long-dead skeletons, dry and dusty, grinning skull to skull; some were mummified by the keen wind, eyes sunk in perpetual bewilderment and some were rotten and new, astonishingly quite new.

They turned again to see themselves, wondering dumbly at what they had seen stretching out infinitely along the wall, all the clasping lovers, no kiss or hand-hold there with either bliss or agony.

And very quietly they kissed as they clung and died there, impaled across the cold spiky barrier, feeling and thought growing more feeble every second.

In the north and in the south a fair-haired woman and a dark-haired man set off slowly to walk towards the wall, love stirring in the innermost recesses of their being.

The Foot

(1967)

CHRISTINE BROOKE-ROSE

The victim to be haunted is female. And beautiful. This makes a difference. She has the habit of confidence, but also a greater adjustment to achieve. In the intact body there is a constant stream of impulses bombarding the cortex from the nerve-ends in the muscles, which bombardment is evenly balanced on both sides. But when the body is no longer intact a neuro-muscular imbalance results which throws additional strain on the sensitized cerebrum and upsets the previous state of equilibrium. It is difficult to estimate at this relatively early stage how far her habit of confidence will counter the despair at the adjustment to be achieved and therefore weaken the imbalance in the stream of impulses reaching the cortical areas.

The victim is female and very beautiful, as far as can be judged at present with her eyes closed peacefully in analgesic slumber unaware of pain. It is easy to forget the full extent of beauty when the eyes are shut and the neuroblasts asleep to agony. Eyes open can bring beauty alive with awareness of pain terror despair or anger, not to mention desire and liquid tenderness or even the alluring invitation down the pathways to the womb the tomb the cavern the ebb and flow of time linked to the sun-devouring moon the monster chasm of death and timelessness that draws man like a magnet from the moment he is conscious of a fall a wrench of umbilical tissue rough manhandling tumbling lying in soft cloud sucking at heaven severed weight of body on stumbling legs and fall, fall through the days and minutes. Eyes open can bring archetypes alive but now they are closed on a white ashen face sheathed in pale lanky hair like dead nerve fibres that conduct no pain along pale lanky limbs except for the right leg amputated above the knee. Pity. A thousand pities bombard the cortex from the nerve-ends in the stump-neuroma where the axons proliferate excitedly and send back false messages of pain that find at present no decoder in the slumbering central image of a limb no longer there. We have, however, no room for pity in the haunting game.

It is a proven scientific fact that women have a higher pain threshold than men. Which makes the task more difficult but interesting. Men are no challenge. Yet even within this distinction the threshold varies from subject to subject and from time to time for there is rhythm in the haunting game as in any other according to stress fatigue drugs general constitution previous equilibrium distraction violent activity including sex and the psychiatrist recommends electroencephalic treatment despite statistics proudly quoted for example out of nineteen cases eight improved six relapsed after improvement three unchanged two worse as if that proved anything and some are unduly sensitive he says in his report. In every case the treatment improved the patient's attitude towards the pain so that he or she was less distressed by it. True, and annoying. But there are ways to re-create distress. Often the treatment altered the nature of the pain he proudly adds and thus in several amputees the position of the phantom limb and its concomitant pain were altered rather than relieved. Yes, there are ways.

Still, they do make the task more and more difficult. In the old days they believed merely in conditioning methods, an empty name for the attempt to raise the threshold simply through the refusal of those in authority to admit the existence of the phantom pain. As if one could refuse to admit the existence of a ghost. They have to admit it now. Unfortunately they also study it, which does make the task more difficult even though they do not wholly understand it yet. Why, for instance, the ghost pain haunts at such an unpredictable rhythm, leaving an amputee in peace for twenty years and suddenly appearing, inexorable, excruciating. Or why it materializes in the phantom shape of the foot only, or the hand, not the whole limb, although the limb is also a phantom and the real pain the stump aches in every neurone. And yet it is obvious that to be effective pain must attack the most active therefore vulnerable part of the central memory-image the extremities once in touch with earth air fire and water, the soles that bear the whole weight of existence as man transmutes his structural archetypes from curled to lying to upright position and learns the shapes of time food light dark play by fingering breasts limbs balls cuddly animals. But there are other reasons. Ghosts must preserve some mystery.

If they can. Certainly knowledge is advancing. White sun, for instance, or audio-analgesia to be more precise can annihilate us if only for a while. But leucotomy is the great enemy, resorted to quite openly in cases of intractable phantom pain. Nice word, intractable, in view of the way we phantoms infiltrate ourselves down the pathways of pain, down the spinothalamic tract to be precise, not that I'm partial to words, they can be enemies too, but I like words that bring alive my task my journey down the pathways of pain, down the spinothalamic tract into which they now however introduce electrodes in a stereotactic procedure to produce a phantom pain and find out where exactly to coagulate. Very dangerous. Obviously, since the phantom is not the real one but electrically raised. The result is only too often spasticism in the other limb on the same side and loss of upward conjugate gaze. Eyes open can bring beauty alive with awareness terror pain despair or anger not to mention the alluring invitation down the pathways to the womb and all the rest. A thirty-year-old woman not as attractive but still desirable and successfully haunted by an excruciating phantom in the foot no longer there was very agitated and importunate said Mr Poole the surgeon but after a leucotomy she became calm, the importunacy vanished and she only referred to the pain when asked if it existed. It is true he innocently proudly adds that she then said it was excruciating. Ghosts must preserve some power.

If they can. There are still ways of lowering the threshold. Severe mental deprivation or retardation for example raise it and the highly intelligent undoubtedly suffer more than the plethoric unimaginative like the last one a man plethoric unimaginative. That was a hopeless attempt. It's best to haunt the intelligent. They are not used to responding fully with their bodies and the shock is greater.

But it also makes the task more difficult in other ways, though interesting. The present victim is not only beautiful, pale of course, ashen pale in all that hair ashen pale from lack of violent activity including sex but intelligent. She thinks about me, thus creating my shape, together with his pain, thus giving me existence as a foot, the prettiest foot I have ever been and perhaps was before the leg was lacerated wrenched and crushed in all that twisted car metal because it's hard to tell whether I once was her real foot or not, so completely do I now achieve identification as her phantom foot slim long and gracefully arched and well sprung above a most shapely big toe. That's where I manage to hurt most. But she thinks intelligently about me, in the full knowledge that I am not really there attached to the long space that is her phantom leg also not there. She winds me round with other thoughts like boring details of hospital routine that loom larger than life or intrinsic worth and wrap each phantom fibre of me like a medullary sheath at times. But at times only for I have my rhythm and several other amputees to haunt which would tend to prove that I never was her personal real foot in a full schedule with necessary rest-periods to withdraw my atoms in quiescence before gathering them up into the neuroblasts that will create me anew within her brain along the spinothalamic tract and the efferent fibres down to the neuroma in the stump where the axons of the severed nerves proliferate wildly and send back false messages to the cortical areas that will soon when the strong tranquillizer dies build up from them the central image of a limb no longer there but wrenched and lacerated crushed and cut now cleanly, surgically away, if cleanly it can be called with such tumourous antheap in the stump. And now she thinks about me, giving me strength, existence, and creating my shape, her slim long phantom foot, her unendurable phantom pain.

She cries quietly. I find this very exciting. The imitation neurones I am now composed of agitate their dendrites like tremulous antennae interlacing intermingling or the frictioning legs of flies that swarm as the cell bodies dance through the synapses and I want her to scream.

But she cries quietly. She is not only beautiful but brave, pale of course ashen pale in all that ashen hair like dead nerve fibres that conduct no pain themselves but sheath the white face crisped in a cramped agony of sharp nails driven into the five bones of the metatarsus and the ball of the foot that only exists within the white matter of the mid-brain as greyish white as her face and as crisped in its creation of my shape with its concomitant pain, dear?

'Yes, nurse. It's very bad. But don't give me another injection. I must learn to deal with it.'

Not if I can help it.

'That's right dear. I wasn't going to. It's time for your percussion soon.'

'Oh no.'

'Oh yes. You know it'll do you good.'

'But it's agony. And it doesn't help at all.'

Alas it does, it is the death of me, although it hurts her real pain in the stump neuroma.

'It's agony at first love. Like wearing the padded cast the day after the operation. But then the pressure gradually deadened the pain, didn't it? It's the same with percussion. You'll see, in time. Like tapping a bad tooth.'

'Temporarily perhaps. But it doesn't cure the tooth does it? And the tooth exists, and is sick. Why should banging my stump with a mallet stop the pain in a foot I merely imagine?'

Her intelligence will be the death of me, despite the lower threshold it creates to help me.

'And why do I get pain in the imagined foot anyway, and not in the whole leg? I imagine the leg too. And the stump hurts like hell. But that's different, it's real pain, so it's bearable, however acute.'

'Yes dear, I know.'

'Do you, nurse? Pain is so personal.'

'Subjective, dear, that's right. You'll be coming on nicely once you recognize that.'

'My foot is an object. Outside myself. It exists.'

'In your mind, love. Only in your mind. Mr Poole explained it to you didn't he?'

'Oh yes, I know. The central nervous system can't get rid of its body-image, it's got so used to it after all those years. Twenty-two years to be precise. As if that helped. Only twenty-two. Why did I have to go with Denis in his crazy car? I didn't even like him. It's so unfair, it's –'

'Now my dear, don't upset yourself. You'll only make it worse.'

'It hurts, it hurts, I can't bear it, nurse, please give me something, I can't bear it.'

She cries much more than quietly now, she shouts, she sobs, she yells, she gasps. I find it very exciting. The imitation neurones I am composed of agitate their dendrites like mad ganglia that arborize the system as the cell bodies dance along the axis cylinder within the fibres of the foot that isn't there, move backwards now, tugging away from the interlaced antennae as if trying to wrench themselves of some submicroscopic umbilical tie anchored into soft tissue, caught into bone, straining, straining to freedom birth and terror of time and space as the impulses race down the fibrils and create me, shape me and I ache strongly, I swell to huge existence that possesses her wholly and loves her loves her loves and hurts her unendurably until the cortical areas can only respond by switching off the supply of blood along the nerves going out of the spinal cord so that she faints.

She looks so beautiful, so white and ashen pale in all that ashen hair like dead nerve fibres that conduct no pain themselves but sheath the white face peaceful now with conjugate upward gaze vanished beyond the slit eyelids to face the darker phantoms of the womb the tomb the cavern the ebb and flow of endless tides linked to the sun-devouring moon monster of chasm death and timelessness that draws the human soul like a magnet from the moment of the first fall wrench of umbilical muscle rough man-handling tumbling lying in soft cloud sucking at heaven severed from weight of body on stumbling legs and fall through days and minutes. Eyes open can bring archetypes alive and love that draws me to her like a magnet as she wakes and there there, love, lie quietly you'll feel better now.

'Yes. Thank you, nurse.'

As if she had done anything.

'Nurse.'

'Yes, love?'

'Is it true that children amputated before the age of four don't get phantom pains? Mr Poole told me.'

They do like to remind us of our powerless spheres. I feel exhausted, impotent.

'Well, if Mr Poole told you it must be true, mustn't it?'

'That doesn't follow. Mr Poole says a lot of things to patients to cheer them up. But like all doctors he's so busy he forgets we're individuals. For instance the other day, during percussion, he said –'

'That reminds me, it's time. Are you all right now, dear?'

She retreats as usual into her obsession with Mr Poole the surgeon the knife-man the castrator. She drowns in Mr Poole, dipping her nerve-ends in soft surrounding tissue as in water oedema, wrapping each phantom fibre of me with a medullary sheath of myelin that winds me round with thoughts of Mr Poole and all that Mr Poole has said in molecular detail to relieve soothe stimulate and occupy. I do not mind however at present being thus wound round cut off castrated as a phantom limb for I have temporarily spent my energy in possessing her so hugely hurtfully and I must rest recuperate my atoms while the rubber mallet knocks at her stump neuroma for ten minutes of time until with each knock several hundred unmyelinated nerve-fibres degenerate and after days weeks months curl up and die. But the real pain in her stump does not concern me, being as she so wisely says real therefore bearable. I merely take advantage of its existence in the early stages to increase my shape my hugeness my hold on her, I borrow its pain returning it with impulse interest. I draw my main strength though from the central image of me, so that after months of intimate relationship I am able to create myself out of this central image without recourse to the pain in the stump which may have vanished almost entirely after years or recur just intermittently according to stress and strain but unrelatedly to my sudden visitations. Ghosts have their own rhythms, must preserve independence, mystery.

I am beginning to miss her. It's always a bad sign when I start analysing my methods of self-creation self-absorption more like. She is herself absorbed away from me in Mr Poole who is gentle manly with silvering hair and sexy eyes he knows just how to use to arouse the right degree of emotional involvement in his patients. He comes into the women's ward saying why haven't you brushed that lovely hair young lady and where's your handbag sweetie there take out your compact and a little lipstick too I like my patients to look feminine even the day after there that's better I thought you were so pretty on the operation table but a little pale as if anyone could look pretty in an oxygen mask. Even the men respond from submerged rivalry for his good looks frustration father-dependence and castration fears well founded as he taps their stumps with a rubber-mallet in percussion therapy talking softly of problems pains and phantoms and get quite annoyed when Dr Willet does it instead.

When is she coming back? Is it ten minutes or ten days since I last possessed her? I am losing track of time, always a ghostly failing when out of sense out of mind. She doesn't think of me. She is absorbed in Mr Poole's silvering hair sexy eyes and soft words like young lady I'm very pleased with you which flow even through the neurilemma across the myelin sheaths of every fibre and send impulses down the unsolid structures of the fibrils past the nodes where somehow they transmute into unformulated other words my little girl my love my sweet good little girl that float their chaotic particles around the entire autonomous system back up the spine into the thalamus with no more than a mild thermal sensation in the phantom foot as I grow jealous at a distance in lost space and time. I should have gone with her. But he would have observed me. And I was tired. And now I am restless at her absence from me.

He is explaining to her in a suave and sexy voice that the phantom pain is related to a central excitatory state with emphasis on the internuncial pool of the spinal cord or in other words my dear the higher sensory centres, with resulting summation of abnormal stimuli and a persistence of the pain pattern due to higher-level involvement. What is summation she asks to hide her confusion at the word involvement. I'm sorry darling oh he calls everyone darling it's his therapeutic way you're so intelligent I forget you're not professional that too is his therapeutic way with her it merely means the total sum, you know, all the abnormal stimuli working together at once. And internuncial well you've heard of a nuncio haven't you, a messenger or ambassador of the Pope, it's the same with the nerves, they send messengers who gather together in the internuncial pool, like a typing pool you know, that's why I'm called Poole, ha, I receive all the nerve messages of all my patients and I sort them out and soothe them, like the pool of Lethe darling, so that they don't hurt any more, you see. For a while at least. Until your next visit.

'You seem intent on building up an emotional dependence in me. If you go on like that I'll get the phantom pain every time, I'm due to see you.'

'Now don't be too intelligent sweetie or you'll make it worse.'

'Why abnormal stimuli working all together? What's abnormal about me?'

'Not you darling. You're a normal healthy lovely girl and you will soon be leading a normal healthy lovely life if you're good and do as I say.'

The words flow through the myelin sheaths of every nerve and send impulses up and down the unsolid structures of the fibrils past the nodes where somehow they transmute to a normal healthy love life not quite formulated as they float in scattered particles slowly around the autonomous system back into the cerebrospinal and drown in the internuncial pool before reaching the thalamus. She lies calm serene almost euphoric on her bed her open eyes alive with liquid tenderness and the alluring invitation down the pathways to the womb the ebb and flow of time linked to the sun-devouring moon white chasm of heaven and timelessness that draws me like a magnet from the moment I am conscious of my rebirth his desire to re-create my shape her phantom foot and devastate her beauty with my aching hugeness as an intractable phantom pain.

She shall love me want me need me despite her intelligence or even because of. She shall desire me to re-create my shape her phantom foot in her mind for the soft-voiced sexy-eyed attention of Mr Poole the knife-man the castrator of that shape once in intimate touch with earth air water mother belly and bearing the whole weight of her existence in upright position on that shape of bone flesh fibre skin deeply engraved within the cellular composition of the left midbrain at the level of the superior colliculus six millimetres lateral to the aqueduct of Sylvius in the region of the pain pathways. She shall cherish her symptoms.

How strong I was on that first day when she came to from dreamless anaesthetic nothingness and wanted to get up convinced her leg her foot were there after all the surgeon having somehow mended soothed plasticized remade the crushed and lacerated limb that now just dully ached through the still slumbering nerves. I watched her wake, so beautiful in her pallor sheathed with pale gold like myelin round dead fibres that conduct no pain. And the astonishment hope wonder in her sleepy siren's eyes that seemed to surface from deep waters moving with the sun-devouring moon great chasm of death and timelessness to which man must return drawn like a magnet from the moment of the fall the wrench of umbilical placenta rough manhandling tumbling lying in soft tissue sucking at the day that streams its minutes into weening separation weight of body on crumbling legs and fall through months and years. Even then I knew in a split atom of time bombarded by her beauty that it would have to be the higher-level involvement for my pains and I felt awed but strong with resulting summation of abnormal stimuli my shape quite hypertrophied though slim still in her mind and gracefully arched the prettiest foot I have ever been and perhaps was before her leg was lacerated crushed in all that twisted car metal.

The optic thalamus in the cerebral cortex was working hard and suddenly awake she saw me clear as I stretched my imitation metatarsus long gracefully arched towards the malleolar prominences on either side of her slim ankle up the shapely shin the rounded knee the dimple in the flesh of the popliteal fossa behind the knee till suddenly she threw back the bedclothes saw the stump bandaged into gaping void and gasped, then started moaning like an animal or a woman about to come. It was very exciting. But annihilating. I had existed so strong so hypertrophied and so sensuously detailed till she saw with her own eyes that I wasn't there and I almost ceased to be. But her terror her suffering as she panted galvanized my impulses into the free nerve-terminations of her pain fibres afferent proprioceptive and she screamed, oh joy ineffable. I knew then that the visio-erotic element of her inner eye would always help me despite her intelligence or perhaps because of.

Words are my enemies. The words of Mr Poole and Dr Willett but especially Mr Poole soft-voiced and sexy-eyed with his demands for lipstick hairbrushing self-confidence vanity and his explanations that soothe strengthen her understanding. She winds me round with words that formulate new thoughts of her mother her boyfriends and her job past present future which wrap each fibre of me like a medullary sheath at times. But only at times for I have my rhythm and although too engrossed obsessed too highly involved now with her to haunt other amputees I need my rest-periods, to ache for her recognition of my existence, of my shape as a foot that belongs to her ineradicably and intimately within her cerebrospinal system bombarding it through all its impulse-bearing tracts with an intractable pain. The real danger of words is that they create thoughts which lead to other thoughts and these if stimulating and distracting and absorbing enough may smother me altogether or knock me out like a percussion mallet until my imitation unmyelin-ated nerve-fibres degenerate curl up and die. If she starts thinking constructively about her future for instance. But there are ways. The words of Mr Poole do have a side-effect that helps me, building up as she so intelligently said an emotional dependence from visit to visit the intelligent recognition of which can in no wise prevent. For his soft-voiced and sexy-eyed attention she too often desires to re-create my phantom shape her foot once in intimate touch with earth air water mother belly and bearing the whole weight of her existence in upright position on that structure of bone flesh fibre skin now pierced with sharp nails driven into the metatarsus and the ball of the foot that only exists as an image deeply engraved within the left midbrain as greyish white as her face and as crisped in its creation of my shape she cherishes with its concomitant phantom pain.

'You are cherishing your symptoms my dear,' says Mr Poole severely with a nevertheless gentle tap on the stump the neuroma almost circumscribed mature now non-proliferating healed and she has never heard the phrase before.

'It means darling that although the phantom pain is undoubtedly real to you the causes are more psychogenic now than physiolo-gical, what we call a functional pain. Don't look so insulted sweetie I'm not saying you're deranged nor that you're malingering. Malingering is very rare in this field. But some patients, who are depressive or hysterical, unconsciously prolong their symptoms even for years and years, and suffer genuine agonies that in the end can only be dealt with by sympathectomy, which is not as you might think darling don't look so frightened the removal of sympathy but the removal of certain nerves or rather ganglia in the sympathetic autonomous nervous system, a small local operation. But you don't want more surgery do you, or, for that matter, a leucotomy, that's much more drastic.'

'What! Never.'

'Well, there you are. That's by way of a playful threat darling since you're not in fact either depressive or hysterical but a normal healthy girl who's had a nasty shock and a nasty operation. Would you like another course of electroencephalic treatment? That gave you some relief didn't it?'

'No.'

'Well, there's a new thing called white sun, a nice poetic name for audio-analgesia, it's fed into the ear over such a range of auditory stimuli it swamps all the receptors in the brain —'

'Shut up!'

'I was hoping you'd say that. All right darling calm down. You want to deal with this yourself. You're a good brave girl. You're doing very well with the new artificial limb, I hear from physio-therapy. That's quite comfortable isn't it? Doesn't hurt? Good. And are you occupying your mind?'

'Yes.'

'Good. What with?'

'Oh, thoughts. Ideas.'

'Now that's not so good. You mustn't get ideas. What thoughts? You should do something. Prepare for ordinary life. We'll be discharging you soon and you must think of that.'

'You just told me thoughts are not so good.'

'Smart girl, you'll be all right. Do you have a job you can go back to?'

'I was a model.'

'Oh. I'm sorry sweetie, you did tell me and so did your mother. Yes. I forgot for a moment.'

'You have so many patients.'

'That's no excuse.'

'As a matter of fact I thought, perhaps, I could write.'

'To whom darling?'

'Just, write. You know, novels.'

'Oh yes. Love stories you mean? Or spies? Why not, there's a lot of money in it. As long as you don't get too excited yourself, tension brings back the phantom you know.'

'Well, I wasn't exactly thinking of love stories.'

No she isn't exactly thinking of love stories or spies although I love her and I spy on her through the symptoms which she cherishes a little for the soft-voiced and sexy-eyed sympathy of the internuncial pool in the spinal cord or in other words my dear my little girl my love my good sweet little girl the higher sensory centres with resulting summation of abnormal stimuli and a persistence of the pain pattern she cherishes due to higher-level involvement fear of sympathectomy and white sun swamping all receptors in her brain. She is thinking of me to write about in order to get me out of her system as they call it not sympathetic or parasympathetic autonomous but cerebrospinal out of her midbrain on to paper instead of aching there fifty-three-and-a-half centimetres away from her stump now circumscribed mature and non-proliferating with a phantom lower leg between though painless but undoubtedly projecting out the pain of sharp nails driven into the metatarsus and the ball of the foot that only exists in the higher sensory centres near the optic thalamus with which she sees me in her inner eye visio-erotically lateral to the aqueduct of Sylvius in the region of the pain pathways until I exist again so strong so hypertrophied and so sensuously detailed that I galvanize my impulses up the free nerve-terminations of her pain fibres afferent proprioceptive and she starts moaning like an animal or a woman in joy ineffable.

I shall not let her get rid of me with words that re-create my shape my galvanizing atoms of agony on mere paper to be read by careless unsuffering millions vicariously and thus dispersed. I shall possess her and possess her again obsessing her absorbing her growing strong on her distress that excites me and re-creates my shape as her sweet phantom foot with its associated pain intractable unendurable and cherished.

She writes however. She has a Biro pen and a small exercise book Denis brought her. He got off with a broken arm worn in a sling for a while and looked like Napoleon short podgy oddly continental with a thin straight wisp from his receding hair down over his brow but constantly smoothed back and patted down as he says how are you dear and the brow contracts a little with guilt concern embarrassment fear removing the sympathy and any love that might have been with two legs. She uses him but not so much as well she might and he brings her fruit and flowers and books she wants about amputation syndromes not magazines full of models and the Biro pen and the small exercise book that stays closed and empty for some time as I continue to possess her again and again growing huge on her distress that excites me in increasing rhythm and re-creates my shape and my obsession with her aching my desire. Despite the increasing rhythm however or because of I need the rest-periods to withdraw my atoms after detumescence before gathering them up into the neuroblasts that will formulate me anew within her brain along the spinothalamic tract and the efferent fibres and she opens meanwhile the small exercise book and in thin impersonal Biro strokes she writes the words she hears like white sun swamping all other receptors in the brain so that the white page slowly engraves itself with the victim to be haunted is female. And beautiful. This makes a difference. She has the habit of confidence, but also a greater adjustment to achieve while I slumber rest in my detumescence. She betrays me.

She isn't thinking of a love-story spy-thriller although she loves me spies on me through the symptoms cherished nor a novel no Proust she à la recherche du pied perdu I also like my little joke I can make cleverer ones than Mr Poole but she starts humbly with a short story that says the victim is female and very beautiful as she knows very well with open eyes that can bring beauty alive with awareness of pain terror despair or anger, not to mention desire and liquid tenderness or even the alluring invitation down the pathways of pain swamped by the white sun of the words she hears, their nuclear cells radiating from the cochlear ganglion of the interior ear in the temporal lobe and round the cerebral cortex to the visual centre in the occipital lobe where the optic chiasm turns me and her whole body upside down until relayed into the parietal lobe and ending in the thalamus where contact pain heat cold localization discrimination recognition of posture merge with the power of responding to different intensities of stimuli so that I drown in merely abstract existence feel knocked out in percussion and bombarded till my imitation unmyelinated nerve-fibres degenerate curl up and die.

It is a proven scientific fact that women have a higher pain threshold than men. Which makes the task more difficult but interesting. All right, let her continue I can bide my time in detumescence until she exhausts herself and begs me to return or re-creates me anew out of the tension from fatigue and emptiness. For even within that distinction the threshold varies from subject to subject and from time to time and there is rhythm in the haunting game as in any other according to stress drugs distraction violent activity including sex and literary creation as with a soldier in combat all senses occupied unaware of wound until his wild ferocity is abated. For there are ways to re-create distress. The electroencephalic treatment she has now prescribed herself may merely alter the nature of the pain and the position of the phantom limb. What fools they are. Variety of position is the spice of intimacy. I find it very exciting. Despite the annihilation through merely abstract existence on the rapidly neuroblasted paper there are still ways of lowering the threshold. Severe mental deprivation for example raises it and the highly intelligent undoubtedly suffer more than the plethoric unimaginative which she certainly is not being at the moment. She thinks about me, thus creating my shape her phantom foot, visually, aurally in words and sensuously in bones flesh skin and neuroblasts that dance along the axis cylinders within the myelin-sheathed fibres of the foot that isn't there except on paper to be read by careless unsuffering millions vicariously and thus dispersed.

I had existed so strong so hypertrophied and so cellularly detailed that her abstract creation will be the death of me unless the electroencephalic treatment she has prescribed herself merely alters my nature my position more or less distant from the stump as a projection of the central body-image in the higher sensory centres in excitatory state galvanizing my impulses into the free nerve-terminations of her pain fibres that tingle afferent propriocept-ive and the imitation neurones I am recomposed of agitate their dendrites like mad ganglia arborizing the system as the cell-bodies dance along the fibres of the foot that isn't there, move backwards now, tugging away from the interlaced antennae as if trying to wrench themselves off some submicroscopic umbilical tie anchored into soft tissue, caught in bone, straining to freedom birth and terror of time and space as the neuroblasts race down the fibrils and create me, shape me and I ache strongly I swell to huge existence that possesses her wholly and loves her loves her loves and hurts her unendurably until she moans and pants like an animal or a woman in joy ineffable and the cortical areas respond by switching off the supply of blood along the nerves leaving the spinal cord and out she passes out.

She looks so beautiful, so white and ashen pale in all that ashen hair like dead nerve-fibres that conduct no pain but sheath the white face peaceful now with conjugate upward gaze vanished beyond the slit eyelids to face the darker phantoms of the womb the tomb the cavern the ebb and flow of internuncial pools linked to the chasm of death and timelessness that draws her like a magnet from the moment of the first fall wrench of umbilical muscle rough manhandling tumbling lying in soft tissue sucking at heaven severed weight of body on crumbling legs and fall through days and minutes. Eyes open can bring archetypes alive and love that draws me like a magnet from the moment of my rebirth in desire to re-create my shape her phantom foot and devastate her beauty with my aching hugeness as an intractable phantom pain.

Yes, there are ways to re-create distress, less often perhaps, which is the way of intimacy, and even haunting has its rhythm decreasing increasing according to stress fatigue drugs general constitution previous equilibrium distraction violent activity including sex and writing. I shall learn to be more discreet, play hard to get perhaps but only play. I cannot live without her and I know her weakness now, I know she needs my love my presence my shape her slim long phantom foot with its concomitant hugeness as a phantom pain.

She cries quietly now. I find this very exciting.

Baby, You were Great

(1967)

KATE WILHELM

John Lewisohn thought that if one more door slammed, or one more bell rang, or one more voice asked if he was all right, his head would explode. Leaving his laboratories, he walked through the carpeted hall to the elevator that slid wide to admit him noiselessly, was lowered gently, two floors, where there were more carpeted halls. The door he shoved open bore a neat sign, Auditioning Studio. Inside he was waved on through the reception room by three girls who knew better than to speak to him unless he spoke first. They were surprised to see him; it was his first visit there in seven or eight months. The inner room where he stopped was darkened, at first glance appearing empty, revealing another occupant only after his eyes had time to adjust to the dim lighting.

John sat in the chair next to Herb Javits, still without speaking. Herb was wearing the helmet and gazing at a wide screen that was actually a one-way glass panel permitting him to view the audition going on in the adjacent room. John lowered a second helmet to his head. It fit snugly and immediately made contact with the eight prepared spots on his skull. As soon as he turned it on, the helmet itself was forgotten.

A girl had entered the other room. She was breathtakingly lovely, a long-legged honey blonde with slanting green eyes and apricot skin. The room was furnished as a sitting room with two couches, some chairs, end tables and a coffee table, all tasteful and lifeless, like an ad in a furniture-trade publication. The girl stopped at the doorway, and John felt her indecision heavily tempered with nervousness and fear. Outwardly she appeared poised and expectant, her smooth face betraying none of the emotions. She took a hesitant step toward the couch, and a wire showed trailing behind her. It was attached to her head. At the same time a second door opened. A young man ran inside, slamming the door behind him; he looked wild and frantic. The girl registered surprise, mounting nervousness; she felt behind her for the door handle, found it and tried to open the door again. It was locked. John could hear nothing that was being said in the room; he only felt the girl's reaction to the unexpected interruption. The wild-eyed man was approaching her, his hands slashing through the air, his eyes darting glances all about them constantly. Suddenly he pounced on her and pulled her to him, kissing her face and neck roughly. She seemed paralyzed with fear for several seconds, then there was something else, a bland nothing kind of feeling that accompanied boredom sometimes, or too complete self-assurance. As the man's hands fastened on her blouse in the back and ripped it, she threw her arms about him, her face showing passion that was not felt anywhere in her mind or in her blood.

'Cut!' Herb Javits said quietly.

The man stepped back from the girl and left her without a word. She looked about blankly, her blouse torn, hanging about her hips, one shoulder strap gone. She was very beautiful. The audition manager entered, followed by a dresser with a gown that he threw about her shoulders. She looked startled; waves of anger mounted to fury as she was drawn from the room, leaving it empty. The two watching men removed their helmets.

'Fourth one so far,' Herb grunted. 'Sixteen yesterday; twenty the day before . . . all nothing.' He gave John a curious look. 'What's got you stirred out of your lab?'

'Anne's had it this time,' John said. 'She's been on the phone all night and all morning.'

'What now?'

'Those damn sharks! I told you that was too much on top of the airplane crash last week. She can't take much more of it.'

'Hold it a minute, Johnny,' Herb said. 'Let's finish off the next three girls and then talk.' He pressed a button on the arm of his chair and the room beyond the screen took their attention again.

This time the girl was slightly less beautiful, shorter, a dimply sort of brunette with laughing blue eyes and an upturned nose. John liked her. He adjusted his helmet and felt with her.

She was excited; the audition always excited them. There was some fear and nervousness, not too much. Curious about how the audition would go, probably. The wild young man ran into the room, and her face paled. Nothing else changed. Her nervousness increased, not uncomfortably. When he grabbed her, the only emotion she registered was the nervousness.

'Cut,' Herb said.

The next girl was brunette, with gorgeously elongated legs. She was very cool, a real professional. Her mobile face reflected the range of emotions to be expected as the scene played through again, but nothing inside her was touched. She was a million miles away from it all.

The next one caught John with a slam. She entered the room slowly, looking about with curiosity, nervous, as they all were. She was younger than the other girls had been, less poised. She had pale-gold hair piled in an elaborate mound of waves on top of her head. Her eyes were brown, her skin nicely tanned. When the man entered, her emotion changed quickly to fear, and then to terror. John didn't know when he closed his eyes. He was the girl, filled with unspeakable terror; his heart pounded, adrenalin pumped into his system; he wanted to scream but could not. From the dim unreachable depths of his psyche there came something else, in waves, so mixed with terror that the two merged and became one emotion that pulsed and throbbed and demanded. With a jerk he opened his eyes and stared at the window. The girl had been thrown down to one of the couches, and the man was kneeling on the floor beside her, his hands playing over her bare body, his face pressed against her skin.

'Cut!' Herb said. His voice was shaken. 'Hire her,' he said. The man rose, glanced at the girl, sobbing now, and then quickly bent over and kissed her cheek. Her sobs increased. Her golden hair was down, framing her face; she looked like a child. John tore off the helmet. He was perspiring.

Herb got up, turned on the lights in the room, and the window blanked out, blending with the wall, making it invisible. He didn't look at John. When he wiped his face, his hand was shaking. He rammed it in his pocket.

'When did you start auditions like that?' John asked, after a few moments of silence.

'Couple of months ago. I told you about it. Hell, we had to,

Johnny. That's the six-hundred-nineteenth girl we've tried out! Six hundred nineteen! All phonies but one! Dead from the neck up. Do you have any idea how long it was taking us to find that out? Hours for each one. Now it's a matter of minutes.'

John Lewisohn sighed. He knew. He had suggested it, actually, when he had said, 'Find a basic anxiety situation for the test.' He hadn't wanted to know what Herb had come up with.

He said, 'Okay, but she's only a kid. What about her parents, legal rights, all that?'

'We'll fix it. Don't worry. What about Anne?'

'She's called me five times since yesterday. The sharks were too much. She wants to see us, both of us, this afternoon.'

'You're kidding! I can't leave here now!'

'Nope. Kidding I'm not. She says no plug up if we don't show. She'll take pills and sleep until we get there.'

'Good Lord! She wouldn't dare!'

'I've booked seats. We take off at twelve thirty-five.' They stared at one another silently for another moment, then Herb shrugged. He was a short man, not heavy but solid. John was over six feet, muscular, with a temper that he knew he had to control. Others suspected that when he did let it go, there would be bodies lying around afterward, but he controlled it.

Once it had been a physical act, an effort of body and will to master that temper; now it was done so automatically that he couldn't recall occasions when it even threatened to flare any more.

'Look, Johnny, when we see Anne, let me handle it. Right?' Herb said. 'I'll make it short.'

'What are you going to do?'

'Give her an earful. If she's going to start pulling temperament on me, I'll slap her down so hard she'll bounce a week.' He grinned happily. 'She's had it all her way up to now. She knew there wasn't a replacement if she got bitchy. Let her try it now. Just let her try.' Herb was pacing back and forth with quick, jerky steps.

John realized with a shock that he hated the stocky, red-faced man. The feeling was new, it was almost as if he could taste the hatred he felt, and the taste was unfamiliar and pleasant.

Herb stopped pacing and stared at him for a moment. 'Why'd she call you? Why does she want you down, too? She knows you're not mixed up with this end of it.'

'She knows I'm a full partner, anyway,' John said.

'Yeah, but that's not it.' Herb's face twisted in a grin. 'She thinks you're still hot for her, doesn't she? She knows you tumbled once, in the beginning, when you were working on her, getting the gimmick working right.' The grin reflected no humor then. 'Is she right, Johnny, baby? Is that it?'

'We made a deal,' John said coldly. 'You run your end, I run mine. She wants me along because she doesn't trust you, or believe anything you tell her any more. She wants a witness.'

'Yeah, Johnny. But you be sure you remember our agreement.' Suddenly Herb laughed. 'You know what it was like, Johnny, seeing you and her? Like a flame trying to snuggle up to an icicle.'

At three-thirty they were in Anne's suite in the Skyline Hotel in Grand Bahama. Herb had a reservation to fly back to New York on the six p.m. flight. Anne would not be off until four, so they made themselves comfortable in her rooms and waited. Herb turned her screen on, offered a helmet to John, who shook his head, and they both seated themselves. John watched the screen for several minutes; then he too put on a helmet.

Anne was looking at the waves far out at sea where they were long, green, undulating; then she brought her gaze in closer, to the blue-green and quick seas, and finally in to where they stumbled on the sand bars, breaking into foam that looked solid enough to walk on. She was peaceful, swaying with the motion of the boat, the sun hot on her back, the fishing rod heavy in her hands. It was like being an indolent animal at peace with the world, at home in the world, being one with it. After a few seconds she put down the rod and turned, looking at a tall smiling man in swimming trunks. He held out his hand and she took it. They entered the cabin of the boat, where drinks were waiting. Her mood of serenity and happiness ended abruptly, to be replaced by shocked disbelief and a start of fear.

'What the hell . . .?' John muttered, adjusting the audio. You seldom needed audio when Anne was on.

'. . . Captain Brothers had to let them go. After all, they've done nothing yet . . .' the man was saying soberly.

'But why do you think they'll try to rob me?'

'Who else is here with a million dollars' worth of jewels?'

John turned it off and said to Herb, 'You're a fool! You can't get away with something like that!'

Herb stood up and crossed the room to stand before a window wall that was open to the stretch of glistening blue ocean beyond the brilliant white beaches. 'You know what every woman wants? To own something worth stealing.' He chuckled, a low throaty sound that was without mirth. 'Among other things, that is. They want to be roughed up once or twice, and forced to kneel . . . Our new psychologist is pretty good, you know? Hasn't steered us wrong yet. Anne might kick some, but it'll go over great.'

'She won't stand for an actual robbery.' Louder, emphasizing it, he added, 'I won't stand for that.'

'We can dub it,' Herb said. 'That's all we need, Johnny, plant the idea, and then dub the rest.'

John stared at his back. He wanted to believe that. He needed to believe it. His voice showed no trace of emotion when he said, 'It didn't start like this, Herb. What happened?'

Herb turned then. His face was dark against the glare of light behind him. 'Okay, Johnny, it didn't start like this. Things accelerate, that's all. You thought of a gimmick, and the way we planned it, it sounded great, but it didn't last. We gave them the feeling of gambling, of learning to ski, of automobile racing, everything we could dream of, and it wasn't enough. How many times can you take the first ski jump of your life? After a while you want new thrills, you know? For you it's been great, hasn't it? You bought yourself a shining new lab and pulled the cover over you and it. You bought yourself time and equipment, and when things didn't go right you could toss it out and start over, and nobody gave a damn. Think of what it's been like for me, kid! I gotta keep coming up with something new, something that'll give Anne a jolt and, through her, all those nice little people who aren't even alive unless they're plugged in. You think it's been easy? Anne was a green kid. For her everything was new and exciting, but it isn't like that now, boy. You better believe it is *not* like that now. You know what she told me last month? She's sick and tired of men. Our little hot-box Annie! Tired of men!'

John crossed to him and pulled him around. 'Why didn't you tell me?'

'Why, Johnny? What would you have done that I didn't do? *I* looked harder for the right guy for her. What would you do for a new thrill for her? I worked for them, kid. Right from the start you said for me to leave you alone. Okay. I left you alone. You ever read any of the memos I sent? You initialed them, kiddo. Everything that's been done, we both signed. Don't give me any of that why-didn't-I-tell-you stuff. It won't work!' His face was ugly red and a vein bulged in his neck. John wondered if he had high blood pressure, if he would die of a stroke during one of his flash rages.

John left him at the window. He had read the memos. Herb knew he had. Herb was right; all he had wanted was to be left alone. It had been his idea; after twelve years of work in a laboratory on prototypes he had shown his ... gimmick ... to Herb Javits. Herb was one of the biggest producers on television then; now he was the biggest producer in the world.

The gimmick was fairly simple. A person fitted with electrodes in his brain could transmit his emotions, which in turn could be broadcast and picked up by the helmets to be felt by the audience. No words or thoughts went out, only basic emotions ... fear, love, anger, hatred ... That, tied in with a camera showing what the person saw, with a voice dubbed in, and you were the person having the experience, with one important difference, you could turn it off if it got to be too much. The 'actor' couldn't. A simple gimmick. You didn't really need the camera and the soundtrack; many users never turned them on at all, but let their own imagination fill in to fit the emotional broadcast.

The helmets were not sold, only rented after a short, easy fitting session. Rent of one dollar a month was collected on the first of the month, and there were over thirty-seven million subscribers. Herb had bought his own network after the second month when the demand for more hours barred him from regular television. From a one-hour weekly show it had gone to one hour nightly, and now it was on the air eight hours a day live, with another eight hours of taped programming.

What had started out as A Day in the Life of Anne Beaumont

was now a life in the life of Anne Beaumont, and the audience was insatiable.

Anne came in then, surrounded by the throng of hangers-on that mobbed her daily – hairdressers, masseurs, fitters, script men . . . She looked tired. She waved the crowd out when she saw John and Herb were there. 'Hello, John,' she said. 'Herb.'

'Anne, baby, you're looking great!' Herb said. He took her in his arms and kissed her solidly. She stood still, her hands at her sides.

She was tall, very slender, with wheat-colored hair and gray eyes. Her cheekbones were wide and high, her mouth firm and almost too large. Against her deep red-gold sun tan her teeth looked whiter than John remembered them. Although too firm and strong ever to be thought of as pretty, she was a very beautiful woman. After Herb released her, she turned to John, hesitated only a moment, and then extended a slim, sun-browned hand. It was cool and dry in his.

'How have you been, John? It's been a long time.'

He was very glad she didn't kiss him or call him darling. She smiled only slightly and gently removed her hand from his. He moved to the bar as she turned to Herb.

'I'm through, Herb,' she said. Her voice was too quiet. She accepted a whisky sour from John, but kept her gaze on Herb.

'What's the matter, honey? I was just watching you, baby. You were great today, like always. You've still got it, kid. It's coming through like always.'

'What about this robbery? You must be out of your mind . . .'

'Yeah, that. Listen, Anne baby, I swear to you I don't know a thing about it. Laughton must have been telling you the straight goods on that. You know we agreed that the rest of this week you just have a good time, remember? That comes over too, baby. When you have a good time and relax, thirty-seven million people are enjoying life and relaxing. That's good. They can't be stimulated all the time. They like the variety . . .' Wordlessly John held out a glass, Scotch and water. Herb took it without looking.

Anne was watching him coldly. Suddenly she laughed. It was a cynical, bitter sound. 'You're not a damn fool, Herb. Don't try to act like one.' She sipped her drink again, continuing to stare at him over the rim of the glass. 'I am warning you, if anyone shows here to rob me, I'm going to treat him like a real burglar. I bought a gun after today's broadcast, and I learned how to shoot when I was only nine or ten. I still know how. I'll kill him. Herb, whoever it is.'

'Baby,' Herb started, but she cut him short.

'And this is my last week. As of Saturday, I'm through.'

'You can't do that, Anne,' Herb said. John watched him closely, searching for a sign of weakness, anything; he saw nothing. Herb exuded confidence. 'Look around, Anne, at this room, your clothes, everything . . . You are the richest woman in the world, having the time of your life, able to go anywhere, do anything . . .'

'While the whole world watches . . .'

'So what? It doesn't stop you, does it?' Herb started to pace, his steps jerky and quick. 'You knew that when you signed the contract. You're a rare girl, Anne, beautiful, emotional, intelligent. Think of all those women who've got nothing but you. If you quit them, what do they do? Die? They might, you know. For the first time in their lives they are able to feel like they're living. You're giving them what no one ever did before, what was only hinted at in books and films in the old days. Suddenly they know what it feels like to face excitement, to experience love, to feel contented and peaceful. Think of them, Anne, empty, with nothing in their lives but you, what you're able to give them. Thirty-seven million drabs, Anne, who never felt anything but boredom and frustration until you gave them life. What do they have? Work, kids, bills. You've given them the world, baby! Without you they wouldn't even want to live any more.'

She wasn't listening. Almost dreamily she said, 'I talked to my lawyers, Herb, and the contract is meaningless. You've already broken it countless times by insisting on adding to the original agreement. I agreed to learn a lot of new things, so they could feel them with me. I did. My God! I've climbed mountains, hunted lions, learned to ski and water ski, but now you want me to die a little bit each week . . . that airplane crash, not bad, just enough to terrify me. Then the sharks. I really do think it was having sharks brought in when I was skiing that did it, Herb. You see, you will kill me. It will happen, and you won't be able to stop it, Herb. Not ever.'

There was a hard, waiting silence following her words. 'No!' John shouted, soundlessly, the words not leaving his mouth. He was looking at Herb. He had stopped pacing when she started to talk. Something flicked across his face, surprise, fear, something not readily identifiable. Then his face went completely blank and he raised his glass and finished the Scotch and water, replacing the glass on the bar. When he turned again, he was smiling with disbelief.

'What's really bugging you, Anne? There have been plants before. You knew about them. Those lions didn't just happen by, you know. And the avalanche needed a nudge from someone. You know that. What else is bugging you?'

'I'm in love, Herb. I want out now before you manage to kill me.' Herb waved that aside impatiently.

'Have you ever watched your own show, Anne?' She shook her head. 'I thought not. So you wouldn't know about the expansion that took place last month, after we planted that new transmitter in your head. Johnny boy here's been busy, Anne. You know these scientist types, never satisfied, always improving, changing. Where's the camera, Anne? Do you ever know where it is any more? Have you even seen a camera in the past couple of weeks, or a recorder of any sort? You have not, and you won't again. You're on now, honey.' His voice was quite low, amused almost. 'In fact the only time you aren't on is when you're sleeping. I know you're in love. I know who he is; I know how he makes you feel; I even know how much money he makes per week. I should know, Anne baby. I pay him.' He had come closer to her with each word, finishing with his face only inches from hers. He didn't have a chance to duck the flashing slap that jerked his head around, and before either of them realized it, he had hit her back. Anne fell back to the chair, too stunned to speak for a moment.

The silence grew, became something ugly and heavy, as if words were being born and dying without utterance because they were too brutal for the human spirit to bear. There was a spot of blood on Herb's mouth where her diamond ring had cut him. He touched it and looked at his finger. 'It's all being taped now, honey, even this,' he said. He returned to the bar, turning his back on her.

There was a large red print on her cheek. Her gray eyes had
turned black with rage; she didn't take her gaze from him.

'Honey, relax,' Herb said after a moment, his voice soft and
easy again. 'It won't make any difference to you in what you do,
or anything like that. You know we can't use most of the stuff,
but it gives the editors a bigger variety to pick from. It was
getting to the point where most of the interesting stuff was going
on after you were off. Like buying the gun. That's great stuff
there, baby. You weren't blanketing a single thing, and it'll all
come through like pure gold.' He finished mixing his drink, tasted
it, and then swallowed most of it. 'How many women have to go
out and buy a gun to protect themselves? Think of them all,
feeling that gun, feeling the things you felt when you picked it up,
looked at it . . .'

'How long have you been tuning in all the time?' she asked.
John felt a stirring along his spine, a tingle of excitement. He
knew what was going out over the miniature transmitter, the
rising crests of emotion she was feeling. Only a trace of them
showed on her smooth face, but the raging interior torment was
being recorded faithfully. Her quiet voice and quiet body were
lies; only the tapes never lied.

Herb felt it too, a storm behind her quietude. He put his glass
down and went to her, kneeling by the chair, taking her hand in
both of his. 'Anne, please, don't be that angry with me. I was
desperate for new material. When Johnny got this last wrinkle
out, and we knew we could record around the clock, we had to
try it, and it wouldn't have been any good if you had known.
That's no way to test anything. You knew we were planting the
transmitter . . .'

'How long?'

'Not quite a month.'

'And Stuart? He's one of your men? He is transmitting also?
You hired him to . . . to make love to me? Is that right?'

Herb nodded. She pulled her hand free and averted her face, not
willing to see him any longer. He got up then and went to the
window. 'But what difference does it make?' he shouted. 'If I
introduced the two of you at a party, you wouldn't think anything
of it. What difference if I did it this way? I knew you'd like each

other. He's bright, like you, likes the same sort of things you do. Comes from a poor family, like yours . . . Everything said you'd get along . . .'

'Oh, yes,' she said almost absently. 'We get along.' She was feeling in her hair, her fingers searching for the scars.

'It's all healed by now,' John said. She looked at him as if she had forgotten he was there.

'I'll find a surgeon,' she said, standing up, her fingers white on her glass. 'A brain surgeon . . .'

'It's a new process,' John said slowly. 'It would be dangerous to go in after them . . .'

She looked at him for a long time. 'Dangerous?'

He nodded.

'You could take it back out . . .'

He remembered the beginning, how he had quieted her fear of the electrodes and the wires. Her fear was that of a child for the unknown and the unknowable. Time and again he had proven to her that she could trust him, that he wouldn't lie to her. He hadn't lied to her, then. There was the same trust in her eyes, the same unshakable faith. She would believe him. She would accept without question whatever he said. Herb had called him an icicle, but that was wrong. An icicle would have melted in her fires. More like a stalactite, shaped by centuries of civilization, layer by layer he had been formed until he had forgotten how to bend, forgotten how to find release for the stirrings he felt somewhere in the hollow, rigid core of himself. She had tried and, frustrated, she had turned from him, hurt, but unable not to trust one she had loved. Now she waited. He could free her, and lose her again, this time irrevocably. Or he could hold her as long as she lived.

Her lovely gray eyes were shadowed with fear and the trust that he had given to her. Slowly he shook his head.

'I can't,' he said. 'No one can.'

'I see,' she murmured, the black filling her eyes. 'I'd die, wouldn't I? Then you'd have a lovely sequence, wouldn't you, Herb?' She swung around, away from John. 'You'd have to fake the story line, of course, but you are so good at that. An accident, emergency brain surgery needed, everything I feel going out to the poor little drabs who never will have brain surgery done. It's very good,' she said admiringly. Her eyes were very black. 'In fact, anything I do from now on, you'll use, won't you? If I kill you, that will simply be material for your editors to pick over. Trial, prison, very dramatic ... On the other hand, if I kill myself ...'

John felt chilled; a cold, hard weight seemed to be filling him. Herb laughed. 'The story line will be something like this,' he said. 'Anne has fallen in love with a stranger, deeply, sincerely in love with him. Everyone knows how deep that love is; they've all felt it, too, you know. She finds him raping a child, a lovely little girl in her early teens. Stuart tells her they're through. He loves the little nymph. In a passion she kills herself. You are broadcasting a real storm of passion, right now, aren't you, honey? Never mind, when I run through this scene, I'll find out.' She hurled her glass at him, ice cubes and orange sections leaving a trail across the room. Herb ducked, grinning.

'That's awfully good, baby. Corny, but after all, they can't get too much corn, can they? They'll love it, after they get over the shock of losing you. And they will get over it, you know. They always do. Wonder if it's true about what happens to someone experiencing a violent death?' Anne's teeth bit down on her lip, and slowly she sat down again, her eyes closed tight. Herb watched her for a moment, then said, even more cheerfully, 'We've got the kid already. If you give them a death, you've got to give them a new life. Finish one with a bang. Start one with a bang. We'll name the kid Cindy, a real Cinderella story after that. They'll love her, too.'

Anne opened her eyes, black dulled now; she was so tight with tension that John felt his own muscles contract and become taut. He wondered if he would be able to stand the tape she was transmitting. A wave of excitement swept him and he knew he would play it all, feel it all, the incredibly contained rage, fear, the horror of giving a death to them to gloat over, and finally, anguish. He would know them all. Watching Anne, he wished she would break then, with him there. She didn't. She stood up stiffly, her back rigid, a muscle hard and ridged in her jaw. Her voice was flat when she said, 'Stuart is due in half an hour. I have to dress.' She left them without looking back.

Herb winked at John and motioned toward the door. 'Want to take me to the plane, kid?' In the cab he said, 'Stick close to her for a couple of days, Johnny. There might be an even bigger reaction later when she really understands just how hooked she is.' He chuckled again. 'By God! It's a good thing she trusts you, Johnny, boy!'

As they waited in the chrome-and-marble terminal for the liner to unload its passengers, John said, 'Do you think she'll be any good after this?'

'She can't help herself. She's too life oriented to deliberately choose to die. She's like a jungle inside, raw, wild, untouched by that smooth layer of civilization she shows on the outside. It's a thin layer, kid, real thin. She'll fight to stay alive. She'll become more wary, more alert to danger, more excited and exciting . . . She'll really go to pieces when he touches her tonight. She's primed real good. Might even have to do some editing, tone it down a little.' His voice was very happy. 'He touches her where she lives, and she reacts. A real wild one. She's one; the new kid's one; Stuart . . . They're few and far apart, Johnny. It's up to us to find them. God knows we're going to need all of them we can get.' His face became thoughtful and withdrawn. 'You know, that really wasn't such a bad idea of mine about rape and the kid. Who ever dreamed we'd get that kind of a reaction from her? With the right sort of build-up . . .' He had to run to catch his plane.

John hurried back to the hotel, to be near Anne if she needed him. He hoped she would leave him alone. His fingers shook as he turned on his screen; suddenly he had a clear memory of the child who had wept, and he hoped Stuart would hurt Anne just a little. The tremor in his fingers increased; Stuart was on from six until twelve, and he already had missed almost an hour of the show. He adjusted the helmet and sank back into a deep chair. He left the audio off, letting his own words form, letting his own thoughts fill in the spaces.

Anne was leaning toward him, sparkling champagne raised to her lips, her eyes large and soft. She was speaking, talking to him, John, calling him by name. He felt a tingle start somewhere deep inside him, and his glance was lowered to rest on her tanned hand in his, sending electricity through him. Her hand trembled when he ran his fingers up her palm, to her wrist where a blue vein throbbed. The slight throb became a pounding that grew, and when he looked again into her eyes, they were dark and very deep. They danced and he felt her body against his, yielding, pleading. The room darkened and she was an outline against the window, her gown floating down about her. The darkness grew denser, or he closed his eyes, and this time when her body pressed against his, there was nothing between them, and the pounding was everywhere.

In the deep chair, with the helmet on his head, John's hands clenched, opened, clenched, again and again.

The Second Inquisition

(1970)

JOANNA RUSS

If a man can resist the influences of his townsfolk, if he can
cut free from the tyranny of neighborhood gossip, the world
has no terrors for him; there is no second inquisition.
— John Jay Chapman

I often watched our visitor reading in the living room, sitting under
the floor lamp near the new, standing Philco radio, with her long,
long legs stretched out in front of her and the pool of light on her
book revealing so little of her face: brownish, coppery features so
marked that she seemed to be a kind of freak and hair that was
reddish black but so rough that it looked like the things my mother
used for scouring pots and pans. She read a great deal, that summer.
If I ventured out of the archway, where I was not exactly hiding but
only keeping in the shadow to watch her read, she would often raise
her face and smile silently at me before beginning to read again, and
her skin would take on an abrupt, surprising pallor as it moved into
the light. When she got up and went into the kitchen with the
gracefulness of a stork, for something to eat, she was almost too tall
for the doorways; she went on legs like a spider's, with long
swinging arms and a little body in the middle, the strange proportions of the very tall. She looked down at my mother's plates and
dishes from a great, gentle height, remarkably absorbed; and asking
me a few odd questions, she would bend down over whatever she
was going to eat, meditate on it for a few moments like a giraffe, and
then straightening up back into the stratosphere, she would pick up
the plate in one thin hand, curling around it fingers like legs, and go
back gracefully into the living room. She would lower herself into
the chair that was always too small, curl her legs around it, become
dissatisfied, settle herself, stretch them out again — I remember so
well those long, hard, unladylike legs — and begin again to read.

She used to ask, 'What is that? What is that? And what is this?' but that was only at first.

My mother, who disliked her, said she was from the circus and we ought to try to understand and be kind. My father made jokes. He did not like big women or short hair – which was still new in places like ours – or women who read, although she was interested in his carpentry and he liked that.

But she was six feet four inches tall; this was in 1925.

My father was an accountant who built furniture as a hobby; we had a gas stove which he actually fixed once when it broke down and some outdoor tables and chairs he had built in the back yard. Before our visitor came on the train for her vacation with us, I used to spend all my time in the back yard, being underfoot, but once we had met her at the station and she shook hands with my father – I think she hurt him when she shook hands – I would watch her read and wish that she might talk to me.

She said, 'You are finishing high school?'

I was in the archway, as usual; I answered yes.

She looked up at me again, then down at her book. She said, 'This is a very bad book.' I said nothing. Without looking up, she tapped one finger on the shabby hassock on which she had put her feet. Then she looked up and smiled at me. I stepped tentatively from the floor to the rug, as reluctantly as if I were crossing the Sahara; she swung her feet away and I sat down. At close view her face looked as if every race in the world had been mixed and only the worst of each kept; an American Indian might look like that, or Ikhnaton from the encyclopedia, or a Swedish African, a Maori princess with the jaw of a Slav. It occurred to me suddenly that she might be a Negro, but no one else had ever seemed to think so, possibly because nobody in our town had ever seen a Negro. We had none. They were 'colored people'.

She said, 'You are not pretty, yes?'

I got up. I said, 'My father thinks you're a freak.'

'You are sixteen,' she said, 'sit down,' and I sat down. I crossed my arms over my breasts because they were too big, like balloons. Then she said, 'I am reading a very stupid book. You will take it away from me, yes?'

'No,' I said.

'You must,' she said, 'or it will poison me, sure as God,' and from her lap she plucked up *The Green Hat: A Romance*, gold letters on green binding, last year's bestseller which I had had to swear never to read, and she held it out to me, leaning back in her chair with that long arm doing all the work, the book enclosed in a cage of fingers wrapped completely around it. I think she could have put those fingers around a basketball. I did not take it.

'Go on,' she said, 'read it, go on, go away,' and I found myself at the archway, by the foot of the stairs with *The Green Hat: A Romance* in my hand. I turned it so the title was hidden. She was smiling at me and had her arms folded back under her head. 'Don't worry,' she said. 'Your body will be in fashion by the time of the next war.' I met my mother at the top of the stairs and had to hide the book from her; my mother said, 'Oh, the poor woman!' She was carrying some sheets. I went to my room and read through almost the whole night, hiding the book in the bedclothes when I was through. When I slept, I dreamt of Hispano-Suizas, of shingled hair and tragic eyes; of women with painted lips who had Affairs, who went night after night with Jews to low dives, who lived as they pleased, who had miscarriages in expensive Swiss clinics; of midnight swims, of desperation, of money, of illicit love, of a beautiful Englishman and getting into a taxi with him while wearing a cloth-of-silver cloak and a silver turban like the ones shown in the society pages of the New York City newspapers.

Unfortunately our guest's face kept recurring in my dream, and because I could not make out whether she was amused or bitter or very much of both, it really spoiled everything.

My mother discovered the book the next morning. I found it next to my plate at breakfast. Neither my mother nor my father made any remark about it; only my mother kept putting out the breakfast things with a kind of tender, reluctant smile. We all sat down, finally, when she had put out everything, and my father helped me to rolls and eggs and ham. Then he took off his glasses and folded them next to his plate. He leaned back in his chair and crossed his legs. Then he looked at the book and said in a tone of mock surprise, 'Well! What's this?'

I didn't say anything. I only looked at my plate.

'I believe I've seen this before,' he said. 'Yes, I believe I have.' Then he asked my mother, 'Have you seen this before?' My mother made a kind of vague movement with her head. She had begun to butter some toast and was putting it on my plate. I knew she was not supposed to discipline me; only my father was. 'Eat your eggs,' she said. My father, who had continued to look at *The Green Hat: A Romance* with the same expression of unvarying surprise, finally said:

'Well! This isn't a very pleasant thing to find on a Saturday morning, is it?'

I still didn't say anything, only looked at my food. I heard my mother say worriedly, 'She's not eating, Ben,' and my father put his hand on the back of my chair so I couldn't push it away from the table, as I was trying to do.

'Of course you have an explanation for this,' he said. 'Don't you?'

I said nothing.

'Of course she does,' he said, 'doesn't she, Bess? You wouldn't hurt your mother like this. You wouldn't hurt your mother by stealing a book that you knew you weren't supposed to read and for very good reason, too. You know we don't punish you. We talk things over with you. We try to explain. Don't we?'

I nodded.

'Good,' he said. 'Then where did this book come from?'

I muttered something; I don't know what.

'Is my daughter angry?' said my father. 'Is my daughter *being rebellious*?'

'She told you all about it!' I blurted out. My father's face turned red.

'Don't you dare talk about your mother that way!' he shouted, standing up. 'Don't you *dare* refer to your mother in that way!'

'Now, Ben —' said my mother.

'Your mother is the soul of unselfishness,' said my father, 'and don't you forget it, missy; your mother has worried about you since the day you were born and if you don't appreciate that, you can damn well —'

'Ben!' said my mother, shocked.

'I'm sorry,' I said, and then I said, 'I'm very sorry, Mother.' My father sat down. My father had a mustache and his hair was parted in the middle and slicked down; now one lock fell over the part in front and his whole face was gray and quivering. He was staring fixedly at his coffee cup. My mother came over and poured coffee for him; then she took the coffeepot into the kitchen and when she came back she had milk for me. She put the glass of milk on the table near my plate. Then she sat down again. She smiled trembling at my father; then she put her hand over mine on the table and said:

'Darling, why did you read that book?'

'Well?' said my father from across the table.

There was a moment's silence. Then:

'Good morning!'

and

'Good morning!'

and

'Good morning!'

said our guest cheerfully, crossing the dining room in two strides, and folding herself carefully down into her breakfast chair, from where her knees stuck out, she reached across the table, picked up *The Green Hat*, propped it up next to her plate and began to read it with great absorption. Then she looked up. 'You have a very progressive library,' she said. 'I took the liberty of recommending this exciting book to your daughter. You told me it was your favorite. You sent all the way to New York City on purpose for it, yes?'

'I don't – I quite –' said my mother, pushing back her chair from the table. My mother was trembling from head to foot and her face was set in an expression of fixed distaste. Our visitor regarded first my mother and then my father, bending over them tenderly and with exquisite interest. She said:

'I hope you do not mind my using your library.'

'No no no,' muttered my father.

'I eat almost for two,' said our visitor modestly, 'because of my height. I hope you do not mind that?'

'No, of course not,' said my father, regaining control of himself.

'Good. It is all considered in the bill,' said the visitor, and looking about at my shrunken parents, each hurried, each spooning in the food and avoiding her gaze, she added deliberately:

'I took also another liberty. I removed from the endpapers certain – ah – drawings that I did not think bore any relation to the text. You do not mind?'

And as my father and mother looked in shocked surprise and utter consternation – at each other – she said to me in a low voice, 'Don't eat. You'll make yourself sick,' and then smiled warmly at the two of them when my mother went off into the kitchen and my father remembered he was late for work. She waved at them. I jumped up as soon as they were out of the room.

'There were no drawings in that book!' I whispered.

'Then we must make some,' she said, and taking a pencil off the whatnot, she drew in the endpapers of the book a series of sketches: the heroine sipping a soda in an ice-cream parlor, show-ing her legs and very chic; in a sloppy bathing suit and big grin, holding up a large fish; driving her Hispano Suiza into a tree only to be catapulted straight up into the air; and in the last sketch landing demure and coy in the arms of the hero, who looked violently surprised. Then she drew a white mouse putting on lipstick, getting married to another white mouse in a church, the two entangled in some manner I thought I should not look at, the lady mouse with a big belly and two little mice inside (who were playing chess), then the little mice coming out in separate envelopes and finally the whole family having a picnic, with some things around the picnic basket that I did not recognize and underneath in capital letters, 'I did not bring up my children to test cigarettes.' This left me blank. She laughed and rubbed it out, saying that it was out of date. Then she drew a white mouse with a rolled-up umbrella chasing my mother. I picked that up and looked at it for a while; then I tore it into pieces, and tore the others into pieces as well. I said, 'I don't think you have the slightest right to –' and stopped. She was looking at me with – not anger exactly – not warning exactly – I found I had to sit down. I began to cry.

'Ah! The results of practical psychology,' she said dryly, gather-ing up the pieces of her sketches. She took matches off the whatnot and set fire to the pieces in a saucer. She held up the smoking match between her thumb and forefinger, saying, 'You see? The finger is – shall we say, perception? – but the thumb is money. The thumb is hard.'

'You oughtn't to treat my parents that way!' I said, crying.

'You ought not to tear up my sketches,' she said calmly.

'Why not! Why not!' I shouted.

'Because they are worth money,' she said, 'in some quarters. I won't draw you any more,' and indifferently taking the saucer with the ashes in it in one palm, she went into the kitchen. I heard her voice and then my mother's, and then my mother's again, and then our visitor's in a tone that would've made a rock weep, but I never found out what they said.

I passed our guest's room many times at night that summer, going in by the hall past her rented room where the second-floor windows gave out onto the dark garden. The electric lights were always on brilliantly. My mother had sewn the white curtains because she did everything like that and had bought the furniture at a sale: a marble-topped bureau, the wardrobe, the iron bedstead, an old Victrola against the wall. There was usually an open book on the bed. I would stand in the shadow of the open doorway and look across the bare wood floor, too much of it and all as slippery as the sea, bare wood waxed and shining in the electric light. A black dress hung on the front of the wardrobe and a pair of shoes like my mother's, T-strap shoes with thick heels. I used to wonder if she had silver evening slippers inside the wardrobe. Sometimes the open book on the bed was Wells's *The Time Machine* and then I would talk to the black glass of the window, I would say to the transparent reflections and the black branches of trees that moved beyond it.

'I'm only sixteen.'

'You look eighteen,' she would say.

'I know,' I would say. 'I'd like to be eighteen. I'd like to go away to college. To Radcliffe, I think.'

She would say nothing, out of surprise.

'Are you reading Wells?' I would say then, leaning against the door jamb. 'I think that's funny. Nobody in this town reads anything; they just think about social life. I read a lot, however. I would like to learn a great deal.'

She would smile then, across the room.

'I did something funny once,' I would go on. 'I mean funny ha-ha, not funny peculiar.' It was a real line, very popular. 'I read *The Time Machine* and then I went around asking people were they Eloi or were they Morlocks; everyone liked it. The point is which you would be if you could, like being an optimist or a pessimist or do you like bobbed hair.' Then I would add, 'Which are you?' and she would only shrug and smile a little more. She would prop her chin on one long, long hand and look into my eyes with her black Egyptian eyes and then she would say in her curious hoarse voice:

'It is you who must say it first.'

'I think,' I would say, 'that you are a Morlock,' and sitting on the bed in my mother's rented room with *The Time Machine* open beside her, she would say:

'You are exactly right. I am a Morlock. I am a Morlock on vacation. I have come from the last Morlock meeting, which is held out between the stars in a big goldfish bowl, so all the Morlocks have to cling to the inside walls like a flock of black bats, some right side up, some upside down, for there is no up and down there, clinging like a flock of black crows, like a chestnut burr turned inside out. There are half a thousand Morlocks and we rule the worlds. My black uniform is in the wardrobe.'

'I knew I was right,' I would say.

'You are always right,' she would say, 'and you know the rest of it, too. You know what murderers we are and how terribly we live. We are waiting for the big bang when everything falls over and even the Morlocks will be destroyed; meanwhile I stay here waiting for the signal and I leave messages clipped to the frame of your mother's amateur oil painting of Main Street because it will be in a museum some day and my friends can find it; meanwhile I read *The Time Machine*.'

Then I would say, 'Can I come with you?' leaning against the door.

'Without you,' she would say gravely, 'all is lost,' and taking out from the wardrobe a black dress glittering with stars and a pair of silver sandals with high heels, she would say, 'These are yours. They were my great-grandmother's, who founded the Order. In the name of Trans-Temporal Military Authority.' And I would put them on.

It was almost a pity she was not really there.

Every year in the middle of August the Country Club gave a dance, not just for the rich families who were members but also for the 'nice' people who lived in frame houses in town and even for some of the smart, economical young couples who lived in apartments, just as if they had been in the city. There was one new, redbrick apartment building downtown, four stories high, with a courtyard. We were supposed to go, because I was old enough that year, but the day before the dance my father became ill with pains in his left side and my mother had to stay home to take care of him. He was propped up on pillows on the living-room daybed, which we had pulled out into the room so he could watch what my mother was doing with the garden out back and call to her once in a while through the windows. He could also see the walk leading up to the front door. He kept insisting that she was doing things all wrong. I did not even ask if I could go to the dance alone. My father said:

'Why don't you go out and help your mother?'

'She doesn't want me to,' I said. 'I'm supposed to stay here,' and then he shouted angrily, 'Bess! Bess!' and began to give her instructions through the window. I saw another pair of hands appear in the window next to my mother's and then our guest – squatting back on her heels and smoking a cigarette – pulling up weeds. She was working quickly and efficiently, the cigarette between her teeth. 'No, not that way!' shouted my father, pulling on the blanket that my mother had put over him. 'Don't you know what you're doing! Bess, you're ruining everything! Stop it! Do it right!' My mother looked bewildered and upset; she passed out of the window and our visitor took her place; she waved to my father and he subsided, pulling the blanket up around his neck. 'I don't like women who smoke,' he muttered irritably. I slipped out through the kitchen.

My father's toolshed and working space took up the farther half of the back yard; the garden was spread over the nearer half, part kitchen garden, part flowers, and then extended down either side of the house where he had fifteen feet or so of space before a white slat fence and the next people's side yard. It was an on-and-offish garden, and the house was beginning to need paint. My mother was working in the kitchen garden, kneeling. Our guest was standing, pruning the lilac trees, still smoking. I said:

'Mother, can't I go, can't I *go*!' in a low voice.

My mother passed her hand over her forehead and called 'Yes, Ben!' to my father.

'Why *can't* I go!' I whispered. 'Ruth's mother and Betty's mother will be there. Why couldn't you call Ruth's mother and Betty's mother?'

'*Not that way*!' came a blast from the living-room window. My mother sighed briefly and then smiled a cheerful smile. 'Yes, Ben!' she called brightly. 'I'm listening.' My father began to give some more instructions.

'Mother,' I said desperately, 'why couldn't you–'

'Your father wouldn't approve,' she said, and again she produced a bright smile and called encouragingly to my father. I wandered over to the lilac trees where our visitor, in her usual nondescript black dress, was piling the dead wood under the tree. She took a last puff on her cigarette, holding it between thumb and forefinger, then ground it out in the grass and picked up in both arms the entire lot of dead wood. She carried it over to the fence and dumped it.

'My father says you shouldn't prune trees in August,' I blurted suddenly.

'Oh?' she said.

'It hurts them,' I whispered.

'Oh,' she said. She had on gardening gloves, though much too small; she picked up the pruning shears and began snipping again through inch-thick trunks and dead branches that snapped explosively when they broke and whipped out at your face. She was efficient and very quick.

I said nothing at all, only watched her face.

She shook her head decisively.

'But Ruth's mother and Betty's mother –' I began, faltering.

'I never go out,' she said.

'You needn't stay,' I said, placating.

'Never,' she said. 'Never at all,' and snapping free a particularly large, dead, silvery branch from the lilac tree, she put it in my arms. She stood there looking at me and her look was suddenly very severe, very unpleasant, something foreign, like the look of somebody who had seen people go off to battle to die, the 'movies' look but hard, hard as nails. I knew I wouldn't get to go anywhere. I thought she might have seen battles in the Great War, maybe even been in some of it. I said, although I could barely speak:

'Were you in the Great War?'

'Which great war?' said our visitor. Then she said, 'No, I never go out,' and returned to scissoring the trees.

On the night of the dance my mother told me to get dressed, and I did. There was a mirror on the back of my door, but the window was better; it softened everything; it hung me out in the middle of a black space and made my eyes into mysterious shadows. I was wearing pink organdy and a bunch of daisies from the garden, not the wild kind. I came downstairs and found our visitor waiting for me at the bottom: tall, bare-armed, almost beautiful, for she'd done something to her impossible hair and the rusty reddish black curled slickly like the best photographs. Then she moved and I thought she was altogether beautiful, all black and rippling silver like a Paris dress or better still a New York dress, with a silver band around her forehead like an Indian princess's and silver shoes with the chunky heels and the one strap over the instep.

She said, 'Ah! don't you look nice,' and then a whisper, taking my arm and looking down at me with curious gentleness, 'I'm going to be a bad chaperone. I'm going to disappear.'

'Well!' said I, inwardly shaking, 'I hope I can take care of myself, I should think.' But I hoped she wouldn't leave me alone and I hoped that no one would laugh at her. She was really incredibly tall.

'Your father's going to sleep at ten,' said my mother. 'Be back by eleven. Be happy.' And she kissed me.

But Ruth's father, who drove Ruth and I and Ruth's mother and our guest to the Country Club, did not laugh. And neither did anyone else. Our visitor seemed to have put on a strange graceful- ness with her dress, and a strange sort of kindliness, too, so that Ruth, who had never seen her but had only heard rumors about

her, cried out, 'Your friend's lovely!' and Ruth's father, who
taught mathematics at high school, said (clearing his throat), 'It
must be lonely staying in,' and our visitor said only, 'Yes. Oh yes.
It is,' resting one immensely long, thin, elegant hand on his
shoulder like some kind of unwinking spider, while his words and
hers went echoing out into the night, back and forth, back and
forth, losing themselves in the trees that rushed past the headlights
and massed blackly to each side.

'Ruth wants to join a circus!' cried Ruth's mother, laughing.

'I do *not*!' said Ruth.

'You *will* not,' said her father.

'I'll do exactly as I please,' said Ruth with her nose in the air,
and she took a chocolate cream out of her handbag and put it in
her mouth.

'You will *not*!' said Ruth's father, scandalized.

'Daddy, you know I will too,' said Ruth, serenely though
somewhat muffled, and under cover of the dark she wormed over
to me in the back seat and passed, from her hot hand to mine,
another chocolate cream. I ate it; it was unpleasantly and piercingly
sweet.

'Isn't it *glorious*?' said Ruth.

The Country Club was much more bare than I had expected, really
only a big frame building with a veranda three-quarters of the way
around it and not much lawn, but there was a path down front to
two stone pillars that made a kind of gate and somebody had
strung the gate and the whole path with colored Chinese lanterns.
That part was lovely. Inside the whole first story was one room,
with a varnished floor like the high school gym, and a punch table
at one end and ribbons and Chinese lanterns hung all over the
ceiling. It did not look quite like the movies but everything was
beautifully painted. I had noticed that there were wicker armchairs
scattered on the veranda. I decided it was 'nice'. Behind the punch
table was a flight of stairs that led to a gallery full of tables where
the grown-ups could go and drink (Ruth insisted they would be
bringing real liquor for 'mixes', although of course the Country
Club had to pretend not to know about that) and on both sides of
the big room French windows that opened onto the veranda and

the Chinese lanterns, swinging a little in the breeze. Ruth was wearing a better dress than mine. We went over to the punch table and drank punch while she asked me about our visitor and I made up a lot of lies. 'You don't know anything,' said Ruth. She waved across the room to some friends of hers; then I could see her start dancing with a boy in front of the band, which was at the other end of the room. Older people were dancing and people's parents, some older boys and girls. I stayed by the punch table. People who knew my parents came over and talked to me; they asked me how I was and I said I was fine; then they asked me how my father was and I said he was fine. Someone offered to introduce me to someone but I said I knew him. I hoped somebody would come over. I thought I would skirt around the dance floor and try to talk to some of the girls I knew, but then I thought I wouldn't; I imagined myself going up the stairs with Iris March's lover from *The Green Hat* to sit at a table and smoke a cigarette or drink something. I stepped behind the punch table and went out through the French windows. Our guest was a few chairs away with her feet stretched out, resting on the lowest rung of the veranda. She was reading a magazine with the aid of a small flashlight. The flowers planted around the veranda showed up a little in the light from the Chinese lanterns: shadowy clumps and masses of petunias, a few of the white ones springing into life as she turned the page of her book and the beam of the flashlight moved in her hand. I decided I would have my cigarette in a long holder. The moon was coming up over the woods past the Country Club lawns, but it was a cloudy night and all I could see was a vague lightening of the sky in that direction. It was rather warm. I remembered something about an 'ivory cigarette holder flaunting at the moon'. Our visitor turned another page. I thought that she must have been aware of me. I thought again of Iris March's lover, coming out to get me on the 'terrace' when somebody tapped me on the shoulder; it was Ruth's father. He took me by the wrist and led me to our visitor, who looked up and smiled vaguely, dreamily, in the dark under the colored lanterns. Then Ruth's father said:

'What do you know? There's a relative of yours inside!' She continued to smile but her face stopped moving; she smiled gently and with tenderness at the space next to his head for the barely perceptible part of a moment. Then she completed the swing of her head and looked at him, still smiling, but everything had gone out of it.

'How lovely,' she said. Then she said, 'Who is it?'

'I don't know,' said Ruth's father, 'but he's tall, looks just like you – beg pardon. He says he's your cousin.'

'*Por nada*,' said our guest absently, and getting up, she shook hands with Ruth's father. The three of us went back inside. She left the magazine and flashlight on the chair; they seemed to belong to the Club. Inside, Ruth's father took us up the steps to the gallery and there, at the end of it, sitting at one of the tables, was a man even taller than our visitor, tall even sitting down. He was in evening dress while half the men at the dance were in business suits. He did not really look like her in the face; he was a little darker and a little flatter of feature; but as we approached him, he stood up. He almost reached the ceiling. He was a giant. He and our visitor did not shake hands. The both of them looked at Ruth's father, smiling formally, and Ruth's father left us; the stranger looked quizzically at me but our guest had already sunk into a nearby seat, all willowiness, all grace. They made a handsome couple. The stranger brought a silver-inlaid flask out of his hip pocket; he took the pitcher of water that stood on the table and poured some into a clean glass. Then he added whisky from the flask, but our visitor did not take it. She only turned it aside, amused, with one finger, and said to me, 'Sit down, child,' which I did. Then she said:

'Cousin, how did you find me?'

'*Par chance*, cousin,' said the stranger. 'By luck.' He screwed the top back on the flask very deliberately and put the whole thing back in his pocket. He began to stir the drink he had made with a wooden muddler provided by the Country Club.

'I have endured much annoyance,' he said, 'from that man to whom you spoke. There is not a single specialized here; they are all half-brained: scattered and stupid.'

'He is a kind and clever man,' said she. 'He teaches mathematics.'

'The more fool he,' said the stranger, 'for the mathematics he thinks he teaches!' and he drank his own drink. Then he said, 'I think we will go home now.'

'Eh! This person?' said my friend, drawing up the ends of her lips half scornfully, half amused. 'Not this person!'

'Why not this person, who knows me?' said the strange man.

'Because,' said our visitor, and turning deliberately away from me, she put her face next to his and began to whisper mischievously in his ear. She was watching the dancers on the floor below, half the men in business suits, half the couples middle-aged. Ruth and Betty and some of their friends, and some vacationing college boys. The band was playing the foxtrot. The strange man's face altered just a little, it darkened; he finished his drink, put it down, and then swung massively in his seat to face me.

'Does she go out?' he said sharply.

'Well?' said our visitor idly.

'Yes,' I said. 'Yes, she goes out. Every day.'

'By car or on foot?' I looked at her but she was doing nothing. Her thumb and finger formed a circle on the table.

'I don't know,' I said.

'Does she go on foot?' he said.

'No,' I blurted suddenly, 'no, by car. Always by car!' He sat back in his seat.

'You would do anything,' he said conversationally. 'The lot of you.'

'I?' she said. 'I'm not dedicated. I can be reasoned with.'

After a moment of silence he said, 'We'll talk.'

She shrugged. 'Why not?'

'This girl's home,' he said. 'I'll leave fifteen minutes after you. Give me your hand.'

'Why?' she said. 'You know where I live. I am not going to hide in the woods like an animal.'

'Give me your hand,' he repeated. 'For old time's sake.' She reached across the table. They clasped hands and she winced momentarily. Then they both rose. She smiled dazzlingly. She took me by the wrist and led me down the stairs while the strange man called after us, as if the phrase pleased him, 'For old time's sake!' and then 'Good health, cousin! Long life!' while the band struck up a march in ragtime. She stopped to talk to five or six people, including Ruth's father who taught mathematics in the high school, and the band leader, and Betty, who was drinking punch with a boy from our class. Betty said to me under her breath, 'Your daisies are coming loose. They're gonna fall off.' We walked through the parked cars until we reached one that she seemed to like; they were all open and some owners left the keys in them; she got in behind the wheel and started up.

'But this *isn't your car!*' I said. 'You can't just—'

'Get in!' I slid in next to her.

'It's after ten o'clock,' I said. 'You'll wake up my father. Who—'

'Shut up!'

I did. She drove very fast and very badly. Halfway home she began to slow down. Then suddenly she laughed out loud and said very confidentially, not to me but as if to somebody else:

'I told him I had planted a Neilsen loop around here that would put half of Greene County out of phase. A dead man's control. I had to go out and stop it every week.'

'What's a Neilsen loop?' I said.

'Jam yesterday, jam tomorrow, but never jam today,' she quoted.

'What,' said I emphatically, 'is a—'

'I've told you, baby,' she said, 'and you'll never know more, God willing,' and pulling into our driveway with a screech that would have wakened the dead, she vaulted out of the car and through the back door into the kitchen, just as if my mother and father had both been asleep or in a cataleptic trance, like those in the works of E. A. Poe. Then she told me to get the iron poker from the garbage burner in the back yard and find out if the end was still hot; when I brought the thing in, she laid the hot end over one of the flames of the gas stove. Then she rummaged around under the sink and came up with a bottle of my mother's Clear Household Ammonia.

'That stuff's awful,' I said. 'If you let that get in your eyes—'

'Pour some in the water glass,' she said, handing it to me. 'Two-thirds full. Cover it with a saucer. Get another glass and another saucer and put all of them on the kitchen table. Fill your mother's water pitcher, cover that, and put that on the table.'

'Are you going to *drink* that?' I cried, horrified, halfway to the table with the covered glass. She merely pushed me. I got everything set up, and also pulled three chairs up to the kitchen table; I then went to turn off the gas flame, but she took me by the hand and placed me so that I hid the stove from the window and the door. She said, 'Baby, what is the specific heat of iron?'

'What?' I said.

'You know it, baby,' she said. 'What is it?'

I only stared at her.

'But you know it, baby,' she said. 'You know it better than I. You know that your mother was burning garbage today and the poker would still be hot. And you know better than to touch the iron pots when they come fresh from the oven, even though the flame is off, because iron takes a long time to heat up and a long time to cool off, isn't that so?'

I nodded.

'And you don't know,' she added, 'how long it takes for aluminum pots to become cold because nobody uses aluminum for pots yet. And if I told you how scarce the heavy metals are, and what a radionic oven is, and how the heat can go *through* the glass and the plastic and even the ceramic lattice, you wouldn't know what I was talking about, would you?'

'No,' I said, suddenly frightened 'no, no, no.'

'Then you know more than some,' she said. 'You know more than me. Remember how I used to burn myself, fiddling with your mother's things?' She looked at her palm and made a face. 'He's coming,' she said. 'Stand in front of the stove. When he asks you to turn off the gas, turn it off. When I say "Now," hit him with the poker.'

'I can't,' I whispered. 'He's too big.'

'He can't hurt you,' she said. 'He doesn't dare; that would be an anachronism. Just do as I say.'

'What are you going to *do*?' I cried.

'When I say "Now",' she repeated serenely, 'hit him with the poker,' and sitting down by the table, she reached into a jam-jar of odds and ends my mother kept on the windowsill and began to buff her nails with a Lady Marlene emery stick. Two minutes passed by the kitchen clock. Nothing happened. I stood there with my hand on the cold end of the poker, doing nothing until I felt I had to speak, so I said, 'Why are you making a face? Does something hurt?'

'The splinter in my palm,' she said calmly. 'The bastard.'

'Why don't you take it out?'

'It will blow up the house.'

He stepped in through the open kitchen door.

Without a word she put both arms palm upward on the kitchen table and without a word he took off the black cummerbund of his formal dress and flicked it at her. It settled over both her arms and then began to draw tight, molding itself over her arms and the table like a piece of black adhesive, pulling her almost down onto it and whipping one end around the table edge until the wood almost cracked. It seemed to paralyze her arms. He put his finger to his tongue and then to her palm, where there was a small black spot. The spot disappeared. He laughed and told me to turn off the flame, so I did.

'Take it off,' she said then.

He said, 'Too bad you are in hiding or you too could carry weapons,' and then, as the edge of the table let out a startling sound like a pistol shot, he flicked the black tape off her arms, returning it to himself, where it disappeared into his evening clothes.

'Now that I have used this, everyone knows where we are,' he said, and he sat down in a kitchen chair that was much too small for him and lounged back in it, his knees sticking up into the air.

Then she said something I could not understand. She took the saucer off the empty glass and poured water into it; she said something unintelligible again and held it out to him, but he motioned it away. She shrugged and drank the water herself. 'Flies,' she said, and put the saucer back on. They sat in silence for several minutes. I did not know what to do; I knew I was supposed to wait for the word 'Now' and then hit him with the poker, but no one seemed to be saying or doing anything. The kitchen clock, which I had forgotten to wind that morning, was running down at ten minutes to eleven. There was a cricket making a noise close outside the window and I was afraid the ammonia smell would get out somehow; then, just as I was getting a cramp in my legs from standing still, our visitor nodded. She sighed, too, regretfully. The strange man got to his feet, moved his chair carefully out of the way and pronounced:

'Good. I'll call them.'

'Now?' said she.

I couldn't do it. I brought the poker in front of me and stood there with it, holding it in both hands. The stranger – who almost had to stoop to avoid our ceiling – wasted only a glance on me, as if I were hardly worth looking at, and then concentrated his attention on her. She had her chin in her hands. Then she closed her eyes.

'Put that down, please,' she said tiredly.

I did not know what to do. She opened her eyes and took the saucer off the other glass on the table.

'Put that down right now,' she said, and raised the glass of ammonia to her lips.

I swung at him clumsily with the poker. I was not sure what happened next, but I think he laughed and seized the end – the hot end – and then threw me off balance just as he screamed, because the next thing I knew I was down on all fours watching her trip him as he threw himself at her, his eyes screwed horribly shut, choking and coughing and just missing her. The ammonia glass was lying empty and broken on the floor; a brown stain showed where it had rolled off the white tablecloth on the kitchen table. When he fell, she kicked him in the side of the head. Then she stepped carefully away from him and held out her hand to me; I gave her the poker, which she took with the folded edge of the tablecloth, and reversing it so that she held the cold end, she brought it down with immense force – not on his head, as I had expected, but on his windpipe. When he was still, she touched the hot end of the poker to several places on his jacket, passed it across where his belt would be, and to two places on both of his shoes. Then she said to me, 'Get out.'

I did, but not before I saw her finishing the job on his throat, not with the poker but with the thick heel of her silver shoe.

When I came back in, there was nobody there. There was a clean, rinsed glass on the drainboard next to the sink and the poker was propped up in one corner of the sink with cold water running on it. Our visitor was at the stove, brewing tea in my mother's brown teapot. She was standing under the Dutch cloth calendar my mother, who was very modern, kept hanging on the wall. My mother pinned messages on it; one of them read 'Be Careful. Except for the Bathroom, More Accidents Occur in the Kitchen Than in Any Other Part of the House.'

'Where –' I said, 'where is – is –'

'Sit down,' she said. 'Sit down here,' and she put me into *his* seat at the kitchen table. But there was no *he* anywhere. She said, 'Don't think too much.' Then she went back to the tea and just as it was ready to pour, my mother came in from the living room, with a blanket around her shoulders, smiling foolishly and saying, 'Goodness, I've been asleep, haven't I?'

'Tea?' said our visitor.

'I fell asleep just like that,' said my mother, sitting down.

'I forgot,' said our visitor. 'I borrowed a car. I felt ill. I must call them on the telephone,' and she went out into the hall, for we had been among the first to have a telephone. She came back a few minutes later. 'Is it all right?' said my mother. We drank our tea in silence.

'Tell me,' said our visitor at length. 'How is your radio reception?'

'It's perfectly fine,' said my mother, a bit offended.

'That's fine,' said our visitor, and then, as if she couldn't control herself, 'because you live in a dead area, you know, thank God, a dead area!'

My mother said, alarmed, 'I beg your par –'

'Excuse me,' said our visitor, 'I'm ill,' and she put her cup into her saucer with a clatter, got up and went out of the kitchen. My mother put one hand caressingly over mine.

'Did anyone . . . insult her at the dance?' said my mother, softly.

'Oh no,' I said.

'Are you sure?' my mother insisted. 'Are you perfectly sure? Did anyone comment? Did anyone say anything about her appearance? About her height? Anything that was not nice?'

'Ruth did,' I said. 'Ruth said she looked like a giraffe.' My mother's hand slid off mine; gratified, she got up and began to gather up the tea things. She put them into the sink. She clucked her tongue over the poker and put it away in the kitchen closet. Then she began to dry the glass that our visitor had previously rinsed and put on the drainboard, the glass that had held ammonia.

'The poor woman,' said my mother, drying it. 'Oh, the poor woman.'

Nothing much happened after that. I began to get my books ready for high school. Blue cornflowers sprang up along the sides of the houses and my father, who was better now, cut them down with a scythe. My mother was growing hybrid ones in the back flower garden, twice as tall and twice as big as any of the wild ones; she explained to me about hybrids and why they were bigger, but I forgot it. Our visitor took up with a man, not a nice man, really, because he worked in the town garage and was Polish. She didn't go out but used to see him in the kitchen at night. He was a thick-set, stocky man, very blond, with a real Polish name, but everyone called him Bogalusa Joe because he had spent fifteen years in Bogalusa, Louisiana (he called it 'Loosiana') and he talked about it all the time. He had a theory, that the colored people were just like us and that in a hundred years everybody would be all mixed up, and you couldn't tell them apart. My mother was very advanced in her views but she wouldn't ever let me talk to him. He was very respectful; he called her 'Ma'am,' and didn't use any bad language, but he never came into the living room. He would always meet our visitor in the kitchen or sometimes on the swing in the back garden. They would drink coffee; they would play cards. Sometimes she would say to him, 'Tell me a story, Joe. I love a good story,' and he would talk about hiding out in Loosiana; he had had to hide out from somebody or something for three years in the middle of the Negroes and they had let him in and let him work and took care of him. He said, 'The coloreds are like anybody.' Then he said, 'The nigras are smarter. They got to be. They ain't nobody's fool. I had a black girl for two years once was the smartest woman in the world. Beautiful woman. Not beautiful like a white, though, not the same.'

'Give us a hundred years,' he added, 'and it'll all be mixed.'

'Two hundred?' said our visitor, pouring coffee. He put a lot of sugar in his; then he remarked that he had learned that in Bogalusa. She sat down. She was leaning her elbows on the table, smiling at him. She was stirring her own coffee with a spoon. He looked at her a moment, and then he said softly:

'A black woman, smartest woman in the world. You're black, woman, ain't you?'

'Part,' she said.

'Beautiful woman,' he said. 'Nobody knows?'

'They know in the circus,' she said. 'But there they don't care. Shall I tell you what we circus people think of you?'

'Of who?' he said, looking surprised.

'Of all of you,' she said. 'All who aren't in the circus. All who can't do what we can do, who aren't the biggest or the best, who can't kill a man barehanded or learn a new language in six weeks or slit a man's jugular at fifteen yards with nothing but a pocket-knife or climb the Greene County National Bank from the first story to the sixth with no equipment. I can do all that.'

'I'll be damned,' said Bogalusa Joe softly.

'We despise you,' she said. 'That's what we do. We think you're slobs. The scum of the earth! The world's fertilizer, Joe, that's what you are.'

'Baby, you're blue,' he said, 'you're blue tonight,' and then he took her hand across the table, but not the way they did it in the movies, not the way they did it in the books; there was a look on his face I had never seen on anyone's before, not the high school boys when they put a line over on a girl, not on grown-ups, not even on the brides and grooms because all that was romantic or showing off or 'lust' and he only looked infinitely kind, infinitely concerned. She pulled her hand out of his. With the same faint, detached smile she had had all night, she pushed back her chair and stood up. She said flatly:

'All I can do! What good is it?' She shrugged. She added, 'I've got to leave tomorrow.' He got up and put his arm around her shoulders. I thought that looked bad because he was actually a couple of inches shorter than she was.

He said, 'Baby, you don't have to go.' She was staring out into the back garden, as if looking miles away, miles away, far away into our vegetable patch or our swing or my mother's hybrids, into something nobody could see. He said urgently, 'Honey, look —' and then, when she continued to stare, pulling her face around so she had to look at him, both his broad, mechanic's hands under her chin, 'Baby, you can stay with me.' He brought his face closer

to hers. 'Marry me,' he said suddenly. She began to laugh. I had
never heard her laugh like that before. Then she began to choke.
He put his arms around her and she leaned against him, choking,
making funny noises like someone with asthma, finally clapping
her hands over her face, then biting her palm, heaving up and
down as if she were sick. It took me several seconds to realize that
she was crying. He looked very troubled. They stood there: she
cried, he, distressed – and I hiding, watching all of it. They began
to walk slowly toward the kitchen door. When they had gone out
and put out the light, I followed them out into the back garden, to
the swing my father had rigged up under the one big tree:
cushions and springs to the ground like a piece of furniture, big
enough to hold four people. Bushes screened it. There was a
kerosene lantern my father had mounted on a post, but it was out.
I could just about see them. They sat for a few minutes, saying
nothing, looking up through the tree into the darkness. The swing
creaked a little as our visitor crossed and uncrossed her long legs.
She took out a cigarette and lit it, obscuring their faces with even
that little glow: an orange spot that wavered up and down as she
smoked, making the darkness more black. Then it disappeared.
She had ground it out underfoot in the grass. I could see them
again. Bogalusa Joe, the garage mechanic, said:

'Tomorrow?'

'Tomorrow,' she said. Then they kissed each other. I liked that;
it was all right; I had seen it before. She leaned back against the
cushions of the swing and seemed to spread her feet in the
invisible grass; she let her head and arms fall back onto the
cushion. Without saying a word, he lifted her skirt far above her
knees and put his hand between her legs. There was a great deal
more of the same business and I watched it all, from the first twist-
ings to the stabbings, the noises, the life-and-death battle in the
dark. The word 'epilepsy' kept repeating itself in my head. They
got dressed and again began to smoke, talking in tones I could
not hear. I crouched in the bushes, my heart beating violently.

I was horribly frightened.

She did not leave the next day, or the next or the next; and she
even took a dress to my mother and asked if she could have it

altered somewhere in town. My school clothes were out, being aired in the back yard to get the mothball smell out of them. I put covers on all my books. I came down one morning to ask my mother whether I couldn't have a jumper taken up at the hem because the magazines said it was all right for young girls. I expected a fight over it. I couldn't find my mother in the hall or the kitchen so I tried the living room, but before I had got halfway through the living room arch, someone said, 'Stop there,' and I saw both my parents sitting on two chairs near the front door, both with their hands in their laps, both staring straight ahead, motionless as zombies.

I said, 'Oh for heaven's sake, what're you—'

'Stop there,' said the same voice. My parents did not move. My mother was smiling her social smile. There was no one else in the room. I waited for a little while, my parents continuing to be dead, and then from some corner on my left, near the new Philco, our visitor came gliding out, wrapped in my mother's spring coat, stepping softly across the rug and looking carefully at all the living room windows. She grinned when she saw me. She tapped the top of the Philco radio and motioned me in. Then she took off the coat and draped it over the radio.

She was in black from head to foot.

I thought 'black', but black was not the word; the word was 'blackness', dark beyond dark, dark that drained the eyesight, something I could never have imagined even in my dreams, a black in which there was no detail, no sight, no nothing, only an awful, desperate dizziness, for her body – the thing was skin-tight, like a diver's costume or an acrobat's – had actually disappeared, completely blotted out except for its outline. Her head and bare hands floated in the air. She said, 'Pretty, yes?' Then she sat cross-legged on our radio. She said, 'Please pull the curtains,' and I did, going from one to the other and drawing them shut, circling my frozen parents and then stopping short in the middle of the quaking floor. I said, 'I'm going to faint.' She was off the radio and into my mother's coat in an instant; holding me by the arm, she got me onto the living room couch and put her arm round me, massaging my back. She said, 'Your parents are asleep.' Then she said, 'You have known some of this. You are a wonderful little pick-up but you get mixed up, yes? All about the Morlocks? The Trans-Temporal Military Authority?'

I began to say 'Oh oh oh oh –' and she massaged my back again.

'Nothing will hurt you,' she said. 'Nothing will hurt your parents. Think how exciting it is! Think! The rebel Morlocks, the revolution in the Trans-Temporal Military Authority.'

'But I – I–' I said.

'We are friends,' she continued gravely, taking my hands, 'we are real friends. You helped me. We will not forget that,' and slinging my mother's coat off onto the couch, she went and stood in front of the archway. She put her hands on her hips, then began rubbing the back of her neck nervously and clearing her throat. She turned around to give me one last look.

'Are you calm?' she said. I nodded. She smiled at me. 'Be calm,' she said softly, '*sois tranquille*. We're friends,' and then she put herself to watching the archway. She said once, almost sadly, 'Friends', and then stepped back and smiled again at me.

The archway was turning into a mirror. It got misty, then bright, like a cloud of bright dust, then almost like a curtain; and then it was a mirror, although all I could see in it was our visitor and myself, not my parents, not the furniture, not the living room.

Then the first Morlock stepped through.

And the second.

And the third.

And the others.

Oh, the living room was filled with giants! They were like her, like her in the face, like her in the bodies of the very tall, like her in the black uniforms, men and women of all the races of the earth, everything mixed and huge as my mother's hybrid flowers but a foot taller than our visitor, a flock of black ravens, black bats, black wolves, the professionals of the future world, perched on our furniture, on the Philco radio, some on the very walls and drapes of the windows as if they could fly, hovering in the air as if they were out in space where the Morlocks meet, half a thousand in a bubble between the stars.

Who rule the worlds.

Two came through the mirror who crawled on the rug, both in diving suits and goldfish-bowl helmets, a man and a woman, fat and shaped like seals. They lay on the rug breathing water (for I saw the specks flowing in it, in and out of strange frills around their necks, the way dust moves in air) and looking up at the rest with tallowy faces. Their suits bulged. One of the Morlocks said something to one of the seals and one of the seals answered, fingering a thing attached to the barrels on its back, gurgling.

Then they all began to talk.

Even if I'd known what language it was, I think it would have been too fast for me; it was very fast, very hard-sounding, very urgent, like the numbers pilots call in to the ground or something like that, like a code that everybody knows, to get things done as fast as you can. Only the seal-people talked slowly, and they gurgled and stank like a dirty beach. They did not even move their faces except to make little round mouths, like fish. I think I was put to sleep for a while (or maybe I just fell asleep) and then it was something about the seal-people, with the Morlock who was seated on the radio joining in – and then general enough – and then something going round the whole room – and then that fast, hard urgent talk between one of the Morlocks and my friend. It was still business, but they looked at *me*; it was awful to be looked at and yet I felt numb; I wished I were asleep; I wanted to cry because I could not understand a word they were saying. Then my friend suddenly shouted; she stepped back and threw both arms out, hands extended and fingers spread, shaking violently. She was shouting instead of talking, shouting desperately about something, pounding one fist into her palm, her face contorted, just as if it was not business. The other Morlock was breathing quickly and had gone pale with rage. He whispered something, something very venomous. He took from his black uniform, which could have hidden anything, a silver dime, and holding it up between thumb and forefinger, he said in perfectly clear English, while looking at me:

'In the name of the war against the Trans-Tempor –'

She had jumped him in an instant. I scrambled up; I saw her close his fist about the dime with her own; then it was all a blur on the floor until the two of them stood up again, as far as they could get from each other, because it was perfectly clear that they hated each other. She said very distinctly, '*I do insist.*' He shrugged. He said something short and sharp. She took out of her own darkness a knife – only a knife – and looked slowly about the room at each person in it. Nobody moved. She raised her eyebrows.

'*Tcha! grozny?*'

The seal-woman hissed on the floor, like steam coming out of a leaky radiator. She did not get up but lay on her back, eyes blinking, a woman encased in fat.

'You?' said my friend insultingly. 'You will stain the carpet.'

The seal-woman hissed again. Slowly my friend walked toward her, the others watching. She did not bend down, as I had expected, but dove down abruptly with a kind of sidewise roll, driving herself into the seal-woman's side. She had planted one heel on the stomach of the woman's diving suit; she seemed to be trying to tear it. The seal-woman caught my friend's knife-hand with one glove and was trying to turn it on my friend while she wrapped the other gloved arm around my friend's neck. She was trying to strangle her. My friend's free arm was extended on the rug; it seemed to me that she was either leaning on the floor or trying to pull herself free. Then again everything went into a sudden blur. There was a gasp, a loud, mechanical click; my friend vaulted up and backward, dropping her knife and clapping one hand to her left eye. The seal-woman was turning from side to side on the floor, a kind of shudder running from her feet to her head, an expressionless flexing of her body and face. Bubbles were forming in the goldfish-bowl helmet. The other seal-person did not move. As I watched, the water began falling in the seal-woman's helmet and then it was all air. I supposed she was dead. My friend, our visitor, was standing in the middle of the room, blood welling from under her hand; she was bent over with pain and her face was horribly distorted but not one person in that room moved to touch her.

'Life –' she gasped, 'for life. Yours,' and then she crashed to the rug. The seal-woman had slashed open her eye. Two of the Morlocks rushed to her then and picked up her and her knife; they were dragging her toward the mirror in the archway when she began muttering something.

'Damn your sketches!' shouted the Morlock she had fought with, completely losing control of himself. 'We are at war; Trans-Temp is at our heels; do you think we have time for dilettantism? You presume on being that woman's granddaughter! We are fighting for the freedom of fifty billions of people, not for your scribble!' and motioning to the others, who immediately dragged the body of the seal-woman through the mirror and began to follow it themselves, he turned to me.

'You!' he snapped. 'You will speak to nobody of this. Nobody!'

I put my arms around myself.

'Do not try to impress anyone with stories,' he added contemptuously, 'you are lucky to live,' and without another look he followed the last of the Morlocks through the mirror, which promptly disappeared. There was blood on the rug, a few inches from my feet. I bent down and put my fingertips in it, and then with no clear reason, I put my fingers to my face.

'— come back,' said my mother. I turned to face them, the wax manikins who had seen nothing.

'Who the devil drew the curtains!' shouted my father. 'I've told you' (to me) 'that I don't like tricks, young lady, and if it weren't for your mother's —'

'Oh, Ben, Ben! She's had a nosebleed!' cried my mother.

They told me later that I fainted.

I was in bed a few days, because of the nosebleed, but then they let me up. My parents said I probably had had anemia. They also said they had seen our visitor off at the railroad station that morning; and that she had boarded the train as they watched her; tall, frizzy-haired, freakish, dressed in black down to between the knees and ankles, legged like a stork and carrying all her belongings in a small valise. 'Gone to the circus,' said my mother. There was nothing in the room that had been hers, nothing in the attic, no reflection in the window at which she had stood, brilliantly lit against the black night, nothing in the kitchen and nothing at the Country Club but tennis courts overgrown with weeds. Joe never came back to our house. The week before school I looked through all my books, starting with *The Time Machine* and ending with *The Green Hat*; then I went downstairs and looked through every book in the house. There was nothing. I was invited to a party; my mother would not let me go. Cornflowers grew around the house. Betty came over once and was bored. One afternoon at the end of summer, with the wind blowing through the empty house from top to bottom and everybody away, nobody next door, my parents in the back yard, the people on the other side of us gone swimming, everybody silent or sleeping or off somewhere – except for someone down the block whom I could hear mowing the lawn – I decided to sort and try on all my shoes. I did this in front of a full-length mirror fastened to the inside of my closet door. I had been taking off and putting on various of my winter dresses, too, and I was putting one particular one away in a box on the floor of the closet when I chanced to look up at the inside of the closet door.

She was standing in the mirror. It was all black behind her, like velvet. She was wearing something black and silver, half-draped, half-nude, and there were lines on her face that made it look sectioned off, or like a cobweb; she had one eye. The dead eye radiated spinning white light, like a Catherine wheel. She said:

'Did you ever think to go back and take care of yourself when you are little? Give yourself advice?'

I couldn't say anything.

'I am not you,' she said, 'but I have had the same thought and now I have come back four hundred and fifty years. Only there is nothing to say. There is never anything to say. It is a pity, but natural, no doubt.'

'Oh please!' I whispered. 'Stay!' She put one foot up on the edge of the mirror as if it were the threshold of a door. The silver sandal she had worn at the Country Club dance almost came into my bedroom: thick-heeled, squat, flaking, as ugly as sin; new lines formed on her face and all over her bare skin, ornamenting her all over. Then she stepped back; she shook her head, amused; the dead eye waned, filled again, exploded in sparks and went out, showing the naked socket, ugly, shocking, and horrible.

'Tcha!' she said, 'my grandma thought she would bring something hard to a world that was soft and silly but nice, and now it's silly and not so nice and the hard has got too hard and the soft too soft and my great-grandma – it is she who founded the order – is dead. Not that it matters. Nothing ends, you see. Just keeps going on and on.'

'But you can't *see*!' I managed. She poked herself in the temple and the eye went on again.

'Bizarre,' she said. 'Interesting. Attractive. Stone blind is twice as good. I'll tell you my sketches.'

'But you don't – you can't –' I said.

'The first,' she said, lines crawling all over her, 'is an Eloi having the Go-Jollies, and that is a bald, fat man in a toga, a frilled bib, a sun-bonnet and shoes you would not believe, who has a crystal ball in his lap and from it wires plugged into his eyes and his nose and his ears and his tongue and his head, just like your lamps. That is an Eloi having the Go-Jollies.'

I began to cry.

'The second,' she went on, 'is a Morlock working; and that is myself holding a skull, like *Hamlet*, only if you look closely at the skull you will see it is the world, with funny things sticking out of the seas and the polar ice caps, and that it is full of people. Much too full. There are too many of the worlds, too.'

'If you'll *stop* –!' I cried.

'They are all pushing each other off,' she continued, 'and some are falling into the sea, which is a pity, no doubt, but quite natural, and if you will look closely at all these Eloi you will see that each one is holding his crystal ball, or running after an animated machine which runs faster than he, or watching another Eloi on a screen who is cleverer and looks fascinating, and you will see that under the fat the man or woman is screaming, screaming and dying.

'And my third sketch,' she said, 'which is a very little one, shows a goldfish bowl full of people in black. Behind that is a smaller goldfish bowl full of people in black, which is going after the first goldfish bowl, and behind the second is a third, which is going after the second, and so on, or perhaps they alternate; that would be more economical. Or perhaps I am only bitter because I lost my eye. It's a personal problem.'

I got to my feet. I was so close I could have touched her. She crossed her arms across her breast and looked down at me; she then said softly, 'My dear, I wished to take you with me; but that's impossible. I'm very sorry,' and looking for the first time both serious and tender, she disappeared behind a swarm of sparks.

I was looking at myself. I had recently made, passionately and in secret, the uniform of the Trans-Temporal Military Authority as I thought it ought to look: a black tunic over black sleeves and black tights. The tights were from a high school play I had been in the year before and the rest was cut out of the lining of an old winter coat. That was what I was wearing that afternoon. I had also fastened a silver curling-iron to my waist with a piece of cord. I put one foot up in the air, as if on the threshold of the mirror, and a girl in ragged black stared back at me. She turned and frantically searched the entire room, looking for sketches, for notes, for specks of silver paint, for anything at all. Then she sat down on my bed. She did not cry. She said to me, 'You look idiotic.' Someone was still mowing the lawn outside, probably my father. My mother would be clipping, patching, rooting up weeds; she never stopped. Someday I would join a circus, travel to the moon, write a book; after all, I had helped kill a man. I had been somebody. It was all nonsense. I took off the curling-iron and laid it on the bed. Then I undressed and got into my middy-blouse and skirt and I put the costume on the bed in a heap. As I walked toward the door of the room, I turned to take one last look at myself in the mirror and at my strange collection of old clothes. For a moment something else moved in the mirror, or I thought it did, something behind me or to one side, something menacing, something half-blind, something heaving slowly like a shadow, leaving perhaps behind it faint silver flakes like the shadow of a shadow or some carelessly dropped coins, something glittering, something somebody had left on the edge of vision, dropped by accident in the dust and cobwebs of an attic. I wished for it violently; I stood and clenched my fists; I almost cried; I wanted something to come out of the mirror and strike me dead. If I could not have a protector, I wanted a monster, a mutation, a horror, a murderous disease, anything! anything at all to accompany me downstairs so that I would not have to go down alone.

Nothing came. Nothing good, nothing bad. I heard the lawn-mower going on. I would have to face by myself my father's red face, his heart disease, his temper, his nasty insistencies. I would have to face my mother's sick smile, looking up from the flowerbed she was weeding, always on her knees somehow, saying before she was ever asked, 'Oh the poor woman. Oh the poor woman.'

And quite alone.

No more stories.

Murder, 1986

(1970)

P. D. JAMES

The girl lay naked on the bed with a knife through her heart. That was the one simple and inescapable fact. No, not simple. It was a fact horrible in its complications. Sergeant Dolby, fighting nausea, steadied his shaking thighs against the foot of the bed and forced his mind into coherence – arranging his thoughts in order, like a child piling brick on coloured brick and holding its breath against the inevitable tumble into chaos. He mustn't panic. He must take things slowly. There was a proper procedure laid down for this kind of crisis. There was a procedure laid down for everything.

Dead. That, at least, was certain. Despite the heat of the June morning the slim, girlish body was quite cold, the rigor mortis already well advanced in face and arms. What had they taught him in Detective School about the onset of rigor mortis, that inexorable if erratic stiffening of the muscles, the body's last protest against disintegration and decay? He couldn't remember. He had never been any good at the more academic studies. He had been lucky to be accepted for the Criminal Investigation Department; they had made that clear enough to him at the time. They had never ceased to make it clear. A lost car; a small breaking and entering; a purse snatch. Send Dolby. He had never rated anything more interesting or important than the petty crimes of inadequate men. If it was something no one else wanted to be bothered with, send Dolby. If it was something the CID would rather not be told about, send Dolby.

And that was exactly how this death would rate. He would have to report it, of course. But it wouldn't be popular news at Headquarters. They were overworked already, depleted in strength, inadequately equipped, forced even to employ him six years after his normal retirement age. No, they wouldn't exactly welcome this spot of trouble. And the reason, as if he didn't know it, was fixed there on the wall for him to read. The statutory notice was pasted precisely over the head of her bed.

He wondered why she had chosen that spot. There was no rule about where it had to be displayed. Why, he wondered, had she chosen to sleep under it as people once slept under a Crucifix? An affirmation? But the wording was the same as he would find on the notice in the downstairs hall, in the lift, on every corridor wall, in every room in the Colony. The Act to which it referred was already two years old:

PRESERVATION OF THE RACE ACT – 1984
Control of Interplanetary Disease
Infection Carriers

All registered carriers of the Disease, whether or not they are yet manifesting symptoms, are required under Section 2 of the above Act to conform to the following regulations . . .

He didn't need to read further. He knew the regulations by heart – the rules by which the Ipdics lived, if you could call it living. The desperate defence of the few healthy against the menace of the many condemned. The small injustices which might prevent the greatest injustice of all, the extinction of man. The stigmata of the Diseased: the registered number tattooed on the left forearm; the regulation Ipdic suit of yellow cotton in summer, blue serge in winter; the compulsory sterilization, since an Ipdic bred only monsters; the rule prohibiting marriage or any close contact with a Normal; the few manual jobs they were permitted to do; the registered Colonies where they were allowed to live.

He knew what they would say at Headquarters. If Dolby had to discover a murder, it would have to be of an Ipdic. And trust him to be fool enough to report it.

But there was no hurry. He could wait until he was calmer, until he could face with confidence whomever they chose to send. And there were things they would expect him to have noticed. He had better make an examination of the scene before he reported. Then, even if they came at once, he would have something sensible to say.

He forced himself to look again at the body. She was lying on her back, eyes closed as if asleep, light brown hair streaming over the pillow. Her arms were crossed over her chest as if in a last innocent gesture of modesty. Below the left breast the handle of a knife stuck out like an obscene horn.

He bent low to examine it. An ordinary handle, probably an ordinary knife. A short-bladed kitchen knife of the kind used to peel vegetables. Her right palm was curved around it, but not touching it, as if about to pluck it out. On her left forearm the registered Ipdic number glowed almost luminous against the delicate skin.

She was neatly covered by a single sheet pulled smooth and taut so that it looked as if the body had been ritually prepared for examination – an intensification of the horror. He did not believe that this childish hand could have driven in the blade with such precision or that, in her last spasms, she had drawn the sheet so tidily over her nakedness. The linen was only a shade whiter than her skin. There had been two months now of almost continuous sunshine. But this body had been muffled in the high-necked tunic and baggy trousers of an Ipdic suit. Only her face had been open to the sun. It was a delicate nut-brown and there was a faint spatter of freckles across the forehead.

He walked slowly around the room. It was sparsely furnished but pleasant enough. The world had no shortage of living space, even for Ipdics. They could live in comfort, even in some opulence, until the electricity, the television, the domestic computer, the micro-oven broke down. Then these things remained broken. The precious skills of electricians and engineers were not wasted on Ipdics. And it was extraordinary how quickly squalour could replace luxury.

A breakdown of electricity in a building like this could mean no hot food, no light, no heating. He had known Ipdics who had frozen or starved to death in apartments which, back in 1980, only six years ago, must have cost a fortune to rent. Somehow the will to survive died quickly in them. It was easier to wrap themselves in blankets and reach for that small white capsule so thoughtfully provided by the Government, the simple painless way out which the whole healthy community was willing for them to take.

But this girl, this female Ipdic PXN 07926431, wasn't living in squalor. The apartment was clean and almost obsessively neat.

The micro-oven was out of order, but there was an old-fashioned electric cooker in the kitchen and when he turned it on the hot plate glowed red. There were even a few personal possessions – a little clutch of seashells carefully arranged on the window ledge, a Staffordshire porcelain figurine of a shepherdess, a child's tea service on a papier-mâché tray.

Her yellow Ipdic suit was neatly folded over the back of a chair. He took it up and saw that she had altered it to fit her. The darts under the breasts had been taken in, the side seams carefully shaped. The hand stitching was neat and regular, an affirmation of individuality, or self-respect. A proud girl. A girl undemoralized by hopelessness. He turned the harsh cotton over and over in his hands and felt the tears stinging the back of his eyes.

He knew that this strange and half-remembered sweetness was pity. He let himself feel it, willing himself not to shrink from the pain. Just so, in his boyhood, he had tentatively placed his full weight on an injured leg after football, relishing the pain in the knowledge that he could bear it, that he was still essentially whole.

But he must waste no more time. Turning on his pocket radio he made his report.

'Sergeant Dolby here. I'm speaking from Ipdic Colony 865. Female Ipdic PXN 07926431 found dead. Room 18. Looks like murder.'

It was received as he had expected.

'Oh, God! Are you sure? All right. Hang around. Someone will be over.'

While he waited he gave his attention to the flowers. They had struck his senses as soon as he opened the door of the room, but the first sight of the dead girl had driven them from his mind. Now he let their gentle presence drift back into his consciousness. She had died amid such beauty.

The apartment was a bower of wild flowers, their delicate sweetness permeating the warm air so that every breath was an intimation of childhood summers, an evocation of the old innocent days. Wild flowers were his hobby. The slow brain corrected itself, patiently, mechanically: wild flowers had been his hobby. But that was before the Sickness, when the words 'flower' and 'beauty' seemed to have meaning. He hadn't looked at a flower with any joy since 1980.

1980. The year of the Disease. The year with the hottest summer for twenty-one years. That summer when the sheer weight of people had pressed against the concrete bastions of the city like an intolerable force, had thronged its burning pavements, had almost brought its transport system to a stop, had sprawled in checkered ranks across its parks until the sweet grass was pressed into pale straw.

1980. The year when there were too many people. Too many happy, busy, healthy human beings. The year when his wife had been alive; when his daughter Tessa had been alive. The year when brave men, travelling far beyond the moon, had brought back to earth the Sickness – the Sickness which had decimated mankind on every continent of the globe. The Sickness which had robbed him, Arthur Dolby, of his wife and daughter.

Tessa. She had been only fourteen that spring. It was a wonderful age for a daughter, the sweetest daughter in the world. And Tessa had been intelligent as well as sweet. Both women in his life, his wife and daughter, had been cleverer than Dolby. He had known it, but it hadn't worried him or made him feel inadequate. They had loved him so unreservedly, had relied so much on his manhood, been so satisfied with what little he could provide. They had seen in him qualities he could never discern in himself, virtues which he knew he no longer possessed. His flame of life was meagre; it had needed their warm breaths to keep it burning bright. He wondered what they would think of him now. Arthur Dolby in 1986, looking once more at wild flowers.

He moved among them as if in a dream, like a man recognizing with wonder a treasure given up for lost. There had been no attempt at formal arrangement. She had obviously made use of any suitable container in the apartment and had bunched the plants together naturally and simply, each with its own kind. He could still identify them. There were brown earthenware jars of Herb Robert, the rose-pink flowers set delicately on their reddish stems. There were cracked tea-cups holding bunches of red clover, meadow buttercups, and long-stemmed daisies; jam jars of white campion and cuckoo flowers; egg cups of birdsfoot trefoil – 'eggs and bacon', Tessa used to call it – and even smaller jars of rue-leaved saxifrage and the soft pink spurs of haresfoot. But, above

all, there were the tall vases of cow-parsley, huge bunches of
strong hollow-grooved stems supporting their umbels of white
flowers, delicate as bridal lace, yet pungent and strong, shedding a
white dust on the table, bed and floor.

And then, in the last jar of all, the only one which held a posy
of mixed flowers, he saw the Lady Orchid. It took his breath
away. There it stood, alien and exotic, lifting its sumptuous head
proudly among the common flowers of the roadside, the white
clover, campion, and sweet wild roses. The Lady Orchid. *Orchis
purpurea*.

He stood very still and gazed at it. The decorative spike rose
from its shining foliage, elegant and distinctive, seeming to know
its rarity. The divisions of the helmet were wine-red, delicately
veined and spotted with purple, their sombre tint setting off the
clear white beauty of the lip. The Lady Orchid. Dolby knew of
only one spot, the fringe of a wood in old Kent County in the
South-east Province, where this flower grew wild. The Sickness
had changed the whole of human life. But he doubted if it had
changed that.

It was then that he heard the roar of the helicopter. He went to
the window. The red machine, like a huge angry insect, was just
bouncing down onto the roof landing pad. He watched, puzzled.
Why should they send a chopper? Then he understood. The tall
figure in the all-white uniform with its gleaming braid swung
himself down from the cockpit and was lost to view behind the
parapet of the roof. But Dolby recognized at once that helmet of
black hair, the confident poise of the head. C. J. Kalvert. The
Commissioner of the Home Security Force in person.

He told himself that it couldn't be true – that Kalvert wouldn't
concern himself with the death of an Ipdic, that he must have
some other business in the Colony. But what business? Dolby
waited in fear, his hands clenched so that the nails pierced his
palms, waited in an agony of hope that it might not be true. But it
was true. A minute later he heard the strong footsteps advancing
along the corridor. The door opened. The Commissioner had
arrived.

He nodded an acknowledgement to Dolby and, without speaking, went over to the bed. For a moment he stood in silence,

looking down at the girl. Then he said, 'How did you get in, Sergeant?'

The accent was on the third word.

'The door was unlocked, sir.'

'Naturally. Ipdics are forbidden to lock their doors. I was asking what you were doing here.'

'I was making a search, sir.'

That at least was true. He had been making a private search.

'And you discovered that one more female Ipdic had taken the sensible way out of her troubles. Why didn't you call the Sanitary Squad? It's unwise to leave a body longer than necessary in this weather. Haven't we all had enough of the stench of decay?'

'I think she was murdered, sir.'

'Do you indeed, Sergeant. And why?'

Dolby moistened his dry lips and made his cramped fingers relax. He mustn't let himself be intimidated, mustn't permit himself to get flustered. The important thing was to stick to the facts and present them cogently.

'It's the knife, sir. If she were going to stab herself, I think she would have fallen on the blade, letting her weight drive it in. Then the body would have been found face downwards. That way, the blade would have done all the work. I don't think she would have had the strength or the skill to pierce her heart lying in that position. It looks almost surgical. It's too neat. The man who drove that knife in knew what he was doing. And then there's the sheet. She couldn't have placed it over herself so neatly.'

'A valid point, Sergeant. But the fact that someone considerately tidied her up after death doesn't necessarily mean that he killed her. Anything else?'

He was walking restlessly about the room as he talked, touching nothing, his hands clasped behind his back. Dolby wished that he would stand still. He said, 'But why use a knife at all, sir? She must have been issued her euthanasia capsule.'

'Not a very dramatic way to go, Dolby. The commonest door for an Ipdic to let life out. She may have exercised a feminine preference for a more individualistic death. Look around this room, Sergeant. Does she strike you as having been an ordinary girl?'

No, she hadn't struck Dolby as ordinary. But this was ground he dare not tread. He said doggedly, 'And why should she be naked, sir? Why take all her clothes off to kill herself?'

'Why, indeed. That shocks you, does it, Dolby? It implies an unpleasant touch of exhibitionism. It offends your modesty. But perhaps she was an exhibitionist. The flowers would suggest it. She made her room into a bower of fragrance and beauty. Then, naked, as unencumbered as the flowers, she stretched herself out like a sacrifice, and drove a knife through her heart. Can you, Sergeant, with your limited imagination, understand that a woman might wish to die like that?'

Kalvert swung round and strode over to him. The fierce black eyes burned into Dolby's. The Sergeant felt frightened, at a loss. The conversation was bizarre. He felt they were playing some private game, but that only one of them knew the rules.

What did Kalvert want of him? In a normal world, in the world before the Sickness when the old police force was at full strength, the Commissioner wouldn't even have known that Dolby existed. Yet here they both were, engaged, it seemed, in some private animus, sparring over the body of an unimportant dead Ipdic.

It was very hot in the room now and the scent of the flowers had been growing stronger. Dolby could feel the beads of sweat on his brow. Whatever happened he must hold on to the facts. He said, 'The flowers needn't be funeral flowers. Perhaps they were for a celebration.'

'That would suggest the presence of more than one person. Even Ipdics don't celebrate alone. Have you found any evidence that someone was with her when she died?'

He wanted to reply, 'Only the knife in her breast.' But he was silent. Kalvert was pacing the room again. Suddenly he stopped and glanced at his watch. Then, without speaking, he turned on the television. Dolby remembered. Of course. The Leader was due to speak after the midday news. It was already 12.32. He would be almost finished.

The screen flickered and the too familiar face appeared. The Leader looked very tired. Even the make-up artist hadn't been able to disguise the heavy shadows under the eyes or the hollows beneath the cheekbones. With that beard and the melancholy, pain-filled face, he looked like an ascetic prophet. But he always had. His face hadn't changed much since the days of his student protest. People said that, even then, he had only really been interested in personal power. Well, he was still under thirty, but he had it now. All the power he could possibly want. The speech was nearly over.

'And so we must find our own solution. We have a tradition in this country of humanity and justice. But how far can we let tradition hamper us in the great task of preserving our race? We know what is happening in other countries, the organized and ceremonial mass suicides of thousands of Ipdics at a time, the humane Disposal Squads, the compulsory matings between computer-selected Normals. Some compulsory measures against the Ipdics we must now take. As far as possible we have relied on gentle and voluntary methods. But can we afford to fall behind while other less scrupulous nations are breeding faster and more selectively, disposing of their Ipdics, re-establishing their techno-logy, looking with covetous eyes at the great denuded spaces of the world? One day they will be repopulated. It is our duty to take part in this great process. The world needs our race. The time has come for every one of us, particularly our Ipdics, to ask ourselves with every breath we draw: have I the right to be alive?'

Kalvert turned off the set.

'I think we can forego the pleasure of seeing once again Mrs Sartori nursing her fifth healthy daughter. Odd to think that the most valuable human being in the world is a healthy fecund female. But you got the message I hope, Sergeant. This Ipdic had the wisdom to take her own way out while she still had a choice. And if somebody helped her, who are we to quibble?'

'It was still murder, sir. I know that killing an Ipdic isn't a capital crime. But the Law hasn't been altered yet. It's still a felony to kill any human being.'

'Ah, yes. A felony. And you, of course, are dedicated to the detection and punishment of felonies. The first duty of a policeman is to prevent crime; the second is to detect and punish the criminal. You learned all that when you were in Detective School, didn't you? Learned it all by heart. I remember reading the first report on you, Dolby. It was almost identical with the last.

"Lacking in initiative. Deficient in imagination. Tends to make errors of judgement. Should make a reliable subordinate. Lacks self-confidence." But it did admit that, when you manage to get an idea into your head, it sticks there. And you have an idea in your head. Murder. And murder is a felony. Well, what do you propose to do about it?'

'In cases of murder the body is first examined by the forensic pathologist.'

'Not this body, Dolby. Do you know how many pathologists this country now has? We have other uses for them than to cut up dead Ipdics. She was a young female. She was not pregnant. She was stabbed through the heart. What more do we need to know?'

'Whether or not a man was with her before she died.'

'I think you can take it there was. Male Ipdics are not yet being sterilized. So we add another fact. She probably had a lover. What else do you want to know?'

'Whether or not there are prints on the knife, sir, and, if so, whose they are.'

Kalvert laughed aloud. 'We were short of forensic scientists before the Sickness. How many do you suppose we have now? There was another case of capital murder reported this morning. An Ipdic has killed his former wife because she obeyed the Law and kept away from him. We can't afford to lose a single healthy woman, can we, Dolby? There's the rumour of armed bands of Ipdics roaming the South-east Province. There's the case of the atomic scientist with the back of his skull smashed in. A scientist, Dolby! Now, do you really want to bother the lab with this petty trouble?'

Dolby said obstinately, 'I know that someone was with her when she picked the flowers. That must have been yesterday — they're still fresh even in this heat, and wild flowers fade quickly. I think he probably came back here with her and was with her when she died.'

'Then find him, Sergeant, if you must. But don't ask for help I can't give.'

He walked over to the door without another glance at the room or at the dead girl, as if neither of them held any further interest for him. Then he turned: 'You aren't on the official list of men encouraged to breed daughters in the interest of the race, are you, Sergeant?'

Dolby wanted to reply that he once had a daughter. She was dead and he wanted no other.

'No, sir. They thought I was too old. And then there was the adverse psychologist's report.'

'A pity. One would have thought that the brave new world could have made room for just one or two people who were unintelligent, lacking in imagination, unambitious, inclined to errors of judgement. People will persist in going their own obstinate way. Goodbye, Dolby. Report to me personally on this case, will you? I shall be interested to hear how you progress. Who knows, you may reveal unsuspected talents.'

He was gone. Dolby waited for a minute as if to cleanse his mind of that disturbing presence. As the confident footsteps died away, even the room seemed to settle itself into peace. Then Dolby began the few tasks which still remained.

There weren't many. First, he took the dead girl's fingerprints. He worked with infinite care, murmuring to her as he gently pressed the pad against each fingertip, like a doctor reassuring a child. It would be pointless, he thought, to compare them with the prints on any of the ordinary objects in the room. That would prove nothing except that another person had been there. The only prints of importance would be those on the knife. But there were no prints on the knife – only an amorphous smudge of whorls and composites as if someone had attempted to fold her hand around the shaft but had lacked the courage to press the fingers firm.

But the best clue was still there – the Lady Orchid, splendid in its purity and beauty, the flower which told him where she had spent the previous day, the flower which might lead him to the man who had been with her. And there was another clue, something he had noticed when he had first examined the body closely. He had said nothing to Kalvert. Perhaps Kalvert hadn't noticed it or hadn't recognized its significance. Perhaps he had been cleverer than Kalvert. He told himself that he wasn't really as stupid as people sometimes thought. It was just that his mind was so easily flustered into incoherence when stronger men bullied or taunted him. Only his wife and daughter had really understood that, had given him the confidence to fight it.

It was time to get started. They might deny him the services of the pathologist and the laboratory, but they still permitted him the use of his car. It would be little more than an hour's drive.

But, before leaving, he bent once more over the body. The Disposal Squad would soon be here for it. He would never see it again. So he studied the clue for the last time – the faint, almost imperceptible circle of paler skin round the third finger of her left hand. The finger that could have worn a ring through the whole of a hot summer day . . .

He drove through the wide streets and sun-filled squares, through the deserted suburbs, until the tentacles of the city fell away and he was in open country. The roads were pitted and unmended, the hedges high and unkempt, the fields a turbulent sea of vegetation threatening to engulf the unpeopled farmlands. But the sun was pleasant on his face. He could almost persuade himself that this was one of the old happy jaunts into the familiar and well-loved countryside of Old Kent.

He had crossed the boundary into the South-east Province and was already looking for the remembered landmarks of hillside and church spire when it happened. There was an explosion, a crack like a pistol shot, and the windshield shattered in his face. He felt splinters of glass stinging his cheeks. Instinctively he guarded his face with his arms. The car swerved out of control and lurched onto the grass verge. He felt for the ignition key and turned off the engine. Then he tentatively opened his eyes. They were uninjured. And it was then he saw the Ipdics.

They came out of the opposite ditch and moved toward him, with stones still in their hands. There were half a dozen of them. One, the tallest, seemed to be their leader. The others shuffled at his heels, lumpy figures in their ill-fitting yellow suits, their feet brown and bare, their hair matted like animals', their greedy eyes fixed on the car. They stood still, looking at him. And then the leader drew his right hand from behind his back, and Dolby saw that it held a gun.

His heart missed a beat. So it was true! Somehow the Ipdics were getting hold of weapons. He got out of the car, trying to recall the exact instructions of such an emergency. Never show fear. Keep calm. Exert authority. Remember that they are inferior, unorganized, easily cowed. Never drop your eyes. But his voice, even to him, sounded feeble, pitched unnaturally high.

'The possession of a weapon by an Ipdic is a capital crime. The punishment is death. Give me that gun.'

The voice that replied was quiet, authoritative, the kind of voice one used to call educated.

'No. First you give me the keys to the car. Then I give you something in return. A cartridge in your belly!'

His followers cackled their appreciation. It was one of the most horrible sounds in the world – the laughter of an Ipdic.

The Ipdic pointed the gun at Dolby, moving it slowly from side to side as if selecting his precise target. He was enjoying his power, drunk with elation and triumph. But he waited a second too long. Suddenly his arm jerked upward, the gun leaped from his grasp, and he gave one high desolate scream, falling into the dust of the road. He was in the first spasm of an Ipdic fit. His body writhed and twisted, arched and contracted, until the bones could be heard snapping.

Dolby looked on impassively. There was nothing he could do. He had seen it thousands of times before. It had happened to his wife, to Tessa, to all those who had died of the disease. It happened in the end to every Ipdic. It would have happened to that girl on the bed, at peace now with a knife in her heart.

The attack would leave this Ipdic broken and exhausted. If he survived, he would be a mindless idiot, probably for months. And then the fits would come more frequently. It was this feature of the Disease which made the Ipdics so impossible to train or employ, even for the simplest of jobs.

Dolby walked up to the writhing figure and kicked away the gun, then picked it up. It was a revolver, a Smith and Wesson .38, old but in good condition. He saw that it was loaded. After a second's thought he slipped it into the pocket of his jacket.

The remaining Ipdics had disappeared, scrambling back into the hedges with cries of anguish and fear. The whole incident was over so quickly that it already seemed like a dream. Only the tortured figure in the dust and the cold metal in his pocket were witnesses to its reality. He should report it at once, of course. The suppression of armed Ipdics was the first duty of the Home Security Force.

He backed the car onto the road. Then, on an impulse, he got out again and went over to the Ipdic. He bent to drag the writhing figure off the road and into the shade of the hedge. But it was no good. Revolted, he drew back. He couldn't bear to touch him. Perhaps the Ipdic's friends would creep back later to carry him away and tend to him. Perhaps. But he, Dolby, had his own problem. He had a murder to solve.

Fifteen minutes later he drove slowly through the village. The main street was deserted but he could glimpse, through the open cottage doors, the garish yellow of an Ipdic suit moving in the dim interior and he could see other yellow-clad figures bending at work in the gardens and fields. None of them looked up as he passed. He guessed that this was one of the settlements which had grown up in the country, where groups of Ipdics attempted to support themselves and each other, growing their own food, nursing their sick, burying their dead. Since they made no demands on the Normals they were usually left in peace. But it couldn't last long. There was no real hope for them.

As more and more of them were overtaken by the last inevitable symptoms, the burden on those left grew intolerable. Soon they too would be helpless and mad. Then the Security Force, the Health Authorities, and the Sanitary Squads would move in, and another colony of the dispossessed would be cleaned up. And it was a question of cleaning up. Dolby had taken part in one such operation. He knew what the final horror would be. But now in the heat of this sun-scented afternoon, he might be driving through the village as he had known it in the days before the Sickness, prosperous, peaceful, sleepy, with the men still busy on the farms.

He left the car at the churchyard gate and slipping the strap of his murder bag over his shoulder, walked up the dappled avenue of elms to the south entrance. The heavy oak door with its carved panels, its massive hinges of hammered iron creaked open at his touch. He stepped into the cool dimness and smelled again the familiar scent of flowers, musty hymn books, and wood polish, saw once again the medieval pillars soaring high to the hammer beams of the roof, and, straining his eyes through the dimness, he glimpsed the carving on the rood screen and the far gleam of the sanctuary lamp.

The church was full of wild flowers. They were the same flowers as those in the dead girl's apartment but here their frail delicacy was almost lost against the massive pillars and the richly carved oak. But the huge vases of cow-parsley set on each side of the chancel steps made a brave show, floating like twin clouds of whiteness in the dim air. It was a church decked for a bride.

He saw a female Ipdic polishing the brass lectern. He made his way up the aisle toward her and she beamed a gentle welcome as if his appearance were the most ordinary event in the world. Her baggy Ipdic suit was stained with polish and she wore a pair of old sandals, the soles peeling away from the uppers. Her greying hair was drawn back into a loose bun from which wisps of hair had escaped to frame the anxious, sun-stained face.

She reminded him of someone. He let his mind probe once again, painfully, into the past. Then he remembered. Of course. Miss Caroline Martin, his Sunday School superintendent. It wasn't she, of course. Miss Martin would have been over seventy at the time of the Sickness. No one as old as that had survived, except those few Tasmanian aborigines who so interested the scientists. Miss Martin, standing beside the old piano as her younger sister thumped out the opening hymn and beating time with her gloved hand as if hearing some private and quite different music. Afterward, the students had gone to their different classes and had sat in a circle around their teachers. Miss Martin had taught the older children, himself among them. Some of the boys had been unruly, but never Arthur Dolby. Even in those days he had been obedient, law-abiding. The good boy. Not particularly bright, but well-behaved. Good, dull, ineffectual. Teacher's pet.

And when she spoke it was with a voice like Miss Martin's.

'Can I help you? If you've come for Evensong services. I'm afraid it isn't until five-thirty today. If you're looking for Father Reeves, he's at the Rectory. But perhaps you're just a visitor. It's a lovely church, isn't it? Have you seen our sixteenth-century reredos?'

'I hoped I would be in time for the wedding.'

She gave a little girlish cry of laughter.

'Dear me, you are late! I'm afraid that was yesterday! But I thought no one was supposed to know about it. Father Reeves said that it was to be quite secret really. But I'm afraid I was very naughty. I did so want to see the bride. After all, we haven't had a wedding here since –'

'Since the Act?'

She corrected him gently, like Miss Martin rebuking the good boy of the class.

'Since 1980. So yesterday was quite an occasion for us. And I did want to see what the bride looked like in Emma's veil.'

'In what?'

'A bride has to have a veil, you know.' She spoke with gentle reproof, taking pity on his masculine ignorance. 'Emma was my niece. I lost her and her parents in 1981. Emma was the last bride to be married here. That was on April 28, 1980. I've always kept her veil and headdress. She was such a lovely bride.'

Dolby asked with sudden harshness the irrelevant but necessary question.

'What happened to her bridegroom?'

'Oh, John was one of the lucky ones. I believe he has married again and has three daughters. Just one daughter more and they'll be allowed to have a son. We don't see him, of course. It wasn't to be expected. After all, it is the Law.'

How despicable it was, this need to be reassured that there were other traitors.

'Yes,' he said. 'It is the Law.'

She began polishing the already burnished lectern, chatting to him as she worked.

'But I've kept Emma's veil and headdress. So I thought I'd just place them on a chair beside the font so that this new bride would see them when she came into church. Just in case she wanted to borrow them, you know. And she did. I was so glad. The bride-groom placed the veil over her head and fixed the headdress for her himself, and she walked up the aisle looking so beautiful.'

'Yes,' said Dolby. 'She would have looked very beautiful.'

'I watched them from behind this pillar. Neither of them noticed me. But it was right for me to be here. There ought to be someone in the church. It says in the prayer book, "In the sight of God and of this congregation." She had a small bouquet of wild flowers, just a simple mixed bunch but very charming. I think they must have picked it together.'

'She carried a Lady Orchid,' said Dolby. 'A Lady Orchid picked by her bridegroom and surrounded by daisies, clover, white campion, and wild roses.'

'How clever of you to guess! Are you a friend, perhaps?'

'No,' said Dolby. 'Not a friend. Can you describe the bridegroom?'

'I thought that you must know him. Very tall, very dark. He wore a plain white suit. Oh, they were such a handsome couple! I wished Father Reeves could have seen them.'

'I thought he married them.'

'So he did. But Father Reeves, poor man, is blind.'

So that was why he risked it, thought Dolby. But what a risk!

'Which prayer book did he use?'

She gazed at him, the milky eyes perplexed. 'Father Reeves?'

'No, the bridegroom. He did handle a prayer book, I suppose?'

'Oh, yes. I put one out for each of them. Father Reeves asked me to get things ready. It was I who decorated the church. Poor dears, it wasn't as if they could have the usual printed service sheets. Emma's were so pretty, her initials intertwined with the bridegroom's. But yesterday they had to use ordinary prayer books. I chose them specially from the pews and put them on the two prayer stools. I found a very pretty white one for the bride and this splendid old book with the brass clasp for the bridegroom. It looked masculine, I thought.'

It lay on the book ledge of the front pew. She made a move to pick it up, but he shot out his hand. Then he dropped his handkerchief over the book and lifted it by the sharp edges of the binding. Brass and leather. Good for a print. And this man's palm would be moist, clammy, perhaps, with perspiration and fear. A hot day; an illegal ceremony; his mind on murder. To love and to cherish until death us do part. Yes, this bridegroom would have been nervous. But Dolby had one more question.

'How did they get here? Do you know?'

'They came by foot. At least, they walked up to the church

together. I think they had walked quite a long way. They were quite hot and dusty when they arrived. But I know how they really came.'

She nodded her unkempt head and gave a little conspiratorial nod.

'I've got very good ears, you know. They came by helicopter. I heard it.'

A helicopter. He knew almost without thinking exactly who was permitted the use of a helicopter. Members of the Central Committee of Government; high ranking scientists and technicians; doctors; the Commissioner of the Home Security Force, and his Deputy. That was all.

He took the prayer book out into the sun and sat on one of the flat-topped gravestones. He set up the prayer book on its end, then unzipped his murder bag. His hands shook so that he could hardly manage the brush and some of the grey powder was spilt and blew away in the breeze. He willed himself to keep calm, to take his time. Carefully, like a child with a new toy, he dusted the book and clasp with powder, gently blowing off the surplus with a small rubber nozzle. It was an old procedure, first practised when he was a young Detective Constable. But it still worked. It always would. The arches, whorls and composites came clearly into view.

He was right. It was a beautiful print. The man had made no effort to wipe it clean. Why should he? How could he imagine that this particular book would ever be identified among the many scattered around the church? How could he suspect that he would ever be traced to this despised and unregarded place? Dolby took out his camera and photographed the print. There must be continuity of evidence. He must leave no room for doubt. Then he classified its characteristics, ready for checking.

There was a little delay at the National Identification Computer Centre when he phoned, and he had to wait his turn. When it came he gave his name, rank, secret code, and the classification of the print. There was a moment's silence. Then a surprised voice asked, 'Is that you, Dolby? Will you confirm your code.'

He did so. Another silence.

'Okay. But what on earth are you up to? Are you sure of your print classification?'

'Yes. I want the identification for elimination purposes.'

'Then you can eliminate, all right. That's the Commissioner. Kalvert, C. J. Hard luck, Dolby! Better start again.'

He switched off the receiver and sat in silence. He had known it, of course. But for how long? Perhaps from the beginning. Kalvert. Kalvert, who had an excuse for visiting an Ipdic Colony. Kalvert, who had the use of a helicopter. Kalvert, who had known without asking that the television set in her room was in working order. Kalvert, who had been too sure of himself to take the most elementary precautions against discovery, because he knew that it didn't matter, because he knew no one would dare touch him. Kalvert, one of the four most powerful men in the country. And it was he, the despised Sergeant Dolby, who had solved the case.

He heard the angry purr of the approaching helicopter without surprise. He had reported the armed attack by the Ipdics. It was certain that Headquarters would have immediately summoned a Squad from the nearest station to hunt them down. But Kalvert would know about the message. He had no doubt that the Commissioner was keeping a watch on him. He would know which way Dolby was heading, would realize that he was danger-ously close to the truth. The armed Squad would be here in time. But Kalvert would arrive first.

He waited for five minutes, still sitting quietly on the gravestone. The air was sweet with the smell of grasses and vibrating with the high-treble midsummer chant of blackbird and thrush. He shut his eyes for a moment, breathing in the beauty, taking courage from its peace. Then he got to his feet and stood at the head of the avenue of elms to wait for Kalvert.

The gold braid on the all-white uniform gleamed in the sun. The tall figure, arrogant with confidence and power, walked unhesitatingly toward him, unsmiling, making no sign. When they were three feet apart, Kalvert stopped. They stood confronting each other. It was Dolby who spoke first. His voice was little more than a whisper.

'You killed her.'

He could not meet Kalvert's eyes. But he heard his reply.

'Yes, I killed her. Shall I tell you about it, Sergeant? You seem to have shown some initiative. You deserve to know part of the truth. I was her friend. That is prohibited by Regulation. She became my mistress. That is against the Law. We decided to get married. That is a serious crime. I killed her. That, as you earlier explained, is a felony. And what are you going to do about it, Sergeant?'

Dolby couldn't speak. Suddenly he took out the revolver. It seemed ridiculous to point it at Kalvert. He wasn't even sure that he would be able to fire it. But he held it close to his side and the curved stock fitted comfortably to his palm, giving him courage. He made himself meet Kalvert's eyes, and heard the Commissioner laugh.

'To kill a Normal is also against the Law. But it's something more. Capital murder, Dolby. Is that what you have in mind?'

Dolby spoke out of cracked lips, 'But why? *Why*?'

'I don't have to explain to you. But I'll try. Have you the imagination to understand that we might have loved each other, that I might have married her because it seemed a small risk for me and would give her pleasure, that I might have promised to kill her when her last symptoms began? Can you, Sergeant Dolby, enter into the mind of a girl like that? She was an Ipdic. And she was more alive in her condemned cell than you have ever been in your life. Female Ipdic PXN 07926431 found dead. Looks like murder. Remember how you reported it, Dolby? A felony. Something to be investigated. Against the Law. That's all it meant to you, isn't it?'

He had taken out his own revolver now. He held it easily, like a man casually dangling a familiar toy. He stood there, magnificent in the sunshine, the breeze lifting his black hair. He said quietly, 'Do you think I'd let any Law on earth keep me from the woman I loved?'

Dolby wanted to cry out that it hadn't been like that at all. That Kalvert didn't understand. That he, Dolby, had cared about the girl. But the contempt in those cold black eyes kept him silent. There was nothing they could say to each other. Nothing. And Kalvert would kill him.

The Squad would be here soon. Kalvert couldn't let him live to tell his story. He gazed with fascinated horror at the revolver held so easily, so confidently, in the Commissioner's hand. And he tightened the grip on his own, feeling with a shaking finger for the trigger.

The armoured car roared up to the churchyard gate. The Squad were here. Kalvert lifted his revolver to replace it in the holster. Dolby, misunderstanding the gesture, whipped up his own gun and, closing his eyes, fired until the last cartridge was spent. Numbed by misery and panic, he didn't hear the shots or the thud of Kalvert's fall. The first sound to pierce his consciousness was a wild screaming and beating of wings as the terrified birds flew high. Then he was aware of an unnatural silence, and of an acrid smell tainting the summer air.

His right hand ached. It felt empty, slippery with sweat. He saw that he had dropped the gun. There was a long mournful cry of distress. It came from behind him. He turned and glimpsed the yellow-clad figure of the female Ipdic, hand to her mouth, watching him from the shadow of the church. Then she faded back into the dimness.

He dropped on his knees beside Kalvert. The torn arteries were pumping their blood onto the white tunic. The crimson stain burst open like a flower. Dolby took off his jacket with shaking hands and thrust it under Kalvert's head. He wanted to say that he was sorry, to cry out like a child that he hadn't really meant it, that it was all a mistake.

Kalvert looked at him. Was there really pity in those dulling eyes? He was trying to speak. 'Poor Dolby! Your final error of judgement.'

The last word was hiccupped in a gush of blood. Kalvert turned his head away from Dolby and drew up his knees as if easing himself into sleep. And Dolby knew that it was too late to explain now, that there was no one there to hear him.

He stood up. The Squad were very close now, three of them, walking abreast, guns at hip, moving inexorably forward in the pool of their own shadows. And so he waited, all fear past, with Kalvert's body at his feet. And he thought for the first time of his daughter. Tessa, whom he had allowed to hide from him because that was the Law. Tessa, whom he had deserted and betrayed. Tessa, whom he had sought at last, but had found too late. Tessa, who had led him unwittingly to her lover and murderer. Tessa, who would never have picked that Lady Orchid. Hadn't he taught her when she was a child that if you picked a wild orchid it can never bloom again?

The Milk of Paradise

(1972)

'JAMES TIPTREE, Jr'

[Alice Sheldon]

She was flowing hot and naked and she straddled his belly in the cuddle-cube and fed him her hard little tits. And he convulsed up and under her and then was headlong on the waster, vomiting.

'Timor! Timor!'

It was not his name.

'Sorry.' He retched up more U4. 'I warned you, Seoul.'

She sat up where he'd thrown her, purely astonished.

'You mean you don't *want* me? But everyone in this station–'

'I'm sorry. I did warn you.' He began to struggle into his gray singlet, long-sleeved, puffed at elbows. 'It's no good. It's never any good.'

'But you're Human. Like me. Aren't you glad you were rescued?'

'Human.' He spat in the waster. 'That's all you can think of.'

She gasped. He was pulling on long gray tights, pleated at knee and ankle.

'What did they *do* to you, Timor?' She rocked on her bottom. 'How did they love you and I can't?' she wailed.

'It's what they were, Seoul,' he said patiently, arranging his dove-gray cuffs.

'Did they look like that?' All gray and shiny? Is that why you wear–'

He turned on her, chunky, gray-covered body, hot eyes in a still face.

'I wear these to conceal my hideous Human body,' he said tightly. 'So I won't make myself sick. Compared to them I was a – a Crot. So are you.'

'Oh-h-h-h–'

His face softened.

'If you could have seen them, Seoul. Tall as smoke, and they were always in music, with . . . something you can't imagine. We haven't –' He stopped tugging at his gray gloves, shuddered. 'Fairer than all the children of men,' he said painfully.

She hugged herself, eyes narrowed.

'But they're dead, Timor. Dead! You told me.'

He went rigid, turned away from her with his hand on his gray slipper.

'How could there be better than Humans?' she persisted. 'Everyone knows there's only Humans and Crots. I don't think it's your crotty Paradise at all, I think –'

He wrenched at the privacy lock.

'Timor, wait! Timor?'

The sound that was not his name followed him into the bright corridors, his feet carrying him blindly on the dry hardness. Fight to breathe evenly, to control the fist that shook him from within.

When he slowed he saw that he was in a part of this station still strange to him. But they were all alike, all like hospital and Trainworld. Parched prisms.

An aged she-Crot wheeled by, grinning vacuously, trailing skin. His stomach churned again at the red scurf. The local Crots were high-grade, equivalent to Human morons. Caricatures. *Subhumans*. Why let them in the stations?

A drone warned him of the air plant ahead and he veered away, passed a flasher: Humans Only. Beyond it was the playroom where he had met Seoul. He found it empty, jagged with rude games and mechanical throats. What the lords of the Galaxy called music. So jealous of their ugliness. He passed the U4 bar, grimaced, and heard water splashing.

It drew him powerfully. There had been water on Paradise . . . such water . . . he came into the station pool.

Two heads shot out of the water, tossed black hair.

'Heyo, the newboy!'

The water was clear and wrong but he felt better.

He stared at the wetness, the olive boy-flesh.

'He flows! Come in, newboy!'

For a moment he held aloof, a gray-clad stranger. Then his body prodded, and he stripped again, showed the hateful dry pink.

'Heyo, he really flows!'

'Ottowa,' one boy told him.

'Hull.' They were twins.

'Timor,' he lied, rolling, sluicing in the wet. He wanted – wanted –

Olive hands on his legs in the bubbling.

'Good?'

'In the water,' he said thickly. They laughed.

'Are you a sub? Come on.'

He flushed, saw it was a joke and followed them.

The pool cube was dim and moist and it was almost good. But their flesh grew greasy-hot and presently he could not do what they wanted.

'He flows nowhere,' the one called Ottowa said.

'You don't –' They were busy with each other. Aching, undrained, he said furiously, 'Humans! Ugly nullhead Humans. You don't know what flowing is.'

They stared at him now, too startled for anger.

'Where are *you* from, newboy?' Ottowa asked.

It was no use, he shouldn't have.

'From Paradise,' he said wearily, pulling on gray silk.

They exchanged looks.

'There's no such planet.'

'There is,' he said. 'There is. There was.' And went out, head averted into the bright wastes. Stilling his face, straightening the short tree of his spine. When would he be in space, allowed simply to do his job? The mindless immensities, the empty stars. Better. *Weave a circle round him thrice and close your eyes with holy dread, for he on honey-dew hath fed and drunk –*

A hand fell on his shoulder from behind.

'So you're the Crot nurseling.'

The old fury lashed him round, fists ready. His eyes went up.

Into dream. He stood gaping his unbelief. But then he saw that the thin black face above his own was Human. Human, not much older than he. But cloud-lean, ghost-graceful, like –

'I'm Santiago. Work to do. Follow me, Crotty.'

Old habit drove his fist, automatically his throat said, 'My-name-is-Timor.'

The dark one twisted lightly, the blow palmed on his shoulder. Contemptuous god-grin.

'Pax, pax.' Black velvet voice. 'Timor, son of the late great Scout Timor. My father's compliments and will you get your ass into the scouter I'm taking out. Sector D needs it as of yesterday and we're short-handed. Your specs say you know how.'

Santiago. His father must be the fat brown stationchief who had greeted him yesterday. How could such a sire –

'Apprentice cert,' his voice was saying.

Santiago nodded and went away without looking back to see that Timor followed.

The scouter was new and of the same model Timor had CRd on. Numbly he moved through the out-system transjection routine, parroting the checks, not daring to look closely at the long figure in the command console.

When they were set to first transit Santiago turned to him.

'Still freaked?'

Timor kept his eyes from the dark magnets.

'Seoul told me a little. I shouldn't have said that, obviously no Crot could raise a man.'

'. . .'

'My father. Wasted me too long. His dear old chum-scout Timor's son, saved from the aliens. Your father and mine spaced together – you'll get all that when you're back. He thinks you're Scout Timor reincarnated. He asked for you, you know.'

'Yes,' Timor got out.

The eyes studied him, hooded.

'It's a good thing he did. Your specs are a little strange.'

'What do you mean?'

'All that sycounsel wad. I expect they had to work you over *completely*. How old were you when you were found?'

'Ten,' said Timor absently. 'What were you doing *with my –*'

'Don't freak. Man going out wants to know who's with him, fair? . . . Ten years with – all right, I won't say it. But if they weren't Crots, what were they? Crots is all we know.'

Timor drew breath. If he could somehow touch understand without words, but he was so tired.

'They were not Crots,' he told the smoke-thin face. 'Compared to them . . .' He turned away.

'You don't want to talk.'

'No.'

'Too bad,' said Santiago lightly. 'We could use a super-race.'

In silence they worked through the transit-change, set the main course parameters and secondary checks. Then Santiago stretched, moved to the lockers.

'Might as well relax and eat now, next transit's not for an hour. Then we can sleep.' With odd, archaic ceremoniousness he opened their food.

Timor realized he was very hungry. And from behind his gut, stabs of a deeper hunger. It seemed good to eat thus with another Human, intimately cocooned in abyssal space. Always before he had been the monitored pupil. Now . . .

He stiffened, summoned scorn.

'U4.'

'No.'

'Try some of this, then. Station's best, I boosted it. You must not have had much rest since you came off Trainworld.'

It was true. Timor took the proffered bulb.

'Where is Sector D?'

'Out toward Deneb. Six transit. They're opening three new systems and we're trying to keep it all supplied.'

They talked a little then, about the station and the weird encapsulated life of Trainworld. Despite himself, Timor felt knots in perilous thaw.

'Music?'

Santiago caught his unguarded wince.

'That wastes you? Your aliens had better music, true?'

Timor nodded.

'They had cities?'

'Oh yes.'

'Real cities? Like Mescalon?'

'More beautiful. Different. With many musics,' he said painfully.

The dark face watched him.

'Where are they now?'

'In Paradise.' Timor shook his head tiredly. 'I mean, the planet was called Paradise. But they're all dead. The scouts who found me had a disease.'

'Bad.'

There was a pause. Then Santiago said musingly, 'There's a spool of planets called paradise something or somebody's paradise. You wouldn't happen to know the coordinates?'

Alarms clattered in Timor's head.

'No!'

'Oh you must have been told.'

'No, no! I forgot. They never –'

'Maybe we could hype you,' Santiago smiled.

'*No!*'

The effort jerked him loose from his stay. As he caught himself clumsily he noticed that the cabin seemed very small, with curious haloes.

'They had cities, you say. Tell me about them.'

He wanted to say it was time for the transit, to stop talking. But he found he was telling the dark ghost about the cities. The cities of his lost world, of Paradise . . .

'– dim ruby light. And music. The music of many, and the mud –'

'*Mud?*'

His heart jolted, raced. Staring mutely at the ghost-angel.

'Oh, keep on the track,' the angel said severely.

Suddenly Timor knew.

'You've drugged me.' Santiago's long lips flickered.

'The people. You say they were beautiful?'

'Fairer than all the children of men,' said Timor helplessly, worlds sliding within him.

'They flowed?'

'They flowed.' Timor's head weaved, tortured. 'More than any Human. More than you.'

'They loved me,' he groaned, reaching his arms to ghosts. 'You look a little like them. Why . . .'

Santiago seemed to be doing something at the console.

'I do?' White teeth made haloes.

'No,' said Timor. Suddenly he was very cool. 'You're only

Human. It's just that you're not pink and you're tall. But you're nothing but a Human. To them, Humans are Crots.'

'Humans are Crots?' Blue-black, knife-face over him, lethal. 'You're trying for it, newboy. So your aliens are something better than Humans? Mere Humans make you vomit? That makes you something very very special. And how convenient, they're all dead, and no one's ever seen it. You know a thing, Timor son of Crot Timor, I think you're lying. You know where it is.'

'No!'

'*Where is it?*'

Timor heard himself yell, saw the ebony mask check and change.

'All right, don't freak. I caught enough of your specs to know the sector they picked you up in. It's not far off course. You said the primary was dim and red, true? Computer will sort it, there can't be too many Class M dwarfs out here.'

He turned away. Timor tried to launch himself to stop him, but his drugged hands were flailing empty bulkhead.

'I am not lying, I am not lying . . .'

The computer was droning.

'– class M Beta primaries Sector Two zero point zed point delta solution one four repeat one four.'

'Ah,' said Santiago. 'Fourteen's too many.' He frowned at Timor, who was now quiet.

'There must be something you know. Some criterion. I want to find this Paradise.'

'They're all dead,' Timor whispered.

'Maybe,' said Santiago. 'Maybe not. And maybe you're lying and maybe not. Either way I want to see it. If the cities are there there'll be things we can use. Or I'll get off for good. Why do you think you're on this trip, newboy? Somebody's hiding something, and I'm going to find it.'

'You can't find it. I won't let you hurt them!' Timor heard his voice break, struggled through shells of unreality. He could see the cabin lights reflected in violet bloom on Santiago's brow. Black stars probed him, golden edged. The face of dream.

'I wouldn't hurt them.' The voice was velvet again. 'Why would I harm Paradise? I want to see them. The cities. We could see the cities together. You could show me.' The dream loomed, swelled closer. Warmth. Melting. 'You could show me.'

'You want to go back, to Paradise.'

Timor's eyes blurred.

'Maybe some of them are still alive. Maybe we could help them.'

Depths shifted to him, oozed scorching springs. 'Santiago . . .' His hands were on richness now, kneading the throb. If it were not so dry, so bright–

The lights dimmed to a blue glow.

'Yes,' Santiago said. His tunic was peeling away, the dark flesh glimmered. 'I would like to share the beauty. You must be very lonely.'

Timor's lips moved, wordless.

'Tell me a little how it was . . . the light . . .'

. . . No, no, no, no, no, no . . .

His mouth was on fire, even his lungs were dry. Somewhere the voder-voice gabbled, quit. His eyes were crusted. 'No, no,' he croaked, his face striking plastic.

'Suck, stupid.'

Liquid gushed in. He sucked greedily and the blue-blackness above him came in focus.

'That wears off. You'll be fine when we get to Paradise.'

'No!' Timor jerked upright, clutching after the long shape that weaved away. He remembered now, the drug and Santiago.

He had been hyped.

The thing that must not, must not ever be.

But Santiago was grinning at him.

'Oh yes, little Timor-whatever-your-name-is. You put out. Those sunless periods. It was a binary, did you know that? Dark-body system. And that cluster you called the Swarm. Computer had it all.'

'You found it? You found Paradise?'

'We're one transit out.'

A cool bursting inside him, fountains of dissolving light unbearable. Santiago had hyped him and found Paradise. He could not believe it.

Slowly he sank back, drank some more, dreamily watching Santiago. Belief grew. They would walk the streets of Paradise. His proud Human would see. The signaller was flashing. Santiago's eyes slid round.

'Recall presignal. But they can't know we've gone off-course.' He shrugged. 'We'll see when the message clears. I'm not turning back.'

'Santiago.' Timor smiled. 'We flowed. I've never said it to a Human before.'

But the black stars came no closer.

'Maybe. I wonder. You said a lot of things. If your Paradise turns out to be a Crot world – Santiago's nostrils wedged. 'A Crot's thing into Humans –

'You'll see. You will see!'

'Maybe.'

The boards chimed for transit, and suddenly Timor's head cleared.

'But they're dead!' he cried. 'I don't want to see it, Santiago. Not all dead. Don't take us there!'

Santiago ignored him, went on setting course. Timor floundered up, pulled at his arms and received a chop that sent him into the stays.

'What's wasting you? Why are you so sure they're all dead?'

Timor's mouth opened, closed. How was he so sure? Armor seemed to be dissolving from his brain. Who had told him that? He had been so young. Could it have been a mistake? A lie?

'In which case,' Santiago's eyes roved the boards, 'would they be friendly?'

'Friendly?' A fearful joy was rising in Timor, perilous, unstoppable. Alive. Was it *possible*? 'Oh, yes.'

'But maybe after that disease,' Santiago persisted. He started a checkrun. 'Just make sure our Ambax is operational.'

Timor hardly heard him, moved like a zombie through the drill. Finally Santiago pushed him at the shower.

'Clean up. In case you meet your friends.'

He seemed to be floating at less than the scouter's nominal gee, roiled by waves of alternate joy and dread. Timor concentrated on the vision of himself and Santiago entering empty cities. No music, but the spires and the . . . his bitter lover would see what a flowing world had been.

They were breaking into the system. To their side a sullen star swelled, eclipsed, reappeared.

'That one. Third out.'

The grav-webs took hold. Timor saw a great star-cluster wheel across the screen. 'The Swarm!'

Paradise. *They were landing on Paradise.*

'Where are the cities?'

'Under the clouds.'

'It's nine-tenths ocean. I don't see any roads. Or fields.'

'That's right. They don't need them. The open spaces are − were just for sport or water-dancing.'

'A hole there. Go down by the sea.'

As the braking bit the signal print-out chattered. Santiago slapped it aside. Overcast churned around them crescendo, thinned. Then the webs grabbed them and they were set down, cooling, in dim ruby light.

Before them the screen showed milky smoothness; sea. With a level shore, and behind them low fronds. And a long crenellated line which fingered Timor's heart. This was not real. This was real.

Santiago was frowning at the message.

'Out of their heads. A *medical* recall?'

Timor scarcely heard him. The cycling lock was a vortex tugging him to the beautiful dimness, the garnet-gleaming light. Real.

'Your moment of truth, newboy.'

The port opened and they went out into Paradise. Healing moisture rushed into Timor's lungs.

'Agh, what a fug. You sure this is breathable?'

'Come on. The city.'

'Where are your spires?'

Twilight, the ground sluiced with sweetness, lapping by the quiet shallow sea. Impatiently, he pulled at Santiago's arm, felt him stumble. Not real.

'Where is the city?'

'Come on.' In dimness they splashed through a grove of short, flabby trees that oozed fruit. The sea curved beside them, barely ankle-deep.

'Is *that* supposed to be a town?'

Timor looked at the low crenellated walls lit only by the dusk. They seemed lower than he remembered, lower and – but he had been a child.

'It's been abandoned, it's crumbled.'

'Mud – *what are those?*'

Gray rotten little things were humping toward them out of the walls, stopping to stare.

'They,' said Timor. 'They must be the – the servants. The workers. I guess they didn't die.'

'They make Crots look Human.'

'No, no.'

'And those are nothing but mud hovels.'

'No,' repeated Timor. He moved forward, pulling his friend who would not see. 'Look, they've just deteriorated.'

'In seven years?'

A low music came to Timor's ears. Three of the lumps were humping closer. All dove-gray like himself, but it was hide, not silk, that bloated at elbows and knees. Gray splayed feet, and between them, under the bags of belly, the giant genitals of two of them leaving triple furrows in the soft mud. The third trailed a central row of great dugs. From their blue-black face holes gentle glubbering sounds.

Dark gems, gold-crusted like the sad eyes of toads met his. The world sideslipped, folded into transparency. The music –

A terrible clamour broke upon him. Timor whirled. The alien beside him was laughing, cruel barking teeth.

'Well, my crotty friend! So this is Paradise!' Santiago yelled, whooped. 'Not even Crots! SUBCROTS!

'Speak to your friends, Crot,' he gasped. 'Answer them!'

But Timor did not understand. A thing was clysming from him, a thing of most careful construction which has almost killed him, dissolving out.

'It is absolutely necessary that this child be totally reconditioned.' He said in a stranger's voice. 'He is Scout Timor's son.' But his words meant nothing to him, for he had heard his name in the music. His true name, name of his babyhood under the soft gray hands and bodies of his first world. The bodies that had taught him love, all in the mud, in the cool mud.

The thing beside him was making hurtful sounds.

'You wanted the beauty!' Timor screamed his last Human words.

And then they were down, tearing and rolling in the sweet mud, gray bodies with him. Until he found that it was no longer fighting but love – love as it always had been, his true flowing, while the voices rose around him the muddied thing under him was dead of drying slipped away in the gray welter, in the music of many, flowing together in Paradise in the dim ruby light.

When it Happens

(1975)

MARGARET ATWOOD

Mrs Burridge is putting up green tomato pickles. There are twelve quarts in each lot with a bit left over, and that is the end of the jars. At the store they tell her there's a strike on at the factory where they get made. She doesn't know anything about that but you can't buy them anywhere, and even before this they were double what they were last year; she considers herself lucky she had those in the cellar. She has a lot of green tomatoes because she heard on the weather last night there was going to be a killer frost, so she put on her parka and her work gloves and took the lantern out to the garden in the pitch dark and picked off all the ones she could see, over three bushels. She can lift the full baskets herself but she asked Frank to carry them in for her; he grumbles, but he likes it when she asks. In the morning the news said the growers had been hit and that would shoot the price up, not that the growers would get any of it themselves, everyone knows it's the stores that make the money.

She feels richer than she did yesterday, but on the other hand there isn't that much you can do with green tomatoes. The pickles hardly made a dint in them, and Frank has said, as he does every year, that they will never eat twenty-four quarts of green tomato pickle with just the two of them and the children gone. Except when they come to visit and eat me out of house and home, Mrs Burridge adds silently. The truth is she has always made two batches and the children never liked it anyway, it was Frank ate them all and she knows perfectly well he'll do it again, without even noticing. He likes it on bread and cheese when he's watching the hockey games, during every commercial he goes out to the kitchen and makes himself another slice, even if he's just had a big meal, leaving a trail of crumbs and bits of pickle from the counter across the floor and over the front room rug to his big chair. It used to annoy Mrs Burridge, especially the crumbs, but now she watches him with a kind of sadness; she once thought their life together would go on forever but she has come to realize this is not the case.

She doesn't even feel like teasing him about his spare tire any more, though she does it all the same because he would miss it if she stopped. 'There you go,' she says, in the angular, prodding, metallic voice she cannot change because everyone expects it from her, if she spoke any other way they would think she was ill, 'you keep on munching away like that and it'll be easy for me to get you out of bed in the mornings, I'll just give you a push and you'll roll all the way down the stairs like a barrel.' And he answers in his methodical voice, pretending to be lazy even though he isn't, 'You need a little fun in life,' as though his pickles and cheese are slightly disreputable, almost like an orgy. Every year he tells her she's made too much but there would be a fuss all right if he went down to the cellar one day and there wasn't any left.

Mrs Burridge has made her own pickles since 1952, which was the first year she had the garden. She remembers it especially because her daughter Sarah was on the way and she had trouble bending down to do the weeding. When she herself was growing up everyone did their own pickles, and their own canning and preserving too. But after the war most women gave it up, there was more money then and it was easier to buy things at the store. Mrs Burridge never gave it up, though most of her friends thought she was wasting her time, and now she is glad she didn't, it kept her in practice while the others were having to learn all over again. Though with the sugar going up the way it is, she can't understand how long anyone is going to be able to afford even the homemade things.

On paper Frank is making more money than he ever has; yet they seem to have less to spend. They could always sell the farm, she supposes, to people from the city who would use it as a weekend place; they could get what seems like a very high price, several of the farms south of them have gone that way. But Mrs Burridge does not have much faith in money; also it is a waste of the land, and this is her home, she has it arranged the way she wants it.

When the second batch is on and simmering she goes to the back door, opens it, and stands with her arms folded across her stomach, looking out. She catches herself doing this four or five times a day now and she doesn't quite know why. There isn't much to see, just the barn and the back field with the row of dead elms Frank keeps saying he's going to cut down, and the top of Clarke's place sticking over the hill. She isn't sure what she is looking for but she has the odd idea she may see something burning, smoke coming up from the horizon, a column of it or perhaps more than one column, off to the south. This is such a peculiar thought for her to have that she hasn't told it to anyone else. Yesterday Frank saw her standing at the back door and asked her about it at dinner; anything he wants to talk to her about he saves up till dinner, even if he thinks about it in the morning. He wondered why she was at the back door, doing nothing at all for over ten minutes, and Mrs Burridge told him a lie, which made her very uneasy. She said she heard a strange dog barking, which wasn't a good story because their own dogs were right there and they didn't notice a thing. But Frank let it pass; perhaps he thinks she is getting funny in her old age and doesn't want to call attention to it, which would be like him. He'll track mud all over her nice shiny kitchen floor but he'd hate to hurt anyone's feelings. Mrs Burridge decides, a little wistfully, that despite his pig-headedness he is a kind and likable man, and for her this is like renouncing a cherished and unquestionable belief, such as the flatness of the earth. He has made her angry so many times.

When the pickles are cool she labels them as she always does with the name and the date and carries them down the cellar stairs. The cellar is the old kind, with stone walls and a dirt floor. Mrs Burridge likes to have everything neat – she still irons her sheets – so she had Frank build her some shelves right after they were married. The pickles go on one side, jams and jellies on the other, and the quarts of preserves along the bottom. It used to make her feel safe to have all that food in the cellar; she would think to herself, well, if there's a snowstorm or anything and we're cut off, it won't be so bad. It doesn't make her feel safe any more. Instead she thinks that if she has to leave suddenly she won't be able to take any of the jars with her, they'd be too heavy to carry.

She comes back up the stairs after the last trip. It's not as easy as it used to be, her knee still bothers her as it has ever since she fell six years ago, she tripped on the second-last step. She's asked Frank a million times to fix the stairs but he hasn't done it, that's what she means by pig-headed. If she asks him more than twice to do something he calls it nagging, and maybe it is, but who's going to do it if he won't? The cold vacant hole at the back of this question is too much for her.

She has to stop herself from going to the back door again. Instead she goes to the back window and looks out, she can see almost the same things anyway. Frank is going towards the barn, carrying something, it looks like a wrench. The way he walks, slower than he used to, bent forward a little – from the back he's like an old man, how many years has he been walking that way? – makes you think, *He can't protect me.* She doesn't think this on purpose, it simply occurs to her, and it isn't only him, it's all of them, they've lost the power, you can tell by the way they walk. They are all waiting, just as Mrs Burridge is, for whatever it is to happen. Whether they realize it or not. Lately when she's gone to the Dominion Store in town she has seen a look on the faces of the women there – she knows most of them, she wouldn't be mistaken – an anxious, closed look, as if they are frightened of something but won't talk about it. They're wondering what they will do, perhaps they think there's nothing they can do. This air of helplessness exasperates Mrs Burridge, who has always been practical.

For weeks she has wanted to go to Frank and ask him to teach her how to use the gun. In fact he has two guns, a shotgun and a twenty-two rifle; he used to like going after a few ducks in the fall, and of course there are the groundhogs, they have to be shot because of the holes they make in the fields Frank drives over on the tractor five or six times a year. A lot of men get injured by overturning tractors. But she can't ask him because she can't explain to him why she needs to know, and if she doesn't explain he will only tease. 'Anyone can shoot a gun,' he'll say, 'all you have to do is pull the trigger . . . oh, you mean you want to hit something, well now, that's different, who you planning to kill?' Perhaps he won't say that; perhaps this is only the way he talked twenty years ago, before she stopped taking an interest in things outside the house. But Mrs Burridge will never know because she will never ask. She doesn't have the heart to say to him, *Maybe you'll be dead. Maybe you'll go off somewhere when it happens, maybe there will be a war.* She can remember the last war.

Nothing has changed outside the window, so she turns away and sits down at the kitchen table to make out her shopping list. Tomorrow is their day for going into town. She tries to plan the day so she can sit down at intervals; otherwise her feet start swelling up. That began with Sarah and got worse with the other two children and it's never really gone away. All her life, ever since she got married, she has made lists of things that have to be bought, sewed, planted, cooked, stored; she already has her list made for next Christmas, all the names and the gifts she will buy for each, and the list of what she needs for Christmas dinner. But she can't seem to get interested in it, it's too far away. She can't believe in a distant future that is orderly like the past, she no longer seems to have the energy; it's as if she is saving it up for when she will have to use it.

She is even having trouble with the shopping list. Instead of concentrating on the paper – she writes on the backs of the used-up days of the page-a-day calendar Frank gives her every New Year's – she is gazing around the kitchen, looking at all the things she will have to leave behind when she goes. That will be the hardest part. Her mother's china, her silver, even though it is an old-fashioned pattern and the silver is wearing off, the egg timer in the shape of a chicken Sarah gave her when she was twelve, the ceramic salt-and-pepper shakers, green horses with perforated heads, that one of the other children brought back from the Ex. She thinks of walking up the stairs, the sheets folded in the chest, the towels stacked neatly on the shelves, the beds made, the quilt that was her grandmother's, it makes her want to cry. On her bureau, the wedding picture, herself in a shiny satin gown (the satin was a mistake, it emphasized her hips). Frank in the suit he has not worn since except to funerals, his hair cut too short on the sides and a surprising tuft at the top, like a woodpecker's. The children when they were babies. She thinks of her girls now and hopes they will not have babies; it is no longer the right time for it.

Mrs Burridge wishes someone would be more precise, so she could make better plans. Everyone knows something is going to happen, you can tell by reading the newspapers and watching the television, but nobody is sure what it will be, nobody can be exact. She has her own ideas about it though. At first it will simply become quieter. She will have an odd feeling that something is wrong but it will be a few days before she is able to pin it down. Then she will notice that the planes are no longer flying over on their way to the Malton Airport, and that the noise from the highway two miles away, which is quite distinct when the leaves are off the trees, has almost disappeared. The television will be non-committal about it; in fact, the television, which right now is filled with bad news, of strikes, shortages, famines, layoffs and price increases, will become sweet-tempered and placating, and long intervals of classical music will appear on the radio. About this time Mrs Burridge will realize that the news is being censored as it was during the war.

Mrs Burridge is not positive about what will happen next; that is, she knows what will happen but she is not positive about the order. She expects it will be the gas and oil: the oil delivery man will simply not turn up at his usual time, and one morning the corner filling station will be closed. Just that, no explanations, because of course they – she does not know who 'they' are, but she has always believed in their existence – they do not want people to panic. They are trying to keep things looking normal, possibly they have already started on this program and that is in fact why things still do look normal. Luckily she and Frank have the diesel fuel tank in the shed, it is three-quarters full, and they don't use the filling station anyway, they have their own gas pump. She has Frank bring in the old wood stove, the one they stored under the barn when they had the furnace and the electricity put in, and for once she blesses Frank's habit of putting things off. She was after him for years to take that stove to the dump. He cuts down the dead elms, finally, and they burn them in the stove.

The telephone wires are blown down in a storm and no one comes to fix them; or this is what Mrs Burridge deduces. At any rate, the phone goes dead. Mrs Burridge doesn't particularly mind, she never liked using the phone much anyway, but it does make her feel cut off.

About now men begin to appear on the back road, the gravel road that goes past the gate, walking usually by themselves, sometimes in pairs. They seem to be heading north. Most of them are young, in their twenties, Mrs Burridge would guess. They are not dressed like the men around here. It's been so long since she has seen anyone *walking* along this road that she becomes alarmed. She begins leaving the dogs off their chains, she has kept them chained at night ever since one of them bit a Jehovah's Witness early one Sunday morning. Mrs Burridge doesn't hold with the Witnesses – she is United – but she respects their perseverance, at least they have the courage of their convictions which is more than you can say for some members of her own church, and she always buys a *Watchtower*. Maybe they have been right all along.

It is about this time too that she takes one of the guns, she thinks it will be the shotgun as she will have a better chance of hitting something, and hides it, along with the shells, under a piece of roofing behind the barn. She does not tell Frank; he will have the twenty-two. She has already picked out the spot.

They do not want to waste the little gasoline they still have left in the pump so they do not make unnecessary trips. They begin to eat the chickens, which Mrs Burridge does not look forward to. She hates cleaning and plucking them, and the angriest she ever got at Frank was the time he and Henry Clarke decided to go into turkey farming. They did it too, despite all she had to say against it, and she had to cope with the turkeys escaping and scratching in the garden and impossible to catch, in her opinion they were the stupidest birds in God's creation, and she had to clean and pluck a turkey a week until luckily the blackhead wiped out a third of the flock, which was enough to discourage them, they sold off the rest at a loss. It was the only time she was actually glad to see Frank lose money on one of his ventures.

Mrs Burridge will feel things are getting serious on the day the electricity goes off and does not come back on. She knows, with a kind of fatalism, that this will happen in November, when the freezer is full of the vegetables but before it is cold enough to keep the packages frozen outside. She stands and looks at the pliofilm bags of beans and corn and spinach and carrots, melting and sodden, and thinks, *Why couldn't they have waited till spring*. It is the waste, of food and also of her hard work, that aggravates her the most. She salvages what she can. During the Depression, she remembers, they used to say those on farms were better off than those in the city, because at least they had food; if you could keep the farm, that is; but she is no longer sure this is true. She feels beleaguered, isolated, like someone shut up inside a fortress, though no one has bothered them, in fact no one has passed their way for days, not even any of the solitary walking men.

With the electricity off they can no longer get the television. The radio stations, when they broadcast at all, give out nothing but soothing music, which Mrs Burridge does not find soothing in the least.

One morning she goes to the back door and looks out and there are the columns of smoke, right where she's been expecting to see them, off to the south. She calls Frank and they stand watching. The smoke is thick and black, oily, as though something has exploded. She does not know what Frank is thinking; she herself is wondering about the children. She has had no news of them in weeks, but how could she? They stopped delivering mail some time ago.

Fifteen minutes later, Henry Clarke drives into the yard in his half-ton truck. This is very unusual as no one has been driving anywhere lately. There is another man with him, and Mrs Burridge identifies him as the man three farms up who moved in four or five years ago. Frank goes out and talks with them, and they drive over to the gas pump and start pumping the rest of the precious gas into the truck. Frank comes back to the house. He tells her there's a little trouble down the road, they are going along to see about it and she isn't to worry. He goes into the back room, comes out with the twenty-two, asks her where the shotgun is. She says she doesn't know. He searches for it, fruitlessly – she can hear him swearing, he does not swear in her presence – until he gives up. He comes out, kisses her goodbye, which is unusual too, and says he'll be back in a couple of hours. She watches the three of them drive off in Henry Clarke's truck, towards the smoke; she knows he will not come back. She supposes she ought to feel more emotional about it, but she is well prepared, she has been saying goodbye to him silently for years.

She re-enters the house and closes the door. She is fifty-one, her feet hurt, and she does not know where she can go, but she realizes she cannot stay here. There will now be a lot of hungry people, those that can make it this far out of the cities will be young and tough, her house is a beacon, signalling warmth and food. It will be fought over, but not by her.

She goes upstairs, searches in the cupboard, and puts on her heavy slacks and her two thickest sweaters. Downstairs she gathers up all the food that will be light enough for her to carry: raisins, cooking chocolate, dried prunes and apricots, half a loaf of bread, some milk powder which she puts into a quart freezer bag, a piece of cheese. Then she unearths the shotgun from behind the barn. She thinks briefly of killing the livestock, the chickens, the heifers and the pig, so no one will do it who does not know the right way; but she herself does not know the right way, she has never killed anything in her life, Frank always did it, so she contents herself with opening the henhouse door and the gate into the back field. She hopes the animals will run away but she knows they probably will not.

She takes one last look around the house. As an afterthought, she adds her toothbrush to the bundle: she does not like the feel of unbrushed teeth. She does not go down into the cellar but she has an image of her carefully sealed bottles and jars, red and yellow and purple, shattered on the floor, in a sticky puddle that looks like blood. Those who come will be wasteful, what they cannot eat themselves they will destroy. She thinks about setting fire to the house herself, before anyone else can do it.

Mrs Burridge sits at her kitchen table. On the back of her calendar page, it's for a Monday, she has written 'Oatmeal' in her evenly spaced public school handwriting that always got a star and has not changed very much since then. The dogs are a problem. After some thought she unchains them, but she does not let them past the gate: at a crucial moment they might give her away. She walks north in her heavy boots, carrying her parka because it is not yet cold enough to put it on, and her package of food and the shotgun which she has taken care to load. She passes the cemetery where her father and mother and her grandmother and grandfather are buried; the church used to be there but it burned down sixteen years ago and was rebuilt closer to the highway. Frank's people are in the other cemetery, his go back to the great-grandfather but they are Anglican, not that he kept it up. There is no one else on the road; she feels a little foolish. What if she is wrong and Frank comes back after all, what if nothing, really, is the matter? 'Shortening' she writes. She intends to make a lemon meringue pie for Sunday, when two of the children are coming up from the city for dinner.

It is almost evening and Mrs Burridge is tired. She is in a part of the country she cannot remember, though she has stayed on the same road and it is a road she knows well; she has driven along it many times with Frank. But walking is not the same as driving. On one side there is a field, no buildings, on the other a woodlot; a stream flows through a culvert under the road. Mrs Burridge kneels down to drink: the water is ice-cold and tastes of iron. Later there will be a frost, she can feel it. She puts on her parka and her gloves, and turns into the forest where she will not be seen. There she will eat some raisins and cheese and try to rest, waiting for the moon to rise so she can continue walking. It is now quite dark. She smells earth, wood, rotting leaves.

Suddenly her eye is caught by a flicker of red, and before she can turn back – how can this happen so quickly? – it takes shape, it is a small fire, off to the right, and two men are crouching near it. They have seen her, too: one of them rises and comes towards her. His teeth bare, he is smiling; he thinks she will be easy, an old woman. He says something but she cannot imagine what it is, she does not know how people dressed like that would talk.

They have spotted her gun, their eyes have fastened on it, they want it. Mrs Burridge knows what she must do. She must wait until they are close enough and then she must raise the gun and shoot them, using one barrel for each, aiming at the faces. Otherwise they will kill her, she has no doubt about that. She will have to be fast, which is too bad because her hands feel thick and wooden; she is afraid, she does not want the loud noise or the burst of red that will follow, she has never killed anything in her life. She has no pictures beyond this point. You never know how you will act in a thing like that until it actually happens.

Mrs Burridge looks at the kitchen clock. On her list she writes

'Cheese', they are eating more cheese now than they used to because of the price of meat. She gets up and goes to the kitchen door.

Angel, All Innocence

(1977)

FAY WELDON

There is a certain kind of unhappiness, experienced by a certain kind of woman married to a certain kind of man, which is timeless: outrunning centuries, interweaving generations, perpetuating itself from mother to daughter, feeding off the wet eyes of the puzzled girl, gaining fresh strength from the dry eyes of the old woman she will become – who, looking back on her past, remembers nothing of love except tears and the pain in the heart which must be endured, in silence, in case the heart stops altogether.

Better for it to stop, now.

Angel, waking in the night, hears sharp footsteps in the empty attic above and wants to wake Edward. She moves her hand to do so, but then stills it for fear of making him angry. Easier to endure in the night the nightmare terror of ghosts than the day-long silence of Edward's anger.

The footsteps, little and sharp, run from a point above the double bed in which Angel and Edward lie, she awake, he sleeping, to a point somewhere above the chest of drawers by the door; they pause briefly, then run back again, tap-tap, clickety-click. There comes another pause and the sound of pulling and shuffling across the floor; and then the sequence repeats itself, once, twice. Silence. The proper unbroken silence of the night.

Too real, too clear, for ghosts. The universe is not magic. Everything has an explanation. Rain, perhaps? Hardly. Angel can see the moon shine through the drawn blind, and rain does not fall on moonlit nights. Perhaps, then, the rain of past days collected in some blocked gutter, to finally splash through on to the rolls of wallpaper and pots of paint on the attic floor, sounding like footsteps through some trick of domestic acoustics. Surely! Angel and Edward have not been living in the house for long. The attic is still unpainted, and old plaster drops from disintegrating laths.

Edward will get round to it sooner or later. He prides himself on his craftsman's skills, and Angel, a year married, has learned to wait and admire, subduing impatience in herself. Edward is a painter – of pictures, not houses – and not long out of art school, where he won many prizes. Angel is the lucky girl he has loved and married. Angel's father paid for the remote country house, where now they live in solitude and where Edward can develop his talents, undisturbed by the ugliness of the city, with Angel, his inspiration, at his side. Edward, as it happened, consented to the gift unwillingly, and for Angel's sake rather than his own. Angel's father Terry writes thrillers and settled a large sum upon his daughter in her childhood, thus avoiding death duties and the anticipated gift tax. Angel kept the fact hidden from Edward until after they were married. He'd thought her an ordinary girl about Chelsea, sometime secretary, sometime barmaid, sometime artist's model.

Angel, between jobs, did indeed take work as an artist's model. That was how Edward first clapped eyes on her; Angel, all innocence, sitting nude upon her plinth, fair curly hair glinting under strong lights, large eyes closed beneath stretched blue-veined lids, strong breasts pointed upwards, stubby pale bush irritatingly and coyly hidden behind an angle of thigh that both gave Angel cramps and spoiled the pose for the students. So they said.

'If you're going to be an exhibitionist,' as Edward complained to her later in the coffee bar, 'at least don't be coy about it.' He took her home to his pad, that handsome, dark-eyed, smiling young man, and wooed her with a nostalgic Sinatra record left behind by its previous occupant; half mocking, half sincere, he sang love words into her pearly ear, his warm breath therein stirring her imagination, and the gentle occasional nip of his strong teeth in its flesh promising passion and pain beyond belief. Angel would not take off her clothes for him: he became angry and sent her home in a taxi without her fare. She borrowed from her flatmate at the other end. She cried all night, and the next day, sitting naked on her plinth, had such swollen eyelids as to set a student or two scratching away to amend the previous day's work. But she lowered her thigh, as a gesture of submission, and felt a change in the studio ambience from chilly spite to warm approval, and she knew Edward had forgiven her. Though she offered herself to multitudes, Edward had forgiven her.

'I don't mind you being an exhibitionist,' Edward said to her in the coffee bar, 'in fact that rather turns me on, but I do mind you being coy. You have a lot to learn, Angel.' By that time Angel's senses were so aroused, her limbs so languid with desire, her mind so besotted with his image, that she would have done whatever Edward wished, in public or in private. But he rose and left the coffee bar, leaving her to pay the bill.

Angel cried a little, and was comforted by and went home with Edward's friend Tom, and even went to bed with him, which made her feel temporarily better, but which she was to regret for ever.

'I don't mind you being a whore,' Edward said before the next studio session, 'but can't you leave my friends alone?'

It was a whole seven days of erotic torment for Angel before Edward finally spent the night with her: by that time her thigh hung loosely open in the studio. Let anyone see. Anyone. She did not care. The job was coming to an end anyway. Her new one as secretary in a solicitor's office began on the following Monday. In the nick of time, just as she began to think that life and love were over, Edward brought her back to their remembrance. 'I love you,' he murmured in Angel's ear. 'Exhibitionist slut, typical, I don't care. I still love you.'

Tap-tap, go the footsteps above, starting off again: clickety-click. Realer than real. No, water never sounded like that. What then? Rats? No. Rats scutter and scamper and scrape. There were rats in the barn in which Angel and Edward spent a camping holiday together. Their tent had blown away: they'd been forced to take refuge in the barn. All four of them. Edward, Angel, Tom and his new girlfriend Ray. Angel missed Edward one night after they all stumbled back from the pub to the barn, and searching for him in the long grass beneath an oak tree, found him in tight embrace with Ray.

'Don't tell me you're hysterical as well as everything else,' complained Edward. 'You're certainly irrational. You went to bed with Tom, after all.'

'But that was before.'

Ah, before, so much before. Before the declarations of love, the abandoning of all defence, all prudence, the surrender of common sense to faith, the parcelling up and handing over of the soul into apparent safe-keeping. And if the receiving hands part, the trusted fingers lose their grip, by accident or by design, why then, one's better dead.

Edward tossed his angel's soul into the air and caught it with his casual hands.

'But if it makes you jealous,' he said, 'why I won't . . . Do you want to marry me? Is that it? Would it make you happier?'

What would it look like when they came to write his biography? Edward Holst, the famous painter, married at the age of twenty-four – to what? Artist's model, barmaid, secretary, crime-writer's daughter? Or exhibitionist, whore, hysteric? Take your choice. Whatever makes the reader happiest, explains the artist in the simplest terms, makes the most successful version of a life. Crude strokes and all.

'Edward likes to keep his options open,' said Tom, but would not explain his remark any further. He and Ray were witnesses at the secular wedding ceremony. Angel thought she saw Edward nip Ray's ear as they all formally kissed afterwards, then thought she must have imagined it.

This was his overture of love: turning Angel in the dark warmth of the marriage bed, Edward's teeth would seek her ear and nibble the tender flesh, while his hand travelled down to open her thighs. Angel never initiated their lovemaking. No. Angel waited patiently. She had tried once or twice, in the early days, letting her hand roam over his sleeping body, but Edward not only failed to respond, but was thereafter cold to her for days on end, sleeping carefully on his side of the bed, until her penance was paid and he lay warm against her again.

Edward's love made flowers bloom, made the house rich and warm, made water taste like wine. Edward, happy, surrounded Angel with smiles and soft encouragement. He held her soul with steady hands. Edward's anger came unexpectedly, out of nowhere, or nowhere that Angel could see. Yesterday's permitted remark, forgiven fault, was today's outrage. To remark on the weather to break an uneasy silence, might be seen as evidence of a complaining nature: to be reduced to tears by his first unexpected biting remark, further fuel for his grievance.

Edward, in such moods, would go to his studio and lock the door, and though Angel (soon learning that to weep outside the door or beat against it, moaning and crying and protesting, would merely prolong his anger and her torment) would go out to the garden and weed or dig or plant as if nothing were happening, would feel Edward's anger seeping out from under the door, darkening the sun, poisoning the earth; or at any rate spoiling her fingers in relation to the earth, so that they trembled and made mistakes and nothing grew.

The blind shakes. The moon goes behind a cloud. Tap, tap, overhead. Back and forth. The wind? No. Don't delude yourself. Nothing of this world. A ghost. A haunting. A woman. A small, desperate, busy woman, here and not here, back and forth, out of her time, back from the grave, ill-omened, bringing grief and ruin: a message that nothing is what it seems, that God is dead and the forces of evil abroad and unstoppable. Does Angel hear, or not hear?

Angel through her fear, wants to go to the bathroom. She is three months pregnant. Her bladder is weak. It wakes her in the night, crying out its need, and Angel, obeying, will slip cautiously out of bed, trying not to wake Edward. Edward needs unbroken sleep if he is to paint well the next day. Edward, even at the best of times, suspects that Angel tossing and turning, and moaning in her sleep, as she will, wakes him on purpose to annoy.

Angel has not yet told Edward that she is pregnant. She keeps putting it off. She has no real reason to believe he does not want babies: but he has not said he does want them, and to assume that Edward wants what other people want is dangerous.

Angel moans aloud: afraid to move, afraid not to move, afraid to hear, afraid not to hear. So the child Angel lay awake in her little white bed, listening to her mother moaning, afraid to move, afraid not to move, to hear or not to hear. Angel's mother was a shoe-shop girl who married the new assistant manager after a six-week courtship. That her husband went on to make a fortune, writing thrillers that sold by the million, was both Dora's good fortune and tragedy. She lived comfortably enough on alimony, after all, in a way she could never have expected, until dying by mistake from an overdose of sleeping pills. After that Angel was brought up by a succession of her father's mistresses and *au pairs*. Her father Terry liked Edward, that was something, or at any rate, he had been relieved at his appearance on the scene. He had feared an element of caution in Angel's soul: that she might end up married to a solicitor or stockbroker. And artists were at least creative, and an artist such as Edward Holst might well end up rich and famous. Terry had six Holst canvasses on his walls to hasten the process. Two were of his daughter, nude, thigh slackly falling away from her stubby fair bush. Angel, defeated – as her mother had been defeated. 'I love you, Dora, but you must understand. I am not *in* love with you.' As I'm in love with Helen, Audrey, Rita, whoever it was: off to meetings, parties, off on his literary travels, looking for fresh copy and new backgrounds, encountering always someone more exciting, more interesting, than an ageing ex-shoe-shop assistant. Why couldn't Dora understand? Unreasonable of her to suffer, clutching the wretched Angel to her alarmingly slack bosom. Could he, Terry, really be the only animation of her flesh? There was a sickness in her love, clearly; unaccompanied as it was by the beauty which lends grace to importunity.

Angel had her mother's large, sad eyes. The reproach in them was in-built. Better Dora's heart had stopped (she'd thought it would: six months pregnant, she found Terry in the housemaid's bed. She, Dora, mistress of servants! What bliss!) and the embryo Angel never emerged to the light of day.

The noise above Angel stops. Ghosts! What nonsense! A fallen lath grating and rattling in the wind. What else? Angel regains her courage, slips her hand out from beneath Edward's thigh preparatory to leaving the bed for the bathroom. She will turn on all the lights and run. Edward wakes; sits up.

'What's that? What in God's name's that?'

'I can't hear anything,' says Angel, all innocence. Nor can she, not now. Edward's displeasure to contend with now; worse than the universe rattling its chains.

'Footsteps, in the attic. Are you deaf? Why didn't you wake me?'

'I thought I imagined it.'

But she can hear them, once again, as if with ears. The same pattern across the floor and back. Footsteps or heartbeats. Quicker and quicker now, hastening with the terror and tension of escape.

Edward, unimaginably brave, puts on his slippers, grabs a broken banister (five of these on the landing – one day soon, some day, he'll get round to mending them – he doesn't want some builder, paid by Angel, bungling the job) and goes on up to the attic. Angel follows behind. He will not let her cower in bed. Her bladder aches. She says nothing about that. How can she? Not yet. Not quite yet. Soon. 'Edward, I'm pregnant.' She can't believe it's true, herself. She feels a child, not a woman.

'Is there someone there?'

Edward's voice echoes through the three dark attic rooms. Silence. He gropes for and switches on the light. Empty, derelict rooms: plaster falling, laths hanging, wallpaper peeling. Floor-boards broken. A few cans of paint, a pile of wallpaper rolls, old newspapers. Nothing else.

'It could have been mice,' says Edward, doubtfully.

'Can't you hear it?' asks Angel, terrified. The sound echoes in her ears: footsteps clattering over a pounding heart. But Edward can't, not any more.

'Don't start playing games,' he murmurs, turning back to warmth and bed. Angel scuttles down before him, into the bath-room; the noise in her head fades. A few drops of urine tinkle into the bowl.

Edward lies awake in bed: Angel can feel his wakefulness, his increasing hostility towards her, before she is so much as back in the bedroom.

'Your bladder's very weak, Angel,' he complains. 'Something else you inherited from your mother?'

Something else, along with what? Suicidal tendencies, alcohol-ism, a drooping bosom, a capacity for being betrayed, deserted and forgotten?

Not forgotten by me, Mother. I don't forget. I love you. Even when my body cries out beneath the embraces of this man, this lover, this husband, and my mouth forms words of love, promises of eternity, still I don't forget. I love you, Mother.

'I don't know about my mother's bladder,' murmurs Angel rashly.

'Now you're going to keep me awake all night,' says Edward. 'I can feel it coming. You know I've nearly finished a picture.'

'I'm not going to say a word,' she says, and then, fulfilling his prophecy, sees fit to add, 'I'm pregnant.'

Silence. Stillness. Sleep?

No, a slap across nostrils, eyes, mouth. Edward has never hit Angel before. It is not a hard slap: it contains the elements of a caress.

'Don't even joke about it,' says Edward, softly.

'But I am pregnant.'

Silence. He believes her. Her voice made doubt impossible.

'How far?' Edward seldom asks for information. It is an act which infers ignorance, and Edward likes to know more than anyone else in the entire world.

'Three-and-a-half months.'

He repeats the words, incredulous.

'Too far gone to do anything,' says Angel, knowing now why she did not tell Edward earlier, and the knowledge making her voice cold and hard. Too far gone for the abortion he will most certainly want her to have. So much for the fruits of love. Love? What's love? Sex, ah, that's another thing. Love has babies: sex has abortions.

But Angel will turn sex into love – yes, she will – seizing it by the neck, throttling it till it gives up and takes the weaker path. Love! Edward is right to be frightened, right to hate her.

'I hate you,' he says, and means it. 'You mean to destroy me.'

'I'll make sure it doesn't disturb your nights,' says Angel, Angel of the bristly fair bush, 'If that's what you're worrying about. And you won't have to support it. I do that, anyway. Or my father does.'

Well, how dare she! Angel, not nearly as nice as she thought. Soft-eyed, vicious Angel.

Slap, comes the hand again, harder. Angel screams, he shouts; she collapses, crawls about the floor – he spurns her, she begs forgiveness; he spits his hatred, fear, and she her misery. If the noise above continues, certainly no one hears it, there is so much going on below. The rustlings of the night erupting into madness. Angel is suddenly quiet, whimpering, lying on the floor; she squirms. At first Edward thinks she is acting, but her white lips and taloned fingers convince him that something is wrong with her body and not just her mind. He gets her back on the bed and rings the doctor. Within an hour Angel finds herself in a hospital with a suspected ectopic pregnancy. They delay the operation and the pain subsides; just one of those things, they shrug. Edward has to interrupt his painting the next afternoon to collect her from the hospital.

'What was it? Hysteria?' he enquires.

'I dare say!'

'Well, you had a bad beginning, what with your mother and all,' he concedes, kissing her nose, nibbling her earlobe. It is forgiveness; but Angel's eyes remain unusually cold. She stays in bed, after Edward has left it and gone back to his studio, although the floors remain unswept and the dishes unwashed.

Angel does not say what is in her mind, what she knows to be true. That he is disappointed to see both her and the baby back safe and sound. He had hoped the baby would die, or failing that, the mother would die and the baby with her. He is pretending forgiveness, while he works out what to do next.

In the evening the doctor comes to see Angel. He is a slight man with a sad face: his eyes, she thinks, are kind behind his pebble glasses. His voice is slow and gentle. I expect his wife is happy, thinks Angel, and actually envies her. Some middle-aged, dowdy, provincial doctor's wife, envied by Angel! Rich, sweet, young and pretty Angel. The efficient secretary, lovable barmaid, and now the famous artist's wife! Once, for two rash weeks, even an art school model.

The doctor examines her, then discreetly pulls down her nightie to cover her breasts and moves the sheet up to cover her crotch. If he were my father, thinks Angel, he would not hang my naked portrait on his wall for the entertainment of his friends. Angel had not known until this moment that she minded.

'Everything's doing nicely inside there,' says the doctor. 'Sorry to rush you off like that, but we can't take chances.'

Ah, to be looked after. Love. That's love. The doctor shows no inclination to go.

'Perhaps I should have a word with your husband,' he suggests. He stands at the window gazing over daffodils and green fields. 'Or is he very busy?'

'He's painting,' says Angel. 'Better not disturb him now. He's had so many interruptions lately, poor man.'

'I read about him in the Sunday supplement,' says the doctor.

'Well, don't tell him so. He thought it vulgarized his work.'

'Did you think that?'

Me? Does what I think have anything to do with anything?

'I thought it was quite perceptive, actually,' says Angel, and feels a surge of good humour. She sits up in bed.

'Lie down,' he says. 'Take things easy. This is a large house. Do you have any help? Can't afford it?'

'It's not that. It's just why should I expect some other woman to do my dirty work?'

'Because she might like doing it and you're pregnant, and if you can afford it, why not?'

'Because Edward doesn't like strangers in the house. And what else have I got to do with my life? I might as well clean as anything else.'

'It's isolated out here,' he goes on. 'Do you drive?'

'Edward needs peace to paint,' says Angel. 'I do drive but Edward has a thing about women drivers.'

'You don't miss your friends?'

'After you're married,' says Angel, 'you seem to lose contact. It's the same for everyone, isn't it?'

'Um,' says the doctor. And then, 'I haven't been in this house for fifteen years. It's in a better state now than it was then. The house was divided into flats, in those days. I used to visit a nice young woman who had the attic floor. Just above this. Four children, and the roof leaked; a husband who spent his time drinking cider in the local pub and only came home to beat her.'

'Why did she stay?'

'How can such women leave? How do they afford it? Where do they go? What happens to the children?' His voice is sad.

'I suppose it's money that makes the difference. With money, a woman's free,' says Angel, trying to believe it.

'Of course,' says the doctor. 'But she loved her husband. She couldn't bring herself to see him for what he was. Well, it's hard. For a certain kind of woman, at any rate.'

Hard, indeed, if he has your soul in his safekeeping, to be left behind at the bar, in the pub, or in some other woman's bed, or in a seat in the train on his literary travels. Careless!

'But it's not like that for you, is it?' says the doctor calmly.

'You have money of your own, after all.'

Now how does he know that? Of course, the Sunday supplement article.

'No one will read it,' wept Angel, when Edward looked up, stony-faced from his first perusal of the fashionable columns. 'No one will notice. It's tucked away at the very bottom.'

So it was. 'Edward's angelic wife Angel, daughter of best-selling crime-writer Terry Toms, has smoothed the path upwards, not just with the soft smiles our cameraman has recorded, but by enabling the emergent genius to forswear the cramped and inconvenient, if traditional, artist's garret for a sixteenth-century farmhouse in greenest Gloucestershire. It is interesting, moreover, to ponder whether a poor man would have been able to develop the white-on-white techniques which have made Holst's work so noticeable: or whether the sheer price of paint these days would not have deterred him.'

'Edward, I didn't say a word to that reporter, not a word,' she said, when the ice showed signs of cracking, days later.

'What are you talking about?' he asked, turning slow, unfriendly eyes upon her.

'The article. I know it's upset you. But it wasn't my fault.'

'Why should a vulgar article in a vulgar newspaper upset me?'

And the ice formed over again, thicker than ever. But he went to London for two days, presumably to arrange his next show, and on his return casually mentioned that he'd seen Ray while he was there.

Angel had cleaned, baked, and sewed curtains in his absence, hoping to soften his heart towards her on his return: and lay awake all the night he was away, the fear of his infidelity so agonizing as to make her contemplate suicide, if only to put an end to it. She could not ask for reassurance. He would throw the fears so neatly back at her. 'Why do you think I should want to sleep with anyone else? Why are you so guilty? Because that's what you'd do if you were away from me?'

Ask for bread and be given stones. Learn self-sufficiency: never show need. Little, tough Angel of the soft smiles, hearing some other woman's footsteps in the night, crying for another's grief. Well, who wants a soul, tossed here and there by teasing hands, over-bruised and over-handled. Do without it!

Edward came home from London in a worse mood than he'd left, shook his head in wondering stupefaction at his wife's baking – 'I thought you said we were cutting down on carbohydrates' – and shut himself into his studio for twelve hours, emerging just once to say – 'Only a mad woman would hang curtains in an artist's studio, or else a silly rich girl playing at artist's wife, and in public at that' – and thrusting the new curtains back into her arms, vanished inside again.

Angel felt that her mind was slowing up, and puzzled over the last remark for some time before realizing that Edward was still harking back to the Sunday supplement article.

'I'll give away the money if you like,' she pleaded through the keyhole. 'If you'd rather. And if you want not to be married to me I don't mind.' That was before she was pregnant.

Silence.

Then Edward emerged laughing, telling her not to be so ridiculous, bearing her off to bed, and the good times were restored. Angel sang about the house, forgot her pill, and got pregnant.

'You have money of your own, after all,' says the doctor.

'You're perfectly free to come and go.'

'I'm pregnant,' says Angel. 'The baby has to have a father.'

'And your husband's happy about the baby?'

'Oh yes!' says Angel. 'Isn't it a wonderful day!'

And indeed today the daffodils nod brightly under a clear sky. So far, since first they budded and bloomed, they have been obliged to droop beneath the weight of rain and mist. A disappointing spring. Angel had hoped to see the countryside leap into energy and colour, but life returned only slowly, it seemed, struggling to surmount the damage of the past: cold winds and hard frosts, unseasonably late. 'Or at any rate,' adds Angel, softly, unheard, as the doctor goes, 'he *will* be happy about the baby.'

Angel hears no more noises in the night for a week or so. There had been misery in the attic room, and the misery had ceased. Good times can wipe out bad. Surely!

Edward sleeps soundly and serenely: she creeps from bed to bathroom without waking him. He is kind to her and even talkative, on any subject, that is, except that of her pregnancy. If it were not for the doctor and her stay in the hospital, she might almost think she was imagining the whole thing. Edward complains that Angel is getting fat, as if he could imagine no other cause for it but greed. She wants to talk to someone about hospitals, confinements, layettes, names – but to whom?

She tells her father on the telephone – 'I'm pregnant.'

'What does Edward say?' asks Terry, cautiously.

'Nothing much,' admits Angel.

'I don't suppose he does.'

'There's no reason *not* to have a baby,' ventures Angel.

'I expect he rather likes to be the centre of attention.' It is the nearest Terry has ever got to a criticism of Edward.

Angel laughs. She is beyond believing that Edward could ever be jealous of her, ever be dependent upon her.

'Nice to hear you happy, at any rate,' says her father wistfully. His twenty-year-old girlfriend has become engaged to a salesman of agricultural machinery, and although she has offered to continue the relationship the other side of marriage, Terry feels debased and used, and was obliged to break off the liaison. He has come to regard his daughter's marriage to Edward in a romantic light. The young bohemians!

'My daughter was an art school model before she married Edward Holst . . . you've heard of him? It's a real Rembrandt and Saskia affair.' He even thinks lovingly of Dora: if only she'd understood, waited for youth to wear itself out. Now he's feeling old and perfectly capable of being faithful to an ex-shoe-shop assistant. If only she weren't dead and gone!

An art school model. Those two weeks! Why had she done it? What devil wound up her works and set poor Angel walking in the wrong direction? It was in her nature, surely, as it was in her mother's, to follow the paths to righteousness, fully clothed.

Nightly, Edward studied her naked body, kissing her here,

kissing her there, parting her legs. Well, marriage! But now I'm pregnant, now I'm pregnant. Oh, be careful. That hard lump where my soft belly used to be. Be careful! Silence, Angel. Don't speak of it. It will be the worse for you and your baby if you do.

Angel knows it.

Now Angel hears the sound of lovemaking up in the empty attic, as she might hear it in hotels in foreign lands. The couplings of strangers in an unknown tongue – only the cries and breathings universal, recognizable anywhere.

The sounds chill her: they do not excite her. She thinks of the mother of four who lived in this house with her drunken, violent husband. Was that what kept you by his side? The chains of fleshy desire? Was it the thought of the night that got you through the perils of the day?

What indignity, if it were so.

Oh, I imagine it. I, Angel, half-mad in my unacknowledged pregnancy, my mind feverish, and the doctor's anecdotes feeding the fever – I imagine it! I must!

Edward wakes.

'What's that noise?'

'What noise?'

'Upstairs.'

'I don't hear anything.'

'You're deaf.'

'What sort of noise?'

But Edward sleeps again. The noise fades, dimly. Angel hears the sound of children's voices. Let it be a girl, dear Lord, let it be a girl.

'Why do you want a girl!' asks the doctor, on Angel's fourth monthly visit to the clinic.

'I'd love to dress a girl,' says Angel vaguely, but what she means is, if it's a girl, Edward will not be so – what is the word – hardly jealous, difficult perhaps. Dreadful. Yes, dreadful.

Bright-eyed Edward: he walks with Angel now – long walks up and over stiles, jumping streams, leaping stones. Young Edward. She has begun to feel rather old, herself.

'I am a bit tired,' she says, as they set off one night for their moonlit walk.

He stops, puzzled.

'Why are you tired?'

'Because I'm pregnant,' she says, in spite of herself.

'Don't start that again,' he says, as if it were hysteria on her part. Perhaps it is.

That night, he opens her legs so wide she thinks she will burst. 'I love you,' he murmurs in her nibbled ear, 'Angel, I love you. I do love you.' Angel feels the familiar surge of response, the holy gratitude, the willingness to die, to be torn apart if that's what's required. And then it stops. It's gone. Evaporated! And in its place, a new strength. A chilly icicle of non-response, wonderful, cheerful. No. It isn't right; it isn't what's required: on the contrary. 'I love you,' she says in return, as usual, but crossing her fingers in her mind, forgiveness for a lie. Please God, dear God, save me, help me save my baby. It is not me he loves, but my baby he hates: not me he delights in, but the pain he causes me, and knows he does. He does not wish to take root in me: all he wants to do is root my baby out. I don't love him. I never have. It is sickness. I must get well. Quickly.

'Not like that,' says Angel, struggling free – bold, unkind, prudish Angel – rescuing her legs. 'I'm pregnant. I'm sorry, but I am pregnant.'

Edward rolls off her, withdraws.

'Christ, you can be a monster. A real ball-breaker.'

'Where are you going?' asks Angel, calm and curious. Edward is dressing. Clean shirt; cologne. Cologne!

'To London.'

'Why?'

'Where I'm appreciated.'

'Don't leave me alone. Please.' But she doesn't mean it.

'Why not?'

'I'm frightened. Here alone at night.'

'Nothing ever frightened you.' Perhaps he is right.

Off he goes; the car breaking open the silence of the night.

It closed again. Angel is alone.

Tap, tap, tap, up above. Starting up as if on signal. Back and forward. To the attic bed which used to be, to the wardrobe which once was; the scuffle of the suitcase on the floor. Goodbye.

I'm going. I'm frightened here. The house is haunted. Someone upstairs, downstairs. Oh, women everywhere, don't think your misery doesn't seep into walls, creep downstairs, and then upstairs again. Don't think it will ever be done with, or that the good times wipe it out. They don't.

Angel feels her heart stop and start again. A neurotic symptom, her father's doctor had once said. It will get better, he said, when she's married and has babies. Everything gets better for women when they're married with babies. It's their natural state. Angel's heart stops all the same, and starts again, for good or bad.

Angel gets out of bed, slips on her mules with their sharp little heels, and goes up the attic stairs. Where does she find the courage? The light, reflected up from the hallway, is dim. The noise from the attic stops. Angel hears only – what? – the rustling noise of old newspapers in a fresh wind. That stops, too. As if a film were now running without sound. And coming down towards Angel, a small tired woman in a nightie, slippers silent on the stairs, stopping to stare at Angel as Angel stares at her. Her face marked by bruises.

'How can I see that,' wonders Angel, now unafraid, 'since there isn't any light?'

She flicks on the switch, hand trembling, and in the light, as she'd known, there is nothing to be seen except the empty stairs and the unmarked dust upon them.

Angel goes back to the bedroom and sits on the bed.

'I saw a ghost,' she tells herself, calmly enough. Then fear reasserts itself: panic at the way the universe plays tricks. Quick, quick! Angel pulls her suitcase out from under the bed – there are still traces of wedding confetti within – and tap-tap she goes, with sharp little footsteps, from the wardrobe to the bed, from the chest of drawers and back again, not so much packing as retrieving, salvaging. Something out of nothing!

Angel and her predecessor, rescuing each other, since each was incapable of rescuing herself, and rescue always comes, somehow. Or else death.

Tap-tap, back and forth, into the suitcase, out of the house.

The garden gate swings behind her.

Angel, bearing love to a safer place.

Night-Side

(1977)

JOYCE CAROL OATES

To Gloria Whelan

6 February 1887. Quincy, Massachusetts. Montague House.

Disturbing experience at Mrs A—'s home yesterday evening. Few
theatrics – comfortable though rather pathetically shabby surroundings – an only mildly sinister atmosphere (especially in contrast to
the Walpurgis Night presented by that shameless charlatan in
Portsmouth: the Dwarf Eustace who presumed to introduce me to
Swedenborg himself, under the erroneous impression that I am a
member of the Church of the New Jerusalem – I!) Nevertheless I
came away disturbed, and my conversation with Dr Moore
afterward, at dinner, though dispassionate and even, at times, a bit
flippant, did not settle my mind. Perry Moore is of course a hearty
materialist, an Aristotelian–Spencerian with a love of good food
and drink, and an appreciation of the more nonsensical vagaries of
life; when in his company I tend to support that general view, as I
do at the University as well – for there is a terrific pull in my
nature toward the gregarious that I cannot resist. (That I do not
wish to resist.) Once I am alone with my thoughts, however, I am
accursed with doubts about my own position and nothing seems
more precarious than my intellectual 'convictions'.

The more hardened members of our Society, like Perry Moore,
are apt to put the issue bluntly: Is Mrs A— of Quincy a conscious
or unconscious fraud? The conscious frauds are relatively easy to
deal with; once discovered, they prefer to erase themselves from
further consideration. The unconscious frauds are not, in a sense,
'frauds' at all. It would certainly be difficult to prove criminal
intention. Mrs A—, for instance, does not accept money or gifts
so far as we have been able to determine, and both Perry Moore

and I noted her courteous but firm refusal of the Judge's offer to send her and her husband (presumably ailing?) on holiday to England in the spring. She is a mild, self-effacing, rather stocky woman in her mid-fifties who wears her hair parted in the center, like several of my maiden aunts, and whose sole item of adornment was an old-fashioned cameo brooch; her black dress had the appearance of having been homemade, though it was attractive enough, and freshly ironed. According to the Society's records she has been a practicing medium now for six years. Yet she lives, still, in an undistinguished section of Quincy, in a neighborhood of modest frame dwellings. The A—s' house is in fairly good condition, especially considering the damage routinely done by our winters, and the only room we saw, the parlor, is quite ordinary, with overstuffed chairs and the usual cushions and a monstrous horsehair sofa and, of course, the oaken table; the atmosphere would have been so conventional as to have seemed disappointing had not Mrs A— made an attempt to brighten it, or perhaps to give it a glamourously occult air, by hanging certain watercolors about the room. (She claims that the watercolors were 'done' by one of her contact spirits, a young Iroquois girl who died in the seventeen seventies of smallpox. They are touchingly garish – mandalas and triangles and stylized eyeballs and even a transparent Cosmic Man with Indian-black hair.)

At last night's sitting there were only three persons in addition to Mrs A—: Judge T— of the New York State Supreme Court (now retired); Dr Moore; and I, Jarvis Williams. Dr Moore and I came out from Cambridge under the aegis of the Society for Psychical Research in order to make a preliminary study of the kind of mediumship Mrs A— affects. We did not bring a stenographer along this time though Mrs A— indicated her willingness to have the sitting transcribed; she struck me as being rather warmly cooperative, and even interested in our formal procedures, though Perry Moore remarked afterward at dinner that she had struck him as 'noticeably reluctant'. She was, however, flustered at the start of the séance and for a while it seemed as if we and the Judge might have made the trip for nothing. (She kept waving her plump hands about like an embarrassed hostess, apologizing for the fact that the spirits were evidently in a 'perverse uncommunicative mood tonight'.)

She did go into trance eventually, however. The four of us were seated about the heavy round table from approximately 6.50 p.m. to 9 p.m. For nearly forty-five minutes Mrs A— made abortive attempts to contact her Chief Communicator and then slipped abruptly into trance (dramatically, in fact: her eyes rolled back in her head in a manner that alarmed me at first), and a personality named Webley appeared. 'Webley's' voice appeared to be coming from several directions during the course of the sitting. At all times it was at least three yards from Mrs A—; despite the semi-dark of the parlor I believe I could see the woman's mouth and throat clearly enough, and I could not detect any obvious signs of ventriloquism. (Perry Moore, who is more experienced than I in psychical research, and rather more casual about the whole phenomenon, claims he has witnessed feats of ventriloquism that would make poor Mrs A— look quite shabby in comparison.) 'Webley's' voice was raw, singsong, peculiarly disturbing. At times it was shrill and at other times so faint as to be nearly inaudible. Something brattish about it. Exasperating. 'Webley' took care to pronounce his final 'g's in a self-conscious manner, quite unlike Mrs A—. (Which could be, of course, a deliberate ploy.)

This Webley is one of Mrs A—'s most frequent manifesting spirits, though he is not the most reliable. Her Chief Communicator is a Scots patriarch who lived 'in the time of Merlin' and who is evidently very wise; unfortunately he did not choose to appear yesterday evening. Instead, Webley presided. He is supposed to have died some seventy-five years ago at the age of nineteen in a house just up the street from the A—s. He was either a butcher's helper or an apprentice tailor. He died in a fire – or by a 'slow dreadful crippling disease' – or beneath a horse's hooves, in a freakish accident; during the course of the sitting he alluded self-pityingly to his death but seemed to have forgotten the exact details. At the very end of the evening he addressed me directly as Dr Williams of Harvard University, saying that since I had influential friends in Boston I could help him with his career – it turned out he had written hundreds of songs and poems and parables but none had been published; would I please find a publisher for his work? Life had treated him so unfairly. His talent – his genius – had been lost to humanity. I had it within my power to help him, he claimed, was I not *obliged* to help him . . . ? He then sang one of his songs, which sounded to me like an old ballad; many of the words were so shrill as to be unintelligible, but he sang it just the same, repeating the verses in a haphazard order:

> *This ae nighte, this ae nighte,*
>   *—Every nighte and alle,*
> *Fire and fleet and candle-lighte,*
>   *And Christe receive thy saule.*
>
> *When thou from hence away art past,*
>   *—Every nighte and alle,*
> *To Whinny-muir thou com'st at last:*
>   *And Christe receive thy saule.*
>
> *From Brig o' Dread when thou may'st pass,*
>   *—Every nighte and alle,*
> *The whinnes sall prick thee to the bare bane:*
>   *And Christe receive thy saule.*

The elderly Judge T—— had come up from New York City in order, as he earnestly put it, to 'speak directly to his deceased wife as he was never able to do while she was living'; but Webley treated the old gentleman in a high-handed, cavalier manner, as if the occasion were not at all serious. He kept saying, *Who is there tonight? Who is there? Let them introduce themselves again — I don't* like *strangers! I tell you I don't* like *strangers!* Though Mrs A—— had informed us beforehand that we would witness no physical phenomena, there were, from time to time, glimmerings of light in the darkened room, hardly more than the tiny pulsations of light made by fireflies; and both Perry Moore and I felt the table vibrating beneath our fingers. At about the time when Webley gave way to the spirit of Judge T——'s wife, the temperature in the room seemed to drop suddenly and I remember being gripped by a sensation of panic – but it lasted only an instant and I was soon myself again. (Dr Moore claimed not to have noticed any drop in temperature and Judge T—— was so rattled after the sitting that it would have been pointless to question him.)

The séance proper was similar to others I have attended. A spirit – or a voice – laid claim to being the late Mrs T——; this spirit addressed the survivor in a peculiarly intense, urgent manner, so that it was rather embarrassing to be present. Judge T— was soon weeping. His deeply creased face glistened with tears like a child's.

Why Darrie! Darrie! *Don't cry! Oh don't cry!* the spirit said. *No one is dead, Darrie. There is no death. No death! . . . Can you hear me, Darrie? Why are you so frightened? So upset? No need, Darrie, no need! Grandfather and Lucy and I are together here – happy together. Darrie, look up! Be brave, my dear! My poor frightened dear! We never knew each other, did we? My poor dear! My love! . . . I saw you in a great transparent house, a great burning house; poor Darrie, they told me you were ill, you were weak with fever; all the rooms of the house were aflame and the staircase was burnt to cinders, but there were figures walking up and down, Darrie, great numbers of them, and you were among them, dear, stumbling in your fright – so clumsy! Look up, dear, and shade your eyes, and you will see me. Grandfather helped me – did you know? Did I call out his name at the end? My dear, my darling, it all happened so quickly – we never knew each other, did we? Don't be hard on Annie! Don't be cruel! Darrie? Why are you crying?*

And gradually the spirit voice grew fainter; or perhaps something went wrong and the channels of communication were no longer clear. There were repetitions, garbled phrases, meaningless queries of *Dear? Dear?* that the Judge's replies did not seem to placate. The spirit spoke of her grave-site, and of a trip to Italy taken many years before, and of a dead or unborn baby, and again of Annie – evidently Judge T—'s daughter; but the jumble of words did not always make sense and it was a great relief when Mrs A— suddenly woke from her trance.

Judge T— rose from the table, greatly agitated. He wanted to call the spirit back; he had not asked her certain crucial questions; he had been overcome by emotion and had found it difficult to speak, to interrupt the spirit's monologue. But Mrs A— (who looked shockingly tired) told him the spirit would not return again that night and they must not make any attempt to call it back.

'The other world obeys its own laws,' Mrs A— said in her small, rather reedy voice.

We left Mrs A—'s home shortly after 9.00 p.m. I too was exhausted; I had not realized how absorbed I had been in the proceedings.

Judge T— is also staying at Montague House, but he was too upset after the sitting to join us for dinner. He assured us, though, that the spirit was authentic – the voice had been his wife's, he was certain of it, he would stake his life on it. She had never called him 'Darrie' during her lifetime, wasn't it odd that she called him 'Darrie' now? – and was so concerned for him, so loving? – and concerned for their daughter as well? He was very moved. He had a great deal to think about. (Yes, he'd had a fever some weeks ago – a severe attack of bronchitis and a fever; in fact, he had not completely recovered.) What was extraordinary about the entire experience was the wisdom revealed: There is no death.

There is no death.

Dr Moore and I dined heartily on roast crown of lamb, spring potatoes with peas, and buttered cabbage. We were served two kinds of bread – German rye and sour-cream rolls; the hotel's butter was superb; the wine excellent; the dessert – crepes with cream and toasted almonds – looked marvelous, though I had not any appetite for it. Dr Moore was ravenously hungry. He talked as he ate, often punctuating his remarks with rich bursts of laughter. It was his opinion, of course, that the medium was a fraud – and not a very skillful fraud, either. In his fifteen years of amateur, intermittent investigations he had encountered far more skillful mediums. Even the notorious Eustace with his levitating tables and hobgoblin chimes and shrieks was cleverer than Mrs A—; one knew of course that Eustace was a cheat, but one was hard pressed to explain his method. Whereas Mrs A— was quite transparent.

Dr Moore spoke for some time in his amiable, dogmatic way. He ordered brandy for both of us, though it was nearly midnight when we finished our dinner and I was anxious to get to bed. (I hoped to rise early and work on a lecture dealing with Kant's approach to the problem of Free Will, which I would be delivering in a few days.) But Dr Moore enjoyed talking and seemed to have been invigorated by our experience at Mrs A—'s.

At the age of forty-three Perry Moore is only four years my senior, but he has the air, in my presence at least, of being considerably older. He is a second cousin of my mother, a very successful physician with a bachelor's flat and office in Louisburg Square; his failure to marry, or his refusal, is one of Boston's perennial mysteries. Everyone agrees that he is learned, witty, charming, and extraordinarily intelligent. Striking rather than conventionally handsome, with a dark, lustrous beard and darkly bright eyes, he is an excellent amateur violinist, an enthusiastic sailor, and a lover of literature – his favorite writers are Fielding, Shakespeare, Horace, and Dante. He is, of course, the perfect investigator in spiritualist matters since he is detached from the phenomena he observes and yet he is indefatigably curious; he has a positive love, a mania, for facts. Like the true scientist he seeks facts that, assembled, may possibly give rise to hypotheses: he does not set out with a hypothesis in mind, like a sort of basket into which certain facts may be tossed, helter-skelter, while others are conveniently ignored. In all things he is an empiricist who accepts nothing on faith.

'If the woman is a fraud, then,' I say hesitantly, 'you believe she is a self-deluded fraud? And her spirits' information is gained by means of telepathy?'

'Telepathy indeed. There can be no other explanation,' Dr Moore says emphatically. 'By some means not yet known to science . . . by some uncanny means she suppresses her conscious personality . . . and thereby releases other, secondary personalities that have the power of seizing upon others' thoughts and memories. It's done in a way not understood by science at the present time. But it will be understood eventually. Our investigations into the unconscious powers of the human mind are just beginning; we're on the threshold, really, of a new era.'

'So she simply picks out of her clients' minds whatever they want to hear,' I say slowly. 'And from time to time she can even tease them a little – insult them, even: she can unloose a creature like that obnoxious Webley upon a person like Judge T— without fear of being discovered. Telepathy . . . Yes, that would explain a great deal. Very nearly everything we witnessed tonight.'

'*Everything*, I should say,' Dr Moore says.

In the coach returning to Cambridge I set aside Kant and my lecture notes and read Sir Thomas Browne: 'Light that makes all things seen, makes some things invisible. The greatest mystery of Religion is expressed by adumbration.'

19 March 1887. Cambridge. 11 p.m.

Walked ten miles this evening; must clear cobwebs from mind.

Unhealthy atmosphere. Claustrophobic. Last night's sitting in Quincy – a most unpleasant experience.

(Did not tell my wife what happened. Why is she so curious about the Spirit World? – about Perry Moore?)

My body craves more violent physical activity. In the summer, thank God, I will be able to swim in the ocean: the most strenuous and challenging of exercises.

Jotting down notes re the Quincy experience:

I. Fraud

Mrs A—, possibly with accomplices, conspires to deceive: she does research into her clients' lives beforehand, possibly bribes servants. She is either a very skillful ventriloquist or works with someone who is. (Husband? Son? The husband is a retired cabinet-maker said to be in poor health; possibly consumptive. The son, married, lives in Waterbury.)

Her stated wish to avoid publicity and her declining of payment may simply be ploys; she may intend to make a great deal of money at some future time.

(Possibility of blackmail? – might be likely in cases similar to Perry Moore's.)

II. Non-fraud

Naturalistic
1. Telepathy. She reads minds of clients.
2. 'Multiple personality' of medium. Aspects of her own buried psyche are released as her conscious personality is suppressed. These secondary beings are in mysterious rapport with the 'secondary' personalities of the clients.

Spiritualistic
1. The controls are genuine communicators, intermediaries between our world and the world of the dead. These spirits give way to other spirits, who then speak through the medium; or

2. These spirits *influence* the medium, who relays their messages using her own vocabulary. Their personalities are then filtered through and limited by hers.

3. The spirits are not those of the deceased; they are perverse, willful spirits. (Perhaps demons? But there are no demons.)

III. Alternative hypothesis

Madness: the medium is mad, the clients are mad, even the detached, rationalist investigators are mad.

~~Yesterday evening at Mrs A—'s home,~~ the second sitting Perry Moore and I observed together, along with Miss Bradley, a stenographer from the Society, and two legitimate clients – a Brookline widow, Mrs P—, and her daughter Clara, a handsome young woman in her early twenties. Mrs A— exactly as she appeared to us in February; possibly a little stouter. Wore black dress and cameo brooch. Served Lapsang tea, tiny sandwiches, and biscuits when we arrived shortly after 6 p.m. Seemed quite friendly to Perry, Miss Bradley, and me; fussed over us, like any hostess; chattered a bit about the cold spell. Mrs P— and her daughter arrived at six-thirty and the sitting began shortly thereafter.

Jarring from the very first. A babble of spirit voices. Mrs A— in trance, head flung back, mouth gaping, eyes rolled upward. Queer. Unnerving. I glanced at Dr Moore but he seemed unperturbed, as always. The widow and her daughter, however, looked as frightened as I felt.

Why are we here, sitting around this table?

What do we believe we will discover?

What are the risks we face . . .?

'Webley' appeared and disappeared in a matter of minutes. His shrill, raw, aggrieved voice was supplanted by that of a creature of indeterminate sex who babbled in Gaelic. This creature in turn was supplanted by a hoarse German, a man who identified himself as Felix; he spoke a curiously ungrammatical German. For some minutes he and two or three other spirits quarreled. (Each declared himself Mrs A—'s Chief Communicator for the evening.)

Small lights flickered in the semi-dark of the parlor and the table quivered beneath my fingers and I felt, or believed I felt, something brushing against me, touching the back of my head. I shuddered violently but regained my composure at once. An unidentified voice proclaimed in English that the Spirit of our Age was Mars: there would be a catastrophic war shortly and most of the world's population would be destroyed. All atheists would be destroyed. Mrs A— shook her head from side to side as if trying to wake. Webley appeared, crying, *Hello? Hello? I can't see anyone! Who is there? Who has called me?* but was again supplanted by another spirit who shouted long strings of words in a foreign language. [Note: I discovered a few days later that this language was Walachian, a Romanian dialect. Of course Mrs A—, whose ancestors are English, could not possibly have known Walachian, and I rather doubt that the woman has even heard of the Walachian people.]

The sitting continued in this chaotic way for some minutes. Mrs P— must have been quite disappointed, since she had wanted to be put in contact with her deceased husband. (She needed advice on whether or not to sell certain pieces of property.) Spirits babbled freely in English, German, Gaelic, French, even in Latin, and at one point Dr Moore queried a spirit in Greek, but the spirit retreated at once as if not equal to Dr Moore's wit. The atmosphere was alarming but at the same time rather manic; almost jocular. I found myself suppressing laughter. Something touched the back of my head and I shivered violently and broke into perspiration, but the experience was not altogether unpleasant; it would be very difficult for me to characterize it.

And then –

And then, suddenly, everything changed. There was complete calm. A spirit voice spoke gently out of a corner of the room, addressing Perry Moore by his first name in a slow, tentative, groping way. *Perry? Perry . . . ?* Dr Moore jerked about in his seat. He was astonished; I could see by his expression that the voice belonged to someone he knew.

Perry . . . ? This is Brandon. I've waited so long for you. Perry, how could you be so selfish? I forgave you. Long ago. You couldn't help your cruelty and I couldn't help my innocence. Perry? My glasses have been broken – I can't see. I've been afraid for so long, Perry, please have mercy

*on me! I can't bear it any longer. I didn't know what it would be like.
There are crowds of people here, but we can't see one another, we don't
know one another, we're strangers, there is a universe of strangers – I can't
see anyone clearly – I've been lost for twenty years, Perry, I've been waiting
for you for twenty years! You don't dare turn away again, Perry! Not
again! Not after so long!*

Dr Moore stumbled to his feet, knocking his chair aside.

'No –. Is it –. I don't believe –.'

Perry? Perry? Don't abandon me again, Perry! Not again!

'What is this?' Dr Moore cried.

He was on his feet now; Mrs A— woke from her trance with a
groan. The women from Brookline were very upset and I must
admit that I was in a mild state of terror, my shirt and my
underclothes drenched with perspiration.

The sitting was over. It was only seven-thirty.

'Brandon?' Dr Moore cried. 'Wait. Where are –? Brandon? Can
you hear me? Where are you? Why did you do it, Brandon? Wait!
Don't leave! Can't anyone call him back –. Can't anyone help
me –'

Mrs A— rose unsteadily. She tried to take Dr Moore's hands in
hers but he was too agitated.

'I heard only the very last words,' she said. 'They're always that
way – so confused, so broken – the poor things –. Oh, what a
pity! It wasn't murder, was it? Not murder! Suicide –? I believe
suicide is even worse for them! The poor broken things, they
wake in the other world and are utterly, utterly lost – they have no
guides, you see – no help in crossing over –. They are completely
alone for eternity –'

'Can't you call him back?' Dr Moore asked wildly. He was
peering into a corner of the parlor, slightly stooped, his face
distorted as if he were staring into the sun. 'Can't someone help
me? . . . Brandon? Are you here? Are you here somewhere? For
God's sake can't someone help!'

'Dr Moore, please, the spirits are gone – the sitting is over for
tonight –'

'You foolish old woman, leave me alone! Can't you see I – I – I
must not lose him –. Call him back, will you? I insist! I insist!'

'Dr Moore, please –. You mustn't shout –'

'I said call him back! At once! *Call him back!*'

Then he burst into tears. He stumbled against the table and hid his face in his hands and wept like a child; he wept as if his heart had been broken.

And so today I have been reliving the séance. Taking notes, trying to determine what happened. A brisk windy walk of ten miles. Head buzzing with ideas. Fraud? Deceit? Telepathy? Madness?

What a spectacle! Dr Perry Moore calling after a spirit, begging it to return – and then crying, afterward, in front of four astonished witnesses.

Dr Perry Moore of all people.

My dilemma: whether I should report last night's incident to Dr Rowe, the president of the Society, or whether I should say nothing about it and request that Miss Bradley say nothing. It would be tragic if Perry's professional reputation were to be damaged by a single evening's misadventure; and before long all of Boston would be talking.

In his present state, however, he is likely to tell everyone about it himself.

At Montague House the poor man was unable to sleep. He would have kept me up all night had I had the stamina to endure his excitement.

There *are* spirits! There have always been spirits!

His entire life up to the present time has been misspent!

And of course, most important of all – there is no death!

He paced about my hotel room, pulling at his beard nervously. At times there were tears in his eyes. He seemed to want a response of some kind from me but whenever I started to speak he interrupted; he was not really listening.

'Now at last I know. I can't undo my knowledge,' he said in a queer hoarse voice. 'Amazing, isn't it, after so many years . . . so many wasted years . . . Ignorance has been my lot, darkness . . . and a hideous complacency. My God, when I consider my deluded smugness! I am so ashamed, so ashamed. All along people like Mrs A— have been in contact with a world of such power . . . and people like me have been toiling in ignorance, accumulating material achievements, expending our energies in idiotic transient things . . . But all that is changed now. Now I know. I *know*. There is no death, as the Spiritualists have always told us.'

'But, Perry, don't you think –. Isn't it possible that –'

'I *know*,' he said quietly. 'It's as clear to me as if I had crossed over into that other world myself. Poor Brandon! He's no older now than he was *then*. The poor boy, the poor tragic soul! To think that he's still living after so many years . . . Extraordinary . . . It makes my head spin,' he said slowly. For a moment he stood without speaking. He pulled at his beard, then absently touched his lips with his fingers, then wiped at his eyes. He seemed to have forgotten me. When he spoke again his voice was hollow, rather ghastly. He sounded drugged. 'I . . . I had been thinking of him as . . . as dead, you know. As dead. Twenty years. Dead. And now, tonight, to be forced to realize that . . . that he isn't dead after all . . . It was laudanum he took. I found him. His rooms on the third floor of Weld Hall. I found him, I had no real idea, none at all, not until I read the note . . . and of course I destroyed the note . . . I had to, you see: for his sake. For his sake more than mine. It was because he realized there could be no . . . no hope . . . Yet he called me cruel! You heard him, Jarvis, didn't you? Cruel! I suppose I was. Was I? I don't know what to think. I must talk with him again. I . . . I don't know what to . . . what to think. I . . .'

'You look awfully tired, Perry. It might be a good idea to go to bed,' I said weakly.

'. . . recognized his voice at once. Oh at once: no doubt. None. What a revelation! And my life so misspent . . . Treating people's *bodies*. Absurd. I know now that nothing matters except that other world . . . nothing matters except our dead, our beloved dead . . . who are *not dead*. What a colossal revelation . . .! Why, it will change the entire course of history. It will alter men's minds throughout the world. You were there, Jarvis, so you understand. You were a witness . . .'

'But –'

'You'll bear witness to the truth of what I am saying?'

He stared at me, smiling. His eyes were bright and threaded with blood.

I tried to explain to him as courteously and sympathetically as possible that his experience at Mrs A——'s was not substantially different from the experiences many people have had at séances. 'And always in the past psychical researchers have taken the position –'

'You were *there*,' he said angrily. 'You heard Brandon's voice as clearly as I did. Don't deny it!'

'– have taken the position that – that the phenomenon can be partly explained by the telepathic powers of the medium –'

'That was Brandon's *voice*,' Perry said. 'I felt his presence, I tell you! *His*. Mrs A—— had nothing to do with it – nothing at all. I feel as if . . . as if I could call Brandon back by myself . . . I feel his presence even now. Close about me. He isn't dead, you see; no one is dead, there's a universe of . . . of people who are not dead . . . Parents, grandparents, sisters, brothers, everyone . . . everyone . . . How can you deny, Jarvis, the evidence of your own senses? You were there with me tonight and you know as well as I do . . .'

'Perry, I don't *know*. I did hear a voice, yes, but we've heard voices before at other sittings, haven't we? There are always voices. There are always "spirits". The Society has taken the position that the spirits could be real, of course, but that there are other hypotheses that are perhaps more likely –'

'Other hypotheses indeed!' Perry said irritably. 'You're like a man with his eyes shut tight who refuses to open them out of sheer cowardice. Like the cardinals refusing to look through Galileo's telescope! And you have pretensions of being a man of learning, of science . . . Why, we've got to destroy all the records we've made so far; they're a slander on the world of the spirits. Thank God we didn't file a report yet on Mrs A——! It would be so embarrassing to be forced to call it back . . .'

'Perry, please. Don't be angry. I want only to remind you of the fact that we've been present at other sittings, haven't we? – and we've witnessed others responding emotionally to certain phenomena. Judge T——, for instance. He was convinced he'd spoken with his wife. But you must remember, don't you, that you and I were not at all convinced . . .? It seemed to us more likely that Mrs A—— is able, through extrasensory powers we don't quite understand, to read the minds of her clients, and then to project certain voices out into the room so that it sounds as if they are coming from other people ... You even said, Perry, that she wasn't a very skillful ventriloquist. You said —'

'What does it matter what, in my ignorance, I said?' he cried. 'Isn't it enough that I've been humiliated? That my entire life has been turned about? Must you insult me as well — sitting there so smugly and insulting *me*? I think I can make claim to being someone whom you might respect.'

And so I assured him that I did respect him. And he walked about the room, wiping at his eyes, greatly agitated. He spoke again of his friend, Brandon Gould, and of his own ignorance, and of the important mission we must undertake to inform men and women of the true state of affairs. I tried to talk with him, to reason with him, but it was hopeless. He scarcely listened to me.

'. . . must inform the world . . . crucial truth . . . There is no death, you see. Never was. Changes civilization, changes the course of history. Jarvis?' he said groggily. 'You see? *There is no death*.'

25 March 1887. Cambridge.

Disquieting rumors re Perry Moore. Heard today at the University that one of Dr Moore's patients (a brother-in-law of Dean Barker) was extremely offended by his behavior during a consultation last week. Talk of his having been drunk — which I find incredible. If the poor man appeared to be excitable and not his customary self, it was not because he was *drunk*, surely.

Another far-fetched tale told me by my wife, who heard it from her sister Maude: Perry Moore went to church (St Aidan's Episcopal Church on Mount Street) for the first time in a decade, sat alone, began muttering and laughing during the sermon, and finally got to his feet and walked out, creating quite a stir. 'What delusions! What delusions!' — he was said to have muttered.

I fear for the poor man' sanity.

31 March 1887. Cambridge. 4 a.m.

Sleepless night. Dreamed of swimming . . . swimming in the ocean . . . enjoying myself as usual when suddenly the water turns thick

. . . turns to mud. Hideous! Indescribably awful. I was swimming nude in the ocean, by moonlight, I believe, ecstatically happy, entirely alone, when the water turned to mud . . . Vile, disgusting mud; faintly warm; sucking at my body. Legs, thighs, torso, arms. Horrible. Woke in terror. Drenched with perspiration: pajamas wet. One of the most frightening nightmares of my adulthood.

A message from Perry Moore came yesterday just before dinner. Would I like to join him in visiting Mrs A— sometime soon, in early April perhaps, on a non-investigative basis . . .? He is uncertain now of the morality of our 'investigating' Mrs A— or any other medium.

4 April 1887. Cambridge.

Spent the afternoon from two to five at William James's home on Irving Street, talking with Professor James of the inexplicable phenomenon of consciousness. He is robust as always, rather irreverent, supremely confident in a way I find enviable; rather like Perry Moore before his conversion. (Extraordinary eyes – so piercing, quick, playful; a graying beard liberally threaded with white; close-cropped graying hair; a large, curving, impressive forehead; a manner intelligent and graceful and at the same time rough-edged, as if he anticipates or perhaps even hopes for recalcitrance in his listeners.) We both find conclusive the ideas set forth in Binet's *Alterations of Personality* . . . unsettling as these ideas may be to the rationalist position. James speaks of a 'peculiarity' in the constitution of human nature: that is, the fact that we inhabit not only our ego-consciousness but a wide field of psychological experience (most clearly represented by the phenomenon of memory, which no one can adequately explain) over which we have no control whatsoever. In fact, we are not generally aware of this field of consciousness.

We inhabit a lighted sphere, then; and about us is a vast penumbra of memories, reflections, feelings, and stray uncoordinated thoughts that 'belong' to us theoretically, but that do not seem to be part of our conscious identity. (I was too timid to ask Professor James whether it might be the case that we do not inevitably own these aspects of the personality – that such phenomena belong as much to the objective world as to our subjective selves.) It is quite possible that there is an element of some indeterminate kind: oceanic, timeless, and living, against which the individual being constructs temporary barriers as part of an ongoing process of unique, particularized survival; like the ocean itself, which appears to separate islands that are in fact not 'islands' at all, but aspects of the earth firmly joined together below the surface of the water. Our lives, then, resemble these islands. . . . All this is no more than a possibility, Professor James and I agreed.

James is acquainted, of course, with Perry Moore. But he declined to speak on the subject of the poor man's increasingly eccentric behavior when I alluded to it. (It may be that he knows even more about the situation than I do – he enjoys a multitude of acquaintances in Cambridge and Boston.) I brought our conversation round several times to the possibility of the *naturalness* of the conversion experience in terms of the individual's evolution of self, no matter how his family, his colleagues, and society in general viewed it, and Professor James appeared to agree; at least he did not emphatically disagree. He maintains a healthy skepticism, of course, regarding Spiritualist claims, and all evangelical and enthusiastic religious movements, though he is, at the same time, a highly articulate foe of the 'rationalist' position and he believes that psychical research of the kind some of us are attempting will eventually unearth riches – revealing aspects of the human psyche otherwise closed to our scrutiny.

'The fearful thing,' James said, 'is that we are at all times vulnerable to incursions from the "other side" of the personality . . . We cannot determine the nature of the total personality simply because much of it, perhaps most, is hidden from us . . . When we are invaded, then, we are overwhelmed and surrender immediately. Emotionally charged intuitions, hunches, guesses, even ideas may be the least aggressive of these incursions; but there are visual and auditory hallucinations, and forms of automatic behavior not controlled by the conscious mind . . . Ah, you're thinking I am simply describing insanity?'

I stared at him, quite surprised.

'No. Not at all. Not at all,' I said at once.

Reading through my grandfather's journals, begun in East Anglia many years before my birth. Another world then. Another language, now lost to us. 'Man is sinful by nature. God's justice takes precedence over his mercy.' The dogma of Original Sin: something brutish about the innocence of that belief. And yet consoling . . .

Fearful of sleep since my dreams are so troubled now. The voices of impudent spirits (Immanuel Kant himself come to chide me for having made too much of his categories − !), stray shouts and whispers I cannot decipher, the faces of my own beloved dead hovering near, like carnival masks, insubstantial and possibly fraudulent. Impatient with my wife, who questions me too closely on these personal matters; annoyed from time to time, in the evenings especially, by the silliness of the children. (The eldest is twelve now and should know better.) Dreading to receive another lengthy letter − sermon, really − from Perry Moore re his 'new position', and yet perversely hoping one will come soon.

I must know.

(Must know *what* . . .?)

I must know.

10 April 1887. Boston. St Aidan's Episcopal Church.

Funeral service this morning for Perry Moore; dead at forty-three.

17 April 1887. Seven Hills, New Hampshire.

A weekend retreat. No talk. No need to think.

Visiting with a former associate, author of numerous books. Cartesian specialist. Elderly. Partly deaf. Extraordinarily kind to me. (Did not ask about the Department or about my work.) Intensely interested in animal behavior now, in observation primarily; fascinated with the phenomenon of hibernation.

He leaves me alone for hours. He sees something in my face I cannot see myself.

The old consolations of a cruel but just God: ludicrous today.

In the nineteenth century we live free of God. We live in the illusion of freedom-of-God.

Dozing off in the guest room of this old farmhouse and then waking abruptly. 'Is someone here? Is someone here?' My voice queer, hushed, childlike. 'Please: is someone here?'

Silence.

Query: Is the penumbra outside consciousness all that was ever meant by 'God'?

Query: Is inevitability all that was ever meant by 'God'?

God – the body of fate we inhabit, then; no more and no less.

God pulled Perry down into the body of fate: into Himself. (Or Itself.) As Professor James might say, Dr Moore was 'vulnerable' to an assault from the other side.

At any rate he is dead. They buried him last Saturday.

25 April 1887. Cambridge.

Shelves of books. The sanctity of books. Kant, Plato, Schopenhauer, Descartes, Hume, Hegel, Spinoza. The others. All. Nietzsche, Spencer, Leibniz (on whom I did a torturous Master's thesis). Plotinus. Swedenborg. *The Transactions of the American Society for Psychical Research.* Voltaire. Locke. Rousseau. And Berkeley: the good Bishop adrift in a dream.

An etching by Halbrech above my desk, The Thames, 1801. Water too black. Inky-black. Thick with mud . . .? Filthy water in any case.

Perry's essay, forty-five scribbled pages. 'The Challenge of the Future.' Given to me several weeks ago by Dr Rowe, who feared rejecting it for the *Transactions* but could not, of course, accept it. I can read only a few pages at a time, then push it aside, too moved to continue. Frightened also.

The man had gone insane.

Died insane.

Personality broken: broken bits of intellect.

His argument passionate and disjointed, with no pretense of objectivity. Where some weeks ago he had taken the stand that it was immoral to investigate the Spirit World, now he took the stand that it was imperative we do so. We are on the brink of a new age . . . new knowledge of the universe . . . comparable to the stormy transitional period between the Ptolemaic and the Copernican theories of the universe ... More experiments required. Money. Donations. Subsidies by private institutions. All psychological research must be channelled into a systematic study of the Spirit World and the ways by which we can communicate with that world. Mediums like Mrs A— must be brought to centers of learning like Harvard and treated with the respect their genius deserves. Their value to civilization is, after all, beyond estimation. They must be rescued from arduous and routine lives where their genius is drained off into vulgar pursuits ... they must be rescued from a clientele that is mainly concerned with being put into contact with deceased relatives for utterly trivial, self-serving reasons. Men of learning must realize the gravity of the situation. Otherwise we will fail, we will stagger beneath the burden, we will be defeated, ignobly, and it will remain for the twentieth century to discover the existence of the Spirit Universe that surrounds the Material Universe, and to determine the exact ways by which one world is related to another.

Perry Moore died of a stroke on the eighth of April; died instantaneously on the steps of the Bedford Club shortly after 2 p.m. Passersby saw a very excited, red-faced gentleman with an open collar push his way through a small gathering at the top of the steps – and then suddenly fall, as if shot down.

In death he looked like quite another person: his features sharp, the nose especially pointed. Hardly the handsome Perry Moore everyone had known.

He had come to a meeting of the Society, though it was suggested by Dr Rowe and by others (including myself) that he stay away. Of course he came to argue. To present his 'new position'. To insult the other members. (He was contemptuous of a rather poorly organized paper on the medium Miss E— of Salem, a young woman who works with objects like rings, articles of clothing, locks of hair, et cetera; and quite angry with the evidence presented by a young geologist that would seem to discredit, once and for all, the claims of Eustace of Portsmouth. He interrupted a third paper, calling the reader a 'bigot' and an 'ignorant fool'.

Fortunately the incident did not find its way into any of the papers. The press, misunderstanding (deliberately and maliciously) the Society's attitude toward Spiritualism, delights in ridiculing our efforts.

There were respectful obituaries. A fine eulogy prepared by Reverend Tyler of St Aidan's. Other tributes. *A tragic loss.* . . . *Mourned by all who knew him.* . . . (I stammered and could not speak. I cannot speak of him, of it, even now. Am I mourning, am I aggrieved? Or merely shocked? Terrified?) Relatives and friends and associates glossed over his behavior these past few months and settled upon an earlier Perry Moore, eminently sane, a distinguished physician and man of letters. I did not disagree, I merely acquiesced; I could not make any claim to have really known the man.

And so he has died, and so he is dead . . .

Shortly after the funeral I went away to New Hampshire for a few days. But I can barely remember that period of time now. I sleep poorly, I yearn for summer, for a drastic change of climate, of scene. It was unwise for me to take up the responsibility of psychical research, fascinated though I am by it; my classes and lectures at the University demand most of my energy.

How quickly he died, and so young: so relatively young.

No history of high blood pressure, it is said.

At the end he was arguing with everyone, however. His personality had completely changed. He was rude, impetuous, even rather profane; even poorly groomed. (Rising to challenge the first of the papers, he revealed a shirt-front that appeared to be stained.) Some claimed he had been drinking all along, for years. Was it possible . . .? (He had clearly enjoyed the wine and brandy in Quincy that evening, but I would not have said he was intemperate.) Rumors, fanciful tales, outright lies, slander . . . It is painful, the vulnerability death brings.

Bigots, he called us. Ignorant fools. Unbelievers – atheists – traitors to the Spirit World – heretics. Heretics! I believe he looked directly at me as he pushed his way out of the meeting room: his eyes glaring, his face dangerously flushed, no recognition in his stare.

After his death, it is said, books continue to arrive at his home from England and Europe. He spent a small fortune on obscure, out-of-print volumes – commentaries on the Kabbala, on Plotinus, medieval alchemical texts, books on astrology, witchcraft, the metaphysics of death. Occult cosmologies. Egyptian, Indian, and Chinese 'wisdom'. Blake, Swedenborg, Cozad. *The Tibetan Book of the Dead*. Datsky's *Lunar Mysteries*. His estate is in chaos because he left not one but several wills, the most recent made out only a day before his death, merely a few lines scribbled on scrap paper, without witnesses. The family will contest, of course. Since in this will he left his money and property to an obscure woman living in Quincy, Massachusetts, and since he was obviously not in his right mind at the time, they would be foolish indeed not to contest.

Days have passed since his sudden death. Days continue to pass. At times I am seized by a sort of quick, cold panic; at other times I am inclined to think the entire situation has been exaggerated. In one mood I vow to myself that I will never again pursue psychical research because it is simply too dangerous. In another mood I vow I will never again pursue it because it is a waste of time and my own work, my own career, must come first.

Heretics, he called us. Looking straight at me.

Still, he was mad. And is not to be blamed for the vagaries of madness.

19 June 1887. Boston

Luncheon with Dr Rowe, Miss Madeleine van der Post, young Lucas Matthewson; turned over my personal records and notes re the mediums Dr Moore and I visited. (Destroyed jottings of a private nature.) Miss van der Post and Matthewson will be taking over my responsibilities. Both are young, quick-witted, alert, with a certain ironic play about their features; rather like Dr Moore in his prime. Matthewson is a former seminary student now teaching physics at the Boston University. They questioned me about Perry Moore, but I avoided answering frankly. Asked if we were close, I said 'No.' Asked if I had heard a bizarre tale making the rounds of Boston salons – that a spirit claiming to be Perry Moore has intruded upon a number of séances in the area – I said honestly that I had not; and I did not care to hear about it.

Spinoza: 'I will analyze the actions and appetites of men as if it were a question of lines, of planes, and of solids.'

It is in this direction, I believe, that we must move. Away from the phantasmal, the vaporous, the unclear; toward lines, planes, and solids.

Sanity.

8 July 1887. Mount Desert Island, Maine

Very early this morning, before dawn, dreamed of Perry Moore: a babbling gesticulating spirit, bearded, bright-eyed, obviously mad. *Jarvis? Jarvis? Don't deny me!* he cried. *I am so . . . so bereft . . .*

Paralyzed, I faced him: neither awake nor asleep. His words were not really *words* so much as unvoiced thoughts. I heard them in my own voice; a terrible raw itching at the back of my throat yearned to articulate the man's grief.

Perry?

You don't dare deny me! Not now!

He drew near and I could not escape. The dream shifted, lost its clarity. Someone was shouting at me. Very angry, he was, and baffled – as if drunk – or ill – or injured.

Perry? I can't hear you –

– our dinner at Montague House, do you remember? Lamb, it was. And crepes with almond for dessert. You remember! You remember! You can't deny me! We were both non-believers then, both abysmally ignorant – you can't deny me!

(I was mute with fear or with cunning.)

– that idiot Rowe, how humiliated he will be! All of them! All of you! The entire rationalist bias, the – the conspiracy of – of fools – bigots – In a few years –. In a few short years –, Jarvis, where are you? Why can't I see you? Where have you gone? –. My eyes can't focus: will someone help me? I seem to have lost my way. Who is here? Who am I talking with? You remember me, don't you?

(He brushed near me, blinking helplessly. His mouth was a hole torn into his pale ravaged flesh.)

Where are you? Where is everyone? I thought it would be crowded here but – but there's no one – I am forgetting so much! My name – what was my name? Can't see. Can't remember. Something very important –

*something very important I must accomplish — can't remember —. Why is
there no God? No one here? No one in control? We drift this way and that
way, we come to no rest, there are no landmarks — no way of judging —
everything is confused — disjointed —. Is someone listening? Would you read
to me, please? Would you read to me? — anything — that speech of
Hamlet's —* 'To be or not' *— a sonnet of Shakespeare's — any sonnet,
anything —* 'That time of year thou may in me behold' *— is that it? —
is that how it begins?* 'Bare ruin'd choirs where the sweet birds once
sang.' *How does it go? Won't you tell me? I'm lost — there's nothing here
to see, to touch — isn't anyone listening? I thought there was someone nearby,
a friend: isn't anyone here?*

(I stood paralyzed, mute with caution: he passed by.)

— 'When in the chronicle of wasted time — the wide world
dreaming of things to come' *— is anyone listening? — can anyone help? —
I am forgetting so much — my name, my life — my life's work — to penetrate
the mysteries — the veil — to do justice to the universe of — of what — what
had I intended? — am I in my place of repose now, have I come home? Why
is it so empty here? Why is no one in control? My eyes — my head — mind
broken and blown about — slivers — shards — annihilating all that's made to
a — a green thought — a green shade — Shakespeare? Plato? Pascal? Will
someone read me Pascal again? I seem to have lost my way — I am being
blown about —. Jarvis, was it? My dear young friend Jarvis? But I've
forgotten your last name — I've forgotten so much —*

(I wanted to reach out to touch him — but could not move,
could not wake. The back of my throat ached with sorrow. Silent!
Silent! I could not utter a word.)

*— my papers, my journal — twenty years — a key somewhere hidden —
where? — ah yes: the bottom drawer of my desk — do you hear? — my desk —
house — Louisburg Square — the key is hidden there — wrapped in a linen
handkerchief — the strongbox is — the locked box is — hidden — my brother
Edward's house — attic — trunk — steamer trunk — initials R. W. M. —
Father's trunk, you see — strongbox hidden inside — my secret journals —
life's work — physical and spiritual wisdom — must not be lost — are you
listening? — is anyone listening? I am forgetting so much, my mind is in
shreds — but if you could locate the journal and read it to me — if you could
salvage it — me — I would be so very grateful — I would forgive you anything,
all of you —. Is anyone there? Jarvis? Brandon? No one? — My journal, my
soul: will you salvage it? Will —*

(He stumbled away and I was alone again.)
Perry–?
But it was too late: I awoke drenched with perspiration.

Nightmare.
Must forget.

Best to rise early, before the others. Mount Desert Island lovely in July. Our lodge on a hill above the beach. No spirits here: wind from the north-east, perpetual fresh air, perpetual waves. Best to rise early and run along the beach and plunge into the chilly water.

Clear the cobwebs from one's mind.

How beautiful the sky, the ocean, the sunrise!

No spirits here on Mount Desert Island. Swimming: skillful exertion of arms and legs. Head turned this way, that way. Eyes half shut. The surprise of the cold rough waves. One yearns almost to slip out of one's human skin at such times . . .! Crude blatant beauty of Maine. Ocean. Muscular exertion of body. How alive I am, how living, how invulnerable; what a triumph in my every breath . . .

Everything slips from my mind except the present moment. I am living, I am alive, I am immortal. Must not weaken: must not sink. Drowning? No. Impossible. Life is the only reality. It is not extinction that awaits but a hideous dreamlike state, a perpetual groping, blundering – far worse than extinction – incomprehensible: so it is life we must cling to, arm over arm, swimming, conquering the element that sustains us.

Jarvis? someone cried. *Please hear me –*

How exquisite life is, the turbulent joy of life contained in flesh! I heard nothing except the triumphant waves splashing about me. I swam for nearly an hour. Was reluctant to come ashore for breakfast, though our breakfasts are always pleasant rowdy sessions: my wife and my brother's wife and our seven children thrown together for the month of July. Three boys, four girls: noise, bustle, health, no shadows, no spirits. No time to think. Again and again I shall emerge from the surf, face and hair and body streaming water, exhausted but jubilant, triumphant. Again and again the children will call out to me, excited, from the day-side of the world that they inhabit.

I will not investigate Dr Moore's strongbox and his secret journal; I will not even think about doing so. The wind blows words away. The surf is hypnotic. I will not remember this morning's dream once I sit down to breakfast with the family. I will not clutch my wife's wrist and say, *We must not die! We dare not die!* – for that would only frighten and offend her.

Jarvis? she is calling at this very moment.

And I say *Yes –? Yes, I'll be there at once.*

Fireflood

(1979)

VONDA N. McINTYRE

Dark moved slowly along the bottom of a wide, swift river, pushing against its current. The clean water made long bubbling strokes over her armor, and round stones scraped against her belly scales. She could live here, hidden in rapids or pools, surfacing every few hours to replenish her internal supplies of oxygen, looking little different from a huge boulder. In time she could even change the color of her armor to conform perfectly to the lighter, grayer rock of this region. But she was moving on; she would not stay in the river long enough to alter her rust-red hue.

Vibrations warned her of rapids. She took more care with her hand- and footholds, though her own mass was her main anchor. Stones rumbling gradually downstream did not afford much purchase for her claws. The turbulence was treacherous and exciting. But now she had to work harder to progress, and the riverbed shifted more easily beneath her. As the water grew swifter it also became more shallow, and when she sensed a number of huge boulders around her, she turned her back to the flow and reared up above the surface to breathe.

The force of the current sent water spraying up over her back, forming a curtain that helped conceal her. She breathed deeply, pumping air through her storage lungs, forcing herself not to exceed her body's most efficient absorption rate. However anxious she was to get underwater again, she would do herself no good if she used more oxygen than she stored during the stop.

Dark's armor, though impenetrable and insensitive to pain, detected other sensations. She was constantly aware of the small point of heat – call it that, she had no more accurate word – in the center of her spinal ridge. It was a radio transceiver. Though she could choose not to hear its incoming messages, it sent out a permanent beacon of her presence that she could not stop. It was meant to bring aid to her in emergencies, but she did not want to be found. She wanted to escape.

Before she had properly caught her breath, she sensed the approach of a helicopter, high above and quite far away. She did not see it: the spray of water glittered before her shortsighted eyes. She did not hear it: the rush of the river drowned out all other sounds. But she had more than one sense that had as yet no name.

She let herself sink beneath the water. An observer would have to watch a single boulder among many to see what had happened. If the searchers had not homed in on the transmitter she could still get away.

She turned upstream again and forged ahead toward the river's source.

If she was very lucky, the helicopter was flying a pattern and had not actually spotted her transmitter at all. That was a possibility, for while it did not quite have the specificity of a laser, it worked on a narrow beam. It was, after all, designed to send messages via satellite.

But the signal did not pass through water and even as the searchers could not detect her, she could not see or feel them through the rough silver surface of the river. Trusting her luck, she continued on.

The country was very different from where she had trained. Though she was much more comfortable underground than underwater, this land was not ideal for digging. She could survive as well beneath liquid, and travel was certainly quicker. If she could not get to the surface to breathe, the time it would take her to stop and extract oxygen directly was about the same. But the character of water was far too constant for her taste. Its action was predictable and its range of temperature was trivial compared to what she could stand. She preferred to go underground, where excitement spiced the exploration. For, though she was slow, methodical, and nearly indestructible, she *was* an explorer. It was just that now she had nowhere to explore.

She wondered if any of her friends had made it this far. She and six others had decided, in secret, to flee. But they offered each other only moral support; each had gone out alone. Twenty more of her kind still remained scattered in their reserve, waiting for assignments that would never come and pretending they had not been abandoned.

Though it was not yet evening, the light faded around her and left the river bottom gray and black. Dark slowly and cautiously lifted her eyes above the water. Her eyes peered darkly from beneath her armor. They were deep blue, almost black, the only thing of beauty about her: the only thing of beauty about her after or before her transformation from a creature who could pass for human to one who could not. Even now she was not sorry to have volunteered for the change. It did not further isolate her; she had always been alone. She had also been useless. In her new life, she had some worth.

The riverbed had cut between tall, thick trees that shut out much of the sunlight. Dark did not know for certain if they would interfere with the radio signal as well. She had not been designed to work among lush vegetation and she had never studied how her body might interact with it. But she did not believe it would be safe for her to take a quiet stroll among the giant cedars. She tried to get her bearings with sun time and body memory. Her ability to detect magnetic fields was worthless here on Earth; that sense was designed for more delicate signals. She closed it off as she might shut her eyes to a blinding light.

Dark submerged again and followed the river upward, keeping to its main branch. As she passed the tributaries that ran and rushed to join the primary channel the river became no more than a stream itself, and Dark was protected only by thin ripples.

She peered out again.

The pass across the ridge lay only a little ahead and above her, just beyond the spring that created the river. To Dark's left lay a wide field of scree, where a cliff and hillside had collapsed. The river flowed around the pile, having been displaced by tons of broken stone. The rubble stretched on quite a way, at least as far as the pass and, if she were lucky, all the way through. It was ideal. Sinking barely underwater, she moved across the current. Beneath her feet she felt the stones change from rounded and water-worn to sharp and freshly broken. She reached the edge of the slope, where the shattered rock projected into the river. On the downstream side she nudged away a few large stones, set herself, and burrowed quickly into the shards.

The fractured crystalline matrix disrupted her echo perception. She kept expecting to meet a wall of solid rock that would push her out and expose her, but the good conditions existed all the way through the pass. Then, on the other side, when she chanced a peek out into the world, she found that the texture of the ground changed abruptly on this side of the ridge. When the broken stone ended, she did not have to seek out another river. She dug straight from the scree into the earth.

In the cool dry darkness, she travelled more slowly but more safely than in the river. Underground there was no chance of the radio signal's escaping to give her away. She knew exactly where the surface was all the time. It, unlike the interface of water and air, did not constantly change. Barring the collapse of a hillside, little could unearth her. A landslide was possible, but her sonar could detect the faults and weaknesses in earth and rock might create a danger.

She wanted to rest, but she was anxious to reach the flyers' sanctuary as quickly as she could. She did not have much farther to go. Every bit of distance might make a difference, for she would be safe after she got inside the boundaries . . . She could be safe there from normal people: what the flyers would do when she arrived she could not say.

Dark's vision ranged much farther through the spectrum than it had when she was human. In daytime she saw colors, but at night and underground she used infrared, which translated to distinguishable and distinctive shades of black. They were supposed to look like colors, but she saw them all as black. They told her what sort of land she was passing through and a great deal about what grew above. Nevertheless, when the sun went down she broke through thick turf and peered around at the forest. The moon had not yet risen, and a nearby stream was almost as dark as ice. The fir trees kept the same deep tone as in bright sunlight. Still, all the colors were black.

Dark breathed deeply of the cold air. It was stuffy underground, though she had not had to switch to reducing her own oxygen. This was for deeper down, in altogether more difficult regions.

The air smelled of moss and ferns, evergreen trees, and weathered stone. But under it all was the sulfurous volcano, and the sweet delicate fragrance of flyers.

Sinking down into the earth once more, Dark travelled on.

The closer Dark got to the volcano, the more jumbled and erratic grew the strata. Lava flows and land movement, glaciers and erosion had scarred and unsettled and twisted the surface and all that lay beneath it. Deep underground Dark encountered a tilted slab of granite, too hard for to her to dig through quickly. She followed it upward, hoping it would twist and fold back down again. But it did not, and she broke through topsoil into the chill silence of a wilderness night. Dirt and pebbles fell away from her shoulder armor. From the edge of the outcropping she looked out, in infrared, over her destination.

The view excited her. The tree-covered slope dropped to tumbled masses of blackened logs that formed the first barrier against intrusion into the flyers' land. Beyond, at the base of the volcano, solidified lava created another wasteland. The molten rock had flowed from the crater down the flank of the mountain; near the bottom it broke into two branches which ran, one to each side, until both ended like true rivers, in the sea. The northern shore was very close, and the pale night-time waves lapped gently on the dim cool beach. To the south the lava had crept through a longer sweep of forest, burning the trees in its path and toppling those beyond its heat, for a much longer distance to the ocean. The wide solid flood and the impenetrable wooden jumble formed a natural barricade. The flyers were exiled to their peninsula, but they stayed there by choice. The humans had no way of containing them short of killing them. They could take back their wings or chain them to the ground or imprison them, but they wished to isolate the flyers, not murder them. And murder it would be if they denied the creatures flight.

The basalt stream glowed with heat retained from the day, and the volcano itself was a softly radiant cone, sparkling here and there where up-wellings of magma approached the surface. The steam rising from the crater shone brightly, and among its clouds shadows soared in spirals along the edges of the column. One of the shadows dived dangerously toward the ground, risking destruction, but at the last moment it pulled up short to soar skyward again. Another followed, another, and Dark realized they were playing a game. Entranced, she hunched on the ridge and watched the flyers play. They did not notice her. No doubt they could see better than she, but their eyes would be too dazzled by the heat's luminous blackness to notice an earthbound creature's armor-shielded warmth.

Sound and light burst upon her like explosions. Clearing the ridge that had concealed it, a helicopter leaned into the air and ploughed toward her. Until this moment she had not seen or heard or sensed it. It must have been grounded, waiting for her. Its searchlights caught and blinded her for a moment, till she shook herself free in an almost automatic reaction and slid across the bare rock to the earth beyond. As she plunged toward the trees the machine roared over her, its backwash blasting up a cloud of dirt and leaves and pebbles. The 'copter screamed upward, straining to miss treetops. As it turned to chase her down again, Dark scuttled into the woods.

She had been careless. Her fascination with the volcano and the flyers had betrayed her, for her stillness must have convinced the humans that she was asleep or incapacitated.

Wondering if it would do any good, she burrowed into the earth. She felt the helicopter land, and then the lighter vibrations of footsteps. The humans could find her by the same technique, amplifying the sounds of her digging. From now on they did not even need her beacon.

She reached a boundary between bedrock and earth and followed its lessened resistance. Pausing for a moment, she heard both movement and its echoes. She felt trapped between sounds, from above and below. She started digging, pushing herself until her work drowned out all other noises. She did not stop again.

The humans could move faster down the steep terrain than she could. She was afraid they would get far enough ahead of her to dig a trench and head her off. If they had enough equipment or construction explosives, they could surround her, or simply kill her with the shock waves of a shaped charge.

She dug violently, pushing herself forward, feeling the debris of her progress slide over her shoulder armor and across her back, filling in the tunnel as quickly as she made it. The roots of living trees, springy and thick, reached down to slow her. She had to dig between and sometimes through them. Their malleable consistency made them harder to penetrate than solid rock, and more frustrating. Dark's powerful claws could shatter stone, but they tangled in the roots and she was forced to shred the tough fibres a few strands at a time. She tired fast, and she was using oxygen far more quickly than she could take it in underground.

Dark slashed out angrily at a thick root. It crumbled completely in a powdery dust of charcoal. Dark's momentum, meeting no resistance, twisted her sideways in her narrow tunnel. She was trapped. The footsteps of the humans caught nearly up to her, and then, inexplicably, stopped. Scrabbling frantically with her feet and one clawed hand, her left front limb wedged uselessly beneath her, she managed to loosen and shift the dirt in the small enclosed space. Finally, expecting the humans to start blasting toward her at any moment, she freed herself.

Despite the ache in her left shoulder, deep under her armor, she increased her pace tremendously. She was beneath the dead trees now, and the dry porous earth contained only the roots of trees that had burned from top to deep underground, or roots riddled with insects and decay. Above her, above ground, the treetrunks lay in an impassable tangle, and that must be why the humans had paused. They could not trench her now.

Gauging her distance to the basalt flow by the pattern of returning echoes, Dark tunneled through the last few lengths of earth. She wanted to go under the stone barrier and come up on the other side in safety. But the echoes proved that she could not. The basalt was much thicker than she had hoped. It was not a single flow but many, filling a deep-cleft valley the gods only knew how far down. She could not go under and she did not have time or strength right now to go through.

It was not the naked sheet of stone that would keep the humans from her, but the intangible barrier of the flyers' boundary. That was what she had to reach. Digging hard, using the last of her stored oxygen, Dark burst up through the earth at the edge of the lava flow and scrambled out onto the hard surface. Never graceful at the best of times, she was slow and unwieldy on land. She lumbered forward, panting, her claws clacking on the rock and scraping great marks across it.

Behind her the humans shouted, as their detectors went off so loudly even Dark could hear them, and as the humans saw Dark for themselves, some for the first time.

They were very close. They had almost worked their way through the jammed treetrunks, and once they reached solid ground again they could overtake her. She scrambled on, feeling the weight of her armor as she never did underground. Its edges dragged along the basalt, gouging it deeply.

Two flyers landed as softly as wind, as milkweed floss, as pollen grains. Dark heard only the rustle of their wings, and when she looked up from the fissured gray rock, they stood before her, barring her way.

She was nearly safe; she was just on the boundary, and once she was over it the humans could not follow. The delicate flyers could not stand up against her if she chose to proceed, but they did not move to let her pass. She stopped.

Like her, the flyers had huge eyes, to extend the spectrum of their vision. Armored brow ridges and transparent shields protected Dark's eyes and almost hid them. The flyers' eyes were protected, too, but with thick black lashes that veiled and revealed them.

'What do you want, little one?' one of the flyers said. Its voice was deep and soft, and it wrapped its body in iridescent black wings.

'Your help,' Dark said. 'Sanctuary.' Behind her, the humans stopped too. She did not know if they still had the legal right to take her. Their steel net scraped along the ground, and they moved hesitantly closer. The black flyer glared, and the human noises ceased. Dark inched forward, but the flyers did not retreat at all.

'Why have you come?' The black flyer's voice withheld all emotion, warmth, or welcome.

'To talk to you,' Dark said. 'My people need your help.'

The raven-winged flyer did not move, except to blink its luminous eyes. But its blue-feathered companion peered at Dark closely, moved a step one way, a step the other, and ruffled the plumage of its wings. The blue flyer's movements were as quick and sharp as those of a bird itself.

'We have no help to offer you,' the black flyer said.

'Let me in, let me talk to you.' Her claws ground against stone as she moved nervously. She could not flee, and she did not want to fight. She could crush the humans or the flyers, but she had not been chosen for her capacity for violence. Her pursuers knew that perfectly well.

Again the nets scraped behind her as the humans moved forward.

'We've only come for her,' one of them said. 'She's a fugitive – we don't want to involve you in any unpleasantness.' The powerful searchlight he carried swept over Dark's back, transfixing the flyers, who turned their faces away. The harsh white illumination washed out the iridescent highlights of the black feathers but brightened the other's wings to the brilliant color of a Stellar's jay.

'Turn out your lights,' the jay said, in a voice as brash and demanding as any real bluejay's. 'It's dawn – you can see well enough.'

The human hesitated, swung the light away, and turned it off. He motioned to the helicopter and its lights faded. As the jay had said, it was dawn, misty and gray and eerie. The flyers faced Dark's adversaries again.

'We have no more resources than you,' the raven flyer said. 'How do you expect us to help you? We have ourselves. We have our land. You have the same.'

'Land!' Dark said bitterly. 'Have you ever seen my land? It's nothing but piles of rotting stone and pits full of rusty water –' She stopped; she had not meant to lose her temper. But she was hunched on the border of captivity, straining toward sanctuary and about to be refused.

'Send her out so we can take her without violating your boundaries. Don't let her cause you a lot of trouble.'

'A little late for such caution,' Jay said. 'Redwing, if we bow to their threats now, what will they do next time? We should let her in.'

'So the diggers can do to our refuge what they did to their own? Pits, and rusting water –'

'It was like that when we came!' Dark cried, shocked and hurt. 'We make tunnels, yes, but we don't destroy! Please hear what I've got to say. Then, if you ask me to go . . . I'll obey.' She made the promise reluctantly, for she knew that once she had lived near the volcano, she would need great will to leave. 'I give my word.' Her voice quivered with strain. The humans muttered behind her; a few steps inside the boundary, a few moments inside and then out – who, besides Dark, would accuse them of entering the flyers' territory at all?

Jay and Redwing glared at each other, but suddenly Jay laughed sharply and turned away. He stepped back and swept one wingtip along the ground, waving Dark into his land. 'Come in, little one,' he said.

Hesitantly, afraid he would change his mind, Dark moved forward. Then, in a single moment, after her long journey, she was safe.

'We have no reason to trust it!' Redwing said.

'Nor any reason not to, since we could just as well be mashed flat between stone and armor. We do have reason not to help the humans.'

'You'll have to send her back,' the leader of the humans said. He was angry; he stood, glowering at the very edge of the border, perhaps a bit over. 'Laws will take her, if we don't now. It will just cost you a lot more in trouble.'

'Take your threats and your noisy machine and get out of here,' Jay said.

'You will be sorry, flyer,' the humans' leader said.

Dark did not really believe they would go until the last one boarded the helicopter and its roar increased, it climbed into the air, and it clattered off into the brightening gray morning.

'Thank you,' Dark said.

'I had ulterior motives,' Jay said.

Redwing stood back, looking at Jay but not at Dark. 'We'll have to call a council.'

'I know. You go ahead. I'll talk to her and meet you when we convene.'

'I think we will regret this,' Redwing said. 'I think we are closer to the humans than to the diggers.' The black flyer leaped into the air, wings outspread to reveal their brilliant scarlet underside, and soared away.

Jay laid his soft hand on Dark's shoulder plate to lead her from the lava to volcanic soil. His skin felt frail, and very warm: Dark's metabolism was slower than it had been, while the flyers' chemistry had been considerably speeded up. Dark was ugly and clumsy next to him. She thought of digging down and vanishing but that would be ill-mannered. Besides, she had never been near a flyer before. Curiosity overcame her. Glancing surreptitiously sideways, beneath the edge of her armor, she saw that he was peeking at her, too. Their gazes met; they looked away, both embarrassed. Then Dark stopped and faced him. She settled back to regard him directly.

'This is what I look like,' she said. 'My name is Dark and I know I'm ugly, but I could do the job I was made for, if they'd let me.'

'I think your strength compensates for your appearance,' the flyer said. 'I'm Jay.' Dark was unreasonably pleased that she had guessed right about his name.

'You never answered Redwing's question,' Jay said. 'Why come *here?* The strip mines –'

'What could you know of strip mines?'

'Other people lived near them before they were given over to you.'

'So you think we should stay there!'

Jay replied to her abrupt anger in a gentle tone. 'I was going to say, this place is nicer than the strip mines, true, but a lot of places nicer than the strip mines are more isolated than we are. You could have found a hidden place to live.'

'I'm sorry,' Dark said. 'I thought –'

'I know. Never mind.'

'No one else like me got this far, did they?'

Jay shook his head.

'Six of us escaped,' Dark said. 'We hoped more than one would reach you. Perhaps I'm just the first, though.'

'That could be.'

'I came to ask you to join us,' Dark said.

Jay looked at her sharply, his thick flaring eyebrows raised in surprise. He veiled his eyes for a moment with the translucent avian membranes, then let them slowly retract.

'Join you? In . . . your preserve?' He was polite enough to call it this time by its official name. Though she had expressed herself badly, Dark felt some hope.

'I misspoke myself,' she said. 'I came . . . the others and I decided to come . . . to ask you to join us politically. Or at least to support us.'

'To get you a better home. That seems only fair.'

'That isn't quite what we're hoping for. Or rather it is, but not the way you mean.'

Jay hesitated again. 'I see. You want . . . what you were made for.'

Dark wanted to nod; she missed the shorthand of the language of the human body, and she found she was unable to read Jay's. She had been two years out of contact with normal humans; or perhaps it was that Jay was a flyer, and his people had made adjustments of their own.

'Yes. We were made to be explorers. It's a useless economy, to keep us on earth. We could even pay our own way after a while.'

Dark watched him closely, but could not tell what he thought. His face remained expressionless; he did not move toward her or away. Then he sighed deeply. That, Dark understood.

'Digger –' She flinched, but inwardly, the only way she could. He had not seemed the type to mock her. '– the projects are over. They changed their minds. There will be no exploring or coloniz-ing, at least not by you and me. And what difference does it make? We have a peaceful life and everything we need. You've been badly used but that could be changed.'

'Maybe,' Dark said, doubting his words. The flyers were beauti-ful, her people were ugly, and as far as the humans were concerned that made every difference. 'But we had a purpose, and now it's gone. Are you happy, living here with nothing to do?'

'We're content. You people are all ready, but we aren't. We'd have to go through as much change again as we already have.'

'What's so bad about that? You've gone this far. You volun-teered for it. Why not finish?'

'Because it isn't necessary.'

'I don't understand,' Dark said. 'You could have a whole new living world. You have even more to gain than we do, that's why we thought you'd help us.' Dark's planned occupation was the exploration of dead worlds or newly formed ones, the places of extremes where no other life could exist. But Jay's people were colonists; they had been destined for a world that was being made over for them, even as they were being suited for what it would become.

'The terraforming is only beginning,' Jay said. 'If we wait until it's complete –'

'But that won't be for generations.'

Jay shrugged. 'We know.'

'You'll never see it!' Dark cried. 'You'll be dead and dust before it changes enough for people like you are now to live on it.'

'We're virus-changed, not constructed,' Jay said. 'We breed true. Our grandchildren may want another world, and the humans may be willing to help them go. But we intend to stay here.' He blinked slowly, dreamily. 'Yes, we *are* happy. And we don't have to work for the humans.'

'I don't care who I work for, as long as I can be something better than a deformed creature,' Dark said angrily. 'This world gives my people nothing and because of that we're dying.'

'Come now,' Jay said tolerantly.

'We're dying!' Dark stopped and rocked back on the edge of her shell so she could more nearly look him in the eye. 'You have beauty all around you and in you, and when the humans see you they admire you. But they're afraid of us! Maybe they've forgotten that we started out human or maybe they never considered us human at all. It doesn't matter. I don't care! But we can't be anything, if we don't have any purpose. All we ask is that you help us make ourselves heard, because they'll listen to you. They love you. They almost worship you!' She paused, surprised by her own outburst.

'Worship us!' Jay said. 'They shoot us out of the sky, like eagles.'

He looked away from her. His gaze sought out clouds, the direction of the sun, for all she knew the eddies of the wind. Dark thought she sensed something, a call or a cry at the very edge of one of her new perceptions. She reached for it, but it eluded her. It was not meant for her.

'Wait for me at sunset,' Jay said, his voice remote. He spread his huge furled wings and sprang upward, the muscles bunching in his short, powerful legs. Dark watched him soar into the sky, a graceful dark blue shape against the cloud-patterned gold and scarlet dawn.

Dark knew she had not convinced them. When he was nothing but a speck she eased herself down again and lumbered up the flank of the volcano. She could feel it beneath her feet. Its long rumbles pulsed through her, at a far lower frequency than she ever could have heard as a human. It promised heat and danger; it excited her. She had experienced no extremes, of either heat or cold, pressure or vacuum, for far too many months.

The ground felt hollow beneath Dark's claws: passages lay beneath her, and lava beaten to a froth by the violence of its formation and frozen by exposure into spongy rock. She found a crevice that would leave no trace of her passing and slid into it. She began to dig, slowly at first, then faster, dirt and pulverized stone flying over her shoulders. In a moment the earth closed in around her.

Dark paused to rest. Having reached the gas-formed tunnels, she no longer had to dig her way through the substance of the mountain. She relaxed in the twisted passage, enjoying the brilliance of the heat and the occasional shining puff of air that came to her from the magma. She could analyze the gases by taste: that was another talent the humans had given her. Vapors toxic to them were merely interesting scents to her. If necessary she could metabolize some gases; the ability would have been necessary in many of the places she had expected to see, where sunlight was too dim to convert, where life had vanished or never evolved and there were no organic chemicals. On the outer planets, in the asteroids, even on Mars, her energy would have come from a tenuous atmosphere, from ice, even from the dust. Out there the challenging extremes would be cold and emptiness, unless she discovered hot, living veins in dying planets. Perhaps now no one would ever look for such activity on the surface of an alien world. Dark had dreamed of the planets of a different star, but she might never get a chance even to see the moon.

Dark sought a living vein in a living world: she moved toward the volcano's central core. Her people had been designed to resist conditions far more severe than the narrow range tolerated by normals, but she did not know if she could survive this great a temperature. Nor did she care. The rising heat drew her toward a heightened state of consciousness that wiped away caution and even fear. The rock walls flowed in the infrared, and as she dug at them, the chips flew like sparks. At last, with nothing but a thin plate of stone between her and the caldera, she hesitated. She was not afraid for her life. It was almost as if she were afraid she *would* survive: afraid the volcano, like all else, would finally disappoint her.

She lashed out with her armored hand and shattered the fragile wall. Steam and vapor poured through the opening, flowing past her. Before she stopped normal breathing she chanced a quick, shallow mouthful and savored the taste and smell, then moved forward to look directly into the crater.

Whatever she had imagined dissolved in the reality. She was halfway up the crater, dazzled from above by light and from below by heat. She had been underground a long time and it was almost exactly noon. Sunlight beat down through clouds of steam, and the gases and sounds of molten rock reached up to her. The currents swirled, hot and hotter, and in the earth's wound a flood of fire burned.

She could feel as well as see the heat, and it pleased her intensely that she would die if she remained where she was. Internal oxygen sustained her: a few deep breaths of the mountain's uncooled exhalations and she would die.

She wanted to stay. She did not want to return to the surface and the probability of rejection. She did not want to return to her people's exile.

Yet she had a duty toward them, and she had not yet completed it. She backed into the tunnel, turned around, and crawled away, hoping someday she could return.

Dark made her way back to the surface, coming out through the same fissure so the land would not change. She shook the dirt off her armor and looked around, blinking, waiting for her eyes to re-accustom themselves to the day. As she rested, colors resolved out of the afterimage dazzle of infrared: the blue sky first, then the deep green trees, the yellow of a scatter of wildflowers. Finally, squinting, she made out dark specks against the crystal clarity of the sky. The flyers soared in small groups or solo, now and again two coming together in lengthy graceful couplings, their wings brushing tips. She watched them, surprised and a little ashamed to be aroused despite herself. For her kind, intercourse was more difficult and more pedestrian. Dark had known how it would be when she volunteered; there was no secret about it. Like most of the other volunteers, she had always been a solitary person. She seldom missed what she had so seldom had, but watching the flyers she felt a long pang of envy. They were so beautiful, and they took everything so for granted.

The winged dance went on for hours, until the sun, reddening, touched mountains in the west. Dark continued to watch, unable to look away, in awe of the flyers' aerial and sexual stamina. Yet she resented their extended play, as well; they had forgotten that an earthbound creature waited for them.

The several pairs of coupled flyers suddenly broke apart, as if on signal, and the whole group of them scattered. A moment later Dark sensed the approach of the humans' plane.

It was too high to hear, but she knew it was there. It circled slowly. Sitting still, not troubling now to conceal the radio-beacon in her spine, Dark perceived it spiraling in, with her as its focus. The plane descended; it was a point, then a silver shape reflecting scarlet sunset. It did not come too close; it did nothing immediately threatening. But it had driven the flyers out of Dark's sight. She hunkered down on the stone promontory, waiting.

Dark heard only the sudden rush of air against outstretched wings as Jay landed nearby. His approach had been completely silent, and intent as she was on the search plane, she had not seen him. She turned her attention from the sky to Jay, and took a few steps toward him. But then she stopped, shamed once more by her clumsiness compared to the way he moved. The flyers were not tall, and even for their height their legs were quite short. Perhaps they had been modified that way. Still, Jay did not lumber. He strode. As he neared her he furled his wings over his back, folding

them one bit at a time, ruffling them to smooth the feathers, folding a bit more. He reminded her not so much of a bird, as of a
spectacular butterfly perched in the wind, flicking his wings
open and closed. When he stopped before her his wings stilled,
each bright-blue feather perfectly placed, framing him from behind. Unconcealed this time by the wings, his body was naked.
Flyers wore no clothes: Dark was startled that they had nothing to
conceal. Apparently they were as intricately engineered as her
own people.

Jay did not speak for so long that Dark, growing uncomfortable,
reared back and looked into the sky. The search plane still circled
loudly.

'Are they allowed to do that?' she said.

'We have no quick way of stopping them. We can protest. No
doubt someone already has.'

'I could send them a message,' she said grumpily. That, after all,
was what the beacon was for, though the message would not contain
the sort of information anyone had ever planned for her to send.

'We've finished our meeting,' Jay said.

'Oh. Is that what you call it?'

Dark expected a smile or a joke, but Jay spoke quite seriously.

'That's how we confer, here.'

'Confer–!' She dropped back to the ground, her claws digging
in. 'You met without letting me speak? You told me to wait for
you at sunset!'

'I spoke for you,' Jay said softly.

'I came here to speak for myself. And I came here to speak for
my kind. I trusted you–'

'It was the only way,' he said. 'We only gather in the sky.'

Dark held down an angry retort. 'And what is the answer?'

Jay sat abruptly on the hard earth, as if he could no longer
support the weight of his wings on his delicate legs. He drew his
knees to his chest and wrapped his arms around them.

'I'm sorry.' The words burst out in a sigh, a moan.

'Call them,' Dark said. 'Fly after them, find them, make them
come and speak to *me*. I will not be refused by people who won't
even face me.'

'It won't help,' Jay said miserably. 'I spoke for you as well as I could, but when I saw I would fail I tried to bring them here. I begged them. They wouldn't come.'

'They wouldn't come . . .' She had risked her life only to have her life dismissed as nothing. 'I don't understand,' she whispered.

Jay reached out and touched her hand: it still could function as a hand, despite her armor and her claws. Jay's hand, too, was clawed, but it was delicate and fine-boned, and veins showed blue through the translucent skin. Dark pulled back the all too solid mass of her arm.

'Don't you, little one?' Jay said, sadly. 'I was so different, before I was a flyer –'

'So was I,' Dark said.

'But you're strong, and you're ready. You could go tomorrow with no more changes and no more pain. I have another stage to go through. If I did it, and then they decided not to send us after all – Dark, I would never be able to fly again. Not in this gravity. There are too many changes. They'd thicken my skin, and regress me again so my wings weren't feathered but scaled – they'd shield my eyes and reconstruct my face for the filters.'

'It isn't the flying that troubles you,' Dark said.

'It is. The risk's too great.'

'No. What troubles you is that when you were finished, you wouldn't be beautiful anymore. You'd be ugly, like me.'

'That's unfair.'

'Is it? Is that why all your people flock around me so willingly to hear what I have to say?'

Jay stood slowly and his wings unfolded above him: Dark thought he was going to sail away off the side of the mountain, leaving her to speak her insults to the clouds and the stones. But, instead, he spread his beautiful black-tipped blue wings, stretched them in the air, and curved them around over Dark so they brushed the ridge of her spine. She shivered.

'I'm sorry,' he said. 'We have grown used to being beautiful. Even I have. They shouldn't have decided to make us in stages, they should have done it all at once. But they didn't, and now it's hard for us, being reminded of how we were.'

Dark stared at Jay, searching for the remnants of how he had been until he became a flyer, understanding, finally, the reasons he had decided to become something other than human. Before, she had only perceived his brilliant plumage, his luminous eyes, and the artificial delicacy of his bones. Now she saw his original proportions, the disguised coarseness of his features, and she saw what he must have looked like.

Perhaps he had not actually been deformed, as Dark had been. But he had never been handsome, or even so much as plain. She gazed at him closely. Neither of them blinked: that must be harder for him, Dark thought. Her eyes were shielded, his were only fringed with long, thick, dark eyelashes.

His eyes were too close together. That was something the virus-forming would not have been able to cure.

'I see,' she said. 'You can't help us, because we might succeed.'

'Don't hate us,' he said.

She turned away, her armor scraping on rock. 'What do you care, if a creature as repellent as I hates you?'

'I care,' Jay said very quietly.

Dark knew she was being unfair, to him if not to his kind, but she had no sympathy left. She wanted to hide herself somewhere and cry.

'When are the humans coming for me?'

'They come when they please,' he said. 'But I made the others promise one thing. They won't ask you to leave till morning. And if we can't find you, then – there's time for you to get away, if you hurry.'

Dark spun around, more quickly than she thought herself able to. Her armor struck sparks, but they glowed only briefly and died.

'Where should I go? Somewhere no one at all will ever see me? Underground, all alone, forever?' She thought of the mountain and its perils, but it meant nothing now. 'No,' she said. 'I'll wait for them.'

'But you don't know what they might do! I told you what they've done to us –'

'I hardly think they'll shoot me out of the sky.'

'Don't joke about it! They'll destroy anything, the things they love and the things they fear . . .'

'I don't care anymore,' Dark said. 'Go away, flyer. Go away to your games, and to your illusions of beauty.'

He glared at her, turned, and sprang into the air. She did not watch him go, but pulled herself completely inside the shadows of her armor to wait.

Sometime during the night she drifted off to sleep. She dreamed of the fireflood: she could feel its heat and hear its roar.

When she awoke, the rising sun blazed directly into her eyes, and the steel blades of a helicopter cut the dawn. She tried and failed to blot out the sound of the humans' machine. She began to shiver, with uncertainty or with fear.

Dark crept slowly down the side of the mountain, toward the border where the humans would land. The flyers would not have to tell her to leave. She wondered if she were protecting herself, or them, from humiliation.

Something touched her and she started, drawing herself tightly into her armor.

'Dark, it's only me.'

She peered out. Jay stood over her with his wings curved around them both.

'You can't hide me,' she said.

'I know. We should have, but it's too late.' He looked gaunt and exhausted. 'I tried, Dark, I did try.'

On the humans' side of the lava flow, the machine landed and sent up a fine spray of dust and rock particles. People climbed out, carrying weapons and nets. Dark did not hesitate.

'I have to go.' She raised her armor up off the ground and started away.

'You're stronger than we are,' Jay said. 'The humans can't come and get you and we can't force you to leave.'

'I know.' The invisible boundary was almost at her feet; she moved reluctantly but steadily toward it.

'Why are you doing this?' Jay cried.

Dark did not answer.

She felt Jay's wingtip brush the edge of her armor as he walked alongside her. She stopped and glanced up at him.

'I'm coming with you,' he said. 'Till you get home. Till you're safe.'

'It's no more safe for you. You can't leave your preserve.'

'Nor could you.'

'Jay, go back.'

'I'll not lose another friend to the humans.'

Dark touched the boundary. As if they were afraid she would still try to escape them, the humans rushed toward her and flung the net over her, pulling in its edges so it caught beneath her armor. They jostled the flyer away from her side.

'This isn't necessary,' she said. 'I'll come with you.'

'Sorry,' one finally said, in a grudging tone. 'It's necessary.'

'Her word's good,' Jay said. 'Otherwise she never would have come out to you at all.'

'What happened to the others?' Dark asked.

One human shrugged.

'Captured,' another said.

'And then?'

'Returned to the sanctuary.'

Dark had no reason not to believe them, simply because they had no reason to spare her feelings if any of her friends were dead.

'You see, Jay, there's no need for you to come.'

'You can't trust them! They'll lie to you for your cooperation and then kill you when I've left you with no witness.'

That could be true; still, she lumbered toward the helicopter, more hindered than helped by the humans' tugging on the steel cables. The blades circled rhythmically over her.

Jay followed, but the humans barred his way.

'I'm going with her,' he said.

She glanced back. Somehow, strangely, he looked even more delicate and frail among the normal humans than he had when she compared him to her own massive self.

'Don't come any farther, flyer.'

He pushed past them. One took his wrist and he pulled away. Two of the humans grabbed him by the shoulders and pushed him over the border as he struggled. His wings opened out above the turmoil, flailing, as Jay fought to keep his balance. A blue feather fluttered free and spiraled to the ground.

Dragging her own captors with her, pulling them by the net-lines as they struggled and failed to keep her on their side, Dark scuttled toward Jay and broke through the group of humans. The flyer lay crumpled on the ground, one wing caught awkwardly beneath him, the other curved over and round him in defense. The humans sprang away from him, and from Dark.

'Jay,' she said. 'Jay . . .'

When she rose, Dark feared his wing was crushed. He winced when he lifted it, and his plumage was in disarray, but, glaring at the humans, he extended and flexed it and she saw to her great relief that he was all right. He glanced down at her and his gaze softened. Dark reached up toward him, and their clawed hands touched.

One of the humans snickered. Embarrassed, Dark jerked her hand away.

'There's nothing you can do,' she said. 'Stay here.'

The net jerked tighter around her, but she resisted it.

'We can't waste any more time,' the leader of her captors said. 'Come on, now, it's time to go.'

They succeeded in dragging her halfway around, and a few steps toward the helicopter, only because she permitted it.

'If you won't let me come with her, I'll follow,' Jay said. 'That machine can't outpace me.'

'We can't control anyone outside your preserve.' Strangely, the human sounded concerned. 'You know the kind of thing that can happen. Flyer, stay inside your boundaries.'

'You pay no heed to boundaries!' Jay cried, as they pulled and pushed Dark the last few paces back into their own territory. She moved slowly, at her own speed, ignoring them.

'Stay here, Jay,' she said. 'Stay here, or you'll leave me with guilt as well as failure.'

Dark did not hear him, if he answered. She reached the 'copter, and steeled herself against the discomfort of its noise and unshielded electrical fields. She managed to clamber up into the cargo hold before they could subject her to the humiliation of being hoisted and shoved.

She looked out through the open door. It was as if the rest of the world were silent, for she could hear and sense nothing but the clamor immediately around her. On the lava ridge, Jay stood still, his shoulders slumped. Suddenly his wings flared out, rose, descended, and he soared into the air. Awestruck once more, Dark watched through the mesh of the net. Jay sailed in a huge circle and glided into the warm updraft of the volcano.

The rotors moved faster, blurring and nearly disappearing. The machine rose with a slight forward lurch, laboring under the weight of the hunting party and Dark as well. At the same time, Jay spiraled upward through the glowing steam. Dark tried to turn away, but she could not. He was too beautiful.

The distance between them grew greater, until all Dark could see was a spark of bright blue appearing, then vanishing, among the columns of steam.

As the helicopter swung round, she thought she saw the spiral of Jay's flight widen, as if he were ignoring the threats the humans had made and cared nothing for warnings, as if he were drifting gently toward the boundaries of his refuge, gradually making up his mind to cross them and follow.

Don't leave your sanctuary, Jay, Dark thought. You don't belong out here.

But then, just before the machine cut off her view, he veered away from the mountain and in one great soaring arc passed over the boundary and into the humans' world.

Wives

(1979)

LISA TUTTLE

A smell of sulphur in the air on a morning when the men had gone, and the wives, in their beds, smiled in their sleep, breathed more easily, and burrowed deeper into dreams.

Jack's wife woke, her eyes open and her little nose flaring, smelling something beneath the sulphur smell. One of those smells she was used to not noticing, when the men were around. But it was all right, now. Wives could do as they pleased, so long as they cleaned up and were back on their proper places when the men returned.

Jack's wife – who was called Susie – got out of bed too quickly and grimaced as the skintight punished her muscles. She caught sight of herself in the mirror over the dressing table: her sharp teeth were bared, and she looked like a wild animal, bound and struggling. She grinned at that, because she could easily free herself.

She cut the skintight apart with scissors, cutting and ripping carelessly. It didn't matter that it was ruined – skintights were plentiful. She had a whole boxful, herself, in the hall closet behind the Christmas decorations. And she didn't have the patience to try soaking it off slowly in a hot bath, as the older wives recommended. So her muscles would be sore and her skintight a tattered rag – she would be free that much sooner.

She looked down at her dead-white body, feeling distaste. She felt despair at the sight of her small arms, hanging limp, thin and useless in the hollow below her ribs. She tried to flex them but could not make them move. She began to massage them with her primary fingers, and after several minutes the pain began, and she knew they weren't dead yet.

She bathed and massaged her newly uncovered body with oil. She felt terrifyingly free, naked and rather dangerous, with the skintight removed. She sniffed the air again and that familiar scent, musky and alluring, aroused her.

She ran through the house – noticing, in passing, that Jack's pet spider was eating the living room sofa. It was the time for building nests and cocoons, she thought happily, time for laying eggs and planting seeds; the spider was driven by the same force that drove her.

Outside the dusty ground was hard and cold beneath her bare feet. She felt the dust all over her body, raised by the wind and clinging to her momentary warmth. She was coated in the soft yellow dust by the time she reached the house next door – the house where the magical scent came from, the house which held a wife in heat, longing for someone to mate with.

Susie tossed her head, shaking the dust out in a little cloud around her head. She stared up at the milky sky and around at all the houses, alien artefacts constructed by men. She saw movement in the window of the house across the street and waved – the figure watching her waved back.

Poor old Maggie, thought Susie. Old, bulging and ugly; unloved and nobody's wife. She was only housekeeper to two men who were, rather unfortunately Susie thought, in love with each other.

But she didn't want to waste time by thinking of wives and men, or by feeling pity, now. Boldly, like a man, Susie pounded at the door.

It opened. 'Ooooh, Susie!'

Susie grinned and looked the startled wife up and down. You'd never know from looking at her that the men were gone and she could relax – this wife, called Doris, was as dolled up as some eager-to-please newlywed and looked, Susie thought, more like a real woman than any woman had ever looked.

Over her skintight (which was bound more tightly than Susie's had been) Doris wore a low-cut dress, her three breasts carefully bound and positioned to achieve the proper, double-breasted effect. Gaily patterned and textured stockings covered her silicone-injected legs, and she tottered on heels three centimetres high. Her face was carefully painted, and she wore gold bands on neck, wrists and fingers.

Then Susie ignored what she looked like because her nose told her so much more. The smell was so powerful now that she could feel her pouch swelling in lonely response.

Doris must have noticed, for her eyes rolled, seeking some safe view.

'What's the matter?' Susie asked, her voice louder and bolder than it ever was when the men were around. 'Didn't your man go off to war with the others? He stay home sick in bed?'

Doris giggled. 'Ooooh, I wish he would, sometimes! No, he was out of here before it was light.'

Off to see his mistress before leaving, Susie thought. She knew that Doris was nervous about being displaced by one of the other wives her man was always fooling around with – there were always more wives than there were men, and her man had a roving eye.

'Calm down, Doris. Your man can't see you now, you know.' She stroked one of Doris's hands. 'Why don't you take off that silly dress and your skintight. I know how constricted you must be feeling. Why not relax with me?'

She saw Doris's face darken with emotion beneath the heavy make-up, and she grasped her hand more tightly when Doris tried to pull away.

'Please don't,' Doris said.

'Come on,' Susie murmured, caressing Doris's face and feeling the thick paint slide beneath her fingers.

'No, don't ... please ... I've tried to control myself, truly I have. But the exercises don't work, and the perfume doesn't cover the smell well enough – he won't even sleep with me when I'm like this. He thinks it's disgusting, and it is. I'm so afraid he'll leave me.'

'But he's gone now, Doris. You can let yourself go. You don't have to worry about him when he's not around. It's safe, it's all right, you can do as you please now – we can do anything we like and no one will know.' She could feel Doris trembling.

'Doris,' she whispered and rubbed her face demandingly against hers.

At that, the other wife gave in, and collapsed in her arms.

Susie helped Doris out of her clothes, tearing at them with hands and teeth, throwing shoes and jewellery high into the air and festooning the yard with rags of dress, stockings and undergarment.

But when Doris, too, was naked, Susie suddenly felt shy and a little frightened. It would be wrong to mate here in the settlement built by men, wrong and dangerous. They must go somewhere else, somewhere they could be something other than wives for a little while, and follow their own natures without reproach.

They went to a place of stone on the far northern edge of the human settlement. It was a very old place, although whether it had been built by the wives in the distant time before they were wives or whether it was natural, neither Susie nor Doris could say. They both felt it was a holy place, and it seemed right to mate there, in the shadow of one of the huge, black, standing stones.

It was a feast, an orgy of life after a season of death. They found pleasure in exploring the bodies which seemed so similar to men but which they knew to be miraculously different, each from the other, in scent, texture and taste. They forgot that they had ever been creatures known as wives. They lost their names and forgot the language of men as they lay entwined.

There were no skintights imprisoning their bodies now, barring them from sensation, freedom and pleasure, and they were partners, not strangers, as they explored and exulted in their flesh. This was no mockery of the sexual act – brutishly painful and brief as it was with the men – but the true act in all its meaning.

They were still joined at sundown, and it was not until long after the three moons began their nightly waltz through the clouds that the two lovers fell asleep at last.

'In three months,' Susie said dreamily. 'We can . . .'

'In three months we won't do anything.'

'Why not? If the men are away . . .'

'I'm hungry,' said Doris. She wrapped her primary arms around herself. 'And I'm cold, and I ache all over. Let's go back.'

'Stay here with me, Doris. Let's plan.'

'There's nothing to plan.'

'But in three months we must get together and fertilize it.'

'Are you crazy? Who would carry it then? One of us would have to go without a skintight, and do you think either of our

husbands would let us slop around for four months without a
skintight? And then when it's born how could we hide it? Men
don't have babies, and they don't want anyone else to. Men kill
babies, just as they kill all their enemies.'

Susie knew that what Doris was saying was true, but she was
reluctant to give up her new dream. 'Still, we might be able to
keep it hidden,' she said. 'It's not so hard to hide things from a
man . . .'

'Don't be so stupid,' Doris said scornfully. Susie noticed that
she still had smears of make-up on her face. Some smears had
transferred themselves to Susie in the night. They looked like
bruises or bloody wounds. 'Come back with me now,' Doris said,
her voice gentle again. 'Forget this, about the baby. The old ways
are gone – we're wives now, and we don't have a place in our
lives for babies.'

'But some day the war may end,' Susie said. 'And the men will
all go back to Earth and leave us here.'

'If that happens,' said Doris, 'then we would make new lives ᶠor
ourselves. Perhaps we would have babies again.'

'If it's not too late then,' Susie said. 'If it ever happens.' She
stared past Doris at the horizon.

'Come back with me.'

Susie shook her head. 'I have to think. You go. I'll be all right.'

She realized when Doris had gone that she, too, was tired,
hungry and sore, but she was not sorry she had remained in the
place of stone. She needed to stay a while longer in one of the old
places, away from the distractions of the settlement. She felt that
she was on the verge of remembering something very important.

A large, dust-coloured lizard crawled out of a hole in the side of
a fallen rock, and Susie rolled over and clapped her hands on it.
But it wriggled out of her clutches like air or water or the wind-
blown dust and disappeared somewhere. Susie felt a sharp pang of
disappointment – she had a sudden memory of how that lizard
would have tasted, how the skin of its throat would have felt,
tearing between her teeth. She licked her dry lips and sat up. In
the old days, she thought, I caught many such lizards. But the old
days were gone, and with them the old knowledge and the old
abilities.

I'm not what I used to be, she thought. I'm something else now – a 'wife', created by man in the image of something I have never seen, something called 'woman'.

She thought about going back to her house in the settlement and of wrapping herself in a new skintight and then selecting the proper dress and shoes to make a good impression on the returning Jack; she thought about painting her face and putting rings on her fingers. She thought about boiling and burning good food to turn it into the unappetizing messes Jack favoured, and about killing the wide-eyed 'coffee fish' to get the oil to make the mildly addictive drink the men called 'coffee'. She thought about watching Jack, and listening to him, always alert for what he might want, what he might ask, what he might do. Trying to anticipate him, to earn his praise and avoid his blows and harsh words. She thought about letting him 'screw' her and about the ugly jewellery and noisome perfumes he brought her.

Susie began to cry, and the dust drank her tears as they fell. She didn't understand how this had all begun, how or why she had become a wife, but she could bear it no longer.

She wanted to be what she had been born to be – but she could not remember what that was. She only knew that she could be Susie no longer. She would be no man's wife.

'I remembered my name this morning,' Susie said with quiet triumph. She looked around the room. Doris was staring down at her hands, twisting them in her lap. Maggie looked half asleep, and the other two wives – Susie didn't remember their names; she had simply gathered them up when she found them on the street – looked both bored and nervous.

'Don't you see?' Susie persisted. 'If I could remember that, I'm sure I can remember other things, in time. All of us can.'

Maggie opened her eyes all the way. 'And what good would that do,' she asked, 'except make us discontented and restless, as you are?'

'What *good* . . . why, if we all began to remember, we could live our lives again – our *own* lives. We wouldn't have to be wives, we could be . . . ourselves.'

'Could we?' said Maggie sourly. 'And do you think the men

would watch us go? Do you think they'd let us walk out of their houses and out of their lives without stopping us? Don't you — you who talk about remembering — don't you remember how it was when the men came? Don't you remember the slaughter? Don't you remember just who became wives, and why? We, the survivors, became wives because the men wouldn't kill us then, not if we kept them happy and believing we weren't the enemy. If we try to leave or change, they'll kill us like they've killed almost everything else in the world.'

The others were silent, but Susie suspected they were letting Maggie speak for them.

'But we'll die,' she said. 'We'll die like this, as wives. We've lost our identities, but we can have them back. We can have the world back, and our lives, only if we take them. We're dying as a race and as a world, now. Being a wife is a living death, just a postponement of the end, that's all.'

'Yes,' said Maggie, irony hanging heavily from the word. 'So?'

'So why do we have to let them do this to us? We can hide — we can run far away from the settlement and hide. Or, if we have to, we can fight back.'

'That's not our way,' said Maggie.

'Then what *is* our way?' Susie demanded. 'Is it our way to let ourselves be destroyed? They've already killed our culture and our past — we have no "way" anymore — we can't claim we do. All we are now is imitations, creatures moulded by the men. And when the men leave — *if* the men leave — it will be the end for us. We'll have nothing left, and it will be too late to try to remember who we were.'

'It's already too late,' Maggie said. Susie was suddenly impressed by the way she spoke and held herself, and wondered if Maggie, this elderly and unloved wife she had once pitied, had once been a leader of her people.

'Can you remember why we did not fight or hide before?' Maggie asked. 'Can you remember why we decided that the best thing for us was to change our ways, to do what you are now asking us to undo?'

Susie shook her head.

'Then go and try to remember. Remember that we made a

choice when the men came, and now we must live with that choice. Remember that there was a good reason for what we did, a reason of survival. It is too late to change again. The old way is not waiting for our return, it is dead. Our world had been changed, and we could not stop it. The past is dead, but that is as it should be. We have new lives now. Forget our restlessness and go home. Be a good wife to Jack – he loves you in his way. Go home, and be thankful for that.'

'I can't,' she said. She looked around the room, noticing how the eyes of the others fell before hers. So few of them had wanted to listen to her, so few had dared venture out of their homes. Susie looked at Maggie as she spoke, meaning her words for all the wives. 'They're killing us slowly,' she said. 'But we'll be just as dead in the end. I would rather die fighting, and take some of them with us.'

'You may be ready to die now, but the rest of us are not,' Maggie said. 'But if you fought them, you would get not only your own death, but the death of us all. If they see you snarling and violent, they will wake up and turn new eyes on the rest of us and see us not as their loving wives but as beasts, strangers, dangerous wild animals to be destroyed. They forget that we are different from them; they are willing to forget and let us live as long as we keep them comfortable and act as wives should act.'

'I can't fight them alone, I know that,' Susie said. 'But if you'll all join with me, we have a chance. We could take them by surprise, we could use their weapons against them. Why not? They don't expect a fight from us – we could win. Some of us would die, of course, but many of us would survive. More than that – we'd have our own lives, our own world, back again.'

'You think your arguments are new,' said Maggie. There was a trace of impatience in her usually calm voice. 'But I can remember the old days, even if you can't. I remember what happened when the men first came, and I know what would happen if we angered them. Even if we managed somehow to kill all the men here, more men would come in their ships from the sky. And they would come to kill us for daring to fight them. Perhaps they would simply drop fire on us, this time being sure to burn out all of us and all life on our world. Do you seriously ask us to bring about this certain destruction?'

Susie stared at her, feeling dim memories stir in response to her words. Fire from the sky, the burning, the killing ... But she couldn't be certain she remembered, and she would rather risk destruction than go back to playing wife again.

'We could hide,' she said, pleading. 'We could run away and hide in the wilderness. The men might think we had died – they'd forget about us soon, I'm certain. Even if they looked for us at first, we could hide. It's our world, and we know it as they don't. Soon we could live again as we used to, and forget the men.'

'Stop this dreaming,' Maggie said. 'We can never live the way we used to – the old ways are gone, the old world is gone, and even your memories are gone, that's obvious. The only way we know how to live now is with the men, as their wives. Everything else is gone. We'd die of hunger and exposure if the men didn't track us down and kill us first.'

'I may have forgotten the old ways, but you haven't. You could teach us.'

'I remember enough to know that what is gone, is gone. To know that we can't go back. Believe me. Think about it, Susie. Try –'

'Don't call me that!'

Her shout echoed in the silence. No one spoke. Susie felt the last of her hope drain out of her as she looked at them. They did not feel what she felt, and she would not be able to convince them. In silence, still, she left them, and went back to her own house.

She waited for them there, for them to come and kill her.

She knew that they would come; she knew she had to die. It was as Maggie had said: one renegade endangered them all. If one wife turned on one man, all the wives would be made to suffer. The look of love on their faces would change to a look of hatred, and the slaughter would begin again.

Susie felt no desire to try to escape, to hide from the other wives as she had suggested they all hide from the men. She had no wish to live alone; for good or ill she was a part of her people, and she did not wish to endanger them nor to break away from them.

When they came, they came together, all the wives of the settlement, coming to act in concert so none should bear the guilt alone. They did not hate Susie, nor did she hate them, but the deadly work had to be done.

Susie walked outside, to make it easier for them. By offering not the slightest resistance, she felt herself to be acting with them. She presented the weakest parts of her body to their hands and teeth, that her death should come more quickly. And as she died, feeling her body pressed, pounded and torn by the other wives, Susie did not mind the pain. She felt herself a part of them all, and she died content.

After her death, one of the extra wives took on Susie's name and moved into her house. She got rid of the spider's gigantic egg-case first thing – Jack might like his football-sized pet, but he wouldn't be pleased by the hundreds of pebble-sized babies that would come spilling out of the egg-case in a few months. Then she began to clean in earnest: a man deserved a clean house to come home to.

When, a few days later, the men returned from their fighting, Susie's man Jack found a spotless house, filled with the smells of his favourite foods cooking, and a smiling, sexily-dressed wife.

'Would you like some dinner, dear?' she asked.

'Put it on hold,' he said, grinning wolfishly. 'Right now I'll take a cup of coffee – in bed – with you on the side.'

She fluttered her false eyelashes and moved a little closer, so he could put his arm around her if he liked.

'Three tits and the best coffee in the universe,' he said with satisfaction, squeezing one of the bound lumps of flesh on her chest. 'With this to come home to, it kind of makes the whole war-thing worthwhile.'

Red as Blood

(1979)

TANITH LEE

The beautiful Witch Queen flung open the ivory case of the magic mirror. Of dark gold the mirror was, dark gold like the hair of the Witch Queen that poured down her back. Dark gold the mirror was, and ancient as the seven stunted black trees growing beyond the pale blue glass of the window.

'*Speculum, speculum*,' said the Witch Queen to the magic mirror. '*Dei gratia.*'

'*Volente deo. Audio.*'

'Mirror,' said the Witch Queen. 'Whom do you see?'

'I see you mistress,' replied the mirror. 'And all in the land. But one.'

'Mirror, mirror, who is it you do not see?'

'I do not see Bianca.'

The Witch Queen crossed herself. She shut the case of the mirror and, walking slowly to the window, looked out at the old trees through the panes of pale blue glass.

Fourteen years ago, another woman had stood at this window, but she was not like the Witch Queen. The woman had black hair that fell to her ankles; she had a crimson gown, the girdle worn high beneath her breasts, for she was far gone with child. And this woman had thrust open the glass casement on the winter garden, where the old trees crouched in the snow. Then, taking a sharp bone needle, she had thrust it into her finger and shaken three bright drops on the ground. 'Let my daughter have,' said the woman, 'hair black as mine, black as the wood of these warped and arcane trees. Let her have skin like mine, white as this snow. And let her have my mouth, red as my blood.' And the woman had smiled and licked at her finger. She had a crown on her head; it shone in the dusk like a star. She never came to the window before dusk: she did not like the day.

She was the first Queen, and she did not possess a mirror.

The second Queen, the Witch Queen, knew all this. She knew how, in giving birth, the first Queen had died. Her coffin had been carried into the cathedral and masses had been said. There was an ugly rumour – that a splash of holy water had fallen on the corpse and the dead flesh had smoked. But the first Queen had been reckoned unlucky for the kingdom. There had been a plague in the land since she came there, a wasting disease for which there was no cure.

Seven years went by. The King married the second Queen, as unlike the first as frankincense to myrrh.

'And this is my daughter,' said the King to his second Queen.

There stood a little girl child, nearly seven years of age. Her black hair hung to her ankles, her skin was white as snow. Her mouth was red as blood, and she smiled with it.

'Bianca,' said the King, 'you must love your new mother.'

Bianca smiled radiantly. Her teeth were bright as sharp bone needles.

'Come,' said the Witch Queen, 'come, Bianca. I will show you my magic mirror.'

'Please, Mamma,' said Bianca softly, 'I do not like mirrors.'

'She is modest,' said the King. 'And delicate. She never goes out by day. The sun distresses her.'

That night, the Witch Queen opened the case of her mirror.

'Mirror. Whom do you see?'

'I see you, mistress. And all in the land. But one.'

'Mirror, mirror, who is it you do not see?'

'I do not see Bianca.'

The second Queen gave Bianca a tiny crucifix of golden filigree. Bianca would not accept it. She ran to her father and whispered, 'I am afraid. I do not like to think of Our Lord dying in agony on His cross. She means to frighten me. Tell her to take it away.'

The second Queen grew wild white roses in her garden and invited Bianca to walk there after sundown. But Bianca shrank away. She whispered to her father, 'The thorns will tear me. She means me to be hurt.'

When Bianca was twelve years old, the Witch Queen said to the King, 'Bianca should be confirmed so that she may take Communion with us.'

'This may not be,' said the King. 'I will tell you, she has not been christened, for the dying word of my first wife was against it. She begged me, for her religion was different from ours. The wishes of the dying must be respected.'

'Should you not like to be blessed by the Church,' said the Witch Queen to Bianca. 'To kneel at the golden rail before the marble altar. To sing to God, to taste the ritual Bread and sip the ritual Wine.'

'She means me to betray my true mother,' said Bianca to the King. 'When will she cease tormenting me?'

The day she was thirteen, Bianca rose from her bed, and there was a red stain there, like a red, red flower.

'Now you are a woman,' said her nurse.

'Yes,' said Bianca. And she went to her true mother's jewel box, and out of it she took her mother's crown and set it on her head.

When she walked under the old black trees in the dusk, the crown shone like a star.

The wasting sickness, which had left the land in peace for thirteen years, suddenly began again, and there was no cure.

The Witch Queen sat in a tall chair before a window of pale green and dark white glass, and in her hands she held a Bible bound in rosy silk.

'Majesty,' said the huntsman, bowing very low.

He was man, forty years old, strong and handsome, and wise in the hidden lore of the forests, the occult lore of the earth. He could kill too, for it was his trade, without faltering. The slender fragile deer he could kill, and the moon-winged birds, and the velvet hares with their sad, foreknowing eyes. He pitied them, but pitying, he killed them. Pity could not stop him. It was his trade.

'Look in the garden,' said the Witch Queen.

The hunter looked through a dark white pane. The sun had sunk, and a maiden walked under a tree.

'The Princess Bianca,' said the huntsman.

'What else?' asked the Witch Queen.

The huntsman crossed himself.

'By our Lord, Madam, I will not say.'

'But you know.'

'Who does not?'

'The King does not.'

'Nor he does.'

'Are you a brave man?' asked the Witch Queen.

'In the summer, I have hunted and slain boar. I have slaughtered wolves in winter.'

'But are you brave enough?'

'If you command it, Lady,' said the huntsman, 'I will try my best.'

The Witch Queen opened the Bible at a certain place, and out of it she drew a flat silver crucifix, which had been resting against the words: *Thou shalt not be afraid for the terror by night . . . Nor for the pestilence that walketh in darkness.*

The huntsman kissed the crucifix and put it about his neck beneath his shirt.

'Approach,' said the Witch Queen, 'and I will instruct you in what to say.'

Presently, the huntsman entered the garden, as the stars were burning up in the sky. He strode to where Bianca stood under a stunted dwarf tree, and he kneeled down.

'Princess,' he said, 'pardon me, but I must give you ill tidings.'

'Give them then,' said the girl, toying with the long stem of a wan, night-growing flower which she had plucked.

'Your stepmother, the accursed jealous witch, means to have you slain. There is no help for it but you must fly the palace this very night. If you permit, I will guide you to the forest. There are those who will care for you until it may be safe for you to return.'

Bianca watched him, but gently, trustingly.

'I will go with you then,' she said.

They went by a secret way out of the garden, through a passage under the ground, through a tangled orchard, by a broken road between great overgrown hedges.

Night was a pulse of deep, flickering blue when they came to the forest. The branches of the forest overlapped and intertwined, like leading in a window, and the sky gleamed dimly through like panes of blue-coloured glass.

'I am weary,' sighed Bianca. 'May I rest a moment?'

'By all means,' said the huntsman. 'In the clearing there, foxes come to play by night. Look in that direction, and you will see them.'

'How clever you are,' said Bianca. 'And how handsome.' She sat on the turf and gazed at the clearing.

The huntsman drew his knife silently and concealed it in the folds of his cloak. He stooped above the maiden.

'What are you whispering?' demanded the huntsman, laying his hand on her wood-black hair.

'Only a rhyme my mother taught me.'

The huntsman seized her by the hair and swung her about so her white throat was before him, stretched ready for the knife. But he did not strike, for there in his hand he held the dark golden locks of the Witch Queen and her face laughed up at him, and she flung her arms about him, laughing.

'Good man, sweet man, it was only a test of you. Am I not a witch? And do you not love me?'

The huntsman trembled, for he did love her, and she was pressed so close her heart seemed to beat within his own body.

'Put away the knife. Throw away the silly crucifix. We have no need of these things. The King is not one half the man you are.'

And the huntsman obeyed her, throwing the knife and the crucifix far off among the roots of the trees. He gripped her to him and she buried her face in his neck, and the pain of her kiss was the last thing he felt in this world.

The sky was black now. The forest was blacker. No foxes played in the clearing. The moon rose and made white lace through the boughs, and through the backs of the huntsman's empty eyes. Bianca wiped her mouth on a dead flower.

'Seven asleep, seven awake,' said Bianca. 'Wood to wood. Blood to blood. Thee to me.'

There came a sound like seven huge rendings, distant by the length of several trees, a broken road, an orchard, an underground passage. Then a sound like seven huge single footfalls. Nearer. And nearer.

Hop, hop, hop, hop. Hop, hop, hop.

In the orchard, seven black shudderings.

On the broken road, between the high hedges, seven black creepings.

Brush crackled, branches snapped.

Through the forest, into the clearing, pushed seven warped, misshapen, hunched-over, stunted things. Woody-black mossy fur, woody-black bald masks. Eyes like glittering cracks, mouths like moist caverns. Lichen beards. Fingers of twiggy gristle. Grinning. Kneeling. Faces pressed to the earth.

'Welcome,' said Bianca.

The Witch Queen stood before a window of glass like diluted wine. She looked at the magic mirror.

'Mirror. Whom do you see?'

'I see you, mistress. I see a man in the forest. He went hunting, but not for deer. His eyes are open, but he is dead. I see all in the land. But one.'

The Witch Queen pressed her palms to her ears.

Outside the window, the garden lay, empty of its seven black and stunted dwarf trees.

'Bianca,' said the Queen.

The windows had been draped and gave no light. The light spilled from a shallow vessel, light in a sheaf, like pastel wheat. It glowed upon four swords that pointed east and west, that pointed north and south.

Four winds had burst through the chamber, and the grey-silver powders of Time.

The hands of the Witch Queen floated like folded leaves on the air, and through dry lips the Witch Queen chanted:

'*Pater omnipotens, mitere digneris sanctum Angelum tuum de Infernis.*'

The light faded, and grew brighter.

There, between the hilts of the four swords, stood the Angel Lucefiel, sombrely gilded, his face in shadow, his golden wings spread and glazing at his back.

'Since you have called me, I know your desire. It is a comfortless wish. You ask for pain.'

'You speak of pain, Lord Lucefiel, who suffer the most merciless pain of all. Worse than the nails in the feet and wrists. Worse than the thorns and the bitter cup and the blade in the side. To be called upon for evil's sake, which I do not, comprehending your true nature, son of God, brother of the Son.'

'You recognize me, then. I will grant what you ask.'

And Lucefiel (by some named Satan, *Rex Mundi*, but nevertheless the left hand, the sinister hand of God's design) wrenched lightning from the ether and cast it at the Witch Queen.

It caught her in the breast. She fell.

The sheaf of light towered and lit the golden eyes of the Angel, which were terrible, yet luminous with compassion, as the swords shattered and he vanished.

The Witch Queen pulled herself from the floor of the chamber, no longer beautiful, a withered, slobbering hag.

Into the core of the forest, even at noon, the sun never shone. Flowers propagated in the grass, but they were colourless. Above, the black-green roof hung down nets of thick green twilight through which albino butterflies and moths feverishly drizzled. The trunks of the trees were smooth as the stalks of underwater weeds. Bats flew in the daytime, and birds who believed themselves to be bats.

There was a sepulchre, dripped with moss. The bones had been rolled out, had rolled around the feet of seven twisted dwarf trees. They looked like trees. Sometimes they moved. Sometimes, something like an eye glittered, or a tooth, in the wet shadows.

In the shade of the sepulchre door sat Bianca, combing her hair.

A lurch of motion disturbed the thick twilight.

The seven trees turned their heads.

A hag emerged from the forest. She was crook-backed, and her head was poked forward, predatory, withered and almost hairless, like a vulture's.

'Here we are at last,' grated the hag, in a vulture's voice.

She came closer and cranked herself down on her knees and bowed her face into the turf and colourless flowers.

Bianca sat and gazed at her. The hag lifted herself. Her teeth were yellow palings.

'I bring you the homage of witches, and three gifts,' said the hag.

'Why should you do that?'

'Such a quick child, and only fourteen years. Why? Because we fear you. I bring you gifts to curry favour.'

Bianca laughed. 'Show me.'

The hag made a pass in the green air. She held a silken cord worked curiously with a plaited human hair.

'Here is a girdle which will protect you from the devices of priests, from crucifix and chalice and the accursed holy water. In it are knotted the tresses of a virgin, and of a woman no better than she should be, and of a woman dead. And here –' a second pass and a comb was in her hand, lacquered blue over green – 'a comb from the deep sea, a mermaid's trinket, to charm and subdue. Part your locks with this, and the scent of ocean will fill men's nostrils and the rhythm of the tides their ears, the tides that bind men like chains. Last,' added the hag, 'that old symbol of wickedness, the scarlet fruit of Eve, the apple red as blood. Bite, and the understanding of Sin, which the serpent boasted of, will be made known to you.' And the hag made her last pass in the air and extended the apple, with the girdle and the comb, towards Bianca.

Bianca glanced at the seven stunted trees.

'I like her gifts, but I do not quite trust her.'

The bald masks peered from their shaggy beardings. Eyelets glinted. Twiggy claws clacked.

'All the same,' said Bianca, 'I will let her tie the girdle on me, and comb my hair herself.'

The hag obeyed, simpering. Like a toad she waddled to Bianca. She tied on the girdle. She parted the ebony hair. Sparks sizzled, white from the girdle, peacock's eye from the comb.

'And now, hag, take a little bit bite of the apple.'

'It will be my pride,' said the hag, 'to tell my sisters I shared this fruit with you.' And the hag bit into the apple, and mumbled the bite noisily, and swallowed, smacking her lips.

Then Bianca took the apple and bit into it.

Bianca screamed – and choked.

She jumped to her feet. Her hair whirled about her like a storm cloud. Her face turned blue, then slate, then white again. She lay on the pallid flowers, neither stirring nor breathing.

The seven dwarf trees rattled their limbs and their bear-shaggy heads, to no avail. Without Bianca's art they could not hop. They strained their claws and ripped at the hag's sparse hair and her mantle. She fled between them. She fled into the sunlit acres of the forest, along the broken road, through orchard, into a hidden passage.

The hag re-entered the palace by the hidden way, and the Queen's chamber by a hidden stair. She was bent almost double. She held her ribs. With one skinny hand she opened the ivory case of the magic mirror.

'*Speculum, speculum. Dei gratia.* Whom do you see?'

'I see you, mistress. And all in the land. And I see a coffin.'

'Whose corpse lies in the coffin?'

'That I cannot see. It must be Bianca.'

The hag, who had been the beautiful Witch Queen, sank into her tall chair before the window of pale cucumber green and dark white glass. Her drugs and potions waited ready to reverse the dreadful conjuring of age the Angel Lucefiel had placed on her, but she did not touch them yet.

The apple had contained a fragment of the flesh of Christ, the sacred wafer, the Eucharist.

The Witch Queen drew her Bible to her and opened it randomly. And read, with fear, the words: *Resurgat*.

It appeared like glass, the coffin, milky glass. It had formed this way. A thin white smoke had risen from the skin of Bianca. She smoked as a fire smokes when a drop of quenching water falls on it. The piece of Eucharist had stuck in her throat. The Eucharist, quenching water to her fire, caused her to smoke.

Then the cold dews of night gathered, and the colder atmospheres of midnight. The smoke of Bianca's quenching froze about her. Frost formed in exquisite silver scrollwork all over the block of misty ice which contained Bianca.

Bianca's frigid heart could not warm the ice. Nor the sunless green twilight of the day.

You could just see her, stretched in the coffin, through the glass. How lovely she looked, Bianca. Black as ebony, white as snow, red as blood.

The trees hung over the coffin. Years passed. The trees sprawled about the coffin, cradling it in their arms. Their eyes wept fungus and green resin. Green amber drops hardened like jewels in the coffin of glass.

'Who is that, lying under the trees?' the Prince asked, as he rode into the clearing.

He seemed to bring a golden moon with him, shining about his golden head, on the golden armour and the cloak of white satin blazoned with gold and blood and ink and sapphire. The white horse trod on the colourless flowers, but the flowers sprang up again when the hooves had passed. A shield hung from the saddle bow, a strange shield. From one side it had a lion's face, but from the other, a lamb's face.

The trees groaned and their heads split on huge mouths.

'Is this Bianca's coffin?' said the Prince.

'Leave her with us,' said the seven trees. They hauled at their roots. The ground shivered. The coffin of ice-glass gave a great jolt, and a crack bisected it.

Bianca coughed.

The jolt had precipitated the piece of Eucharist from her throat.

In a thousand shards the coffin shattered, and Bianca sat up. She stared at the Prince, and she smiled.

'Welcome, beloved,' said Bianca.

She got to her feet and shook out her hair, and began to walk toward the Prince on the pale horse.

But she seemed to walk into a shadow, into a purple room; then into a crimson room whose emanations lanced her like knives. Next she walked into a yellow room where she heard the sound of crying which tore her ears. All her body seemed stripped away; she was a beating heart. The beats of her heart became two wings. She flew. She was a raven, then an owl. She flew into a sparkling pane. It scorched her white. Snow white. She was a dove.

She settled on the shoulder of the Prince and hid her head under her wing. She had no longer anything black about her, and nothing red.

'Begin again now, Bianca,' said the Prince. He raised her from his shoulder. On his wrist there was a mark. It was like a star. Once a nail had been driven in there.

Bianca flew away, up through the roof of the forest. She flew in at a delicate wine window. She was in the palace. She was seven years old.

The Witch Queen, her new mother, hung a filigree crucifix

around her neck. 'Mirror,' said the Witch Queen. 'Whom do you see?'

'I see you, mistress,' replied the mirror. 'And all in the land. I see Bianca.'

Sur

(1982)

URSULA K. LE GUIN

A Summary Report of the *Yelcho* Expedition to the Antarctic, 1909–1910

Although I have no intention of publishing this report, I think it would be nice if a grandchild of mine, or somebody's grandchild, happened to find it some day; so I shall keep it in the leather trunk in the attic, along with Rosita's christening dress and Juanito's silver rattle and my wedding shoes and finneskos.

The first requisite for mounting an expedition – money – is normally the hardest to come by. I grieve that even in a report destined for a trunk in the attic of a house in a very quiet suburb of Lima I dare not write the name of the generous benefactor, the great soul without whose unstinting liberality the *Yelcho* Expedition would never have been more than the idlest excursion into daydream. That our equipment was the best and most modern – that our provisions were plentiful and fine – that a ship of the Chilean Government, with her brave officers and gallant crew, was twice sent halfway round the world for our convenience: all this is due to that benefactor whose name, alas! I must not say, but whose happiest debtor I shall be till death.

When I was little more than a child my imagination was caught by a newspaper account of the voyage of the *Belgica*, which, sailing south from Tierra del Fuego, became beset by ice in the Bellingshausen Sea and drifted a whole year with the floe, the men aboard her suffering a great deal from want of food and from the terror of the unending winter darkness. I read and reread that account, and later followed with excitement the reports of the rescue of Dr Nordenskjold from the South Shetland Isles by the dashing Captain Irizar of the *Uruguay*, and the adventures of the *Scotia* in the Weddell Sea. But all these exploits were to me but forerunners of the British National Antarctic Expedition of 1902–1904, in the *Discovery*, and the wonderful account of that expedition by Captain Scott. This book, which I ordered from London and reread a thousand times, filled me with longing to see with my own eyes that strange continent, last Thule of the South, which lies on our maps and globes like a white cloud, a void, fringed here and there with scraps of coastline, dubious capes, supposititious island, headlands that may or may not be there: Antarctica. And the desire was as pure as the polar snows: to go, to see – no more, no less. I deeply respect the scientific accomplishments of Captain Scott's expedition, and have read with passionate interest the findings of physicists, meteorologists, biologists, etc.; but having had no training in any science, nor any opportunity for such training, my ignorance obliged me to forego any thought of adding to the body of scientific knowledge concerning Antarctica; and the same is true for all the members of my expedition. It seems a pity; but there was nothing we could do about it. Our goal was limited to observation and exploration. We hoped to go a little farther, perhaps, and see a little more; if not, simply to go and to see. A simple ambition, I think, and essentially a modest one.

Yet it would have remained less than an ambition, no more than a longing, but for the support and encouragement of my dear cousin and friend Juana – (I use no surnames, lest this report fall into strangers' hands at last, and embarrassment or unpleasant notoriety thus be brought upon unsuspecting husbands, sons, etc.). I had lent Juana my copy of *The Voyage of the Discovery*, and it was she who, as we strolled beneath our parasols across the Plaza de Armas after Mass one Sunday in 1908, said, 'Well, if Captain Scott can do it, why can't we?'

It was Juana who proposed that we write Carlota – in Valparaiso. Through Carlota we met our benefactor, and so obtained our money, our ship, and even the plausible pretext of going on retreat in a Bolivian convent, which some of us were forced to employ (while the rest of us said we were going to Paris for the winter season). And it was my Juana who in the darkest moments remained resolute, unshaken in her determination to achieve our goal.

And there were dark moments, especially in the early months of

The map in the attic

1909 – times when I did not see how the Expedition would ever become more than a quarter ton of pemmican gone to waste and a lifelong regret. It was so very hard to gather our expeditionary force together! So few of those we asked even knew what we were talking about – so many thought we were mad, or wicked, or both! And of those few who shared our folly, still fewer were able, when it came to the point, to leave their daily duties and commit themselves to a voyage of at least six months, attended with not inconsiderable uncertainty and danger. An ailing parent; an anxious husband beset by business cares; child at home with only ignorant or incompetent servants to look after it: these are not responsibilities lightly to be set aside. And those who wished to evade such claims were not the companions we wanted in hard work, risk, and privation.

But since success crowned our efforts, why dwell on the setbacks and delays, or the wretched contrivances and downright lies that we all had to employ? I look back with regret only to those friends who wished to come with us but could not, by any contrivance, get free – those we had to leave behind to a life without danger, without uncertainty, without hope.

On the seventeenth of August 1909 in Punta Arenas, Chile, all the members of the Expedition met for the first time: Juana and I, the two Peruvians; from Argentina, Zoe, Berta, and Teresa; and our Chileans, Carlota and her friends Eva, Pepita, and Dolores. At the last moment I had received word that Maria's husband, in Quito, was ill, and she must stay to nurse him, so we were nine, not ten. Indeed, we had resigned ourselves to being but eight, when, just as night fell, the indomitable Zoe arrived in a tiny pirogue manned by Indians, her yacht having sprung a leak just as it entered the Strait of Magellan.

That night before we sailed we began to get to know one another; and we agreed, as we enjoyed our abominable supper in the abominable seaport inn of Punta Arenas, that if a situation arose of such urgent danger that one voice must be obeyed without present question, the unenviable honor of speaking with that voice should fall first upon myself: if I were incapacitated, upon Carlota: if she, then upon Berta. We three were then toasted as 'Supreme Inca', 'La Araucana', and 'The Third Mate', among a lot of laughter and cheering. As it came out, to my very great pleasure and relief, my qualities as a 'leader' were never tested; the nine of us worked things out amongst us from beginning to end without any orders being given by anybody, and only two or three times with recourse to a vote by voice or show of hands. To be sure, we argued a good deal. But then, we had time to argue. And one way or another the arguments always ended up in a decision, upon which action could be taken. Usually at least one person grumbled about the decision, sometimes bitterly. But what is life without grumbling, and the occasional opportunity to say, 'I told you so'? How could one bear housework, or looking after babies, let alone the rigors of sledge-hauling in Antarctica, without grumbling? Officers – as we came to understand aboard the *Yelcho* – are forbidden to grumble; but we nine were, and are, by birth and upbringing, unequivocally and irrevocably, all crew.

Though our shortest course to the southern continent, and that originally urged upon us by the captain of our good ship, was to the South Shetlands and the Bellingshausen Sea, or else by the South Orkneys into the Weddell Sea, we planned to sail west to the Ross Sea, which Captain Scott had explored and described, and from which the brave Ernest Shackleton had returned only the previous autumn. More was known about this region than any other portion of the coast of Antarctica, and though that more was not much, yet it served as some insurance of the safety of the ship, which we felt we had no right to imperil. Captain Pardo had fully agreed with us after studying the charts and our planned itinerary; and so it was westward that we took our course out of the Strait next morning.

Our journey half round the globe was attended by fortune. The little *Yelcho* steamed cheerily along through gale and gleam, climbing up and down those seas of the Southern Ocean that run unbroken round the world. Juana, who had fought bulls and the far more dangerous cows on her family's *estancia*, called the ship '*la vaca valiente*', because she always returned to the charge. Once we got over being seasick we all enjoyed the sea voyage, though oppressed at times by the kindly but officious protectiveness of the captain and his officers, who felt that we were only 'safe' when huddled up in the three tiny cabins which they had chivalrously vacated for our use.

We saw our first iceberg much farther south than we had looked for it, and saluted it with Veuve Clicquot at dinner. The next day we entered the ice pack, the belt of floes and bergs, broken loose from the land ice and winter-frozen seas of Antarctica, which drifts northward in the spring. Fortune still smiled on us: our little steamer, incapable, with her unreinforced metal hull, of forcing a way into the ice, picked her way from lane to lane without hesitation, and on the third day we were through the pack, in which ships have sometimes struggled for weeks and been obliged to turn back at last. Ahead of us now lay the dark gray waters of the Ross Sea, and beyond that, on the horizon, the remote glimmer, the cloud-reflected whiteness of the Great Ice Barrier.

Entering the Ross Sea a little east of Longitude West 160°, we came in sight of the Barrier at the place where Captain Scott's party, finding a bight in the vast wall of ice, had gone ashore and sent up their hydrogen-gas balloon for reconnaissance and photography. The towering face of the Barrier, its sheer cliffs and azure and violet water-worn caves, all were as described, but the location had changed: instead of a narrow bight there was a considerable bay, full of the beautiful and terrific orca whales playing and spouting in the sunshine of that brilliant southern spring.

Evidently masses of ice many acres in extent had broken away from the Barrier (which – at least for most of its vast extent – does not rest on land but floats on water) since the *Discovery*'s passage in 1902. This put our plan to set up camp on the Barrier itself in a new light; and while we were discussing alternatives, we asked Captain Pardo to take the ship west along the Barrier face towards Ross Island and McMurdo Sound. As the sea was clear of ice and quite calm, he was happy to do so, and when we sighted the smoke plume of Mount Erebus, to share in our celebration – another half case of Veuve Clicquot.

The *Yelcho* anchored in Arrival Bay, and we went ashore in the ship's boat. I cannot describe my emotions when I set foot on the earth, on that earth, the barren, cold gravel at the foot of the long volcanic slope. I felt elation, impatience, gratitude, awe, familiarity. I felt that I was home at last. Eight Adélie penguins immediately came to greet us with many exclamations of interest not unmixed with disapproval. 'Where on earth have you been? What took you so long? The Hut is around this way. Please come this way. Mind the rocks!' They insisted on our going to visit Hut Point, where the large structure built by Captain Scott's party stood, looking just as in the photographs and drawings that illustrate his book. The area about it, however, was disgusting – a kind of graveyard of seal skins, seal bones, penguin bones, and rubbish, presided over by the mad, screaming gulls. Our escorts waddled past the slaughterhouse in all tranquillity, and one showed me personally to the door, though it would not go in.

The interior of the hut was less offensive, but very dreary. Boxes of supplies had been stacked up into a kind of room within the room; it did not look as I had imagined it when the *Discovery* party put on their melodramas and minstrel shows in the long winter night. (Much later, we learned that Sir Ernest had re-arranged it a good deal when he was there just a year before us.) It was dirty, and had about it a mean disorder. A pound tin of tea was standing open. Empty meat tins lay about; biscuits were spilled on the floor; a lot of dog turds were underfoot – frozen, of course, but not a great deal improved by that. No doubt the last occupants had had to leave in a hurry, perhaps even in a blizzard. All the same, they could have closed the tea tin. But housekeeping, the art of the infinite, is no game for amateurs.

Teresa proposed that we use the hut as our camp. Zoe counter-proposed that we set fire to it. We finally shut the door and left it as we had found it. The penguins appeared to approve, and cheered us all the way to the boat.

McMurdo Sound was free of ice, and Captain Pardo now proposed to take us off Ross Island and across to Victoria Land, where we might camp at the foot of the Western Mountains, on dry and solid earth. But those mountains, with their storm-darkened peaks and hanging cirques and glaciers, looked as awful as Captain Scott had found them on his western journey, and none of us felt much inclined to seek shelter among them.

Aboard the ship that night we decided to go back and set up our base as we had originally planned, on the Barrier itself. For all available reports indicated that the clear way south was across the level Barrier surface until one could ascend one of the confluent glaciers to the high plateau which appears to form the whole interior of the continent. Captain Pardo argued strongly against this plan, asking what would become of us if the Barrier 'calved' – if our particular acre of ice broke away and started to drift northward. 'Well,' said Zoe, 'then you won't have to come so far to meet us.' But he was so persuasive on this theme that he persuaded himself into leaving one of the *Yelcho*'s boats with us when we camped, as a means of escape. We found it useful for fishing, later on.

My first steps on Antarctic soil, my only visit to Ross Island, had not been pleasure unalloyed. I thought of the words of the English poet:

> Though every prospect pleases,
> And only Man is vile

But then, the backside of heroism is often rather sad; women and servants know that. They know also that the heroism may be no less real for that. But achievement is smaller than men think. What is large is the sky, the earth, the sea, the soul. I looked back as the ship sailed east again that evening. We were well into September now, with ten hours or more of daylight. The spring sunset lingered on the twelve thousand foot peak of Erebus and shone rosy gold on her long plume of steam. The steam from our own small funnel faded blue on the twilit water as we crept along under the towering pale wall of ice.

On our return to 'Orca Bay' – Sir Ernest, we learned years later, had named it the Bay of Whales – we found a sheltered nook where the Barrier edge was low enough to provide fairly easy access from the ship. The *Yelcho* put out her ice anchor, and the next long, hard days were spent in unloading our supplies and setting up our camp on the ice, a half kilometer in from the edge: a task in which the *Yelcho*'s crew lent us invaluable aid and interminable advice. We took all the aid gratefully, and most of the advice with salt.

The weather so far had been extraordinarily mild for spring in this latitude; the temperature had not yet gone below -20° Fahrenheit, and there was only one blizzard while we were setting up camp. But Captain Scott had spoken feelingly of the bitter south winds on the Barrier, and we had planned accordingly. Exposed as our camp was to every wind, we built no rigid structures above ground. We set up tents to shelter in while we dug out a series of cubicles in the ice itself, lined them with hay insulation and pine boarding, and roofed them with canvas over bamboo poles, covered with snow for weight and insulation. The big central room was instantly named Buenos Aires by our Argentineans, to whom the center, wherever one is, is always Buenos Aires. The heating and cooking stove was in Buenos Aires. The storage tunnels and the privy (called Punta Arenas) got some back heat from the stove. The sleeping cubicles opened off Buenos Aires, and were very small, mere tubes into which one crawled feet first; they were lined deeply with hay and soon warmed up one's body warmth. The sailors called them 'coffins' and 'wormholes', and looked with horror on our burrows in the ice. But our little warren or prairie-dog village served us well, permitting us as much warmth and privacy as one could reasonably expect under the circumstances. If the *Yelcho* was unable to get through the ice in February, and we had to spend the winter in Antarctica, we certainly could do so, though on very limited rations. For this coming summer, our base – Sudamérica del Sur, South South America, but we generally called it the Base – was intended merely as a place to sleep, to store our provisions, and to give shelter from blizzards.

To Berta and Eva, however, it was more than that. They were its chief architect-designers, its most ingenious builder-excavators, and its most diligent and contented occupants, forever inventing an improvement in ventilation, or learning how to make skylights, or revealing to us a new addition to our suite of rooms, dug in the living ice. It was thanks to them that our stores were stowed so handily, that our stove drew and heated so efficiently, and that Buenos Aires, where nine people cooked, ate, worked, conversed, argued, grumbled, painted, played the guitar and banjo, and kept the Expedition's library of books and maps, was a marvel of comfort and convenience. We lived there in real amity; and if you simply had to be alone for a while, you crawled into your sleeping hole head first.

Berta went a little farther. When she had done all she could to make South South America livable, she dug out one more cell just under the ice surface, leaving a nearly transparent sheet of ice like a greenhouse roof; and there, alone, she worked at sculptures. They were beautiful forms, some like a blending of the reclining human figure with the subtle curves and volumes of the Weddell seal, others like the fantastic shapes of ice cornices and ice caves. Perhaps they are there still, under the snow, in the bubble in the Great Barrier. There where she made them they might last as long as stone. But she could not bring them north. That is the penalty for carving in water.

Captain Pardo was reluctant to leave us, but his orders did not permit him to hang about the Ross Sea indefinitely, and so at last, with many earnest injunctions to us to stay put — make no journeys — take no risks — beware of frostbite — don't use edge tools — look out for cracks in the ice — and a heartfelt promise to return to Orca Bay on the twentieth of February, or as near that date as wind and ice would permit, the good man bade us farewell, and his crew shouted us a great goodbye cheer as they weighed anchor. That evening, in the long orange twilight of October, we saw the topmast of the *Yelcho* go down the north horizon, over the edge of the world, leaving us to ice, and silence, and the Pole.

That night we began to plan the Southern Journey.

The ensuing months passed in short practice trips and depot-laying. The life we had led at home, though in its own way strenuous, had not fitted any of us for the kind of strain met with in sledge-hauling at ten or twenty degrees below freezing. We all needed as much working-out as possible before we dared undertake a long haul.

My longest exploratory trip, made with Dolores and Carlota, was south-west towards Mount Markham, and it was a nightmare — blizzards and pressure ice all the way out, crevasses and no view of the mountains when we got there, and white weather and sastrugi all the way back. The trip was useful, however, in that we could begin to estimate our capacities; and also in that we had started out with a very heavy load of provisions, which we depoted at 100 and 130 miles SSW of Base. Thereafter other parties pushed on farther, till we had a line of snow cairns and depots right down to Latitude 83° 43′, where Juana and Zoe, on an exploring trip, had found a kind of stone gateway opening on a great glacier leading south. We established these depots to avoid, if possible, the hunger that had bedevilled Captain Scott's Southern Party, and the consequent misery and weakness. And we also established to our own satisfaction – intense satisfaction – that we were sledge-haulers at least as good as Captain Scott's husky dogs. Of course we could not have expected to pull as much or as fast as his men. That we did so was because we were favored by much better weather than Captain Scott's party ever met on the Barrier; and also the quantity and quality of our food made a very considerable difference. I am sure that the fifteen percent of dried fruits in our pemmican helped prevent scurvy; and the potatoes, frozen and dried according to an ancient Andean Indian method, were very nourishing yet very light and compact – perfect sledging rations. In any case, it was with considerable confidence in our capacities that we made ready at last for the Southern Journey.

The Southern Party consisted of two sledge teams: Juana, Dolores, and myself; Carlota, Pepita, and Zoe. The support team of Berta, Eva, and Teresa set out before us with a heavy load of supplies, going right up on to the glacier to prospect routes and leave depots of supplies for our return journey. We followed five days behind them, and met them returning between Depot Ercilla and Depot Miranda (see map). That 'night' – of course there was no real darkness – we were all nine together in the heart of the level plain of ice. It was the fifteenth of November, Dolores's birthday. We celebrated by putting eight ounces of pisco in the hot chocolate, and became very merry. We sang. It is strange now to remember how thin our voices sounded in that great silence. It was overcast, white weather, without shadows and without visible horizon or any feature to break the level; there was nothing to see at all. We had come to that white place on the map, that void, and there we flew and sang like sparrows.

After sleep and a good breakfast the Base Party continued north, and the Southern Party sledged on. The sky cleared presently. High up, thin clouds passed over very rapidly from south-west to north-east, but down on the Barrier it was calm and just cold enough, five or ten degrees below freezing, to give a firm surface for hauling.

On the level ice we never pulled less than eleven miles, seventeen
kilometers, a day, and generally fifteen or sixteen miles, twenty-
five kilometers. (Our instruments, being British made, were cal-
ibrated in feet, miles, degrees Fahrenheit, etc., but we often
converted miles to kilometers because the larger number sounded
more encouraging.) At the time we left South America, we knew
only that Mr Shackleton had mounted another expedition to the
Antarctic in 1908, had tried to attain the Pole but failed, and had
returned to England in June of the current year, 1909. No
coherent report of his explorations had yet reached South America
when we left; we did not know what route he had gone, or how
far he had got. But we were not altogether taken by surprise
when, far across the featureless white plain, tiny beneath the
mountain peaks and the strange silent flight of the rainbow-fringed
cloud wisps, we saw a fluttering dot of black. We turned west
from our course to visit it: a snow heap nearly buried by the
winter's storm – a flag on a bamboo pole, a mere shred of
threadbare cloth – an empty oilcan – and a few footprints standing
some inches above the ice. In some conditions of weather the
snow compressed under one's weight remains when the surrounding soft snow melts or is scoured away by the wind; and so these
reversed footprints had been left standing all these months, like
rows of cobbler's lasts – a queer sight.

We met no other such traces on our way. In general I believe
our course was somewhat east of Mr Shackleton's. Juana, our
surveyor, had trained herself well and was faithful and methodical
in her sightings and readings, but our equipment was minimal – a
theodolite on tripod legs, a sextant with artificial horizon, two
compasses, and chronometers. We had only the wheel meter on
the sledge to give distance actually travelled.

In any case, it was the day after passing Mr Shackleton's
waymark that I first saw clearly the great glacier among the
mountains to the south-west, which was to give us a pathway
from the sea level of the Barrier up to the altiplano, ten thousand
feet above. The approach was magnificent: a gateway formed by
immense vertical domes and pillars of rock. Zoe and Juana had
called the vast ice river that flowed through that gateway the
Florence Nightingale Glacier, wishing to honor the British, who

had been the inspiration and guide of our expedition; that very brave and very peculiar lady seemed to represent so much that is best, and strangest, in the island race. On maps, of course, this glacier bears the name Mr Shackleton gave it, the Beardmore.

The ascent of the Nightingale was not easy. The way was open at first, and well marked by our support party, but after some days we came among terrible crevasses, a maze of hidden cracks, from a foot to thirty feet wide and from thirty to a thousand feet deep. Step by step we went, and step by step, and the way always upward now. We were fifteen days on the glacier. At first the weather was hot, up to 20°F, and the hot nights without darkness were wretchedly uncomfortable in our small tents. And all of us suffered more or less from snowblindness just at the time when we wanted clear eyesight to pick our way among the ridges and crevasses of the tortured ice, and to see the wonders about and before us. For at every day's advance more great, nameless peaks came into view in the west and south-west, summit beyond summit, range beyond range, stark rock and snow in the unending noon.

We gave names to these peaks, not very seriously, since we did not expect our discoveries to come to the attention of geographers. Zoe had a gift for naming, and it is thanks to her that certain sketch maps in various suburban South American attics bear such curious features as 'Bolivar's Big Nose', 'I Am General Rosas'. 'The Cloudmaker', 'Whose Toe?' and 'Throne of Our Lady of the Southern Cross'. And when at last we got up onto the altiplano, the great interior plateau, it was Zoe who called it the pampas, and maintained that we walked there among vast herds of invisible cattle, transparent cattle pastured on the spindrift snow, their gauchos the restless, merciless winds. We were by then all a little crazy with exhaustion and the great altitude – twelve thousand feet – and the cold and the wind blowing and the luminous circles and crosses surrounding the suns, for often there were three or four suns in the sky, up there.

That is not a place where people have any business to be. We should have turned back; but since we had worked so hard to get there, it seemed that we should go on, at least for a while.

A blizzard came with very low temperatures, so we had to stay in the tents, in our sleeping bags, for thirty hours, a rest we all needed; though it was warmth we needed most, and there was no warmth on that terrible plain anywhere at all but in our veins. We huddled close together all that time. The ice we lay on was two miles thick.

It cleared suddenly and became, for the plateau, good weather: twelve below zero and the wind not very strong. We three crawled out of our tent and met the others crawling out of theirs. Carlota told us then that her group wished to turn back. Pepita had been feeling very ill; even after the rest during the blizzard, her temperature would not rise above 90°. Carlota was having trouble breathing. Zoe was perfectly fit, but much preferred staying with her friends and lending them a hand in difficulties to pushing on towards the Pole. So we put the four ounces of pisco which we had been keeping for Christmas into the breakfast cocoa, and dug out our tents, and loaded our sledges, and parted there in the white daylight on the bitter plain.

Our sledge was fairly light by now. We pulled on to the south. Juana calculated our position daily. On the twenty-second of December, 1909, we reached the South Pole. The weather was, as always, very cruel. Nothing of any kind marked the dreary whiteness. We discussed leaving some kind of mark or monument, a snow cairn, a tent pole and flag; but there seemed no particular reason to do so. Anything we could do, anything we were, was insignificant, in that awful place. We put up the tent for shelter for an hour and made a cup of tea, and then struck '90° Camp'. Dolores, standing patient as ever in her sledging harness, looked at the snow; it was so hard frozen that it showed no trace of our footprints coming and she said, 'Which way?'

'North,' said Juana.

It was a joke, because at that particular place there is no other direction. But we did not laugh. Our lips were cracked with frostbite and hurt too much to let us laugh. So we started back, and the wind at our backs pushed us along, and dulled the knife edges of the waves of frozen snow.

All that week the blizzard wind pursued us like a pack of mad dogs. I cannot describe it. I wished we had not gone to the Pole. I think I wish it even now. But I was glad even then that we had left no sign there, for some man longing to be first might come some day, and find it, and know then what a fool he had been, and break his heart.

We talked, when we could talk, of catching up to Carlota's party, since they might be going slower than we. In fact they had used their tent as a sail to catch the following wind and had got far ahead of us. But in many places they had built snow cairns or left some sign for us; once Zoe had written on the lee side of a ten-foot sastruga, just as children write on the sand of the beach at Miraflores, 'This Way Out!' The wind blowing over the frozen ridge had left the words perfectly distinct.

In the very hour that we began to descend the glacier, the weather turned warmer, and the mad dogs were left to howl forever tethered to the Pole. The distance that had taken us fifteen days going up we covered in only eight days going down. But the good weather that had aided us descending the Nightingale became a curse down on the Barrier ice, where we had looked forward to a kind of royal progress from depot to depot, eating our fill and taking our time for the last three hundred odd miles. In a tight place on the glacier I lost my goggles – I was swinging from my harness at the time in a crevasse – and then Juana had broken hers when we had to do some rock climbing coming down to the Gateway. After two days in bright sunlight with only one pair of snow goggles to pass amongst us, we were all suffering badly from snowblindness. It became acutely painful to keep lookout for landmarks or depot flags, to take sightings, even to study the compass, which had to be laid down on the snow to steady the needle. At Concolorcorvo Depot, where there was a particularly good supply of food and fuel, we gave up, crawled into our sleeping bags with bandaged eyes, and slowly boiled alive like lobsters in the tent, exposed to the relentless sun. The voices of Berta and Zoe were the sweetest sound I ever heard. A little concerned about us, they had skied south to meet us. They led us home to Base.

We recovered quite swiftly, but the altiplano left its mark. When she was very little, Rosita asked if a dog 'had bitten Mama's toes'. I told her 'yes, a great, white, mad dog named Blizzard!' My Rosita and my Juanito heard many stories when they were little, about that fearful dog and how it howled, and the transparent cattle of the invisible gauchos, and a river of ice eight thousand feet high called Nightingale, and how Cousin Juana drank a cup of tea standing on the bottom of the world under seven suns, and other fairy tales.

We were in for one severe shock when we reached Base at last. Teresa was pregnant. I must admit that my first response to the poor girl's big belly and sheepish look was anger – rage – fury. That one of us should have concealed anything, and such a thing, from the others! But Teresa had done nothing of the sort. Only those who had concealed from her what she most needed to know were to blame. Brought up by servants, with four years' schooling in a convent, and married at sixteen, the poor girl was still so ignorant at twenty years of age that she had thought it was 'the cold weather' that made her miss her periods. Even this was not entirely stupid, for all of us on the Southern Journey had seen our periods change or stop altogether as we experienced increasing cold, hunger, and fatigue. Teresa's appetite had begun to draw general attention; and then she had begun, as she said pathetically, 'to get fat'. The others were worried at the thought of all the sledge-hauling she had done, but she flourished, and the only problem was her positively insatiable appetite. As well as could be determined from her shy references to her last night on the hacienda with her husband, the baby was due at just about the same time as the *Yelcho*, the twentieth of February. But we had not been back from the Southern Journey two weeks when, on 14 February, she went into labor.

Several of us had borne children and had helped with deliveries, and anyhow most of what needs to be done is fairly self-evident; but a first labor can be long and trying, and we were all anxious, while Teresa was frightened out of her wits. She kept calling for her José till she was as hoarse as a skua. Zoe lost all patience at last and said, 'By God, Teresa, if you say "José!" once more I hope you have a penguin!' But what she had, after twenty long hours, was a pretty little red-faced girl.

Many were the suggestions for that child's name from her eight proud midwife-aunts: Polita, Penguina, McMurdo, Victoria . . . But Teresa announced, after she had had a good sleep and a large serving of pemmican, 'I shall name her Rosa – Rosa del Sur,' Rose of the South. That night we drank the last two bottles of Veuve Clicquot (having finished the piscos at 88° 30′ South) in toasts to our little Rose.

On the nineteenth of February, a day early, my Juana came down into Buenos Aires in a hurry. 'The ship,' she said, 'the ship has come,' and she burst into tears – she who had never wept in all our weeks of pain and weariness on the long haul.

Of the return voyage there is nothing to tell. We came back safe.

In 1912 all the world learned that the brave Norwegian Amundsen had reached the South Pole; and then, much later, came the accounts of how Captain Scott and his men had come there after him, but did not come home again.

Just this year, Juana and I wrote to the captain of the *Yelcho*, for the newspapers have been full of the story of his gallant dash to rescue Sir Ernest Shackleton's men from Elephant Island, and we wished to congratulate him, and once more to thank him. Never one word has he breathed of our secret. He is a man of honor, Luis Pardo.

I add this last note in 1929. Over the years we have lost touch with one another. It is very difficult for women to meet, when they live so far apart as we do. Since Juana died, I have seen none of my old sledge-mates, though sometimes we write. Our little Rosa del Sur died of the scarlet fever when she was five years old. Teresa had many other children. Carlota took the veil in Santiago ten years ago. We are old women now, with old husbands, and grown children, and grandchildren who might someday like to read about the Expedition. Even if they are rather ashamed of having such a crazy grandmother, they may enjoy sharing in the secret. But they must not let Mr Amundsen know! He would be terribly embarrassed and disappointed. There is no need for him or anyone else outside the family to know. We left no footprints, even.

Peter and the Wolf

(1982)

ANGELA CARTER

At length the grandeur of the mountains becomes monotonous; with familiarity, the landscape ceases to provoke awe and wonder and the traveller sees the alps with the indifferent eye of those who always live there. Above a certain line, no trees grow. Shadows of clouds move across the bare alps as freely as the clouds themselves move across the sky.

A girl from a village on the lower slopes left her widowed mother to marry a man who lived up in the empty places. Soon she was pregnant. In October, there was a severe storm. The old woman knew her daughter was near her time and waited for a message but none arrived. After the storm passed, the old woman went up to see for herself, taking her grown son with her because she was afraid.

From a long way off, they saw no smoke rising from the chimney. Solitude yawned round them. The open door banged backwards and forwards on its hinges. Solitude engulfed them. There were traces of wolf-dung on the floor so they knew wolves had been in the house but left the corpse of the young mother alone although of her baby nothing was left except some mess that showed it had been born. Nor was there a trace of the son-in-law but a gnawed foot in a boot.

They wrapped the dead in a quilt and took it home with them. Now it was late. The howling of the wolves mutilated the approaching silence of the night.

Winter came with icy blasts, when everyone stays indoors and stokes the fire. The old woman's son married the blacksmith's daughter and she moved in with them. The snow melted and it was spring. By the next Christmas, there was a bouncing grandson. Time passed. More children came.

When the eldest grandson, Peter, reached his seventh summer, he was old enough to go up the mountain with his father, as the men did every year, to let the goats feed on the young grass. There Peter sat in the new sunlight, plaiting the straw for baskets, until he saw the thing he had been taught most to fear advancing silently along the lea of an outcrop of rock. Then another wolf, following the first one.

If they had not been the first wolves he had ever seen, the boy would not have inspected them so closely, their plush, grey pelts, of which the hairs are tipped with white, giving them a ghostly look, as if they were on the point of dissolving at the edges; their sprightly, plumely tails; their acute, inquisitive masks.

Then Peter saw that the third wolf was a prodigy, a marvel, a naked one, going on all fours, as they did, but hairless as regards the body although hair grew around its head.

The sight of this bald wolf so fascinated him that he would have lost his flock, perhaps himself been eaten and certainly been beaten to the bone for negligence had not the goats themselves raised their heads, snuffed danger and run off, bleating and whinnying, so that the men came, firing guns, making hullabaloo, scaring the wolves away.

His father was too angry to listen to what Peter said. He cuffed Peter round the head and sent him home. His mother was feeding this year's baby. His grandmother sat at the table, shelling peas into a pot.

'There was a little girl with the wolves, granny,' said Peter. Why was he so sure it had been a little girl? Perhaps because her hair was so long, so long and lively. 'A little girl about my age, from her size,' he said.

His grandmother threw a flat pod out of the door so the chickens could peck it up.

'I saw a little girl with the wolves,' he said.

His grandmother tipped water into the pot, got up from the table and hung the pot of peas on the hook over the fire. There wasn't time, that night, but, next morning, very early, she herself took the boy back up the mountain.

'Tell your father what you told me.'

They went to look at the wolves' tracks. On a bit of dampish ground they found a print, not like that of a dog's pad, much less

like that of a child's footprint, yet Peter worried and puzzled over
it until he made sense of it.

'She was running on all fours with her arse stuck in the air . . .
therefore . . . she'd put all her weight on the ball of her foot,
wouldn't she? And splay out her toes, see . . . like that.'

He went barefoot in summer, like all the village children; he
inserted the ball of his own foot in the print, to show his father
what kind of mark he would have made if he, too, always ran on
all fours.

'No use for a heel, if you run that way. So she doesn't have a
heel-print. Stands to reason.'

At last his father made a slow acknowledgement of Peter's
powers of deduction, giving the child a veiled glance of disquiet.
It was a clever child.

They soon found her. She was asleep. Her spine had grown so
supple she could curl into a perfect C. She woke up when she
heard them and ran, but somebody caught her with a sliding
noose at the end of a rope; the noose over her head jerked tight
and she fell to the ground with her eyes popping and rolling. A
big, grey, angry bitch appeared out of nowhere but Peter's father
blasted it to bits with his shotgun. The girl would have choked if
the old woman hadn't taken her head on her lap and pulled the
knot loose. The girl bit the grandmother's hand.

The girl scratched and fought until the men tied her wrists and
ankles together with twine and slung her from a pole to carry her
back to the village. Then she went limp. She didn't scream or shout,
she didn't seem to be able to, she made only a few dull, guttural
sounds in the back of her throat, and, though she did not seem to
know how to cry, water trickled out of the corners of her eyes.

How burned she was by the weather! Bright brown all over;
and how filthy she was! Caked with mud and dirt. And every inch
of her chestnut hide was scored and scabbed with dozens of scars
of sharp abrasions of rock and thorn. Her hair dragged on the
ground as they carried her along; it was stuck with burrs and it
was so dirty you could not see what colour it might be. She was
dreadfully verminous. She stank. She was so thin that all her ribs
stuck out. The fine, plump, potato-fed boy was far bigger than
she, although she was a year or so older.

Solemn with curiosity, he trotted behind her. Granny stumped alongside with her bitten hand wrapped up in her apron. Once the girl was dumped on the earth floor of her grandmother's house, the boy secretly poked at her left buttock with his forefinger, out of curiosity, to see what she felt like. She felt warm but hard. She did not so much as twitch when he touched her. She had given up the struggle; she lay trussed on the floor and pretended to be dead.

Granny's house had one large room which, in winter, they shared with the goats. As soon as it caught a whiff of her, the big tabby mouser hissed like a pricked balloon and bounded up the ladder that went to the hayloft above. Soup smoked on the fire and the table was laid. It was now about supper-time but still quite light; night comes late on the summer mountain.

'Untie her,' said the grandmother.

Her son wasn't willing at first but the old woman would not be denied, so he got the breadknife and cut the rope round the girl's ankles. All she did was kick, but when he cut the rope round her wrists, it was as if he had let a fiend loose. The onlookers ran out of the door, the rest of the family ran for the ladder to the hayloft but Granny and Peter both ran to the door, to shoot the bolt, so she could not get out.

The trapped one knocked round the room. Bang – over went the table. Crash, tinkle – the supper dishes smashed. Bang, crash, tinkle – the dresser fell forward upon the hard white shale of crockery it shed in falling. Over went the meal barrel and she coughed, she sneezed like a child sneezes, no different, and then she bounced around on fear-stiffened legs in a white cloud until the flour settled on everything like a magic powder that made everything strange. Her first frenzy over, she squatted a moment, questing with her long nose and then began to make little rushing sorties, now here, now there, snapping and yelping and tossing her bewildered head.

She never rose up on two legs; she crouched, all the time, on her hands and tiptoes, yet it was not quite like crouching, for you could see how all fours came naturally to her as though she had made a different pact with gravity than we have, and you could see, too, how strong the muscles in her thighs had grown on the mountain, how taut the twanging arches of her feet, and that indeed, she only used her heels when she sat back on her haunches. She growled; now and then she coughed out those intolerable, thick grunts of distress. All you could see of her rolling eyes were the whites, which were the bluish, glaring white of snow.

Several times, her bowels opened, apparently involuntarily. The kitchen smelled like a privy yet even her excrement was different to ours, the refuse of raw, strange, unguessable, wicked feeding, shit of a wolf.

Oh, horror!

She bumped into the hearth, knocked over the pan hanging from the hook and the spilled contents put out the fire. Hot soup scalded her forelegs. Shock of pain. Squatting on her hindquarters, holding the hurt paw dangling piteously from its wrist before her, she howled, in high, sobbing arcs.

Even the old woman, who had contracted with herself to love the child of her dead daughter, was frightened when she heard the girl howl.

Peter's heart gave a hop, a skip, so that he had a sensation of falling; he was not conscious of his own fear because he could not take his eyes off the sight of the crevice of her girl-child's sex, that was perfectly visible to him as she sat there square on the base of her spine. The night was now as dark as, at this season, it would go – which is to say, not very dark; a white thread of moon hung in the blond sky at the top of the chimney so that it was neither dark nor light indoors yet the boy could see her intimacy clearly, as if by its own phosphorescence. It exercised an absolute fascination upon him.

Her lips opened up as she howled so that she offered him, without her own intention or volition, a view of a set of Chinese boxes of whorled flesh that seemed to open one upon another into herself, drawing him to an inner, secret place in which destination perpetually receded before him, his first, devastating, vertiginous intimation of infinity.

She howled.

And went on howling until, from the mountain, first singly, then in a complex of polyphony, answered at last voices in the same language.

She continued to howl, though now with a less tragic resonance.

Soon it was impossible for the occupants of the house to deny to themselves that the wolves were descending on the village in a pack.

Then she was consoled, sank down, laid her head on her forepaws so that her hair trailed in the cooling soup and so closed up her forbidden book without the least notion she had ever opened it or that it was banned. Her heavy eyelids closed on her brown, bloodshot eyes. The household gun hung on a nail over the fireplace where Peter's father had put it when he came in but when the man set his foot on the top rung of the ladder in order to come down for his weapon, the girl jumped up, snarling and showing her long yellow canines.

The howling outside was now mixed with the agitated dismay of the domestic beasts. All the other villagers were well locked up at home.

The wolves were at the door.

The boy took hold of his grandmother's uninjured hand. First the old woman would not budge but he gave her a good tug and she came to herself. The girl raised her head suspiciously but let them by. The boy pushed his grandmother up the ladder in front of him and drew it up behind them. He was full of nervous dread. He would have given anything to turn time back, so that he might have run, shouting a warning, when he first caught sight of the wolves, and never seen her.

The door shook as the wolves outside jumped up at it and the screws that held the socket of the bolt to the frame cracked, squeaked and started to give. The girl jumped up, at that, and began to make excited little sallies back and forth in front of the door. The screws tore out of the frame quite soon. The pack tumbled over one another to get inside.

Dissonance. Terror. The clamour within the house was that of all the winds of winter trapped in a box. That which they feared most, outside, was now indoors with them. The baby in the hayloft whimpered and its mother crushed it to her breast as if the wolves might snatch this one away, too; but the rescue party had arrived only in order to collect their fosterling.

They left behind a riotous stench in the house, and white tracks of flour everywhere. The broken door creaked backwards and forwards on its hinges. Black sticks of dead wood from the extinguished fire were scattered on the floor.

Peter thought the old woman would cry, now, but she seemed unmoved. When all was safe, they came down the ladder one by one and, as if released from a spell of silence, burst into excited speech except for the mute old woman and the distraught boy. Although it was well past midnight, the daughter-in-law went to the well for water to scrub the wild smell out of the house. The broken things were cleared up and thrown away. Peter's father nailed the table and the dresser back together. The neighbours came out of their houses, full of amazement; the wolves had not taken so much as a chicken from the hen-coops, not snatched even a single egg.

People brought beer into the starlight, and schnapps made from potatoes, and snacks, because the excitement had made them hungry. That terrible night ended up in one big party but the grandmother would eat or drink nothing and went to bed as soon as her house was clean.

Next day, she went to the graveyard and sat for a while beside her daughter's grave but she did not pray. Then she came home and started chopping cabbage for the evening meal but had to leave off because her bitten hand was festering.

That winter, during the leisure imposed by the snow, after his grandmother's death, Peter asked the village priest to teach him to read the Bible. The priest gladly complied; Peter was the first of his flock who had ever expressed any interest in learning to read.

The boy became very pious, so much so that his family were startled and impressed. The younger children teased him and called him 'Saint Peter' but that did not stop him sneaking off to church to pray whenever he had a spare moment. In Lent, he fasted to the bone. On Good Friday, he lashed himself. It was as if he blamed himself for the death of the old lady, as if he believed he had brought into the house the fatal infection that had taken her out of it. He was consumed by an imperious passion for atonement. Each night, he pored over his book by the flimsy candlelight, looking for a clue to grace, until his mother shooed him off to sleep.

But, as if to spite the four evangelists he nightly invoked to protect his bed, the nightmare regularly disordered his sleep. He tossed and turned on the rustling straw pallet he shared with two little ones.

Delighted with Peter's precocious intelligence, the priest started to teach him Latin. Peter visited the priest as his duties with the herd permitted. When he was fourteen, the priest told his parents that Peter should now go to the seminary in the town in the valley where the boy would learn to become a priest himself. Rich in sons, they spared one to God, since his books and his praying made him a stranger to them. After the goats came down from the high pasture for the winter, Peter set off. It was October.

At the end of his first day's travel, he reached a river that ran from the mountain into the valley. The nights were already chilly; he lit himself a fire, prayed, ate bread and cheese his mother had packed for him and slept as well as he could. In spite of his eagerness to plunge into the white world of penance and devotion that awaited him, he was anxious and troubled for reasons he could not explain to himself.

In the first light, the light that no more than clarifies darkness like egg shells dropped in cloudy liquid, he went down to the river to drink and to wash his face. It was so still he could have been the one thing living.

Her forearms, her loins and her legs were thick with hair and the hair on her head hung round her face in such a way that you could hardly make out her features. She crouched on the other side of the river. She was lapping up water so full of mauve light that it looked as if she were drinking up the dawn as fast as it appeared yet all the same the air grew pale while he was looking at her.

Solitude and silence; all still.

She could never have acknowledged that the reflection beneath her in the river was that of herself. She did not know she had a face; she had never known she had a face and so her face itself was the mirror of a different kind of consciousness than ours is, just as her nakedness, without innocence or display, was that of our first parents, before the Fall. She was hairy as Magdalen in the wilderness and yet repentance was not within her comprehension.

Language crumbled into dust under the weight of her speechlessness.

A pair of cubs rolled out of the bushes, cuffing one another. She did not pay them any heed.

The boy began to tremble and shake. His skin prickled. He felt he had been made of snow and now might melt. He mumbled something, or sobbed.

She cocked her head at the vague, river-washed sound and the cubs heard it, too, left off tumbling and ran to burrow their scared heads in her side. But she decided, after a moment, there was no danger and lowered her muzzle, again, to the surface of the water that took hold of her hair and spread it out around her head.

When she finished her drink, she backed a few paces, shaking her wet pelt. The little cubs fastened their mouths on her dangling breasts.

Peter could not help it, he burst out crying. He had not cried since his grandmother's funeral. Tears rolled down his face and splashed on the grass. He blundered forward a few steps into the river with his arms held open, intending to cross over the other side to join her in her marvellous and private grace, impelled by the access of an almost visionary ecstasy. But his cousin took fright at the sudden movement, wrenched her teats away from the cubs and ran off. The squeaking cubs scampered behind. She ran on hands and feet as if that were the only way to run towards the high ground, into the bright maze of the uncompleted dawn.

When the boy recovered himself, he dried his tears on his sleeve, took off his soaked boots and dried his feet and legs on the tail of his shirt. Then he ate something from his pack, he scarcely knew what, and continued on the way to the town; but what would he do at the seminary, now? For now he knew there was nothing to be afraid of.

He experienced the vertigo of freedom.

He carried his boots slung over his shoulder by the laces. They were a great burden. He debated with himself whether or not to throw them away but, when he came to a paved road, he had to put them on, although they were still damp.

The birds woke up and sang. The cool, rational sun surprised him; morning had broken on his exhilaration and the mountain now lay behind him. He looked over his shoulder and saw, how, with distance, the mountain began to acquire a flat, two-dimensional look. It was already turning into a picture of itself, into the postcard hastily bought as a souvenir of childhood at a railway station or a border post, the newspaper cutting, the snapshot he would show in strange towns, strange cities, other countries he could not, at this moment, imagine, whose names he did not yet know, places where he would say, in strange languages, 'That was where I spent my childhood. Imagine!'

He turned and stared at the mountain for a long time. He had lived on it for fourteen years but he had never seen it before as it might look to someone who had not known it as almost a part of the self, so, for the first time, he saw the primitive, vast, magnificent, barren, unkind simplicity of the mountain. As he said goodbye to it, he saw it turn into so much scenery, into the wonderful backcloth for an old country tale, tale of a child suckled by wolves, perhaps, or of wolves nursed by a woman.

Then he determinedly set his face towards the town and tramped onwards, into a different story.

'If I look back again,' he thought with a last gasp of superstitious terror, 'I shall turn into a pillar of salt.'

The Pits beneath the World

(1983)

MARY GENTLE

A wind stirs the blue grass of the Great Plains. The flat land stretches out to the perfect circle of the horizon. There is not a rock or tree to break the monotony. Seventeen moons burn in a lilac sky. A blue-giant sun is setting, its white dwarf companion star hangs in the evening sky.

The small figure stands waist-deep in the grass. She aches from running bent over in a crouch. Now she straightens, biting back a gasp at the pain.

Shrill chittering and whistling noises come from the distance. Seen!

Up until today she's been sorry that she's small for her age. Now she's glad. Only a small human could lie concealed in the Plains grass. She edges away and crawls on, hands and knees stained blue by the grass sap.

Behind her, the whistling of the Talinorian hunting party begins again.

There is no doubt: she is their quarry.

When did it go wrong? Pel Graham wondered. The Talinorians are our friends. What happened?

She was hurt and bewildered as well as afraid.

It had all been fine until two days ago . . .

There! – the Talinorian whistled – The *chelanthi*! –

Pel peered ahead between its sheaf of stalked eyes. Far out across the Great Plain, grass rippled where no wind blew.

'Hold on!' called Pel's mother, riding high astride the glittering carapace of another Talinorian, Baltenezeril-lashamara.

With a clatter of shell the Talinorian hunting party edged down the side of the cliff. Pel clung as Dalasurieth-rissanihil lurched under her, body-suckers clutching the rock as they moved down the almost vertical surface. The long segmented body rippled.

'Faster!' she yelled, and then remembering that the human voice had too low a frequency for the Talinorian's sensors, tapped the message out on the alien's eye-carapace. The stalked eyes retreated briefly under the hard shell. Pel had learned to interpret this as amusement.

Now they went more slowly. The Talinorians were better suited to rocky cliffs and scarps. Only for the traditional *chelanthi* hunts did they venture down onto grassland.

Pel waved to her mother, and to the other members of the Earth scientific expedition honoured to ride in the Talinorian hunt. It was a time of relaxation. They must have finished negotiating, Pel thought, not very interested. She did not want to leave Talinor yet.

The wind blew her hair in her eyes. She turned her head, seeing the rocky 'coast' behind them. Clusters of rock rose starkly out of the flat grassland. It was impossible to think of them as anything but islands, jutting out of a grass ocean. On the rocking-gaited Talinorian, Pel felt like a ship at sea. Hunting the beasts of the ocean, the *chelanthi*.

– We're falling behind –

The other unburdened Talinorians were faster. Dalasurieth-rissanihil slowed still further.

The 'islands' they had left were small, and in a natural condition. They were covered with bush-berry-trees, the purple fruit hanging down in long strings; and with the *cureuk* flowers that folded up when touched. Mothbirds flew only in this hour between the blue sun's rising and the white sun's following, when they again roosted. A multitude of singing insects nested in the crevices of the rock, and the nights were bright with luminous starflies. It was different from Talinor-Prime, Pel thought, where the expedition had set down the shuttle.

– They have made a kill –

– Where? –

Pel stared ahead over Dalasurieth-rissanihil's carapace, but saw nothing in detail. If she admitted the truth she preferred riding to hunting, and wasn't sorry to miss the end.

A wisp of smoke coiled up ahead.

– Dala', look! –

– Stray laserbeam. Don't they realize what a grass fire might do?' –

Dalasurieth-rissanihil sounded, as far as she could tell, furious.

– I thought you had to use spears? –

– Tradition demands it. The leader will have something to say to them back at Prime! –

Pel saw the Talinorians put the fire out before it could spread. Others carried the scaly *chelanthi* slung across their patterned carapaces, held in place by their forked scorpion-tails. Clusters of thin jointed arms waved excitedly.

– Will you stay for the hunt tomorrow? –

– I have to go home. It's my –. The click and whistle language failed her. – It's a party. The northern team should be back. And besides, it's my . . . –

She couldn't find a word for 'birthday', and struggled to make it clear. Dalasurieth-rissanihil rattled its forked tail.

– So you will have been alive eleven seasons of your home world? That is a long time to be adult. I had thought you younger –

Privately she laughed. Aliens were often stupid about the most obvious things. Except, she thought, I don't suppose it is obvious to them; not even an eleventh birthday . . .

– How old are you, Dala'? –

– I have been adult three seasons –

Pel couldn't be bothered to translate that into Earth-standard years. She knew it wasn't long.

– Yes, but how long ago were you born? I mean, I'm not adult. Not exactly. I don't come of age until I'm fourteen –

– You are not adult? –

– No, not yet; I told you. Oh, you don't understand –

They were turning back towards the islands and Talinor-Prime. Dalasurieth-rissanihil was unusually silent on the way back across the plain, and she wondered if she had offended him.

Talinor-Prime. An 'island' in a grassland 'ocean', but this island was a continent. Big enough to take a flyer three days to cross it. A rock plateau a few metres higher than the surrounding plain, and with a totally different ecology – as Pel's xeno-biologist mother was very prone to telling her. More important from Pel's point of view, Talinor-Prime held the city and the starship landing-field.

It was noon before they arrived. The two suns – blue Alpha and white Beta – blazed together in the sky. Pel had a black and a purple shadow following her on the carved rock walkway.

'Ready for the party tomorrow?' her mother asked.

'You bet. Are the others back yet?'

'Not yet. I'm expecting them to call in soon.'

The long arthropod bodies of the Talinorians glided past them on low trollies. Some preferred the powered walkways that riddle the rock of Prime. They were too low for an adult human to enter without stooping, but Pel was small enough to stand upright in them.

They turned down another walkway and saw the starfield between the wasp-nest dwellings of the Talinorians. Pel looked through the view-grills as they walked. She liked the inside of the 'nests', with their powered valve-doors and beam-operated equipment. Talinorian manipulative limbs weren't strong, but they were good at delicate work. Their great love was glass, which their formulae made stronger than anywhere else in the galaxy. Sculptured, woven in filaments, blown into spheres and cubes and octagons, the ornaments glittered in the light of the two suns; and Talinor-Prime chimed as the wind blew.

'Pel!'

Pel ran out from staring through a view-grill. She caught up as they began to walk across the vast expanse of the starfield. The blue-grey rock was hot underfoot.

'Tell me,' her mother said, 'what do you and Dala' talk about?'

'Oh . . . things,' Pel shrugged.

'I'm sorry in a way that there are no other kids with this expedition. I always wonder if it's fair to bring you on these trips. But since there are just the two of us . . .'

Pel made a rude noise. 'Try and stop me coming with you,' she invited. 'Anyway, it's training – for the future.'

Her mother laughed.

The starfield was on a long spit of 'island' jutting out into the grassland. At that time there were no other sharp ships there. Pel looked at the squat dirty shuttle with affection. It would be great to have the other half of the team back with the ship.

I wonder if they brought me any presents? she thought; and didn't answer when her mother asked her what she was grinning at.

Blue Alpha's dawn light stretched her shadow far behind her on the rocks. The morning smelled clean, spicy. A cool wind blew out of the south. Pel scrambled down the long spit towards the edge of the grassland. Mothbirds beat their fragile wings round her, bright against the amethyst sky.

She could just have waited on the shuttle. But Pel preferred to keep watch in the open, and wait for the ship's return.

Something whirred past her ear.

She swatted at it automatically. Glancing round, she saw some Talinorians on the slope above her, and recognized one of them as Dalasurieth-rissanihil.

A shadow flicked her face.

The spear clattered on the rock beside her.

Pel sprang up. The red line of a laser kicked the rock into molten steam. While she watched, Dalasurieth-rissanihil raised the gun and took aim again.

She took a flying leap off the rocks, running as fast as she could through the grass. It slowed her, but she managed to reach the cover of a rock overhang.

Another party of Talinorians waited beyond it.

She swerved out into the open, running like a hare. Arms and legs pumping, lungs burning; she fell into a stride that took her far out into the blue grassland.

It dawned on her as she fell into the scant cover that the grass afforded, far from Talinor-Prime, that those first shots had not been meant to kill. Only to start her running. Only to force her out into the grass ocean, where killing might take place honourably with glass-tipped hunting spears.

She put her head down, gripped her knees, and tried to stop shaking. When the first panic subsided, bewilderment remained. Then it hardened into a cold determination.

Pel Graham looked back to the distant cliffs of Prime. She thought, Somehow I'll get back. I'll make them pay. Somehow I'll find out . . . Dalasurieth-rissanihil – *why?*

She heard the hunting party in the distance.

*

Evening found her still further away, driven out of sight of Prime. The islands were specks on the horizon. If it had not been for the gentle ridges and undulations of the ground here, she would have been spotted long ago. Now she clung to cover under an alien sky. The grassland went from aquamarine to azure to indigo as Beta set.

The expedition will come looking, Pel thought. I only have to stay free until the shuttle flies over and finds me. I bet they're already on their way –

The grass rustled.

Pel flopped down on her stomach. A blunt muzzle pushed along the reed-bladed grass. A *chelanthi*. Its low flexible body was covered in mirror-scales, camouflaging it. She saw tiny eyeclusters almost hidden under the muzzle. The actual mouth was further back, between the front pairs of legs. As she watched, it began to crop the grass.

Aren't they meat-eaters? Pel wondered.

A scaly hide brushed her arm. She shot back, biting off a yell. The *chelanthi* raised its muzzle, eye-stalks wavering reproachfully. Pel stifled laughter. It scuttled off past the first *chelanthi*. She followed it.

The ridge concealed a dip beyond. The hollow was pitted with holes, among which many *chelanthi* were grazing. They seemed harmless. They probably were . . .

Another *chelanthi* emerged from one of the pits. They must burrow deep, Pel thought. How else would they hide from the Talinorians?

A long whistle sounded through the gathering twilight. She thought, what if the hunters have heat-seeking equipment? That'll show up human body-heat miles off when it's dark . . .

Pel Graham grinned. It was a crazy idea she had. Good, but crazy; still, she might be a little crazy herself by now. There was every excuse for it.

The *chelanthi* did not object when Pel crept into one of the pits beside them. It was dry, earth trodden down hard, and surprisingly roomy. She lay sheltered among their warm scaly bodies, hidden from anything on the grassland above.

The blue sun set in an ocean-coloured sky. The few stars of the galaxy's rim burned in lonely splendour. The moons rose, all seventeen of Talinor's satellites. Sometimes their varying orbits made them appear in clusters, but now they hung in a string of crescents. Pel Graham slept fitfully in the warm night. The Talinorian hunting party passed five miles to the west.

Morning came chill. Disturbed out of one pit when the *chelanthi* went to graze, Pel crawled into another. It had only one occupant. This *chelanthi* made a racheting noise like a broken clock and nipped at her hand. Pel backed out in an undignified scramble.

She watched. The *chelanthi* was busy at the mouth of that pit. It appeared to be stringing a substance from glands under its body. The stubby forepaws gripped the pit's mouth, and Pel saw that it was beginning to weave a web over it.

She listened, but heard no sound of the hunt.

I'm safe here. At least I'm hidden. But I have to get back to Prime. I have to warn them!

The day wore on. Pel was extremely bored by the *chelanthi*. True, they did her no harm. They did nothing except crop the grass. The webbed pit remained closed, and she was not sure if the *chelanthi* inside were sleeping, hibernating, or dead. Hourly the mass of its hidden body became more shapeless.

Unless the Talinorians stumbled across her, the *chelanthi* would hide her. They camouflaged her against long-distance night sensors, and in the day radiation from the two suns made long-distance sensing impossible.

It was not until then that it occurred to her; if she was hidden from Talinorian sensors, she must also be hidden from those of the Earth expedition.

The second evening came. The blue giant Alpha eclipsed the white dwarf Beta as the suns set. Pel was hungrier than she had ever thought it possible to be. Thirst made her drink the water that collected on the flat-bladed grass, and hope that it didn't carry infection.

She was even more determined to get back to Talinor-Prime. It was think of that, or panic, and she didn't dare panic.

The *chelanthi* gave up grazing and headed for the pits.

Pel thought about the webbed pit, she hadn't looked at it in a while. She walked over to it.

As she watched, the webbing over the pit's entrance twitched. It bulged as if something beneath it were trying to get out. Pel stepped back rapidly.

The webbing reared up and split. Something sharp, grey, and glistening protruded. It twitched again, slitting the web still further. A multitude of thin, many-jointed and hard-shelled limbs followed, gripping the sides of the pit. A carapace emerged. Under it, clustered eye-stalks waved. The body heaved itself up onto the grass, segment by armoured segment, disclosing the suckers on the underside. The patterned shell gleamed. Last to leave the pit was the forked scorpion-tail.

Pel stared.

The young Talinorian looked round at the grass-eating *chelanthi*, at Pel Graham who stood frozen with astonishment, and clicked and whistled softly. As it scuttled off it said – Don't you know that there are some things it's better for you not to see? –

It changes everything! Pel thought.

The grass was harsh under her hands and knees. She followed the line of a low ridge. The pits and the broken web were far behind her. She knew that the new-born Talinorian would betray her to the hunting party as soon as it found them.

White Beta rose, and the plains flooded with colour. A little warmth came back to Pel as she moved.

It spoke, it was a *chelanthi*, and it – changed.

It had looked very like Dalasurieth-rissanihil, who was only three seasons 'adult'.

Shrilly in the distance came the whistle of the hunters. Abandoning the *chelanthi*, she had abandoned safety.

I will get back to Prime! she told herself.

She saw something flash in the morning sky like a thrown coin.

'Hey! Hey, shuttle!'

They'll never hear me, never see me, never sense me . . . If there was any way I could mark myself out . . .

Fire would have been best, but she had no way to set the grass lands on fire. And then she remembered the *chelanthi* hunt.

Deliberately Pel stood up and ran to the crown of the ridge. She waved both arms over her head, semaphoring wildly.

The shrilling of the hunters was louder, much louder.

As fleet as fear could make her, she ran. A laserbeam licked redly out to her left, and even through her exhaustion she had time for a grin of triumph.

A line of grass burst into crackling fire. The shuttle's course veered wildly. It began to descend.

Pel could hardly breathe. The world was going red and black round her. But she staggered over the ramp a hundred yards ahead of her pursuers and fell into her mother's arms.

The Talinorian hunting party dwindled below.

'That took some sorting out. You musn't blame them,' Pel's mother turned away from the computer console. 'It's not uncommon in nature to have a larval stage, after all. Even on Earth, moths and butterflies ... And until they change they're quite unintelligent. Just animals, really.'

'Did you tell them?' Pel asked. 'About – children?'

Outside the shuttle's viewport, Talinor-Prime sparkled in the light of two suns. The wind ruffled the grasslands.

'It's a great step forward in understanding each other.' She put her hand on Pel's shoulder. 'You see, when you said you weren't adult –'

'They thought it was all right to hunt me down?'

'Don't be bitter. Worlds are different places.' She turned her back. 'If they'd hurt *you* . . .'

Pel knew what that note in her mother's voice meant. Lightly she said, 'I'm all right.'

'I know you are, love.'

But you don't understand, she thought. Dalasurieth-rissanihil was my friend . . .

'Were you afraid? Oh, that's a stupid question . . . it was a brave thing you did, Pel.'

'Will they stop the hunting?'

'You don't have to be afraid. Not now it's been made clear to everyone.'

'No.' Pel shook her head impatiently. 'The *chelanthi* hunting. Will you stop that?'

'You know we can't interfere in alien worlds.' Her mother sat down at the console. 'You get some rest. I'm going to pilot us in.'

The door irised shut. Back in the main body of the shuttle, Pel stared out of the port. Hunger, exhaustion; she has been told that these will pass.

Two suns cast the descending shuttle's double shadow on the landing-field. She remembers the endless grassland like a great sea.

She remembers Talinor-Prime jutting up in headlands and cliffs and peaks. And she remembers the pits beneath the world, and the *chelanthi* as they nuzzled at her in their sleep.

She sits down and hides her face in her hands.

Pel Graham is thinking of the other children.

Two Sheep

(1983)

JANET FRAME

Two sheep were travelling to the saleyards. The first sheep knew that after they had been sold their destination was the slaughter-house at the freezing works. The second sheep did not know of their fate. They being driven with the rest of the flock along a hot dusty valley road where the surrounding hills leaned in a sun-scorched wilderness of rock, tussock and old rabbit warrens. They moved slowly, for the drover in his trap was in no hurry, and had even taken one of the dogs to sit beside him while the other scrambled from side to side of the flock, guiding them.

'I think,' said the first sheep who was aware of their approaching death, 'that the sun has never shone so warm on my fleece, nor, from what I see with my small sheep's eye, has the sky seemed so flawless, without seams or tucks or cracks or blemishes.'

'You are crazy,' said the second sheep who did not know of their approaching death. 'The sun is warm, yes, but how hot and dusty and heavy my wool feels! It is a burden to go trotting along this oven shelf. It seems our journey will never end.'

'How fresh and juicy the grass appears on the hill!' the first sheep exclaimed. 'And not a hawk in the sky!'

'I think,' replied the second sheep, 'that something has blinded you. Just look up in the sky and see those three hawks waiting to swoop and attack us!'

They trotted on further through the valley road. Now and again the second sheep stumbled.

'I feel so tired,' he said. 'I wonder how much longer we must walk on and on through this hot dusty valley?'

But the first sheep walked nimbly and his wool felt light upon him as if he had just been shorn. He could have gambolled like a lamb in August.

'I still think,' he said, 'that today is the most wonderful day I have known. I do not feel that the road is hot and dusty. I do not notice the stones and grit that you complain of. To me the hills have never seemed so green and enticing, the sun has never seemed so warm and comforting. I believe that I could walk through this valley forever, and never feel tired or hungry or thirsty.'

'Whatever has come over you?' the second sheep asked crossly. 'Here we are, trotting along hour after hour, and soon we shall stand in our pens in the saleyards while the sun leans over us with its branding irons and our overcoats are such a burden that they drag us to the floor of our pen where we are almost trampled to death by the so dainty feet of our fellow sheep. A fine life that is. It would not surprise me if after we are sold we are taken in trucks to the freezing works and killed in cold blood. But,' he added, comforting himself, 'that is not likely to happen. Oh no, that could never happen! I have it on authority that even when they are trampled by their fellows, sheep do not die. The tales we hear from time to time are but malicious rumours, and those vivid dreams which strike us in the night as we sleep in the sheltered hills, they are but illusions. Do you not agree?' he asks the first sheep.

They were turning now from the valley road, and the saleyards were in sight, while drawn up in the siding on the rusty railway lines, the red trucks stood waiting, spattered inside with sheep and cattle dirt and with white chalk marks, in cipher, on the outside. And still the first sheep did not reveal to his companion that they were being driven to certain death.

When they were jostled inside their pen the first sheep gave an exclamation of delight.

'What a pleasant little house they have let to us! I have never seen such smart red-painted bars, and such four-square corners. And look at the elegant stairway which we will climb to enter those red caravans for our seaside holiday!'

'You make me tired,' the second sheep said. 'We are standing inside a dirty pen, nothing more, and I cannot move my feet in their nicely polished black shoes but I tread upon the dirt left by sheep which have been imprisoned here before us. In fact I have never been so badly treated in all my life!' And the second sheep began to cry. Just then a kind elderly sheep jostled through the flock and began to comfort him.

'You have been frightening your companion, I suppose,' she said angrily to the first sheep. 'You have been telling horrible tales of our fate. Some sheep never know when to keep things to themselves. There was no need to tell your companion the truth, that we are being led to certain death!'

But the first sheep did not answer. He was thinking that the sun had never blessed him with so much warmth, that no crowded pen had ever seemed so comfortable and luxurious. Then suddenly he was taken by surprise and hustled out a little gate and up the ramp into the waiting truck, and suddenly too the sun shone in its true colours, battering him about the head with gigantic burning bars, while the hawks congregated above, sizzling the sky with their wings, and a pall of dust clung to the barren used-up hills, and everywhere was commotion, pushing, struggling, bleating, trampling.

'This must be death,' he thought, and he began to struggle and cry out.

The second sheep, having at last learned that he would meet his fate at the freezing works, stood unperturbed now in the truck with his nose against the wall and his eyes looking through the slits.

'You are right,' he said to the first sheep. 'The hill has never seemed so green, the sun has never been warmer, and this truck with its neat red walls is a mansion where I would happily spend the rest of my days.'

But the first sheep did not answer. He had seen the approach of death. He could hide from it no longer. He had given up the struggle and was lying exhausted in a corner of the truck. And when the truck arrived at its destination, the freezing works, the man whose duty it was to unload the sheep noticed the first lying so still in the corner that he believed it was dead.

'We can't have dead sheep,' he said. 'How can you kill a dead sheep?'

So he heaved the first sheep out of the door of the truck onto the rusty railway line.

'I'll move it away later,' he said to himself. 'Meanwhile, here goes with this lot.'

And while he was so busy moving the flock, the first sheep, recovering, sprang up and trotted away along the line, out the gate of the freezing works, up the road, along another road, until he saw a flock being driven before him.

'I will join the flock,' he said. 'No one will notice, and I shall be safe.'

While the drover was not looking, the first sheep hurried in among the flock and was soon trotting along with them until they came to a hot dusty road through a valley where the hills leaned in a sun-scorched wilderness of rock, tussock, and old rabbit warrens.

By now he was feeling very tired. He spoke for the first time to his new companions.

'What a hot dusty road,' he said. 'How uncomfortable the heat is, and the sun seems to be striking me for its own burning purposes.'

The sheep walking beside him looked surprised.

'It is a wonderful day,' he exclaimed. 'The sun is warmer than I have ever known it, the hills glow green with luscious grass, and there is not a hawk in the sky to threaten us!'

'You mean,' the first sheep replied slyly, 'that you are on your way to the saleyards, and then to the freezing works to be killed.'

The other sheep gave a bleat of surprise.

'How did you guess?' he asked.

'Oh,' said the first sheep wisely. 'I know the code. And because I know the code I shall go around in circles all my life, not knowing whether to think that the hills are bare or whether they are green, whether the hawks are scarce or plentiful, whether the sun is friend or foe. For the rest of my life I shall not speak another word. I shall trot along the hot dusty valleys where the hills are both barren and lush with spring grass.

'What shall I do but keep silent?'

And so it happened, and over and over again the first sheep escaped death, and rejoined the flock of sheep who were travelling to the freezing works. He is still alive today. If you notice him in a flock, being driven along a hot dusty road, you will be able to distinguish him by his timidity, his uncertainty, the frenzied expression in his eyes when he tries, in his condemned silence, to discover whether the sky is at last free from hawks, or whether they circle in twos and threes above him, waiting to kill him.

Relics

(1985)

ZOË FAIRBAIRNS

The Managing Director of Universal Magazines has invited me to lunch in his office and forgotten to get me any. I did wonder, when I walked in at the agreed time and found him coming to the end of a box of *foie gras* sandwiches, but I didn't say anything and now I know: I am not to be fed because he wants to get cracking.

'What I have to say is in the strictest confidence.'

Greg Sargent loves secrets, so I nod solemnly.

'I'm going to make you an offer. If you accept, the news will be released by us at the appropriate time. If you refuse – and you are daft enough – you're not to tell anyone that I asked you.'

'Isn't that what they say when they offer someone an OBE?'

'Don't be such a damn fool. How would I know? It's about that magazine of yours, *Women's Action*.'

He always calls it that magazine of mine even though it's years since I left the collective. I thought it went a bit too far. Now it goes even farther, but I still read it. So does Greg. It fascinates him. He's had his own personal subscription from the beginning, separate from the office copy that Unimag always takes of any publication presuming to survive outside its imperial boundaries. It is an embarrassing fact that Greg owns one of the few complete, bound collections of back numbers in existence. He reads it meticulously – often more meticulously than I do – a fact with which he loves to taunt me. For instance, I once remarked that I'd quite enjoyed a particular film and he said, 'Well, you do surprise me. That magazine of yours said it was quite seriously flawed.'

And on another occasion he looked up from a feature article and enquired, 'How is political lesbianism different from the other kind?'

Today he says, 'It's going to fold. I assume from your expressionless expression that you know already.'

I must watch my mouth. *Women's Action* goes much too far but I love it. I do not propose to admit to this powerful man that I too have heard rumours, the most alarming of which is that the magazine owes several thousand pounds to the Inland Revenue and cannot pay.

Greg doesn't care whether I admit it or not.

'We're going to buy it,' he says. 'Clear all the debts and relaunch.'

'They've agreed to sell to *you*?'

'I haven't asked them yet.'

'Don't get too excited, then. Things would have to get a lot worse before the collective would let it trot out as a stablemate of *Unicorn* and *Women's Nest*.'

'If you wanted to run features criticizing *Women's Nest* or *Unicorn*, you could,' he says. 'Do them good.'

'Doing them good wasn't quite . . . what do you mean, *you*?'

'I want you to be editor.'

'Now listen, Greg.'

'No, you listen. That little magazine's got potential and it's not just me who thinks so. My ad manager's waiting for me to fire the gun. He's got this scheme. For the first six months anyone who takes a full-price page in two of our other women's magazines will get the same ad half-price in *Today's Women's Action*. I've broken a few pencils on that title I can tell you, but today's woman's going to buy it. This'll age you and your friends on the *collective*: today's school-leaver was four – *four* – when you started. Today's woman isn't fighting men, she knows she's got them right here.'

He presses his thumb down hard on his desk-top in illustration.

'These advertisements, Greg –'

'You think today's woman can't laugh and turn the page if there's a silly ad? Well, she can. Not that she won't thank the advertisers in passing for keeping the price down for her and her less fortunate sisters who are on the dole. She *cares*. So don't go all prim with me about make-up. You think I wouldn't like to put make-up on some mornings? You'll have as many editorial pages as you've got now and I'll be relying on you to preserve the unique character of the magazine. Keep us straight. Tell me where to get off if necessary. If you don't, I'll fire you. I'm as much of a feminist as the next man, but I'm a businessman and I don't make donations to good causes, I make investments, and the fact that we're having this conversation should prove to you that you can stop fighting because you've won. Stop laughing.'

'Greg. Do me a favour. Phone up *Women's Action* now and ask to speak to the editor. You'll soon hear what they think about hierarchies.'

'Their line is dead,' he says. 'Non-payment I expect. Run without an editor, can they? Can they run without a telephone too?'

'I'm not going to listen to this any more, it's irresponsible. Those women'll put out a welcome mat for the bailiffs rather than agree to what you're proposing.'

'Welcome them into their homes, will they?'

'What do you mean?'

'That so-called collective of yours isn't a proper limited company, is it? So it'll come down to individuals.'

'It'll be blood out of a stone.' Will it, though? Salaries on the magazine have always been tiny, but some of the collective have other jobs. They may have savings, houses, cars. They'll be cleaned out to pay taxes to the government and still there'll be no magazine.

'Greg, the magazine isn't mine to sell or refuse to sell. Make them your offer and see what they say. If and when you're the owner, ask me again if I want to be editor.'

'No,' he says. 'You misunderstand. We're not making any offer *unless* you'll be editor. Come on, you can't freelance on the fringes for ever. You must be nearly forty. I am. Come in from the cold and bring your magazine with you. Hey, didn't I invite you for lunch?'

'I've never been to the camp at the base before. I've meant to but I've always been too busy.'

Today is the day of the dragon festival. 'Dragon', according to the handouts, means to see clearly. In what language, I wonder, but that is a petty thought. If dragon festival day is the day for seeing clearly, perhaps I will see what I must do.

The women are going to make an eight-mile dragon and wind

her round the base. She will then be sent on a world tour to embrace other bases. How do you make an eight-mile dragon?

'Please take your bits of dragon to Green Gate and start sewing them together!'

Bits of dragon! Sewing! I stare in horror at the woman with the megaphone. I never learned to sew, despite having had a skilled and irascible teacher in Sister St Laur. I remember the art room on Thursday afternoons. I used to fidget and pick at a grubby sampler, listening to Sister St Laur's bible stories, which were far more interesting. I looked up one day and discovered I was the only girl still working on a sampler. Everyone else in my class was making a dress! I couldn't understand it. Was it one of those things that happens to other girls in the school holidays, like starting their periods or having holes made in their ears? It seemed better to get on with my sampler and say nothing. But now here I am surrounded by women with beautiful home-made tapestries, quilts, shawls and tablecloths, and I have nothing.

Somebody gives me a lime-green leaflet.

'Whatever your contribution, welcome! We cannot all go over the fence! We cannot all leave our homes! Whether you have been here two hours or two years, you are one of us!'

I have been here twenty minutes, but the perimeter fence is eight miles long, so if I walked round it I will be one of them by the time I get back to the beginning.

Under the high noon sun the ground is baked and cracked and tinder dry in places, hazardously slushy in others. Where the mud is worst, a causeway has been improvised: planks, poles, wire-netting, carpet. It must be crossed with care, one person at a time clinging to the fence for balance, and here and there little groups of women gather, smiling with shy friendliness, waiting for each other.

We are shadowed by soldiers inside the wire. They keep up a commentary over their walkie-talkie radios, in their odd, staccato language.

'Six females proceeding in a westerly direction. Over.'

I yearn for such language, in which everything is simple. Shall I stop a group and say, 'Listen, I've been made this offer, what do you think I should do?' But Greg has made my silence a condition of his keeping the offer open.

'One female proceeding in an easterly direction. Over.'

Beyond the wire and its gibbering sentries the base is flat and empty, the only movement the heat shimmering. In the far distance an aircraft takes off, swallowed up in the sky before its brief roar is even audible. There are foxgloves tangled up in the barbed wire and like Winnie the Pooh I make up a little hum as I walk and this is what I hum:

> Tangled up in the barbed wire,
> Tangled up in the foxgloves,
> Tangled up in the barbed wire,
> Tangled up in the foxgloves.

Which becomes:

> Tangled up in the firewood,
> Tangled up in the shit pits,
> Tangled up in the Green Gate,
> Tangled up in the Blue Gate.

'Appears to be making up a poem. Over.'

> Tangled up in the car park,
> Tangled up in the death's head,
> Tangled up in the fig tree,
> Tangled up in the chessboard.

It isn't a chessboard, it's Sister St Laur, decorating the fence. She paddles deftly on her knees through piles of brightly-coloured rags, her black and white rosary beads clicking a rhythm like mine. She has made a lushly magnificent image of a fig tree, burst figs hang like open green and black mouths with white gums and seedy red teeth. I rush at her, shouting:

'Why can't I sew?'

'Because I can't either.'

'How can you say that when you've made this?'

'Appear to be having an argument about a fig tree. Over.'

'This,' scoffs Sister St Laur, 'is not sewing.' She demonstrates. All she is doing is to weave the rags through the mesh of the fence, tucking the loose ends into the inside.

'Appear to be, er –'

'Oh *do* be quiet,' says Sister St Laur to the soldier. 'I am trying to teach this child her bible.'

She lets me weave brown rags into the earth around the tree's roots. I hate this sort of work and time refuses to pass. The sun hangs obstinately overhead still signifying noon, but the women's leaflet said that I must serve two hours before I count as one of them. I am tired of brown rags, but Sister St Laur will not allow me to work on the tree itself until I am more skilled and can recite verbatim from the relevant gospel. I can only paraphrase.

'Didn't Jesus want figs and there weren't any? So he put a curse on the tree.'

'Exactly. Disgraceful. "He found nothing on it but leaves for the time of figs was not yet." Didn't stop him, though, did it? If the tree had sprouted figs out of season he wouldn't have liked that either, which just goes to show –'

The sky is split by the scream of a siren. The soldier jabbers into his radio and the radio jabbers back. The earth is shaking. Hordes of women rush past bearing bits of dragon, screaming, 'The convoys are going out! Stop them! Stop them!' Deathly-white slipstreams criss-cross the vociferous skies, the fig tree is putting out dead arms to cut itself down. The arms are the arms of soldiers in thick protective clothing. They have bolt-cutters in their hands. They clip and wrench until the tree hangs only by a hinge in the wire, and no barrier remains between us the women and them the soldiers. The air is rigid with wings, the rags of the tree are dead in the mud. Sister St Laur is doing a little dance of rage. The soldiers are coming to get us.

'Into the shelters,' they shout. 'Get into the shelters!'

'You're letting *us* into the shelters?'

'We'll need you for after,' say the soldiers. 'Why d'you think we've kept you handy?'

I won't enter their shelter. I won't walk willingly to my own death. But I'm not being asked to, I'm being offered a chance to survive. My feet teeter at the top of a staircase of a thousand steps. I have never been afraid of heights, but depths I cannot stand. This can't be it. This can't be death. I had hoped there would be a resignation, a quiet closing-down when it finally came. But my sense, my faculties are putting on fireworks: *See what we can do.*

Don't close us down. Don't, don't! The soldier has me in an arm-lock
and all I can feel is the sweetness of contact, contact with warm
flesh that has living blood running through it. My eyes glorify in
the flaming light; the rumbles and roars are music, my brain can
still think. Why didn't we realize? We knew there were shelters.
We knew there were plans for rebuilding the world afterwards.
We knew that soldiers and politicians, senior police officers and
town clerks were to be preserved. How did it escape our attention
that such groups were unlikely to contain women of childbearing
age and consequently other arrangements would have to be made?

Will we be together, those of us who are brought down into
their shelter? Will we be able to plan? The underground room is
cold and full of confusion. I can't see who else is here. It's not one
of these bureaucrats' shelters we've heard about, with desks and
telephones and wall-charts. There's nothing like that. But there's
food for a long siege: rows and rows of deep-freeze cabinets.

'Get in,' my captor says, lifting a lid. 'It won't be no worse than
falling asleep in the snow. Nice and cosy you'll be, better than up
there.'

He puts me into a deep-freeze cabinet. There is one last gleam
of rainbow light through the whiskers of ice before the lid comes
down and all is darkness. My ears are lined with frost and when I
hear more thumps I cannot tell whether they are the sounds of
other lids closing, or the bunker collapsing on top of me, or
people being shot. The soldier has lied, it isn't nice and cosy at all;
I'm freezing.

'I knew it, I knew it, I knew there would be some left
somewhere!'

Somebody has lifted my lid. I can't see who it is through all the
ice, but the voice sounds male and I am uneasy. I have no illusions
as to what I have been preserved for. Whether it is the fear
associated with this thought that causes the frost in my eyes to
melt I cannot say, but I am able to make him out: a short creature
of scholarly bearing with a file of notes under his arm, a clipboard
in his hands and an expression of intense intellectual excitement on
his face. Apart from an over-large head he looks physiologically
normal, but I can't see clearly.

To my irritation, he offers me a visiting-card. What am I supposed to do with it? My arms are still pinned to my sides and the print is too small to read. Does he suppose that it is normal for women to be coated in ice? The heat of my anger clears sufficient space for me to move my lips and shout,

'Defrost! Defrost!'

'Good gracious, silly of me, I really am most frightfully sorry, it's the excitement —'

I feel a switch go, and soon I stand dripping before him. He places his card on the edge of the cabinet and steps back. I pick it up. It says:

MR CONSTABLE
DEPARTMENT OF RELICS

'Your name?' he asks.

'I think it's . . . it used to be . . . it's no good . . .'

'No-Good?' he repeats, referring to his file.

'I mean, I can't remember.'

'Don't worry, I have a collection of women's names and very pretty some of them are too, like you if I may say so.'

He beams and blushes and bows as he says this, as if he has been practising. Pretty! I look down at myself and feel my face. I am certainly well preserved.

'Mr Constable, how old am I?'

His blush deepens. 'This is hardly the time or the place . . . before I even know your name . . .'

'Have you got a towel?'

Again he misunderstands and consults his list, muttering:

'"A-Towel". I don't have that, but I have "Scrubber"'.

'That was never a name, Mr Constable, it was a job. I should like to get dry.'

'Then come up into the sunshine!'

He points towards the staircase. Light is filtering down, but I am starting to remember something that makes me anxious.

'Is that really sunlight?'

'Oh yes.'

'It's not a nuclear winter, then?'

'On the contrary,' beams Mr Constable. 'Please. After you.'

His distant courtesy intensifies my loneliness. I ask if we might not look in the other cabinets first.

'All in good time. I want to show you where you will be kept.'

'What are those?' He points at my face.

'Tears, Mr Constable.'

'I have heard of those.'

'Mr Constable. I'm sorry, but – it's been such a long time since I've seen anybody and such terrible things have happened. Would it be possible for you to *greet* me in some way before you do your research?' I offer my hand for a handshake; I long to hold a human hand, but he steps back, at once shocked and reassuring.

'I understand your anxiety,' he says. 'But nobody is going to touch you.'

We are walking together through clear, brilliant air. I keep my eyes down in order not to have to take in too many horrors at once: but the turf under my feet is perfectly green with not so much as a puddle or a patch of mud, and the only sound is bird-song. I allow myself to glance about. There is no sign of weapons, soldiers, aircraft, destruction or danger of any kind, but of course I cannot yet see clearly. He has brought me to an arrangement of benders and tents, neat but uninhabited.

'This is where you will live,' he says.

'How?'

'Precisely as you please. Mine is a ministry for preservation, not control, and we rely on you to recreate your historic way of life from which we in the human race may learn to live as you lived, in peace. I think you will find that my research has enabled me to anticipate most of your wants, though not without opposition from my committees. "Where *are* these creatures for whom you want public funds to reconstruct the Peace Camp, Mr Constable?" I have been asked down the years. But I have soldiered on – I beg your pardon, *struggled* on – sure in my heart that one day I would find you. Let me show you round. This is where the fence comes closest to the Viewing Platforms so it might be best to begin your decorations here. Let me have a list of the materials you will require, wool, photographs, and so forth. That part of the fence over there is for you to cut down. Well, it would be a pity to cut down what you have decorated, wouldn't it? Whenever you cut it down it will be restored within twenty-four hours so you will be able to cut it down again. This is probably the point at which the fence is easiest for you to climb – after you – and this is where you may dance.'

'Are there missiles under there?'

'Goodness no. They are on the moon, out of harm's way.'

The birds are still singing but I can't see them. Now Mr Constable is singing too.

'Tangled up in the fox-gloves, tangled up in the barbed wire, tangled up in the . . .'

'What's that?'

'I thought you would recognize it. Isn't it one of your songs?'

'It began to be. It was never finished.'

'We have them all in the archive. You can't kill the spi-i-rit, she is like a . . .' He catches my glare and stops. 'I am doing my best,' he says huffily. 'You must forgive me if I make the occasional gaffe. And now . . . now that you understand the situation, shall we go and melt your friends?'

Sister St Laur is a head and a half taller than Mr Constable. As she brushes herself down she showers him with sharp icicles.

'I say!' he protests.

'Piss off,' says Sister St Laur.

'You'll have to be polite to him,' I remonstrate in a whisper. 'What choice do we have?'

'We have all the choices in the world. As I was saying before I was interrupted, fig trees are always in the wrong, so it doesn't matter what we do. Who is this little twerp?'

'I don't understand it, I don't understand it,' mutters Mr Constable to himself. 'The clothing suggests a nun but . . .'

'Nun nothing. Let's play chess.'

She takes off her head-dress and a layer of her skirt. She arranges squares on a sheet of ice, then starts to make pieces and pawns. I advise Mr Constable to get on with defrosting the others. One by one they come out of their cabinets, weighed down and immobilized by their icy shrouds. But once Mr Constable has explained about the Department of Relics, the renewable fence, the Viewing Platforms and the missiles on the moon, no further action is required to melt them. They stand before him like a row of blowtorches.

'If you think we are going up there to be made an exhibition of!'

'Come and play chess,' calls Sister St Laur. 'The Queen is the most powerful piece on the board.'

'Ladies, ladies,' says Mr Constable tremulously. Behind his hand he whispers to me, 'Is that what I should call them?'

'What do you mean, *them*? I am one of them.'

'Oh, no, you are not like them. They are not real peace women, are they? They must be the ones who only came for the day. Better than nothing, though, better than nothing. Ladies, women, girls, sisters. I must ask you now to follow me to the camp which has been prepared for you. You have my personal guarantee of safety and privacy, other than . . .'

'The purpose of the game,' explains Sister St Laur, 'is to checkmate, that is, trap the king. It is not difficult, the king can hardly move. Once the king has been disposed of, the game is over.'

'. . . other than on the occasional Open Day, which would be arranged with your full . . .'

'It used to be the rule that white moved first, giving black a built-in disadvantage, but there is no reason for us to stick to that rule, or any other.'

'All right!' shouts Mr Constable. 'Play chess! Stay down here! See if I care. You are not what I was looking for in any case! But be warned! I shall make a full report to my committees! Not everyone is as committed to your preservation as I . . . have been.'

Shaking his enormous head, more in sorrow than in anger, he climbs the stairs alone. Sister St Laur is setting out her pieces and the other women are improvising rules for a form of chess in which queens and pawns can only triumph and colour is irrelevant. I am tempted to join them but I am afraid for our safety. I pursue the sulky Mr Constable. At last he allows me to mollify him. He suggests that I come to the city. There will probably be sufficient interest in me, he says, to take the minds of his committees off the disappointment they will undoubtedly feel when they hear what the others are like.

*

High above the rows of sharp-edged boxes that constitute the
city, gleams the Reliquary: round as a rollerball, white as the
moon, it hovers on legs so thin as to be almost invisible. We
enter through an automatic opening and are conveyed along a
corridor. There is no need to walk, the floors move. Open
escalators criss-cross and radiate in circular tiers: glass-walled lifts
whisper up and down, bearing huge-headed staring replicas of Mr
Constable.

'My committee,' he says, 'waiting to meet you.'

'Show me round first.'

'Very well. But we musn't be long.'

'Please,' say the notices, 'go slowly to adjust your eyes to the
light. Be as quiet as possible. Follow the arrows. Do not take
pushchairs. Beware of pickpockets.'

I looked quizzically at Mr Constable: Pushchairs? Babies then?

'Indeed. Embryos can be grown in any bodily cavity.' And he
taps his head.

A tortoise eats leaves behind glass, watching me. It pokes out
its pink tongue. Another flash of pink causes me to spin round to
where a sting-ray is pressing its gorgeous rose-coloured belly
against the inside of its tank. An elephant limps an endless circle,
its foot tethered to a stake.

'By slightly restricting her liberty,' Mr Constable explains, 'we
can give her much greater freedom, train her better and make her
life more interesting in the long term. After the meeting I should
like to show you my research archive. It may be that there is some
help you can give me, identifying documents, and so forth. Some
of them are very puzzling.'

I am starting to cry.

'What's the matter?' he asks tenderly.

'I'm so lonely.'

'What does that mean? How can I help?'

'Just take me away from here.'

It is night-time when we reach the point where the city ends and
the wilderness begins. We walk in silence through the dead,
treeless rubble, the warm moonlit dark. The moon is brighter than
I remember it, as if it were on fire. I suggest that we stop in a

cave. After my long ice age I feel needy and tender and sharply alive. I hold out my arms to Mr Constable.

'Oh no,' he says primly. 'It would be an act of conquest.'

'It doesn't have to be.'

'I knew I should have asked you to explain those documents to me!'

'We were never all the same, Mr Constable. You have to understand that, even if it does spoil your research.'

After a little coaxing he creeps into me like a cat. He is a joy to teach. He has never dreamed that such things are possible. Through the waves of our ecstasy I seem to see the moon explode, but I cannot see clearly when I am doing this.

I certainly thought it was *our* ecstasy. But when we yawn out naked in the morning with its odd patchy light, the moon vanished, the sun racing with clouds, he says:

'I cannot think what came over me.'

I avoid the obvious riposte. Flippancy would not be appreciated. He is metaphysically troubled, as one often is on the first occasion.

'We will look upon it as a relic,' he says at last and with some relief.

'But wasn't it good for you?'

'Penetration, invasion, war . . .'

'You want to start a war?'

'That is not what *I* feel but the others are not all like me.'

'I wasn't planning to do it with the others, Mr Constable.'

'I would like,' he admits, 'to snuggle against you and sleep for ever.'

'Well then! And listen. I have been calculating at what point in my menstrual cycle the world ended. I think I may have a child!'

He stares at my head, aghast. Smiling in gentle reproof, I directed his glance lower down. He refuses to look. He straightens his shoulders and pulls on his clothes. He throws my clothes at me, none too gently.

'We must return to the city,' he says. 'I have betrayed a trust.'

'But it was my idea!'

'The trust of my committee. They will be *furious*.'

He seems terrified. He appears to have thought of a remedy, and calms down. Speaking very slowly, he says:

'I have a suggestion to make. If you agree, I shall inform the committee. If you refuse – and I am sure you are too sensible – you're not to tell anyone that I asked you.'

'Isn't that what they used to say when they ... Oh, never mind.'

'We will say that the recent event was proposed by me as participant-observation research. In furtherance of this research you will give birth in the Reliquary. Women are my subject as you know. But I don't do favours, I do research, and the fact that we're having this conversation should prove to you that you can stop fighting because you've won. *Stop laughing.*'

He tries to restrain me from running off but it is easy to escape from the little twerp. Finding my way back to the place where the women are is more difficult. Forty days and forty moonless nights pass before I am home.

I chuckle to find the camp deserted, the fence undecorated, the silo undanced-upon. They must still be playing chess in the shelter. As I descend the steps, though, my optimism takes on an edge of unease.

The air is very cold. Bits of makeshift chess pieces litter the steps. There is no one about. The lids of the cabinets are down, the switches locked to freeze.

With effort I can raise the lids but I cannot throw the switches. The women have been violently flung back into cold storage. Their postures of struggle are frozen in blocks of ice.

For a long time I am immobilized by despair. Then it occurs to me that sooner or later, one way or another, my womb is going to bring forth warm water or warm blood or both. Either will serve to start the melting process.

The cold, cranial obstetrics of the relic collectors will not have allowed for this! We will have to wait of course, but not for too long.

Actually we hardly have to wait at all. To pass the time I start to talk to myself, recounting the various offers I have received. My words seem to arouse strong emotions inside the deep freeze cabinets, because with growls and roars and gushes of water the ice breaks and the women sit up as one and shout with incredulous laughter:

'He wanted you to do *what?*'

Thanks to Carol Sarler, Elsbeth Lindner, Jen Green, Robyn Rowland and Sarah Lefanu for help with this story; also to Sunderland Polytechnic for hosting me as Writer in Residence, 1983–1985.

The Evening and the Morning and the Night

(1987)

OCTAVIA E. BUTLER

When I was fifteen and trying to show my independence by getting careless with my diet, my parents took me to a Duryea-Gode disease ward. They wanted me to see, they said, where I was headed if I wasn't careful. In fact, it was where I was headed no matter what. It was only a matter of when: now or later. My parents were putting in their vote for later.

I won't describe the ward. It's enough to say that when they brought me home, I cut my wrists. I did a thorough job of it, old Roman style in a bathtub of warm water. Almost made it. My father dislocated his shoulder breaking down the bathroom door. He and I never forgave each other for that day.

The disease got him almost three years later – just before I went off to college. It was sudden. It doesn't happen that way often. Most people notice themselves beginning to drift – or their relatives notice – and they make arrangements with their chosen institution. People who are noticed and who resist going in can be locked up for a week's observation. I don't doubt that that observation period breaks up a few families. Sending someone away for what turns out to be a false alarm ... Well, it isn't the sort of thing the victim is likely to forgive or forget. On the other hand, not sending someone away in time – missing the signs or having a person go off suddenly without signs – is inevitably dangerous for the victim. I've never heard of it going as badly, though, as it did in my family. People normally injure only themselves when their time comes – unless someone is stupid enough to try to handle them without the necessary drugs or restraints.

My father ... killed my mother, then killed himself. I wasn't home when it happened. I had stayed at school later than usual, rehearsing graduation exercises. By the time I got home, there were cops everywhere. There was an ambulance, and two attendants were wheeling someone out on a stretcher – someone covered. More than covered. Almost . . . bagged.

The cops wouldn't let me in. I didn't find out until later exactly what had happened. I wish I'd never found out. Dad had killed Mom, then skinned her completely. At least, that's how I hope it happened. I mean I hope he killed her first. He broke some of her ribs, damaged her heart. Digging.

Then he began tearing at himself, through skin and bone, digging. He had managed to reach his own heart before he died. It was an especially bad example of the kind of thing that makes people afraid of us. It gets some of us into trouble for picking at a pimple or even for daydreaming. It has inspired restrictive laws, created problems with jobs, housing, schools . . . The Duryea-Gode Disease Foundation has spent millions telling the world that people like my father don't exist.

A long time later, when I had gotten myself together as best I could, I went to college – to the University of Southern California – on a Dilg scholarship. Dilg is the retreat you try to send your out-of-control DGD relatives to. It's run by controlled DGDs like me, like my parents while they lived. God knows how any controlled DGD stands it. Anyway, the place has a waiting list miles long. My parents put me on it after my suicide attempt, but chances were, I'd be dead by the time my name came up.

I can't say why I went to college – except that I had been going to school all my life and I didn't know what else to do. I didn't go with any particular hope. Hell, I knew what I was in for eventually. I was just marking time. Whatever I did was just marking time. If people were willing to pay me to go to school and mark time, why not do it?

The weird part was, I worked hard, got top grades. If you work hard enough at something that doesn't matter, you can forget for a while about the things that do.

Sometimes I thought about trying suicide again. How was it I'd had the courage when I was fifteen but didn't have it now? Two DGD parents – both religious, both as opposed to abortion as they were to suicide. So they had trusted God and the promises of modern medicine and had a child. But how could I look at what had happened to them and trust anything?

I majored in biology. Non-DGDs say something about our disease makes us good at the sciences – genetics, molecular biology, biochemistry . . . That something was terror. Terror and a kind of driving hopelessness. Some of us went bad and became destructive before we had to – yes, we did produce more than our share of criminals. And some of us went good – spectacularly – and made scientific and medical history. These last kept the doors at least partly open for the rest of us. They made discoveries in genetics, found cures for a couple of rare diseases, made advances in the fight against other diseases that weren't so rare – including, ironically, some forms of cancer. But they'd found nothing to help themselves. There had been nothing since the latest improvements in the diet, and those came just before I was born. They, like the original diet, gave more DGDs the courage to have children. They were supposed to do for DGDs what insulin had done for diabetics – give us a normal or nearly normal life span. Maybe they had worked for someone somewhere. They hadn't worked for anyone I knew.

Biology. School was a pain in the usual ways. I didn't eat in public anymore, didn't like the way people stared at my biscuits – cleverly dubbed 'dog biscuits' in every school I'd ever attended. You'd think university students would be more creative. I didn't like the way people edged away from me when they caught sight of my emblem. I'd begun wearing it on a chain around my neck and putting it down inside my blouse, but people managed to notice it anyway. People who don't eat in public, who drink nothing more interesting than water, who smoke nothing at all – people like that are suspicious. Or rather, they make others suspicious. Sooner or later, one of those others, finding my fingers and wrists bare, would fake an interest in my chain. That would be that. I couldn't hide the emblem in my purse. If anything happened to me, medical people had to see it in time to avoid giving me the medications they might use on a normal person. It isn't just ordinary food we have to avoid, but about a quarter of a *Physicians' Desk Reference* of widely used drugs. Every now and then there are news stories about people who stopped carrying their emblems – probably trying to pass as normal. Then they have an accident. By the time anyone realizes there is anything wrong, it's too late. So I wore my emblem. And one way or another, people got a look at it or got the word from someone who had. 'She *is*!' Yeah.

At the beginning of my third year, four other DGDs and I decided to rent a house together. We'd all had enough of being lepers twenty-four hours a day. There was an English major. He wanted to be a writer and tell our story from the inside – which had only been done thirty or forty times before. There was a special-education major who hoped the handicapped would accept her more readily than the able-bodied, a pre-med who planned to go into research, and a chemistry major who didn't really know what she wanted to do.

Two men and three women. All we had in common was our disease, plus a weird combination of stubborn intensity about whatever we happened to be doing and hopeless cynicism about everything else. Healthy people say no one can concentrate like a DGD. Healthy people have all the time in the world for stupid generalizations and short attention spans.

We did our work, came up for air now and then, ate our biscuits, and attended classes. Our only problem was house-cleaning. We worked out a schedule of who would clean what when, who would deal with the yard, whatever. We all agreed on it; then, except for me, everyone seemed to forget about it. I found myself going around reminding people to vacuum, clean the bathroom, mow the lawn . . . I figured they'd all hate me in no time, but I wasn't going to be their maid, and I wasn't going to live in filth. Nobody complained. Nobody even seemed annoyed. They just came up out of their academic daze, cleaned, mopped, mowed, and went back to it. I got into the habit of running around in the evening reminding people. It didn't bother me if it didn't bother them.

'How'd you get to be housemother?' a visiting DGD asked.

I shrugged. 'Who cares? The house works.' It did. It worked so well that this new guy wanted to move in. He was a friend of one of the others, and another pre-med. Not bad looking.

'So do I get in or don't I?' he asked.

'As far as I'm concerned, you do,' I said. I did what his friend should have done – introduced him around, then, after he left, talked to the others to make sure nobody had any real objections. He seemed to fit right in. He forgot to clean the toilet or mow the lawn, just like the others. His name was Alan Chi. I thought Chi was a Chinese name, and I wondered. But he told me his father was Nigerian and that in Ibo, the word meant a kind of guardian angel or personal god. He said his own personal god hadn't been looking out for him very well to let him be born to two DGD parents. Him too.

I don't think it was much more than that similarity that drew us together at first. Sure, I liked the way he looked, but I was used to liking someone's looks and having him run like hell when he found out what I was. It took me a while to get used to the fact that Alan wasn't going anywhere.

I told him about my visit to the DGD ward when I was fifteen – and my suicide attempt afterward. I had never told anyone else. I was surprised at how relieved it made me feel to tell him. And somehow his reaction didn't surprise me.

'Why didn't you try again?' he asked. We were alone in the living room.

'At first, because of my parents,' I said. 'My father in particular. I couldn't do that to him again.'

'And after him?'

'Fear. Inertia.'

He nodded. 'When I do it, there'll be no half measures. No being rescued, no waking up in a hospital later.'

'You mean to do it?'

'The day I realize I've started to drift. Thank God we get some warning.'

'Not necessarily.'

'Yes, we do. I've done a lot of reading. Even talked to a couple of doctors. Don't believe the rumors non-DGDs invent.'

I looked away, stared into the scarred, empty fireplace. I told him exactly how my father had died – something else I'd never voluntarily told anyone.

He sighed. 'Jesus!'

We looked at each other.

'What are you going to do?' he asked.

'I don't know.'

He extended a dark, square hand, and I took it and moved closer to him. He was a dark, square man – my height, half again my weight, and none of it fat. He was so bitter sometimes, he scared me.

'My mother started to drift when I was three,' he said. 'My father only lasted a few months longer. I heard he died a couple of years after he went into the hospital. If the two of them had had any sense, they would have had me aborted the minute my mother realized she was pregnant. But she wanted a kid no matter what. And she was Catholic.' He shook his head. 'Hell, they should pass a law to sterilize the lot of us.'

'They?' I said.

'You want kids?'

'No, but –'

'More like us to wind up chewing their fingers off in some DGD ward.'

'I don't want kids, but I don't want someone else telling me I can't have any.'

He stared at me until I began to feel stupid and defensive. I moved away from him.

'Do you want someone else telling you what to do with your body?' I asked.

'No need,' he said. 'I had that taken care of as soon as I was old enough.'

This left me staring. I'd thought about sterilization. What DGD hasn't? But I didn't know anyone else our age who had actually gone through with it. That would be like killing part of yourself – even though it wasn't a part you intended to use. Killing part of yourself when so much of you was already dead.

'The damned disease could be wiped out in one generation,' he said, 'but people are still animals when it comes to breeding. Still following mindless urges, like dogs and cats.'

My impulse was to get up and go away, leave him to wallow in his bitterness and depression alone. But I stayed. He seemed to want to live even less than I did. I wondered how he'd made it this far.

'Are you looking forward to doing research?' I probed. 'Do you believe you'll be able to –'

'No.'

I blinked. The word was as cold and dead a sound as I'd ever heard.

'I don't believe in anything,' he said.

I took him to bed. He was the only other double DGD I had ever met, and if nobody did anything for him, he wouldn't last much longer. I couldn't just let him slip away. For a while, maybe we could be each other's reasons for staying alive.

He was a good student – for the same reason I was. And he seemed to shed some of his bitterness as time passed. Being around him helped me understand why, against all sanity, two DGDs would lock in on each other and start talking about marriage. Who else would have us?

We probably wouldn't last very long, anyway. These days, most DGDs make it to forty, at least. But then, most of them don't have two DGD parents. As bright as Alan was, he might not get into medical school because of his double inheritance. No one would tell him his bad genes were keeping him out, of course, but we both knew what his chances were. Better to train doctors who were likely to live long enough to put their training to use.

Alan's mother had been sent to Dilg. He hadn't seen her or been able to get any information about her from his grandparents while he was at home. By the time he left for college, he'd stopped asking questions. Maybe it was hearing about my parents that made him start again. I was with him when he called Dilg. Until that moment, he hadn't even known whether his mother was still alive. Surprisingly, she was.

'Dilg must be good,' I said when he hung up. 'People don't usually . . . I mean . . .'

'Yeah, I know,' he said. 'People don't usually live long once they're out of control. Dilg is different.' We had gone to my room, where he turned a chair backward and sat down. 'Dilg is what the others ought to be, if you can believe the literature.'

'Dilg is a giant DGD ward,' I said. 'It's richer – probably better at sucking in the donations – and it's run by people who can expect to become patients eventually. Apart from that, what's different?'

'I've read about it,' he said. 'So should you. They've got some new treatment. They don't just shut people away to die the way the others do.'

'What else is there to do with them?' *With us*.

'I don't know. It sounded like they have some kind of . . . sheltered workshop. They've got patients doing things.'

'A new drug to control the self-destructiveness?'

'I don't think so. We would have heard about that.'

'What else could it be?'

'I'm going up to find out. Will you come with me?'

'You're going up to see your mother.'

He took a ragged breath. 'Yeah. Will you come with me?'

I went to one of my windows and stared out at the weeds. We let them thrive in the backyard. In the front we mowed them, along with the few patches of grass.

'I told you my DGD-ward experience.'

'You're not fifteen now. And Dilg isn't some zoo of a ward.'

'It's got to be, no matter what they tell the public. And I'm not sure I can stand it.'

He got up, came to stand next to me. 'Will you try?'

I didn't say anything. I focused on our reflections in the window glass – the two of us together. It looked right, felt right. He put his arm around me, and I leaned back against him. Our being together had been as good for me as it seemed to have been for him. It had given me something to go on besides inertia and fear. I knew I would go with him. It felt like the right thing to do.

'I can't say how I'll act when we get there,' I said.

'I can't say how I'll act, either,' he admitted. 'Especially . . . when I see her.'

He made the appointment for the next Saturday afternoon. You make appointments to go to Dilg unless you're a government inspector of some kind. That is the custom, and Dilg gets away with it.

We left L.A. in the rain early Saturday morning. Rain followed us off and on up the coast as far as Santa Barbara. Dilg was hidden away in the hills not far from San José. We could have reached it faster by driving up I–5, but neither of us were in the mood for all that bleakness. As it was, we arrived at 1 p.m. to be met by two armed gate guards. One of these phoned the main building and verified our appointment. Then the other took the wheel from Alan.

'Sorry,' he said. 'But no one is permitted inside without an escort. We'll meet your guide at the garage.'

None of this surprised me. Dilg is a place where not only the patients but much of the staff has DGD. A maximum security prison wouldn't have been as potentially dangerous. On the other hand, I'd never heard of anyone getting chewed up here. Hospitals and rest homes had accidents. Dilg didn't. It was beautiful – an old estate. One that didn't make sense in these days of high taxes. It had been owned by the Dilg family. Oil, chemicals, pharmaceuticals. Ironically, they had even owned part of the late, unlamented Hedeon Laboratories. They'd had a briefly profitable interest in Hedeonco: the magic bullet, the cure for a large percentage of the world's cancer and a number of serious viral diseases – and the cause of Duryea-Gode disease. If one of your parents was treated with Hedeonco and you were conceived after the treatments, you had DGD. If you had kids, you passed it on to them. Not everyone was equally affected. They didn't all commit suicide or murder, but they all mutilated themselves to some degree if they could. And they all drifted – went off into a world of their own and stopped responding to their surroundings.

Anyway, the only Dilg son of his generation had had his life saved by Hedeonco. Then he had watched four of his children die before Doctors Kenneth Duryea and Jan Gode came up with a decent understanding of the problem and a partial solution: the diet. They gave Richard Dilg a way of keeping his next two children alive. He gave the big, cumbersome estate over to the care of DGD patients.

So the main building was an elaborate old mansion. There were other, newer buildings, more like guest-houses than institutional buildings. And there were wooded hills all around. Nice country. Green. The ocean wasn't far away. There was an old garage and a small parking lot. Waiting in the lot was a tall old woman. Our guard pulled up near her, let us out, then parked the car in the half-empty garage.

'Hello,' the woman said, extending her hand. 'I'm Beatrice Alcantara.' The hand was cool and dry and startlingly strong. I thought the woman was DGD, but her age threw me. She appeared to be about sixty, and I had never seen a DGD that old. I wasn't sure why I thought she was DGD. If she was, she must have been an experimental model – one of the first to survive.

'Is it Doctor or Ms?' Alan asked.

'It's Beatrice,' she said. 'I am a doctor, but we don't use titles much here.'

I glanced at Alan, was surprised to see him smiling at her. He tended to go a long time between smiles. I looked at Beatrice and couldn't see anything to smile about. As we introduced ourselves, I realized I didn't like her. I couldn't see any reason for that either, but my feelings were my feelings. I didn't like her.

'I assume neither of you have been here before,' she said, smiling down at us. She was at least six feet tall, and straight.

We shook our heads. 'Let's go in the front way, then. I want to prepare you for what we do here. I don't want you to believe you've come to a hospital.'

I frowned at her, wondering what else there was to believe. Dilg was called a retreat, but what difference did names make?

The house close up looked like one of the old-style public buildings – massive, baroque front with a single, domed tower reaching three stories above the three-story house. Wings of the house stretched for some distance to the right and left of the tower, then cornered and stretched back twice as far. The front doors were huge – one set of wrought iron and one of heavy wood. Neither appeared to be locked. Beatrice pulled open the iron door, pushed the wooden one, and gestured us in.

Inside, the house was an art museum – huge, high-ceilinged, tile-floored. There were marble columns and niches in which sculpture stood or paintings hung. There was other sculpture displayed around the rooms. At one end of the rooms there was a broad staircase leading up to a gallery that went around the rooms. There more art was displayed. 'All this was made here,' Beatrice said. 'Some of it is even sold from here. Most goes to galleries in the Bay Area or down around L.A. Our only problem is turning out too much of it.'

'You mean the patients do this?' I asked.

The old woman nodded. 'This and much more. Our people

work instead of tearing at themselves or staring into space. One of them invented the p.v. locks that protect this place. Though I almost wish he hadn't. It's gotten us more government attention than we like.'

'What kind of locks?' I asked.

'Sorry, Palmprint-voiceprint. The first and the best. We have the patent.' She looked at Alan. 'Would you like to see what your mother does?'

'Wait a minute,' he said. 'You're telling us out-of-control DGDs create art and invent things?'

'And that lock,' I said. 'I've never heard of anything like that. I didn't even see a lock.'

'The lock is new,' she said. 'There have been a few news stories about it. It's not the kind of thing most people would buy for their homes. Too expensive. So it's of limited interest. People tend to look at what's done at Dilg in the way they look at the efforts of *idiots savants*. Interesting, incomprehensible, but not really important. Those likely to be interested in the lock and able to afford it know about it.' She took a deep breath, faced Alan again. 'Oh, yes, DGDs create things. At least they do here.'

'Out-of-control DGDs.'

'Yes.'

'I expected to find them weaving baskets or something – at best. I know what DGD wards are like.'

'So do I,' she said. 'I know what they're like in hospitals, and I know what it's like here.' She waved a hand toward an abstract painting that looked like a photo I had once seen of the Orion Nebula. Darkness broken by a great cloud of light and color. 'Here we can help them channel their energies. They can create something beautiful, useful, even something worthless. But they create. They don't destroy.'

'Why?' Alan demanded. 'It can't be some drug. We would have heard.'

'It's not a drug.'

'Then what is it? Why haven't other hospitals –?'

'Alan,' she said. 'Wait.'

He stood frowning at her.

'Do you want to see your mother?'

'Of course I want to see her!'

'Good. Come with me. Things will sort themselves out.'

She led us to a corridor past offices where people talked to one another, waved to Beatrice, worked with computers ... They could have been anywhere. I wondered how many of them were controlled DGDs. I also wondered what kind of game the old woman was playing with her secrets. We passed through rooms so beautiful and perfectly kept it was obvious they were rarely used. Then at a broad, heavy door, she stopped us.

'Look at anything you like as we go on,' she said. 'But don't touch anything or anyone. And remember that some of the people you'll see injured themselves before they came to us. They still bear the scars of those injuries. Some of those scars may be difficult to look at, but you'll be in no danger. Keep that in mind. No one here will harm you.' She pushed the door open and gestured us in.

Scars didn't bother me much. Disability didn't bother me. It was the act of self-mutilation that scared me. It was someone attacking her own arm as though it were a wild animal. It was someone who had torn at himself and been restrained or drugged off and on for so long that he barely had a recognizable human feature left, but he was still trying with what he did have to dig into his own flesh. Those are a couple of the things I saw at the DGD ward when I was fifteen. Even then I could have stood it better if I hadn't felt I was looking into a kind of temporal mirror.

I wasn't aware of walking through that doorway. I wouldn't have thought I could do it. The old woman said something, though, and I found myself on the other side of the door with the door closing behind me. I turned to stare at her.

She put her hand on my arm. 'It's all right,' she said quietly. 'That door looks like a wall to a great many people.'

I backed away from her, out of her reach, repelled by her touch. Shaking hands had been enough, for God's sake.

Something in her seemed to come to attention as she watched me. It made her even straighter. Deliberately, but for no apparent reason, she stepped toward Alan, touched him the way people do sometimes when they brush past – a kind of tactile 'Excuse me.' In that wide, empty corridor, it was totally unnecessary. For some reason, she wanted to touch him and wanted me to see. What did she think she was doing? Flirting at her age? I glared at her, found myself suppressing an irrational urge to shove her away from him. The violence of the urge amazed me.

Beatrice smiled and turned away. 'This way,' she said. Alan put his arm around me and tried to lead me after her.

'Wait a minute,' I said, not moving.

Beatrice glanced around.

'What just happened?' I asked. I was ready for her to lie – to say nothing happened, pretend not to know what I was talking about.

'Are you planning to study medicine?' she asked.

'What? What does that have to do –?'

'Study medicine. You may be able to do a great deal of good.' She strode away, taking long steps so that we had to hurry to keep up. She led us through a room in which some people worked at computer terminals and others with pencils and paper. It would have been an ordinary scene except that some people had half their faces ruined or had only one hand or leg or had other obvious scars. But they were all in control now. They were working. They were intent but not intent on self-destruction. Not one was digging into or tearing away flesh. When we had passed through this room and into a small, ornate sitting room, Alan grasped Beatrice's arm.

'What is it?' he demanded. 'What do you do for them?'

She patted his hand, setting my teeth on edge. 'I will tell you,' she said. 'I want you to know. But I want you to see your mother first.' To my surprise, he nodded, let it go at that.

'Sit a moment,' she said to us.

We sat in comfortable, matching upholstered chairs, Alan looking reasonably relaxed. What was it about the old lady that relaxed him but put me on edge? Maybe she reminded him of his grandmother or something. She didn't remind me of anyone. And what was that nonsense about studying medicine?

'I wanted you to pass through at least one workroom before we talked about your mother – and about the two of you.' She turned to face me. 'You've had a bad experience at a hospital or a rest home?'

I looked away from her, not wanting to think about it. Hadn't the people in that mock office been enough of a reminder? Horror film office. Nightmare office.

'It's all right,' she said. 'You don't have to go into detail. Just outline it for me.'

I obeyed slowly, against my will, all the while wondering why I was doing it.

She nodded, unsurprised. 'Harsh, loving people, your parents. Are they alive?'

'No.'

'Were they both DGD?'

'Yes, but . . . yes.'

'Of course. Aside from the obvious ugliness of your hospital experience and its implications for the future, what impressed you about the people in the ward?'

I didn't know what to answer. What did she want? Why did she want anything from me? She should have been concerned with Alan and his mother.

'Did you see people unrestrained?'

'Yes,' I whispered. 'One woman. I don't know how it happened that she was free. She ran up to us and slammed into my father without moving him. He was a big man. She bounced off, fell, and . . . began tearing at herself. She bit her own arm and . . . swallowed the flesh she'd bitten away. She tore at the wound she'd made with the nails of her other hand. She . . . I screamed at her to stop.' I hugged myself, remembering the young woman, bloody, cannibalizing herself as she lay at our feet, digging into her own flesh. Digging. 'They try so hard, fight so hard to get out.'

'Out of what?' Alan demanded.

I looked at him, hardly seeing him.

'Lynn,' he said gently. 'Out of what?'

I shook my head. 'Their restraints, their disease, the ward, their bodies . . .'

He glanced at Beatrice, then spoke to me again. 'Did the girl talk?'

'No. She screamed.'

He turned away from me uncomfortably. 'Is this important?' he asked Beatrice.

'Very,' she said.

'Well . . . can we talk about it after I see my mother?'

'Then and now.' She spoke to me. 'Did the girl stop what she was doing when you told her to?'

'The nurses had her a moment later. It didn't matter.'

'It mattered. Did she stop?'

'Yes.'

'According to the literature, they rarely respond to anyone,' Alan said.

'True.' Beatrice gave him a sad smile. 'Your mother will probably respond to you, though.'

'Is she . . .?' He glanced back at the nightmare office. 'Is she as controlled as those people?'

'Yes, though she hasn't always been. Your mother works with clay now. She loves shapes and textures and —'

'She's blind,' Alan said, voicing the suspicion as though it were fact. Beatrice's words had sent my thoughts in the same direction. Beatrice hesitated. 'Yes,' she said finally. 'And for . . . the usual reason. I had intended to prepare you slowly.'

'I've done a lot of reading.'

I hadn't done much reading, but I knew what the usual reason was. The woman had gouged, ripped, or otherwise destroyed her eyes. She would be badly scarred. I got up, went over to sit on the arm of Alan's chair. I rested my hand on his shoulder, and he reached up and held it there.

'Can we see her now?' he asked.

Beatrice got up. 'This way,' she said.

We passed through more workrooms. People painted; assembled machinery; sculpted in wood, stone; even composed and played music. Almost no one noticed us. The patients were true to their disease in that respect. They weren't ignoring us. They clearly didn't know we existed. Only the few controlled-DGD guards gave themselves away by waving or speaking to Beatrice. I watched a woman work quickly, knowledgeably, with a power saw. She obviously understood the perimeters of her body, was not so dissociated as to perceive herself as trapped in something she needed to dig her way out of. What had Dilg done for these people that other hospitals did not do? And how could Dilg withhold its treatment from the others?

'Over there we make our own diet foods,' Beatrice said, pointing through a window toward one of the guest-houses. 'We permit more variety and make fewer mistakes than the commercial pre-parers. No ordinary person can concentrate on work the way our people can.'

I turned to face her. 'What are you saying? That the bigots are right? That we have some special gift?'

'Yes,' she said. 'It's hardly a bad characteristic, is it?'

'It's what people say whenever one of us does well at something. It's their way of denying us credit for our work.'

'Yes. But people occasionally come to the right conclusions for the wrong reasons.' I shrugged, not interested in arguing with her about it.

'Alan?' she said. He looked at her.

'Your mother is in the next room.'

He swallowed, nodded. We both followed her into the room.

Naomi Chi was a small woman, hair still dark, fingers long and thin, graceful as they shaped the clay. Her face was a ruin. Not only her eyes but most of her nose and one ear were gone. What was left was badly scarred. 'Her parents were poor,' Beatrice said. 'I don't know how much they told you, Alan, but they went through all the money they had, trying to keep her at a decent place. Her mother felt so guilty, you know. She was the one who had cancer and took the drug ... Eventually, they had to put Naomi in one of those state-approved, custodial-care places. You know the kind. For a while, it was all the government would pay for. Places like that ... well, sometimes if patients were really troublesome – especially the ones who kept breaking free – they'd put them in a bare room and let them finish themselves. The only things those places took good care of were the maggots, the cockroaches, and the rats.'

I shuddered. 'I've heard there are still places like that.'

'There are,' Beatrice said, 'kept open by greed and indifference.' She looked at Alan. 'Your mother survived for three months in one of those places. I took her from it myself. Later I was instrumental in having that particular place closed.'

'You took her?' I asked.

'Dilg didn't exist then, but I was working with a group of

controlled DGDs in L.A. Naomi's parents heard about us and asked us to take her. A lot of people didn't trust us then. Only a few of us were medically trained. All of us were young, idealistic, and ignorant. We began in an old frame house with a leaky roof. Naomi's parents were grabbing at straws. So were we. And by pure luck, we grabbed a good one. We were able to prove ourselves to the Dilg family and take over these quarters.'

'Prove what?' I asked.

She turned to look at Alan and his mother. Alan was staring at Naomi's ruined face, at the ropy, discolored scar tissue. Naomi was shaping the image of an old woman and two children. The gaunt, lined face of the old woman was remarkably vivid — detailed in a way that seemed impossible for a blind sculptress.

Naomi seemed unaware of us. Her total attention remained on her work. Alan forgot about what Beatrice had told us and reached out to touch the scarred face.

Beatrice let it happen. Naomi did not seem to notice. 'If I get her attention for you,' Beatrice said, 'we'll be breaking her routine. We'll have to stay with her until she gets back into it without hurting herself. About half an hour.'

'You can get her attention?' he asked.

'Yes.'

'Can she . . .?' Alan swallowed. 'I've never heard of anything like this. Can she talk?'

'Yes. She may not choose to, though. And if she does, she'll do it very slowly.'

'Do it. Get her attention.'

'She'll want to touch you.'

'That's all right. Do it.'

Beatrice took Naomi's hands and held them still, away from the wet clay. For several seconds Naomi tugged at her captive hands, as though unable to understand why they did not move as she wished.

Beatrice stepped closer and spoke quietly. 'Stop, Naomi.' And Naomi was still, blind face turned toward Beatrice in an attitude of attentive waiting. Totally focused waiting.

'Company, Naomi.'

After a few seconds, Naomi made a wordless sound.

Beatrice gestured Alan to her side, gave Naomi one of his hands. It didn't bother me this time when she touched him. I was too interested in what was happening. Naomi examined Alan's hand minutely, then followed the arm up to the shoulder, the neck, the face. Holding his face between her hands, she made a sound. It may have been a word, but I couldn't understand it. All I could think of was the danger of those hands. I thought of my father's hands.

'His name is Alan Chi, Naomi. He's your son.' Several seconds passed.

'Son?' she said. This time the word was quite distinct, though her lips had split in many places and had healed badly. 'Son?' she repeated anxiously. 'Here?'

'He's all right, Naomi. He's come to visit.'

'Mother?' he said.

She re-examined his face. He had been three when she started to drift. It didn't seem possible that she could find anything in his face that she would remember. I wondered whether she remembered she had a son.

'Alan?' she said. She found his tears and paused at them. She touched her own face where there should have been an eye, then she reached back toward his eyes. An instant before I would have grabbed her hand. Beatrice did it.

'No!' Beatrice said firmly.

The hand fell limply to Naomi's side. Her face turned toward Beatrice like an antique weather-vane swinging around. Beatrice stroked her hair, and Naomi said something I almost understood. Beatrice looked at Alan, who was frowning and wiping away tears.

'Hug your son,' Beatrice said softly.

Naomi turned, groping, and Alan seized her in a tight, long hug. Her arms went around him slowly. She spoke words blurred by her ruined mouth but just understandable.

'Parents?' she said. 'Did my parents . . . care for you?' Alan looked at her, clearly not understanding.

'She wants to know whether her parents took care of you,' I said.

He glanced at me doubtfully, then looked at Beatrice.

'Yes,' Beatrice said. 'She just wants to know that they cared for you.'

'They did,' he said. 'They kept their promise to you, Mother.'

Several seconds passed. Naomi made sounds that even Alan took to be weeping, and he tried to comfort her.

'Who else is here?' she said finally.

This time Alan looked at me. I repeated what she had said.

'Her name is Lynn Mortimer,' he said. 'I'm . . .' He paused awkwardly. 'She and I are going to be married.'

After a time, she moved back from him and said my name. My first impulse was to go to her. I wasn't afraid or repelled by her now, but for no reason I could explain, I looked at Beatrice.

'Go,' she said. 'But you and I will have to talk later.'

I went to Naomi, took her hand.

'Bea?' she said.

'I'm Lynn,' I said softly.

She drew a quick breath. 'No,' she said. 'No, you're . . .'

'I'm Lynn. Do you want Bea? She's here.'

She said nothing. She put her hand to my face, explored it slowly. I let her do it, confident that I could stop her if she turned violent. But first one hand, then both, went over me very gently.

'You'll marry my son?' she said finally.

'Yes.'

'Good. You'll keep him safe.'

As much as possible, we'll keep each other safe. 'Yes,' I said.

'Good. No one will close him away from himself. No one will tie him or cage him.' Her hand wandered to her own face again, nails biting in slightly.

'No,' I said softly, catching the hand. 'I want you to be safe, too.'

The mouth moved. I think it smiled. 'Son?' she said.

He understood her, took her hand.

'Clay,' she said. Lynn and Alan in clay. 'Bea?'

'Of course,' Beatrice said. 'Do you have an impression?'

'No!' It was the fastest that Naomi had answered anything. Then, almost childlike, she whispered. 'Yes.'

Beatrice laughed. 'Touch them again if you like, Naomi. They don't mind.'

We didn't. Alan closed his eyes, trusting her gentleness in a way I could not. I had no trouble accepting her touch, even so near my eyes, but I did not delude myself about her. Her gentleness could turn in an instant. Naomi's fingers twitched near Alan's eyes, and I spoke up at once, out of fear for him.

'Just touch him, Naomi. Only touch.'

She froze, made an interrogative sound.

'She's all right,' Alan said.

'I know,' I said, not believing it. He would be all right, though, as long as someone watched her very carefully, nipped any dangerous impulses in the bud.

'Son!' she said, happily possessive. When she let him go, she demanded clay, wouldn't touch her old-woman sculpture again. Beatrice got new clay for her, leaving us to soothe her and ease her impatience. Alan began to recognize signs of impending destructive behavior. Twice he caught her hands and said no. She struggled against him until I spoke to her. As Beatrice returned, it happened again, and Beatrice said, 'No, Naomi.' Obediently Naomi let her hands fall to her sides.

'What is it?' Alan demanded later when we had left Naomi safely, totally focused on her new work – clay sculptures of us. 'Does she only listen to women or something?'

Beatrice took us back to the sitting room, sat us both down, but did not sit down herself. She went to a window and stared out. 'Naomi only obeys certain women,' she said. 'And she's sometimes slow to obey. She's worse than most – probably because of the damage she managed to do to herself before I got her.' Beatrice faced us, stood biting her lip and frowning. 'I haven't had to give this particular speech for a while,' she said. 'Most DGDs have the sense not to marry each other and produce children. I hope you two aren't planning to have any – in spite of our need.' She took a deep breath. 'It's a pheromone. A scent. And it's sex-linked. Men who inherit the disease from their fathers have no trace of the scent. They also tend to have an easier time with the disease. But they're useless to us as staff here. Men who inherit from their mothers have as much of the scent as men get. They can be useful here because the DGDs can at least be made to notice them. The same for women who inherit from their mothers but not their fathers. It's only when two irresponsible DGDs get together and produce girl children like me or Lynn that you get someone who can really do some good in a place like this.' She looked at me. 'We are very rare commodities, you and I. When you finish school you'll have a very well paid job waiting for you.'

'Here?' I asked.

'For training, perhaps. Beyond that, I don't know. You'll probably help start a retreat in some other part of the country. Others are badly needed.' She smiled humorlessly. 'People like us don't get along well together. You must realize that I don't like you any more than you like me.'

I swallowed, saw her through a kind of haze for a moment. Hated her mindlessly – just for a moment.

'Sit back,' she said. 'Relax your body. It helps.'

I obeyed, not really wanting to obey her but unable to think of anything else to do. Unable to think at all. 'We seem,' she said, 'to be very territorial. Dilg is a haven for me when I'm the only one of my kind here. When I'm not, it's a prison.'

'All it looks like to me is an unbelievable amount of work,' Alan said.

She nodded. 'Almost too much.' She smiled to herself. 'I was one of the first double DGDs to be born. When I was old enough to understand, I thought I didn't have much time. First I tried to kill myself. Failing that, I tried to cram all the living I could into the small amount of time I assumed I had. When I got into this project, I worked as hard as I could to get it into shape before I started to drift. By now I wouldn't know what to do with myself if I weren't working.'

'Why haven't you . . . drifted?' I asked.

'I don't know. There aren't enough of our kind to know what's normal for us.'

'Drifting is normal for every DGD sooner or later.'

'Later, then.'

'Why hasn't the scent been synthesized?' Alan asked. 'Why are there still concentration-camp rest-homes and hospital wards?'

'There have been people trying to synthesize it since I proved what I could do with it. No one has succeeded so far. All we've been able to do is keep our eyes open for people like Lynn.' She looked at me. 'Dilg scholarship, right?'

'Yeah. Offered out of the blue.'

'My people do a good job keeping track. You would have be contacted just before you graduated or if you dropped out.'

'Is it possible,' Alan said, staring at me, 'that she's already doing it? Already using the scent to . . . influence people?'

'You?' Beatrice asked.

'All of us. A group of DGDs. We all live together. We're all controlled, of course, but . . .' Beatrice smiled. 'It's probably the quietest house full of kids that anyone's ever seen.'

I looked at Alan, and he looked away. 'I'm not doing anything to them,' I said. 'I remind them of work they've already promised to do. That's all.'

'You put them at ease,' Beatrice said. 'You're there. You . . . well, you leave your scent around the house. You speak to them individually. Without knowing why, they no doubt find that very comforting. Don't you, Alan?'

'I don't know,' he said. 'I suppose I must have. From my first visit to the house, I knew I wanted to move in. And when I first saw Lynn, I . . .' He shook his head. 'Funny, I thought all that was my idea.'

'Will you work with us, Alan?'

'Me? You want Lynn.'

'I want you both. You have no idea how many people take one look at one workroom here and turn and run. You may be the kind of young people who ought to eventually take charge of a place like Dilg.'

'Whether we want to or not, eh?' he said.

Frightened, I tried to take his hand, but he moved it away. 'Alan, this works,' I said. 'It's only a stopgap, I know. Genetic engineering will probably give us the final answers, but for God's sake, this is something we can do now!'

'It's something *you* can do. Play queen bee in a retreat full of workers. I've never had any ambition to be a drone.'

'A physician isn't likely to be a drone,' Beatrice said.

'Would you marry one of your patients?' he demanded. 'That's what Lynn would be doing if she married me – whether I become a doctor or not.'

She looked away from him, stared across the room. 'My husband is here,' she said softly. 'He's been a patient here for almost a decade. What better place for him . . . when his time came?'

'Shit!' Alan muttered. He glanced at me. 'Let's get out of here!' He got up and strode across the room to the door, pulled at it, then realized it was locked. He turned to face Beatrice, his body language demanding she let him out. She went to him, took him by the shoulder, and turned him to face the door. 'Try it once more,' she said quietly. 'You can't break it. Try.'

Surprisingly, some of the hostility seemed to go out of him. 'This is one of those p.v. locks?' he asked.

'Yes.'

I set my teeth and looked away. Let her work. She knew how to use this thing she and I both had. And for the moment, she was on my side.

I heard him make some effort with the door. The door didn't even rattle. Beatrice took his hand from it, and with her own hand flat against what appeared to be a large brass knob, she pushed the door open.

'The man who created that lock is nobody in particular,' she said. 'He doesn't have an unusually high IQ, didn't even finish college. But sometime in his life he read a science-fiction story in which palmprint locks were a given. He went that story one better by creating one that responded to voice or palm. It took him years, but we were able to give him those years. The people of Dilg are problem solvers, Alan. Think of the problems you could solve!'

He looked as though he were beginning to think, beginning to understand. 'I don't see how biological research can be done that way,' he said. 'Not with everyone acting on his own, not even aware of other researchers and their work.'

'It *is* being done,' she said, 'and not in isolation. Our retreat in Colorado specializes in it and has – just barely – enough trained, controlled DGDs to see that no one really works in isolation. Our patients can still read and write – those who haven't damaged themselves too badly. They can take each other's work into account if reports are made available to them. And they can read material that comes in from the outside. They're working, Alan. The disease hasn't stopped them, *won't* stop them.' He stared at her, seemed to be caught by her intensity – or her scent. He spoke as though his words were a strain, as though they hurt his throat. 'I won't be a puppet. I won't be controlled . . . by a goddamn smell!'

'Alan –'

'I won't be what my mother is. I'd rather be dead!'

'There's no reason for you to become what your mother is.'

He drew back in obvious disbelief.

'Your mother is brain-damaged – thanks to the three months she spent in that custodial-care toilet. She had no speech at all when I met her. She's improved more than you can imagine. None of that has to happen to you. Work with us, and we'll see that none of it happens to you.'

He hesitated, seemed less sure of himself. Even that much flexibility in him was surprising. 'I'll be under your control or Lynn's,' he said.

She shook her head. 'Not even your mother is under my control. She's aware of me. She's able to take direction from me. She trusts me the way any blind person would trust her guide.'

'There's more to it than that.'

'Not here. Not at any of our retreats.'

'I don't believe you.'

'Then you don't understand how much individuality our people retain. They know they need help, but they have minds of their own. If you want to see the abuse of power you're worried about, go to a DGD ward.'

'You're better than that, I admit. Hell is probably better than that. But . . .'

'But you don't trust us.'

He shrugged.

'You do, you know.' She smiled. 'You don't want to, but you do. That's what worries you, and it leaves you with work to do. Look into what I've said. See for yourself. We offer DGDs a chance to live and do whatever they decide is important to them. What do you have, what can you realistically hope for that's better than that?'

Silence. 'I don't know what to think,' he said finally.

'Go home,' she said. 'Decide what to think. It's the most important decision you'll ever make.'

He looked at me. I went to him, not sure how he'd react, not sure he'd want me no matter what he decided.

'What are you going to do?' he asked.

The question startled me. 'You have a choice,' I said. 'I don't. If she's right . . . how could I not wind up running a retreat?'

'Do you want to?'

I swallowed. I hadn't really faced that question yet. Did I want to spend my life in something that was basically a refined DGD ward? 'No!'

'But you will.'

'. . . Yes.' I thought for a moment, hunted for the right words. 'You'd do it.'

'What?'

'If the pheromone were something only men had, you would do it.'

That silence again. After a time he took my hand, and we followed Beatrice out to the car. Before I could get in with him and our guard-escort, she caught my arm. I jerked away reflexively. By the time I caught myself, I had swung around as though I meant to hit her. Hell, I did mean to hit her, but I stopped myself in time. 'Sorry,' I said with no attempt at sincerity.

She held out a card until I took it. 'My private number,' she said. 'Before seven or after nine, usually. You and I will communicate best by phone.'

I resisted the impulse to throw the card away. God, she brought out the child in me.

Inside the car, Alan said something to the guard. I couldn't hear what it was, but the sound of his voice reminded me of him arguing with her — her logic and her scent. She had all but won him for me, and I couldn't manage even token gratitude. I spoke to her, low-voiced.

'He never really had a chance, did he?'

She looked surprised. 'That's up to you. You can keep him or drive him away. I assure you, you *can* drive him away.'

'How?'

'By imagining that he doesn't have a chance.' She smiled faintly. 'Phone me from your territory. We have a great deal to say to each other, and I'd rather we didn't say it as enemies.'

She had lived with meeting people like me for decades. She had good control. I, on the other hand, was at the end of my control. All I could do was scramble into the car and floor my own phantom accelerator as the guard drove us to the gate. I couldn't look back at her. Until we were well away from the house, until we'd left the guard at the gate and gone off the property, I couldn't make myself look back. For long, irrational minutes, I was convinced that somehow if I turned, I would see myself standing there, gray and old, growing small in the distance, vanishing.

(*Learning about*) *Machine Sex*

(1988)

CANDAS JANE DORSEY

A naked woman working at a computer. Which attracts you most? It was a measure of Whitman that, as he entered the room, his eyes went first to the unfolded machine gleaming small and awkward in the light of the long-armed desk lamp; he'd seen the woman before.

Angel was the woman. Thin and pale-skinned, with dark nipples and black pubic hair, and her face hidden by a dark unkempt mane of long hair as she leaned over her work.

A woman complete with her work. It was a measure of Angel that she never acted naked, even when she was. Perhaps especially when she was.

So she has a new board, thought Whitman, and felt his guts stir the way they stirred when he first contemplated taking her to bed. That was a long time ago. And she knew it, felt without turning her head the desire, and behind the screen of her straight dark hair, uncombed and tumbled in front of her eyes, she smiled her anger down.

'Where have you been?' he asked, and she shook her hair back, leaned backward to ease her tense neck.

'What is that thing?' he went on insistently, and Angel turned her face to him, half-scowling. The board on the desk had thin irregular wings spreading from a small central module. Her fingers didn't slow their keyboard dance.

'None of your business,' she said.

She saved the input, and he watched her fold the board into a smaller and smaller rectangle. Finally she shook her hair back from her face.

'I've got the option on your bioware,' he said.

'Pay as you go,' she said. 'New house rule.'

And found herself on her ass on the floor from his reflexive, furious blow. And his hand in her hair, pulling her up and against the wall. Hard. Astonishing her with how quickly she could hurt how much. Then she hurt too much to analyze it.

'You are a bitch,' he said.

'So what?' she said. 'When I was nicer, you were still an asshole.'

Her head back against the wall, crack. Ouch.

Breathless, Angel: 'Once more and you never see this bioware.' And Whitman slowly draws breath, draws back, and looks at her the way she knew he always felt.

'Get out,' she said. 'I'll bring it to Kozyk's office when it's ready.'

So he went. She slumped back in the chair, and tears began to blur her vision, but hate cleared them up fast enough, as she unfolded the board again, so that despite the pain she hardly missed a moment of programming time.

Assault only a distraction now, betrayal only a detail: Angel was on a roll. She had her revenge well in hand, though it took a subtle mind to recognize it.

Again: 'I have the option on any of your bioware.' This time, in the office, Whitman wore the nostalgic denims he now affected, and Angel her street-silks and leather.

'This is mine, but I made one for you.' She pulled it out of the bag. Where her board looked jerry-built, this one was sleek. Her board looked interesting; this one packaged. 'I made it before you sold our company,' she said. 'I put my best into it. You may as well have it. I suppose you own the option anyway, eh?'

She stood. Whitman was unconsciously restless before her.

'When you pay me for this,' she said, 'make it in MannComp stock.' She tossed him the board. 'But be careful. If you take it apart wrong, you'll break it. Then you'll have to ask me to fix it, and from now on, my tech rate goes up.'

As she walked by him, he reached for her, hooked one arm around her waist. She looked at him, totally expressionless. 'Max,' she said, 'it's like I told you last night. From now on, if you want it, you pay. Just like everyone else.' He let her go. She pulled the soft dirty white silk shirt on over the black leather jacket. The complete rebel now.

'It's a little going away present. When you're a big shot in MannComp, remember that I made it. And that you couldn't even take it apart right. I guarantee.'

He wasn't going to watch her leave. He was already studying the board. Hardly listening, either.

'Call it the Mannboard,' she said. 'It gets big if you stroke it.' She shut the door quietly behind herself.

It would be easier if this were a story about sex, or about machines. It is true that the subject is Angel, a woman who builds computers like they have never been built before outside the human skull. Angel, like everyone else, comes from somewhere and goes somewhere else. She lives in that linear and binary universe. However, like everyone else, she lives concurrently in another universe less simple. Trivalent, quadrivalent, multivalent. World without end, with no amen. And so, on.

They say a hacker's burned out before he's twenty-one. Note the pronoun: he. Not many young women in that heady realm of the chip.

Before Angel was twenty-one – long before – she had taken the cybernetic chip out of a Wm Kuhns fantasy and patented it; she had written the program for the self-taught AI the Bronfmanns had bought and used to gain world prominence for their Mann-Comp lapboard; somewhere in there, she'd lost innocence, and when her clever additions to that AI turned it into something the military wanted, she dropped out of sight in Toronto and went back to Rocky Mountain House, Alberta, on a Greyhound bus.

It was while she was thinking about something else – cash, and how to get some – that she had looked out of the bus window in Winnipeg into the display window of a sex shop. Garter belts, sleazy magazines on cheap coated paper with dayglo orange stickers over the genitals of bored sex kings and queens, a variety of ornamental vibrators. She had too many memories of Max to take it lightly, though she heard the laughter of the roughnecks in the back of the bus as they topped each others' dirty jokes, and thought perhaps their humour was worth emulating. If only she could.

She passed her twentieth birthday in a hotel in Regina, where she stopped to take a shower and tap into the phone lines, checking for pursuit. Armed with the money she got through automatic transfer from a dummy account in Medicine Hat, she rode the bus the rest of the way ignoring the rolling of beer bottles under the seats, the acrid stink of the on-board toilet. She was thinking about sex.

As the bus roared across the long flat prairie she kept one hand on the roll of bills in her pocket, but with the other she made the first notes on the program that would eventually make her famous.

She made the notes on an antique NEC lapboard which had been her aunt's, in old-fashioned BASIC – all the machine would support – but she unravelled it and knitted it into that artificial trivalent language when she got to the place at Rocky and plugged the idea into her Mannboard. She had it written in a little over four hours on-time, but that counted an hour and a half she took to write a new loop into the A1. (She would patent that loop later the same year and put the royalties into a blind trust for her brother, Brian, brain-damaged from birth. He was in Michener Centre in Red Deer, not educable; no one at Bronfmann knew about her family, and she kept it that way.)

She called it Machine Sex; working title.

Working title for a life; born in Innisfail General Hospital, father a rodeo cowboy who raised rodeo horses, did enough mixed farming out near Caroline to build his young second wife a big log house facing the mountain view. The first baby came within a year, ending her mother's tenure as teller at the local bank. Her aunt was a programmer for the University of Lethbridge, chemical molecular model analysis on the University of Calgary mainframe through a modem link.

From her aunt she learned BASIC, Pascal, COBOL and C; in school she played the usual turtle games on the Apple IIe; when she was fourteen she took a bus to Toronto, changed her name to Angel, affected a punk hairstyle and the insolent all-white costume of that year's youth, and eventually walked into Northern Systems, the company struggling most successfully with bionics at the time, with the perfected biochip, grinning at the proper young men in their grey three-piece suits as they tried to find a bug in it anywhere. For the first million she let them open it up; for the next five she told them how she did it. Eighteen years old by the phony records she'd cooked on her arrival in Toronto, she was free to negotiate her own contracts.

But no one got her away from Northern until Bronfmann bought Northern lock, stock and climate-controlled workshop. She had been sleeping with Northern's boy-wonder president by then for about a year, had yet to have an orgasm though she'd learned a lot about kinky sex toys. Figured she'd been screwed by him for the last time when he sold the company without telling her; spent the next two weeks doing a lot of drugs and having a lot of cheap sex in the degenerate punk underground; came up with the A1 education program.

Came up indeed, came swaggering into Ted Kozyk's office, president of Bronfmann's MannComp subsidiary, with that jury-rigged Mannboard tied into two black-box add-ons no bigger than a bar of soap, and said, 'Watch this.'

Took out the power supply first, wiped the memory, plugged into a wall outlet and turned it on.

The bootstrap greeting sounded a lot like Goo.

'Okay,' she said, 'it's ready.'

'Ready for what?'

'Anything you want,' she said. By then he knew her, knew her rep, knew that the sweaty-smelling, disheveled, anorectic-looking waif in the filthy, oversized silk shirt (the rebels had affected natural fabrics the year she left home, and she always did after that, even later when the silk was cleaner, more upmarket, and black instead of white) had something. Two weeks ago he'd bought a company on the strength of that something, and the board Whitman had brought him just yesterday, even without the software to run on it, had been enough to convince him he'd been right.

He sat down to work, and hours later he was playing Go with an A1 he'd taught to talk back, play games, and predict horse races and the stock market.

He sat back, flicked the power switch and pulled the plug, and stared at her.

'Congratulations,' she said.

'What for?' he said; 'you're the genius.'

'No, congratulations, you just murdered your first baby,' she said, and plugged it back in. 'Want to try for two?'

'Goo,' said the deck. 'Dada.'

It was her little joke. It was never a feature on the MannComp A-One they sold across every MannComp counter in the world.

But now she's all grown up, she's sitting in a log house near Rocky Mountain house, watching the late summer sunset from the big front windows, while the computer runs Machine Sex to its logical conclusion, orgasm.

She had her first orgasm at nineteen. According to her false identity, she was twenty-three. Her lover was a delegate to Mann-Comp's annual sales convention; she picked him up after the speech she gave on the ethics of selling Ais to high school students in Thailand. Or whatever, she didn't care. Kozyk used to write her speeches but she usually changed them to suit her mood. This night she'd been circumspect, only a few expletives, enough to amuse the younger sales representatives and reassure the older ones.

The one she chose was smooth in his approach and she thought, well, we'll see. They went up to the suite MannComp provided, all mod cons and king-size bed, and as she undressed she looked at him and thought, he's ambitious, this boy, better not give him an inch.

He surprised her in bed. Ambitious maybe, but he paid a lot of attention to detail.

After he spread her across the universe in a way she had never felt before, he turned to her and said, 'That was pretty good, eh, baby?' and smiled a smooth little grin. 'Sure,' she said, 'it was okay,' and was glad she hadn't said more while she was out in the ozone.

By then she thought she was over what Whitman had done to her. And after all, it had been simple enough, what he did. Back in that loft she had in Hull, upstairs of a shop, where she covered the windows with opaque mylar and worked night and day in that twilight. That night as she worked he stood behind her, hands on her shoulders, massaging her into further tenseness.

'Hey, Max, you know I don't like it when people look over my shoulder when I'm working.'

'Sorry, baby.' He moved away, and she felt her shoulders relax just to have his hands fall away.

'Come on to bed,' he said. 'You know you can pick that up whenever.'

She had to admit he was being pleasant tonight. Maybe he too was tired of the constant scrapping, disguised as jokes, that wore at her nerves so much. All his efforts to make her stop working, slow her down so he could stay up. The sharp edges that couldn't be disguised. Her bravado made her answer in the same vein, but in the mornings, when he was gone to Northern, she paced and muttered to herself, reworking the previous day until it was done with, enough that she could go on. And after all what was missing? She had no idea how to debug it.

Tonight he'd even made some dinner, and touched her kindly. Should she be grateful? Maybe the conversations, such as they were, where she tried to work it out, had just made it worse–.

'Ah, shit,' she said, and pushed the board away. 'You're right, I'm too tired for this. *Demain.*' She was learning French in her spare time.

He began with hugging her, and stroking the long line along her back, something he knew she liked, like a cat likes it, arches its back at the end of the stroke. He knew she got turned on by it. And she did. When they had sex at her house he was without the paraphernalia he preferred, but he seemed to manage, buoyed up by some mood she couldn't share; nor could she share his release.

Afterward, she lay beside him, tense and dissatisfied in the big bed, not admitting it, or she'd have to admit she didn't know what would help. He seemed to be okay, stretched, relaxed and smiling.

'Had a big day,' he said.

'Yeah?'

'Big deal went through.'

'Yeah?'

'Yeah, I sold the company.'

'You what?' Reflexively moving herself so that none of her body touched his.

'Northern. I put it to Bronfmann. Megabucks.'

'Are you joking?' but she saw he was not. 'You didn't, I didn't . . . Northern's *our* company.'

'My company. I started it.'

'I made it big for you.'

'Oh, and I paid you well for every bit of that.'

She got up. He was smiling a little, trying on the little-boy grin. No, baby, she thought, not tonight.

'Well,' she said, 'I know for sure that this is my bed. Get out of it.'

'Now, I knew you might take this badly. But it really was the best thing. The R&D costs were killing us. Bronfmann can eat them for breakfast.'

R&D costs meant her. 'Maybe. Your clothes are here.' She tossed them on the bed, went into the other room.

As well as sex, she hadn't figured out betrayal yet either; on the street, she thought, people fucked you over openly, not in secret.

This, even as she said it to herself, she recognized as romantic and certainly not based on experience. She was street-wise in every way but one: Max had been her first lover.

She unfolded the new board. It had taken her some time to figure out how to make it expand like that, to fit the program it was going to run. This idea of shaping the hardware to the software had been with her since she made the biochip, and thus made it possible and much more interesting than the other way around. But making the hardware to fit her new idea had involved a great deal of study and technique, and so far she had had limited success.

This reminded her again of sex, and, she supposed, relationships, although it seemed to her that before sex everything had been on surfaces, very easy. Now she had sex, she had had Max, and now she had no way to realize the results of any of that. Especially now, when Northern had just vanished into Bronfmann's computer empire, putting her in the position again of having to prove herself. What had Max used to make Bronfmann take the bait? She knew very clearly: Angel, the Northern Angel, would now become the MannComp Angel. The rest of the bait would have been the A1; she was making more of it every day, but couldn't yet bring it together. Could it be done at all? Bronfmann had paid high for an affirmative answer.

Certainly this time the bioware was working together. She began to smile a little to herself, almost unaware of it, as she saw how she could interconnect the loops to make a solid net to support the program's full and growing weight. Because, of course, it would have to learn as it went along – that was basic.

Angel as metaphor; she had to laugh at herself when she woke from programming hours later, Max still sleeping in her bed, ignoring her eviction notice. He'll have to get up to piss anyway, she thought; that's when I'll get him out. She went herself to the bathroom in the half-dawn light, stretching her cramped back muscles and thinking remotely, well, I got some satisfaction out of last night after all: the beginnings of the idea that might break this impasse. While it's still inside my head, this one is mine. How can I keep it that way?

New fiscal controls, she thought grimly. New contracts, now that Northern doesn't exist any more. Max can't have this, what-ever it turns into, for my dowry to MannComp.

When she put on her white silks – leather jacket underneath, against the skin as street fashion would have it – she hardly knew herself what she would do. The little board went into her bag with the boxes of pills the pharmaceutical tailor had made for her. If there was nothing there to suit, she'd buy something new. In the end, she left Max sleeping in her bed; so what? she thought as she reached the highway. The first ride she hitched took her to Toronto, not without a little tariff, but she no longer gave a damn about any of that.

By then the drugs in her system had lifted her out of a body that could be betrayed, and she didn't return to it for two weeks, two weeks of floating in a soup of disjointed noise, and always the program running, unfolding, running again, unfolding inside her relentless mind. She kept it running to drown anything she might remember about trust or the dream of happiness.

When she came home two weeks later, on a hot day in summer with the Ottawa Valley humidity unbearable and her body tired, sore and bruised, and very dirty, she stepped out of her filthy silks in a room messy with Whitman's continued inhabitation; furious, she popped a system cleanser and unfolded the board on her desk. When he came back in she was there, naked, angry, working.

*

A naked woman working at a computer. What good were cover-ups? Watching Max after she took the new A1 up to Kozyk, she was only triumphant because she'd done something Max could never do, however much he might be able to sell her out. Watching them fit it to the bioboard, the strange unfolding machine she had made to fit the ideas only she could have, she began to be afraid. The system cleanser she'd taken made the clarity inescapable. Over the next few months, as she kept adding clever loops and twists, she watched their glee and she looked at what telephone numbers were in the top ten on their modem memories and she began to realize that it was not only business and science that would pay high for a truly thinking machine.

She knew that ten years before there had been Pentagon programmers working to model predatory behaviour in A1s using Prolog and its like. That was old hat. None of them, however, knew what they needed to know to write for her bioware yet. No one but Angel could do that. So, by the end of her nineteenth year, that made Angel one of the most sought after, endangered ex-anorectics on the block.

She went to conferences and talked about the ethics of selling A1s to teenagers in Nepal. Or something. And took a smooth salesman to bed, and thought all the time about when they were going to make their approach. It would be Whitman again, not Kozyk, she thought; Ted wouldn't get his hands dirty, while Max was born with grime under his nails.

She thought also about metaphors. How, even in the new street slang which she could speak as easily as her native tongue, being screwed, knocked, fucked over, jossed, dragged all meant the same thing: hurt to the core. And this was what people sought out, what they spent their time seeking in pick-up joints, to the beat of bad old headbanger bands, that nostalgia shit. Now, as well as the biochip, Max, the A1 breakthrough, and all the tailored drugs she could eat, she'd had orgasm too.

Well, she supposed it passed the time.

What interested her intellectually about orgasm was not the lovely illusion of transcendence it brought, but the absolute binary predictability of it. When you learn what to do to the nerve endings, and they are in a receptive state, the program runs like kismet. Warm boot. She'd known a hacker once who'd altered his bootstrap messages to read 'warm pussy'. She knew where most hackers were at; they played with their computers more than they played with themselves. She was the same, otherwise why would it have taken a pretty-boy salesman in a three-piece to show her the simple answer? All the others, just like trying to use an old MS-DOS disc to boot up one of her Mann lapboards with crystal RO/RAM.

*

Angel forgets she's only twenty. Genius is uneven. There's no substitute for time, that relentless shaper of understanding. Etc. Etc. Angel paces with the knowledge that everything is a phase, even this. Life is hard and then you die, and so on. And so, on.

One day it occurred to her that she could simply run away.

This should have seemed elementary but to Angel it was a revelation. She spent her life fatalistically; her only successful escape had been from the people she loved. Her lovely, crazy grandfather; her generous and slightly avaricious aunt; and her beloved imbecile brother: they were buried deep in a carefully forgotten past. But she kept coming back to Whitman, to Kozyk and Bronfmann, as if she liked them.

As if, like a shocked dog in a learned helplessness experiment, she could not believe that the cage had a door, and the door was open.

She went out the door. For old times' sake, it was the bus she chose; the steamy chill of an air-conditioned Greyhound hadn't changed at all. Bottles – pop and beer – rolling under the seats and the stench of chemicals filling the air whenever someone sneaked down to smoke a cigarette or a reef in the toilet. Did anyone ever use it to piss in? She liked the triple seat near the back, but the combined smells forced her to the front, behind the driver, where she was joined, across the country, by an endless succession of old women, immaculate in their fortrels, who started conversations and shared peppermints and gum.

She didn't get stoned once.

The country unrolled strangely: sex shop in Winnipeg, bank machine in Regina, and hours of programming alternating with polite responses to the old women, until eventually she arrived, creased and exhausted, in Rocky Mountain House.

Rocky Mountain House: a comfortable model of a small town, from which no self-respecting hacker should originate. But these days, the world a net of wire and wireless, it doesn't matter where you are, as long as you have the information people want. Luckily for Angel's secret past, however, this was not a place she would be expected to live – or to go – or to come from.

An atavism she hadn't controlled had brought her this far. A rented car took her the rest of the way to the ranch. She thought only to look around, but when she found the tenants packing for a month's holiday, she couldn't resist the opportunity. She carried her leather satchel into their crocheted, frilled guest room – it had been her room fifteen years before – with a remote kind of satisfaction.

That night, she slept like the dead – except for some dreams. But there was nothing she could do about them.

Lightning and thunder. I should stop now, she thought, wary of power surges through the new board which she was charging as she worked. She saved her file, unplugged the power, stood, stretched, and walked to the window to look at the mountains.

The storm illuminated the closer slopes erratically, the rain hid the distances. She felt some heaviness lift. The cool wind through the window refreshed her. She heard the program stop, and turned off the machine. Sliding out the back-up capsule, she smiled her angry smile unconsciously. When I get back to the Ottawa Valley, she thought, where weather never comes from the west like it's supposed to, I'll make those fuckers eat this.

Out in the corrals where the tenants kept their rodeo horses, there was animal noise, and she turned off the light to go and look out the side window. A young man was leaning his weight against the reins-length pull of a rearing, terrified horse. Angel watched as flashes of lightning strobed the hackneyed scene. This was where she came from. She remembered her father in the same struggle. And her mother at this window with her, both of them watching the man. Her mother's anger she never understood until now. Her father's abandonment of all that was in the house, including her brother, Brian, inert and restless in his oversized crib.

Angel walked back through the house, furnished now in the

kitschy western style of every trailer and bungalow in this country-side. She was lucky to stay, invited on a generous impulse, while all but their son were away. She felt vaguely guilty at her implicit criticism.

Angel invited the young rancher into the house not only because this is what her mother and her grandmother would have done. Even Angel's great-grandmother, whose father kept the stopping house, which meant she kept the travellers fed, even her spirit infused in Angel the unwilling act. She watched him almost sullenly as he left his rain gear in the wide porch.

He was big, sitting in the big farm kitchen. His hair was wet, and he swore almost as much as she did. He told her how he had put a trailer on the north forty, and lived there now, instead of in the little room where she'd been invited to sleep. He told her about the stock he'd accumulated riding the rodeo. They drank Glenfiddich. She told him her father had been a rodeo cowboy. He told her about his university degree in agriculture. She told him she'd never been to university. They drank more whiskey and he told her he couldn't drink that other rot gut any more since he tasted real Scotch. He invited her to see his computer. She went with him across the yard and through the trees in the rain, her bag over her shoulder, board hidden in it, and he showed her his computer. It turned out to be the first machine she designed for Northern – archaic now, compared with the one she'd just invented.

Fair is fair, she thought drunkenly, and she pulled out her board and unfolded it.

'You showed me yours, I'll show you mine,' she said.

He liked the board. He was amazed that she had made it. They finished the Scotch.

'I like you,' she said. 'Let me show you something. You can be the first.' And she ran Machine Sex for him.

He was the first to see it: before Whitman and Kozyk who bought it to sell to people who already have had and done everything; before David and Johnathon, the Hardware Twins in MannComp's Gulf Islands shop, who made the touchpad devices necessary to run it properly; before a world market hungry for the kind of glossy degradation Machine Sex could give them bought it in droves from a hastily created – MannComp-subsidiary – numbered company. She ran it for him with just the automouse on her board, and a description of what it would do when the hardware was upgraded to fit.

It was very simple, really. If orgasm was binary, it could be programmed. Feed back the sensation through one or more touch-pads to program the body. The other thing she knew about human sex was that it was as much cortical as genital, or more so: touch is optional for the turn-on. Also easy, then, to produce cortical stimuli by programmed input. The rest was a cosmetic elaboration of the premise.

At first it did turn him on, then off, then it made his blood run cold. She was pleased by that: her work had chilled her too.

'You can't market that thing!' he said.

'Why not? It's a fucking good program. Hey, get it? Fucking good.'

'It's not real.'

'Of course it isn't. So what?'

'So, people don't need that kind of stuff to get turned on.'

She told him about people. More people than he'd known were in the world. People who made her those designer drugs, given in return for favors she never granted until after Whitman sold her like a used car. People like Whitman, teaching her about sexual equipment while dealing with the Pentagon and CSIS to sell them Angel's sharp angry mind, as if she'd work on killing others as eagerly as she was trying to kill herself. People who would hire a woman on the street, as they had her during that two-week nightmare almost a year before, and use her as casually as their own hand, without giving a damn.

'One night,' she said, 'just to see, I told all the johns I was fourteen. I was skinny enough, even then, to get away with it. And they all loved it. Every single one gave me a bonus, and took me anyway.'

The whiskey fog was wearing a little thin. More time had passed than she thought, and more had been said than she had intended. She went to her bag, rummaged, but she'd left her drugs in Toronto, some dim idea at that time that she should clean up her act. All that had happened was that she had spent the days so tight with rage that she couldn't eat, and she'd already cured herself of that once; for the record, she thought, she'd rather be stoned.

'Do you have any more booze?' she said, and he went to look. She followed him around his kitchen.

'Furthermore,' she said, 'I rolled every one of them that I could, and all but one had pictures of his kids in his wallet, and all of them were teenagers. Boys and girls together. And their saintly dads out fucking someone who looked just like them. Just like them.'

Luckily, he had another bottle. Not quite the same quality, but she wasn't fussy.

'So I figure,' she finished, 'that they don't care who they fuck. Why not the computer in the den? Or the office system at lunch hour?'

'It's not like that,' he said. 'It's nothing like that. People deserve better.' He had the neck of the bottle in his big hand, was seriously, carefully pouring himself another shot. He gestured with both bottle and glass. 'People deserve to have – love.'

'Love?'

'Yeah, love. You think I'm stupid, you think I watched too much TV as a kid, but I know it's out there. Somewhere. Other people think so too. Don't you? Didn't you, even if you won't admit it now, fall in love with that guy Max at first? You never said what he did at the beginning, how he talked you into being his lover. Something must have happened. Well, that's what I mean: love.'

'Let me tell you about love. Love is a guy who talks real smooth taking me out to the woods and telling me he just loves my smile. And then taking me home and putting me in leather handcuffs so he can come. And if I hurt he likes it, because he likes it to hurt a little and he thinks I must like it like he does. And if I moan he thinks I'm coming. And if I cry he thinks it's love. And so do I. Until one evening – not too long after my *last* birthday, as I recall – he tells me that he has sold me to another company. And this only after he fucks me one last time. Even though I don't belong to him any more. After all, he had the option on all my bioware.'

'All that is just politics.' He was sharp, she had to grant him that.

'Politics,' she said, 'give me a break. Was it politics made Max able to sell me with the stock: hardware, software, liveware?'

'I've met guys like that. Women too. You have to understand that it wasn't personal to him, it was just politics.' Also stubborn. 'Sure, you were naive, but you weren't wrong. You just didn't understand company politics.'

'Oh, sure I did. I always have. Why do you think I changed my name? Why do you think I dress in natural fibres and go through all the rest of this bullshit? I know how to set up power blocs. Except in mine there is only one party – me. And that's the way it's going to stay. Me against them from now on.'

'It's not always like that. There are assholes in the world, and there are other people too. Everyone around here still remembers your grandfather, even though he's been retired in Camrose for fifteen years. They still talk about the way he and his wife used to waltz at the Legion Hall. What about him? There are more people like him than there are Whitmans.'

'Charlotte doesn't waltz much since her stroke.'

'That's a cheap shot. You can't get away with cheap shots. Speaking of shots, have another.'

'Don't mind if I do. Okay, I give you Eric and Charlotte. But one half-happy ending doesn't balance out the people who go through their lives with their teeth clenched, trying to make it come out the same as a True Romance comic, and always wondering what's missing. They read those bodice-ripper novels, and make that do for the love you believe in so naively.' Call her naive, would he? Two could play at that game. 'That's why they'll all go crazy for Machine Sex. So simple. So linear. So fast. So uncomplicated.'

'You underestimate people's ability to be happy. People are better at loving than you think.'

'You think so? Wait until you have your own little piece of land and some sweetheart takes you out in the trees on a moonlit night and gives you head until you think your heart will break. So you marry her and have some kids. She furnishes the trailer in a five-room sale grouping. You have to quit drinking Glenfiddich because she hates it when you talk too loud. She gets an allowance every month and crochets a cozy for the TV. You work all day out in the rain and all evening in the back room making the books balance on the outdated computer. After the kids come she gains weight and sells real estate if you're lucky. If not she makes things out of recycled bleach bottles and hangs them in the yard. Pretty soon she wears a nightgown to bed and turns her back when you slip in after a hard night at the keyboard. So you take up drinking again and teach the kids about the rodeo. And you find some square-dancing chick who gives you head out behind the bleachers one night in Trochu, so sweet you think your heart will break. What you gonna do then, mountain man?'

'Okay, we can tell stories until the sun comes up. Which won't be too long, look at the time; but no matter how many stories you tell, you can't make me forget about that thing.' He pointed to the computer with loathing.

'It's just a machine.'

'You know what I mean. That thing in it. And besides, I'm gay. Your little scenario wouldn't work.'

She laughed and laughed. 'So that's why you haven't made a pass at me yet,' she said archly, knowing that it wasn't that simple, and he grinned. She wondered coldly how gay he was, but she was tired, so tired of proving power. His virtue was safe with her; so, she thought suddenly, strangely, was hers with him. It was unsettling, and comforting at once.

'Maybe,' he said. 'Or maybe I'm just a liar like you think everyone is. Eh? You think everyone strings everyone else a line? Crap. Who has the time for that shit?'

Perhaps they were drinking beer now. Or was it vodka? She found it hard to tell after a while.

'You know what I mean,' she said. 'You should know. The sweet young thing who has AIDS and doesn't tell you. Or me. I'm lucky so far. Are you? Or who sucks you for your money. Or josses you 'cause he's into denim and Nordic looks.'

'Okay, okay. I give up. Everybody's a creep but you and me.'

'And I'm not so sure about you.'

'Likewise, I'm sure. Have another. So, if you're so pure, what about the ethics of it?'

'What *about* the ethics of it?' she asked. 'Do you think I went through all that sex without paying attention? I had nothing else to do but watch other people come. I saw that old cult movie, where the aliens feed on heroin addiction and orgasm, and the woman's not allowed orgasm so she has to OD on smack. Orgasm's more decadent than shooting heroin? I can't buy that, but there's something about a world that sells it over and over again. Sells the thought of pleasure as a commodity, sells the getting of it as if it were the getting of wisdom. And all these times I told you about, I saw other people get it through me. Even when someone finally made me come, it was just a feather in his cap, an accomplishment, nothing personal. Like you said. All I was was a program, they plugged into me and went through the motions and got their result. Nobody cares if the AI finds fulfilment running their damned data analyses. Nobody thinks about depressed and angry Mannboard ROMs. They just think about getting theirs.

'So why not get mine?' She was pacing now, angry, leaning that thin body as if the wind were against her. 'Let me be the one who runs the program.'

'But you won't be there. You told me how you were going to hide out, all that spy stuff.'

She leaned against the wall, smiling a new smile she thought of as predatory. And maybe it was. 'Oh, yes,' she said. 'I'll be there the first time. When Max and Kozyk run this thing and it turns them on. I'll be there. That's all I care to see.'

He put his big hands on the wall on either side of her and leaned in. He smelled of sweat and liquor and his face was earnest with intoxication.

'I'll tell you something,' he said. 'As long as there's the real thing, it won't sell. They'll never buy it.'

Angel thought so too. Secretly, because she wouldn't give him the satisfaction of agreement, she too thought they would not go that low. *That's right*, she told herself, *trying to sell it is all right — because they will never buy it.*

But they did.

A woman and a computer. Which attracts you most? Now you don't have to choose. Angel has made the choice irrelevant.

In Kozyk's office, he and Max go over the ad campaign. They've already tested the program themselves quite a lot; Angel knows this because it's company gossip, heard over the cubicle walls in the washrooms. The two men are so·absorbed that they don't notice her arrival.

'Why is a woman better than a sheep? Because sheep can't cook. Why is a woman better than a Mannboard? Because you haven't bought your sensory add-on.' Max laughs.

'And what's better than a man?' Angel says; they jump slightly. 'Why, your MannComp touchpads, with two-way input. I bet you'll be able to have them personally fitted.'

'Good idea,' says Kozyk, and Whitman makes a note on his lapboard. Angel, still stunned though she's had weeks to get used to this, looks at them, then reaches across the desk and picks up her prototype board. 'This one's mine,' she says. 'You play with yourselves and your touchpads all you want.'

'Well, you wrote it, baby,' said Max. 'If you can't come with your own program . . .'

Kozyk hiccoughs a short laugh before he shakes his head. 'Shut up, Whitman,' he says. 'You're talking to a very rich and famous woman.'

Whitman looks up from the simulations of his advertising storyboards, smiling a little, anticipating his joke. 'Yeah. It's just too bad she finally burned herself out with this one. They always did say it gives you brain-damage.'

But Angel hadn't waited for the punch-line. She was gone.

Prodigal Pudding

(1988)

SUNITI NAMJOSHI

There was once a cat who lived in a house and was loved by her mistress, but only on Mondays. Love had been rationed. The mistress of the cat believed in moderation. But the cat herself remained unconvinced. 'O Mistress,' she said, 'O Purveyor of All Pleasures, O Sole Source of Solace and Delight.' 'What?' asked the mistress. 'Well,' said the cat, 'O Sole Source of Salmon and Suchlike, Mondays are good, but the other days are wretched. Nobody can live on Mondays alone.' 'Are you complaining?' enquired the mistress. 'Oh no,' said the cat, 'but there used to be a time when you loved me on Tuesdays and Wednesdays and frequently on Thursdays.' 'Very well,' said the mistress, 'I shall consider the matter. But today is a Tuesday you must understand.' So the cat went away. The next morning the mistress of the cat greeted the cat with the following words: 'O Pudding, O Cat, O Delectable Dish, O My Precocious Piglet and My Heart's Delight, good morning.' 'What happened?' asked the cat. 'Well,' said the mistress, 'I love you so much that in the goodness of my heart I have decided to accede to your request. Since you say that you cannot live on a diet of Mondays, I have decided to give you Wednesdays instead.' The cat went away and thought for a while. Then she came back. 'Thank you,' she said, and they spent the day cooing and clucking and purring and petting and all that. But on Thursday morning the cat wasn't there, nor on Friday. She wasn't there on Saturday or Sunday or Monday or Tuesday. On Wednesday morning the cat reappeared. 'O Prodigal Pudding,' cried the mistress sweetly though she was absolutely furious and wanted to shout, only it was Wednesday, 'where have you been?' 'I've been thinking,' said the cat, 'I see that you're right. One day in seven is more than enough. So I'll see you on Wednesdays and love you then.' 'You can't do that,' roared the mistress. 'Yes, I can,' said the cat, 'and you mustn't roar.' 'But it's outrageous,' said the mistress, 'to have to make do with a Once-a-Week Cat. O Pleasant Pussy Cat, O My Sweet and Generous Darling, won't you reconsider?'

'Well, all right,' said the cat. 'In future I'll visit you on Mondays instead.'

Boobs

(1989)

SUZY McKEE CHARNAS

The thing is, it's like your brain wants to go on thinking about the miserable history mid-term you have to take tomorrow, but your body takes over. And what a body! You can see in the dark and run like the wind and leap parked cars in a single bound.

Of course you pay for it next morning (but it's worth it). I always wake up stiff and sore, with dirty hands and feet and face, and I have to jump in the shower fast so Hilda won't see me like that.

Not that she would know what it was about, but why take chances? So I pretend it's the other thing that's bothering me. So she goes, 'Come on, sweetie, everybody gets cramps, that's no reason to go around moaning and groaning. What are you doing, trying to get out of school just because you've got your period?'

If I didn't like Hilda, which I do even though she is only a stepmother instead of my real mother, I would show her something that would keep me out of school forever, and it's not fake, either.

But there are plenty of people I'd rather show that to.

I already showed that dork Billy Linden.

'Hey, Boobs!' he goes, in the hall right outside Homeroom. A lot of kids laughed, naturally, though Rita Frye called him an asshole.

Billy is the one that started it, sort of, because he always started everything, him with his big mouth. At the beginning of term, he came barrelling down on me hollering, 'Hey, look at Bornstein, something musta happened to her over the summer! What happened, Bornstein? Hey, everybody, look at Boobs Bornstein!'

He made a grab at my chest, and I socked him in the shoulder, and he punched me in the face, which made me dizzy and shocked and made me cry, too, in front of everybody.

I mean, I always used to wrestle and fight with the boys, being that I was strong for a girl. All of a sudden it was different. He hit me hard, to really hurt, and the shock sort of got me in the pit of my stomach and made me feel nauseous, too, as well as mad and embarrassed to death.

I had to go home with a bloody nose and lie with my head back and ice wrapped in a towel on my face and dripping down into my hair.

Hilda sat on the couch next to me and patted me. She goes, 'I'm sorry about this, honey, but really, you have to learn it sometime. You're all growing up and the boys are getting stronger than you'll ever be. If you fight with boys, you're bound to get hurt. You have to find other ways to handle them.'

To make things worse, the next morning I started to bleed down there, which Hilda had explained carefully to me a couple of times, so at least I knew what was going on. Hilda really tried extra hard without being icky about it, but I hated when she talked about how it was all part of these exciting changes in my body that are so important and how terrific it is to 'become a young woman'.

Sure. The whole thing was so messy and disgusting, worse than she had said, worse than I could imagine, with these black clots of gunk coming out in a smear of pink blood – I thought I would throw up. That's just the lining of your uterus, Hilda said. Big deal. It was still gross.

And plus, the *smell*.

Hilda tried to make me feel better, she really did. She said we should 'mark the occasion' like primitive people do, so it's something special, not just a nasty thing that just sort of falls on you.

So we decided to put poor old Pinkie away, my stuffed dog that I've slept with since I was three. Pinkie is bald and sort of hard and lumpy, since he got in the washing machine by mistake, and you would never know he was all soft plush when he was new, or even that he was pink.

Last time my friend Gerry-Anne came over, before the summer, she saw Pinky laying on my pillow and though she didn't say anything, I could tell she was thinking that was kind of babyish. So I'd been thinking about not keeping Pinky around any more.

Hilda and I made him this nice box lined with pretty scraps

from her quilting class, and I thanked him out loud for being my friend for so many years, and we put him up in the closet, on the top shelf.

I felt terrible, but if Gerry-Anne decided I was too babyish to be friends with any more, I could end up with no friends at all. When you have never been popular since the time you were skinny and fast and everybody wanted you on their team, you have that kind of thing on your mind.

Hilda and Dad made me go to school the next morning so nobody would think I was scared of Billy Linden (which I was) or that I would let him keep me away just by being such a dork.

Everybody kept sneaking funny looks at me and whispering, and I was sure it was because I couldn't help walking funny with the pad between my legs and because they could smell what was happening, which as far as I knew hadn't happened to anybody else in Eight A yet. Just like nobody else in the whole grade had anything real in their stupid training bras except me, thanks a lot.

Anyway I stayed away from everybody as much as I could and wouldn't talk to Gerry-Anne, even, because I was scared she would ask me why I walked funny and smelled bad.

Billy Linden avoided me just like everybody else, except one of his stupid buddies purposely bumped into me so I stumbled into Billy on the lunch-line. Billy turns around and he goes, real loud, 'Hey, Boobs, when did you start wearing black and blue make-up?'

I didn't give him the satisfaction of knowing that he had actually broken my nose, which the doctor said. Good thing they don't have to bandage you up for that. Billy would be hollering up a storm about how I had my nose in a sling as well as my boobs.

That night I got up after I was supposed to be asleep and took off my underpants and T-shirt that I sleep in and stood looking at myself in the mirror. I didn't need to turn a light on. The moon was full and it was shining right into my bedroom through the big dormer window.

I crossed my arms and pinched myself hard to sort of punish my body for what it was doing to me.

As if that could make it stop.

No wonder Edie Siler had starved herself to death in the Tenth Grade! I understood her perfectly. She was trying to keep her body down, keep it normal-looking, thin and strong, like I was too, back when I looked like a person, not a cartoon that somebody would call 'Boobs'.

And then something warm trickled in a little line down the inside of my leg, and I knew it was blood and I couldn't stand it any more. I pressed my thighs together and shut my eyes hard, and I did something.

I mean I felt it happening. I felt myself shrink down to a hard core of sort of cold fire inside my bones, and all the flesh part, the muscles and the squishy insides and the skin, went sort of glowing and free-floating, all shining with moonlight, and I felt a sort of shifting and balance-changing going on.

I thought I was fainting on account of my stupid period. So I turned around and threw myself on my bed, only by the time I hit it, I knew something was seriously wrong.

For one thing, my nose and my head were crammed with these crazy, rich sensations that it took me a second to even figure out were smells, they were so much stronger than any smells I'd ever smelled. And they were – I don't know – *interesting* instead of just stinky, even the rotten ones.

I opened my mouth to get the smells a little better, and heard myself panting in a funny way as if I'd been running, which I hadn't, and then there was this long part of my face sticking out and something moving there – my tongue.

I was licking my chops.

Well, there was this moment of complete and utter panic. I tore around the room whining and panting and hearing my toenails clicking on the floorboards, and then I huddled down and crouched in the corner because I was scared Dad and Hilda would hear me and come to find out what was making all this racket.

Because I could hear them. I could hear their bed creak when one of them turned over, and Dad's breath whistling a little in an almost snore, and I could smell them too, each one with a perfectly clear bunch of smells, kind of like those desserts of mixed ice-cream they call a medley.

My body was twitching and jumping with fear and energy, and

my room – it's a converted attic-space, wide but with a ceiling that's low in places – my room felt like a jail. And plus, I was terrified of catching a glimpse of myself in the mirror. I had a pretty good idea of what I would see, and I didn't want to see it.

Besides, I had to pee, and I couldn't face trying to deal with the toilet in the state I was in.

So I eased the bedroom door open with my shoulder and nearly fell down the stairs trying to work them with four legs and thinking about it, instead of letting my body just do it. I put my hands on the front door to open it, but my hands weren't hands, they were paws with long knobbly toes covered with fur, and the toes had thick black claws sticking out of the ends of them.

The pit of my stomach sort of exploded with horror, and I yelled. It came out this wavery 'wooo' noise that echoed eerily in my skull-bones. Upstairs, Hilda goes, 'Jack, what was that?' I bolted for the basement as I heard Dad hit the floor of their bedroom.

The basement door slips its latch all the time, so I just shoved it open and down I went, doing better on the stairs this time because I was too scared to think. I spent the rest of the night down there, moaning to myself (which meant whining through my nose, really) and trotting around rubbing against the walls trying to rub off this crazy shape I had, or just moving around because I couldn't sit still. The place was thick with stinks and these slow-swirling currents of hot and cold air. I couldn't handle all the input.

As for having to pee, in the end I managed to sort of hike my butt up over the edge of the slop-sink by Dad's workbench and let go in there. The only problem was that I couldn't turn the taps on to rinse out the smell because of my paws.

Then about three a.m. I woke up from a doze curled up in a bare place on the floor where the spiders weren't so likely to walk, and I couldn't see a thing or smell anything either, so I knew I was okay again even before I checked and found fingers on my hands again instead of claws.

I zipped upstairs and stood under the shower so long that Hilda yelled at me for using up the hot water when she had a load of washing to do that morning. I was only trying to steam some of the stiffness out of my muscles, but I couldn't tell her that.

It was real weird to just dress and go to school after a night like that. One good thing, I had stopped bleeding after only one day, which Hilda said wasn't so strange for the first time. So it had to be the huge greenish bruise on my face from Billy's punch that everybody was staring at.

That and the usual thing, of course. Well, why not? *They* didn't know I'd spent the night as a wolf.

So Fat Joey grabbed my book bag in the hallway outside science class and tossed it to some kid from Eight B. I had to run after them to get it back, which of course was set up so the boys could cheer the bouncing of my boobs under my shirt.

I was so mad I almost caught Fat Joey, except I was afraid if I grabbed him, maybe he would sock me like Billy had.

Dad had told me, 'Don't let it get you, kid, all boys are jerks at that age.'

Hilda had been saying all summer, 'Look, it doesn't do any good to walk around all hunched up with your arms crossed, you should just throw your shoulders back and walk like a proud person who's pleased that she's growing up. You're just a little early, that's all, and I bet the other girls are secretly envious of you, with their cute little training bras, for Chrissake, as if there was something that needed to be *trained*.'

It's okay for her, she's not in school, she doesn't remember what it's like.

So I quit running and walked after Joey until the bell rang, and then I got my book bag back from the bushes outside where he threw it. I was crying a little, and I ducked into the girls' room.

Stacey Buhl was in there doing her lipstick like usual and wouldn't talk to me like usual, but Rita came bustling in and said somebody should off that dumb dork Joey, except of course it was really Billy that put him up to it. Like usual.

Rita is okay except she's an outsider herself, being that her kid brother has AIDS, and lots of kids' parents don't think she should even be in the school. So I don't hang around with her a lot. I've got enough trouble, and anyway I was late for math.

I had to talk to somebody, though. After school I told Gerry-Anne, who's been my best friend on and off since Fourth Grade. She was off at the moment, but I found her in the library and I told her I'd had a weird dream about being a wolf. She wants to be a psychiatrist like her mother, so of course she listened.

She told me I was nuts. That was a big help.

That night I made sure the back door wasn't exactly closed, and then I got in bed with no clothes on – imagine turning into a wolf in your underpants and T-shirt – and just shivered, waiting for something to happen.

The moon came up and shone in my window, and I changed again, just like before, which is not one bit like how it is in the movies – all struggling and screaming and bones snapping out with horrible cracking and tearing noises, just the way I guess you would imagine it to be, if you knew it had to be done by building special machines to do that for the camera and make it look real; if you were a special effects man, instead of a werewolf.

For me, it didn't have to look real, it was real. It was this melting and drifting thing, which I got sort of excited by this time. I mean it felt – interesting. Like something I was doing, instead of just another dumb body-mess happening to me because some brainless hormones said so.

I must have made a noise. Hilda came upstairs to the door of my bedroom, but luckily she didn't come in. She's tall, and my ceiling is low for her, so she often talks to me from the landing.

Anyway I'd heard her coming, so I was in bed with my whole head shoved under my pillow, praying frantically that nothing showed.

I could smell her, it was the wildest thing – her own smell, sort of sweaty but sweet, and then on top of it her perfume, like an ice-pick stuck in my nose. I didn't actually hear a word she said, I was too scared, and also I had this ripply shaking feeling inside me, a high that was only partly terror.

See, I realized all of a sudden, with this big blossom of surprise, that I didn't have to be scared of Hilda, or anybody. I was strong, my wolf-body was strong, and anyhow one clear look at me and she would drop dead.

What a relief, though, when she went away. I was dying to get out from under the weight of the covers, and besides I had to sneeze. Also I recognized that part of the energy roaring around inside me was hunger.

They went to bed – I heard their voices even in their bedroom, though not exactly what they said, which was fine. The words weren't important any more, I could tell more from the tone of what they were saying.

Like I knew they were going to do it, and I was right. I could hear them messing around right through the walls, which was also something new, and I have never been so embarrassed in my life. I couldn't even put my hands over my ears, because my hands were paws.

So while I was waiting for them to go to sleep, I looked myself over in the big mirror on my closet door.

There was this big wolf head with a long slim muzzle and a thick ruff around my neck. The ruff stood up as I growled and backed up a little.

Which was silly of course, there was no wolf in the bedroom but me. But I was all strung out, I guess, and one wolf, me in my wolf-body, was as much as I could handle the idea of, let alone two wolves, me and my reflection.

After that first shock, it was great. I kept turning one way and another for different views.

I was thin, with these long, slender legs but strong, you could see the muscles, and feet a little bigger than I would have picked. But I'll take four big feet over two big boobs any day.

My face was terrific, with jaggedy white ripsaw teeth and eyes that were small and clear and gleaming in the moonlight. The tail was a little bizarre, but I got used to it, and actually it had a nice plumey shape. My shoulders were big and covered with long, glossy-looking fur, and I had this neat colouring, dark on the back and a sort of melting silver on my front and underparts.

The thing was, though, my tongue, hanging out. I had a lot of trouble with that, it looked gross and silly at the same time. I mean, that was *my tongue*, about a foot long and neatly draped over the points of my bottom canines. That was when I realized that I didn't have a whole lot of expressions to use, not with that face, which was more like a mask.

But it was alive, it was my face, those were my own long black lips that my tongue licked.

No doubt about it, this was *me*. I was a werewolf, like in the movies they showed over Halloween weekend. But it wasn't anything like your ugly movie werewolf that's just some guy loaded up with pounds and pounds of make-up. I was *gorgeous*.

I didn't want to just hang around admiring myself in the mirror, though. I couldn't stand being cooped up in that stuffy, smell-crowded room.

When everything settled down and I could hear Dad and Hilda breathing the way they do when they're sleeping, I snuck out.

The dark wasn't very dark to me, and the cold felt sharp like vinegar, but not in a hurting way. Every place I went, there were these currents like waves in the air, and I could draw them in through my long wolf nose and roll the smell of them over the back of my tongue. It was like a whole different world, with bright sounds everywhere and rich, strong smells.

And I could run.

I started running because a car came by while I was sniffing at the garbage bags on the curb, and I was really scared of being seen in the headlights. So I took off down the dirt alley between our house and the Morrisons' next door, and holy cow, I could tear along with hardly a sound, I could jump their picket fence without even thinking about it. My back legs were like steel springs and I came down solid and square on four legs with almost no shock at all, let alone worrying about losing my balance or twisting an ankle.

Man, I could run through that chilly air all thick and moist with smells, I could almost fly. It was like last year, when I didn't have boobs bouncing and yanking in front even when I'm only walking fast.

Just two rows of neat little bumps down the curve of my belly. I sat down and looked.

I tore open garbage bags to find out about the smells in them, but I didn't eat anything from them. I wasn't about to chow down on other people's stale hotdog-ends and pizza crusts and fat and bones scraped off their plates and all mixed in with mashed potatoes and stuff.

When I found places where dogs had stopped and made their mark, I squatted down and pissed there too, right on top. I just wiped them *out*.

I bounded across that enormous lawn around the Wanscombe place, where nobody but the oriental gardener ever sets foot, and walked up the back and over the top of their BMW, leaving big fat paw-prints all over it. Nobody saw me, nobody heard me, I was a shadow.

Well, except for the dogs, of course.

There was a lot of barking when I went by, real hysterics, and at first I was really scared. But then I popped out of an alley up on Ridge Road, where the big houses are, right in front of about six dogs that run together. Their owners let them out all night and don't care if they get hit by a car.

They'd been trotting along with the wind behind them, checking out all the garbage bags set out for pick-up the next morning. When they saw me, one of them let out a yelp of surprise, and they all skidded to a stop.

Six of them. I was scared. I growled.

The dogs turned fast, banging into each other in their hurry, and trotted away.

I don't know what they would have done if they met a real wolf, but I was something special, I guess.

I followed them.

They scattered and ran.

Well, I ran too, and this was a different kind of running. I mean, I stretched, and I raced, and there was this joy. I chased one of them.

Zig, zag, this little terrier kind of dog tried to cut left and dive under the gate of somebody's front walk, all without a sound – he was running too hard to yell, and I was happy running quiet.

Just before he could ooze under the gate, I caught up with him and without thinking I grabbed the back of his neck and pulled him off his feet and gave him a shake as hard as I could, from side to side.

I felt his neck crack, the sound vibrated through all the bones of my face.

I picked him up in my mouth, and it was like he hardly weighed a thing. I trotted away holding him up off the ground, and under a bush in Baker's Park I held him down with my paws and I bit into his belly, that was still warm and quivering.

Like I said, I was hungry.

The blood gave me this rush like you wouldn't believe. I stood there a minute looking around and licking my lips, just sort of panting and tasting the taste because I was stunned by it, it was like eating honey or the best chocolate malted you ever had.

So I put my head down and chomped that little dog, like shoving your face into a pizza and inhaling it. God, I was *starved*, so I didn't mind that the meat was tough and rank-tasting after that first wonderful bite. I even licked blood off the ground after, never mind the grit mixed in.

I ate two more dogs that night, one that was tied up on a clothes-line in a cruddy yard full of rusted out car-parts down on the South side, and one fat old yellow dog out snuffling around on his own and way too slow. He tasted pretty bad, and by then I was feeling full, so I left a lot.

I strolled around the park, shoving the swings with my big black wolf nose, and I found the bench where Mr Granby sits and feeds the pigeons every day, never mind that nobody else wants the dirty birds around crapping on their cars. I took a dump there, right where he sits.

Then I gave the setting moon a goodnight, which came out quavery and wild. 'Loo-loo-loo!' And I loped toward home, springing off the thick pads of my paws and letting my tongue loll out and feeling generally super.

I slipped inside and trotted upstairs, and in my room I stopped to look at myself in the mirror.

As gorgeous as before, and only a few dabs of blood on me, which I took time to lick off. I did get a little worried – I mean, suppose that was it, suppose having killed and eaten what I'd killed in my wolf shape, I was stuck in this shape forever? Like, if you wander into a fairy castle and eat or drink anything, that's it, you can't ever leave. Suppose when the morning came I didn't change back?

Well, there wasn't much I could do about that one way or the other, and to tell the truth, I felt like I wouldn't mind; it had been worth it.

When I was nice and clean, including licking off my own bottom, which seemed like a perfectly normal and nice thing to do at the time, I jumped up on the bed, curled up, and corked right off. When I woke up with the sun in my eyes, there I was, my own self again.

It was very strange, grabbing breakfast and wearing my old sweatshirt that wallowed all over me so I didn't stick out so much, while Hilda yawned and shuffled around in her robe and slippers and acted like her and Dad hadn't been doing it last night, which I knew different.

And plus, it was perfectly clear that she didn't have a clue about what *I* had been doing, which gave me a strange feeling.

One of the things about growing up which they're careful not to tell you is, you start having more things you don't talk to your parents about. And I had a doozie.

Hilda goes, 'What's the matter, are you off Sugar Pops now? Honestly, Kelsey, I can't keep up with you! And why can't you wear something nicer than that old shirt to school? Oh, I get it: disguise, right?'

She sighed and looked at me kind of sad but smiling, her hands on her hips. 'Kelsey, Kelsey,' she goes, 'if only I'd had half of what you've got when *I* was a girl – I was flat as an ironing board, and it made me so miserable, I can't tell you.'

She's still real thin and neat-looking, so what does she know about it? But she meant well, and anyhow I was feeling so good I didn't argue.

I didn't change my shirt, though.

That night I didn't turn into a wolf. I laid there waiting, but though the moon came up, nothing happened no matter how hard I tried, and after a while I went and looked out the window and realized that the moon wasn't really full any more, it was getting smaller.

I wasn't so much relieved as sorry. I bought a calendar at the school book sale two weeks later, and I checked the full moon nights coming up and waited anxiously to see what would happen.

Meantime, things rolled along as usual. I got a rash of zits on my chin. I would look in the mirror and think about my wolf-face, that had beautiful sleek fur instead of zits.

Zits and all I went to Angela Durkin's party, and next day Billy Linden told everybody that I went in one of the bedrooms at

Angela's and made out with him, which I did not. But since no grown-ups were home and Fat Joey brought grass to the party, most of the kids were stoned and didn't know who did what or where anyhow.

As a matter of fact, Billy once actually did get a girl in Seven B high one time out in his parents' garage, and him and two of his friends did it to her while she was zonked out of her mind, or any way they said they did, and she was too embarrassed to say anything one way or the other, and a little while later she changed schools.

How I know about it is the same way everybody else does, which is because Billy was the biggest boaster in the whole school, and you could never tell if he was lying or not.

So I guess it wasn't so surprising that some people believed what Billy said about me. Gerry-Anne quit talking to me after that. Meantime Hilda got pregnant.

This turned into a huge discussion about how Hilda had been worried about her biological clock so she and Dad had decided to have a kid, and I shouldn't mind, it would be fun for me and good preparation for being a mother myself later on, when I found some nice guy and got married.

Sure. Great preparation. Like Mary O'Hare in my class, who gets to change her youngest baby sister's diapers all the time, yick. She jokes about it, but you can tell she really hates it. Now it looked like it was my turn coming up, as usual.

The only thing that made life bearable was my secret.

'You're laid back today,' Devon Brown said to me in the lunchroom one day after Billy had been especially obnoxious, trying to flick rolled up pieces of bread from his table so they would land on my chest. Devon was sitting with me because he was bad at French, my only good subject, and I was helping him out with some verbs. I guess he wanted to know why I wasn't upset because of Billy picking on me. He goes, 'How come?'

'That's a secret,' I said, thinking about what Devon would say if he knew a werewolf was helping him with his French: *loup*, *manger*.

He goes, 'What secret?' Devon has freckles and is actually kind of cute-looking.

'A *secret*,' I go, 'so I can't tell you, dummy.'

He looks real superior and he goes, 'Well, it can't be much of a secret, because girls can't keep secrets, everybody knows that.'

Sure, like that kid Sara in Eight B who it turned out her own father had been molesting her for years, but she never told anybody until some psychologist caught on from some tests we all had to take in Seventh Grade. Up till then, Sara kept her secret fine.

And I kept mine, marking off the days on the calendar. The only part I didn't look forward to was having a period again, which last time came right before the change.

When the time came, I got crampy and more zits popped out on my face, but I didn't have a period.

I changed, though.

The next morning they were talking in school about a couple of prize miniature Schnauzers at the Wanscombes that had been hauled out of their yard by somebody and killed, and almost nothing left of them.

Well, my stomach turned a little when I heard some kids describing what Mr Wanscombe had found over in Baker's Park, 'the remains', as people said. I felt a little guilty, too, because Mrs Wanscombe had really loved those little dogs, which somehow I didn't think about at all when I was a wolf the night before, trotting around hungry in the moonlight.

I knew those Schnauzers personally, so I was sorry, even if they were irritating little mutts that made a lot of noise.

But heck, the Wanscombes shouldn't have left them out all night in the cold. Anyhow, they were rich, they could buy new ones if they wanted.

Still and all, though. I mean, dogs are just dumb animals. If they're mean, it's because they're wired that way or somebody made them mean, they can't help it. They can't just decide to be nice, like a person can. And plus, they don't taste so great, I think because they put so much junk in commercial dog-foods – anti-worm medicine and ashes and ground-up fish, stuff like that. Ick.

In fact after the second Schnauzer I had felt sort of sick and I didn't sleep real well that night. So I was not in a great mood to start with; and that was the day that my new brassiere disappeared while I was in gym. Later on I got passed a note telling me where to find it; stapled to the bulletin board outside the Principal's office, where everybody could see that I was trying a bra with an underwire.

Naturally, it had to be Stacey Buhl that grabbed my bra while I was changing for gym and my back was turned, since she was now hanging out with Billy and his friends.

Billy went around all day making bets at the top of his lungs on how soon I would be wearing a D-cup.

Stacey didn't matter, she was just a jerk. Billy mattered. He had wrecked me in that school forever, with his nasty mind and his big, fat mouth. I was past crying or fighting and getting punched out. I was boiling, I had had enough crap from him, and I had an idea.

I followed Billy home and waited on his porch until his mom came home and she made him come down and talk to me. He stood in the doorway and talked through the screen door, eating a banana and lounging around like he didn't have a care in the world.

So he goes, 'Whatcha want, Boobs?'

I stammered a lot, being I was so nervous about telling such big lies, but that probably made me sound more believable.

I told him that I would make a deal with him: I would meet him that night in Baker's Park, late, and take off my shirt and bra and let him do whatever he wanted with my boobs if that would satisfy his curiosity and he would find somebody else to pick on and leave me alone.

'What?' he said, staring at my chest with his mouth open. His voice squeaked and he was practically drooling on the floor. He couldn't believe his good luck.

I said the same thing over again.

He almost came out onto the porch to try it right then and there. 'Well, shit,' he goes, lowering his voice a lot, 'why didn't you say something before? You really mean it?'

I go, 'Sure,' though I couldn't look at him.

After a minute he goes, 'Okay, it's a deal. Listen, Kelsey, if you like it, can we, uh, do it again, you know?'

I go, 'Sure. But Billy, one thing: this is a secret, between just you and me. If you tell anybody, if there's one other person hanging around out there tonight—'

'Oh no,' he goes, real fast, 'I won't say a thing to anybody, honest. Not a word, I promise!'

Not until afterward, of course, was what he meant, which if there was one thing Billy Linden couldn't do, it was keep quiet if he knew something bad about another person.

'You're gonna like it, I know you are,' he goes, speaking strictly for himself as usual. 'Jeez. I can't believe this!'

But he did, the dork.

I couldn't eat much for dinner that night, I was too excited, and I went upstairs early to do homework, I told Dad and Hilda.

Then I waited for the moon, and when it came, I changed.

Billy was in the park. I caught a whiff of him, very sweaty and excited, but I stayed cool. I snuck around for a while, as quiet as I could — which was real quiet — making sure none of his stupid friends were lurking around. I mean, I wouldn't have trusted just his promise for a million dollars.

I passed up half a hamburger lying in the gutter where somebody had parked for lunch next to Baker's Park. My mouth watered, but I didn't want to spoil my appetite. I was hungry and happy, sort of singing inside my own head, 'Shoo, fly, pie, and an apple-pandowdie . . .'

Without any sound, of course.

Billy had been sitting on a bench, his hands in his pockets, twisting around to look this way and that way, watching for me — for my human self — to come join him. He had a jacket on, being it was very chilly out.

He didn't stop to think that maybe a sane person wouldn't be crazy enough to sit out there and take off her top leaving her naked skin bare to the breeze. But that was Billy all right, totally fixed on his own greedy self and without a single thought for anybody else. I bet all he could think about was what a great scam this was, to feel up old Boobs in the park and then crow about it all over school.

Now he was walking around the park, kicking at the sprinkler-heads and glancing up every once in a while, frowning and looking sulky.

I could see he was starting to think that I might have stood him up. Maybe he even suspected that old Boobs was lurking around watching him and laughing to herself because he had fallen for a trick. Maybe old Boobs had even brought some kids from school with her to see what a jerk he was.

Actually that would have been pretty good, except Billy probably would have broken my nose for me again, or worse, if I'd tried it.

'Kelsey?' he goes, sounding mad.

I didn't want him stomping off home in a huff. I moved up closer, and I let the bushes swish a little around my shoulders.

He goes, 'Hey, Kelse, it's late, where've you been?'

I listened to the words, but mostly I listened to the little thread of worry flickering in his voice, low and high, high and low, as he tried to figure out what was going on.

I let out the whisper of a growl.

He stood real still, staring at the bushes, and he goes, 'That you, Kelse? Answer me.'

I was wild inside, I couldn't wait another second. I tore through the bushes and leaped for him, flying.

He stumbled backward with a squawk — 'What!' — jerking his hands up in front of his face, and he was just sucking in a big breath to yell with when I hit him like a demo-derby truck.

I jammed my nose past his feeble claws and chomped down hard on his face.

No sound came out of him except this wet, thick gurgle, which I could more taste than hear because the sound came right into my mouth with the gush of his blood and the hot mess of meat and skin that I tore away and swallowed.

He thrashed around, hitting at me, but I hardly felt anything through my fur. I mean, he wasn't so big and strong laying there on the ground with me straddling him all lean and wiry with wolf-muscle. And plus, he was in shock. I got a strong whiff from below as he let go of everything right into his pants.

Dogs were barking, but so many people around Baker's Park have dogs to keep out burglars, and the dogs make such a racket all the time, that nobody pays any attention. I wasn't worried. Anyway, I was too busy to care.

I nosed in under what was left of Billy's jaw and I bit his throat out.

Now let him go around telling lies about people.

His clothes were a lot of trouble and I really missed having hands. I managed to drag his shirt out of his belt with my teeth, though, and it was easy to tear his belly open. Pretty messy, but once I got in there, it was better than Thanksgiving dinner. Who would think that somebody as horrible as Billy Linden could taste so *good*?

He was barely moving by then, and I quit thinking about him as Billy Linden any more. I quit thinking at all, I just pushed my head in and pulled out delicious steaming chunks and ate until I was picking at tidbits, and everything was getting cold.

On the way home I saw a police car cruising the neighborhood the way they do sometimes. I hid in the shadows and of course they never saw me.

There was a lot of washing up to do in the morning, and when Hilda saw my sheets she shook her head and she goes, 'You should be more careful about keeping track of your period so as not to get caught by surprise.'

Everybody in school knew something had happened to Billy Linden, but it wasn't until the day after that that they got the word. Kids stood around in little huddles trading rumors about how some wild animal had chewed Billy up. I would walk up and listen and add a really gross remark or two, like part of the game of thrilling each other green and nauseous with made-up details to see who would upchuck first.

Not me, that's for sure. I mean, when somebody went on about how Billy's whole head was gnawed down to the skull and they didn't even know who he was except from the bus pass in his wallet, I got a little urpy. It's amazing the things people will dream up. But when I thought about what I had actually done to Billy, I had to smile.

It felt totally wonderful to walk through the halls without having anybody yelling, 'Hey, Boobs!'

There are people who just plain do not deserve to live. And the same goes for Fat Joey, if he doesn't quit crowding me in science lab, trying to get a feel.

One funny thing, though, I don't get periods at all any more. I get a little crampy, and my breasts get sore, and I break out more than usual – and then instead of bleeding, I change.

Which is fine with me, though I take a lot more care now about how I hunt on my wolf nights. I stay away from Baker's Park. The suburbs go on for miles and miles, and there are lots of places I can hunt and still get home by morning. A running wolf can cover a lot of ground.

And I make sure I make my kills where I can eat in private, so no cop car can catch me unawares, which could easily have happened that night when I killed Billy, I was so deep into the eating thing that first time. I look around a lot more now when I'm eating a kill, I keep watch.

Good thing it's only once a month that this happens, and only a couple of nights. 'The Full Moon Killer' has the whole State up in arms and terrified as it is.

Eventually I guess I'll have to go somewhere else, which I'm not looking forward to at all. If I can just last until I can have a car of my own, life will get a lot easier.

Meantime, some wolf nights I don't even feel like hunting. Mostly I'm not as hungry as I was those first times. I think I must have been storing up my appetite for a long time. Sometimes I just prowl around and I run, boy do I run.

If I am hungry, sometimes I eat from the garbage instead of killing somebody. It's no fun, but you do get a taste for it. I don't mind garbage as long as once in a while I can have the real thing fresh-killed, nice and wet. People can be awfully nasty, but they sure taste sweet.

I do pick and choose, though. I look for people sneaking around in the middle of the night, like Billy, waiting in the park that time. I figure they've got to be out looking for trouble at that hour, so whose fault is it if they find it? I have done a lot more for the burglary problem around Baker's Park than a hundred dumb 'watchdogs', believe me.

Gerry-Anne is not only talking to me again, she has invited me to go on a double-date with her. Some guy she met at a party invited her, and he has a friend. They're both from Fawcett Junior High across town, which will be a change. I was nervous, but finally I said yes. We're going to the movies next weekend. My first real date! I am still pretty nervous, to tell the truth.

For New Year's, I have made two solemn vows.

One is that on this date I will not worry about my chest, I will not be self-conscious, even if the guy stares.

The other is, I'll never eat another dog.

If the Word was to the Wise

(1990)

CAROL EMSHWILLER

It is written that what is written shall be done as it is written, and that the sacred books and secret words shall remain sacred and secret. It is written that what is written shall be the law of the land and that those who rule the words shall be the leaders of the land. It is written that the leaders shall live in the towers and turrets of the library, and that they shall heed the words of the books therein and shall take an oath to do so. Since the library opens on Monday, Monday is the first day of a possible five-day communion with books, so Monday will be a sacred and a joyful day, and on that day the flags of the library will fly.

The word for word will be word, and the word for library will be library, and the word for law will be law and it will be obeyed.

The library is the tallest building in the city. No other building is ever to be as tall or as magnificent. It has nine white towers where eighty pale blue flags fly. Inside, silks hang along the walls. Alabaster lamps in niches give the interior a soft, mysterious glow in keeping with the mysteries of the words. In summer, the bronze doors that face east are opened at dawn in order that the first light should penetrate deep into the malachite lobby. Anyone can enter, but over the door there is a warning:

BEWARE ALL YE WHO ENTER FOR HERE IS UNDERSTANDING
BEYOND ALL UNDERSTANDING.

In the several sub-basements of the library there are two safes. One contains the secret, sacred writings of the laws of the written word which are the laws of the library and the laws of the land. This safe is opened frequently in order for the members of the central book committee to refer to the written word. The other safe is larger and more secure. This one contains the banned books. Someone did, they said, enter this safe many years ago and read, they said, several pages of lewd and anti-library writings. They said he even wrote down what he had read, but that was found and burned, and the person was not killed, not confined, but deprived of communication. His tongue was split and his upper teeth pulled out, the tendons of the thumb and fingers of both hands were cut so that writing was out of the question also. This was so long ago that no one today, they said, remembers exactly what that safe contains, and we thank God for that. We had, they said, wiped out, once and for all, all the evil books by appropriating them and locking them up. We lived, therefore, in harmony and with only good words.

The princes of the library are housed in the sub-basements also, for they are the ones who guard the safes. I was one of them. (It's an honor and a privilege and I took pride in walking about the library and being called prince.) We were the ones who saw to it that those who visited the safe that contained the words of the laws were qualified to do so and had permission from the chairman of the central book committee. Of course there was no permission, ever, for visiting the banned books, even for the members of the book committee. They said the only possible reason for entering that room would be in order to bring more books in, and this hadn't happened in all the time since I had become a prince of the library.

None of us princes has ever entered either of these rooms, though we know the combination, but we guard each other as much as we guard anyone, and we've made vows. I had never been tempted to enter the safes, nor had I allowed myself to wonder what could be in those rooms in all my eighteen years of service. (I came here as a boy of fifteen, having sworn the oaths, and being, already, six foot tall, and having, already, learned to take words seriously.)

But then there was Josephine. She was older than she looked, but I liked it that she was my age. I wouldn't have known what to do with her if she had been a teenager, which is the age she looked. I had lived so much of my life among the princes that I'd lost the 'family' touch. I'd forgotten what it was like to have people of your own. Josephine took the lead. She went after what she wanted. She offered me a captaincy and a space of my own on the eighteenth floor and she had the power to get it for me. At least she said she did, and I believed her because she was the daughter of the head librarian. It was not as powerful a position as if she were the daughter of the chairman of the central book committee, but still her mother was a person to be reckoned with and I thought might actually have the power to do as Josephine said she could. Josephine said the room would have to be small, pieced out of someone else's apartment, and it might not look towards the river, but inwards towards the towers (which I would find – I would *still* find – as beautiful as any outside view could be, for the white, glazed tiles of the towers reflect the colors of the sky and so are endlessly changing and, on sunny Mondays when the flags fly, I can't think of anything I'd rather look out at. Eighty! Imagine that. Eighty blue flags.)

The view from Josephine's balcony was exciting in a different way. Daytimes the river is full of sailing vessels (some quite large), and skiffs and barges – often library barges full of books, some-times small boats rowed by several princes such as myself, but in the service of some lesser library. At night the lanterns on the far banks looked as though they were lit up for a festival. It's a view not many princes of the library have been privileged to see. I was grateful for it. In fact I wasn't sure I wanted an apartment on the eighteenth floor. I just wanted Josephine and that things should stay as they were.

I wasn't sure what Josephine wanted. Perhaps she didn't know herself. I often thought she chose me not because of me at all, but because I was a prince and had access to forbidden rooms. Any prince would have done as well. She even told me so to my face, laughing at me, but then she would take it back – say that that was her idea at first, but that it wasn't any more – that she loved me for me. I didn't know what to believe, but actually I didn't care, as long as I had the privileges of her balcony and bedroom.

You might think that I would regret the promises I made to her in our moments of passion, but what else had I to give? She already had everything and she gave so much to me, including the river view and boats and lights along the shore. What could I give her but my one and only gift, access to words which we had probably forgotten the meanings of, let alone how to pronounce them – access to excesses neither of us could imagine in our wildest conjectures.

Yet for all this, she was an innocent – in many ways as innocent as she looked. Perhaps her desire to see forbidden documents was out of that same innocence. How could she foresee, being who she was, words that might be dangerous – that might harm?

It was this innocence that lured me. I especially liked it in her voice. She sang, but not professionally. Her voice wasn't powerful enough. It was fluty, breathy, young . . . She never suspected that her voice was too small to ever amount to anything. She was even innocent of the fact that she couldn't carry a tune and that her rhythms were often off in odd ways. She made the rounds but no one hired her. Yet her voice was to my taste. It was all of a piece with her pale beauty. Like her voice, which no one thought worth listening to but me, no one but me thought she was beautiful. Perhaps she could read this in my eyes. Perhaps this was why she picked me.

Though it was she who tempted me, I knew full well that if the thing was done, I couldn't blame her for it. And it was I who had sworn the oaths, not she.

I didn't rush into it. I asked her, over and over, why anyone would want to see subversive books, least of all she. Didn't we already have more than enough words? More than enough concepts? More, in fact, than we could handle as it was? More than any one person could learn about in a lifetime? We already had ideas that ought to be voiced only in the privacy of one's own home, and we had words for no other purpose than to be said in anger; there were even books that came in plain brown wrappers. Why would anyone want or need even more outrageous ideas than we had?

'Because they're there,' she always said. 'Because they exist.'

I told her she shouldn't be overawed by what she didn't know. I said she ought to learn to live with a little bit of ignorance. I tickled her toes as I said it. She would think I was just teasing, but I wasn't. 'Might just as well,' I said, 'write down wrong words and things not true, so that what is written is lies.' Even as I said it, I felt I had blasphemed.

Josephine turned away and looked out the window to the far side of the river, squinting. I stopped stroking and tickling her feet and we were silent for a long time.

We were lying sideways across her hammock, I facing upriver, she, facing down. My boots were on the floor, my cap of honor carefully on top of them. The cap was the pale blue of the library – the honorable blue of honorable words.

Suddenly we turned to hold each other for comfort, and the holding turned into caresses, and she said (and it wasn't the first time), 'What lewd things do you suppose they have in that safe about how to make love? What evil ways that we can't even think of?' And we began to think of the ways and to laugh, and then we tried to find the ways: backwards, forwards, upside down, until we fell out of the hammock (and it wasn't the first time).

Afterwards Josephine wondered if everything in the safe might be hilarious, but I said that was unlikely.

At that time I wasn't sure if I would open the secret safe for her or not. In fact I really thought I wouldn't. I didn't want anything to change. I stalled her. I kept questioning her. But then things changed.

Normally Josephine's mother never bothered to come down to her daughter's apartment. Normally Josephine's mother never bothered with her daughter at all. I wondered about this sometimes, but then I knew that the head librarian had a busy schedule. And then Josephine was a grown-up – in her thirties as I was. Yet I did think that she and her mother might have been friends and talked now and then, but they never did that I knew of. But then her mother did come and it was clear that she had come in anger, for she bounded in, slammed the door and shouted for Josephine, whom she called Joe. (Josephine was so unlike a 'Joe' that I was almost as shocked by that as I was by what happened afterwards.)

We never did find out what that first anger was about because she was even angrier when she found me there, naked, and her daughter dressed in what was, essentially, nothing but mosquito netting. (We had been, again that day, playing the same game of 'What is written in the forbidden safe?')

'Not worthy of the word,' she said. 'Either of you.' And to Josephine, 'Must you pick lovers from the gutter?'

I thought she hadn't noticed my uniform and my cap on my boots beside the couch. 'I'm a prince of the library,' I said.

'Rats,' she said, 'from the cellars. That's what everybody calls you.'

Of course it wasn't the first time I'd heard this. We even called ourselves cellar rats sometimes, but I never expected to hear it from the very people who were the bosses of our bosses, people we considered our kings and queens, and for whom we were the princes. Here was one of the very ones who had told us we were princes and should conduct ourselves as such, saying, 'Rat, rat, rat . . .' I was not only shocked by that, but also by the fact that one of the leaders of the library could be so out of control.

When she could catch her breath, she told Josephine that she might at least have had a smidgen of dignity for the sake of her mother and her mother's job, and then she turned to me and told me that if she found me on any floor higher than the first basement she would have me de-capped and forbidden to wear library blues ever again.

That I couldn't be on or above the ground floor meant I had no access to the library books which occupied the first seven floors of the library. We princes had access to all seven floors if we were so inclined, which was more than most citizens had. I had (I realized it right then) not taken advantage of my privileges, and now access to 'understanding beyond all understanding' was out of the question to me forever.

And then there was the fragrance of the library on those days when incense burned in the lower halls! And the soft light from the alabaster lamps! Often I sat among the books, not to read, but to be in the silence and the glow. And I knew I was welcome – that the patrons of the words liked to see the princes come and sit with them. They would smile and call me prince. The library was, in a way, father and mother to me after I had left that distant village in order to come here to be a prince.

What Josephine's mother said also meant that I had no access to the elevators that took me up to Josephine's rooms.

And how could Josephine's mother say we were rats to everybody? When I walked the streets I could see the whole world of words knew we were word-proper men in responsible positions. I was thinking it would serve Josephine's mother right if her daughter *did* enter that safe and if she *did* read whatever there was in there that was the most lewd and the most subversive. I no longer had any desire to save either myself or Josephine from her crazy wishes. In fact I hoped she would be caught and her mother shamed by it. And yet I did . . . I really did love Josephine. But I wanted her to share my fate – to be dragged down with me so we would still be together one way or another. I was partly banned and partly cursed, why not both of us completely cursed? Or blessed as the case may be. 'Then shall your eyes be opened and ye shall be as Gods.' Our eyes will be opened and we will know what is to be known.

Josephine's mother said she would talk to Josephine later – that she had to leave right then because she couldn't stand the sight of me.

As I dressed, I told Josephine to meet me in a lower hall the next night . . . that we would go into the safe. That we might as well do it, and it would have to be now or never.

She looked frightened, but I thought she was more frightened of her mother than of any forbidden room. She said she would be there, but I could see the desire for it had left her. It wasn't a game any more. I wasn't sure if she'd be there or not, but I thought that if she was, it would be a sign that she cared about me – that she could be with me without the tickling and the giggling and the pretending, and that she could defy her mother for my sake.

And she was there. She was even early, waiting for me. I couldn't help but smile – though I was worried about my future, which didn't look good no matter what happened now. She came into my arms as if she really loved me and we held each other a long time. It wasn't dangerous for us in those lower corridors. It wasn't that unusual for princes to bring girlfriends here. There were few places a prince could take someone where they could be alone for a while. We wouldn't be noticed when other princes came by.

After we had held each other long enough to soak up comfort and courage, I told her my plan. It wouldn't be hard if I could be quick with the combination. Things were quite lax, actually. We princes were serious about our guarding, but it had been decades since anyone had tried to get into those safes without authorization. We put in our time, dutifully, but we didn't expect confrontations. Changing of the guards took place in a front hallway some distance from the safes and the ceremony had, in recent years, evolved into an elaborate rite which we princes felt was worthy of the word and of the library. We liked the pomp of it. Josephine and I would simply wait in an adjoining hall listening to the clump, clump of the guards until they clumped away for the ceremony.

But just as the footsteps faded and Josephine and I were about to make a run for the safe, there was a squeak and grind, and, not three feet from where we were standing, a section of a malachite panel seemed to split and out came the head of the central book committee and hurried to the safe. If he'd looked about anxiously he'd have caught us, but he seemed sure of himself as though he'd done this so often he no longer thought much about it. It took him only a second to open the door. He bypassed all the compli- cated turnings of the dials and simply pulled a single small lever and the safe opened. He is a bulky man, but graceful for all that and he slid in sideways and the door shut behind him silently.

Josephine and I looked at each other as though the world had turned upside down which, for us, it had. We hesitated only a few moments and then we followed, using the same little lever. The door swung open and we were in. Only when the door closed behind us did we wonder how we would be able to get out of there. As it happened that was taken care of.

It was a large nondescript room and nobody was in it. There were only a few book racks along the walls and these were more than half empty, the books that remained lying helter-skelter on the shelves without dignity. There were several mismatched long tables and a few cast off chairs, none of them worthy of the library. (We princes had better than these in our barracks.) On the tables there were several books lying as though recently put down. Some were open and turned over, their backs broken. There were even some on the floor, corners bent from having been dropped and pages dog-eared. Neither of us had ever seen books that had been treated this way. Though there was dust everywhere, there were signs of recent use, clean spots and smudged spots. Obviously people read here. We turned to some of the books to see what they were about. What we glanced at didn't seem to have anything new to us: bondage, rape, sex with animals ... We'd heard of these before. But we didn't want to spend much time with the books. We were too worried about where the head of the book committee might have gone and when he would be coming back. There were no good hiding places in that room.

We found the secret door by the smeared place along the wall where many dusty hands had worked another lever. You could see, along the floor, that one of the bookcases used to be pulled over to cover it but, obviously, nobody bothered with that any more. Above this door someone had pencilled rather carelessly the same words that were over the library doors:

> BEWARE ALL YE WHO ENTER FOR HERE IS UNDERSTANDING
> BEYOND ALL UNDERSTANDING.

Behind the door I thought I could hear the sound of running water and strange cries. Also I thought I heard a horse whinny, and birds, and laughter, and I remembered what Josephine had said about it, maybe, being hilarious, and I felt the prickle of gooseflesh along my arms.

All through this Josephine and I had kept looking at each other, frightened and awed, not knowing what to think. And now we looked at each other again. She nodded. 'We've gone so far,' she said, 'one more thing won't make any difference.' I pulled the lever then and the door opened. It was as thick as a safe door. As it opened the sounds came clear. Yes, water, shouting, squeals, but not a single word.

Inside was a garden ... a jungle ... Fountains, hanging plants, bushes, huge ferns. Great purplish lights overhead, and people – all naked, all pawing at each other, making animal sounds and laughing hysterically. Here were the élite of the library – even Josephine's mother – scorning the word and living out the forbidden secrets of the forbidden safe. There was a horse and a goat. There was a peacock making dreadful squawks, but no more dreadful than the squawks of the people. There were yaps, yowls, howls, caws, caterwaulings, and great ha-has. They, at least, found it hilarious.

Josephine and I quickly took off our clothes in order that we might hide among the naked bodies and not be found out. Josephine pulled her hair down to cover her face as much as she could and we stood there, holding hands, knowing that all the words we had learned were lies – that the word was not the word as we understood it – that things were not done according to what was written, or, at least not according to any writing we knew of.

Of course being naked didn't hide us for long. Josephine's mother recognized her at once. We were seized and, in a drunken, laughing frenzy, knives were brought out, and hammers, and pliers. All the people looked as though they finally had, in us, what they'd been waiting for and hoping for for a long time. I saw Josephine's mother give the first blow that knocked out her front teeth, screaming at her the only words I heard in that place at all. 'Stupid,' she yelled, 'Crazy, crazy. You could have been down here any time you wanted if you'd picked a proper lover from the right class of person. You could have been down here with the best of us any night you wanted to, wordless.' You might think this was the end of words for Josephine and me, but I have someone who knows my signals, even after all these years, she still knows. My mother reads my eyes and lips, counts taps, knows my gestures. She writes it out and I nod yes or no. Then she will tell.

And Josephine and I still have each other. Our eyes say all that needs to be said.

Trial by Teaspoon

(1992)

LYNDA RAJAN

She wasn't what you'd call a very nice sort of person, my friend
Mrs McBride. Well, she wasn't really my friend, come to that,
though she thought she was of course. I'd known her, on and off,
more off than on, in fact, for nearly fifty years. Ever since she
married my Angus's best friend's cousin and had her first, five
months later, in the same week as I had my Venetia. Sort of drew
us together, that did. And then they moved in to the house next
door when old Mr McKay passed away. We shared our troubles in
those days. God knows we had enough of them. It was harder for
her than for me, naturally, after her Donald ran off and left her
with three kids, and not even for another woman. She could have
weathered that. But he just couldn't stand Nettie McBride any
longer, so they said. Though she said it was good riddance and
she was better off without him. He always seemed a decent
enough chap to me – but you never know what goes on behind
people's front doors, do you?

What really got me about Nettie was her mean-spiritedness.
She'd borrow a cup of sugar and give you half a cup back. She
would leave your washing hanging out in the rain, even though
she knew you were out and it was nearly dry. And she'd torment
her children – and mine, until I put a stop to it – in nasty little
ways, like the 'joke' she'd play on them with the teaspoon. We'd
be sitting there, round the table, having a cup of tea, the kids all
ranged round beside us, and she'd scoop a spoonful of sugar and
stir it into her tea, sort of thoughtfully, and then she'd take the
spoon out, and press it down on the back of one of their hands.
Red hot it was, and wouldn't they yelp? They'd leap up from the
table, tears in their eyes, and shout 'What did you do that for?'
and she'd laugh, her loud harsh laugh, and say 'I was only joking.
Can't you take a joke?' and look at me and wink, as if I was in it

with her. And I'd glare at her, but she wouldn't care, just carry on laughing at us having no sense of humour. The kids kept away from her after she'd done that a couple of times, but there was always some innocent, some friend of theirs for her to play the trick on.

Or she'd say 'Don't look now, but there's a nightingale (or a wren, or a parrot) on the fence,' and you wouldn't know whether to look or not, wanting to see it but not wanting to frighten it away; so you'd miss it and she would have one up on you because she'd seen it and you hadn't.

Silly little things, I know, but it was the way she did them that made them seem important. Like the time she said, 'Don't look now, but your Venetia's kissing that Hamilton boy behind the lamp-post,' and I did look, and wished I hadn't because Venetia saw me, and thought I was spying on her, and wouldn't speak to me for two days, and didn't stop kissing the Hamilton boy anyway, judging by what happened later.

It was as though Nettie McBride liked to have some kind of hold over you, to know something you didn't, to gloat at your discomfort. Power, I suppose. Though what good it did her I shall never know. We fell out over the lamp-post business and I didn't speak to her again for months, not till she came round with the bootees and bonnet she'd knitted, and even that was sort of triumphal, though it was difficult to put a finger on exactly. And that's how it's been between us over the years, times of a kind of neighbourliness and times of nodding in the street, or not even that.

But after my Angus passed over, two years and three months ago now, she began to call in to see me quite regularly. At first it was to offer help with the funeral arrangements and then to give advice on how to cope without a man, giving me the benefit, if that's the word, of all her years of managing alone. To be honest, I was glad of her company at the beginning. So many of the people I thought were my friends seemed to evaporate when Angus died. They didn't know what to say, or seemed to be embarrassed in my company, and after the funeral was over they just drifted away and got on with their own lives. It was as if I just didn't exist for them any more. I was the same person, but to them I was somehow different. I'll never understand that. Almost as though I had died as well, in a funny sort of way.

Anyway, whatever you might say about Nettie, she kept on coming round, even if it was to organize my life in a way I didn't want it to be organized. Her children had left home years before, and I suppose she was lonely. But I hadn't realized quite how lonely until one day she casually mentioned her plan to me. 'This house is too big for you, Elspeth,' she said. 'It'll be a liability in a few years' time when you can't get upstairs or manage the garden.' It was a bit of a shock, her saying that: pulled me up short, you could say. I was managing perfectly alright, and couldn't really imagine not being able to. After all, Venetia and her husband were always happy to help if I needed someone to clip the hedge, or paint the kitchen ceiling. I said as much to Nettie. She smiled in a patronizing sort of way and said something about them having a family of their own to look after, and not wanting to come chasing up here at my beck and call all the time. As though I was always making a nuisance of myself, which I certainly am not.

'Anyway,' she said, 'I've had a word with the council and they think it's a very good idea.' What was a good idea? Had she been carrying on talking while I was being indignant about what she'd said before and I'd missed it? She hadn't finished. 'It would mean a young family could have my house, and everyone would move up the housing list. The council were very pleased about it. Of course, you could go into their sheltered housing, which would have the same effect, but I thought we would make a good team, you and me. And as I'm a bit more nimble than you, I could have the upstairs rooms.' And then the penny dropped. I stared at Nettie, aghast. She was still talking. 'So the lady from the housing department is coming round here to discuss it with you, tomorrow morning, if that's alright.' It damn well wasn't alright and she knew it. But she had the council on her side, and I had the uncomfortable feeling that I was being outmanoeuvred. A very clever strategist was Nettie McBride. But not quite as clever as me, I like to think.

'Well, Nettie,' I said, turning on my helpless victim voice that I know brings out the worst in her, 'I have to say that it takes a bit of getting used to, that idea. Why don't we have a cup of tea and talk it over before we make any hasty decisions.' I walked over to the stove and struck a match under the kettle. Opening the dresser door, I took out three of my best cups and saucers, and gave them a good polish with the corner of my apron, watching her all the while out of the corner of my eye. I could see the suspense was getting to her; she couldn't make out what I was going to say next. I got the feeling she had rehearsed this little scene before she came round: and that it wasn't going exactly according to plan. I swirled the old tea-leaves round the pot and emptied them into the bucket I keep for compost just outside the back door. The kettle began to whistle and I measured out four caddy-spoons of tea – 'One each and one for the pot,' I said, and poured the boiling water over it. We sat down at the table. It reminded me of the old days, when the children had gathered around us, squabbling for the custard creams amongst the garibaldis.

'Who's the other cup for?' asked Nettie, 'Are you expecting someone? You didn't say.' I glanced at her – enigmatically, I think you would have called it. 'Only Angus,' I said, 'He always comes in for his tea at this time. Needs it after working on the allotment all the afternoon.' She looked at me as though I was mad. 'Don't look now,' I continued, taking a spoonful of sugar from the basin and stirring it into my tea, 'but there he is coming up the path.' A strangled gulp constricted Nettie's throat as she tried to decide whether or not to turn round and look. Curiosity got the better of her, and, at the same time, temptation completely overcame me. As she craned her head round to the window, I removed the spoon from my tea and laid it gently on the back of her sunspotted hand.

I don't think I have ever seen anyone move quite so fast or scream quite so loudly as Nettie did then. In one sweeping movement she scooped up her handbag and shot out of the back door as if her shoes were on fire. As I watched, she skidded to a halt and stepped to the left, then to the right, as if trying to avoid someone who was doing the same.

'Oh, stop it, Nettie!' I called out, 'I was only joking, you know me. Can't you take a joke?'

A stocky figure in a familiar blue anorak and pompom hat drifted through Nettie's shuddering form, floated upwards for several feet and then hovered whilst carefully pouring the contents of my compost bucket over Nettie's beige felt hat. She shrieked in a frenzy of fear and fury and scuttled down the path, dripping potato peelings and tea-leaves as she went.

'I've always wanted to do that,' he said, parking himself down in his usual chair. 'Is this my cup?'

'Oh, Angus!' I laughed till my buttons popped. 'It is so good to have you back. And not a moment too soon!'

Nettie McBride moved into sheltered housing soon after that. I won't be joining her just yet. Angus and I are perfectly happy as we are for the time being.

In the Green Shade of a Bee-Loud Glade

(1993)

L. A. HALL

I was always glad to return to the island heart of the Sanctuary, whether I'd been walking its bounds or leaving it to visit the Watchtower, or, as now, the depot. The bag of provisions I'd collected was slung over my shoulder as I reached the causeway; the waves of the sea-loch lapped against it, the tide turning, ready to divide it once more from the mainland. I paused for a moment, the water not yet anywhere near high enough for me to need to race across lest I be cut off here on the wrong shore.

It was quiet: only the lapping of the small waves broke the silence, and perhaps, almost below the threshold of hearing, the faint distant hum of bees. No bird-song; no sound at all of bird or animal life. I raised my eyes to look for the flash of pink on the other side where the hoopoes were nesting. Perhaps the occasional visitor they had always been, given this mild summer. Or, dared I hope, because of climatic changes a more regular migrant?

I looked across to the headlands, the Watchtower dark against the blue sky streaked here and there with wisps of cloud. Sun glinted like gold-dust on the water. Ahead of me across the already narrowing causeway the glades were green. But no sign of birds, of squirrels. No movement but leaves ruffled by the light breeze.

The silence continued: strange. I had thought it one of those sudden moments of quiet on a summer's afternoon, when the only sounds are those of inanimate nature, the soft soughing of breeze and rustle of foliage – the breathing of the universe.

I shook myself and set off, the water swirling almost to the narrow track where I set my feet. Only when I reached the far side did I see the signs that something was wrong.

Grass crushed down, bushes torn up, trees scarred, ruts of red earth bleeding through the green. Not footprints: the marks of wheels. I shivered, freezing for a moment, and then dropped the bag behind a bush while I got off the track in a hurry, moving cautiously between the trees, ready to drop flat and hide, my ears straining for any sound. But still nothing but the constant lapping of the rising tide.

Should I turn back? Would I be trapped on the island with whatever had already despoiled its margin? Yet the quiet, sinister though it was, reassured me. I could not imagine that whatever had gouged up the ground in that way had done it silently. Nevertheless, I retained caution in my progress to the central glade.

And paused at its edge, studying the scene.

The hut still stood. The garden had been torn up in a brutal but haphazard fashion. On the grass in front of me lay the mangled pink body of one of the hoopoes, stained with blood, once living beauty destroyed and turned to horror.

My stomach heaved, sour matter rising into my throat, but I swallowed it back, the taste continuing to burn in my mouth as I circled the glade, not yet venturing into the open. No human to be seen: only torn corpses of birds and small animals, which had been too tame and trusting to be shy or wary. I had misled them about the beneficence of my kind, and I had done wrong. They had died, cruelly.

Slowly, timidly, I crossed the despoiled glade to the hut. The door was shut as I had left it. I stretched out my hand to the doorknob and drew it back. It had not been locked: why should it have been? This was a Sanctuary, a precious enclave of biodiversity of which I was privileged to be Warden. Who . . . what . . . My stomach heaved again at this contemplation of the unthinkable.

I edged around the hut to the window. The interior was empty, and to all appearance untouched. I opened the door and stumbled over to the chair, falling into it, letting my head drop forward to the table, as sobs welled forth, shaking my body with their intensity.

At length I sat up, wiped my smeary face on my sleeve. The bees! I hadn't even thought of the bees. Those essential factors in the ecosystem, the producers of the honey I delivered to the depot, or turned into mead for that not exactly forbidden if not

exactly licensed trade with the Watchtower. What had happened
to the bees?

I staggered, aching, leaden-footed, through the trees to the
dozen hives at the water's edge. But I could tell that – whatever,
whoever – had not come this far: the signs of damage only
extended to the glade and no further.

There was a gentle humming from the hives. Without veil and
smoke, I dared not venture nearer. I dropped to my knees. The
old superstition, passingly mentioned in the old book from which
I'd learnt such apiary craft as I knew. Telling the bees of disasters.
'Oh bees,' I whispered, 'oh bees,' as I recounted the tale of my
return to the island.

Only then did I skirt round the hives to the lake-edge, to bathe
my filthy sweaty face with water salt as the tears I had cried, but
cool and clear where those had been hot and sticky.

I looked up. Had I heard the cries of birds? Yes. They had not
all been destroyed, some had escaped and they were coming back.
Perhaps, in the undergrowth or the treetops, I would find birds
and animals that had relearnt the ancestral skills of self-preservation
that my too tactful presence had effaced.

What had happened here, today, was petty by comparison with
the eco-crimes that had defaced and deformed our world, I knew.
Yet how? – who . . .? Could the Sanctuary ever be the same?
Would – this – happen again?

The next day I took the boat across to the Watchtower on the
headland, loath as I was to leave the Sanctuary. It was the only
way I could think of to contact the outside world. A message left
at the depot might not be collected for days yet. And surely this –
incident – should be reported, even though there was so much to
do, unsystematic though the despoliation had been. The wanton
careless casual nature of the destruction was perhaps more chilling
than more calculated malice: the herb garden torn up because it
was the first thing encountered within the glade, and easily done;
the henhouse had not been found, was my guess, and the hut left
untouched in spite of its unlocked door.

I rowed steadily across the loch in a light wind, looking back.
From this aspect one could not discern any violation.

I beached the boat and took out the flagons of mead (these had gone unnoticed inside the hut), before I climbed the steep stone steps to the gateway of the Tower. Handing the flagons to the sentry on guard, I said 'Compliments of the Warden of the Sanctuary to the Commander, and could I have a minute or two of his time?' I knew that only one flagon would reach the Commander, and that the other would find its way to the guardroom.

I waited, leaning against the harsh chilly stone wall: no moss or lichen ever grew on Watchtower walls, let alone grass or flowers. Probably the garrison kept them scoured. One of the necessary compromises that had to be made (one could not have Watchtower walls weakened) like the vast latifundia which were the only feasible means of feeding the population. Only in these scattered Sanctuaries could biodiversity, complex eco-systems, be lovingly nurtured. Our future, our hopes.

'Come on up.' The sentry beckoned from the top of the steps, gesturing me up towards the Commander's room.

He stood up as I entered. 'Warden. To what do I owe this pleasure?'

'Scarcely a pleasure.' I sat down. 'Something – or someone – got onto the island while I was visiting the depot yesterday and . . .' I gulped, swallowed again, 'did damage. K–killed things. Are–c–can . . . could anyone have got across from beyond the Pale?'

Some emotion flickered across his face, and was smoothed away. Raising bushy greying eyebrows he said 'Raiders from beyond the Pale? I hardly think so, Warden. The life of Guardians is less dramatic than you imagine, I can assure you that there's no one unauthorized this side of the Pale in our sector, or for ten miles the other side.'

'They had wheels, from the way the ground was churned up. They tore up the garden – birds and animals killed. Yesterday. While I was at the depot.' ˙

He smiled indulgently. 'I assure you, the Watchtowers ensure that no one from the wrong side gets across the Pale. You can trust us.'

'Then how do you explain what happened?'

He leant across the space between our chairs, and patted my

arm. I flinched – months of solitude had made me uneasy around even one other person, while a tag-end of disturbing memory flickered across my mind and was gone. He drew back a little, perhaps discerning my distaste for too close a proximity. 'My dear Warden: you're all alone in your Sanctuary. Perhaps in your solitude you drink a little too much of the excellent mead you brew? Smoke too much of those – interesting – herbs you cultivate, or nibble on those – unusual – mushrooms? I admire you, Warden, and those like you: I could never stand the strain of such isolation and solitude myself. Who is to blame you if occasionally you . . . indulge yourself?'

I stared at him. Surely he must know that one was chosen a Warden for one's fitness for the niche, as everyone was allocated to their most suitable occupation. How could he think solitude too much for me when to be in a room with one other person made me sweat, my muscles tense uncomfortably? Why should I need to dull my senses against the rich life of the Sanctuary? And even if I did hold a private revel, as I did from time to time, how was it conceivable that one chosen as a Warden could wantonly destroy life? What could I say? Even if I were to beg him to come to the island (and was that even allowable?) to see the damage, doubtless he could concoct some explanation to satisfy himself.

'Don't they ever allow you a leave of absence?' asked the Commander kindly. 'Get back to civilization for a bit, have a break.' He stood up and laid a hand – meant to be reassuring or sympathetic, but nearly making me scream – on my shoulder. 'Take things easy. And thank you for the mead. You wouldn't have . . .?'

Automatically I took the small packet out of the inner pocket of my jerkin. 'Be cautious with it. It's pretty strong.'

He gave a knowing chuckle. It was clear that I was dismissed as fanciful, wits turned by prolonged solitude and probably over-indulgence in substances too readily available to a Warden.

As I rowed back across the loch it dawned on me that asserting the impenetrable nature of the Pale might have been a face-preserving lie. Had that been the cause of that sudden flicker of emotion before his face smoothed to bland reassurance? Maybe raiders could sneak across unnoticed: after all, I had often idly wondered why the Watchtower was so angled that its best lines of sight were out to sea, not over the land. Certainly there were patrols, but if no good watch could be kept for unauthorized movements, might not raiders manage to enter the settled lands? This partially reassured me: the Commander might not wish to disclose the Guardians' deficiencies to an outsider, but surely, now alerted, he would make every effort to locate and trap them.

Surely.

As I rowed back to the island I saw the solitary grebe swimming on the waters of the loch. Such a magnificent bird. I wondered, was it consciously lonely for a mate, for the release of its spectacular mating display? Or would it only know once instinct was triggered? This speculation depressed me. For all I knew it was the last great crested grebe left. Never again the mating dance of which I had read. It struck me, as it had before, that it ought to make sense for the Wardens of Sanctuaries to be able to communicate with one another. Suppose, in one of the others, another lonely grebe swam round and round, waiting for a mate to unlock the ceremony?

Maybe this was considered. Our reports, presumably, were collated . . . somewhere . . . and points such as this noted. Maybe there were simply no other grebes left. My job was to observe, to study, to note, to cherish and nurture biodiversity here in this Sanctuary.

I pulled the boat up well above the tide-line and paused by the hives, to whisper, superstitiously, to the bees about the day's happenings, invoking some power I knew not what. As I straightened up I heard noises: from the direction of the central glade. A crash as of a door being broken in (though the hut door had not been locked, would have opened at a touch), tearing rending noises, the clucking of panicked hens, smashing sounds. I shinned up the nearest tree, and hoped that whoever, whatever, it was would not think to look up to the treetops.

I was not particularly careful to conceal myself, to move with especial silence, but doubted that anyone could hear much above the noise that was being made. As I reached the edge of the clearing a sheaf of torn paper fluttered past my nose. They were tearing up the books: the rare, precious books, casting pages up in handfuls. I rested in the crotch of the tree, my cheek against the bark of the branch, scarcely daring even to breathe, hidden, I hoped, by the leaves, watching.

They were not in uniform, but . . . The close-cropped heads, the well-nourished, muscular bodies. Not raiders. Would raiders from beyond the Pale wear such clothes: good quality fabric well-sewn, clean, not ragged – I thought not. Guardians, off duty, I guessed – the pair of immense two-wheelers propped up at the far edge of the glade were such as Guardians rode on patrol. These, the clothes, might be stolen, but I thought not. My – visitors – were too like Guardians I had seen at the Watchtower for there to be much doubt that they were anything else.

I tried not to shudder at the coarse banter they tossed to and fro. Could Guardians, those supposed to protect me, the Sanctuaries, the rest of the civilized lands, speak thus?

They had kicked over the recycling hopper and strewn the contents broadcast, destroying hours of careful sorting. Not purely wanton damage this time, I registered, making sense of their obscenity-splattered comments. They were looking for something: liquor, or any other intoxicant, which (so it seemed) they were denied (or simply rationed more than they liked). I watched them as they even delved into the composter, complaining loudly at the smell as they carelessly interrupted its organic processes.

Finally, failing to find what they were looking for after much foul-mouthed search, and occasional random kicks of frustration, they mounted the two-wheelers, a pair on each. Burning fuel's acrid tang fouled the sweet air of the glade as they drove off, crashing rudely over bushes, brushing carelessly close by the trees in their path. I listened to the vile racket dwindling into the distance and finally silence.

I vomited: gobbets splashed down the tree in which I perched precariously, quivering, revolted. As I climbed down, clumsy, scratching myself, breaking twigs, I made a mental apology to the tree for these indignities I was putting upon it.

Stumbling, falling, running into trees, I finally reached the beehives. 'Oh, bees, what am I going to do?'

That night, nervous, bone-tired, fearing sleep's oblivion, half-awake, half-asleep, I found half-memory and half-dream bringing back a lulling voice, coming from a face – that was not quite clear. Myself wrapped in a blanket – tactile sensation of its roughness against bare skin, rubbing abraded patches – slumped in a chair. Bland grey room. No windows.

Words about finding the appropriate niche. The damage done by the wrong organism in the wrong niche. The place where one did not only not damage but did good. The right place. Not punishment. Finding the right niche.

Gratitude, black fear-cloud lifting.

Fear?

The blanket. The bare skin. Abrasions. My slumping posture.

I came stark awake, shaking.

Tumbling thoughts, torn scraps of memory.

Why punish and confine, or waste, someone who could be of use? Give them something that they'll find engrossing: alone, unable to generate or communicate any dangerous ideas. Somebody has to cherish while meticulously observing and recording these tiny enclaves of biodiversity, after all.

Tidy. Like the geometric fields of the latifundia, Watchtowers scoured clean of everything green and growing. Biodiversity carefully contained.

I tried to get the garden straightened, replanting pulled-up roots, resetting knocked-down poles, in an attempt to restore some kind of order. Did pride or vanity keep me from flight, or lack of a place to run? I paused, a bunch of earthy radishes in my hand, as the crude mechanical roar of the two-wheelers rose above the birdsong, the sound of waves, the hum of bees. Screeching and crashing through the trees, shouts and laughter. Birds took off in a flurry of wings. The rabbits browsing at the edge of the glade a second ago: gone too. Squirrels raced for the highest treetops. They had learnt very quickly.

My hand hurt and I realized that I was gripping the handle of the hoe. The hoe. I looked down at it – a weapon. Why not hoe into halberd? If they found me not entirely unarmed and unprotected . . .

I waited, the hoe resting on the ground before me, as the

machines crashed into the glade and choked into silence. Shouted cross-talk died into sullenness as they saw me. Slowly they dismounted. They looked at me, and I looked at them. The work in the Sanctuary had made me fitter than the city ever had, but had not given me muscles like theirs, even had I had height to match theirs: and had I had both, still I was only one.

There was a pause, as they took in this new, unexpected, factor. And I continued to look at them, until, with a sudden sick stab in the stomach, I *saw*. Out here, patrolling the Pale, those differently disruptive than myself of the good order of cities or latifundia. Guardians.

Oh, perhaps not all Guardians were such exiles, but the Pale would be the place to send them. The place where they could do least damage, and maybe some good.

Like me, the cast-out, the refuse of a tidy society.

No such recognition of our similar plights appeared to be crossing the minds of the invaders. I was an inconvenience, something hostile but probably not very dangerous, something which . . . My mind processed the various possibilities in a microsecond. I tightened my grip on the hoe and hoped that my shudder had not been observed.

They shuffled forward, forming a menacing group. I was glad that I had the hut at my back. Another frozen pause. Were they waiting for me to do something – a gesture of surrender, of submission? Did I imagine that that might make any difference?

Not really.

They started to close in. I made a swipe with the hoe, catching one of them across the shins. Higher, I thought – aim higher. I lunged, and one went down with a scream: a lucky hit, I had been thrusting blindly, not aiming.

Three hostile growls raised hair on my nape.

Three, angry, still on their feet, and no cover for me. If I ran, tried to elude them . . . Boat, perhaps? Get away, on the water – I made another thrust with the hoe and ran blindly through the gap that made.

They were too close behind me, no hope of losing them in the woods, by getting up into a tree maybe, but there was no chance, no time to do more than keep on running, just that bit ahead of them blundering on my trail, panting obscenities. How escape?

I burst into the open. No time to drag the boat to the water's edge, push it out, row to safety. I dodged between the hives and into the water. Could they swim?

Already thigh deep, I struck out. Beyond this beach the shore shelved steeply; it might just deter them—

Screams. Agonized screams of unnaturally high pitch. Still swimming, I glanced back over my shoulder. A black buzzing cloud occluded the invaders. Dim shadows within it, they writhed and contorted.

The bees. The bees had risen. To my defence, or simply because they had been disturbed? Anyway they had driven off my pursuers, stumbling, cursing, limping back into the woods.

I trod water, watching the shore, for a long time after the roar of departing two-wheelers had dwindled into silence, before I dared to return to land. The island was deserted. They had gone, and I did not think that they would be back. If they survived: I had read that sometimes people died of bee-stings, especially in such quantity.

But whether the invaders lived or not, the bees had died. They had died in defending the Sanctuary. Weeping I fell to my knees, carelessly among the hives to which the survivors were returning. 'Oh, bees, I am sorry. Oh, bees, what shall I do?'

I looked at the solitary water-bird in the middle of the loch. Maybe the grebe had once had a mate. Did the memory of that triumphant celebration linger? Turning away, I walked back to the hut.

Taking one last look inside, I closed the door. I had filled one small bag with my personal necessities. I looked around the glade, where no one would have guessed at any disturbance, unless they noticed the heap of freshly-dug earth where I had buried the innocent casualties.

I could not, would not stay. Even if I thought my peace might now continue undisturbed, which seemed unlikely, I could not stay. Not once realization had dawned of how I had been seduced.

In the city I had been part of a team sorting through old books, old documents for anything that might be useful, finding the value that might be in discarded rubbish. Sometimes we found things

that could be used, but also we found things that told how things
had once been, that there were other ways of running things that
were not (as we had always been told) necessarily worse. We
talked about these, we generated new ideas, we spread our
thoughts.

Alone and scattered we were as sterile as the solitary grebe,
neuter as worker-bees serving the hive-queen.

I thought it probable that someone of no great size, no lumber-
ing muscular creature like the Guardians, used to walking softly
and carefully through woods, might slip unnoticed across the Pale
– since they spent more time watching the sea, for boats slipping
down the coast, away, to – whatever there might be, beyond the
Pale. Nevertheless, I was not heading in that direction.

I would return to the city. Like it or not, it was my niche,
where, with a little luck, I might be able to sow a few seeds, cross-
pollinate a thought or two, graft idea to idea.

Of course, next time the end might not be mere exile. It was a
risk I accepted.

Death in the Egg

(1994)

ANN OAKLEY

Melanie Howard had never had a mother. Her father used to joke that the quality of his fathering made up for this. As a father, he was, as most of them are, well-intentioned, but he was also at times obtuse, insensitive, and quite overly heavy-handed. He suffered from the common misapprehension that he could mould his daughter as he saw fit, and not as she did. That if only he said and did the requisite things, she would turn out pleasant-looking, well-mannered, tidy, kind to animals and old people, reasonably work-oriented, and cautious in love – a regular good little citizen, in fact.

But at sixteen Melanie Howard is none of these things. Her hair hangs in a greasy curtain either side of a pale, unwashed face. Water is her enemy, the dark her friend. Whenever she can, she squashes beetles and picks the legs off spiders. This summer on holiday in Spain, she enjoyed flattening with her sandals a large, innocent toad, leaving its legs sprawled unsymmetrically across the steamy tarmac of the road. The only subject she shows any talent in at school is CDT, which to the uninitiated means she's developing quite a flair for bevelling the edges of bookcases, not to mention flirting with the CDT teacher, a socially mobile ex-garage mechanic with herpes genitalis called Anthony Ruffini.

Melanie and her father, Raymond, live in a small town on the flat marshland of Essex. Raymond is a solicitor. They live in Essex because Raymond thought it would be easier to be a single father there than in a number of other places, including the metropolis. Besides, Raymond's own mother and father, a solid bungalow-dwelling duo, live not far away, and there have been occasions on which the help and advice of Mr and Mrs Howard senior have been invaluable to Raymond, and thus, it was hoped, to young Melanie. 'She's like a rose that needs pruning,' complains Mrs Howard senior, who is much given to gardening metaphors. 'More like a weed, if you ask me,' mutters her husband from behind his cabbages. 'The prickly sort you'd be advised to handle with gloves on.'

Raymond loved Melanie, but this didn't help particularly. The word 'love' was like water to Melanie – something to be eschewed at nearly all costs. 'But I do love you, Melanie!' her father would exclaim in self-defence and despairingly of her latest escapade. 'Love's not enough,' young Melanie would say – it was the title of a pop-song famous at the time. And: 'Why can't I go to a late-night film in London? I don't see what's wrong with staying up all night and coming back on the train in the morning.' Or: 'It's no skin off your nose if I leave school and go on the dole, is it?' And: 'Don't take your sexual hang-ups out on me, father. I'm on the pill, and it's none of your business what I do!'

'What did she say, dear?' Mrs Howard senior had come to choose some new curtains for the drawing-room in her son's house, and had unfortunately picked up a bit of this latest exchange. But she was also a little deaf, so Raymond was able to make some excuse and retreat to his den – a little caramel room under the stairs thick with old legal papers – wringing his hands in proverbial despair.

Things went from bad to worse. Finally, one day, Raymond acknowledged that his daughter, the much-loved greasy dark-haired Melanie, *was* out of control, and not in a way that could be remedied by pruning. He discussed the problem with his colleagues at McQueen, Howard and Chandlers in Saffron Walden, but the colleagues all seemed to have children doing similar things. The main difference was that they all had wives who were handling it for them, and Melanie didn't have a mother. Raymond tried to talk to his own mother about it – about the general problem of Melanie – but either she didn't hear or she didn't want to listen. His father told him to go and find a mother for Melanie, but that was nothing new: he'd been saying that for years. 'It's no use, Dad,' said Raymond mournfully; 'Good mothers are hard to find. Particularly for someone like Melanie.'

In the end Raymond telephoned a man he knew at the local university, a professor of psychology called Jeffrey Quark. Jeffrey was a sycophantic and pretentious Canadian who'd gone into cognitive psychology after having failed with a lumber business, and having visited an astrologer in Vancouver who told him to. Professor Jeffrey Quark was never at a loss for words, which is not quite the same as having a gift for them, but most people couldn't tell the difference.

'Send her to an analyst, Raymond,' Jeffrey advised, having listened ad nauseam to Raymond's account of Melanie's wrong-doings. 'She never had a mother, did she? I expect that's it.'

Jeffrey gave Raymond the name of an analyst who lived over a hardware store in Saffron Walden. Dr Freundlich was Austrian, and lived in Saffron Walden because he'd married an infertile opera singer whose roots were in those parts. His consulting room had two windows facing different directions, one looking over the local cemetery, the other over the gardens of the public library. Books and bodies. Dead matter, anyway.

Melanie wouldn't go to see Dr Freundlich, of course she wouldn't. 'A shrink!' she'd screamed at Raymond. 'Why me? Why not you? Your generation invented shrinks, you should use them!'

Mrs Howard senior, sitting hemming some nice Laura Ashley curtains, wanted to know what a shrink was. Raymond phoned Jeffrey again. 'Try bribery,' Jeffrey advised this time. It took a degree in cognitive psychology to come up with tricks like that.

'What do you want most in the world, Mel?' Raymond asked his daughter, who was etching her left eye with kohl at the time. A sandalwood joss stick powdered the cover of her GCSE maths textbook, and an open jar of chocolate spread nearby boasted a light covering of fungus on its dark turbid surface.

'What?'

'Turn the music down, Mel.' Raymond repeated his question: 'If you could have what you most want, what would it be?'

'For you to get off my back, Dad,' was what she said. 'To lead my own life.'

'Yes, but apart from that,' persisted Raymond patiently.

'A rottweiler?' said Melanie hopefully. 'A microwave of my very own?'

'You know what I feel about dogs and radiation,' replied Raymond sternly.

'Okay, okay. Okay. I was just trying it on. I only mentioned animals and technology as I'm not too fond of humans at the moment. What do you want me to do, Dad? Whatever it is, I won't do it unless you let me leave school and go to work on the plastic flower counter at Woolworths.'

'Okay, okay,' said Raymond repetitively, and sighing. 'But in turn you go to see Dr Freundlich twice a week for six months. Minimum.'

After four visits, Dr Freundlich rang Raymond up. 'Zis muzzer,' he began 'zat Melanie did not 'ave . . .'

'I thought you might mention that,' said Raymond. 'What has she said, Melanie? Are you getting on well?'

'Vell enough,' grunted Dr Freundlich in his best Saffron Walden German accent. Actually Melanie hadn't said a word, yet. But that was only to be expected, in view of the recalcitrant and deeply layered nature of the problem. 'I do not zeenk,' pronounced Dr Freundlich carefully, 've vill make progress until ve 'ave confronted ze muzzer kvestion.'

'You want me to tell her?' asked Raymond nervously.

'Vat eez zere to tell 'er, Mr Howard?'

'Quite a lot,' ventured Raymond, after a short pause, and thinking a little guiltily of the short story on this subject he *had* told Melanie long ago, when she was a malleable little girl.

'It happened like this, you see,' said Raymond, a few days later. He'd visited Woolworths and invited Melanie out for lunch. She chose to go to the Happy Eater.

'It happened like this. I always meant to tell you, but it got more and more difficult the longer I left it. I don't find these things easy, you know.'

'Go on Dad, I've only got half an hour.' Melanie had become surprisingly punctual since she'd got her Woolworths job.

'Well your mother – yes, of course you did have one – and I were on holiday in France. It was November. We were staying in a little hotel by the A15. Your mother was French. She was a French maid. She had wonderful copper-coloured hair. It was very, very misty – it often is at that time of year.' He paused, watching Melanie eating her cheeseburger. 'We'd been there a couple of days,' he continued, while Melanie munched, flat green pickles easing their way squashily out of the sides of her white bun. 'Your mother went out for a walk. It was a Sunday morning. It was the hunting season.' Raymond swallowed, as Melanie did, but there was nothing but an imaginary lump in his throat.

'She went out for a walk, but she never came back. I never knew what happened. As I said, it was the hunting season, so it could have been a farmer. There were a lot of them out with their guns that day. Rifles, and camouflage jackets. So the rabbits wouldn't recognize them, you understand. The men went hunting and the women went looking for mushrooms.' Raymond's voice trailed off. He wasn't sure in how much detail Dr Freundlich wanted him to tell Melanie this story.

Melanie wiped her hands on the Happy Eater paper napkin, and looked at her watch, and then at him. 'So the tale about adoption, about how you picked me out from this place full of babies, and I was the only one who wasn't crying, and I had this funny little upstanding hair you fell in love with, wasn't true? I didn't think it was, fathers aren't generally fit to adopt. Go on then, what happened next, Dad? All you've said is that my mother went out for a walk one day. Where was I? I wasn't a rabbit or a mushroom, so where do I figure in this narrative?'

'It isn't very nice, dear,' he murmured apologetically.

'Life isn't nice,' said Melanie philosophically. 'Come on, Dad, get on with it.'

'Are you sure you're not upset?' he queried again.

'Not unduly. Not yet,' said the redoubtable Melanie, picking up her milkshake and cleaning out the bottom of the glass with a noisy hoovering action.

'The police found her five days later. She was pregnant, that was where you came in. I thought she was only five or six months pregnant – she was always very vague about dates and places and times, your mother. It went with the hair. And she wasn't very big.' Raymond thought of Melanie's mother's little waist, hardly swelled by pregnancy, and of her white, milky thighs, receptive even now, through the mists of his memory and the lunchtime smoke of the Saffron Walden Happy Eater.

'It was the most remarkable thing. The baby – you – were still alive. She was lying under an oak tree. Where in another season there would have been truffles. They took her to the hospital in Meulan, and did a Caesarean. A postmortem birth, they called it. I'd never heard of it before. You were alive, but your mother was dead. They said they'd never known a case like it. Normally the baby only lives for a few minutes after its mother dies, you see. But you, you had . . .'

'Kept going all that time,' finished Melanie, 'under the oak tree.'

'Well yes.'

'Yuck,' she said graphically. 'Is that all?' She poked her striped straw around amongst the cerise remnants in the bottom of her milkshake glass.

'Are you sure you're not upset?' her father asked again. 'Perhaps now you can understand why I didn't tell you before?'

'No and no,' said Melanie. 'You should have told me. Secrets hurt more than true stories. Though I have to say this one doesn't sound true. Not really.' She sucked on her straw, her beautiful white teeth stained with bits of pink.

'That's right,' said Raymond thoughtfully. 'It doesn't, really, does it? That's one reason I never told you before. I didn't think you'd believe it. I might as well have told you you're a child from outer space! But whatever you are, Mel,' said her father anxiously and quickly, lest there should be any misunderstanding between them, 'whatever you are, wherever you come from, you're very dear to me. Very precious. Very precious indeed.' He thought his eyes might have been wet as he said this.

'Okay, Dad, don't upset yourself.' Melanie patted her father on the shoulder. 'Thanks for telling me. I've got to go back to work now. The girl who's taken over from me has got to go visit her old man in the Scrubs this p.m.'

Raymond blanched at the company his daughter was keeping. He walked her down the High Street, and tried to kiss her goodbye outside the dry cleaners next door.

'The big news is I was a postmortem birth,' Melanie told Dr Freundlich the following Friday, looking out over the cemetery. They were the very first words she'd spoken to him. 'At least according to my father's account of the matter. I think you should be seeing him instead of me. Either that or I come from another planet. No wonder I'm so mixed up. What do you think, Mr Shrink?'

Dr Freundlich grunted.

'Well said. It's made me think, though. About mothers and babies and about parents and children. Maybe none of us really belong to one another. We only think we do. Thereby of course creating work for the likes of you. No, don't bother to comment, I can't stand your grunts, they remind me of pigs looking for truffles. Not that I've ever heard pigs looking for truffles. Nor did my dear mother, she died in the wrong season.

'Or *was* it the wrong season? I've been doing some research since my father's disclosures in the Happy Eater, Dr Freundlich. I even finally utilized the symbolic power of our little sessions, squeezed in here between the cemetery and the library. I took a walk in the cemetery at night, and the dead souls talked to me – it was a lot more interesting than talking to the living. And then, in the full light of day, I went to the library and struck up a relationship with the librarian, who is another sort of medium in her spare time, and together we discovered that in that season in France and also in England, particularly, for some reason, in Essex, there were other cases like mine. That is, like what happened to my mother and me. There were also a few reported in northern Norway and in Italy. Of young women found dead with babies ready to be born far further advanced in their gestations than they ought to have been. So there's a whole breed of us, Dr Freundlich. What do you make of that? Isn't it exciting? I suppose you realize one of the things it means? It means we're not human, after all. I never understood why I felt so little in common with my dear father. I thought it was because he's a bit of a stuffed shirt – he never even got himself another woman after my mother died, though I do suspect him of one or two concealed and probably none-too-savoury peccadilloes. But now I understand the true meaning of what they call the generation gap. It's more than that. It's a species gap, you see.'

Dr Freundlich felt he needed to communicate with Melanie Howard's father about this, and some time later Raymond Howard rang his friend Professor Jeffrey Quark to let him know what had happened about Melanie and her problem behaviour. Jeffrey was reading a paper for the Research Grants Board of the Economic and Social Research Council at the time, a dense proposal from a fellow psychologist to model conversational analysis on computers. In the interests of pretending he liked it, but so as to ensure that the chap wouldn't get the money, Jeffrey gave it an alpha minus.

'I had to have her committed, Jeffrey,' said Raymond, sadly. 'Well, compulsorily detained as a disturbed young person – that's the jargon. Ever since I told her the truth about her mother she's been quite uncontrollable. She started to do the queerest things. She ate some of the flowers in mother's garden. It reminded me of the toad she squashed that summer in Spain. That's what I said to the social worker, on reflection there have been signs of something being not quite right for a while. She took to stealing road signs as well – you know, those ones that show a man grappling with an umbrella. She burnt her schoolbooks and sprayed my den with shaving foam.' Raymond shuddered at the memory: his little haven had looked like a coffee cream cake. 'But that was nothing to the things she *said*. I couldn't bear to repeat them to you, Jeffrey. It seems she developed the belief that she wasn't human, so she didn't have to stick to ordinary rules of politeness and so on. Telling her about her origins unbalanced her. I never should have done it. It was Dr Freundlich's fault. Why did you make me send her to him, Jeffrey?'

Jeffrey Quark didn't tell Raymond that this was only one of many things he habitually got wrong, and this included his grading of the proposal on computerized conversational analysis, which, if the truth were told, was a load of cobblers really. 'Look on the bright side, Raymond,' advised Jeffrey, in what seemed a slightly cavalier fashion, though he often had to talk to himself in exactly the same vein. 'Think how much easier your life'll be now without Melanie to worry about. The world's your oyster. You can stay at the office late, go up to town . . .'

Raymond Howard isn't consoled. He wants his daughter back, whatever her species. Dr Freundlich starts a new book called *The Fantasy of being an Adolescent* based on the case-history of Melanie. And in a mental hospital overlooking the Essex marshes, Melanie Howard composes a short story called 'Death in the Egg', in the company of her sisters who claim familiarity with sounds and sights they've never heard or seen, thereby proving that some young people are a different species from everyone else.

Kay and Phil

(1994)

LUCY SUSSEX

'I know that this may sound quite ridiculous but the writer
had very much the character of a visitant.'
                    – From a letter describing Katharine Burdekin

Midnight, 1961, in Point Reyes, California. Not a creature was
stirring, except in the small cabin, its one lighted window like a
wakeful eye. Suddenly that eye blinked – and standing before the
bright curtain was a figure, tall and thin as a shadow puppet. It
paused, huddling the folds of a long robe tightly to it, its head
moving back and forth questioningly. From within the cabin, the
noise of a book closing cut through the rural night like a pistol
shot. The visitor nodded, and moved soundlessly towards the
cabin door.

Phil called this place the 'hovel', though it was really a haven,
the place away from home where he wrote. Tonight, though, he
was not seated at the Royal typewriter but lolling in the one
armchair, a pile of books at his elbow. He had Goebbels' *Diaries*,
Alan Bullock on Hitler, *The Tibetan Book of the Dead*, anthologies
of Japanese poetry, and on top, the black-backed twin volumes of
the *I Ching*. You do too much research, his wife Anne had said
over dinner. Like heck, he had thought. Now he wondered if she
was right. Maybe I should just go ahead with the book. We need
the money, don't we? All those goddamned bills . . .

No, he thought. This has gotta be good. If I slip up anywhere,
it'll show, and we'll have no sale then, no cash for the cars and the
cat food and the kids' teeth.

Behind him, he heard the sound of a discreet, very low cough.
He turned his head to see, standing by the door, what he at first
took to be his mother. Dorothy shouldn't be here, he thought –

last I heard she was on vacation. And why is she dressed in her nightclothes?

Then he remembered that his mother never wore pajamas, let alone striped flannelette ones such as showed through the slit in the mannish woollen dressing gown, nor plain slippers, without heels. The tall, thin, elderly woman standing in front of the closed door was a stranger.

'Forgive me for interrupting you at your work,' she said.

An English voice. It put him in mind of movies he had seen during the war years, Laurence Olivier, Vivien Leigh ... those well-bred tones, ineffably polite. Almost without thinking, he stood, offering her his chair.

'No, no,' she said, moving towards his desk. 'The typing chair will do.'

Phil started to say that the chair was currently occupied by Beulah, a little half-wild stray who lashed out at anyone who tried to pet her. But the woman merely scooped up the cat and placed her atop the desk, beside the typewriter.

'Oh,' he said, finally speaking. For he knew then that his visitor was extraordinary, even beyond her appearing in his hovel in what was hardly visiting dress. Should he bow to her, kneel to her?

'Ma'am, who, or what, are you? Only an angel coulda got that close to Beulah and come away in one piece.'

She smiled. 'I'm not an angel. I'm Kay.'

'Phil.' He started to put out his hand, then withdrew, nervously. 'I'm not a ghost either,' she added. 'Although close to it, these last five years. I had what the doctor called an aneurysm. He said I wouldn't last the week, so I did, and more! But I've been bedridden all that time.'

She crossed one leg over the other, a slipper dangling nearly off her topmost foot and for the first time he noticed that her white, prominently veined feet were soft, without calluses.

'Being confined like that, one needs some form of compensation. So my spirit ... wanders. I hadn't left England since the 1920s, well, not bodily. But in the last few years, how I've travelled! To Versailles, where I set a novel I wrote from my friend Margaret (an American, like you, Phil), my friend Margaret's notes; to Berlin, where Margaret's husband reported on the Nazis for the

Guardian newspaper; even to Sydney, Australia, a place I hated, though it was there that the cosmic finger first touched me and I wrote my maiden novel, in six weeks! That was the most time it took, with all my books.'

She fell silent, but Phil made no response. Hesitantly, she said: 'Please forgive an old woman for her ramblings.'

'No, Ma'am —'

'Kay,' she corrected gently.

'Kay, I was just thinking that writing as though God had tapped you on the shoulder is like my way of working. Night and day, at speed.'

And on speed, he thought, but I can't say that to an old lady. You can't tell a Grandmom that you've been taking drugs to keep up your writing schedule, just to support that expensive habit, a family.

'I wrote that way,' she said, nodding. 'But no more, not since my illness. No more books. A relief, perhaps, since after the war my agent couldn't place a single work of mine . . .'

'Jesus!' said Phil, thinking of his own unsold novels. Then suddenly remembering whom he was addressing, he looked at Kay plaintively. If swearing bothered her, it didn't show in that lined, pale face. A little reassured, he said:

'I think . . . we have things in common.'

'I could sense that.'

'Sense?'

'A sixth, possibly even seventh sense. You see, Phil, I was lying in my bed in Suffolk, under the best eiderdown, and suddenly I *knew* that someone was thinking about a novel of mine. That's rare these days — I've been quite forgotten. So I came to see who it was.'

She leaned forward, scrutinizing his face. He tried to arrange it into something seemly, under the pressure of that intense gaze, but knew that it expressed only bafflement.

'Hey, I was just sitting here, thinking about all the books I'd read, in order to write just one of my own . . . and none of them —'

Here he gestured at the stack.

'— none of them were by a Kay.'

'I was only Kay for two books,' she said quickly. 'For the rest I used all of my christian name. Katharine. Katharine Burdekin.'

'Sorry, but it means nothing to me.'

'I also used a pseudonym. War was near, and being anti-fascist could have been dangerous, for my family and friends.' She was silent for a moment, then added shyly: 'Very few people know this. I was Murray Constantine.'

This is hell, thought Phil. She's an old lady, what's more she's a writer, so how can I hurt her feelings by telling her she's got the wrong guy?

It must have showed in his face, for Kay looked momentarily uncertain. Then she shot at him: *Swastika Night*!

'Oh,' said Phil. 'I read that book ten, fifteen, years back. But it was by a man . . .'

'Murray Constantine. Me.'

She smiled. Damn her, thought Phil, suddenly irate. How dare she bother me when I'm trying to work? He didn't even remember *Swastika Night*, apart from the title. But she had bent down, and was examining the stack of source material.

'Ah,' she said, straightening. 'That nasty little man's diaries. Bullock's *Hitler*. Those I understand. But the Tibetan book?'

'I am creating a world,' he said, 'in which Germany and Japan won the war.'

'As I did in *Swastika Night*!'

She's right! thought Phil. It's slowly coming back, that novel, and how it began . . . in a sorta Nazi Church, hundreds of years in the future.

'Kay, until now I had no conscious thought of your book.'

'Subconscious, then. Never underestimate it.'

'No,' said Phil. 'I never would.' He eyed her nervously. Was he about to be accused of planning plagiarism? But her expression was thoughtful rather than angry.

'There would be differences in how we would envisage such a world,' she said, swinging one foot. 'You are fortunate to be writing well after the defeat of fascism. In 1936 it seemed an all too possible future. Now it is merely an alternative for you to toy with, fictionally.'

Phil got to his feet, stung. 'Hey! I'm not playing with anything.

I'm serious!' He gestured wildly, inarticulately, then froze – because at the tip of his index finger a window had suddenly opened up, as if one of his stepdaughters had snipped an illustration from the *National Geographic*, leaving a neat hole in the glossy paper, so that in flipping through the magazine he had found the page depicting the home of a Pilgrim father cutting to the following photo-feature on Tahiti. There, in his cabin, was a large square of bright blue sky, with a vapour trail across it.

'Aargh,' he said, and withdrew his hand hurriedly. The window remained, floating in mid-air.

Kay had risen. 'My fault, I'm afraid. Things like this happen when I go abroad. I suppose it's so improbable that a sickly old Englishwoman should wander via the astral plane that attendant improbabilities follow hard upon . . .'

She shuffled up to the square and gazed into it. 'The view from an office,' she commented.

Phil neared, and cautiously peeked over her bony shoulder. He saw a room very high up, dominated by a glass wall, showing San Franciscan sky and the Golden Gate bridge. In the foreground was visible one corner of a shiny hardwood desk and by the window hung a scroll, of beautiful paper, with Oriental characters writ large upon it. He smiled in recognition. 'That's Tagomi's office.'

'Tagomi?'

'He's in the book I'm planning.'

She turned her head, and he saw a glint of excitement in those old eyes. 'Shall we take a closer look?'

She reached out one hand to the bottom of the window, which moved downward at her touch, until it reached the floor. There it stayed, and Kay unbent, breathing heavily. Their feet, in Kay's slippers and Phil's sneakers, were only inches from the threshold.

'What does one do now?' she said, and Phil, without knowing why he did so, slipped his hand around hers. It was lukewarm to the touch, and so dry he imagined that if she rubbed her hands they would sound like dead leaves on the sidewalk. Thus joined, they took a deep breath and stepped into . . .

Soft expensive carpet. With the shock, perhaps of finding something so mundane, they disengaged, Phil standing still, Kay almost skipping to the window. 'Why,' she said, 'it's like a picture postcard. "Wish you were here" – with that bridge on the verso.'

'It's Golden Gate, in San Francisco,' Phil said.

'I never went there. Is this much like . . .' She paused. 'How it really is?'

'Like enough,' said Phil.

'Beautiful,' she said. 'Very beautiful. What is that big structure there, to the left, the shell, with one side open?'

He made his feet move slowly across the carpet until he stood by her side, his nose almost touching the glass.

'Golden Poppy stadium,' he said after a moment. 'For baseball.'

'How everything is golden, in this America!' she said.

'This Japanese America,' he said.

She gave him a sidelong look. 'I had that too,' she said. 'Not that I tried hard to imagine it. I concentrated more on Nazi Germany.'

Phil was staring down at the view. Either the ships in the Bay were moving very slowly, or their engines had stopped, despite the long plumes of smoke from the funnels. And what about the cars he could see at the base of the building? They weren't parked, or in a traffic jam, yet they were immobile.

He glanced at his watch, and saw the hands moving. It was 12.30 a.m. California time. What of the clocks here? He looked around, trying to find one and suddenly noticed that seated at the desk was a small Japanese man.

'Tagomi!' he said, and heard a gasp, as Kay saw him too. Tagomi made no response; he didn't even seem to breathe.

'Is he dead?' That was Kay.

'I don't think so.' Phil walked around the desk, stopping behind Tagomi. The Japanese was bowed over an open drawer, one hand inside it, arrested in the act of turning the key of a small teakwood box. Phil looked at Tagomi's wrist, and saw that the smallest hand on the Seiko watch was still.

'We're beyond . . . time,' he said.

'Or perhaps outside it, in this world of yours,' said Kay. 'Here, you are God.'

'Gee, I suppose I am,' said Phil. The idea scared him.

Kay joined him behind the desk. 'What's in the box? Do you think we could have a God's eye view?'

'If you must,' said Phil. Open! he thought at the box. Tagomi's hand moved very slightly, completing the turn of the key, and reaching down, Phil flicked the lid of the box back. There, on a bed of crimson silk, lay –

'A Cowboy gun,' said Kay. 'Like little boys have.'

'It's a US 1860 Civil War Colt .44,' said Phil.

'Really?' Kay sounded impressed.

'No,' Phil admitted. 'It's a fake. But Tagomi doesn't know that. The gun's a prized possession, to him and his Japanese friends. They collect authentic American artefacts.'

'But you said it wasn't real.'

'Well yeah, there's a flourishing trade in fakes by Americans, who sell them to the Japanese . . .'

'Then the Japanese must be stupid, to be hoodwinked like that,' she said flatly.

'No, they're not stupid,' he said, echoing her pronunciation, so that he said 'stew-pid' rather than 'stoo-pid'. 'They're very intelligent and high-minded and civilized.'

'In my book,' she said, 'I had one of the Nazis say the only mental characteristic of the Japanese was ape-like imitativeness.'

'And what was the response to that?'

'That he was a little prejudiced, perhaps.'

'A little? Listen lady, during the war I thought much like your Nazi. I punched the wall when I heard about Pearl Harbour and almost cheered when I saw the old Jap market gardener, who hawked vegetables up and down the neighbourhood, dragged off to the internment camp. But then I met this Jewish guy, who'd been interned himself in China. He said there were no ovens in that camp. And, get this: when the Germans requested that the Japs turn their machine guns on the Jews, they refused!'

'I didn't know that,' she said. 'My only contact with the Orient was in the ports to and from Australia. I must admit that I didn't like what I saw.'

There was a short silence.

'The Japanese would have had little contact with the Jews,' she said. 'Not enough to feel threatened, to incite xenophobia, the fear of the other.'

'Fear of the other,' said Phil, chewing over the idea.

'The person who is different from you. Who, by being so, makes you so insecure, uncertain that your right is the divine right, as you believe. And if they will not be like you, they must be suppressed, confined, finally exterminated. That is what lies behind all racism and . . .'

Her voice trailed off. What was she about to say? thought Phil. Something important, I can tell that. But her gaze was fixed on Tagomi's outstretched hand.

'Phil, I don't want to alarm you unneccessarily, but I think your Tagomi moved a little, all by himself. Towards the gun.'

Phil bent down and stared at Tagomi's hand. It was then he noticed how beautiful it was, the golden skin finely grained, the fingers long and tapering towards the well-shaped nails. I made that? he thought.

'I was always nervous of guns,' Kay was saying, 'even before I became a pacifist.'

He glanced up at her, then back at the hand. In that instant, it seemed, something changed. While my attention was away, he thought, Tagomi started to reach for his trusty Colt. He doesn't like me here. He wants to lead a dull life, with that dumpy wife of his (on the desktop there was a photo of the woman, looking, in her kimono, like a bolster with a sash tied around it). He doesn't need Nazi hitmen in his office, nor all the other things I've planned for him. So he's trying to shoot first and ask questions later.

He gazed at that round Oriental face, but found it inscrutable. If Tagomi can hear us, he thought, he's not letting on. But I'm not going to stay around and find out.

'Let's get outa here,' he said, standing upright. Kay nodded emphatically. They clasped hands again, and without taking their gaze from Tagomi stepped to one side of the desk and backward – and found themselves standing on the wooden floor of the hovel. Before them was the window. I gotta close it, he thought, before Tagomi comes gunning after us. But how?

'What did you do?' he asked, 'to make it big enough for us to go through?'

'I'm really not sure. Does it make sense to say that I tugged on something that wasn't there?'

Phil put one finger to the bottom of the window. It didn't feel as if he was touching anything, but the vista suddenly snapped shut like a rollerblind.

In the shock he released Kay and she took a step sideways. After a moment she said:

'In retrospect, I believe we imagined that man reaching for his gun. Like children alone in a dark barn. Did that shadow move? Ooh, it's the bogeyman!'

'Tagomi isn't a bogeyman,' said Phil, with a sudden urge to defend his creation. 'He's one of the good guys. It'll almost destroy him to use his prized gun on the Nazis.'

She clapped her hands. 'What an original touch! Cowboys and Indians with the Reich! I would never have thought of it.'

'Then it's not in your book?' said Phil, pleased.

'No.' She gave an impish smile. 'That is all your own work. But I'll tell you something that maybe, just maybe isn't. In *Swastika Night* I had a Samurai who collected American traditional tunes. He preserved "Shenandoah", for instance. It seems to me that he is not so far away from your Tagomi and his friends, with their guns, and their cowboy hats, I imagine, and fringed leather trousers.'

No way, thought Phil, am I going to tell her that Tagomi buys a Mickey Mouse watch. Because she'd laugh, and I swear, though she may be old, and a woman, and sick, and half a ghost – I swear that I'd punch her as hard as I could.

'Okay,' he said, to change the subject. 'I'm not going to argue that one. It might be that the seed that made my Japanese collectors of American artefacts came from you. But if it did, then it was a pretty small seed. I'd have to see a lot more of your Nazi world to believe any sort of plagiarism.'

'I wasn't suggesting that. More of an influence.'

'Oh yeah? Prove it!'

She looked at him. 'You mean, conjure up one's book, like you did?'

'That's right, lady.'

She put her head on one side, thinking. 'You became angry. So angry that your arms flailed out, pointing at thin air, which suddenly parted, showing the Otherworld. Phil, I doubt if I could do that. I was brought up to be genteel, by my parents, my governess, and Cheltenham Ladies' College. Though I grew up to be something quite different from what they intended, the training lingers.'

She closed her eyes. 'I cannot show anger. I will have to summon my novel, not unconsciously as you did, but by an effort of will.'

She clasped her hands. There was a long silence, broken only by a distant owl hoot. Phil wandered over to Beulah. Her paws twitched, she poked out a sliver of rough pink tongue. He wished she'd let him pet her. Maybe, if he really worked on it . . .

He glanced over his shoulder at Kay, who was frowning in agonized concentration. Suddenly her hands unclasped, the palms moving apart jerkily, as if forced. Between them he could glimpse grey, formless matter. She was trembling now, the motion so violent that it seemed she would inadvertently crush what she held. He took two big steps across the room, and caught hold of her wrists, steadying her. Slowly, their combined strength brought her imaginary world into the ordinary reality of his hovel.

He could see that this window was different from his, being fuzzy around the edges, showing not sky but instead heavy dark masonry and two or three unlit glass bulbs, cone-shaped, as if from an electric candelabra. Her hands pulled further apart and now he could see the false candles, and below them a metal wall bracket, it was cast in the form of a swastika.

Kay moaned and her hands went limp. He drew her gently away from the window, which remained, no bigger than a trapdoor, but solidly there, as had been the threshold into Tagomi's office. Still with her eyes closed, she whispered:

'It's such a sad world, that I made.'

Phil peered into it again. It looked more solemn, to him, like an Episcopal church, if you ignored the repellent shape of the bracket. 'Hey!' he said. 'Open your eyes.'

She did. 'Ah,' she said. 'Where I began. In Germany, in the seventh century of the Third Reich. We are looking into a Nazi place of worship, built in the shape of a swastika –'

Phil could remember that vaguely from the novel.

'– where a service is in progress,' finished Kay. With an

obvious effort she dragged her gaze from the window and faced him.

'Phil, back in your San Francisco, we became fearful that the Samurai Tagomi would shoot us down, despite him being a good man. Here, we will be intruding on a sacred ceremony, performed by men, who if not evil in themselves, are devoted to an evil creed. It will be particularly unsafe for me.'

'You're afraid,' said Phil. Damn it, hadn't it been dangerous for him too, back in Tagomi's office, a demiurge faced with his flesh-and-blood creation?

'No, I am merely recalling that we panicked.'

She was staring at the window again. He too was increasingly drawn to it. I betcha anything there's music with the service, he thought. It's the best thing about the Germans – their sublime feeling for sound. I wanna hear the tunes, even though they're Nazi.

'This is your world,' he said unkindly. 'It's up to you to keep it under control, okay?'

Kay said nothing, merely ducked her head down to the level of the window. She paused, then thrust forward, the top of her body vanishing into the scene as if she were a horror movie ghost. Phil hastily grabbed the tail of her dressing gown, and was half led, half drawn into the opening scene of a book that was mostly haze in his memory.

He found himself kneeling on cold flagstone, clutching an old woman's skirt. He released it and glanced around him. They were halfway up a flight of stairs, the only light from a high, barred window.

He looked at Kay, who shrugged. 'Down, I think. It's over twenty years since I was in this world.'

He stood, and followed her down the steps to a small square space, with two exits. One, presumably leading to the outside, was barred by a thick wooden door, braced with metal, securely locked; the other only by a green velvet curtain, dependent from massive brass rings. Kay drew the fabric slightly away from one wall and yellow light fell upon her, gilding her fine white hair. She paused, peering between cloth and stone, then boldly pulled back all the curtain.

Revealed was another swastika candelabra, lit this time, illuminating two human backs, stock-still in front of an elaborate keyboard. A church organ, thought Phil, and seated at it were the organist, a woman with mouse-brown hair and a young girl, with the same drab colouring, a page-turner. Kay took a few steps forward; he followed. Now they were gazing over the musicians' heads, into a vaulted space, very high, but narrow. Though he could barely see the arched roof, against the opposite wall was a kettledrum, and leaning over it, a burly figure, sticks poised to strike. There was a choir too, all in long, flowing robes, like gospel singers, their mouths half open, as if about to sing.

At the centre of the building, where its four arms met, stood an aged and dignified man, wearing a black cloak, over a tunic as blue as the San Franciscan sky, with silver swastikas on the collar. Around him were the congregation, who had risen from simple wooden chairs, their mouths also agape.

'Frozen like that, they do look absurd,' murmured Kay.

Phil knew ministers, and he did not doubt the calm authority of the man in black and sky-blue. What bothered him, though, was that the swastikas were accompanied by the flowing hair and beard of an old testament prophet. What is the guy, he wondered, a beatnik? The drummer was similarly hirsute, as were the choir and congregation. Bearded like hillbillies, the lot of them. The only exceptions were the children in the congregation, a very pretty blonde girl in the front row of the choir, and the sisters? mother and daughter? at the organ. He looked down at the two mousy heads below him and realized suddenly that he was in error: though the organist had hair as long as Anne's, *he* also sported a straggly goatee.

Kay goofed, he decided. The Nazis would never let their hair grow like that – they'd think it effeminate. But he could hear, barely above a whisper, her voice again:

'The old man is the Knight von Hess, the feudal leader of this district. I suspect that he may be rather like your Samurai Tagomi, a noble man in an ignoble system, although he himself would reject any comparison with the Japanese. It was he who compared them to apes.'

Phil was looking at the congregation. 'Who's the young man in the second row, with the broad, ruddy face, and the protuberant blue eyes?'

Kay turned her head. 'Clever you,' she said. 'That's Hermann, another main character.'

'He sticks out because he's gawping at the chick singer. When the service is over, is he gonna ask Goldilocks for a date?'

'Goldilocks is a boy.'

'The faggot!'

'They all are.'

He stared at her. You may look like a sweet old lady, he thought, but hoo boy! you certainly don't think like one.

'Is that the reason for the long hair?'

'No. Even before the war certain sections of the Nazi party were identifying with pagan mythology. I merely extended the concept to their religion and their personal appearance, having them bearded and tressed like Thor and Wotan. And . . .'

A slightly mischievous expression crept across her face.

'But perhaps I will let you see for yourself. If we could find a secluded nook in this church, somewhere where we could see without being observed ourselves, I might be able to start the action of the novel. I feel a curious desire to hear the choir, vile though their lyrics are. I should know – I wrote them myself.'

'Behind the curtain?' said Phil.

'We couldn't see anything there. I wonder about the steps, though. Might they lead to a vantage point?'

Before he could reply she had answered herself. 'Of course! How could I forget, not that I made use of it in the book. The Hitler miracle plays!'

'What?'

'They would have been performed in the church, and the scenes where Hitler and Goebbels are addressed by the Divine Thunderer, from Heaven where the heroes live, require gods. Upstairs!'

She darted out of the alcove, her passage nearly smothering him in the voluminous folds of the curtain. He extricated himself, and followed. She was nimble on the stairs, so much so that he worried for her. What if she has another an . . . whatever-it-is, here? he thought, as they passed the window, with its comforting view of hovel and sleeping black cat. Will I be trapped in a Nazi world?

But he said nothing, and they came to a landing cum props room with, heaped in it, horned papier mâché helmets, wooden spears, even a breastplate, its gilt beginning to flake and peel. The room was closed on one side by another curtain, blue this time. Kay marched up to the slit in the centre of the curtain and drew it aside a smidgen.

'Yes,' she said. 'I was right!'

Looking down through the lips of dusty blue cloth he could see the choir, the congregation and the grizzled head of von Hess.

'There's a platform out there,' he said.

'Too visible. We will be safer behind the curtain.'

She sat down on the cold stone, regaining her breath. Phil did likewise, feeling vulnerable and wishing that they could be closer to their exit.

After a while Kay said: 'You may find this strange, but I am not entirely sure how to get things moving.'

'Concentrate,' he said. 'Or maybe snap your fingers.'

He acted out his words, then regretted it, for the sound was fearfully loud in this quiet place. Kay smiled, cautiously lifted her hand, then repeated his motion.

Music. First ther was an organ chord, deep and sonorous, then a roll on the drums, as loud as if Kay's Divine Thunderer were within the church. Phil looked down and saw the Knight had turned towards the west of the building, with the congregation following suit. A massed choir of male voices sang out: '*Ich glaube!*'

'Their Creed!' said Kay, speaking loudly into his ear, for the singing soared towards the gods at awesome volume. They believe, Phil thought, they must really believe, to sing like that. That singer, the blond boy, what a pure soprano! It put him in mind of an angel, a Wagnerian angel. Pity about the tune though. And the arrangement. It sounded like the duller bits of Beethoven and Wagner shook around in a barrel with some Bavarian drinking songs. This is supposed to be seven hundred years in the future, he thought. Surely German music would have progressed in that time. What about Schoenberg and the other avant-garde composers? Then he recollected that they had mostly been Jewish and the Nazis had abominated their work.

What were they singing about now? He caught the word

'exploded' and on cue the organ and the drums cut in again, augmenting the sound to a thunderous roar. The figures below lifted their arms stiffly in the Nazi salute and he felt a pang of distaste.

'What was that crescendo for?' he said into Kay's ear. She turned her head, and, her lips almost against his earlobe, said: 'Adolf Hitler, their Christ. They were saying he was not born of woman, but exploded from the head of the Thunderer.'

It sounded crazy to Phil. He shut up and listened to the rest of the Creed, which contained some familiar names, with Stalin and Lenin execrated, Goebbels and Goering praised, bizarre in that mass-like setting. At the end the Knight turned back towards the east, and the congregation sat, the sound of their chairs on the stone floor jarring and discordant. There was a long silence, then the Knight, after a cough as polite and soft as Kay's, began to intone, in beautiful courtly German. Phil mentally translated the words:

> As a woman is above a worm
> So is a man above a woman.

What? he thought. That wasn't in the Nazi ideology. They were keen on *Kinder, Küche, Kirche*; but I don't think they were misogynists. Hitler had Eva Braun. Goebbels was a womanizer. Most of the others were family men. Maybe it's got something to do with Kay making them homosexual. He turned, intending to ask, but she was intent on the service.

He said nothing, listening to that elegant voice, that could make such bloodthirsty sentiments sound poetic. There was stuff now about race defilement – that figured, then something about Hitler and the Thunderer. Apparently they formed a Duality. While he was still trying to work that out, the Knight finished, coughed again, and saluted the congregation. The ceremony was over.

'Is that it?' he whispered to Kay. Below, the singers were moving out of their seats with military precision. They formed a neat bloc in front of the choir-stalls, then marched, in formation, down the aisle. The drummer and the pair at the organ followed, and after a pause, the congregation.

He nudged Kay, still wanting an answer. She shook her head.

The Knight, Phil suddenly noticed, was not among the marchers. 'Where is the old man?' he asked, and she replied: 'In the Hitler Chapel, resting. He has another service to conduct shortly.'

At the same time Phil heard, from far below, shouting, of which he caught only the final imprecation not to dawdle. He sat back, watching the church empty, until only two brawny men remained, who were collecting the wooden chairs and stacking them against the walls. Then they too left. What now? wondered Phil.

Then he heard sounds below, shuffling and whimpers, and a body of people came slowly into sight, not marching, but straggling. They were all dressed in jacket and trousers of an ugly dun-brown, and their downcast heads were shaved.

Jesus! thought Phil, appalled at this mass of ugliness. The Knight had reappeared and was walking, shoulders back, head erect, towards the mass of brown, which as he neared emitted shrill, terrified cries. Another bearded man, carrying a big stick, moved among the crowd; eddying like a sheepdog he brought them to a halt, a disorganized clump halfway up the church. When all stood still he saluted the Knight and marched quickly out of the church. Far below huge doors slammed.

'I hadn't thought of it until now,' Kay murmured, 'but they could, in theory, while alone in the church with the Knight, tear him to pieces.'

'You mean the ones with the shaved heads? Are they from a concentration camp?'

'They live in a cage, yes.'

'What are they? Jews? Communists?'

'Listen to them!' said Kay. The Knight had stopped, yet the screams continued. Phil traced one of the thin sounds to a short figure, its naked head almost too big for its puny body. Why, that's a boy! he thought, then almost immediately spotted another, his head half buried in the lap of an elderly adult. It's kids who are screaming, he realized, indignant. What's the old man think he's doing, scaring those little guys like that?

The form of what was unmistakably a pregnant woman, despite the shaved head, and the unfeminine, unflattering garb, caught his eye. Shouldn't she be sitting down? he thought. She doesn't look too good. He could distinguish other full-bellied figures in the crowd, and had started to make a count before he became distracted by the number of people who were weeping – children, the pregnant females, old folk, young adults, they were snivelling or sobbing or howling unrestrainedly.

He glanced at Kay, and saw her eyes were damp. Embarrassed, he looked back down again and suddenly became aware that besides the factor of dress in common, all were narrow-shouldered and slight. Though none wore dresses or makeup, below him was a company of –

'Women,' said Kay, and below her the Knight shouted: '*Frauen!*' Phil jumped at the sound of that deep voice, but felt, besides the physical reaction, a more profound shock. Kay was regarding him intensely again.

'Phil,' she said, 'didn't you remember the Women's Worship from my book?'

He hadn't, until now, because those shaven heads, that abject misery, had upset him so much that he had put *Swastika Night* out of his conscious memory.

'No,' he said truthfully.

'You must have had some inkling from what von Hess said. Or from the men-only ceremony.'

'I thought I saw some girls,' he said, recalling the page-turner, and a few beardless faces among the congregation.

'Immature boys,' she said. 'You sat through the service and never noticed the absence of women!'

She had an all too familiar look on her face. He had seen it on Dorothy, his mother; on Anne; and on his other two wives. It said: Men!

'That's right,' he said aggressively. 'But you confused me with the longhairs. Hey, what have you got, some sorta hair fetish? Why shave the women?'

'They can't be allowed to be beautiful,' she said sadly. 'Because they are only kept for breeding. They are worms, remember? A beautiful woman has power over men, and in this world women are powerless. The society depends upon it. This service reinforces the message, by telling them it is their sacred duty to be submissive and bear sons.'

'You got one helluva warped vision!' he said. 'I read all about the Nazis for my book, and they never put women in camps, unless they were Communist, or Jewish, or . . .'

'Feminists,' she finished. 'In 1932 Hitler suppressed the German organizations for women.'

'Yeah, but they wanted to work outside the home and —'

He froze, thinking of the argument this remark would have provoked at home. 'I didn't mean that,' he said quickly. 'But Kay, this stuff is paranoid. And I don't see how it can work. How do the Nazis make sure they all grow up faggots? Teenage boys go crazy about girls — they make holes in the walls of changing rooms, they . . .'

'Ssh,' said Kay, suddenly very still herself. Phil glanced down again and saw only the Knight calmly addressing the women. 'Relax,' he said. 'Nobody heard.'

'But I can hear!' she whispered, and suddenly he understood: coming from the stairwell was the faint but unmistakable creak of a heavy door's hinges. It was followed by soft, ascending footsteps.

'Hermann once hid in the church when he was a lad, to sneak a look at the Women's Worship,' she said. 'He's well past that now, but some of the boys in the congregation wouldn't be. Even though the punishment is to be publicly shamed and beaten insensible.'

'To the window!' said Phil, scrambling to his feet. She was having trouble rising, so he offered her a hand up, feeling again her dry skin and now the lightness of her body, as if her very bones were hollow. They started down the staircase, leaping and stumbling —

But they were too late. 'Gott in Himmel!' said a husky voice, and they saw, halfway up the stairs, the young page-turner, transfixed by the window in front of him, the hole in his reality. He glanced above it, at Phil and Kay, and his spotty chin dropped even more. That man had a beard, but his greying dark hair was cut so close to his skull that he could have been a woman. And behind him was another man, venerable as the Knight, with a fine head of hair, yet beardless as a boy! The big iron key he had stolen dropped from his sweaty fingers and clattered down the stairs.

'This wasn't in the book,' panted Kay.

'I know, I remember it perfectly now. The noise that key's making! Von Hess'll hear! Kay, snap your fingers!'

She did, but without a sound. 'I was never good at that sort of thing,' she said apologetically.

Women weren't, in Phil's experience. He supplied the sound himself, but of course nothing happened.

The boy saw movement in the window, and the mask of a small black cat appeared, only inches, it seemed, from his face. It showed sharp teeth and hissed noiselessly at him. He took a step back, then ducked, for Phil, pausing only to yell: 'Get outa the way, Beulah!' made a mad dive at the window.

Phil landed in a heap, not at the bottom of the stairs, but on a wooden floor. Seconds later Beulah inflicted a set of deep scratches on the back of his hand.

'You're risking a trip to Naziland!' he growled, then felt a slipper in the small of his back. 'Oh I'm sorry,' said an English voice, and Kay stepped into the hovel.

'Get rid of it!' he said. She obliged, putting both hands around the gap, through which, as he rolled aside and stood, he could see the boy, fleeing down the stairs lickety-split.

'I hope he doesn't hurt himself,' said Kay.

'I don't care,' was Phil's reply. Kay was exerting herself, pushing at the space, but it looked no smaller. 'You need help?' he asked, but she shook her head firmly. The veins on her neck stuck out, her face reddened . . . and slowly the window dwindled between her palms. She held them together finally, in the gesture of prayer, then relaxed with a flourish, as though washing her hands of the Nazi world.

There was a long silence, during which he returned to his armchair, and just sat, drained. Kay remained standing, looking very old and ill.

'Why?' he said finally. 'Why make the Nazis treat women like that? It's . . . horrible.'

'It's not so far removed from the real situation of women throughout the centuries,' she said. 'And the germs of it are present in the Nazi writings. I believed when I wrote my book, though not many agreed with me, that the Nazis were capable of exterminating the Jews. And after that, what next? The Nazi system fed upon hate, it needed an enemy. Why not the oldest?'

'The oldest?' he repeated, thinking: I don't hate women, although I don't get on with Dorothy, and things with Anne aren't so good now . . .

She sighed. 'I was married once.'

'I've done it three times,' he said glumly.

'You amaze me. After I left my husband, I made sure that I never again lived with a person of the opposite sex. It's too hard, Phil, being with someone who is human, like you, but oh, so different!'

Is it ever, thought Phil.

'We fear the other, who is not like us, but is necessary for the continuance of the race. If not for that, I suspect men would have exterminated women long ago.'

'That's too dark, Kay,' he said. 'I can't accept that. I think we'll hafta agree to differ there.'

'As we do with our separate visions of the fascist world?' she said.

'Yeah!' and they shook on it. Her hand felt ethereal, as if a gust of wind would blow her spinning up into the air. She can't stay here much longer, Phil realized.

'I'm glad I dropped by,' she said, the words incongruous, the sort of thing he associated with women's tea parties. 'Your book looked most interesting. If I live to see it published, I'll ask my companion to buy a copy for me.'

If it's published, thought Phil, but merely said: 'Thanks.'

She smiled. 'And I think I did, just a bit, influence you.'

'Yeah,' he said. 'I guess I was thinking about the book, before you came.'

'Goodbye,' she said, but made no move. She's the guest, Phil thought, and she wants me to escort her outside. So he got up, and opened the door for her; she stepped out into the Californian night.

'Thank you, Phil, for showing me your book.'

'And thanks for showing me yours. Goodbye, Kay.'

She turned and began to walk away, so he closed the door. That was one weird lady, he thought, with relief. He could hear the faint flap of her slippers, one step, two steps . . . then silence.

He flung the door open again; but saw only country darkness.

'Kay!' he shouted, but there was no answer. He shut out the night, feeling acute loss.

Wonder what she looked like when she was young, he thought. From her eyes and brows, she had dark hair. I like that on a woman. She might even have been beautiful.

His gaze fell on another dark gal, Beulah, who had settled herself in his armchair. 'Watch it, cat,' he said. 'I could take you by the tail and cast you into a Nazi church service.'

The fuss that'd cause, Beulah falling, claws out, and hissing, into the midst of those poor downtrodden women.

'Or into the office of a good friend of mine, Mr Nobusuke Tagomi.'

At the thought of Tagomi his head turned and he contemplated the space in the hovel where the first window had been. He put out an arm, pointing at the non-existent space. Nothing happened. He repeated the action, more forcefully, but got the same result.

He turned again, to look at the typewriter. Jesus, I'm tired, he thought, but sleep can come later. He walked over to the desk, opened the top drawer and took out a small bottle. There were two pills left. He gulped them down, without water, then took the cover off the Royal typewriter. Then he spent some time searching for paper, which he placed within easy reach of his typing chair. He sat down and rolled the top-most sheet into the machine.

I gotta get back to Tagomi, he thought, but without Kay, there's only one way I can reach him. It's not as spectacular, sure, as pointing at the air and watching the fabric of the world roll down, but it's tried and true. Here I go!

He began typing his novel.

Notes on the Authors

AIKEN, JOAN [Delano]. Born Britain, 1924. Her literary career began when she wrote for BBC Radio in 1944. Her first books were for children and several, including *All You've Ever Wanted* (1953) and *More than You Bargained for* (1955), were collections of fantasy stories. She has also written successful thrillers, which often contain a dash of fantasy and horror, and some of her best adult fantasy tales are collected in *The Windscreen Weepers* (1969).

ATWOOD, MARGARET. Born Canada, 1939. A novelist, poet and critic, who has become a dominant figure of Canadian literature, she has written a long list of outstanding novels and short stories exploring the lives and emotions of women. *The Handmaid's Tale* (1986) is a bleak depiction of a future world where women are denied control over any part of their lives.

BAILEY, HILARY. Born Britain, 1936. Her first stories were published in the mid 1960s in the innovative *New Worlds* magazine, which she went on to edit in 1974–5. Since then she has written occasional SF/fantasy/horror stories as well as more mainstream works. Her most recent novel is a fantasy: *Frankenstein's Bride* (1995).

BOWEN, ELIZABETH [Dorothea Cole]. Born Ireland; 1899–1973. A prominent author of short stories and novels such as *The Heat of the Day* (1949) and *Eva Trout* (1968), she often made use of the supernatural to create fear. 'The Demon Lover' is ranked as a major contribution to the short story genre.

BRACKETT, LEIGH [Douglass]. Born USA; 1915–1978. An author of mysteries as well as fantasy and science fiction, she wrote space operas such as *The Sword of Rhiannon* (1953); many other novels, including *Alpha Centauri – or Die!* and the Skaith series; and short stories. She co-wrote such classic screenplays as *The Big Sleep* and *The Empire Strikes Back*.

BROOKE-ROSE, CHRISTINE. Born Switzerland, 1923. Novelist, critic and academic (she was Professor of American Literature at the University of Paris VIII), she championed the French *nouveau roman* and new trends in French literary criticism to English-speaking readers. These concerns are reflected in her experimental fictions, including the novels *Out* (1964), *Between* (1968) and *Thru* (1975), which, like her short stories, contain many elements of fantasy and humour.

BUTLER, OCTAVIA E[stelle]. Born USA, 1947. 'I began writing fantasy and science fiction because these seemed to be the genres in which I could be freest, most creative.' Her series of Patternist novels create an ambitious future history, which starts in 1690 in *Wild Seed* (1980) and deals with issues of power through a group of people developing psionic abilities. *Kindred* (1979) tells the story of a young black woman transported back in time and into slavery.

CARRINGTON, LEONORA. Born Britain, 1917. Educated at English convent schools, at the age of nineteen Carrington attended the first Surrealist exhibition in London, was electrified by it, soon afterwards met Max Ernst and fled with him to France. There she painted and began writing her unique fictions. During the War she suffered a breakdown and was rescued from a Madrid asylum by her former nanny, who arrived in a submarine. Carrington eventually settled in Mexico and continued her work as a Surrealist painter and writer.

CARTER, ANGELA [Olive, née Stalker]. Born Britain; 1940–1994. A writer of novels, short stories, essays, poetry and plays, she developed to extraordinary effect the 'neo-Gothic' tradition and gave new dimensions to old fairy tales. A concern with the social construction of gender permeates her work, notably in *The Magic Toyshop* (1967) and the post-apocalyptic *Heroes and Villains* (1969).

CHARNAS, SUZY MCKEE. Born USA, 1939. As well as the dystopias *Walk to the End of the World* (1974) and *Motherlines* (1979), she has written a novel about a vampire disguised as an anthropology professor, a number of short stories, and 'urban fantasies' for young adults. The content of her work is often controversial.

DORSEY, CANDAS JANE. Born Canada, 1952. A writer of SF novels and short stories, she established her reputation with *Machine Sex . . . and Other Stories* (1988), in which she portrays the impact on women of a technology that is organized by men.

DU MAURIER, DAPHNE. Born Britain; 1907–1989. Famous for novels such as *Jamaica Inn* (1936) and *Rebecca* (1938) (filmed, as was her short story 'The Birds', by Alfred Hitchcock), she created an atmosphere of suspense and fear in her work, which raises serious questions about the nature of good and evil.

EMSHWILLER, CAROL [née Fries]. Born USA, 1921. The author of over one hundred short stories of SF and fantasy, which often employ poetic or experimental forms, such as the much-anthologized 'Sex and/or Mr Morrison', she has also written a surrealist fantasy novel, *Carmen Dog* (1988).

FAIRBAIRNS, ZOË. Born Britain, 1948. A campaigner for CND, she has written works that have made a valuable contribution to the peace movement. Her fiction includes the feminist dystopia *Benefits* (1979), as well as a number of short tales of fantasy.

FRAME, JANET [Paterson]. Born New Zealand, 1924. As told in her books of autobiography, *To the Island* and *An Angel at my Table*, she spent many years in psychiatric hospitals and was mistakenly diagnosed as a schizophrenic. There is an edge of fantasy to much of her fiction, especially the short stories in *You are Now Entering the Human Heart* (1983).

GENTLE, MARY. Born Britain, 1956. One of the newer writers of fantasy, her first two novels (*Golden Witchbreed* and *Ancient Light*) depict a genderless society in the tradition of Le Guin. She is now writing stories about a world in which magic works as well as science.

HALL, L[eslie] A[nn]. Born Britain, 1949. A professional archivist who has also written scholarly studies of sex in history, such as *Hidden Anxieties: Male Sexuality 1900–1950* (1991), she has privately written fantasy and SF stories from an early age and has recently completed her first novel.

HENDERSON, ZENNA. Born USA; 1917–1983. A teacher for most of her life, Henderson's stories and novels often concern themselves with child–adult relationships, and the warmth and gentle tone of her writing contrast with the macho space fiction of the period. Her most popular stories are those about 'The People', extraterrestrials with psychic gifts who are hiding in the American Midwest. These are all in *The People Collection* (1991).

JACKSON, SHIRLEY. Born USA; 1919–1965. Best known for her brutal story 'The Lottery' (1948) and for novels like *The Haunting of Hill House* (1959) and *We have Always Lived in the Castle* (1962), her work has been described as 'New Gothic', evoking the alienation and horror of modern life.

JAMES, P[hyllis] D[orothy]. Born Britain, 1920. Acclaimed for her achievements in revitalizing the detective story genre with her Adam Dalgleish books, which have received critical praise and won commercial success, P. D. James has also written on true crime in *The Maul and the Pear Tree* (1971). *The Children of Men* (1992) is a novel set in the future.

'KAVAN, ANNA' [Helen Edmonds, née Woods]. Born France; 1901–1968. Having travelled frequently in her early years, she began to write in Burma under the name of Helen Ferguson and produced six realist novels. By World War II she was divorced, a heroin addict, and embarking on a long history of mental illness. Stories like 'Asylum Piece' and 'Mr Dog Head' from this period are surrealistic and nightmarish, culminating in *Ice* (1967), which has been hailed as an SF classic.

LEE, TANITH. Born Britain, 1947. She is a leading writer of fantasy, exploring myth and dreams in such novels as *Birthgrave* (1975) and *Quest for the White Witch* (1979), as well as in children's books and erotic tales. Some of her stories are collected in *Red as Blood* (1983) and *The Gorgon* (1985).

LE GUIN, URSULA K[roeber]. Born USA, 1929. Her fantastic stories and novels, especially *The Left Hand of Darkness* (1969), *The Dispossessed* (1974) and *The Word for World is Forest* (1976), blend a high degree of storytelling with a serious attempt to address contemporary problems of gender, society and ecology. See *The Language of the Night* (1979) for her thoughtful comments on fantasy in general and on her own work.

McCAFFREY, ANNE [Inez]. Born USA, 1948. A prolific author of historical, romantic and Gothic novels as well as science fiction and fantasy, she has achieved most success as the creator (in such novels as *Dragonflight* and *Dragonsdawn*) of Pern, a planet of telepathic dragons and their riders. Her home in Ireland is called Dragonhold.

McINTYRE, VONDA N[eel]. Born USA, 1948. Using SF to explore the possibility of a non-sexist society, she has written several novels and short stories, some of which are collected in *Fireflood* (1979). Her other work includes the novel *Dreamsnake* (1978), various *Star Trek* novelizations and *Aurora: Beyond Equality*, an important anthology of fantasy edited with Susan J. Anderson in 1976.

NAMJOSHI, SUNITI. Born India, 1941. Her unconventional fiction includes *Feminist Fables* (1981) and *The Conversations of a Cow* (1985), in which an Indian lesbian cow appears to her and takes her on an extraordinary journey.

OAKLEY, ANN. Born Britain, 1944. A sociologist, she is also a highly successful author of novels, short stories and autobiography. Her fiction has moved increasingly away from the realism of earlier novels like *The Men's Room* (1988) to a blend of realism and fantasy that 'play[s] around with the interface between "nature" and "culture".'

OATES, JOYCE CAROL. Born USA, 1938. A prolific novelist, short story writer, poet and critic, she has written fiction that ranges from naturalistic stories of everyday lives to Gothic nightmares. The trilogy comprising *A Garden of Earthly Delights* (1967), *Expensive People* (1968) and *Them* (1969) is a chronicle of three American families from different classes spanning a long time-scale. Oates has also taught at various universities.

RAJAN, LYNDA. Born Britain, 1946. An academic and writer of short stories, her use of fantasy enables her to probe the secrecy and misunderstandings of relationships.

REED, KIT [née Craig]. Born USA, 1954. Her work spans several genres: she has written realistic novels such as *The Better Part* (1967) and *Fort Privilege* (1985), as well as more impressionistic works and fantasy/SF. Her short stories are perhaps better known than her novels. Her focus is usually people and the impact of technology on their lives.

RUSS, JOANNA. Born USA, 1937. An author of fiction and feminist and literary criticism, she emerged in the 1960s as an important writer of SF's New Wave. Her fantasy novel *The Female Man* (1975) is now considered a classic.

SAXTON, JOSEPHINE [née Howard]. Born Britain, 1935. One of the small band of British women writers who began to experiment with speculative fiction in the 1960s, she has written five novels, starting with *The Heiros Gamos of Sam and An Smith* (1969). All of these – like her stories – employ elements of SF and fantasy, often to humorous or satirical effect.

SPARK, MURIEL [Sarah]. Born Scotland, 1918. An author of critical works on Mary Shelley and the Brontës, her novels include *The Prime of Miss Jean Brodie* (1961) and *The Mandelbaum Gate* (1965). While she consciously used anti-realist techniques later in her writing career, some of the stories in *The Go-Away Bird* (1958) reveal her early ability to efface the line between reality and the unreal.

SUSSEX, LUCY. Born New Zealand, 1957. She moved to Australia in 1971 after periods of living in France and England, working as an author and researcher. She has edited anthologies and written for children (*The Peace Garden*) and teenagers, mainly in the SF and fantasy genres, and has been instrumental in the rediscovery of some nineteenth-century women writers, such as Mary Fortune. Her collection of fantastic stories, *My Lady Tongue and Other Tales*, was published in 1990 in Australia.

'TIPTREE, JAMES, Jr' [Alice Sheldon, née Bradley, also wrote as 'Racoona Sheldon']. Born USA; 1915–1987. A highly regarded author of fantasy and SF, most readers and many critics assumed that she was a man until her true identity was revealed in 1977.

Her novels, *Up the Walls of the World* (1978) and *Brightness Falls from the Air* (1985), and her many short stories explore the cruelty caused by differences of race and gender.

TUTTLE, LISA. Born USA, 1952. She has written many distinctive SF, fantasy and horror short stories, some of which are collected in *A Spaceship Built of Stone* (1987). She has also edited a collection of women's horror stories called *Skin of the Soul* (1992).

WELDON, FAY [née Birkinshaw]. Born Britain, 1931. A prominent author of novels, short stories, plays and screenplays, she wrote the horror novel *The Life and Loves of a She-Devil* (1984) and *The Cloning of Joanna May* (1989), a fantasy about four cloned women created by genetic engineering. Her work has been said to depict 'a savage, unstoppable sex war in which women, often cruel to each other, have the moral advantage . . .'

WILHELM, KATE [Gertrude, née Meredith]. Born USA, 1928. One of the female SF writers who began to attract attention in the 1960s with stories and novels such as *The Killer Thing* (1967), Wilhelm later turned away from pure SF towards speculative fiction and more mainstream writing in novels like *Fault Lines* (1977), a woman's disordered recollections of her life.